Beware of Chicken

— BOOK 3 —

— BOOK 3 —

CASUALFARMER

Podium

Cover and interior art by Tsuu

ISBN: 978-1-0394-5228-2

Published in 2024 by Podium Publishing
www.podiumaudio.com

To my sister,

who helped me immensely during

the editing process for this book.

BEWARE OF CHICKEN

— BOOK 3 —

There is nothing that captures the soul of cultivation more truly than a tournament.

It is the place where every cultivator gathers, from far and wide. They come to lay claim to priceless treasures. They come to bring glory to their Sects. They come to test themselves, against the best the world has to offer!

The roar of the crowds fills their ears! The heat of combat sets fire to their veins! For only in battle is one's cultivation *truly* tested!

There, in the arena, all of their strengths and all of their weaknesses are laid bare. The victor's star will surely rise, while the defeated are consigned to ignominy.

Peerless treasures can be found at the auctions, and new techniques can be gleaned from competitors.

Friendships are forged—as are grudges that can rage for a thousand years.

So rise from your comfortable homes and secluded Sects! Go out into the world, for glory awaits!

CHAPTER 1

SUFFERING FROM SUCCESS

My hands drifted along the wood, taking in the form. There was, as always, something so profoundly relaxing about sitting down and working with my hands . . . most of the time. Mechanics had never been my forte, but woodworking? It was one of the things I had been good at, in another life. A bit of an old-fashioned thing, to be sure, like knitting, but it helped pass the time and let everything wash away.

It was a little odd for things to suddenly be so quiet. Tigu, Xiulan, Ri Zu, and the Xong brothers had left last week for the tournament in the Dueling Peaks. I had gotten used to Tigu doing something strange, shouting and boasting. But they hadn't been gone for so long that I was missing them yet. I just hoped that going to the tournament would be something they enjoyed, rather than something that they would regret.

I knocked twice on the wood under my fingers. *No jinxing my friends, please, whatever fates are out there.*

The week after my friends had left had been generally filled with the most boring part of farming. Bookkeeping, and looking at what I had to do for the next harvest. Last year I had been alone and had to do a lot more work to prepare the land—I had actually planted earlier this year than last year, by nearly two full months. That was combined with the topography of my property. The hills were a bit smaller around here, so they didn't block the sun as much as they did in Hong Yaowu, or most places around Verdant Hill.

That meant that the plants grew just slightly faster too. Farming wasn't something that was exact. The harvest could happen in a rather large time frame, and this year it just happened to be a lot earlier than last year. Harvesting just at the end of summer, rather than so close to the Mid-Autumn Festival. It was something to think on for next year.

Should I delay planting by a little? It would spread out the work a bit more at the beginning of the season, but that means I might not be free to head over to Hong Yaowu to help out like I normally do, I thought.

But maybe this time for harvest was better. There was a bit less rain this time of year too, and the rice was still drying. Less rain did make things easier—because it still needed to be husked and polished, and that was the most labour-intensive part. Even as a cultivator, I would need help, and I was waiting until after the tournament to get started, because this would be all hands on deck.

Mostly because I had done the math.

I had done the math . . . and it was still a little mind-boggling and intimidating. The oldest form of wealth was the amount of crops you had. When I came here, I'd had the idea that I would be a subsistence farmer, just taking what I needed. I would have enough money and resources for some comforts, but nothing grand.

Instead, I was rich in the oldest sense. Going by last year's yields . . .

2,656. Two thousand, six hundred, fifty-six.

Two thousand six hundred fifty-six forty-kilogram bags of rice.

Give or take a few.

That was on par with the other places' full-on industrial farming operation yields.

It was a strange, abstract thing, trying to visualise the stacks of rice bales . . . but I gave it my best shot.

Which was also why I was working on this project.

I took a step back and looked down at my old cart, patting it affectionately. It was a good tool and still had plenty of years left in it. I was actually kind of attached to it. This cart had been with me since Pale Moon Lake City and had served faithfully, even with all the abuse. My old gal would have broken a long time ago without Qi.

It turned my eyes from the old beater to my new hot rod, the behemoth resting quietly in my front yard.

Qi-reinforced axles. Solid branch construction on the wheel spokes. Smooth, hand-sanded finish. It was less a cart and more of a boat with wheels, and it looked as sturdy as a fortress. A painted maple leaf and wheat/rice symbol was painted on the back. *Our* symbol.

And yet even with this giant cart, I'd still have to make at least seven trips to transport all the rice I wanted to sell. I'd have to make an entire fleet of the things.

Taking a deep breath, I slapped my hands onto my thighs. My work here was done for today.

I had an important appointment.

Rising, I walked past the little saplings, which had begun poking up from the peach pits Washy had brought home. They were growing out of the small courtyard, next to the trees Xiulan had given us for a wedding present. We already had some peach trees already fruiting, but hey, I would never say no to more. And I think these may have been a different type than we already had. They felt a little strange and had been oddly finicky to even get this far.

When I got to the living room, I rapped twice on the windowsill, and Meimei perked up from where she was writing out a truly *vast* shopping list. Both Noodle the snake and Peppa the pig were working with her.

"Ready, Meimei?" I asked her, and she nodded happily, glancing at the two attending to her. Peppa snorted indulgently, and Noodle closed his good eye, letting out a hiss of good-natured amusement.

I collected the hamper and the blanket, then held out my arm as my wife approached. She took it with a smile, and we set off across the property. Big D inclined his head to us on our way out, before turning back to whatever he'd been talking about with Babe and Yin.

Our boar and dragon were chilling in the river. Washy's long, sinuous body was unspooled into the river while he basked on a rock, and the small hill that was Chunky rose out of the center of the deeper part, covered in water plants and frogs.

Meimei let go of my arm and, with a hop, alighted on the small hill in the river. Her limbs windmilled for a moment before she caught herself, then spun around to grin at me.

I looked up at her just as Chunky's head breached the river, reeds and water plants hanging off his tusks. He chuffed happily, chewing on some of the water reeds and covered in mud from rooting along the bottom.

A single leap took me after her, and then we hopped to the other side of the river. I had built a bridge . . . but this was more fun.

From there, it was a short trek to the top of our toboggan hill, where we took a seat under one of the trees. It had a nice bough on it that looked like a good place for a swing or a treehouse. I set out the blanket and unpacked our lunch. Tomatoes, some sandwiches, and some tea.

"It's coming along well. I'll need to do some more research on prices, but we'll definitely have enough to purchase whatever we need. I never knew glass required so much stuff," she mused, before she took a big bite of a raw tomato slice. She let out a little sound of contentment. "I *swear* these things are addictive."

I smiled and took my own slice, already having had the seeds removed—I needed them for next year. While tomatoes were technically perennials, they would definitely die if they were left out all winter.

"I'll have to get the Lord Magistrate something nice for finding these," I agreed. "And you're sure you don't want to come?"

Meimei bobbed her head, her eyes gleaming. "Father is coming around again. We're going to be adding to the archives, the most any Hong has done in over a hundred years, if the records are right!" The genuine joy and excitement in her voice from actually getting to contribute to the scrolls she had once read obsessively was rather cute.

She was already off, talking about how the Lowly Spiritual Herbs seemed to accelerate the effects of other medicines, or at least the young shoots did. The older ones seemed to increase potency.

I listened as we ate, but it was rather clear I would need to do a lot more reading on how the human body worked.

I just let her talk, listening and occasionally asking questions on what she had found.

But eventually we lapsed into silence. At some point, she had climbed into my lap and now stared out over the property.

"You're going to be going soon?" she asked me.

"Yeah. That crystal is starting to look a bit sketchier, so we'll have to go see if it can be fixed." I hadn't wanted to go to Pale Moon Lake City *quite* yet . . . but it was looking like I had to. A sudden downturn in the crystal's condition was forcing my hand. "I'll see if I can dry out some of the rice with Qi, then head out after checking in with the Magistrate."

She nodded.

"If you do end up going and checking the tournament out while you're down there, give everyone my love," she stated.

Ha. I had been considering it. I still didn't particularly want to go and see a place in full "cultivator mode," but . . . well, my friends were there. The least I could do was check it out.

"So go and have a nice trip down to Pale Moon Lake City. Your lady wife shall hold the home while you're gone," she said haughtily before looking up and giving me a cheeky grin.

I laughed. "Well, would my lady wife do me the honour of concluding the day by catching frogs with me?" I asked.

Meimei broke down into giggles, then stood, hiking up her skirt.

We got muddy. We got wet. We got into a splashing war as we chased down the croaking amphibians, seeing who could catch the fattest and dumbest-looking frog.

Growing old is mandatory. Growing *up* is optional.

And I totally won, by the way. My frog was bigger, and I had the recording crystal picture to prove it.

↔

It started out as a lovely day. His wife had woken him up with a song he hadn't heard in years, the piece requiring more dexterity than she could usually manage. Her serenade had filled the hall, her fingers working with regained grace that was still improving day by day.

He purposefully stayed quiet for a while so he could listen, silently thanking little Meiling for her gift.

Then he was brought a letter from his son, who was in Pale Moon Lake City, studying for his civil service exams. It had been two years already since he had sent his son to learn, and he and his wife had a wonderful time together as he read the words of their dutiful son aloud. His son spoke on his education and his adventures in the capital. His wife rolled her eyes at his dreamy recounting of some noble girl.

"Takes after his father," his lady jabbed good-naturedly.

It was a simple, mundane letter, but it was good to hear from him again. Hopefully, they would see him again soon, before he received his first position. He wished for his son to succeed on his own merits, but just in case, something had been arranged.

He was quite energetic as he did his sword forms that day. The blade always felt awkward and heavy in his hand, yet the guards always looked on in admiration. Not that they knew much about swordplay either. They worked with spears and bows, but the sword was part of the image, so he diligently practised with it. He would never be good, but it was expected he could at least give a show of knowing what he was doing.

It also helped keep his body in good condition. If he wasn't careful, he would get fat, and that was *certainly* not part of his image. So he ran a few laps, just in case he had to flee from somebody or something. His stamina was quite good, if he did say so himself.

He cleansed his body afterwards. A perk of being the Magistrate was not having to gather the water like he used to. Then the servants brought him and his wife a fine meal.

The next task was organising the men for the time of the harvest. Another year's end was only a few months away.

That was then when things took a slight downturn. The cultivator arrived, with an absolute monstrosity of a cart. An entire team of oxen would be required to pull it, such was its size. It was a fortress on wheels!

The man was all smiles as he politely requested an audience and brought to the Magistrate several bales of rice, so that the Lord Magistrate could appraise them as he had promised.

The Lord Magistrate stared at what was before him. He picked up a grain. He rolled it in between his fingers. He used the viewing glass to look at it in exacting detail. There was a slight pearlescence to it. Under the scope of the viewing glass, it looked like a gemstone, polished to a sheen and reflecting some of the light.

The sight was astounding. The slight sweet scent, even dried like this, was mouthwatering.

This was not silver-grade rice. No, it went beyond that into something else entirely.

He carefully put the grain down, his face schooled into a mask of calm. It was nearly twice the size of the grain from last year, though slightly shorter and wider.

"I must apologise, but Verdant Hill cannot afford rice of this quality," he finally said to the cultivator.

Rou Jin frowned. "Well . . . *that's* inconvenient. It's really that much better?"

"It is. We simply can't afford rice of this quality. Even accounting for the mistake last year . . . there aren't enough favours in this world this Magistrate can give you to make up the difference," The Lord Magistrate said.

Jin scratched his chin.

"Well, if it's *that* much more, then I won't burden you with it. Pale Moon Lake or the Azure Jade Trading Company it is, then," Rou Jin said with a shrug. "Thanks for checking it out for me."

His smile appeared quite genuine.

"Thank you again, for everything. Especially the tomatoes. Hopefully I've repaid you enough. And Meimei sends her love, Lady Wu," the cultivator continued. The Lord Magistrate's wife smiled and waved at the man.

"Have a good day, my dear," she said with a soft smile. The cultivator nodded, then exited the room.

Leaving behind eight bags of gold-grade rice. As well as an assortment of fruits, vegetables, and more Seven Fragrance Jewel herbs.

The Lord Magistrate slumped in his seat and pinched his nose.

How absolutely reasonable and unreasonable at the same time.

This was almost as bad as the reports from the Gutter of a Chicken Demon going around taking down sheep rustlers. He thought Bi De had returned to his home; why were there still reports of a Chicken Demon?

There was a rustling as his wife got out a peach. Its aroma was heady, filling the room with a seductive scent.

She held the juicy, glistening, tempting fruit of a demon out to him.

He grabbed it and took a bite.

It was the best peach he had ever had.

↔

I sighed as I looked at my rice. Well, it kind of sucked that I couldn't sell things here. It looked like I was going to be heading to Pale Moon Lake City sooner rather than later.

But . . . well, something good can come of this too, I guess. I had been waffling about actually going and seeing the tournament. I guess this was the kick in the pants to get me heading south.

Well, I guess that was it then. To Pale Moon Lake City . . . and maybe to the tournament. I wondered how my friends were doing—hells, they must have already been in the city by now!

CHAPTER 2

THE GREAT LAKE

The chill from Cloudrest Ridge seeped into Gou Ren's bones as he trudged towards its peak. His boots crunched slightly in the fine powder that lay atop it even in the middle of summer. Gou Ren really didn't know why anybody called this massive thing a hill. Maybe it was the shape, a gentle dome that had been easy to ascend, save for its height.

"And here we are!" his brother, Yun Ren, declared as they stopped ascending and the entire thing levelled out.

"Whoa . . ." Gou Ren muttered, staring out at the absolutely enormous lake that stretched out before them before disappearing into the horizon on either side.

He had seen the images, of course, but it was so *different* in person.

"Big!" Tigu agreed, hopping up so she could sit on his shoulders and get a better view. Her legs dangled on either side of Gou Ren's head.

The sun made the fields shine and shimmer in verdant hues, while the enormous lake reflected the light like a giant mirror; a sun was high above, and a sun was captured in its depths. Ships plied the waters, their little dots concentrated around Pale Moon Lake City's harbor.

"Your images almost do it justice," Xiulan said, her breath frosting in front of her. Yun Ren, who was smiling down at the scene, whipped around, his face a mixture of shock and offence . . . before he saw the little smile on Xiulan's face and settled for glaring at her.

Gou Ren smirked. His older brother was still having a bit of trouble adjusting to Xiulan's newfound mischievous streak.

"But you are correct. The view is spectacular, Yun Ren. Thank you for leading us in this direction," Xiulan stated, as she gazed upon the lake. "I would like to see it from the back of Wa Shi."

Yun Ren nodded vigorously. "Imagine the view!" he agreed.

Gou Ren looked back down, then prodded Tigu off his shoulders as he left the two of them to wax poetic about the scenery.

The trip had been pretty uneventful so far as they ran down from the north. It was still so weird that he could run this fast, but other than the speed nothing about the trip had been exciting. It felt like they were just on a hunting trip back home with the addition of an overly excitable sibling tagging along. Tigu would often shoot off to investigate something or go to pluck a medicinal herb Ri Zu had shown her. Her pack was getting steadily heavier with her findings, much to Ri Zu's amusement.

Their diversions were either that, or them stopping at some manner of waterfall so Yun Ren could record images. In the evenings, they camped under the stars and swapped stories over the fire.

Mostly, the stories were his brother complaining about a fox Spirit Beast. Gou Ren wanted to meet him. Anything that could annoy his brother so much should receive his warmest regards.

Each day they awoke with the sun and set off for another day of running—though most mornings he had to pry his brother and Tigu off him. People using him as a source of warmth never changed, though it was a little awkward waking up to Tigu sprawled across his chest. She acted a lot like the kids in the village when she was sleepy, so it was rather easy to put her into that category.

He was getting used to it.

Their route steadily took them southeast. While they traveled, Gou Ren could feel something change in his bones. He could taste it in the air. The sun felt slightly different on his skin. He was the farthest south he had ever been in his life, and the thought of seeing the city filled him with excitement.

He ducked a second before something whistled over his head, barely dodging the snowball Tigu had thrown at him—only to get pelted by a much smaller snowball a second later.

Tigu laughed, her hands on her hips, while Ri Zu from her perch on Tigu's head tossed another tiny snowball up and down in her paw.

They were all rather wet when they finally arrived on the main road, skidding down from the mountain to join the masses of people flowing along the main highway into Pale Moon Lake City. The road was twice the size of the one they had built back home, and worn from the thousands who traversed it. Gou Ren's head craned around as he took in the veritable river of humanity. There were even designated sections for people, and others for carts, organising what should have been absolute chaos. The left side of the road was traffic heading towards the city, while the right was moving away.

They entered the gates. The guards inspected them for a brief moment but otherwise did not make any moves from their posts. Yun Ren waved to one in particular, who hesitantly waved back.

"Nice guy! Gave me directions when I came here the first time!" he shouted to the others over the din.

Xiulan had apparently not been here too many times, so Yun Ren led the way, walking with purpose, while they all followed. The city didn't exactly smell pleasant, and his nose wrinkled as he followed after his brother.

"Pale Moon Lake City is the mortal capital of the Azure Hills. However, Grass Sea City is the heart of cultivators' affairs," she had explained to him when he'd asked about it before.

The city itself was a teeming mass of shouting and food stalls, of hundreds—no, thousands—of workers. Fishermen, street sweepers, butchers, and shopkeepers, all going about their business and talking over each other. He felt himself slowing as he took it all in.

Gou Ren was startled out of his country-boy gaping by a hand clapping gently on his shoulder. He blushed at Xiulan's amused smile, and she pushed him along, guiding him back onto the path behind his brother. Gou Ren tried to pay attention after that, but Tigu didn't bother. She simply held on to the end of Xiulan's sleeve as they walked, her eyes wide and her head swivelling back and forth to take in the city. She dodged easily around the press of bodies but still kept her hand on Xiulan as they pushed through the crowd.

There was a little black head peeking out of the back of Tigu's shirt—Ri Zu sniffed rapidly at the city's air, her eyes equally excited.

Gou Ren shook his head and tried to ignore some of the more enticing sights. Luckily, it didn't take them too long to push through the crowd.

His brother was walking with confidence as they approached the rich part of the city. The streets here were pristine, well cleaned, and wide, as the buildings increased in size and height.

I'm definitely going to build one of those, he thought as he stared at the multilayered tower. It just looked so *cool.*

Eventually, they came to a walled compound, with two guards standing at the entrance. The walls were high and filled with detailed carvings of crystals and chunks of glittering rock.

Yun Ren walked directly towards one of the guards, who seemed to recognise him—and then the man suddenly winced as something started buzzing rapidly underneath his shirt. He tapped it rapidly, and it stopped.

"Here to see Miss Biyu again, Master Yun Ren?" the guard asked.

"You got it! How ya been, Maoli?" his brother said genially, and the guard gave a tentative smile in response. The other guard just looked a bit shocked as Yun clasped the guard's arm in greeting.

"You brought some friends along this time? You just need to sign in; the Masters and Miss Biyu have given you leave to enter the compound." The guard looked up at them all—though when his eyes landed on Xiulan, he froze, his mouth dropping open.

Xiulan's smile turned slightly brittle.

Gou Ren stepped into the man's field of view, causing him to start in surprise. He then shook his head, his face still crimson. Maoli coughed before pulling out a ledger.

They signed their names and walked into the compound. Gou Ren ignored Xiulan ruffling his hair, the woman smiling brightly at him.

They entered the courtyard. It was incredibly beautiful, filled with fragrant trees and pristine benches, and was surrounded by a two-story building with green roof tiles and multiple doors. A few people in thick cloaks with an odd design were milling about, sitting around, and talking, with their odd masks hanging down over their chests.

"You know where she lives?" Gou Ren asked.

His brother nodded and scratched his cheek. "Ah . . . yeah, I helped her move in. She used to live in a different compound, but she impressed some of the crystal masters, so she got a bigger one."

Gou Ren glanced up at the building, and then around at the number of people in it. It was interesting. He didn't know if he would ever want to live in this strange building, but the idea was neat.

His brother walked over to one of the ground-floor doors when they got inside and knocked on it loudly.

There was a muffled squeak, and some shuffling a moment later.

A girl with fluffy, messy brown hair peeked around the slightly open doorframe, like she had just pulled the thick hood and goggles from her head.

"Who . . . ?" she asked, and then her eyes widened further.

"Hey, Biyu," Yun Ren said with a smile. There was none of the normal exaggerated casualness like when he tried to talk to the girls in Verdant Hill. Instead, he just looked happy to see her.

The door opened fully. "Yun!" Biyu chirped out while beaming at Yun Ren. Her eyes darted over Yun Ren, then settled on the crystal around his neck.

"It still works?" she asked eagerly.

"Like a dream," Yun Ren replied.

The girl let out a happy sound. "I can't wait to take a look at it, make sure everything still functions the way it's supposed—actually, never mind, you have to see this!" she said eagerly, grabbing Yun Ren's arm and pulling him into the house . . . which left the rest of them out on the step.

Gou Ren turned to Xiulan and Tigu, who shrugged. After a moment, they followed in after them.

Inside, it was a small house that was *way* more decorated than Gou Ren was expecting. There were potted plants and bright paint on the wall in the entryway and kitchen—as well as what looked like posters for various plays. Gou Ren smirked when he saw one for the Demon-Slaying Orchid displayed prominently. An open door led to a bedroom that had a plush-looking bed and a line of dolls on shelves attached to the walls. But the biggest place by far was a larger area that was fully dedicated to what looked to be a workshop. There were chisels and files neatly organised on the desk, along with glass lenses. Tigu perked up as she saw the carving tools.

"I was working on this! The Masters just said I could do whatever I wanted, so look! The Crystal Pane Mark Two!" Biyu rattled off, as she showed Yun Ren a crystal that looked a lot like his own, though this one had a slight circular protrusion on the front. His brother's eyes were intent as he picked it up.

"Yeah, it's a bit heftier, but . . . oh, hey, that's interesting. It's like a focusing lens! It zooms in!" his brother exclaimed as the protrusion on the front seemed to twist.

Biyu puffed out her chest with pride. "It took me a while, but I got it! Now I want to see what images you've taken with the other one!"

His brother grinned, clearly about to project some images.

Gou Ren rolled his eyes, then coughed—both his brother and his "friend" jumped at the noise, shoving away from each other and blushing.

"I-I-I-I'm s-sorry, hon-honoured guests!" Biyu stuttered out, her face flushed as she realised what she had done. "This one is Biyu—just Biyu! Please partake of my hospitality, limited though it may be!"

"Gou Ren. This fool's brother." He introduced himself, bowing in greeting and smiling. "Nice to meet the girl he wouldn't shut up about."

Both of them flushed at that. Biyu glanced at Yun Ren with affection as his brother studiously looked away.

"Rou Tigu!" Tigu said, before going back to examining the tiny chisels and files as well as the minute crystal shavings. "Oho? You're quite skilled! We must trade pointers on carving, Just Biyu!"

"And I am Cai Xiulan," the woman introduced herself.

Biyu paused at Xiulan's introduction.

"Like . . . the Demon-Slaying Orchid?" she asked. Xiulan's lips quirked into a smile. She was still wearing the rough clothes from the farm and didn't look like any of the portraits of her.

"Yes," Xiulan replied.

"Okay, it's a very pretty name . . . and it's nice to meet you all!" Biyu smiled nervously, obviously still a bit embarrassed at completely disregarding them at first. Now acting as a much better host, she got them all seated at the table. It was a bit difficult finding room for them all, and getting the tea ready in the cramped space, but Biyu didn't seem to mind the number of people in the house. "So!" Gou Ren asked. "How did . . . *this* happen."

Biyu smiled. "After he bought his recording crystal, he came back the next day to show me all the images he took. He bought me a meal to thank me for my work. It gave me a few more ideas, so I took them to Master Fang! He was already quite happy with my progress, so . . . Well, he said I should live in the main compound. So Yun helped me move everything, and then we went out for dinner again . . ."

"Love at first sight?" Gou Ren ribbed—and both of them immediately blushed again.

"For all of his complaints about Senior Sister, Yun Ren seems to be quite the romantic as well," Xiulan mused.

"*Shaddup*," Yun Ren grunted, glaring at both of them, while Biyu just fiddled with the hem of her cloak.

Yun sat up and clapped his hands. "But yeah, stuff aside, I actually wanted to see if you could help us, Biyu. My friend has a crystal, but it's a bit . . . broken?"

The red on her cheeks faded, and Biyu sat up straighter.

The moment the image of the crystal formed on the wall, her eyes sharpened, gaining an almost predatory look of intent.

"That is beyond me. It's a wonder it hasn't exploded already," she muttered, looking closely at the warped crystal. "Old, too. See those facets? We call that the Ancestors' Style. We don't really use it anymore. It's for crystals a lot more powerful than what we normally get. And . . . well, it's impractical doing facets that way. Even the most minute of shakes in your hand could disrupt the formation you're imposing on it. Master Fang has cut a crystal in that style, and it took him ten years! He said I *might* be able to do one, after looking at my work, but . . ." She shrugged.

Yun Ren hummed as he lazed on the couch, his knees knocking against Gou Ren's just as they usually did. "Fair enough. Do you know anybody else who could help us?" he asked.

Biyu nodded. "I can talk to Master Fang directly. He's the only one here right now, on account of the tournament, so if he can't help you . . ." she said apologetically. "He'd want to examine it, if nothing else. And he might let me watch him really work." Her eyes shone at that, the same glint Yun got when he was recording, or that Meimei did when talking about medicine.

Gou Ren understood why his brother liked her.

"Thanks, Biyu. Jin and Bi De are good friends, you know? Just thought I'd ask for them," Yun Ren said.

The woman nodded, seriously, before seeming to remember that she was their host again. "Ah! Can I treat you to a meal? I'd like to get to know all of you better!"

"Sounds great!" Gou Ren cheered.

Free food? Hells yeah.

CHAPTER 3

SO CLOSE, YET SO FAR

In the end, Biyu had insisted on guiding them around the city. She was a bit over-eager and acted like she was full of confidence . . . but she kept glancing back at them like she didn't *quite* know what to do.

Gou Ren guessed she had never really played guide for so many people before.

"The city is arranged like the spokes of a wheel, so if you ever get lost, just walk to one of the main streets and go from there," she explained as they strolled through the wealthier part of the city. "You don't go through any alleys unless you were born in that ward, or if you have a death wish, since the gangs are a bit bad in some parts. But that's probably not a problem for any of you guys . . ." She trailed off. She hadn't actually directly brought up the fact that any of them were cultivators yet. Gou Ren did catch a muttered "Didn't you say she was a cat?" from Biyu to Yun Ren, but she seemed to be doing her best not to pry.

"But . . . well, those Plum Blossom guys are supposed to be taking over? Nobody really knows much about them, other than that they're co-opting or driving out every other gang," she mused. "I don't really keep up with any of that beyond what I hear everyone else saying, since I'm too busy. I still haven't seen that production by the Jade Dragon Troupe of the Demon-Slaying Orchid," she said, now grumbling to herself.

"Oh? I saw the posters in your home. You enjoy such plays?" Xiulan asked.

Biyu nodded. "I worked on some of the crystals they're using! I really want to see how they work in the actual show!" she said, her eyes shining.

Gou Ren snorted with amusement, and Biyu flushed. "You two are *exactly* alike," he said with a grin, shoving at his brother.

"Indeed, they are quite similar," Xiulan stated, amused.

Biyu tilted her face down and started playing with a strand of her hair.

"So, how long are you all going to be in Pale Moon Lake City? I know the tournament is soon . . ." Biyu asked after recovering her composure.

"We were planning to stay a single night, after asking about the crystal for Master Jin," Xiulan answered for them. "We must arrive at the Dueling Peaks soon."

Biyu considered that. She glanced at one of the large, lavish buildings she was heading towards, then looked back to Yun Ren. Her eyes firmed and she seemed to come to a decision.

"Then . . . I have *just* the place to eat!" she said with a little smile. "Well, if you like the kind of stuff Yun likes, at least! It will really give you a taste of the city!"

So they passed by the high-end establishments, restaurants that looked more like mansions than places where food could be served, and continued on past the wealthy districts, and back into the outer city.

He eyed the heavy crowds, but for the most part as soon as people noticed their party, they moved out of the way—they moved especially quickly after a single glance at the thick cloak and gloves Biyu was still wearing, even in the summer heat. Even the guards nodded respectfully when she passed. It was a bit weird, if Gou Ren was honest. People bowing to you just because of who you worked for. Biyu didn't seem to notice, though.

They had headed right for the docks, and in particular, a stand run by an old man who greeted Biyu like an old friend.

"This place is really good," Yun Ren said. "My first time in the city, we went to one of the more expensive places, but it was pretty meh. The prices were obscene!"

"I would like to try one of those more expensive places at least once, just to see what they're like, but I'm sure this is good too. Is she okay taking us around like this?" Gou Ren asked. "She seems a bit . . . flustered."

His brother shrugged. "She's spent most of her life studying. She likes it. But not too many friends, yeah? She wanted to make a good impression, and ain't too sure how to, I think." Gou Ren nodded. "You like her, though?" Yun Ren suddenly asked.

"Yeah, she's nice. Mom and Dad will like her too," Gou Ren replied, and he meant it. She seemed like the kind of girl their mother would like. Driven and hardworking.

Yun Ren rolled his eyes. "Yeah, yeah, we both know what Mom thinks every gal should be like. I'll go help her get the stuff over."

They didn't sit near the stall. Biyu led them a bit farther on, to a set of tables near a wall that looked out over the water, setting down several plates.

"This is a Pale Moon Lake specialty!" Biyu said, putting down the plate.

"It's green," Gou Ren commented, cocking his head to the side as the rest of the table leaned in to look at the dish with interest.

"Yup! They use a kind of watergrass that grows in the lake to make the noodles that colour!" Biyu informed them.

Gou Ren shrugged, then took a bite. It was certainly an interesting flavour. Slightly sour, slightly spicy from black pepper. The meat was a freshwater crab that was quite a bit larger than he'd been expecting, thick pieces of claw and leg meat peppered with vegetables.

Xiulan had a contemplative look on her face as she chewed. "One for Wa Shi, I think," she whispered, and Gou Ren nodded. He'd have to come back this way, or see if he could get some of the grass for the greedy fish. "Thank you for taking us to this place, Biyu."

The woman blushed and scratched at the back of her head, obviously pleased by the appreciation.

They were seated near the docks, on a raised section that looked out into the lake. It was a bit quieter and less crowded here, but below them was still a whirlwind of activity. The ships were huge—massive barges laden down with ores, or smaller boats coming in with loads of fish. It was a hustle and bustle that Gou Ren wasn't quite sure he liked. Tigu seemed to be twitching slightly as she tried to take in everything going on at once.

There was a bit of a commotion, so Gou Ren glanced down at the docks, where a bunch of men were chasing an otter that had stolen a fish. Gou Ren chuckled at the scene, then looked up at the seemingly endless blue expanse that took up the entire horizon.

"I grew up in this ward," Biyu said wistfully as she stared out over the lake. "Father owned his own boat, and Mother had a shop. I like just coming down here sometimes. It's a bit hard to visit them now that they're on the north end of the lake. Taking a weeklong boat ride up there isn't my idea of fun, but it's better than a three-week walk."

They sat together in companionable silence as the breeze flowed over them.

"Thanks for letting me show you around," Biyu said, scratching her cheek absent-mindedly. She looked a bit awkward still, but she now had a happy smile on her face.

"We shall be relying on your knowledge more, if you would allow us, Biyu," Xiulan replied quietly. "I would like to examine the archives of the city, though I understand one needs some manner of documentation?"

Biyu nodded. "We can use mine if you want," she offered.

"I wish to see the chisels of this place, and to witness the crystal carvers!" Tigu declared.

'And we shall require knowledge of the herb merchants,' a little voice squeaked, as Ri Zu crawled out from her position on Tigu's back and bowed. *'Forgive Ri Zu for not introducing herself earlier.'*

Biyu's owlish eyes widened, and they flicked to Yun Ren before turning back to Ri Zu. "Nice to . . . meet you?" she asked.

The rat nodded, as Biyu stared for a moment longer before recomposing herself.

"Not that weird," she whispered to herself. "Like Master Fang's monkey, but smarter!" She perked up again. "So! Let's go and see what else the city has to offer!"

↔

Lu Ri, Senior Disciple of the Cloudy Sword Sect, was not a happy man. In fact, he was a rather annoyed man. His informant's messages about the village in the north had been a bit garbled, and had to be re-sent multiple times, but *eventually* he had the picture. The Magistrate of Verdant Hill had been quite reluctant to speak of Jin Rou and had seemed outright confused about the name. But he did know *something* about him.

Jin Rou had been there. Lu Ri's own investigation had confirmed his presence in Verdant Hill; the annoying slug of a cultivator of the Shrouded Mountain Sect had been beaten by him. But had he truly left? There were still rumours coming from the north regarding goods of superlative quality. Everybody else Lu Ri's man had interviewed said that Jin Rou had moved on—that there was another cultivator called "Sister Medical Fairy" who lived in the north.

The question was whether Jin Rou had stayed.

How vexing. Lu Ri had two choices: visit this Sister Medical Fairy in the north and see if she had any more clues . . . or try his luck at the Dueling Peaks Tournament, where every cultivator in the province would be. And possibly where Jin Rou was heading to, if he had left the north.

North or west? It was a decision he had to make, yet both decisions would take time. If he went north, he could possibly miss the tournament. If he went to the tournament, there was the chance that Jin Rou wasn't there at all.

Lu Ri sighed.

This required tea and pastries with the wonderful syrup to *truly* make the correct choice. So he went to his preferred establishment and ordered his treat.

Instead, he was treated to the master of the establishment coming out and bowing deeply to him, all while sweating heavily.

"My deepest apologies, Master Cultivator. The last of the syrup was . . . recently purchased. There is nothing that we can do at this time, other than offer our most sincere regrets that we cannot serve you."

The blow was a minor one, yet it still hurt.

Ah, it was always a shame when something finite came to an end.

He took a deep, soothing breath as the sensor stone rattled so much it nearly cracked.

It was not the man's fault.

So he simply had tea that day. He had tea, as he pondered his choices.

□

"And then . . . like this," Biyu said, looking through the lens at the crystal. Her fingers barely moved as she carved off tiny portions. Tigu was watching her intently, her eyes focused, considering this new way of carving.

"I see! A formation within carvings, how interesting!" Tigu declared.

Yun Ren smiled at the scene. Tigu had on Biyu's goggles and it looked rather amusing, as his . . . well, his *friend* coached the cat through the very basics of crystal carving.

She was both patient and kind. His cheeks heated up a bit.

She had gotten more comfortable as the day went on, pointing out the little things in the city. From the slightly different clothing styles from each ward, to the way the buildings were built, to the story about the rather vicious gang feud that happened when she was little that set most of the slums on fire.

Or her complaints about how the current Lord Magistrate rarely addressed any real problems in the city.

Yun Ren got a bit of a new appreciation for the Patriarch of Verdant Hill. He couldn't imagine the Lord Magistrate letting any of that shit slide.

His brother was yawning, slumped against the side of the couch. He looked exhausted. Xiulan, on the other hand, was eagerly reading the scroll she'd copied from the archives with Ri Zu on her shoulder—the one Meimei had found all those years ago.

His brother yawned again. "We should prolly go," Gou Ren muttered. "Got a long run tomorrow."

Xiulan paused in her reading and looked out the window.

"Indeed. I thank you for your hospitality, Biyu," Xiulan said courteously.

Everybody else started packing up, but Yun Ren himself had something to do.

"I'll catch up in a sec, yeah?" Yun Ren told them. His brother nodded. "We're going to the inn Biyu told us was good."

They waved their goodbyes, but for the moment, Yun Ren stayed.

Biyu collapsed onto the couch.

"Too much!" she moaned. "I guided the Demon-Slaying Orchid around the city! Why didn't you tell me she was your friend! You just called her Lanlan!" she grumbled into the cushion.

Yun Ren laughed as he picked up her legs and sat on the couch, rubbing some of the knots out.

"She doesn't like too much attention. I think she was happy you didn't pry."

"She's even more beautiful than the plays say she is. Unfair," Biyu muttered petulantly.

"One of the prettiest girls I ever met," Yun Ren agreed. "About as pretty as you."

Biyu whined into the cushion. "Like she'd put up with you anyway, ass," Biyu jabbed.

Yun laughed as they sat together.

"I got somethin' for ya. A friend gave it to me, said I should give it to you. I don't know what it is, but . . ."

Biyu perked up as he pulled open his pack, revealing the crystal.

Her eyes widened to comical proportions.

"Oh," she squeaked out. "A storage crystal."

"Is it something good?" he asked. Wide eyes turned to Yun Ren.

"These don't exist in the Azure Hills. There isn't enough Qi to form a spatial crystal!" Her voice was slightly faint.

"Spatial crystal? That certainly sounds impressive."

"They're used to make spatial rings! It's been centuries since there's been even *fragments* for us to look at!"

"Cool. Looking forward to seeing what you do with it!"

Yun Ren rose and sauntered off, leaving Biyu to stare uncomprehendingly at what he had just left in her house.

"Yun!" she shouted after him. "Yun, you can't just—I can't accept—"

"See ya later, Little Owl!" he called instead, still facing away so she couldn't see the blush on his face.

"*Thank you!*" she shouted out.

He raised his arm, waving her goodbye.

Yun Ren was in a good mood as he wandered the streets, skipping and humming to himself, but then something caught his interest.

He hopped up onto the roof next to his brother. Gou Ren turned to him with a raised eyebrow.

"Good night?" he asked.

"Yup!" Yun Ren said cheerily. "But what about you? I thought you were tired," he asked his brother.

Gou Ren shrugged, then tilted his piece of paper towards him. A sketch of the city.

"Got stuck in my head. Wanted to draw a bit more before we left." Gou Ren's brush absently tapped the image of a tower. One he looked like he was in the process of redesigning.

Yun Ren smiled at his brother.

"Gonna need to be better at math if you're going for architecture," Yun Ren ribbed.

His brother didn't rise to the bait, simply pondering things.

Ah, he's serious, then.

"I'll take a couple images for ya. Just point out which ones you want, yeah?" Yun Ren said.

His brother smiled at him, eyes lighting up.

CHAPTER 4

THE CURSE OF NOODLE SHOPS

The Grass Sea. It had taken another week to get to it from Pale Moon Lake City, and now it stretched out before them even as their stride ate the li before them.

Tigu knew vaguely what the "sea" was, despite never having seen anything like it. She just *knew*. Images flashed in her head of an endless expanse of water, and of her own Master's descriptions. She knew that Pale Moon Lake was close, but compared to what she knew of the ocean, it was but a drop of water.

If that was the case, then the Grass Sea was aptly named. The forests abruptly thinned, the hills grew shorter and fatter, and all that was left was a vast, green expanse. The breeze smelled vaguely sweet from the thousands of meadow flowers that poked up, and the sun shone intently on their backs, much stronger than it was back home. There were barely any rocks, making the hills look far smoother than they should be.

Blue sky and green grass, as far as the eye could see. It was a striking sight, and Disciple Yun Ren's crystal chimed repeatedly while he captured the view. They had been running for most of the day now, across the hills instead of braving the congested road. Tigu had expected the number of people to decrease as they left the city, not *increase*. Every village they passed was at a minimum twice the size of Hong Yaowu, while the towns were larger and denser than Verdant Hill!

Truly, there were a great many people in this world!

With a hop, she alighted on Disciple Gou Ren's pack so she could get a better view, squinting at the horizon and the endless grass fields.

"It goes on forever. Is it all like this?" Tigu asked the Blade of Grass as she flopped backwards, dangling on Gou Ren's back. Disciple Gou Ren made a noise of irritation as her legs fixed around his neck, and Ri Zu squeaked with outrage when she nearly fell out of Tigu's shirt.

Xiulan was startled out of her contemplation at the question, having been deep in thought. While they'd gotten steadily closer to their goal, she had grown quieter. Not morose, but she had been thinking about something.

Yet she did not seem overly concerned, and now her face brightened slightly, shaking her head as Tigu dangled upside down.

"Not all, Tigu," she explained. "Although most of the grass is like this, there are different kinds of grass. The grass near the Misty Lake can grow to be twice as tall as a man. The Bloodgrass of the Bonepile is as scarlet as its namesake, and Wrecker Thicket is full of blades as wide as a man's wrist and as sharp as a knife."

Tigu listened intently, her mind conjuring all sorts of interesting images. Gou Ren made another noise of irritation, then grabbed her legs and flipped her so she was stomach down on his shoulder like a bag of rice.

"Will you show us one day?" Tigu asked, completely unbothered by the rough handling.

Xiulan nodded firmly. "Of course. We shall travel these lands if you wish it, as honoured guests and friends of the Verdant Blade Sect!" she declared, before her gaze seemed to wander off. "Though . . . I am a bit concerned about how my Sect Elders shall act. I'm sure it is nothing to fear, but I do not wish for Master Jin's generosity to be tested, should they get . . . ideas about our relationship," she said, then let out a sigh.

Tigu didn't know how to respond to that. It was outside her experiences, but the thought of some man trying to pressure her Master and Mistress made her uneasy.

"But enough ill thoughts. I shall speak with them and make sure nothing like that happens," Xiulan assured her.

Tigu nodded. If the Blade of Grass said she would do this, then she would do this! "Tell us about the tournament!" Tigu asked, putting the other conversation out of her mind.

Xiulan nodded. "The Dueling Peaks Tournament begins in the Earthly Arena, the largest arena in the Azure Hills, where they conduct the opening ceremony and the judgement. Each cultivator there declares their Sect and places their hands upon the Heavenly Ascension Stone, which reveals the cultivator's cultivation level to all present. Then the tournament bouts begin. It is single elimination, with a loss removing the competitor from the tournament. In each round, the arena is raised one level, using the power of the Masters and the strength of those who have lost."

Gou Ren paused. "Wait, they *pull it up the mountain*?" he asked, incredulous. "With people inside it?"

"Yes. Each round raises the arena closer to the heavens, until at the last, the tournament sits atop the Dueling Peaks. It's . . . not particularly fun to be a part of the pulley team. Having to lift the entire arena, as well as a hundred thousand people, is a bit difficult," Xiulan confessed. "Though I suppose it is good strength training? They used to use artifacts, but those broke around two thousand years ago, so it is with strength that the arena now rises!"

Tigu could see it. Standing atop a mountain, facing Xiulan . . . It sounded most enjoyable!

"Are there any limits? Like . . . strength limits, or age limits or something?" Yun Ren asked.

"The only limits are that one must actually be a cultivator and be born in the Azure Hills. Tournaments in other provinces may say that one must be of a certain cultivation level . . . but in truth the Azure Hills are too weak to put any such stipulation," Xiulan stated.

"What about the Hill of Torment?" Tigu asked.

"That is a separate event, after the first bouts. I do not believe I will be entering the hill this year. There would be nothing of value for me to find."

"Eh, really? But you said there were a bunch of monsters you could fight in there!"

"There are indeed; feral Spirit Beasts to fight, and ancient ruins to explore."

"I'm gonna enter that part!" Tigu stated with conviction.

Xiulan chuckled at her enthusiasm. "Well, I'll direct you to make the proper procedures. It's a bit confusing for newcomers. Let's have a meal in that town. It is the last stop before the Dueling Peaks. We should be able to see the tournament grounds soon."

Xiulan pointed at the dark spot on the horizon, and they adjusted their course, heading for the walls.

As they grew closer, Tigu could see the walls were roughly hewn of the same light grey stone that littered the ground back home. Most buildings around here were made of that stone, as there didn't seem to be too many trees. The guards at the gate—or *guard* to be exact—looked utterly bored and exhausted. He barely glanced at the four of them as they entered, studiously ignoring their existence.

The town itself was absolutely packed with people. Although there were obviously fewer people here than in Pale Moon Lake City, it was a denser, more crowded place. Tigu had abandoned her position on Gou Ren's back as they pushed their way through the crowd.

"Let's go there, I've had food from there before," the Blade of Grass stated, pointing to a noodle shop.

Tigu's head swivelled—and she immediately spotted something interesting. A man with a long blue spear upon his back talking to another woman, who wore a rather excessive amount of silk robes.

Other cultivators.

Tigu felt her blood pump faster as she recalled her Master's wisdom.

"Ha! We head towards an exciting place!" she cheered.

Xiulan paused, and turned back to Tigu. *"The noodle shop?"* she asked, baffled.

"Yeah! Our Master says that when cultivators gather at a restaurant, a fight or an altercation shall inevitably break out!" Tigu declared. "He said to dive behind the counter and watch!"

Xiulan chucked. "Come, now, I'm sure he meant that as a joke . . ." She trailed off, her brow furrowing. "Well, there was that time with the Young Mistress of Misty Lake, Xianghua, or there was also the time with that Young Master, and . . ."

The Blade of Grass paused. She opened her mouth and closed it again. She pondered for a moment more.

"*Huh*," she finally muttered, looking mildly concerned.

"So . . . are we still heading over there?" Disciple Gou Ren asked.

"It *should* be fine?" Disciple Xiulan responded, though she looked a bit less confident than she had before. "It doesn't happen *every* time."

They opened the door, and their party walked in. And indeed, as expected, it was full of cultivators! Tigu could feel their intent as they glanced at the newcomers. Their eyes ghosted over Tigu for the most part, lingered for a moment upon her Brother Disciples, before finally alighting on the Blade of Grass . . . and staying there. The jaw of one of the men dropped, and they began to mutter. Tigu could hear them remarking on her beauty and wondering who she was.

What an odd bunch! Tigu thought, amused.

Tigu's eyes flicked around excitedly as Xiulan and Yun Ren went to put in their orders. She saw a man who had a large hammer and a nice body, almost like her Master's!

There is Blue-Spear Guy! And that one has a rather pretty-looking hairpin! The craftsmanship is quite good! Gold, with small, translucent pieces of glass or rock forming the spaces in the wings—

"It is rude to stare," the woman scolded, her eyes narrow as she looked at Tigu. Her Qi swirled about her slightly.

Ah! She's right! It is rude to stare, my Master and Mistress taught me that! Tigu scolded herself for forgetting her lessons.

"Sorry!" Tigu apologised, just as her Master had instructed. "I was just admiring your hairpin! Wonderful craftsmanship!"

The other woman looked at her strangely, like she hadn't quite been expecting her response or the conversation to go that way.

"Well, I suppose even a yokel has some eye for quality," she muttered.

"This one is Rou Tigu! Who are you?" she offered politely.

The woman stared at her. "You're a strange one" was all she said before turning back around.

How rude!

Another man from a table nearby, slim and wearing a grey robe, snorted. "Look at this brat, staring at jewelry without a care in the world!" he chortled. "If you go into the tournament with that attitude, girl, you're going to get hurt."

He smirked. His green Qi coiled around him, and intent brushed up against her senses. It was an unpleasant, minor distraction.

Tigu cocked her head to the side. Her back twitched at the small amount of challenge in his tone, but she carefully put it off to the side, remembering her lessons.

"Thank you for the warning!" she allowed. "But I don't think I'm in any danger!" De-escalation! Exactly like she had been taught!

The man's eye twitched. Disciple Gou Ren snorted, and the woman let out a short, sharp laugh as well.

The Green Man's intent flared more as he stood.

Tigu's eyes narrowed. Oh! She was supposed to show her strength!

Tigu's own intent flared. Her Qi manifested in a shroud of blue power.

The room fell into silence. The Green Man's face went pure white, as blood drained from it. She could hear his heart suddenly hammering in his chest.

"See? I'm not in any danger at all!" she stated.

"Yes, miss, no danger at all," the man replied, then swallowed thickly.

Tigu nodded as he sat back down.

"Forgive my earlier rudeness, miss. My name is Yinxia Qiao," the woman with the hairpin said, turning around entirely to greet Tigu politely. She was sweating a bit for some reason.

"Nice to meet you," Tigu responded. "Say, do you come here often?"

"My Sect lies around these parts, yes," the woman answered immediately.

"Do you think we're gonna see any fights?" she asked hopefully.

The woman looked around at the suddenly subdued atmosphere.

"No, miss, I . . . do not believe so."

Tigu frowned. Was her Master wrong? She kind of wanted to see how these people fought . . .

But nothing happened. Everybody just . . . sat there.

"Did we miss something?" Yun Ren asked when he and Xiulan came back with the food.

CHAPTER 5

THE DUELING PEAKS

Boring!" Tigu muttered. "They were *boring*!"

Xiulan chuckled at her antics, amused the girl was still this upset even after leaving the noodle shop three hours prior. Xiulan was glad that their trip to the noodle bar had been uneventful. She had been a bit worried—hearing Master Jin's statement about restaurants and cultivators had shaken her. Through her own experience, it would seem that his words rang true. How many times had she seen a fight break out over something in a restaurant?

"Maybe next time don't scare 'em so bad," Junior Brother snarked. "Man looked like he was about to shit himself."

Xiulan had felt Tigu's intent often enough. The arrogant, furious gaze of an apex predator deciding you were prey combined with Tigu's own instincts. It was quite a bracing feeling.

It got the heart pumping pleasantly, and it injected just a bit of seriousness into their spars. Yet nothing came of it. Aside from the glances from the other patrons, they had been left alone to eat and no altercation had taken place.

This was much to Tigu's disappointment. The girl had been complaining as much as Gou Ren normally did, petulant and pouty that there had been no entertainment, uncaring or oblivious to the eyes that had followed them out. Xiulan would be concerned, normally. Insulting another cultivator was sure to create a grudge, but the man had no identifying markings on him and she didn't know his name, so he likely didn't have any Sect behind him, preventing him from retaliating.

At least the noodles had been as good as she remembered them from several years ago.

"Hey, is there a reason we're travelling with the crowd this time?" Yun Ren asked, glancing around at the throng of carts they were weaving through.

Xiulan smiled, checking the position of the sun. She knew *about* where they were, and the timing should be perfect.

"Some consideration for you, Junior Brother. We'll be leaving the road soon. At that hill there," she informed him.

Yun Ren's eyes sharpened. Intrigued by the cryptic answer, he obligingly followed after her.

They turned off the road where she said they would and trekked up the hill. Through their walk, the sky darkened, dyeing itself with the colours of sunset.

They crested the grassy hill and gazed upon the Dueling Peaks.

Two mountains stood tall and proud, jutting into the sky. Near mirrors of each other in height and width.

Perhaps once, long ago, it had been *one* mountain. Perhaps some ancient cultivator had cleaved it in two, yet there were no records of it. Just the two sheer faces pointing towards each other. Ropes spanned the gap, and from them hundreds of flags and pendants fluttered in the wind. They flew the symbols of the attending Sects and merchant trading companies, and the flags of the Crimson Phoenix Empire itself.

And on the ground filling the bottom of the gap in the two mountains was the Earthly Arena, silhouetted by the setting sun. This time of year it was framed perfectly between the twin peaks as the last golden rays disappeared behind the horizon. It cast the town and buildings and caravans that sprawled out from the base of the mountain in sharp relief. The grass below them, dyed orange and gold by the light, swayed in ripples as the wind blew, tousling their hair and soothing some of the fading sun's bite.

The most important cultural center for the cultivators of the Azure Hills. It was striking in its beauty, and even from this far away they could feel both the charged atmosphere and the Qi that saturated the earth—the most she had felt since leaving Fa Ram.

Xiulan had always enjoyed this view. She knew few who did not comment at least once upon the beauty of the sunset between the mountains. The Framed Sun Sect was even said to have based their cultivation style on this ancient mount and the way that it held the sun between the two peaks.

There was the chiming of a recording crystal. An awed squeak from Ri Zu. Tigu's eyes sparkled in the light, and Gou Ren just stared, his lips slowly forming into a smile.

"Thanks for the view, Lanlan," Yun Ren whispered.

After a little while, they descended into the town around the Dueling Peaks and went to their accommodations for the evening.

"Does your Sect own this place or somethin'?" Gou Ren asked, clearly trying not to gawk at the intricate architecture and carved reliefs that decorated the pillars outside. It was an opulent palace, in the middle of a small town.

There was gold and lacquered wood in abundance, and Gou Ren inspected one of the joint works with interest.

Xiulan shook her head, handing a jade slip with the symbol of her Sect on it to the clerk. The man bowed as he received it. His immaculate silk robes were unruffled, his sole job to greet incoming guests. The payment would be delivered from the Sect's accounts later, now that they were so close to the heartland. "We shall be meeting them on the morrow. The Young Mistress must be looking her best when she returns." She said the last part with exasperation, but in truth she was looking forward to a bath.

"Masters, Mistresses, if it pleases you, follow this servant," one of the attendants—a rather plain-looking woman with an impassive face—said, bowing in servitude. She held out an arm to direct them to the room Xiulan had booked. They were silent as ghosts, trained to be barely seen, and heard less.

Xiulan nodded along as she held a letter out to another servant: a message informing her father that she would be meeting him tomorrow.

It was rather amusing, how awkward her companions looked. Both of her Junior Brothers had their heads swivelling around, taking in the opulent building as they ascended the stairs. Gou Ren even thanked the female servant, which typically wasn't done in this sort of establishment. The woman appeared startled and raised her sleeves to cover her mouth, her face red.

Gou Ren didn't notice, already walking into the room with interest.

"We shall require no further attendance besides the food tonight," Xiulan instructed the woman, who jerked her eyes away from Junior Brother's behind, nodding rapidly.

"Do you not need the bath heated, Mistress?" the woman asked, and Xiulan shook her head.

"We shall do that ourselves."

The woman nodded, bowing to the will of her customer.

Xiulan examined the room. There were four large beds, a well-appointed common area, and a small balcony, able to be open to the night air but shielded from view. They had an adjoining room to bathe in, separated by a screen and stocked with some oils and soaps.

Soon enough, Xiulan was sighing in contentment. She had used Master Jin's technique to heat the bath with her Qi, and after a quick scrub-down with the heated water, she allowed Ri Zu to do her work. There was a slight tingling as the needles entered her back, followed by relief.

Ri Zu had learned from Senior Sister well, and she was having Tigu help manipulate Xiulan's body.

'Pull up, yes, like that!' Ri Zu instructed Tigu as the girl rolled Xiulan's ankle. *'Any spot that catches?'*

Tigu shook her head. "Everything moves perfectly!" she declared.

'Ri Zu was not expecting much change anyway. Master made sure of our bodies' conditions before we left!' the rat stated, before she gently removed the needles.

Xiulan settled into the bath, warmed through Qi, and let out another breath as Tigu leaned back against Xiulan's chest.

It was too bad they didn't have any of Master Jin's branches. She had surprisingly come to enjoy the feeling of them hitting her back, and they did wonders for circulation. Instead, she contented herself with looking up at the mountain; Tigu allowed Ri Zu to use her hand as a platform, the rat fastidiously scrubbing herself clean as she always did.

Xiulan sighed, then got out the scented oils, as well as the soaps, and began the process of cleaning her own hair. Tigu helped, but it was an involved process.

Back at her Sect, the maids helped her. At Fa Ram, Senior Sister had taken up that duty, and she was by far the most skilled. Tigu? Well, it got done eventually. Especially once Tigu started poking her in the side, chattering about how interesting the mountain looked. A far cry from the silent girls who had previously attended to the Young Mistress, speaking in whispers if they had to talk at all.

And Tigu took entirely too much delight in seeing if she could tickle her when she washed Xiulan's back.

She was also *considerably* less understanding when Xiulan pinned her down and exacted revenge.

Xiulan was still grinning at the pouting Tigu as they exited the bath, their hair still damp.

"Geez. You two splash out all the water?" Gou Ren demanded, turning around to glare at them before his eyes widened with shock. He coughed, looking away. "That robe is *way* too small for you," he grunted, his face a bit red.

Xiulan glanced down at her robe. Indeed, it was . . . but neither of the brothers were gazing at her as they once had.

She chuckled at Yun Ren, who was pointedly looking at his recording crystal. His eyes would twitch to the side occasionally, but they never strayed to her.

She pulled the robe closed a bit more, out of consideration.

"I require some assistance, Junior Brother," she asked, and held out a comb.

Gou Ren sighed, but obligingly got up.

"Seriously? First my brother, then my mom, then Meimei and Meihua . . ." he grumbled. "I never have any time for my own hair!"

His skilled hands worked through her locks, then Tigu's, and then, to his loud exasperation, Ri Zu's fur, before he could finally take his own bath, where she could hear him grumbling about the amount of water left.

His mood did improve after he had bathed, and the rest of his foul mood was mollified as Xiulan returned the favour for his hair.

They ate the meal the servants brought to them, talking and laughing together. The Xong brothers argued about something that wasn't important, but she took Gou Ren's side anyway.

That night, when they went to sleep . . . Tigu was once more her companion.

Xiulan yawned, and pulled the smaller girl close.

□

I hefted the last sack into the loaded cart.

"Everybody ready?" I asked. The rooster, the snake, and the rabbit all nodded.

I nodded back, then turned to the ones who would see us off to Pale Moon Lake City.

"Take care of Meimei for me, 'kay?" I joked to the lad. Little Xian nodded resolutely, while his sister rolled her eyes. Pops looked similarly amused.

Chunky chortled at his enthusiasm before nudging the boy. His eyes lit up, and they both dashed off.

"Got the list?" she asked, and I nodded, holding up our shopping list that was more the size of a scroll. "Then . . . have a good trip, my dear husband."

She smiled at me, and the whole world contracted to just her.

Our lips met in a goodbye kiss, and it wasn't . . . particularly chaste, judging by the way Pops coughed. We both stuck our tongues out at him, and he rolled his eyes in response.

"See you soon, Meimei," I told my wife.

"Come back safely, Jin," she whispered back.

I still had a silly little grin as I got behind the cart's bar and hefted.

Three hundred bags of Qi-dried rice. Twelve tons wasn't *too* bad, when you got down to it.

The cart rocked into motion as the disciples on top of the cart bowed to those they were leaving behind.

One foot in front of the other, to Pale Moon Lake.

Gotta find parts for a still, repair a crystal, and see what those guys who were looking for me were all about. The Magistrate said that their accents were from the south, so Pale Moon Lake City was probably the best place to start.

I was a bit nervous about it . . . but, well, the Lord Magistrate thought they were normal dudes, not cultivators. *If they were normal people, it might be because I forgot to pay a tax or something. Hopefully, anyway.*

CHAPTER 6

THE YOUNG MISTRESS

Xiulan's clothes shimmered in the light. Her skin was pale and flawless, like she hadn't been out in the sun the entire summer. Her lips were red and inviting. Her hair was braided immaculately, silky locks that otherwise cascaded down her back.

It was a production. An image projected to the world with her clothes and her bearing . . . but she didn't mind this one. This one was real. Not a mask that had been put on for a falsehood.

It looked *right*.

She turned from the mirror to her companions. Yun Ren was just staring out the window, while Tigu and Ri Zu were looking intently at the drawings Junior Brother was doing with a ruler, leaning over his shoulder as he muttered something about arches.

"I shall be two hours or so in making my report to my Sect," she informed them. "It's best if I explain things to them alone at first."

Yun Ren looked up from the window. "So we just wait around here, then?" he asked, and she shook her head.

"Why would you have to just wait around? To be cooped up in here and waiting wouldn't be productive. The tournament begins tomorrow, but there is still much to experience today. I shall come find you when I am finished."

Her friends all glanced at each other and shrugged.

"See ya later, then." Gou Ren waved at her. "Good luck with your Sect stuff."

Xiulan's lips quirked into a small smile at his fond tone.

"I will see you all soon," she declared as she descended from the room, her two jade-green swords floating openly behind her.

"Good morning, honoured custom . . . er . . ." The woman at the front counter paused midbow as she beheld Xiulan. Her eyes widened in awe, and her mouth opened slightly. "Demon-Slaying Orchid . . ." she whispered to herself.

"The accommodations were excellent. My compliments to the Master of the establishment," she said, then turned for the entrance.

"Ah . . . um . . . Yes, Lady Cai! Thank you for your words, Lady Cai!" she managed to get out as Xiulan exited the inn.

The streets were already bustling in the early-morning light, yet she found none that impeded her path. The people in the streets parted as if they were water before a ship. Whispers of "Demon-Slaying Orchid" followed her as she walked towards the mountain. Some eyes were awed. Some eyes were narrowed in concentration, watching her.

Her pace was calm and unhurried. The stares . . . they didn't matter. They didn't bother her anymore.

It was actually rather nice, walking through the town, smelling the cooking fires that made delicacies from all over the Azure Hills.

Yet her leisurely walk did not last forever.

A group approached her, wearing the colours of her Sect. They walked openly and with purpose, with one man in the lead.

"We pay our respects to the Young Mistress!" they shouted as one, their fists clasped in front of them as they bowed. Their leader, Bolin, who had joined the Sect a decade and a half ago, offered her the deepest one.

"I have returned. It is good to see you all again," she said, and she meant it.

They looked like they had been doing well. Xiulan inclined her head, and the group formed up around her, allowing her to lead as she followed the path.

The one who walked closest to her spoke.

"Did you have a good trip, Young Mistress?" Bolin asked. He was older than her, yet he was still "Junior Brother." He had previously been one of her tails, before she had lost him.

"It was quite the adventure," she stated simply, gracing him with a smile. "What about you, Junior Brother? I do hope it wasn't spent entirely in the wilderness, or being sent on errands for the Elders . . ."

She hoped Bolin hadn't been searching for her the entire time—or heavens forbid, been punished. She could not admit that she had evaded their eyes on purpose, because of her promise to Master Jin to let him remain unbothered. Such a thing would be tantamount to admitting that she was hiding something, and acting like she didn't know what they had been doing gave them both some cover.

A branch of peace.

Bolin smiled at her, accepting her reconciliation. "Thank you for your concern, Young Mistress, but all was well." He probably hadn't spent too long looking for her after she disappeared. He'd done his best to perform the task his Elder set for him . . . but no one could blame him for losing the Young Mistress who eclipsed his cultivation. "We had much work to do though. The Plum Blossom's Shadow . . . They've been around only six months, yet they've come very far. Someone of immense talent is controlling them."

Xiulan filed that away for later, since they were now approaching the gates of the compound.

"The Elders wish for a private audience immediately," he stated simply. "They're a bit upset that you cut it so close, and Elder Yi is Elder Yi."

"Thank you for the warning." It was quite kind of him to give her that much.

Bolin accepted her thanks, moving forwards to open the enormous, heavy gate to the courtyard for her. He paused, turning back to her.

"Was it worth it?" Bolin asked.

Xiulan did not even have to think. She turned directly to face him. "Yes."

Bolin let out a pleased breath, then bowed his head.

The gates opened.

"We pay our respects to the Young Mistress!" The greeting roared out.

Two rows of five men stood, their hands clasped before them in a martial salute: the cultivators of her Sect who had been spared to travel to the Dueling Peaks. Their numbers had been cut down by Sun Ken, so these were all who were left. There were the older members of her Sect, who looked at her with pride—those who had stalled in the First Stage of the Initiate's Realm, never to rise higher.

Next came the favoured. Her Junior Brothers and Sisters, those whom she had taught.

Those who had the most potential out of all of their new members. The four of them stood at attention as well, smiles bright on their faces. They now bowed to her, overjoyed at her return.

Finally, there were mortals, and the servants were slightly behind them. Some of the servants she had known since she was first aware of her surroundings. Mortals whose families had served the Verdant Blade Sect for untold generations.

She recognised all of them, even out of the corners of her eyes. Granny Ping, the brothers Dai and Bai, and the weaver Muling. The kindly old grandmother, who had once snuck her sweets.

But . . . she did not truly know that much about them, did she? They looked so happy to see her, yet she had repaid them poorly for their devotion. Rarely were they allowed entrance to the heart of the Sect, but they performed most of the vital duties.

There were as many of them here as the number of people who lived in Hong Yaowu.

Yet she knew another village better than her own people.

It was a slightly sobering thought. But one that sounded right. *Her* people.

She would have to rectify this as soon as the opportunity presented itself.

Her head held high, she entered the Elders' chamber. The five Elders were sitting on their knees on cushions, watching her intently as she bowed her head to them in greeting.

"Cai Xiulan pays her respects to the Elders of the Verdant Blade," she stated, raising her head and meeting the gazes of her Elders. The mood was tense. Her father's gaze was searching, but she could tell he was relieved to see her. The others seemed relieved as well, but Elder Yi was frowning.

"Cutting it close, Daughter," her father said, looking mildly amused. "But I have never known you to be late. Are you all satisfied with this, brothers?" he asked the room.

"Indeed. The Verdant Blade's dutiful daughter is ever reliable," Elder Han stated, stroking his beard and nodding.

Some of the tension drained. There were a few amused smiles, but most seemed satisfied that she was among them.

All except Elder Yi.

"I am pleased that she is here . . . but . . . where have you *been*, Young Mistress?" he rumbled, his eyes sharp. "After such accolades, one would expect you to continue racking up merit and for your name to continue to spread. But after you visited Grass Sea City, there was a remarkable lack of news."

Her father frowned at Elder Yi. The man was always harsh and humorless, suspicious and almost, Xiulan would say, *paranoid*. He was always concerned with the Sect's capabilities and how they were perceived by others.

That pressure often came down on Xiulan, as the man pushed and prodded at her to remain upright and honourable.

After she had returned from Fa Ram for the first time, it had grown even worse. It was he who had organised a lot of her demonstrations, he who had pressed her to take more students, and he who had gotten her to tell stories of Sun Ken's death.

"Well, do you have an answer for us, Young Mistress?" he asked.

"Yi!" her father began to rebuke, but another of the Elders spoke up.

"I must confess some interest as well," Elder Jibai said idly. "And I am also curious if you have found any more of that rice."

There were more nods. Her father glared. But even he could not completely shut down all other Elders if they wished to know.

All of the Elders had their attention upon her. Perhaps at one time she would have stumbled over her words to explain herself.

Now she felt no such urge. She felt calm and at peace. Her power was as placid as a lake, and thus it was hard to see how deep it was.

So she enlightened them.

She let out a breath as her own power swelled. It filled the room. Her father's jaw dropped. Elder Yi's eyes widened as he coughed. Power equal to theirs filled the room—the Profound Realm.

"I have been in deep meditation and training with a Hidden Master," she stated simply. "Is that not sufficient?"

There was silence as they digested her strength.

"My honourable father, our Sect Master, knew my intentions, for the Hidden Master wished not to be disturbed."

"So, what did this Hidden Master get in return for this generosity?" Elder Yi asked leadingly.

Xiulan frowned at the insinuation.

"My purity is intact, if that is what you are asking," she shot back. She brought out the jar of maple syrup and placed it upon the table. Once more there was a shocked silence, as the Elders beheld the simple glazed clay bottle. The simple, unassuming bottle that was *full* of Qi.

"He wishes for an amicable relationship with us. And that we take care of his disciples while they are here." All knew that Hidden Masters were either the greatest allies or the most terrible enemies. She would have liked to keep the syrup for herself . . . but she knew it would bring Master Jin his peace.

There were noises of interest. It was much more understandable that a man was asking for a favour from them.

Even though he was not. Even though a reward for this was not on his mind.

"So you have gained us a new ally, Cai Xiulan," Elder Han said, stroking his beard and staring at the syrup. His eyes were focused completely upon it as he took short breaths, tasting the scent that made him swallow, for his mouth was watering. Even Elder Yi could barely keep his eyes off the prize.

"He wishes for his seclusion, but he is also willing to sell his goods to us. We should keep such things quiet, should we not, to retain access to them?" Xiulan asked, putting it to the Elders' decision.

There was another set of nods. Elder Han laughed at the thought.

"Indeed, my daughter," Cai Xi Kong stated, smiling at her. "In fact, brothers, should my daughter, who already has a good relationship with our mysterious master, continue it? It would bring us great things, would it not?"

The Elders stared at the bottle of syrup, and one by one they nodded.

Even Elder Yi, as grudging as it was.

"And so it shall be. We shall all show respect to the disciples of this Hidden Master," her father said, smiling at her. "But now, we must discuss our strategy for the tournament. My daughter, I would like to hear your insights . . ."

Xiulan grimaced internally. She had hoped that this would be a rather short interview.

I hope everyone else is having a much better time than I am, she thought.

↔

Gou Ren was *not* having a particularly good time. Oh, it had started well enough. The town . . . almost city . . . *place* was incredibly interesting. The countless thousands of sights and smells had been intoxicating. It was like the festivals at Verdant Hill, yet a thousand times more.

They had perused the stalls, and eaten some food, and generally had a good time . . . until the crowds started getting worse. Then Gou Ren had stopped, because a scroll had caught his eye, and when he looked up again, everybody was gone.

So now he was wandering idly through the streets of the market, searching for his brother and Tigu. He had already doubled back a few times.

He snorted in irritation as he pushed through the people. Lots of silk clothes here, but for the most part, there were actually a lot of normal people. *Most* were normal people, actually, come from all over the Azure Hills to set up shop and sell things.

Gou Ren shook his head in frustration, and he decided to get out of the crowded area and press into a side street. They had been travelling closer to the mountain, so maybe his friends were that way . . . ?

He was studying the crowd when he noticed an old man who was walking backwards, looking around, a bit confused. The man hit an intersection, but instead of pausing to look around, he continued going . . . and went right into the path of a woman in a blue dress with a cloud pattern on it.

The old man fell, shocked at the sudden resistance, and kicked up a bit of dust.

Gou Ren frowned as the woman put her hands on her hips, glowering down at the fallen grandfather.

"Look at this dirt everywhere, old man," the woman sneered. "Wandering around with your head in the clouds . . . You're courting death!"

She reached for the old man, and Gou Ren's blood ran cold. Bad stories Meimei had told him about cultivators swirled unpleasantly.

Wait, is she actually going to—?

His body began to move as she grasped the back of the old man's robe, her eyes disdainful. She lifted him into the air—

And set him back down, and began to strike the dirt from his robes.

"Look at this! You court death, gawking as you do! Foolish, impudent! You *dare* to not pay attention in this place?"

Just as she spoke, a heavy cart rolled past, its driver clearly not paying attention as he argued with his partner. If the old man hadn't bumped into the woman, he probably would have gotten run over.

The man seemed utterly bewildered and began to try to bow awkwardly, while the woman's hands swiftly danced over the old man's hips, checking a bit like Meimei did for any contusions.

"Thank you, Young Miss—" the man tried, but the beautiful woman *harrumphed*, glaring at him.

"Hmph! You might die if you continue to act in this way! Your bones would be shattered, your organs ruptured, and you would perish unmourned in a ditch!"

Gou Ren stared at the scene as the woman pushed the old man on his way.

There was almost certainly a better way for all that to have been said. The woman watched the old man go . . . and then turned back to the crowd, pointing at Gou Ren. Her storm-grey eyes were narrowed in anger, and her lips pulled into a scowl.

"And *you*! Who are you to gaze upon me with such eyes?" She raised a haughty brow. "Come, and face this Young Mistress!"

Gou Ren stepped forwards. "Ah . . . sorry. A bit of a misunderstanding, miss," he apologised.

The woman glared at him, looking directly into his eyes, before she suddenly blinked. She stared at him, her eyes flicking all over his face with what seemed like confusion. Then her own face flushed slightly, and coughed.

"A misunderstanding? Tell me, how could one ever misunderstand this Young Mistress?"

"I thought you were gonna hurt him," he muttered, deciding on the truth. She couldn't be too bad if she had helped out that old man, could she?

"Oho? And you would have stood against me if that was the case?" she demanded.

"Yeah," Gou Ren replied bluntly.

The woman paused, seeming taken aback by his words. She bit her lip as she stared at his face again. She was nearly as tall as he was, with a willowy figure, a sword strapped to her waist, and a strange contraption on her back, which at first he had mistaken for a pack.

"You are a fool twice over for your words! I don't hate it! Liu Xianghua, the Young Mistress of the Misty Lake Sect, approves of your foolishness!"

Xianghua? wait—

"Xiulan's friend?" he blurted out, remembering the story Xiulan had told about the woman.

The woman recoiled as if he had just slapped her, but also seemed oddly *happy* to have been called Xiulan's friend.

"Friend? I, who ascended to the Fourth Stage of the Initiate's Realm to challenge her once more? Nay, we are fated rivals! Our battle will be legendary!" She posed, one hand on her hip and a fist raised to the sky. "Naturally, I shall emerge victorious. And who are you, to know me through the Blade of Grass?" she demanded.

"Her um . . . friend . . . ? Xong Gou Ren. Nice to meet you?"

He bowed to the strange woman.

She stared at him, her head cocked to the side. "*Cai Xiulan* calls you *friend*?"

"More like . . . Junior Brother," he admitted. "Uh. Listen, I gotta find my friends, so . . . bye?" he managed, backing away.

"I see!" the woman declared, and quickly fell into step beside him.

Gou Ren glanced at her nervously.

"I shall aid you, of course," she stated, refusing to look at him.

What a strange *woman.*

CHAPTER 7

WAYWARD COMPANION

The meeting with the Elders had gone on for far longer than Xiulan would have liked. After the discussion of the tournament, they had moved on to sampling the syrup . . . which was a bit amusing, especially when her honourable father had groaned with pleasure.

It appeared they had something in common. Though his was more a deep grumble of contentment than her undignified sounds. It was still rather embarrassing, however. She would have to try harder to control herself.

Senior Sister had said it was endearing, but Xiulan still tried to keep a tight grip on it.

"I think this concludes all that needs to be spoken of," her father stated.

The rest of the Elders nodded.

"Then this meeting is adjourned. Bring the Hidden Master's disciples to be introduced. Tomorrow, we shall make the name Verdant Blade resound throughout the Azure Hills just as it did when you slew Sun Ken! The star that is our Sect is on the ascent."

The Elders were in agreement, satisfied smiles upon their faces.

The meeting was then adjourned and Xiulan dismissed.

She walked out of the building, thinking upon what had transpired. She would likely be made an Elder for her accomplishment, though she was still a bit concerned about Elder Yi. The plan was to have her friends stay with her here at the Sect compound and partake of her hospitality . . .

"Senior Sister?"

She was startled from her introspection by a hopeful voice. She raised her head to gaze upon a familiar face.

An Ran, one of the disciples that she had personally taught. Behind her stood several others, those chosen for the tournament . . . and all of them were her students.

She felt a small welling of pride at that. They had taken what she had said to heart, focusing on improving themselves.

"Junior Sister, it is good to see you. Your bearing has improved—I see it in your eyes," she said. "To see you all in good spirits is a blessing."

The disciples perked up at her words, relief flooding them.

"We just wished to welcome you back, Senior Sister. And to thank you for your guidance." An Ran spoke for all of them, her smile bright.

To think that she had been annoyed training them several months ago. What sort of teacher would be angry about eager students?

Perhaps it had been from the looks they gave her, so full of awe. The admiration had felt undeserved before. A stinging betrayal of the memory of those who fell.

It was different now. Their eyes did not make her feel bile climbing her throat this time. Instead, she felt calm.

Xiulan smiled at them, and there was a little intake of breath from the disciples.

The meeting with the Elders had gone on for a while, but there was still time before she had to return. "Thank you for greeting me. I'm proud to have such diligent Juniors. Would you do me the honour of showing me how far you've grown?"

The Junior Disciples brightened as she moved to await them in the arena.

She noted in all of them an undercurrent of tension, and a bit of a lack of focus. Worry, nervousness, and fear lay upon their minds, likely from the fact that they were about to participate in the tournament.

She would have to rectify that.

"An Ran. You first, please," she called. Her eager Junior practically skipped to stand in front of her, drawing her blade. She was not at the level that she could make it float yet, but her stance spoke of her progress.

They bowed to each other . . . and then the clash of blades began.

There was something different about it. Before, she'd still needed to focus upon her movements. She'd still had to consider herself.

Now her body flowed. She could devote all her time and effort to her students, to move their bodies and make them better. A little tap here. A small shift there.

Her students were silent as they watched with wide eyes.

A sword clattered to the ground.

"You have improved, An Ran," Xiulan said. "The holes in your defence have closed, and your increasing skill shows your dedication to your path."

"Thank you for your pointers, Senior Sister!" the girl shouted, bowing to her.

"Huyi. You next, please," she called, and the young man stepped up. He had unfortunate eyes—like those of a dead fish—but Xiulan knew his consideration for his fellows.

The young man bowed, and she began with him.

→

Their session was, by necessity, short. But Xiulan had seen what she needed to see, and they took her instruction like a sapling taking root, eagerly absorbing what she had given them.

"All of you have grown. Be proud of your accomplishments," she told them, even as they sat in various states of exhaustion.

The disciples smiled at each other.

"Senior Sister, do you have any other advice for us?" Xi Bu asked, the shortest of them asked, his voice a deep rumble despite his stature and young-looking face.

"Go into this tournament with your mind upon your future growth, rather than your current limitations. This tournament is but another lesson, and what you learn from it is the true prize."

The disciples nodded, their gazes considering. It was a bit of strange advice, rather than what they'd likely been expecting: showing the world their glory.

However, it was something they needed to hear. They were under enough pressure already.

An Ran especially was considering what Xiulan said, her brow furrowed.

"Now I must go, but I shall be back tonight. Meditate and rest, for it would do you no good to hurt yourself before the tournament."

The disciples chorused their assent. Satisfied with what she had accomplished, Xiulan returned to the town at the feet of the Dueling Peaks.

↔

"See him?" Yun Ren shouted up at Tigu, who stood on his shoulders.

"No!" she called back, before hopping down onto the road with a frown. She bit her lip as her eyes searched fruitlessly.

The day had started well enough after Xiulan had left. They had decided to go to the outskirts and then work their way in, which had been a bit of a mistake.

Honestly, there were actually a lot more people than Yun Ren had been expecting here. Merchant caravans poured in, erecting pop-up shops or stalls. The roads were a whirlwind of activity . . . but everybody seemed to be concentrated in the outskirts. The only people he saw walking towards the mountain were those with nicer clothes.

But that was mostly irrelevant at the moment.

Yun Ren raised an eyebrow at Tigu, who caught his eye before studiously looking away, pretending she was still searching the crowd.

"Tigu," he said, and the girl slumped a little, turning to face him directly, her head held high but resigned.

'This is Ri Zu's fault. She smelled medicinal herbs this way.' The rat's nose was poking out of Tigu's shirt, and she was wringing her hands together.

"No, I disobeyed the Master's orders and got too excited," Tigu muttered, as the two of them awaited his judgement.

Yun Ren sighed, tugging at his ponytail. He didn't *do* scolding. He left that to Meimei. But here he was, the arbiter of justice for a very guilty-looking Tigu.

It was kind of annoying that she'd run off. But he had known she was doing something kind of dumb and chased after her, stopping outside a shop closer to the mountain. She had been a bit embarrassed then . . . and then even more so when Yun Ren realised that his brother wasn't right behind them.

Even retracing their steps hadn't turned him up, which was when Tigu went from slightly guilty to worried, and then to ashamed.

Yun Ren chopped his hand into Tigu's head. The girl blinked curiously at the light blow.

"Are you gonna do it again?" he asked.

"No, I shall not," Tigu stated with conviction. Having something unfortunate happen often got lessons to stick, so he had a feeling he wouldn't have to keep too much of an eye on her.

"Then there's no sense worrying about it. Gou is gonna be fine." His little bro could take care of himself.

"Indeed! Our fellow disciple is more than a match for any challenge!" Tigu said, reassuring herself.

Yun Ren pondered for a moment.

"You mentioned smell, Ri Zu. Do you have anything?" he asked. The rat sniffed the air and shook her head with a grimace.

'There are so many people, even Disciple Gou Ren's smell does not stand out,' Ri Zu squeaked at him.

Yun Ren sighed again.

Their search was largely fruitless, so they continued their walk through the overcrowded outskirts, to the less-crowded streets, and eventually he decided to just head over to their meeting place.

"My friends!" They heard a shout, and Yun Ren turned, seeing Xiulan approach them with a smile. She looked a little tired, and her eyes searched for Gou. When she failed to see him, she frowned.

Yun Ren shrugged, as Tigu tried to hide behind him. "There was a bit of an incident, and we were just trying to find him," he replied. "Gou might have gone to the meeting spot? We weren't planning on going there till a bit later, but . . ."

Xiulan nodded, looking a little concerned as they headed to the restaurant across town. It was a more opulent place, like the inn, but for some reason most of the seating was out the back, in little gazebos.

Yun Ren breathed a sigh of relief as he saw his brother's back. Then he saw that his brother was sitting with someone.

A woman.

A woman who was leaning forwards slightly, her eyes fixed on his dear baby brother. Yun Ren stopped walking forwards as he laid eyes on the classical beauty wearing a fine blue dress.

Tigu's eyes widened happily as she saw Gou Ren, and she made to rush off to greet their wayward companion. There was a brief urge to let Tigu gear up for a tackling hug in front of the woman Gou Ren had just met . . . but Yun Ren was a kind and generous brother—he caught Tigu's shirt, stopping her cold.

"Eh?" Tigu asked, looking up, confused.

"Let my little bro work his magic, yeah?" he said, smiling proudly. *Go get 'em, champ!* He mentally cheered his little bro on.

Which was when the last person he expected to ruin things stepped forwards.

↔

"And *that* is how I defeated the Young Master of the Azure Horizon Sect!" Xianghua boasted as she finished her story. "I threw some medicine at his feet and pitied him for his weakness! He was most incensed! His face went as red as a cherry! It was the Blade of Grass that taught me that insult!"

Gou Ren nodded, surprisingly engrossed. He was still a *little* unsure of what to make of the woman. They had wandered around together for a while until Gou Ren got tired of searching and went to the restaurant they had said they would meet up at.

He assumed that the girl would leave after that, but instead she had sat down with him, and out of politeness, Gou Ren had started trying to make conversation.

Conversation that had somehow ended up with her telling a story about how she defeated somebody last month in a battle.

And then fixed him up, which made the guy *angry* for some reason? As angry as Xianghua was when Xiulan "went easy on her" the last time they fought.

Gou Ren *really* didn't get cultivators. Xianghua described every act of decency she did as an insult.

"What about yourself, Xong Gou Ren, what manner of martial exploits have you?" she suddenly asked, as if she'd just realised she had been the only one talking for the better part of an hour.

Gou Ren was about to say none. But if Xiulan was her "eternal rival . . ."

"I kicked Xiulan into the river once," he said, joking. The woman's eyes widened.

"You landed a blow upon *Cai Xiulan*?" she stated, shifting around the bench they were sitting on slightly and getting closer to him. Her eyes were wide and impressed.

"Ah, no it was . . . kind of a surprise attack . . . ?" he said, floundering.

Instead of looking at him with disdain, she now seemed even *more* impressed.

"That is quite the feat! Perhaps, after the tournament, we shall trade pointers sometime . . . ?" she asked leadingly.

Gou Ren shrugged. It would be a bit like sparring with Xiulan—and then a shadow loomed over him.

"Liu Xianghua. What are your intentions with my Junior Brother?" Xiulan asked. She was smiling, and it was anything but happy.

Yun Ren was farther back, looking apologetic for some reason, while Tigu looked concerned.

He felt a hand touch his arm.

"I am merely speaking with your Junior Brother, Cai Xiulan," Xianghua stated, a smirk in her voice. "You act like I shall steal him away!"

Xiulan twitched, and a vein in her forehead pulsed.

Xianghua laughed.

"Oh? That is a fantastic expression, Cai. I hope to see it more often." The woman abruptly stood. "It was adequate meeting you, Xong Gou Ren. But your companions have arrived, and I cannot stand to stay in this woman's presence until I have defeated her! I shall see you at the tournament, Cai Xiulan!" she declared in a loud voice, drawing the attention of everyone in the restaurant, before leaving in a storm of silk.

Gou Ren raised an eyebrow, before shrugging. *A bit dramatic, that.*

"Took you guys long enough," he sighed as they sat down. His brother shrugged, while Tigu started mumbling out apologies.

Xiulan, on the other hand, looked annoyed.

"Steal him away?" she grumbled. "You can do *much* better than that woman, Junior Brother! I'll warn her off bothering you."

Gou Ren raised an eyebrow at the declaration, but Xiulan was deep in thought.

"An Ran perhaps . . . ? She has a much better disposition . . ." she muttered to herself.

Gou Ren looked to his brother, who just raised his hands helplessly.

CHAPTER 8

REMEMBER TO READ THE FINE PRINT

Tigu slurped her soup, in a good mood again. Disciple Gou Ren had forgiven her for wandering off, bonking her on the head like Yun Ren had done, before transitioning to tousling her hair. Her Juniors were quite forgiving of her mistakes!

The food wasn't particularly good, though. She considered the taste, inspecting it for any qualities Wa Shi would like . . . and finding none. Shrugging, she turned back to the conversation that was ongoing with her fellow disciples.

"So, you gonna meet up with her again?" Yun Ren asked around a mouthful of food. His smile was wide. "We saw some places you could take her. Need my help to find a spot to woo your lady?"

He looked *entirely* too amused.

Surprisingly, it was Xiulan who answered, even as Disciple Gou Ren's brow furrowed in irritation.

"Junior Brother can do much better. Xianghua is too . . . too . . ." She seemed to struggle with her words. Like she couldn't quite find anything *truly* wrong with the other woman.

Tigu didn't know why. Was not their goal to aid their Junior Brother? He'd seemed quite comfortable with the woman, so they must have enjoyed each other's company.

Xiulan had also spoken of the great battle she had had against the woman. That meant Xianghua was strong! Sure, she had lost in the end, but so had Tigu! This Xianghua woman might be worthy of having her brother's attention.

"I think it shall be a fine idea!" Tigu declared. "You should meet with her again!" Xiulan shot her a look of utter betrayal.

Hmph! They were rivals! Though the Blade of Grass thought Tigu would follow her blindly and discard a fine woman for no reason? How impudent! If Tigu backed this contender, she already had a head start!

Gou Ren sighed.

"Where are we headed next?" he said, changing the subject.

"Registration," Xiulan said authoritatively. "While my Sect handles things for me, Tigu needs to reserve her place for tomorrow." She seemed glad for the shift in conversation. "Then we have until sunset before we are expected at the manor.

I have arranged your stay with my Sect," she said, her voice betraying a slight hint of nervousness.

"I shall render judgement on the other Blades of Grass!" Tigu declared.

Xiulan snorted and shook her head.

They finished their meal, then set off into the wide avenues.

"It's arranged a bit like Pale Moon Lake, with the rings," Disciple Gou Ren noted as they got closer to the mountain.

"Yes. The outer rings are mostly for the mortals. The common folk are the farthest out. Then the merchants, then the nobles, and finally the cultivators," Xiulan explained.

Tigu looked around with interest. The buildings on the outskirts were simple affairs, but they quickly transitioned into two-story structures, and now there were entire walled compounds. All had symbols and colours presented proudly upon their closed gates but . . . well, Tigu might have been expecting a *bit* more.

It looked mostly like the city. Yet there weren't any fights breaking out, nor people challenging each other.

The locals, however, were much more colourful than even the noble city folk, wearing long silk robes or standing around with their weapons on full display.

Yet there was something . . . *off.*

"Why is it so quiet?" Tigu asked.

"Last-minute preparations," the Blade of Grass stated. "Most will be within their compounds, in meditation, or receiving instruction. However, as the tournament progresses, things tend to become a bit looser."

"One big party, huh?" Yun Ren asked.

"I suppose. I have never attended. Xianghua tried to drag me out once, four years ago, but I needed to train more . . ." Xiulan trailed off and shrugged.

Disciple Yun Ren and Gou Ren looked at each other and nodded. The grins they sported spoke of mischief.

They continued walking to the mountain. Built into the side of it was their destination: an enormous stone vault with the character for "azure" carved into it.

"Here we are. That way is registration. The rest are administrative buildings," Xiulan said, and Tigu nodded, setting off towards the doors.

"Anything interesting around here?" Yun Ren asked.

"There are some interesting carvings, said to have been done by the First Emperor," Xiulan started to say, but Tigu wasn't really paying attention. Instead, her eyes were on the door. She grinned at it. She was ready. She could not *wait* to be in this room!

Tigu squared her shoulders, straightened her back, and pushed open the doors.

"I am here to join the tournament!" she announced, her voice booming off the vaulted ceiling.

There was a pause as *everybody* turned to look at her. The room wasn't very full. There were a few people, all hunched over desks, and several official-looking men with veils over their faces.

She heard Xiulan snort from behind her, and amused noises came from the brothers.

She had expected some manner of preliminary bout, or tough-looking masters gazing down upon her. Instead, they all appeared a bit like Uncle Xian. Scholars and clerks, one and all.

One of the men coughed politely.

Tigu turned her attention to him.

"Number three can see you, miss," the nasal voice told her.

Tigu turned to where he was pointing.

"Ah. Thanks," Tigu said as she approached. The man seemed pleasantly surprised, then took a piece of chalk and marked something on a board on his desk. The category in which he made that mark was nearly empty, while the other was so full it had nearly gone off the board.

"I am here to register," she informed man number three.

He nodded politely and deposited a stack of paper before her.

It was rather large.

"It is the code of conduct, young miss, as well as the necessary dispensations all tournaments are required to include, as of the Cloudy Sky Decree, issued in the five thousand one hundred sixty-seventh year of the Crimson Phoenix Empire."

Tigu stared at the papers.

"Thank you. I shall fill these out." She picked up the stack of papers and made her way to an open seat but paused when the door banged open.

"I, Zang Wei, have come to register for the tournament!" a voice boomed off the walls.

Everybody turned to look at the boy. His face went a bit red.

There was a polite cough, and the boy turned to the man at the front.

"Number four can see you, sir," the nasal voice stated, sending the boy on his way.

→

"In accordance with the previous statements this body shall require all contestants to maintain a . . ." Tigu's finger paused at the courtly character.

'Virtuous bearing. That character is rare. They mostly use this,' Ri Zu squeaked as she looked at the paper. Her little finger traced the character on Tigu's neck, which she did recognise.

"Thanks," she muttered, and got back to reading.

This whole registration business was a chore. And not the fun kind of chore, like sleeping on—guarding the sheep, or even Ri Zu's lessons. This was just a bunch of boring reading and writing.

Who knew tournaments needed so much paperwork? She could almost hear Pi Pa chiding her that of course such an undertaking would require much accounting.

The man who had given her this actually seemed a bit surprised that she was sitting down to fully read it. The other guy had just signed everything and left, the fool.

She would not shirk from this. Mistress and Pi Pa had told her to read everything she was given before she signed anything.

She had already messed up once today, running ahead of Yun Ren like she had promised not to; so, with that failure in mind, she sat and read everything.

No killing, unless it was by accident. No assaulting the spectators. Once this form was signed all fights would be confined to designated areas . . .

Most of the stipulations seemed fairly straightforward. There was even a place where fighters could go and receive a free meal once a day, "Courtesy of Chao Baozi."

Tigu stretched after reading the last portion. She made sure everything was in order, affixed her signature to the documents, and returned to the front.

The man examined the documents, then nodded. He reached into his desk and brought out what looked like a necklace before handing it over.

"Here is your jade token. Do not lose it. As the official gong sounds tomorrow, bring it to the western entrance. The eastern entrance will remain closed and will not accept you. The northern and southern entrances are for spectators only. At the fourth gong, the gates will close, and the judging will start. If you are not here by then, you will be disqualified. Do you understand everything you have been told?" The man with the veil covering his face droned on, like he had said the same speech far too many times already.

Tigu nodded her head and took the jade piece. It was about the size of her palm, bright green and carved with the image of the Dueling Peaks.

"We wish you luck in the tournament tomorrow, Rou Tigu. May the heavens favour you." And with that, she was dismissed. When she walked away, she saw that her fellow disciples were all waiting for her. Gou Ren was drawing in his scroll again, while Yun Ren held his crystal in one hand. He was swapping his thumb over it, an interested look on his face, as the images hovered slightly above it. He was sweating slightly, intent and concentrating, as Xiulan watched.

"That took a while," Xiulan said, looking up at her. "Was there a problem?" Tigu shook her head and held up the token. Ri Zu had disappeared back down her shirt. "Excellent. We still have time; was there anything in particular you wanted to see?"

'Medicinal herbs,' Ri Zu said.

"Well, then, this way to the medicinal herbs," Xiulan declared, and they stepped out into the air once more.

It was late afternoon now while they headed back to the merchants' quarter. The building they came to was large and stately. It smelled like herbs—quite like the Mistress, if Tigu was honest.

Ri Zu squealed with excitement when they entered the shop. Only her little head peeked out, her nose shaded by Tigu's hair and sniffing excitedly. Disciple

Gou Ren's footsteps echoed as he walked on the marble floors, which contrasted with the rest of their silent footsteps.

There was row, upon row, upon row of shelves, each with immaculately lacquered drawers. A pressed version of what was inside them was on the front between two panes of glass.

Tigu had only seen Hong Xian's storage before. Although it was diligently maintained, it was nothing compared to this vast room. Curiously, the air was much cooler than outside.

Tigu supposed it might have something to do with the odd blue crystals in the wall, which seemed to be giving off cold air.

Ri Zu pinched Tigu's neck. She rolled her eyes and stepped forwards.

'Hot-Touch Petals! Two Element Flower roots! Ah! Antbane fungus!' Her little voice chittered away as they passed each drawer. *'Ri Zu has only read of some of these! Oh, Master will be very-very overjoyed! Now, what are the price . . . es . . .'* Ri Zu trailed off.

She stared at the sign with the prices. Tigu stared at it too.

Were those numbers in the right place? It seemed like there were one or two too many.

Tigu pulled open her coin pouch and checked the amount.

"Well, we can get one of these," Tigu said.

Ri Zu looked in the pouch, then squeaked something most uncharitable about the owners of this shop.

"This is nuts," Yun Ren muttered as he approached them. "I thought the prices in Pale Moon Lake City were bad, but this . . ." He shook his head, as Ri Zu squeaked her agreement.

"Is everything all right?" Xiulan asked.

'Expensive!' Ri Zu said.

Xiulan stared at the prices.

"Oh!" she said, realising their predicament. "Do not concern yourself." She pulled out the token with the symbol of her Sect on it. "Let your Senior Sister take care of it!" Despite their protests, the Blade of Grass was quite insistent.

As Xiulan concluded their shopping, Yun Ren waited near the front of the shop, chewing his lip.

"We can't have her buy us everything," Yun Ren muttered, staring out of the large window.

Tigu shrugged, not seeing the problem. "She is a fellow disciple, is she not?" Tigu asked, looking back to where Xiulan was speaking with a man in fine robes. "What's ours is hers; what's hers is ours."

Yun Ren didn't answer.

Tigu turned back to him. He was studying a man on the street who had just handed a painting to a well-dressed lady. He had several pieces of paper beside him, and a few portraits of people's faces. There was a list beside him, saying how much each level of detail for a portrait cost.

Yun Ren stared at the price. He glanced at Xiulan, and then his recording crystal. Then he grinned, showing all his teeth.

□

"So, what do you think the Young Mistress's companions are like?" Huyi asked as he oiled his blade.

An Ran looked up from tending to her own sword. It was a wonderful jade colour, the same as Senior Sister's. They were seated together as they always were—the "Orchid's Petals," as they were called in the Sect. It was a name An Ran wore with pride, but her fellows were a bit more ambivalent about it. They said it wasn't *manly* enough.

Yet they still proclaimed their membership, standing above the others of the Sect, as well as the fresh recruits, who had poured in after hearing of the Demon-Slaying Orchid.

They had been hurting with the loss of so many of their cultivators to Sun Ken, but the fresh blood ensured that the Verdant Blade would not wither.

Xi Bu, the short young man who looked more like a boy, scratched his chin, considering the question. "Powerful. Serene. Like our Senior Sister," he decreed in his usual taciturn manner.

An Ran agreed. They surely would be. Senior Sister was a paragon of virtue. Kind, good, and so beautiful. Her journey had only seen her grow even more elegant! Her skin was like the purest jade, her complexion soft as resin. Her movements had been breathtaking before but were utterly *captivating* now. Her eyes saw every gap in their form, every mistake and imperfection in their work. Her body flowed like a dance as she adjusted their stances, and already An Ran felt her body move with more grace, an imperfect mirror to her Senior Sister—even as she directed them into better forms through little tops of her foot or adjusting their stances.

It was humbling and enlightening at the same time, to face such a woman. To be a part of her Sect and receive her personal tutelage.

"I agree. They must be something special, to warrant Senior Sister's regard," An Ran decreed.

"Oi, oi, I think I see them!" Li shouted from his position hidden on the roof.

"Places, everybody. We must show them the hospitality of our Sect," An Ran commanded. Her fellows nodded—one must always show their best face to visitors.

She saw her Senior Sister as she entered first. Her refined features were pulled into a small, amused smile. Her blue eyes sparkled like sapphires.

An Ran prepared to receive the guests of the Young Mistress. The Young Mistress, to her knowledge, had never brought any visitors around before. *These people who had earned her regard must be of the highest quality! Just as elegant, just as profound—*

"Ah, so this is your home, Blade of Grass?" a brash, excited, and *young* female voice called, staring around at the walls. A girl wearing only a too-large and well-used gi, along with bandages around her chest, walked in, chewing on a candied peach. She had a set of markings on her cheeks, and big yellow eyes.

Her skin was dark, her hair and eyes were wild, and she had dirt on her toes, utterly shattering any elegant image An Ran had expected. She even had a country accent!

The others were just as strange. A fox-faced man was giggling to himself as he patted a pouch bulging with coins. He had a scarf around his neck and was wearing the clothes of *tribesmen*, of all things. How far had the Young Mistress travelled to meet people from outside the Empire?

The last was tall. His face was stern as his eyes took in the courtyard. His shirt was open at the front, exposing an expanse of muscle. He looked just as wild and unrestrained as the girl, ambling about without any grace at all.

These were the companions of the Mistress? These . . . these *ruffians*?

"Hello!" a bright and cheery voice shouted right in front of An Ran's face. She recoiled. Instead of a demure greeting from a well-spoken lady, a brash, sassy child shoved herself into An Ran's space. "This one is Rou Tigu! I greet you, Smaller Blade of Grass!"

"We greet the Young Mistress's honoured guests . . ." she managed to get out.

CHAPTER 9

THE SMALLER BLADE OF GRASS

An Ran and her fellows managed to recover their composure after the boisterous girl's greeting, then led them to the prepared room.

None of her Senior Sister's companions were what they had expected. Rou Tigu, as she had introduced herself, fairly skipped along, her eyes taking in as much as she could as they walked through the courtyard to the separated entertaining room. The other two were more sedate but were obviously keeping an eye on their Junior.

Huyi snorted, his dead-fish eyes on the back of the girl's head. "Reminds me of my little sister," he drawled. Her other companions kept their thoughts to themselves. As she opened the door for their guests, all of the guests' eyes became interested in the interior. At the fine cushions and lacquered tables, the room was set up on a bit of a short notice to entertain them.

They entered the room, and one of her companions called for a servant to bring the food.

An Ran left the head of the table to the Young Mistress and bowed to the honoured guests.

"We apologise that the Sect Master and the Elders cannot meet you this time; they are at the dinner finalizing the tournament structure. Please, allow us to introduce ourselves further, as we are to be at your disposal tonight. This one is An Ran."

"Hisho Huyi," the disciple said from beside her. He was slouching a bit, so Ran would scold him later, though none of their guests seemed concerned.

"Xi Bu," the shortest and youngest stated, his deep voice resonating through the room.

"Lee Li," their last member called excitedly. His spiky, bright-green hair was pulled into a ponytail, and his green Verdant Blade uniform was a bit rumpled from his time on the roof.

"Together, we are the Orchid's Petals," An Ran said, bowing once more. "Please, honoured guests, if you require anything do not hesitate to ask."

"The Orchid's Petals?" Tigu asked, clearly confused.

"I aided them in their training, and they have grown wonderfully," the Young Mistress explained, though she seemed a little embarrassed. "So the mortals and some of the other disciples here began calling them that."

The orange-haired girl perked up.

"Aha! My sparring partner's students? I shall show them how to land blows on you better, Blade of Grass. Prepare yourself!" she declared boisterously.

An Ran recoiled at the words that passed her lips. This little girl, landing blows on the Young Mistress? Her *sparring partner*?

"She lands blows on Senior Sister?" Li whispered incredulously.

The Young Mistress chuckled at the statement.

"I am sure they would appreciate your guidance, Tigu," she replied, then smiled at all of them. "It is good to experience how others fight and learn new movements. Tigu is a powerful foe . . . and a good training partner."

An Ran frowned at the younger girl. If the Young Mistress said so, it must be true, but An Ran was still skeptical.

"Ah! Right, I'm supposed to show you my strength!" Tigu declared.

There was a burst of Qi and intent. The Orchid's Petals froze, their sweat travelling upwards on their faces from the sheer pressure. An Ran could barely breathe as she felt the vast, predatory presence gaze upon her.

As soon as it appeared, it was gone.

The two men and the Young Mistress looked unaffected.

An Ran swallowed. "We would be honoured to trade pointers with you, Young Mistress Rou."

The girl preened as Senior Sister shook her head with amusement. "Come, let us all sit and relax before the tournament tonight," she declared.

It was a little bit awkward at first. An Ran, at a slight nudge from Senior Sister, had ended up beside the man who was called Gou Ren. He smiled sheepishly at her and gave her a nod.

An Ran inclined her head slightly, as the decorum manual dictated, her face impassive. The man seemed a bit amused by it.

Yet the tension was still there. These unknown people, who had been travelling with their Young Mistress.

"So . . . how did you end up meeting Senior Sister?" Li asked, ever quick to drop decorum. He glanced at Senior Sister, who nodded at the topic.

"Master and Mistress healed her after she collapsed from her wounds!" Tigu said, nodding authoritatively.

An Ran bit her lip. So *that* was why Senior Sister had come back looking unharmed. Sun Ken was Sun Ken. The battle must have been truly legendary, and not even graceful Senior Sister could have escaped completely unscathed—but to hear she had collapsed, and only been saved through a quirk of fate, was worrying.

"Yeah, she was pretty beat up," Gou Ren stated. "What did Meimei say? Her intestines were nearly exposed? Not to mention all that Demonic Qi . . ."

"She was better by morning, though. Barely recognised her!" the fox-faced boy finished.

And how powerful was their master, to have healed the wounds and purged Demonic Qi in a single night? It took Ty An a bit over a week to repair a bone after it had been broken.

"Yes. Master Jin and Senior Sister saved my life," Cai Xiulan said wistfully. "I owe them much."

Her fond smile broke through the awkwardness far more than any words.

Xi Bu clasped his hands in front of him. "Thank you for aiding our Young Mistress, then," he stated, bowing. "I look forward to an honourable bout in the ring."

The fox-faced boy blinked. "Ha? Oh, it's just Tigu in the tournament. Me and my brother are just here to watch."

Of course, there had to be another statement that defied belief.

"You do not wish for the fame, or the pills awarded to those who go far?" Huyi asked, incredulous.

"Not really. We're just here to cheer on Tigu and Xiulan," the man beside her said with a sigh. "As for the other stuff, I don't think we need it."

How blunt a declaration of power! An Ran swallowed, and resolved to learn more.

□

Lu Ban was in an increasingly foul mood as the day progressed. When he'd first travelled to the Azure Hills from the Sea of Snow, he hadn't really noticed the lack of Qi in the province. His attention had been consumed with stabilizing his cultivation.

But now? In the carriage with its yoked spirits, carrying them tirelessly onwards, he could feel it. The lack of Qi was stifling.

It added irritation upon irritation. It scratched and gnawed, and took a small measure of his concentration just to keep his Qi inside his body at times—like the very air was attempting to drink him dry.

Even though over the course of the year he had achieved much merit . . . this was still something he had to do.

"Scout the Dueling Peaks Tournament for talent."

It was a fool's errand. It was an *insult*, to be sent once more to this gods-forsaken province, where that utter bastard Rou Jin had humiliated him. He was at the fourth stage of the Profound Realm already! He shouldn't have had to do make-work like this!

But when he brought the matter directly to the Elders . . . he was rebuffed. Rebuffed with cold eyes, even as this body's father complained. His "father" assured him that this was the last indignity he would have to suffer for his "youthful indiscretion."

Youthful indiscretion now, rather than "great shame."

He glared out the windows of the carriage.

Back to the Azure Hills. Back to his original stumbling block.

In his mind he cursed his true Master for even suggesting the place for stabilizing his technique. *"It is safe, and you need time"* were the man's last, rasping words before Lu Ban had found himself cold and alone again.

It would have been better to climb back up the mountains and brave the dangers there. Spirit Beasts and terrible weather would have been much preferable to *that bastard.* His fingers throbbed at the memory.

Or perhaps it was fate conspiring against him? He had received a healthy helping of fortune after meeting his Master. Perhaps this was fate trying to balance the scales.

And *that man* was obviously important, to have some expert searching for him—an expert who could invade one of the Shrouded Mountain's fortresses to interrogate a Young Master.

He told himself it had been mostly surprise that had shocked him into inaction. The man was far above himself, yet he likely could not have slain Lu Ban in a single blow. But his cursed instincts from his time on the streets told him it was safer to roll over and give the man what he wanted than to fight. He would have to master those instincts better, so it would not happen again.

That, and he had corrected a deficiency in his own defences. Five talismans that would enable him to escape certain death. Talismans that would utterly negate a blow from a cultivator in the Earth Realm; even a cultivator in the Sky Realm could be foiled by all five.

It had taken all of the resources he had amassed, and a gift from this body's father. But if he ever ran into the man with the hole in his hat, or *Jin,* he would survive—survive and bring down the might of Shrouded Mountain upon them.

He sighed again. The only bonus was the fact that he had no real minder for this mission. Instead, he had six subordinates, who were annoyed as he was about coming to this weak place.

Still, even if he couldn't cultivate normally with the lack of Qi, he should be able to improve his main technique. There would be enough people to feed on: their blood and potential. Even if they were weak, quantity had a quality all of its own.

It took several more hours before they finally arrived; once there, he strode out of the carriage and into a pavilion meant to receive him.

It was utterly inadequate. The treasures they displayed were worthless, and the organisers not worth his time, as they droned on and made empty platitudes, thanking the Shrouded Mountain for deigning to glance in their direction. The cultivators of this land were just as pathetic as their treasures. Their Masters and Elders . . . he could defeat all of them with one hand tied behind his back.

Absolutely pathetic.

Like he would have come if he had not been forced to. He was the highest-ranking disciple of the Shrouded Mountain to venture to this place in decades.

Sometimes his Sect even sent mortals as the main delegation, who would pass judgement upon the cultivators of this land.

There was a formal dinner, with himself at the head table. He was surrounded on all sides by ants, as they tried to curry favour with him and extolled the virtues of his Sect. They puffed themselves up. They said that their disciples were sure to impress—Lu Ban sorely doubted that claim.

A single one of their number being admitted to the Shrouded Mountain Sect would be a great honour and would prove their abilities to the weak people of this province. It was honestly amusing how their "greatest talent" would likely be used as a street sweeper or a bed warmer.

They took his smirk to mean that he was enjoying himself, instead of smiling at their utter delusion. Perhaps he *would* elevate one of these worms, just to upset the power balance of these Sects.

It was a most amusing idea. One of the pretty ones. Or perhaps he would conquer a Sect's Elder? That, too, was appealing. Dinner ended with him in a slightly better mood, and then he was to tour the Earthly Arena.

It was in that tour he discovered *one* thing of value in this worthless province.

It was not the stage that impressed him. It was not its construction, having only rudimentary barriers to protect the audience, and even those were failing in some sections.

No, it was how the stage was lifted to the heavens. The defeated were forced to raise up the victors. In that, the Azure Hills had made a wonder. A place where your lessers were both figurative and literal stepping-stones.

He would have to implement the idea back at the Sect!

Finally, he was allowed to leave the annoying weaklings behind, and he was admitted to the guest mansion. Another disappointment. It was old and ugly. But at least the brothels were nearby.

He stared out over the quiet town as day turned to night.

And made clear his intent to have copious amounts of alcohol in his box for the boredom that was sure to follow.

CHAPTER 10

THE VERDANT BLADE SECT

An Ran stared with interest at the image of Pale Moon Lake City from the top of the mountain. She had never actually been before. None of them had, never truly venturing out of the Grass Sea, and the only city they had visited was Grass Sea City. They were radically different places. Grass Sea City had all but consumed the Twin Snake Rivers on which it was situated, sprawling out across the land without rhyme or reason. Pale Moon Lake City, on the other hand, looked utterly tiny compared to the enormous circular lake it had been built upon.

"This thing is very useful," Li said, examining the wafer of crystal in Yun Ren's hand. "Why has nobody thought to do such a thing before?"

Yun Ren shrugged. "The crystal was defective. Nobody wanted it because it couldn't record moving images or sound. But having something this size able to record still images? It's perfect."

"Whoever made this must be one skilled beyond measure," Xi Bu stated.

Yun Ren's chest puffed out with pride. "I can put you in touch, yeah? It's *way* cheaper than a full crystal."

"You'd do that for us?" Huyi asked, leaning in. He absently moved a piece on the game board. Tigu stared blankly at it, then let out a noise of anger and frustration. She fell backwards and started kicking her legs, scratching at her head. An Ran thought she heard what sounded like squeaking laughter coming from the girl, but it was a bit hard to tell. Huyi snorted, yet something approaching a smile crawled across his face, softening his rotten eyes to something almost handsome.

"'Course I can." Yun Ren nodded. "I'll put in a good word!"

"Cheers for Brother Yun Ren!" Li exclaimed, then filled Yun Ren's cup. There was a snort from beside her as the wild Gou Ren looked on. He held up a bottle, and she nodded, so he poured her a drink. They wouldn't be drinking much tonight—they were strictly rationed on account of the first bouts tomorrow, much to the boy's disappointment.

And a bit to An Ran's. The plum wine was *very* good. And the company was acceptable, at the very least, though she would be keeping a close eye on the men. Tigu obviously reminded Huyi of his little sister, while the boys were . . . well, they were all right, An Ran supposed. Yun Ren was very eager to show off his amazing images, and while Gou Ren chimed in occasionally, he seemed content to simply sit and watch his brother's presentation.

Senior Sister had gone out of the room for a moment, saying she needed to speak to the servants.

"So . . . what's life like in the Sect, anyway? I've heard a bit from Xiulan, but I was wondering what you thought about it?" Gou Ren asked her.

An Ran was startled at the question. A bit was because they were overly familiar with Senior Sister—they just called her by her given name! But An Ran was a good host, so she entertained his question. "We train our martial spirit, and contemplate the Mysteries of the Verdant Blade Scripture," she said. "There is always some manner of chore to be done too, but those aren't so bad. Not when one is so strong and enduring."

An Ran really couldn't imagine going back to being a mortal. Not that she was exactly an immortal herself, only at the Second Stage of the Initiate's Realm, but it certainly was nice.

Gou Ren laughed. "Yeah, I never get tired of lifting up rocks, or carrying in barrels of water like they're nothing!"

An Ran smiled at his honest joy. Really, she had tried speaking to another cultivator from a different Sect about the more mundane things in life, and she had gotten a sneer in response. Where was their wonder at this strength?

"Yourself?" she asked politely.

Gou Ren smiled. "It's hard at times . . . but I think these are some of the best days of my life." His grin was infectious.

Indeed. These days *were* the best days of An Ran's life. Aside from listening to Xi Bu's mind-bending riddles, tolerating Huyi's acidic tongue, and dealing with whatever damn fool idea Li got into his head. But these were minor distractions. Within the peaceful confines of the Verdant Blade Sect, and learning from Senior Sister's movements . . . the days were a treasure. To learn from her inspiration even more so.

Gou Ren was very different than An Ran had thought—

She caught herself. *No! In the stories, that was how they caught you! Luring you in by being personable! They were still men! They traveled around with Senior Sister, and no one could resist her beauty! Surely they were toads lusting after swan's flesh!*

"And this is Biyu," Yun Ren said with pride. The image was of him with his arm around a fluffy woman. Both were sporting small smiles. "She's . . . well, she's we're . . . *Ya know?*"

"Ah? Look at this bastard, showing off!" Huyi complained. Xi Bu smirked, while Li clapped him on the back.

The image was of an owlish-looking girl, with a soft smile on her face as she stood with Yun Ren. Their contentment was obvious.

Okay, maybe *he* wasn't lusting after her . . . she glanced at Gou Ren, who still had been nothing but a gentleman.

"Disciple Gou Ren! Disciple Gou Ren! I require your assistance!" Tigu whined, slamming into the man, who rolled his eyes. She glared at Huyi from the place she'd just taken in Gou Ren's lap.

"Ha! You bullying our Tigu?" the man demanded jokingly. Huyi snorted.

"Yes! Fish Eyes tried to throw the game!" Tigu whined, and her fellow disciple spluttered. An Ran nearly choked, while Li just burst out laughing. "He won't use his full power!"

Gou Ren laughed, standing up. "I see. So you want me to see if I can draw out his true might?"

Tigu nodded eagerly. "He has defeated me! But you can regain our honour!"

He settled down on the other side of the game board, Tigu leaning over his shoulder. The rest of the disciples quickly migrated to that side of the board, leaving Huyi alone against Gou Ren.

Well, Huyi *did* always win when they played. An Ran even found part of her traitorous heart yearning for Huyi to be defeated. He gloated annoyingly when he won.

She mulled over her options. She could either support her fellow disciple or . . . An Ran deliberately walked over to sit down on the side opposite Huyi.

He looked very offended, with everyone arrayed against him.

Gou Ren turned out to be quite good at the game. "You use old men's tricks!" Huyi complained as a piece snapped into place, taking one of Huyi's.

They watched the game go back and forth, tricks and traps and feints. It wasn't particularly high level, by any means. An Ran had seen a game between two of the Elders once before, with their consummate attacks and defences. This was a dirty pub brawl in comparison.

The game wound down. Huyi clicked his tongue.

"Draw?" Gou Ren offered.

Huyi considered the board.

"Draw," he agreed.

"Oh? You youngsters seem like you're enjoying yourselves," a strong, rich voice An Ran knew stated.

An Ran and the rest of her fellows shot to their feet at the Sect Master's entrance. The powerful man stood in the doorway, his green robes immaculate, four swords floating behind him, each in a beautiful green scabbard. With him stood his daughter, the Young Mistress, amusement dancing in her eyes.

"We greet Sect Master Xi Kong!" they shouted as one.

He nodded his head and raised his hand in dismissal as he gazed upon Senior Sister's companions. His presence filled the room, not oppressive, not focusing, but inquisitive.

"I bid you welcome to our home, honoured guests," he declared, clasping his fists in front of him. "I must admit you are all not at all what I expected," he stated, gazing upon the tribal and wild garb that was most prominent. "Yet my daughter vouches for you, so as these disciples said, you may partake of our hospitality as long as you wish, honoured guests."

All of their guests had risen to their feet and showed the Sect Master proper deference. Even Tigu, who bowed her head at the right angle and was the picture of a lady, if only for a moment.

"Thank you for your hospitality," they intoned. The Sect Master nodded in acknowledgement. He stroked his beard. His gaze lingered for a moment upon the men, who straightened slightly under his eyes, before turning to Tigu and raising an eyebrow at her rather blatant stare.

The orange-haired girl smiled. "Your eyes are as pretty as the Blade of Grass's! I see where she gets it from!" the girl declared.

Crystal-blue eyes widened. An Ran could not even voice her shock.

The Sect Master stared for a moment at the earnest statement, and then he laughed. It was deep and rich, filling the room. An Ran had never heard the Master sound so amused.

"Ah! I have never had anyone compliment my eyes, save for my wife! I thank you for your words, little one," he chuckled, shaking his head. "Your orange hair is as vibrant as a tiger's fur, and I am certain you are just as fierce!"

Tigu grinned.

"I shall not keep you from your last moments of peace before the tournament. I bid you all a good night, and may your hard work reap you your rewards. Daughter, I place everything in your capable hands."

Senior Sister bowed. "I shall meet your expectations as best as I am able, Honoured Father."

He nodded one last time, then departed.

Everyone in the room slumped.

"I can't believe you said that!" Li exclaimed, clearly impressed by her fortitude.

"The heavens favour fools, it seems," Xi Bu muttered, though he was smirking.

The others went back to their game, but An Ran stayed behind a bit. She looked to Senior Sister, who was watching them with a small smile on her face.

She looked at them just like An Ran remembered her mother staring, her smile set in place as her children got along and helped each other.

An Ran blushed at such warmth being directed at her, and flushed even further when Senior Sister gestured her over.

"Are you enjoying yourself, Junior Sister?" she asked quietly.

"Yes, Senior Sister. Your companions are . . . unique," An Ran answered.

"A bit strange, you mean?" Senior Sister asked, amusement dancing in her eyes.

"Yes."

Senior Sister chuckled, then turned back to where the boys and Tigu were arranged in a circle, playing cards. The goal seemed to be for the numbered cards to add up to twenty-one. It was a simple game, but it looked fun.

They all watched intently as Yun Ren flipped another card.

"Twenty-two! Your gamble failed, Head of Grass!" Tigu cackled.

Li swore, and Senior Sister chuckled as he threw his arms up and fell over backwards, kicking his legs. An Ran sighed at his antics.

"Better luck next time, Head of Grass," Huyi said, a shit-eating grin on his face.

"Your skills must improve, Head of Grass," Xi Bu stated blandly.

"The good kind of strange, though," Xiulan whispered fondly.

"Blade of Grass! Smaller Blade of Grass! What are you doing, skulking about!" Tigu shouted, waving them over.

"Shall we?" Senior Sister asked.

What could An Ran do but say yes?

And when they did retire for the night, she slept quite well.

→

The next morning, the nervousness had come back in full force. Li had the jitters, while Huyi was even more acidic than normal. An Ran tried to keep herself from snapping at them, but even she was feeling the strain.

Their guests, however, appeared none the worse for wear. Tigu was bouncing up and down with a smile on her face, while Yun Ren fiddled with his crystal and Gou Ren tried to get the orange-haired girl to calm down.

She glanced around the room. Senior Sister was setting up some knives and several pots. An Ran felt a flash of irritation. Just where were the servants? And why was the Young Mistress preparing this? It was unacceptable!

"It took a bit to convince them last night, but they gave in eventually," she heard Senior Sister say to Yun Ren. She seemed to be preparing for something. The man nodded.

Knives rose into the air.

The table went silent.

An Ran could make a single practice artifact wobble slightly. On a good day, she could levitate it a finger's breadth above the floor.

Now, however, she beheld a symphony. A dance. A martial formation that never erred.

Used for cooking.

None spoke until the food was finished, and there were plates set in front of them.

"Thanks for making breakfast, Xiulan," Gou Ren said.

"You are welcome. I hope this gives you strength to make it through the day," she said, nodding her head.

The Young Mistress of the Sect, her Senior Sister, had taken time to craft them all a meal. How blessed by the heavens were they? How benevolent was their Young Mistress?!

"Our Young Mistress is too generous," Xi Bu whispered.

Huyi and Li just started stuffing their faces.

Only An Ran remained staring. Even as her mouth watered.

A chopstick prodded her in the side, startling her.

"Come now, eat up . . . Smaller Blade of Grass," Senior Sister chided, an amused lilt in her voice. An Ran flushed at the nickname, though she supposed it wasn't too bad being directly compared to Senior Sister. At least Tigu didn't call her Fish Eyes, like she called Huyi.

She hesitantly put a bite into her mouth. It was delicious.

□

"Okay, so we're going *here* for the spectator portion . . . And Tigu, you're over here, okay?" Yun Ren said.

"Yes, west gate!" she shouted.

The gong sounded, and she took off.

Senior Sister watched her go, then turned back to her Junior Disciples.

Cai Xiulan took a little breath and turned from the warm Senior Sister to the stately Young Mistress. Yet even as she put on the mask that was her armour against the world, her gaze wasn't quite as cold or dispassionate as it once was.

An Ran picked up the flag bearing the symbol of their Sect.

Her Juniors fell into step behind her, the Young Mistress at their head.

The mortal servants cheered, waving flags and dropping flower petals upon them, following behind as they entered the rapidly crowding streets.

The first day of the tournament had begun.

CHAPTER 11

THE EARTHLY ARENA

'Tigu! Tigu, head-turn back! You stupid-fool! You scurry-ran off too quickly! Take Ri Zu back to other Family-Clan!'

Ri Zu's strident voice hollered as Tigu darted around the crowds in the pre-dawn light. The town had seemingly transformed overnight. The taller buildings rained petals from strange-looking baskets, and there were even more cloth banners and flags! The streets were already lined with crowds, gazing on them and shouting names as they watched the people with flags march their way to the Earthly Arena. It was loud, with shouting and cheers. The air was full of the smell of food being fried and served from stands along the way.

It just was all so exciting!

'Tigu!' Ri Zu yipped again. Her little nails dug into Tigu's back, slightly painful for the first time. Normally she resided in the back of Tigu's shirt, but right now she was squeaking *directly* into Tigu's ear.

"Nope! Master said we must be punctual! If you wish to go back to the others, you can go alone. Are you not working on your ability to hide in the shadows?" Tigu asked her tiny companion.

'Master also said to not take unnecessary risks if one can help it!' Ri Zu squeaked, managing to get her strange accent under control.

"Is introducing yourself to the Blade of Grass's Petals too much of a risk?" Tigu asked.

Ri Zu shifted uncomfortably as her nails retracted from Tigu's skin. She went silent, and Tigu slowed. It was getting a bit too crowded anyway.

Tigu awaited Ri Zu's reason for hiding away. Was she simply that dedicated to refining her abilities? None of the Petals had noticed her, as far as Tigu could tell.

'Master's story about cultivators were . . . no. Ri Zu cannot blame them.' There was a great sigh. *'Ri Zu is just nervous. And after meeting Biyu . . . it is hard. It is like you said. They look at you differently. What is the point of Ri Zu being there, if only to be stared at like an oddity?'*

There was frustration there. Frustration Tigu understood. She sighed, then slowed her stride a bit more. They still had plenty of time—maybe she *had* been a bit overeager.

Ri Zu sighed again. *'And Ri Zu could smell pills. Especially upon the Sect Master. They were different, less acrid smelling, yet they were there. They . . . they smelled like Chow Ji.'*

Tigu frowned. "I do not believe the Petals have nefarious ends."

'Ri Zu knows. Ri Zu just couldn't . . . Ri Zu was scared,' the rat said, sounding disappointed in herself. *'Look at Ri Zu. Her mouth is big, and she squeaks mightily, yet she still hides away from the world.'*

Tigu's finger found Ri Zu's nose with a harsh flick. Ri Zu squeaked and snorted with outrage.

"*Hmph*! I have acknowledged you, Bi De has acknowledged you, yet you say this manner of things? Have you not trained hard? Are you not a member of Fa Ram? If they have foul intent, or poison pills, then that just means you have to defeat them like you did Chow Ji, no?"

Ri Zu said nothing, but Tigu was fairly certain the quiet one was thinking.

"What did Master and Mistress say about trying?" Tigu asked.

'Try and fail, rather than not try at all,' Ri Zu muttered petulantly. Her little fist reached out and boxed Tigu's ear. Ha! It did not hurt at all! *'Very well! Ri Zu shall keep you safe from poisons! Now hurry up! That was the second gong!'*

Tigu's eyes widened at the reverberating tone, deeper than the first, making her chest feel like it was vibrating.

She shot off to the west once again.

"And if you feel like you don't belong, and if you still can't get people to treat you as you wish, just become human! Though they may still dislike your personality—you *are* rather annoying!"

Ri Zu once more said nothing. Though there was a menacing aura that dripped out of the little rat, which got Tigu's heart pumping pleasantly and a cold sweat dripping down her back.

She would *most certainly* be checking her food, though.

The crowds thinned as they neared the western gate. Tigu could already see it, the massive edifice of stone that looked to go through one of the mountains so they could reach the arena within. Everything was just so big here! It was a bit silly, really. Why would they drill through the mountain, when it was already split in two?

Tigu shook her head at the thought of it. As she drew closer, there were fewer people lining the streets. Tigu saw one boy from the marching cultivators bow his head slightly as an older woman kissed him on both cheeks. Another man raised both his arms, egging on a rough-looking group of people who hooted and hollered for him. Others were alone, their eyes set as they approached the gate. The scent of flowers mixed with the feeling of tension and determination. Tigu rolled back her shoulders and strode forwards.

The gate was flanked by two statues, coiling dragons that entwined over their heads, staring down imperiously at all who would walk beneath their stern gaze.

More veiled clerks stood at the entryway. Tigu waited in the small line that formed at the gate, hopping from foot to foot with excitement. One of the older men looked back at her. Tigu offered him a smile, yet the man only scoffed, shaking his head.

Rude.

It did not take long for her to get to the front, where the clerk accepted her jade token with a small nod.

"Thank you for your service!" Tigu told the clerk as she walked in. She could sense the amusement from the man.

Slowly, the drums, the horns, and the cheers of the crowds faded, until all that was left was silence when Tigu got to the waiting room. It was a wide, vaulted stone room, full of ancient carvings on the walls, and lit with crystals. It was a spartan place, with only a few benches to sit. It was about half full with participants, nearly a hundred people in the room. Against one wall were the clerks, who were writing things down and speaking quietly to each other. Nearly every person looked at her as she entered, their eyes probing. The atmosphere was focused and tense, and few were talking.

There was a dull rumble a moment later as the entire mountain seemed to vibrate.

The third gong sounded.

Tigu felt a smile spread actress her face. It was nearly time! She could barely wait!

She glanced around. The atmosphere was tense. Few looked relaxed enough for her to approach, so she went to sit by a wall, waiting for it all to begin.

The fourth gong sounded a few minutes later, so deep and rumbling that Tigu felt her bones vibrate, even in the mountain.

The conversations all ceased as one of the official-looking men stood. He approached a small, raised platform and stood atop it, gazing down at the assembled cultivators.

He brought his fist to his mouth and issued forth a polite cough.

"This Humble Servant of His Imperial Majesty greet—" the nasal voice began. He was cut off by the sound of pounding feet, as a panicked-looking boy finished his mad dash into the hall, skidding to a stop.

Oh, that's . . . Zang Wei? she thought, recognising the boy.

He let out a breath in obvious relief, then flushed when he realised everybody was looking at him.

The man on the stand cleared his throat again, starting again as if nobody had interrupted.

"This Humble Servant of His Imperial Majesty greets the cultivators who have assembled here today. On behalf of His Imperial Majesty's Sects, and the Azure Hills, we thank you for your contribution. Now, as you all know, the opening ceremonies will commence shortly, and for that there is a small piece of production.

Normally, one walks in with their Sect, but as you are all independent cultivators, we shall do this instead. I would ask you all to line up—see these markings upon the floor? Stand upon them, if you would. Those who are shorter in the front."

There was some shuffling, and some grumbling, but lining up went remarkably smoothly. Tigu found herself in the front, as one of the shortest there. Only one boy was shorter, and he looked even younger than Tigu!

The man on the podium nodded his head.

"The opening ceremony shall start soon. First is the judging, then the preliminary bout, which shall cut your numbers in half." His voice was cold and dispassionate as he gazed upon them all from behind his veil.

"Tomorrow, all who have registered, win or lose, may attempt to brave the Hill of Torment. It holds both treasure and dangers in equal measure. Those within may find the key to victory, or may find only injury and swift defeat."

A final gong sounded.

"May the heavens favour you this day," the man said, then turned to look up at a seam of crystal that was set into the wall.

"Once, every eight years, is this Grand Summit called!" a voice boomed through the halls. Tigu jumped, then squinted at the crystal the sound was emanating from. "We have no number for this tournament, as it has been practised since before there were any records to describe it! This is a place of battle, where our ancestors once dueled for glory!"

"Honoured guests! Honoured combatants! Today, we shall witness the purest form of cultivation! Today, we shall witness the path of ascension! With this azure sky as our witness! With His Imperial Majesty's eyes in attendance! Today, we witness the very heights of glory our Azure Hills commands! The place that shall see our younger generation rise as far as they may climb! The Dueling Peaks Grand Summit!"

There was a dull, rumbling roar.

One of the veiled men stepped in front of them, carrying a white flag with the character for "azure" upon it.

"Forwards behind me, please," the man said, and their group of one hundred began their march.

"These lone sparks seek the heavens by forging their own path!" the voice boomed, as Tigu stepped out through the last portion into the Earthly Arena.

It was dazzling, with the sun just poking up over the walls of the arena—thousands of eyes were upon her. Tigu nearly froze at the shouts, heckling, and cheers of good fortune.

The clerk with the flag marched forwards to the other end of the arena, where there was a giant banner with a phoenix upon it. The banner of the Empire. He raised the white flag high and drove it into the ground beneath it.

There were more cheers. Tigu glanced to the stands and managed to pick out the Xong brothers. Gou Ren was waving, and Yun Ren was looking through his recording crystal. Tigu waved up at them, and several other people in the stands waved back, laughing.

"They have travelled alone and forged their own paths admirably. *But will it be enough?*" the voice asked. Tigu glanced over to one of the sections, where there was a slightly rotund man standing on a pedestal of green crystal, his arms spread as he spoke into a crystal growth that came up to near his mouth.

"In their way lies the Sects! The virtuous, the noble, the profound of these Azure Hills!"

The crowd leaned forwards. To Tigu, it appeared this moment was what many had been waiting for.

The gates flew open once more, revealing the flags of the Sects.

"The experts of Grand Ravine! The undisputed power of the Azure Hills! The legendary Grand Ravine Sect!"

Hide drums thundered as the people hammered their instruments, wide-brimmed hats covering their faces. Their clothes were a riot of colour, and they looked like they had the same designs on them that the Xong brothers had—but Tigu heard some people voicing their displeasure. These people were obviously not liked by everyone! Ten cultivators marched in. They wore bandanas, and their skin was covered in geometric shapes. Tigu's eyes widened. They had drawn on themselves! It looked quite interesting! The man at their head strode in like he owned the place, his eyes flicking over them and landing for a brief moment on Tigu before he frowned and moved on.

"The ever-inscrutable Misty Lake Sect!" The Xianghua lady strode in at the head of a small group, one hand arrogantly on her hip. Her strange pack was glowing slightly, dull red light shining through vents on the side. A section of the stands began to shout and stomp their feet. Many of them were wearing reed hats, and several had long bargepoles that they slammed onto the ground. They marched to the front of the arena, where the azure flag stood, and the flag-bearer slammed it into the ground, adding the swirling symbol under the phoenix.

"The brave, the bold! Hermetic Iron!" A man who looked quite similar to her Master strode in, a massive hammer strapped across his back and with gauntlets adorning his arms. He had one man beside him, who was tall and lanky looking, and both looked grim and resolute.

The ringing of metal on metal thundered—Tigu blinked as she saw what was making the noise. *Have those people brought* anvils *up into their section?*

More and more names were called. Groups of people strode in, flags fluttering in the breeze. And at each name, another section of the arena added their voice. Some seemed to house only a few people. Others had many that would shout and chant their names.

"The slayers of Sun Ken! The rising stars! The jade swords! *The Verdant Blade!*" the man boomed.

They marched forwards in unison, and the crowd gasped. Tigu smiled at the entrance. The Blade of Grass was in fine form today! She looked absolutely at peace, even under the eyes of so many.

Tigu waved and the Blade of Grass gave her a smile. Tigu heard the other two people beside her gasp. One seemed to stagger, and Zang Wei's face flushed so red Tigu wondered if he was all right.

The entire arena was vibrating at this point, and it was getting a little hard to think. Tigu felt Ri Zu curl up into a little ball and hold her ears. Tigu's eyes darted all around. She saw the other Sects coming in. The people wearing strange clothes in the stands. Those in the isolated boxes, wearing fanciful clothes, staring down. One in particular looked kind of bored as he took a swig from a bottle. His eyes were sharp—Tigu got a bit of a bad feeling about the man.

"The Framed Sun!" the announcer's voice thundered for the last time as four people wearing reds and golds added the final flag.

"And all are here to be judged." The crowds kept cheering as another section of the arena opened up. From it came ten men, carrying a stone twice the size of Master's and Mistress's favourite rock. It was jet black and polished to nearly a mirror shine.

The cheers and calls reached a fever pitch—until with a resounding *thud*, the giant stone came to a rest in the center of the arena.

Abruptly, the cheering cut out, and silence reigned.

"Come! The honour of the first to be judged! This year, as drawn by lots: the Misty Lake Sect!"

Xianghua smirked as she and her three fellows approached the stone. All bowed first to it, then to the flag . . . and then the woman with the strange contraption on her back pressed her hands to the stone.

It hummed and rumbled, before it began to change colour. It shifted, and then the bottom seemed to start to fill with water and mist, rising partially up the stone, until a strange pictogram formed.

It looked a bit like the character for "man," with a strange box beside him.

"Liu Xianghua! The Fourth Stage of the Initiate's Realm!" the announcer's voice boomed.

The woman turned and brushed some of her hair behind her in an elegant movement, staring down imperiously at the rest of them. Several people groaned or gnashed their teeth as her power was revealed—but the people in the stands were going nuts. Cheers and howls resounded as the bargepoles slammed into the ground again.

Muttering swept through the arena.

"Fourth Stage?"

"A true power."

"Ones to look out for."

The next one pressed his hands to the stone. The mist swirled and shifted, draining a bit, and another pictogram appeared.

"Han Bao! Second Stage of the Initiate's Realm!"

There was some more muttering, but more subdued this time. One person beside Tigu was taking notes.

There came a slight shuffling form Tigu's shirt.

'This feels like it is going to take a long while,' Ri Zu muttered.

Tigu glanced around at all the people.

Yes, it probably was. And from the look of things, her group would be going last.

She sighed and shook her head.

Some of the excitement drained away, but it was kind of interesting watching all the pretty colours swirl on the stone. The Framed Sun people seemed to have a tiny sun rise on the stone, before it formed into another "man" character, with what Tigu was beginning to think was a number. The number two.

But . . . well, Initiate and three seemed to be the average, for the people who were at the heads of their processions.

Only a member of the Grand Ravine, "Strongest Sect in the Grass Sea," had another in the Fourth Stage of the Initiate's Realm.

Tigu yawned.

As more cultivators approached the stone, some people started selling meals in the stands. Tigu wished she had something to chew on.

Eventually, it was time for Xiulan's turn.

She stepped up as the crowd hushed again, then pressed her hand to the stone.

The black stone shuddered. Blades of grass swarmed up from its base, completely taking over the blank, black stone. It grew in waves, surging up, and up, until the entire stone was green.

Slowly, a *new* pictogram formed.

A strange, swirling circle, and a dash.

"P-P-Pr-Profound Realm? " the man stuttered.

The crowd grew deathly silent. The man who'd made Tigu feel a bit unsettled seemed to choke on his drink. Another old man in a different box brought his hands to his mouth, then seemed to start coughing. Xianghua's jaw dropped. Her eyes went wide, a look of shock spreading across her face.

"Ha!" she boomed. "As expected of that woman! But power shall not be enough!"

Her voice quavered, which ruined the words' forced bravado, but it broke the sudden quiet.

The crowd exploded, and Tigu picked at her ear at the sudden roar.

There was even a pause to the whole proceedings, as some man came out to check the stone and then nod at the man announcing things.

And it continued. Though nobody seemed to be paying much attention after that. Everybody was muttering, or talking about "the Demon-Slaying Orchid."

Finally, though, after the Sects went, it was finally their turn to be judged. A few more First Stage Initiates, and even a person who it came up blank for, to the jeers of the crowd.

Tigu touched the stone. What looked like massive rents cut across it, until another symbol formed.

"Rou Tigu! Fifth Stage!" the announcer man shouted. The crowd once more howled.

With a shrug, she stepped off the stage, ignoring everybody staring at her.

I hope the fights start soon—or they at least get us something to eat, I'm hungry! she thought as she walked back to her place.

CHAPTER 12

CULTURE SHOCK

As he stared around at the chatter, the exclamations, and the sheer excitement in the crowd, Gou Ren realised that he still didn't really *get* cultivation. Jin had explained the basics to them, of course. About how cultivators ascended in realms and got more powerful, but none of them had been too interested in the details at the time. He had heard the stories too. But thinking about the Spiritual Realm or the Earth Realm, or whatever the realms were, he didn't know *exactly* where everything landed. Most of the stories just kind of mentioned this stuff offhand, and he didn't exactly read them himself. He would just sit down in front of Meimei when she had a scroll in hand, she'd give him the stink eye, and then she'd start reading aloud whatever story she was currently on.

All he knew was that the Profound Realm must be pretty impressive, to have people spitting out their drinks. That one old man in the box across the arena had coughed so hard he spat out blood.

Gou Ren hoped he was all right.

"I'm guessing Xiulan's rank is pretty good?" he muttered to his brother, who shrugged. He didn't seem too concerned and was busy watching the odd stone shift colours. It was pretty neat.

"P-pretty good?" he heard a man sitting beside them splutter at his comment. "That's amazing, especially for the Azure Hills!"

Gou Ren turned to the man. He had long, slightly greasy hair and looked downright offended by Gou Ren's statement. His robe had a number of patches on it, and he had a small brush along with a pad of paper on his lap. The man looked the Xong brothers up and down, his eyes lingering on Gou Ren's headband and Yun Ren's scarf.

"You boys from up north?" he guessed.

Gou Ren nodded, a bit surprised at the man's insight. "Yeah. It's our first time watching something like this."

The man's eyes went from accusatory to wide with enthusiasm.

"First time at a tournament! Well, allow this Tao the Traveller to enlighten you. You know the realms, correct?"

"Initiate, Profound, Spirit?" Yun Ren answered, leaning in curiously. "I think Heavenly and Earth go in there somewhere."

The man nodded his head. "Half right. Initiate, Profound, Spiritual, Earth, Sky, Imperial, and the last that we know of is the Heavenly, or Divine Realm, with five minor stages between each realm. A cultivator's power in each step grows exponentially."

"So they just get stronger and stronger?" Gou Ren asked, nodding.

"Well, there are also other differences. Other provinces say that Profound is when you become a 'true' cultivator, as that is when the body truly begins to change. An Initiate, they say, is just a mortal with power! Your flesh is just flesh. Your bones, just bones. In the Profound Realm, your body begins to harden and grow beyond what you are at your birth. In other provinces, for a youth tournament like this, Profound would likely be the requirement for entry. I know that in the Immortal Flame Tournament in the Imperial Capital, one must be at *least* in the Spiritual Realm."

The man had started wagging his finger, excitedly gesticulating as he talked, a bit like Meimei when she went entirely too deep into an explanation on medicine. He glanced at his brother, who rolled his eyes at the explanation, but neither of them interrupted.

"In the Spiritual Realm, your soul strengthens! It becomes a thing you can make tangible, to armour yourself entirely and ward off attacks. It is also when most cultivators create their cores, a mass of solidified Qi that is the catalyst for further ascension. At the Earth Realm, their body is completely remade: their skin turns to jade and their bones transform into the hardest of metals! In the Sky Realm, a cultivator creates their domain, imposing their spirit upon the world like the Cloudy Sword Sect's Raging Cloudy Sword Formation!"

Finally, the man seemed to be finished, his eyes gleaming.

"What about the Imperial and Heavenly ones?" Gou Ren asked out of curiosity.

Tao the Traveller shrugged. "I don't know much, other than they are the realms of overwhelming power. They say the Endless Ocean was made by a cultivator in the Divine Realm—that our continent was once twice the size but was shattered by a single punch! It's amazing, isn't it?"

Gou Ren grinned. To be able to split a continent in a single punch sounded so awesome—and then he paused and thought about it for a second. In his mind, he hefted a rock onto his back that would need every man in the village to lift. He remembered Jin's sad smile, his eyes serious as he asked:

"What do you want to do with power?"

Gou Ren clenched his hand into a fist. He could grind rocks to dust by *squeezing* them. What would happen to a *person*?

He shook his head, shoving the thoughts away, and focusing again on the stone.

"But you boys are in for a treat!" Tao continued. "There's something special about these bouts. Like the fact that us mortals can actually see the cultivators still move! The tournament in the Howling Fang Mountains I went to, well, all I could see were the flashes from the techniques!"

Gou Ren raised an eyebrow.

"Why go watch it, then?" he asked

"Why would I not! It was an amazing experience," Tao declared, his eyes shining with passion. "I may not have any proper meridians of my own, but I do get to see wonders like this! And in my home province as well."

Gou Ren glanced at his brother, and they both shrugged.

"You know much about this arena?" he asked.

Tao grinned. "Of course! See that gong up there?" he asked, pointing. "That is the Thunder of the Earth! Treasure of the Earthly Arena . . ."

The voice from below echoed, as the man launched into an explanation. The gong was a lot more interesting!

↔

"Zang Wei! Second Stage of the Initiate's Realm!" Bai Huizong boomed. The Resounding Crystal Dais beneath him hummed as it took his words and echoed them for all to hear, though his voice was strained from how much he had shouted earlier. He was still excited, however, and his tone reflected that. There was always a feeling of immense power when he stood here, his voice thundering like he was some manner of cultivator himself. He captured the minds of all who heard him.

Bai Huizong, His Imperial Majesty's Director of Spiritual Ascension Affairs for the Azure Hills, loved his job—even if his title was far grander than his duties actually entailed.

He was a glorified tourney host most of the time. The Sects often wanted a "neutral" observer for these multi-Sect events, and who better than one of their technical overlords, as they were supposedly beholden to the Crimson Phoenix Empire. The Sects did their business, and like most in his position, as long as they committed no treasonous offence he looked the other way when they were less than ideal in their behaviour. What could he do, anyway? He was just a mortal.

"Zei Lin, First Stage of the Initiate's Realm!" he thundered, as the final person stepped away from the stone.

To his surprise, there was only a single mortal who had tried to sneak in this year. A record! Normally, the Judgement Stone was there to weed out those with weak cultivation, but at this tournament there was technically no rule preventing them from participating. Such was the weakness of the Azure Hills, but they tended to get brutalized rather badly in the first round.

Except for once, where a tricky lad had managed to defeat an Initiate of the First Stage, albeit through the ring-out rule that was implemented in the preliminaries. A sorry business, that. The cultivator took his own life out of shame. The boy, who bowed out after his single victory, had later been found beaten to death by what most assumed were the cultivator's sectmates. The killers had never been found.

"Now that all have been judged, we shall assign the brackets!" he said, gesturing to the set of tables by the walls. His men were already in position, and the rest of the labourers were preparing to cordon off the separate rings for the preliminary bouts.

Bai Huizong stepped off the Resounding Crystal Dais and took the cloth that was offered by his assistant, mopping his damp forehead. It did take a bit out of him to use the device, and the sun's rays were getting him quite hot.

He glanced around at the stands. Normally, this small preparatory period would have most people start to wander off, to go and bet, or to start to file out for some food after the long opening ceremony. Not so this time. Everyone in attendance was still glued to their seats, discussing the outcome of the judging stage. The crowds were positively buzzing, and he could see those in the private seats discussing things excitedly, or in the cases of the Sects looking increasingly worried.

Huizong could not blame them.

Profound Realm. A cultivator in her twenties had ascended to the Profound Realm. Such a thing just did not happen in the Azure Hills! The first in nearly a thousand years, if he remembered his history of the summit correctly.

Huizong was supposed to be impartial, but he couldn't help but enjoy this development. He would have to direct his company to make more Demon-Slaying Orchid dolls. They were already a hit, but this would surely bring him riches untold!

And the other surprise, Rou Tigu—an independent, no less! A girl coming out of nowhere with such a high cultivation was something straight out of a story. The "official" tournament report would surely be a best seller this year as well.

Huizong looked idly at the brackets as they started to form. They were already mostly decided. The Sects would never stand for their Young Masters and Mistresses knocking each other out in the preliminaries, so pitting them against those of their own Sect was right out.

Indeed, Cai Xiulan was matched against a member of the Framed Sun Sect. It would have been a horrid mismatch even before she fought Sun Ken.

Now? It was an *execution*.

He sat calmly in his seat as the rest of the matches were assigned. He drank some of the fine wine set nearby, wetting his parched throat. The vast stone colosseum was showing its age, but it was still grand and awe-inspiring. An edifice from before recorded history. The people sat in rows on stone benches, rising up into the sky. The Sect Masters were in their boxes, staring down at the grounds with frowns on their faces, stern and calculating.

"Sir. Starting bets are in," one of his men whispered. "As expected, Cai Xiulan is the front-runner, and our earnings are looking *very* good this year."

Huizong smiled. "Excellent news. Any outliers?"

"No, sir. Everything seems to be proceeding as it should be."

"Good." He glanced at the completed bracket. "And close the betting soon. We'll be starting shortly."

His clerk bowed, then strode away. Huizong glanced to the arena, which had been sectioned off into sixteen separate areas, each with its own proctor. The first round was done in batches.

Huizong stood and stretched. He cleared his throat before stepping back onto the Resounding Crystal Dais.

"The stages are set! The combatants are ready! They shall abide by all virtues and bring only glory to themselves and their Sects!" His voice boomed out once more. All eyes were upon ring three, where Cai Xiulan stood calmly before her opponent. "Victory in this round is by ring-out or submission!"

The contestants bowed to each other.

Huizong raised his hand. The men on top of the colosseum, on the west-facing mountain, shouted a command. A striker—a single piece of wood that was thicker around than ten trees lashed together—was pulled back by hundreds of labourers. It was said there were once glowing characters upon the gong and the striker, but they had long since faded and been replaced by paint.

The men held their position on top of the arena. The sun glinted off the dull grey metal of the gong, impossibly ancient and still unmarred, despite thousands of years of use.

Huizong lowered his hand sharply.

The men heaved the striker forwards, right into the center of the gong. A force that could surely shatter the gates of Pale Moon Lake City in a single blow hammered into the center of the gong.

The sound was indescribable, the strange shape of the arena and the mountains making it reverberate and harmonize.

"Begin!" he commanded.

The first bouts started.

And one of them ended.

The Junior of the Framed Sun Sect was outside the arena.

Cai Xiulan stood, her eyes calm and serene, with her palm on the boy's chest.

She had not even drawn her blades. There was a slight cloud of dust from where the boy's feet had tried to dig in and failed. In any other case, this would be a humiliating, devastating loss.

Instead, the boy looked relieved as the Young Mistress of the Verdant Blade Sect pulled her hand back and bowed, gracing him with a smile. The boy's face flushed, and he looked dazed, though he managed his own gesture of respect in return.

The crowds, predictably, went wild. There was another eruption of cheering as the masses praised the Young Mistress's restraint and benevolence. Mercy, as always, was the domain of the strong. The recording crystals of the Sects were surely focused upon her, and they would likely be reviewing their recordings feverishly, searching for anything that they might use as an advantage.

The boy even received conciliatory looks from his sectmates on the sidelines, the Young Master of the Sect simply patting his shoulder.

It was a bit disappointing to know the winner before even the tournament really began, but that was life sometimes. He only hoped that there was one who could provide her with enough challenge to give the crowd a good show.

The next set of bouts had nothing so exciting. Liu Xianghua, who would have made waves for being at the Fourth Stage of the Initiate's Realm, now seemed almost to be forgotten. She had a pensive look on her face, distracted, but it was still not enough to stop her from expertly slamming the pommel of her sword into her opponent's head, knocking him out.

The other fights, in comparison, were mostly quite tame. Swords clashed, and there was some blood and broken bones, but largely, they were expected outcomes. The crowd above shouted their enjoyment, cheering and whooping as sixteen more fights were conducted at once.

The next bout had Rou Tigu versus one of the Juniors of the Hermetic Iron Sect.

The wild-looking girl was bouncing from foot to foot, her eyes narrow as the man drew out a one-handed hammer and slammed his fist into the plates on his chest. He was looking nervous—which was understandable as he faced off against a woman three stages above him.

The gong sounded.

Rou Tigu shot forwards to slam her fist into the boy's chest plate. He staggered backwards at the blow, though the girl took no steps to chase him further or capitalise on the opening.

Instead, planting her hands on her hips, she shouted something at the boy. Then she went in again, sending out a light jab to his face that rocked his head to the side. Then she retreated, watching him with narrowed eyes. She played with him like a cat with a mouse.

The crowd, of course, loved it. They laughed and jeered as she danced around the taller boy, striking him with impunity.

What a vicious little creature, toying with him so! Huizong could only imagine what insults she was shouting at her opponent and what abuse he was suffering!

Off to the side, the Young Master of the Hermetic Iron Sect had to be restrained, his face flushed red in anger, clearly indignant on the behalf of the injury inflicted to his Junior.

Huizong could almost see the finals now. The serene Cai Xiulan versus the wild Rou Tigu. The villainous, mocking girl versus the noble Verdant Blade!

He sat back to watch the show.

↔

Tigu struggled to hold back a yawn as she started to repeat the same moves. She had been so excited for her first bout, ready for the enjoyable time that was to come. And then the Blade of Grass had finished her fight in the time it took her to blink. And as she had stared around at the others, at the fighters she was supposed to play with, they—well, they disappointed.

This one looked promising enough, with his armour and his mallet, but the way he swung it was so strange. Halfway between a man who used a mallet to carve stone, and Uncle Che, with his hammering of iron. She supposed that may be the case, as he had many interesting engravings upon his armor and hammer. The fight may not be interesting, but the carvings were. They were pleasing to the eye, and that soothed some of her irritation.

He was a tall, lanky one, and when Tigu tested his defenses, she nearly threw him out of the arena! It was shocking! *Ri Zu* put up a better fight than him! So Tigu had switched tracks, and treated the interaction like a sparring session.

At least he was learning. Tigu's hand flashed out, and this time, the boy managed to interpose his hammer. His eyes widened in pride and accomplishment.

She nodded and pushed. The boy skidded backward and tripped, falling out of the arena. Perhaps, if she came to another tourney, he would put up a better fight the next time?

She bowed, as a "virtuous bearing" demanded, and the boy bowed back.

"Worry not about this loss, Junior Brother. I shall repay her a hundred-fold for what she did!" a voice boomed. There were a couple of shouts, and a commotion from off to the side.

"And it appears the Young Master of the Hermetic Iron Sect has taken to the field!" the fat man on the podium shouted excitedly.

Tigu turned as a man approached, and her eyes widened. He had a small splattering of freckles on his cheeks, but his form. Oh, his form was intriguing!

He was the right height, his muscles defined, his form cut perfectly. With his engraved armor, and his bearing, he would make a fine sculpture! Not as fine a sculpture as her Master, but she would still ask him later. He was the only one so far who tickled her urge to craft.

The man had one arm reaching back to his hammer, when her opponent stepped in front of him.

"She was telling me how to properly block her blows!" her opponent, Lanky Hammer, exclaimed. "We were trading pointers, and she was most kind to me, Senior Brother."

The tall man paused, his eyes roving all over her opponent's body, checking for damage.

"She spent the entire time telling me that my blocking was inefficient, and that to properly disrupt a faster foe, I needed to have a looser stance. The second to last hit, before she removed me from the arena . . . was the same as her first. I managed to block it," Lanky Hammer said proudly. As he should be! Tigu had taught him, which naturally made him just slightly superior to others here!

The big man still looked a bit confused and his face, which had been a dark red, took on a more pleasing bronze shade.

"Is this true?" he asked Tigu.

"Yes! His carvings were quite pleasing, and though it was a boring fight, I decided to trade pointers with him. Perhaps next time, he will pose a better challenge," she said with a shrug.

She looked all over the freckled man's body. He was covered in light scars and carvings. He would make an excellent subject!

Slowly, a tentative smile formed on his face.

"I thank you for taking care of my junior, then," he said, bowing slightly.

Tigu smiled back. "Your freckles and muscles are quite pleasing! You remind me of my master! I hope to meet you in combat later,"—*What could be a good name for this one?*—"Handsome Man!"

Yes, that one worked. He was certainly far more appealing than any of the others here. So tiny and thin! Not worth sculpting at all!

The man's face went red again, his jaw dropped. Tigu waved goodbye to them both, and wandered back to her section.

But she couldn't ignore how much her shirt was shaking, nor the little squeaks of mirth.

"Hm? What is so funny, Ri Zu?" she asked.

CHAPTER 13

RAISING THE STAKES

Tigu yawned as the last bouts started. The person who had their stone show up blank was almost absently pushed out of the ring by the Handsome Man, who appeared deep in thought, with his face still a bit red, though he was constantly sneaking glances at Tigu.

Ri Zu would not explain why she should not call him "Handsome Man," only that it was inappropriate.

Tigu shrugged, then glanced around. All of the Petals had made it through the first match, and were looking mighty pleased with themselves as they stood beside the Blade of Grass.

There was a shout from the crowd as the loud one, Zang Wei, suddenly shifted and the man who had been pummeling him went flying out of the arena.

He panted harshly but managed to raise his arms in victory.

The gong sounded, and the combatants were directed to line up once more, though the losers were separated. Some of them had tears in their eyes. Others were hunched and tired-looking. They were injured and beaten. But some of the defeated fighters still had steel in their spine.

Tigu didn't exactly know what she should feel for them. A large part of her scoffed at their weakness. Another part, one that had been steadily growing during her time in human form, felt an odd sort of sympathy. She knew what it was like to be defeated again and again.

The participants stood behind one of the veiled men, who led them out of the arena to the sound of half cheers and half jeers.

"Give thanks to the defeated!" the voice boomed, and the crowd began to stomp their feet. "And all in the stands, sit and brace yourselves!"

The gong began to sound. Each thunderous strike set the whole stadium vibrating.

Then there was an odd grating sound, and the entire stadium *heaved*. Some of the competitors staggered.

The ground rumbled. The mountain groaned . . . and the Earthly Arena began to rise.

"Heave!" the crowd shouted. The gong sounded, and they inched up again.

"Heave!" Another shudder. The crowd pounded their feet.

"Heave!" The entire stadium groaned . . . and not a single *crack* or sound of falling rock echoed, as the Earthly Arena rose.

"Heave!" they roared one final time. There was a shuddering, grinding sound.

The arena stopped moving, something locking into place beneath their feet.

"Give thanks to the Masters! Give thanks to the defeated!" the voice boomed. "For it is with their strength that the great arena rises!"

Tigu, this time, cheered with the rest of the crowd. *That was quite exhilarating!*

The man cleared his throat as the defeated ones walked in. They were sweaty and exhausted-looking, most of them stripped of their shirts, as they lined up once more.

Some seemed confused as they were given water and several of the aides wiped their sweat with towels. They clearly hadn't been expecting anything but jeers for being defeated.

"And now, honoured combatants and guests, with the First Ascension of the Earthly Arena, we shall reveal the brackets!" the voice boomed once more.

The air above the arena spluttered to life and fuzzed. Tigu rubbed her eyes as slowly, haltingly, a giant image formed. It winked out of existence for a brief few seconds before forming again. Then it spiraled around in a giant orb, showing names and lines travelling towards the center.

Tigu pouted. She was on the opposite side of the chart to the Blade of Grass! Would she truly have to wait so long to have some fun? Her next opponent was one from that Grand Ravine place.

She shook her head as the crowd continued to cheer.

"Now, tomorrow is the Hill of Torment, and there will also be an auction held in the Azure Jade Trading Company's halls! The bouts will resume in two days, at the same time as they commenced today! Being late is grounds for disqualification!"

With that, they were dismissed. There was another room on the side of the mountain, one with a spiral staircase, that she was directed through until she was back onto the streets.

She wandered out with the rest of the competitors through the gates; once through she yawned again, stretching, as the rest of them gave her a wide berth.

'So? You have won your first bout. Was it what you were hoping for?' Ri Zu asked.

"Not really," Tigu replied. She kicked at the ground, then wandered over to the other entrance. She supposed it was nice to have different people to fight. But it wasn't anything special. *Hopefully, the Hill of Torment tomorrow will be fun.*

She sighed, looking up at the sky. Her fellow disciples had told her they would meet her here after the match.

She was only waiting for a couple of minutes before she heard a small commotion in one of the alleyways nearby. Two people were shouting at each other, and it sounded quite aggressive.

"Should I see what that is?" she asked.

'I suppose,' Ri Zu squeaked, poking her little nose out and raising her eyebrow at Tigu.

"I'm not running off this time! I'll be back here in a second!" Tigu said more to herself than Ri Zu, who rolled her eyes. Tigu walked forwards, towards the raised voices.

A ragged-looking man and his group were surrounding Zang Wei, who was glaring back. Tigu remembered the man fighting, but his friends had all been in the stands—and Tigu didn't think any of them were cultivators.

"I think there may be a little accident if you don't bow out, boy. It's for your own good!" the lead man said, leering.

Zang Wei's eyes narrowed.

"Well, maybe *you* might suffer an accident!" he thundered back, getting into a martial stance. *Why were they fighting? Did they not—*

Tigu remembered Zang Wei flipping to the end and signing the sheet, not reading it at all.

How foolish.

Tigu frowned at the scene and debated letting them continue, but finally sighed and decided to speak up.

"That will disqualify you, fools," she stated, irritated. Everybody paused.

The ragged man whirled, a snarl on his face, before it slid off as Tigu stepped out of the shadows. He quickly waved his hand, and his group stopped surrounding the loud Zang Wei.

"One must always act with a virtuous bearing. Fighting outside the specified grounds shall lead to immediate disqualification. Did *neither* of you read the forms they got us to sign?" she demanded.

Both of them paled, then glanced at each other and back to her. "I, uh, can't read," the rough-looking man muttered.

"The courtly characters are hard," Zang Wei agreed. "But . . . everybody else was signing it, so it was probably fine?"

Indeed, the courtly characters were hard, but that was no excuse!

Tigu shrugged.

"Competitors get free food from Chao Baozi too," she said blandly.

Both of them perked up at that.

"A fortuitous encounter," Zang Wei muttered to himself, before bowing. "Thank you for enlightening me, Fairy Sister! Would you do me the honour of dining with me?" he asked brightly.

"Oi! No, eat with us, Big Sis!" the man in rags tried. "The Farrow Gang owes ya, yeah?"

"No. Go about your business, Loud Boy, Rags," she replied, deciding on both of their names. Her curiosity satisfied, she began to walk away.

The rough-looking man spluttered, while the men behind him looked a bit offended.

"Look at that, you ugly Rags, you scared that icy beauty away!"

"Ha, you loud little shit, I'm going to beat your teeth into the back of your throat in the ring!" the big man snarled. "Be grateful she interfered, and that these rules are foolish!"

Tigu glanced back. They were arguing with each other as they travelled in the same direction, the group of people trailing behind them.

With a shrug, she wandered back to the meeting spot—just in time for her fellow disciples to round the corner.

"Where is the Blade of Grass?" she asked.

"She was told to bring the rest of the students directly to the manor," Yun Ren said. "So they're all going there, though we got some time to kill, if you want."

Tigu nodded. "I get free food at Chao Baozi," she told them.

Both brothers started stroking imaginary beards sagely. "Never turn down free food," they said in unison, and set off.

"So what did you say to that hammer guy?" Disciple Gou Ren asked, as they strolled through the streets towards the restaurant.

"Oh? I said I would see the Handsome Man later," she said, ignoring Gou Ren's sudden coughing fit and the return of Ri Zu's chittering laughter. "His muscles and freckles are quite nice, and I would like to carve him!"

Yun Ren stared at her and then burst into laughter, ruffling her hair.

Tigu *still* didn't see what was so funny about it.

They kept bugging her about it for a long time, even during their dinner. It was a bit annoying, but at least the meat buns were good. She felt quite refreshed after eating them.

She would have to come here tomorrow! Like her fellow disciples had said, free food was never to be turned down!

They returned to the compound of the Verdant Blade, and Tigu drifted off to sleep. She wondered what her Master would think. And what he was doing right now.

They were probably having an exciting time!

↔

Bi De stood on the front of the great travelling fortress-coop as it trundled down the road, making for Pale Moon Lake City. The wind caressed his feathers while a song drifted on the breeze.

Steady, twanging tones drifted out of his Great Master's "Ban Jo" as he sat on top of the rice. He hummed along to a tune only he knew, a straw hat pulled low over his eyes and a stalk of grain in his mouth.

Miantiao was beside him, basking in the sun on the tarp-covered rice bags.

His Great Master had been in an odd mood since they set off. Half nervousness, half excitement. He seemed convinced that something strange or bad would happen on the road, his eyes searching for some manner of hidden danger.

It was such that Bi De had redoubled his own watch, flying high and circling around at night, looking for anything that could cause his Great Master such distress.

But as the days dragged on, his Great Master managed to relax. He took calming breaths in the morning, and spent longer than usual doing his morning stretches, but his mood *did* improve.

His Great Master raised his hand in greeting as another cart came the other way on the road. Its occupants stared incredulously at the sight, their eyes wide. One of the older men looked into his bottle with concern before shaking his head and studiously ignoring them.

Bi De's Great Master chuckled as he kept strumming his instrument.

"You okay down there?" he asked, sitting up and glancing at the front of the cart.

'Hell yeah!' Yin panted as she strained against the ropes, pulling them onwards. *'Strength training, for the rematch against Senior Sister!'* the rabbit enthused.

Their Great Master nodded. "Well, whenever you want to switch back, call me. Don't want you to hurt yourself," he said, before leaning back again.

He'd seemed quite surprised when Yin had asked to pull the cart this morning. Bi De's Great Master had obviously been intending to carry them the entire way. And while Yin was obviously much slower than their Master, he allowed it.

His Great Master did eventually take back over, after scolding a panting Yin for pushing herself too hard. It was not so much the weight as it was the awkward way she had to pull their load.

His hand ruffled the rabbit's fur, and she leaned back into the touch gladly, giggling slightly.

Bi De's Master shook his head, then set off at a faster pace.

Yin stared at his back as she settled in beside Miantiao. She turned to Bi De, her eyes full of warmth.

'Thank you for bringing us, Bi De!' she cheered.

Bi De smiled at her as they journeyed onwards.

They stopped for the night not long after. His Great Master stretched and yawned.

"Getting a bit heavier, it feels like," he muttered, experimentally lifting the cart. He did not seem overly concerned, however. He made them their meal before he drifted off to sleep on top of the sacks of rice.

Bi De was getting ready to join him when he noticed a movement in the forest. His eyes narrowed, and he went to investigate, Yin beside him.

"Quick in and out, yeah?" a voice stated confidently.

"Are you sure about this? How did he get it here—he doesn't have any oxen!"

"It doesn't matter, we'll call the rest of the boys!"

"But what if he's . . . *ya know?*" the man muttered nervously.

"What, *a cultivator*? They don't travel these roads!" the other scoffed.

Bi De had heard enough. He coughed politely while Yin smiled brilliantly.

Both men whirled. Then, they paused, staring incredulously at them both. There was a moment of silence.

"Huh? *A chicken?*" the more assertive one demanded.

"And a bunny?" the other muttered.

There was a brief moment of violence.

The less assertive one was rather quick to lead them to his comrades.

The next morning, the Great Master stared blankly at the pile of groaning men.

He took a breath and let it out.

"Good job," he stated and scratched behind Yin's ears.

They reached the gates of the city the next day.

CHAPTER 14

THE CRYSTAL DEAL

Yes, sir. You may store your wares here. I swear upon the honour of the Pale Moon Lake City Guard that none shall lay a hand upon it," the guard said as he handed me a note with a seal on it. He and his fellows saluted me respectfully. "This will be where your wares will be stored." He pointed to a storage area on the map, near one of the guardhouses.

"Thanks. You boys have a good day, now!" I called out to them. They bowed once again, then took the bandits to the temporary holding cells. The bandits were apparently a newer group, but there had already been complaints about them. They were originally a gang from the city that had been pushed out into the countryside.

If I had a nickel for every time I had to take people to the police after arresting them, I'd have two nickels. Which isn't a lot, but it is a bit strange that it happened twice.

With a shrug, I headed over to the place the guards had directed me to, lugging the cart. It had been a bit funny to see the looks on their faces as I wandered in pulling this monstrosity, with a bunch of beaten-up bandits tied up on it. The men still seemed a bit shell-shocked and had been silent the entire trip. The guards were quite polite, though they'd all appeared caught by surprise. I think they were slacking off, because they had something that was emitting a dull buzz, like an alarm clock, and all of them were shooting it nervous glances.

It was strange being in Pale Moon Lake City again, but I suppose it was nice. I hadn't really looked around too much when I was here the last time, since I'd been running from the Cloudy Sword Sect. I had gotten in and out as fast as I could, on a rainy, miserable day. This Pale Moon Lake City was much livelier than that one, and while I didn't particularly like the smell, I did want to at least explore this time. The buildings looked fantastic, in all their tiered glory. It was a living, breathing, ancient city. One with parks and pavilions sprinkled throughout it. Surprisingly, it was very clean. The wide avenues were clear of trash or dung, for the most part, with the worst of it being confined to the slums we'd passed by outside the walls.

It was a little irritating getting the cart through the streets, though, and I would be glad to have somewhere to store it. My muscles weren't sore, but I was getting pretty tired mentally. Which made sense, really. Going to Verdant Hill wasn't exactly that long a trip, so I guess fatigue never really had time to build up.

The people at the depot were efficient. They took the note, then immediately led me to a windowless warehouse with a thick, heavy set of iron doors, where my cart was locked up tight.

And then it was off into the city, heading to the Crystal Emporium, with a rabbit stuffed down the front of my shirt, a snake curled around my arm, and a chicken on my shoulder. They were all eager and excited to accomplish their mission, the crystal secure in my pack.

Mengde's Crystal Emporium was pretty easy to find, especially with Yun Ren's directions. If the enormous columns and gold filigree in the doors hadn't been enough of a giveaway, the shop was *massive*. The obvious crystals surrounding it really drove home how "fantasy" this section of the city was. That, and the giant palace visible nearby that was probably as big as half the Forbidden City of Beijing. Seriously, I think the Imperial Government was compensating for something.

I opened the door, the sound of another buzzer greeting us as we walked in. A man at the front perked up—

"Hey, long time no see!" I called to him, and his eyes widened. It was the guy who had come to Verdant Hill to sell me my first crystal! He did a bit of a double take at the animals on me, before shaking his head.

"Ah, honoured customer!" he said, glancing at the clattering device. It was making quite the racket. He tapped it once, which apparently turned it off. "Is everything well with your purchase?"

I waved him off. "Everything is perfect. I'm actually here to see Biyu?" I asked. The man nodded, but I caught some grumbling about "lucky geniuses."

He went to the back, leaving me alone for a moment in the nearly empty shop. I took the time to gawk at the crystals. Some of them were faintly luminescent. A few of the crystals were stored in special stone cases, and others were simply in lacquered boxes. Honestly? They looked a bit like fake plastic, which was kind of funny.

"Um, Master Jin?" a soft voice asked, and I turned. Biyu looked exactly like the pictures Yun Ren had taken of her. Wide eyes, fluffy hair, and a tentative smile.

"Yeah, that's me! Nice to finally meet you, Biyu!" I said, exchanging bows with the woman. Her eyes flicked to Bi De, then to Yin, and sparked for a brief moment with childish joy before she got it under control.

"Master Jin, Bi De, Master Fang awaits. He wishes to meet as soon as you are able, if it pleases you," she said formally, and Big D ruffled his feathers happily at the acknowledgement.

"I'm good to meet now, if he's ready," I told her. She nodded once, determination coming over her features.

"This way, then, please!" she said, and turned, leading me through the building and out the back.

The building was pretty big, and there was an entire courtyard behind it. One filled with trees, and even a stream stocked with koi.

"I've seen the images, but this place is really nice," I said, making conversation.

Biyu jumped a little at my words, looking a bit awkward. I knew her type well, from both experience and Yun Ren's stories. Biyu was a bit of an introvert, it seemed.

"Uh, it's lovely, isn't it?" she said, smiling tentatively.

"Yeah. I'd like to have worked in a place this nice, back before I became a farmer. Sweeping the streets kinda sucked!"

Biyu seemed a bit shocked at my words, and then a commiserating smile came over her face.

"Sorry for adding to the woes of the street sweepers. Before this, I was with my mother gutting fish."

I chuckled, having successfully disarmed some of her nervousness.

"Bit of a big change, eh? But a good one. Yun Ren said you got promoted recently?"

"Ah, yes, it's been very busy, especially after Yun's gift. It's so . . . so interesting, all the ancient styles!" she enthused, her eyes shining. "And Master Fang is very happy with how I'm progressing! And . . . um, sorry. I know of Bi De, but you two are?" she politely asked my other two companions. I smiled at the earnest question.

'Noodle,' the snake said in greeting. Or rather, he said "Miantiao," which *meant* "noodle."

'Yin!' the rabbit said, introducing herself.

Biyu's smile went all wobbly as Yin hopped up to her, bowing. The woman let out a little squeak, and her eyes started to sparkle as she beheld Yin. That's kind of cute. "If I may be so bold, Yin, you are very beautiful!" she said, and the rabbit preened. Now that the introductions were done, Biyu led us to a slightly smaller building, nestled against the back wall in the normal style of multiple buildings in a courtyard. One that was the most ornamented out of the lot. It looked old.

"Anything I should know before meeting your Master?" I asked.

She seemed to think for a moment. "I don't think so?" she replied nervously. "He has always been kind to me, but . . ." She trailed off.

I nodded. "Well, thanks for the help. Dinner tonight, my treat? I got some embarrassing stories of Yun Ren, directly from his mom."

Biyu's face flushed red, and then she laughed, knocking on the door a moment later.

"Master Fang," she called.

"Enter," an aged voice answered.

Biyu opened the door.

The house was simpler than I had been expecting, considering the outside of it. There was a fine seating area in the center, but for the most part the house was a workshop. Massive tables and racks of tools dominated the room, with what looked like hundreds of shelves with tomes lining the walls.

It was the house of someone absolutely dedicated to their craft, with the bare minimum of comfort. The man's bed was directly next to a workbench. There was just enough space left over for him to entertain a guest if he had to.

I got thc feeling that it was also a statement to meet me here in his home. He could have probably met me in a fancy restaurant or something; instead, he'd invited me to enter the heart of his domain. The proof of his craft and dedication surrounded us.

"So, you are the one who has been so good to our Crystal Emporium," the old voice stated, and as he walked forwards I got my first look at Master Fang. He looked . . . a bit stereotypical, if I'm honest. The man had a wizened face like old leather that had been left out in the sun for too long, and one of those thin mustaches that hung down to his chest. His eyes, however, were still as sharp as daggers. He wore the exact same thick cloak, gloves, and goggles as Biyu did with nothing to denote his superior rank.

"Mengde Fang greets the Master Cultivator," the old man said respectfully, bowing low.

I nodded, clasping my own hands in front of me and returning his gesture of respect.

"Thank you for meeting with us," I said. Yin hopped out of my shirt and Big D flapped down to bow as well. Noodle stayed where he was, observing. The man's eyes focused on them intently, and then his gaze drifted back to me.

He didn't seem surprised to see them. In fact, he offered them polite nods.

Huh. Noodle's coils tightened slightly on my arm.

Biyu herself bowed, then made to leave as I sat down on the couch on the other side of the table.

"Stay, little stone," he commanded, taking a seat himself. Biyu sat beside her master on the couch.

"I understand you come to us with a problem, Master Cultivator?" he asked.

I nodded and glanced at Big D, who nodded as well.

"Yeah, I wanted to see if this could be fixed." I pulled out my pack and, careful to avoid touching the crystal, opened it and set it on the table. The crystal had certainly seen better days, but it wasn't flickering too badly at the moment. It simply sat there, with the shards of other crystals sticking out of it.

Master Fang's eyes widened as he stared at the flickering crystal. He swallowed thickly and let his eyes trace over its form. Biyu too was just staring, almost like she was having a religious experience.

"Wonderous . . ." Master Fang breathed. "In all my years . . . may I?" he asked, and I nodded.

He pulled his goggles over his eyes and stood, walking around the table. "These sections are grown into it. Six thousand years?" he muttered, as he looked closely at the spokes. "More? I have not seen this variation of the Azure Ancient Style. Its facets are much more complex than one normally sees."

He kept muttering about spokes and faceting, until he suddenly whistled.

There was a shuffling sound, and from the back of the house strode a creature. If I had never seen the creature in the Before, I probably would have been shocked. Its face was free of fur and pale blue, with a lack of a nose that reminded me vaguely of a skull. Beady eyes that were almost black peered at us, and orange fur surrounded its face.

A golden snub-nosed monkey. It cocked its head to the side, staring at us, before handing over a strange tool to the man.

Its eyes were still a bit dull. Well trained, instead of a Spirit Beast.

Master Fang was completely transfixed by the crystal. He waved his strange tool over the top of it and around it, pausing to mark down numbers that I had no idea what they meant.

His breathing slowly got faster, and Biyu's eyes went wider and wider at whatever the crystal maker was writing down.

"Imperfections, here, here, and here," he muttered, writing. "Microfractures in the fourth cardinal quadrant. Contamination from the other crystal is . . . severe. Integrity is failing, but most of the storage is intact, just shorting with the Qi Break here." He spoke quickly, jotting down his notes.

Until he abruptly stopped, staring at what he had written, then glanced back at the crystal. "Formation within a formation, how . . . ? No, such a thing *is* possible, but the control needed is . . ." He paused.

"Biyu, retrieve for me the reference books from the vault," he commanded, and pulled out a key, handing it to the owlish girl. She nodded, her eyes wide, and went to do as bid.

The man sank back into the couch, looking like he had just run a marathon. His hands were shaking as he pulled off his goggles.

He looked at the crystal, then turned back to us and bowed low.

"This Mengde Fang thanks the Master Cultivator and his companions for allowing him to examine their crystal," he whispered, and began chewing on his lip as his eyes locked on the crystal. "This would help explain so much . . ." he muttered.

Master Fang sat quietly, lost in his thoughts. I didn't want to interrupt, so we waited for a bit until Biyu returned. She came back a few minutes later with a few old and dusty-looking scrolls that Master Fang immediately opened, his eyes flowing feverishly over the letters while he occasionally said a number that Biyu dutifully wrote down.

After about an hour of us sitting and watching both of them work, Fang finally spoke again.

"Master Cultivator. While the crystal is unstable, this Mengde Fang believes it can be fixed. With the entire resources of our Crystal Emporium, I estimate it shall take thirty years, provided the heavens favour us," he stated matter-of-factly. "Should you choose to entrust this duty to us, we shall carry it out to the end."

Thirty years?!

Big D recoiled in shock pretty much in tandem with me.

"Is there . . . any faster way?" I asked.

"The detail is too fine. A master could work on such a crystal perhaps for two consecutive hours before his concentration began to slip. It requires absolute focus, and commitment, lest something go wrong. Perhaps a cultivator could do it faster," he admitted. "But first they would have to learn the ancient style of the Azure Hills. Which is a task that would take several years itself . . . provided we were willing to open the vaults to such a scholar."

I grimaced. Ancient copyright, huh? I frowned at the crystal. Well, it's going to take a long-ass time. Will Big D even be alive in thirty years?

I scratched at my head as Big D looked at the crystal with frustration. It was like a corrupted hard drive with all your work. If only we had some backups, or some way to transfer it or . . .

I paused.

"Is there any way to just get whatever is stored inside it out?" I asked. "Like, transferred to another crystal?"

Master Fang frowned.

"That *may* be possible," he said at last. "But we would need another crystal of this quality. I know of one held by one who is ill-inclined to help . . . but he may." He glanced at his pet monkey, then at Big D. He looked conflicted, his eyes flicking once to the crystal.

"We have our secrets, but in light of this discovery, I think Master Gen would be amenable to being bothered."

He wanted to study it. To work on it. I could see the ill-disguised hunger.

'We merely require the knowledge,' Big D stated, speaking for the first time. *'Should we retrieve what we need, we shall entrust the empty vessel to you.'*

Master Fang didn't seem shocked at the voice. Instead, he took a deep breath.

"I must speak to my fellows, as well as Master Gen," he finally said. He rose and bowed once again. We collected the crystal, then left with Biyu.

Big D was obviously frustrated with the outcome. And I was a bit too. Seriously, *thirty years* to repair it? Hopefully we would be able to do at least something with it earlier than that.

We were all a bit quiet as we pondered the predicament.

Biyu took me to a tasty noodle shop, and even if she was a bit nervous, she was good enough company. I kind of really wanted to tousle her hair, but I knew I shouldn't. It was just so fluffy!

At the end of the day, we came back to the Crystal Emporium, where Master Fang was waiting for us.

"Master Gen will meet with you, but you must travel to meet him, for he cannot travel the distance in his age. This one apologises for the inconvenience," Fang stated, handing over a sheet of paper.

A map of an area that looked close to the Dueling Peaks. Well, I guess I was *definitely* visiting now, after I got everything else done. It'd be fun to surprise my friends.

CHAPTER 15

THE DAY OF "FUN"

We were in the streets the next morning as the sun came up. I had some stuff to do before we could head to the Dueling Peaks. Since I was already in the city, I wanted to finish everything up first before I left. Big D, Yin, and Noodle had been invited back to the Crystal Emporium, so that Master Fang could better explain to them what he would be doing to the crystal, if the transfer idea didn't pan out. The snake had a bit of an issue, though. He had seemed a bit bothered last night, but it was only now that he was bringing it up.

"I'm pretty certain he doesn't mean you any harm," I told the snake.

'Hisss reaction wasss suspiciousss,' the snake hissed. *'Where was his shock? All others have expresssed at least* something.*'*

I guess he had a point. Master Fang hadn't really had any reaction to the Spirit Beasts that had come into his home, and seemed completely at ease with Big D talking to him.

"Why don't you just ask him?" I returned. "You just went quiet while we were in there. For all you know, he's met a Spirit Beast before . . . if he stays shifty, *then* it's a little suspicious, yeah, but if he answers, then it's better, right?"

The snake paused, then snorted. *'Jussst ask? I suppose it is that sssimple.'*

Big D clucked with amusement. We met Biyu on the road outside her house. My "kids" got dropped off with their host.

"I can . . . uhhhh, carry you, if you want?" Biyu offered to Noodle as she saw his kinked back, but her eyes kept darting to Yin.

The snake raised his good eyebrow, looking amused. *'Thank you, dear,'* he said and slowly slithered up one of Biyu's arms. *'Accept the kind woman's offer, Yin.'*

The rabbit cocked her head to the side, and with a shrug she hopped into Biyu's arms.

The woman looked inordinately happy with the fluffy bunny in her arms, a rooster on her shoulder, and a snake surreptitiously rolling his eye at me from her arm.

I kind of wanted to see what Master Fang would say about the crystals, but I also needed to see if I could actually sell this year's rice harvest.

So that left the Azure Jade Trading Company.

I had changed into the nice coat Meimei had gotten for me when she came back from cleaning the well at Verdant Hill. With a wave at my "kids," I went to get some of the rice and another couple of maple syrup jugs I had brought along from the secured storage area. The guards were quick and attentive, though one of them kept tapping at a stone pendant on the door and glancing at me. It looked like the entry buzzer that the Crystal Emporium had.

It was apparently on the fritz or something, because it didn't buzz me in. I snorted at that—things always broke down at the most inopportune times. I wondered what tech support was like here. Did they ask if you'd turned it off and on again? Still, the guys let me in, even without their doohickey going off.

With a few bags over my shoulder, I set off to the Azure Jade Trading Company headquarters. It was easy to find, with the murals of their symbol all around, and the absolutely gigantic building that they owned.

There were carved dragons on the side of the doors, and it was painted shades of vibrant blues and greens.

The front counter was pretty busy. It was part reception, part warehouse, and there were all manner of goods on display here. There were clothes, and what looked like beds, as well as rings and necklaces. It seemed like a small mall, or maybe a strange kind of IKEA?

Meh. Nothing that I needed.

"Rou Jin, here to see Guan Bo," I said to the well-dressed woman at the receptionist desk.

The receptionist's eyes flicked across my form, lingering on my freckles, my tanned skin, and my coat. It was a bit of a contrast to her fine clothes, uniform, and pale skin from working indoors. She looked at something on the desk before she raised a delicate eyebrow.

"One moment, please, sir," she said, with just a hint of a patronizing tone. Her eyes dutifully went to her scroll, then widened with surprise when she saw my name on it. "I'm sorry, sir, I need to inform my superiors," she said and went into the back.

Guan Bo came dashing out a few minutes later.

"Master Jin! So good to see you!" he declared with genuine cheer, bowing respectfully when he came out. "How may our Azure Jade Trading Company aid you today?"

I smiled, then held out one of the bags of rice.

"Got some stuff to sell," I said, patting the jug as well.

Guan Bo's eyes gleamed, and I sighed internally. *Yay, negotiations with a merchant. Those were* always *fun.*

I braced for combat, following Bo into the battleground of his choosing.

↔

Blood splattered, as another shrieking, mindless beast threw itself at her. Six more of its packmates went for different points on her body in a coordinated attack.

Blades of Qi shredded them a moment before Tigu flipped over a sudden blast of fire and arrows that shot from the walls.

'Left! On your left!' Ri Zu squeaked, drawing Tigu's attention to another beast as it seemingly materialized from the walls and jumped at Tigu, its maw wide.

Rou Tigu laughed and slammed an axe-kick into its skull, sending it to the ground. She landed for a brief moment, then immediately had to move again.

She bounced off the wall right when the ground opened up beneath her feet and landed on the other side. She glanced back at the spiked pit. That one had been quite tricky!

"I am glad you decided to accompany me this day, Ri Zu!" Tigu declared. Indeed, it had been a bit of a surprise that her companion had willingly come to this place, but Tigu was glad her words had had an effect on the rat!

Ri Zu squeaked, still a bit unused to the praise, and buried herself in Tigu's hair.

Tigu laughed, skipped through the halls to the end of the little maze, and tapped the table of stone that was resting there.

There was a bottle on this table, one full of pills. She picked the dusty thing up and looked at the little blue and green pellets.

"How long have these been down here to get so dusty?" she asked Ri Zu, who shrugged.

'A long while, Ri Zu thinks. They've probably lost their potency anyway. Medicine only lasts so long,' Ri Zu said.

Tigu put the bottle back down and turned back to return to the surface. She hopped over the pit, plucked some more arrows out of the air, and pushed her way past the two halves of a rock that had fallen from the ceiling. She exited up into the mist-filled air and the dark, grasping branches that blotted out the sun's rays.

Tigu could see just fine.

The Hill of Torment was proving to be a great distraction. The Smaller Blade of Grass had explained it to her as they had lined up in the morning, telling her that about a hundred people would be entering. "The closest thing the Azure Hills has to a hidden realm," An Ran had said of the mist-shrouded hill in the middle of a ravine. It had been dark and foreboding, and everybody else had been nervous as they stepped into the swirling mist.

It had whited out her vision for a moment, and then they were on the hill.

After that, all of the other contestants had run off in different directions, racing into the depths of the hill to find "treasures." Even the Petals had split up, going their separate ways in what looked like a prearranged search pattern.

So Tigu went exploring, picking a direction that felt right, and found her first vault. There had been a pit trap, spikes that shot from the ceiling, and an area that had holes in the wall that dribbled out a bit of oil that failed to ignite.

It had been an amusing distraction. The next location's traps had been better thought out. Then this one had had the strange, screaming Spirit Beasts in it, burrowed into the walls.

They were interesting. A good test of awareness and ability.

She wished the Blade of Grass were here, but Xiulan's father had ordered her to rest for the main tournament, saying that nothing in the hill would be useful for her.

While the fights weren't that interesting, the little vaults were. She wanted to challenge the Blade of Grass and see who could clear more of them!

She wandered through the dark forest. Occasionally, she would hear shouts of combat, or more screeches of beasts, but everything seemed well in hand.

Tigu came to an odd dip in the hill, then paused. She glanced over it for a moment and frowned.

There was something about this one, something that triggered her instincts. She searched up and down it, until she found an odd groove, then *pulled.*

The hill made a grinding sound as it opened.

A foul air blew out of the tunnel.

Grinning, Tigu descended into the pit, hoping for an actual challenge.

↔

"Ha! Truly, we have the luck of the heavens on our side, Loud Boy!" the bastard Rags enthused to Zang Wei.

He glared at the taller, rough man as Rags held up the pill bottle.

Truly, they *were* lucky. Somebody was opening up these vaults, defeating the traps and the Spirit Beasts, and then ignoring the treasure. It boggled the mind! There was still the occasional monster they had to kill patrolling around, but the vast majority had already been defeated.

"Here, one for each of us. Never tell your boss he isn't a kind and generous soul!"

"You aren't my boss, Rags," he bit out.

"Aww, don't be like that! We drank together, Loud Boy!" the rough man cheered.

They had . . . only because he'd gotten challenged to a drinking contest, like a fool. Waking up with his cheek on Rags's chest had been mortifying.

Zang Wei grumbled. If Rags weren't so persistent, and good in a fight, he'd have tried to abandon the bastard long ago. But alas, they had saved each other's lives on this dangerous, cursed hill.

And he might need some backup for the next part. Zang Wei remembered the ancient map he had found, and the warning about the guardian.

They exited the vault with the Initiate Soul Refining Pills and continued through the Hill of Torment. It was a fine prize. Zang Wei led them in the vague direction of the spot on the map. He would need to find the lever to open the secret hiding spot—

He paused at the open hole, his heart sinking.

Rags, on the other hand, just laughed.

"Lucky again!" he called, eagerly descending.

Once more, the traps were all sprung, the guardians defeated.

And when they came upon the final room, both of them gaped in shock. Webbing covered the walls, along with acid burns and glowing green blood. There was a corpse, a massive, dismembered Five Venom Spider, still twitching.

And a woman, standing in the middle of the carnage.

Rou Tigu turned to them, a small splash of green blood on her cheek. Her yellow eyes pierced them both. But instead of the cold disdain that had been there when she'd first beheld them, her eyes were now wild with bloodlust and satisfaction.

"Loud Boy. Rags," she said in greeting, holding up a spider leg as thick as Zang Wei's biceps. "Do you think this is edible?"

CHAPTER 16

THE WAR OF WORDS

"Come in, come in, Master Jin!" Guan Bo the merchant called out to the cultivator as he sat down at his desk. Master Jin took a seat in a plush chair in front of the desk. Servants rushed in after the pair of men to attend to them. A pot of steaming water was placed down on a side table, along with a selection of pastries and fine sweetmeats. Juices chilled by a frost crystal and rice wine in a carafe warmed to perfection completed the exquisite selection.

In truth, Guan Bo had heard about a man entering the city with a giant cart yesterday and made the deduction himself that it was Master Jin. However, he did not dare presume to approach the cultivator before the man was ready to speak. Guan Bo had assumed the cultivator would approach at his leisure, if at all, though he'd been hopeful he would have another rewarding meeting. So he had cleared most of his schedule, then given the staff and servants the depictions of Rou Jin's strong cultivation and heroic frame, along with his name. He even had a room prepared in his home. There were, after all, many tales of cultivators suddenly appearing in the night, and so he had striven to be ready to accommodate the man.

It was bad luck that the man had arrived when Guan Bo was doing one of the few tasks he had to personally attend to, but at least he did not seem upset about having needed to wait.

The merchant carefully studied the cultivator's expression as he took his seat. The freckled man held a bag over his shoulder and another of those glorious jars sure to be filled with maple syrup. Both had a mark on them, half maple leaf and half rice stalk. He put both precious containers down and smiled at Guan Bo.

"Master Jin, have you been well?" Guan Bo asked as they made themselves comfortable.

The cultivator nodded. "I have been excellent. This has been a wonderful year, and my wife is with child," Master Jin said with a happy grin.

"How wonderful! Please, permit our company to send you a gift in this auspicious time!" he said aloud. Then he thought, *Something suitable for a first child. Perhaps another dress for his beautiful wife? Or something for the household?*

Master Jin looked both surprised and pleased by the offering and nodded. "And yourself? How have you been?"

"Never better. My wife was quite pleased with my return, and my company was delighted with my acquisitions. I was actually preparing another caravan to go up north, though if you're already here, we may conduct negotiations at your leisure."

Master Jin picked up a pastry and took a bite, humming at the taste. Guan Bo's mind whirled, trying to figure out how to take their current relationship further. He was obviously a man who valued his wife, if the first thing he stated was her pregnancy. Perhaps Bo could introduce Rou Jin to his own family?

"So, how has the maple syrup been selling?" he asked after he'd finished swallowing.

"Excellently, Master Jin! Your statement of its value at Verdant Hill was, of course, correct. Half of one jar was used as a sampler, and then the Jade Dragon restaurant purchased the second jar for one hundred eighty silver coins, and the third sold for two hundred."

Prices that had given him some favour. Guan Bo, always seen as one of the less skilled of his family's merchants, had suddenly acquired a venture that could prove immensely profitable. A good contact with a cultivator, and a very pricey and suddenly-in-demand good. His star was on the rise!

The cultivator nodded, mulling over the prices. It was over twice that which had been paid to him, but there was no way Guan Bo was going to mislead him about that. After the success of the Royal Jade Dragon restaurant, the others were clamouring for more of the golden liquid. "What did the travel expenses look like?" he asked, and Guan Bo nodded. It was the right sort of question.

The month-long travel time, the guards, and the wagons all did start to add up. "The expenses were thirty silver coins, Master Jin." Though most of that was the guards, and the losses he'd incurred waiting around in the town. He would most certainly be able to cut that down. "Of course, in light of this product's success, we are most assuredly willing to renegotiate prices," Guan Bo reassured the cultivator. "Does one hundred twenty coins sound acceptable at this time?"

If Master Jin were a mortal, Guan Bo's trading company likely would have attempted to keep the purchasing price at eighty. Cultivators, however, demanded a different approach.

And keeping the cultivator happy was a priority.

Master Jin considered the price, then nodded. "That should be fine," he decided. "Though I did not come here just for the syrup. I have a few other things to sell, as well as a request."

Guan Bo could feel his eyes light up.

"Of course, of course. What is it you wish for us to aid you with, Master Jin?" he said eagerly.

"I know the Imperial Government normally buys rice . . . but what exactly are the rules about selling higher grades?" he asked.

Rice? That wasn't quite what Guan Bo had been expecting, but he dutifully answered anyway.

"Silver and above are considered commodities, instead of an Imperial Essential, and may be sold like any other good to whomever the seller pleases," he stated. "While the prices of the three standard grades are ironclad . . . the spiritual grades tend to be much more fluid, due to rarity. silver-grade rice is on the cusp of regulation and has a generally fixed price."

"That does make sense." Master Jin nodded, then held up the rice bag he had brought in with him. "So, how much would something like this sell for? The Lord Magistrate said it would be too expensive for them to purchase at Verdant Hill."

Guan Bo nodded. Most likely silver-grade rice, then, but he took the bag anyway. Having a supplier for silver-grade rice was something one had to look out for. It grew so rarely in their hills that it had to be imported.

"Ah, it has been a long, long while since this Guan Bo has graded rice!" he said. He stood, getting out his lens and his scale—all pieces he had been trained with but rarely got to use.

He set himself up, aligning the scale and making sure the lens was in proper order, as the cultivator took out some grains from his bag. Even a quick glance at the rice revealed its quality.

Excitedly, he took a grain of rice from the cultivator. Silver-grade, grown here in the Azure Hills, instead of imported from without! A miracle of miracles.

He stared at the fat grain, its polished sheen, and its faint, pearlescent glimmer.

Guan Bo did not need his scales and lenses. He *knew* silver-grade rice. He ate it once upon the Mid-Autumn Festival, and once upon the new year every year, a gift from his family.

This was not silver-grade rice.

"A full bag of this?" he eventually managed to ask.

"Actually, I've got three hundred bags in the cart," Master Jin said, simply jerking his thumb over his shoulder.

Three hundred?! Guan Bo almost swallowed his tongue in shock.

"It was all I could fit in the cart. I'll have to make half a dozen trips or so just to get everything down here . . ." he grumbled.

Eighteen hundred bags of gold-grade rice. *At least.*

Their largest order ever for silver-grade rice had been a hundred bags for the Lord Magistrate of Pale Moon Lake City.

Guan Bo could feel himself getting light-headed. His forehead grew damp as sweat started beading uncontrollably. He took a breath and did his best to calm himself.

"I . . . excuse me, Master Jin, I must . . . I must go and speak to my superiors."

The cultivator nodded, stretching his arms above his head.

"No problem. Do what you have to," he stated.

Guan Bo stood. As soon as he was out of the room and the door closed behind him, he broke into a sprint.

The upper members of the Azure Jade Trading Company sat at the Azure Jade table. It was a single piece of polished jade shaped by master craftsmen into a table wide enough to seat thirty people. The table reflected a soft blue glow interspersed with veins of white and green.

Master Jin had been surprisingly accommodating about the need for a private meeting and was currently touring warehouses. His guide had been instructed to take him *wherever* he wished to go, even if it was normally off limits to outsiders. Guan Bo was a bit nervous as he waited. The true source of his nerves was the slight buzz that filled the air.

Six of their number were at the head of the room, their hands pressed against the transmission stone. The sound was fuzzy, and the connection would occasionally break, but it had to be done.

"I see. You were right to contact me," an aged female voice echoed from the stone. While Guan Bo's grandfather was officially the head of the company, and a fine businessman, every member of the family knew that his grandmother, Shan Daiyu, was the one who made most of the heavy decisions. She was currently at the Dueling Peaks, holding their auction in the heart of the Grass Sea.

There was a brief pause as she thought things over.

"Yinxue, Ping, head to the Howling Fang Mountains and Yellow Rock Plateau. Leverage some of our contacts there," she commanded decisively, her voice like a whip—it startled Bo to attention. "Begin immediately."

"Yes, Honoured Mother," his uncles barked, making the gesture of respect, even though she wasn't able to see them. Grandmother had always had that kind of effect on people.

"Li, take over managing the shipments to Grass Sea City."

"As you say, Honoured Grandmother," a cousin obediently agreed.

"Liquidate what we need to. Accommodate his demands accordingly. We will be his primary contact. Make sure this happens." The woman rattled off commands.

Guan Bo knew that gold-grade rice was big, but for his grandmother to go so far . . . well, the *entirety* of the Azure Jade Trading Company was being mobilized.

"Little Bo, you said he was married?" The voice turned its attention to him.

"Yes, Grandmother," he squeaked out. "A peerless beauty."

"Hmm. In the end, he is but a man," she eventually decided. "Chyou. See if you can deepen our relationship with him. You will become our primary contact."

Guan Bo's sister flushed for a brief moment as the request was made, but it swiftly faded.

"Yes, Grandmother," she said, and Guan Bo saw the calculation in her eyes. His sister always did remind him of their old lady.

"And . . . what shall I do?" Guan Bo asked.

"You will be rewarded handsomely, Little Bo. You have done well, but we shall take things from here."

Ah. In truth, he'd been expecting to be removed from his position, but the confirmation that it was happening still hurt. He knew the decision was final. Guan Bo sank into his chair and sighed.

So much for his rising star, and his plans. He'd be shuffled off to another post.

↔

The Trading Company eventually got back to me. I was actually a little nervous, walking into what was essentially a board meeting. A bunch of steely-eyed merchants wanting what I had put me a little on edge.

Honestly? I hadn't been taking this as seriously as I should have been, in retrospect. I was still just assuming that my "good rice" would mean I got paid a bit more, so having the Azure Hills equivalent of a Fortune 500 company shit itself and then call an emergency meeting was a bit beyond what I'd been expecting.

So with a brief breath, I walked into the lions' den.

It was like something out of a period drama. There were several older gentlemen, all seated when I arrived, who rose and greeted me the moment I entered. They were a bit stereotypical-looking, long hair tied into a topknot with a few mustaches on some of the otherwise bare faces. There was also a younger woman, who seemed about Bo's age, maybe in her early twenties, seated to the right of the old man at the front and center.

She was eye-catching and had a bit of a resemblance to Bo. Her lips were painted red, and her face was pale. Her green eyes were framed in rose eye shadow, and her unusual red hair was done up in an elaborate braid.

Guan Bo was off to the side, nearly at the end of the line of people. Farther in the corner, the only man with a table sat with a pad of paper and a brush, ready to take notes.

As one, the men and woman of the Azure Jade Trading Company bowed, the lowest I had ever seen somebody go beside Xiulan after we'd saved her life.

"We, the Azure Jade Trading Company, greet Master Jin," they intoned.

Am I supposed to bow here too?

"Master Jin, thank you for your time. We hope that we have not unduly infringed upon it," the old man said, his head still lowered.

I shrugged. "It hasn't been too long."

The men and singular woman raised their heads in perfect unison. "We thank you for your consideration," one of the men said. " This one is Guan Xi, head of operations while my honoured grandfather and Master of the Azure Jade Trading Company is indisposed at the Dueling Peaks. He begs your forgiveness for not being present."

"There is nothing to forgive," I said simply.

Xi's eyes brightened just slightly, a smile coming across his features. The man in the corner, I noticed, was writing down everything we said. A scribe for our business meeting, I guess.

"I have requested your attention to clarify a few matters. While our Guan Bo is a fine member of our company, the value of the goods you propose to exchange requires the oversight of one of a higher rank in the company. One with more experience, and of a higher position. Our Master, Guan Ping, offers to conduct business himself, when he returns. In the meantime, if it pleases you, we would assign one better suited to accommodating you."

All of them bowed their heads again—including Guan Bo, who had a resigned look on his face.

I considered it. Business was all about relationships, really. Now, I wasn't much of a calculating man, but it was always better to do business with somebody who owes you a favour.

"Guan Bo has been great. I'm fine if our relationship continues as it is," I said. The old man was the picture of serene grace, but Bo's head snapped up, his eyes wide with shock and gratitude.

If he wasn't my friend before, he certainly was now.

"As you desire, Master Jin," the old man said, stroking his beard. "I am sure you see the value in our Guan Bo. And should you desire anything else, our Guan Chyou will be our point of contact, if it pleases you. She will be available at all times to meet your needs."

The woman offered me a warm, pretty smile and a deep bow.

I nodded absently. *Kinda like a secretary, or Bo's assistant?*

"Then, Master Jin, we will proceed with negotiations."

I swallowed as I faced the united front. The members of the trading company versus a street rat and a farm boy.

In the end, I'd like to think I gave a good battle. I certainly gave it my best shot. We settled on the price of fifty silver coins per bag. Nearly ten times the amount of a bag of even silver-grade rice, which was itself ten times the price of blue grade. The price alone was a good one: if I sold my entire harvest, I would have more money than I knew what to do with. Hell, even just these bags were more than enough to basically retire with.

I guess Meimei will be getting a bit of a bigger library than she bargained for.

But, as always, sometimes the most valuable thing isn't the main, direct price of goods you get.

It's the *perks.*

Preferred shipping of goods. Inroads to suppliers. Information. The Lord Magistrate was a goddamn wizard for getting me tomatoes, but he was, at the end of the day, a man in a remote location.

Hell, I didn't even have to pay for any inns I stayed at anymore. Like . . . ever. The Trading Company would be footing the bill.

To use another modern analogy, I was getting wined and dined, then taken golfing. Something novel to both parts of my past. I'll admit, it was a little nice getting my ass kissed. An effective business tactic, to make somebody feel more important than they were.

We both got a set of the contracts, written by the scribe. Nothing seemed out of order, so we concluded our business for the day, and then I got taken to a fancy restaurant for a feast.

And I may have had a bit much to drink, considering Chyou kept filling my glass, and the men of the company kept toasting me.

"To your health, Master Jin!" one of the men called, and I obligingly drained the drink, nodding to the man. As I set down the cup, Chyou attentively refilled it. I nodded my thanks, and she bowed her head before I took another bite of the food. This place was pretty good, and everything had gone bright and pleasantly bubbly. Bo was already sheets to the wind and passed the hell out.

I leaned back with contentment, popping another dumpling in my mouth. Maybe I *had* drunk a bit much, but after describing my interest in alcohol, the company had brought a lot of drinks out for me. Including one special one that they said was like a thousand years old or something, but the memory of it was a tiny bit fuzzy. It was real good, though.

I noticed a shadow watching me from the roof and nodded to Big D. The rooster bowed his head, then left. I was touched he had been trying to look out for me.

Which reminded me that I should probably get to bed soon.

I waved to the big-shot guy, who nodded. "We have rooms available, should it please you," he said, still remarkably sober.

I mulled it over for a second before agreeing. *I'd get the rest of the guys in the morning.*

"This way, Master Jin," Chyou said, and I got up to follow her. We walked in silence for most of the way, Chyou beside me. She had been pretty quiet, aside from occasionally giggling at something I said.

"So, you're going to be my guide in the morning too?" I asked Chyou.

"Yes, sir," Chyou replied as we reached the building. She got out a set of keys, unlocking the door and revealing a well-furnished room.

"Of course, Master Jin, I am here to see to your *every* need." There was an inflection in her voice that was slightly flirty. I wasn't sure I liked it.

I frowned a bit at the insinuation, and the woman's flirty smile immediately fell from her face. Ah, crap. I didn't mean for that to happen. Things were hard enough for women in this world. Getting assigned as a secretary and told to flirt with the big-shot customer probably *sucked.*

The happy buzz faded. I didn't want her to have to walk on eggshells around me, so I thought for a second.

"How familiar are you with medical scrolls?" I asked.

The woman paused, seemingly surprised at the question.

"Not too familiar, but I know many who are, Master Jin," she said tentatively.

"'S all good! Could you get a list for me, of what most of them think are the essentials?" I asked. There, now she could help me with something I needed, where she wouldn't have to interact with me for a while.

She seemed a little confused, her eyes narrowing slightly. Curiosity, and something cunning, lurked in those eyes before her smile returned in full force.

"Of course, Master Jin. I shall have it prepared for you," she agreed. "Do you need me for anything else tonight?"

"Nah. G'night. Thanks for the room, yeah?" I waved her off.

I slid into the bed as the door closed. I'd have a lot to do tomorrow, getting the rest of the stuff I needed, and having Noodle help me with the glass stuff. But at least I wouldn't have to go searching around for suppliers, with an army of merchants eager to get me discounts and direct me where to go.

CHAPTER 17

HEAVEN DOESN'T ALWAYS SHAKE

"Me next! Me next!" a woman exclaimed, her eyes wide and eager.

"Of course, my lady! Which background would you like?" Yun Ren said in what he probably thought was a suave voice.

It took all Gou Ren had not to snort.

Gou Ren kept his face carefully blank, though, as he held up two boards full of images. It was supposed to be a day of exploring, with Tigu gone at the Hill of Torment and Xiulan resting at her Sect.

Instead, Gou Ren's brother had talked him into helping with a new business venture. Something Yun Ren had been up late at night preparing for.

The first time Yun Ren had sold his images, it had been a quick sale. He approached a person on the street and offered. That was all well and good, but it was an annoying way to do business, constantly walking up to people and asking if you could take their portrait.

His brother grinned as a flash of light came from his hands and crystal.

"There you are, my lady, a beautiful portrait for a *beautiful* woman," he said cheerfully. The crowd gasped as he turned around the image, cast onto the piece of stone.

Well, it was two images. A landscape, and then a second overlaid on top of that, so she looked like she was sitting in a field of flowers.

Let it never be said Gou Ren's brother was unimaginative, or slow to exploit an opportunity to make money.

The heavy coins clinked into Yun Ren's hand as more people crowded around, begging to be next.

Gou Ren kept an eye on his brother. He could see the sweat on Yun Ren's forehead, and he was shaky on his feet, so he was almost certainly overdoing it with using his Qi.

But he was beaming and his eyes were bright with joy. He wasn't even counting the money anymore, just depositing the coins into the safe beside him so he could get to work on the next image. He was already looking like he was going to call up his next customer when Gou Ren loudly cleared his throat.

"I must apologise, dear customers, but the Image Master needs his rest." He pitched his voice so it could be heard, booming out over the clamouring crowd. Everybody startled at the sound, even Yun Ren, who finally seemed to notice his shaking hands. He flushed when he realised how inattentive he had been to his reserves.

"One more!" Yun Ren declared, and the crowd cheered. "You, sir!" he said, pointing to a young man a bit farther back. "How about you? You've been here a while!"

The young man—a boy really, not that Gou Ren could talk—came forwards a bit awkwardly. Gou Ren winced when he noticed the crutches and his limp leg. His clothes were of fine quality, and he had short, slightly wavy hair. He almost looked a bit familiar. Had Gou Ren seen him before?

His brother, however, just nodded as the boy selected a background. A few flashes of light later, the boy was sitting atop Cloudrest Ridge, with Pale Moon Lake City stretching out behind him. His grin brightened, and he bowed.

The crowd grumbled at the attraction closing, but nobody actually got pushy. They all obligingly dispersed.

Gou Ren helped his brother clean up. "I wonder how Tigu is doing?" Yun Ren asked absently as he picked up some more of the stone slabs. They were actually from the Verdant Blade Sect. The disciples had to punch through them as part of their training, or so An Ran had said. They had given Yun Ren a set when he had asked earlier that morning.

Tigu had easily put her fist through an entire stack before they had left to set up, just to see what the training was like, before leaving with Ri Zu.

"She's either having a lot of fun—or that hill is going to be littered with statues of naked Jin," Gou Ren snarked as he picked up one of the other signs.

His brother burst out laughing. "Really, she still does that?"

Gou Ren shrugged. "She mostly puts pants on them now. I nearly pissed myself when I hopped onto a big rock out back on the farm and came face to face with Jin's bits."

His brother kept laughing.

They finished cleaning up, though his brother was still a little unsteady on his feet.

"I actually think I'm gonna take a nap or something," Yun Ren sighed. "That was a bit more intense than I thought it would be. The auction is soon, right?"

"A few hours still."

"I'll go and see if Lanlan is out of her meeting, then. She looked a bit annoyed earlier."

Gou Ren grimaced. She had been smiling like Meimei did when she was in a particularly vicious mood after a servant had called her up to the Elders at the gate right when they were about to leave. They had offered to wait for her, but she had waved them off. "I'll take this stuff, then—don't look at me like that, I'm good to carry it. You, however, can take some of my load for me," Yun Ren said.

Gou Ren's hand jerked up as he caught a bag full of coins.

"Thanks for holdin' the signs, yeah?"

Gou Ren rolled his eyes as he felt how heavy the pouch was. "It doesn't need to be this much."

"La-di-da-di-da, can't hear you, too tired," his brother sang as he walked away, carrying his signs with him.

Gou Ren sighed and started walking in a random direction. The entire place was bustling. There were tons of people on the street headed into packed teahouses. He had some time to kill, so he wandered around for a bit. He checked out some more of the stalls and found a nice-looking hammer—until he saw the price.

He'd never complain that Yao Che was overcharging for his work again. Sure, the engraved hammer he'd been looking at was pretty, but if he wanted a fancy hammer all done up, he'd just buy a normal one and ask Tigu to engrave it.

He grabbed a bite to eat, and kept up his pace, but paused when something caught his eye. The boy with crutches who had bought the image from Yun Ren had tripped, dropping the stone tablet. The stone wasn't broken, at least, but the boy's face was twisted into a grimace as he clutched at his leg. No one moved to help him, all stepping around him without giving him a second glance.

Gou Ren frowned at everybody passing the kid by, before heading over.

"You need some help?" he asked.

The boy startled at the sound of Gou Ren's voice, then looked up at his proffered hand. He stared at it almost suspiciously before reaching out and allowing Gou Ren to lift him to his feet.

"Thanks," he mumbled, glaring at his limp leg.

"No trouble. The stone is a bit heavy, especially with one hand, yeah?" The boy nodded reluctantly. It looked like the admission pained him. "How about you tell me where you're going, and I'll bring it along for you?"

The boy's eyes narrowed and his mouth set in a firm line.

"I don't need pity," he said, more to himself than Gou Ren, it seemed. Gou Ren considered just leaving it, but the kid was probably around thirteen or so. He remembered being that age and how it felt.

"Of course you don't, honoured customer," Gou Ren said. "Just offering to help out our customer, yeah?"

The boy mulled his offer over a moment before looking away. "Okay." He whispered.

Sheesh, the kid has some pride, he thought.

They set off towards where the cultivator houses were. It was a silent journey, with the boy not offering to speak to Gou at all. Gou Ren kept pace with the quiet boy, who kept sneaking glances at him while pretending to look straight ahead.

Eventually, the boy spoke.

"This is far enough." He bit his lip and looked to the side. "Thank you, sir. What did you say your name was?"

"Xong Gou Ren. Yourself?"

The boy nodded his head. "Bowu." The boy's lips quirked into a smile. "And fear not! This Young Master shall repay you a hundredfold."

Gou Ren rolled his eyes at the boy's earnest grin. *Really,* Young Master*?* The kid certainly thought highly of himself.

"Yeah, yeah. Have a good day, kid," he said, waving him away, then setting off.

He suddenly paused and turned around, looking at the open door as the boy hobbled inside. He reached into his pocket and took out the piece of paper Xianghua had given him.

The symbol on the door matched.

Gou Ren shook his head. Things weren't *that* much of a coincidence, were they?

He glanced up at the sun and set off again. It was time to go to an auction.

□

"And this piece is sold! We thank the Framed Sun Sect for their patronage!" Xiulan watched as the woman running the auction finalized the sale. She wore traditional garb for a merchant and had brilliant red hair that was put up in a carefully tied knot. Her expressive eyes had some wrinkles, but despite the signs of age she looked quite beautiful.

"For the next piece, we have five Initiate Earth-Element pills! Refined in Yellow Rock Plateau!" she yelled out. There were noises of interest from around the room.

Xiulan sat primly in her seat as she watched the proceedings from the second level reserved for the Sects. The rest of the Elders were in their positions, but they were off to the side in a more open area. Beside her, both Junior Brother Gou Ren and Yun Ren sat looking mostly bored at the proceedings.

"Is this it?" Gou Ren asked, frowning. "It's just a bunch of those 'cores,' some grass, and a few pills. Ain't there supposed to be like . . . heavens-shaking treasures or something?"

They had been quite excited at the start, though their enthusiasm had waned as the proceedings went on. Xiulan privately thought they had heard a few too many stories, but she could not blame them. They were still farm boys.

"If there were heavens-shaking treasures at every auction, I think the heavens would fall down," Xiulan said. The brothers let out snorts of laughter. "It is a fairly normal auction, all told. Some things are useful for us, some things we do not need. And normally, 'heavens-shaking treasures' come at the end anyway."

The brothers nodded.

The pills were sold after a brief bidding war, the losers glaring at the winners, and the room dimmed slightly.

"Now we have come to the moment you have *all* been waiting for. We originally had another item for you today, but this just came in, and we, the Azure Jade Trading Company, could not help but share it!"

She held up a jade slip, with the symbol of the Azure Jade Trading Company on it.

"We would not normally auction off objects without first presenting them to you, but we are the Azure Jade Trading Company! We swear upon our honour that we will deliver these items without fail!"

There was more murmuring as the crowd speculated.

The woman paused, letting the moment settle. "We, the Azure Trading Company, present to you esteemed customers five bags of gold-grade rice. Received from a patron of our illustrious company. We would like to offer you the first bags of gold-grade rice to grace this province in a thousand years!"

The murmuring ceased. Eyes sharpened.

"The bidding begins at two hundred fifty silver coins!"

Hands went up. The woman smiled, showing teeth.

The Xong brothers glanced at each other.

"Rice?" Gou Ren asked, confused.

Hands kept launching up. Noble mortals battled with Sect Masters for the honour of purchasing the bounty.

Yun Ren's eyes opened completely as the price kept going up. "That's some expensive rice. Bet it's not as good as Jin's."

Gou Ren shook his head. "Sucker's bet!"

↔

"Kind of a wash, eh?" Gou Ren muttered to his brother.

"Yeah. I dunno what I expected," Yun Ren muttered back as they waited at the gate for Tigu to return. Xiulan was waiting with them, along with a few other people. The area was surprisingly empty.

Gou Ren squinted into the darkness, the sun having long since set—

Movement.

"Hey, I think I see them!" Yun Ren said, perking up.

At the front of the procession was a flash of orange hair, the giant smile on Tigu's face plainly noticeable. Gou Ren raised his hand to wave.

Then he saw the people behind her.

Xiulan's students, along with two people he didn't know, trudged along. In contrast to the smiling, orange-haired girl, the rest of them looked exhausted and sweaty, with minor wounds and bandages covering their bodies. On top of that, Li and An Ran looked vaguely traumatized.

Gou Ren raised an eyebrow at Tigu and the makeshift basket full of odd, black . . . He squinted.

They looked like enormous spider legs.

"We found a nest! And they taste good! It was great!" Tigu enthused. She shoved a goopy leg into his hand.

Gou Ren stared blankly at it.

At least she hadn't set it outside his door, like the village cat normally did.

CHAPTER 18

THE SPIDER INCIDENT

An Ran reflected upon her day as she walked back to the manor with her fellows. They were all silent, contemplating what had happened and staring at Tigu with evaluating eyes.

They'd known Tigu was strong, but seeing the depths of her power was enlightening. Yet that was not the main thing on their minds.

Tigu gesticulated wildly, and the small Spirit Beast rat on her shoulder would either nod her head or bat at the girl's ear.

Senior Sister glanced at the rat, yet there was no surprise on her face. Which meant she'd known about it beforehand. She seemed completely at ease, even as An Ran's mind whirled.

An Ran rubbed at the bandages on her wounds. Whatever the Spirit Beast had put on it, it itched a bit.

A Spirit Beast had tended to her wounds. An Ran had barely even seen a Spirit Beast before the Hill of Torment. And Tigu had one that tended to wounds?

"And how did this all happen, Junior Sister?" the Young Mistress asked as she stared at An Ran, her eyes concerned. She startled, tearing her eyes away from the rat.

Swallowing thickly, An Ran began to recount her day.

←

It had started off well enough. In the morning, An Ran had watched Tigu excitedly look through a scroll on the monsters of the Hill of Torment, pointing to the various drawn pictures and declaring them worthy foes, while Senior Sister had explained the spiritual nature of the hill to her.

She had even come to see them off, along with the two brothers. An Ran was fairly certain nothing untoward would happen. In the single day that she'd known them, they had comported themselves well despite their rustic origins.

"Go, and return safely," Senior Sister had said warmly to the Petals, while Gou Ren had pulled Tigu into a headlock and Yun Ren ruffled her hair as their farewells.

It was so very easy to forget that the strange girl could trade blows with Senior Sister when she acted like this.

All of the Petals had steeled themselves, then set off to the misty hill.

They had already decided upon a searching pattern that kept them close enough to come to each other's aid if things went wrong, each of them carrying a horn in case of a true emergency. It was no transmission stone, but using one of those upon the hill would be an exercise in futility, as the strange eddies of Qi disrupted any attempt to speak.

Their search had not been particularly fruitful. The dark, obscuring trees and occasional Ripper attacks left her blood thundering in her veins, despite attempting to mimic Senior Sister's serene presence.

Though the enemies only came in packs of twos or threes, which was odd. Senior Sister had said that the average pack size was generally in the dozens.

For hours they had searched, occasionally calling out to each other to confirm their locations. At one point, An Ran encountered a member of the Misty Lake Sect, but after a tense moment their nominal ally had just nodded and gone on their way. Until at last, she had received some fortune: a small patch of Spiritual Grass, hidden under a fallen tree. She had collected every sprig, carefully uprooting the entire patch. A modest reward, but a reward nonetheless.

Just as she'd finished putting the sprigs in her pack, she heard the alarm sound.

It was to only be used in emergencies, and An Ran redoubled her pace.

She dashed through the trees, leaping over fallen branches. Huyi dashed from the side, his eyes grim, while Xi Bu formed up on her other side, his gaze sharp and focused.

The horn choked out another blare, as they pinpointed his position, erupting into the clearing.

They could barely believe their eyes at what they beheld. Li tossed his horn aside, his face panicked. The man-sized Five Venom Spider hissed. Li's blade met iron-hard carapace as legs speared at him relentlessly, and virulent poison dripped from the spider's fangs. After a moment of shock at seeing the beast, An Ran steeled herself, just like Senior Sister would, and prepared for combat.

"Go!" An Ran shouted, snapping them out of their stupor. She got two nods in response.

[Verdant Blade Sword Arts, First Form: A Single Blade of Grass]

Huyi leapt onto the creature's back, attempting to get his sword in between the armour plates, while An Ran and Xi Bu aimed for the joints. The spider was fast, however. It screamed and thrashed, spoiling their blows. Swords skittered off the solid carapace as the beast reacted. Legs that were as sharp as lances lashed out, scoring a small gash along An Ran's arm, while Huyi was thrown into a tree.

However, the beast was outnumbered. Carefully, methodically, they managed to wear it down. Repeated strikes began to make small gashes in the spider's armour.

An Ran finally managed to drive her blade into a gap on the spider's knee, sending the beast shrieking and staggering away. Xi Bu slid on his knees underneath the creature, then struck upwards, burying his blade in the gaps in its armour.

The spider screeched again as the blades found purchase. An Ran repeated Huyi's maneuver, leaping onto the thrashing thing's back to get her blade in between the plates of chitin in its abdomen.

The Five Venom Spider let loose one last shriek as ichor spilled from its wounds, and then it perished.

They had to push it off Xi Bu, who was absolutely covered in ichor. A moment later she realised they all were.

An Ran couldn't help it. She started giggling. "You have the same colour hair as Li now," she told the small boy, managing to get a grin out of the normally stoic member of their group.

Sweaty and shaken, Li said, "I thank my fellow disciples for their help," as serious as An Ran had ever heard him. He was covered in scratches from the battle, and blood flowed from a large gash on his cheek.

But he was alive. She nodded at his gratitude, and Xi Bu clapped his hand on Li's shoulder. An Ran turned to Huyi to hear his normally snarky response, but her fellow Petal was not smiling, or even paying attention to their rescued fellow. He was simply staring up at the canopy, his dead-fish eyes wide.

An Ran glanced up at where he was looking in the pitch-black branches as they rattled in the breeze—

But there was no wind.

The canopy was shaking. Ruby eyes burned in the darkness and there came the clicking of hundreds of armoured legs.

"We need to go. Now," Huyi said with a calm that belied their situation.

Fleeing and showing one's back to the enemy was often considered shameful. An Ran and her fellow disciples ran without hesitation.

The surging tide of chitin was not to be denied. The smaller, faster spiders flung themselves at the cultivators. The disciples turned and swung. The spiders exploded into green gore as the Petals cut them down. They were lucky the smaller spiders' carapaces were not hard enough yet to resist blades.

But it slowed their escape down.

The heavier, lumbering forms descended from the trees, letting out keening shrieks as they thundered towards the disciples.

An Ran wondered, for a brief moment, why the beasts screamed. Normal spiders didn't make any noise at all.

They could not run. Basic pack instincts sent some of the smaller spiders skittering past, dropping down on sticky webs to cut off the retreat. They had to turn. They *had* to fight.

They moved as best they could into a defensive formation, guarding each other.

And then she was fighting for her life. Her sword struck downwards as a smaller spider jumped at her knees. She dodged around legs that were like spears and drove her sword up into the maw of one of the creatures. Around her the battle raged.

"I hate spiders!" Li screamed hysterically, though his form was still remarkably crisp, even with the whites of his eyes showing in panic. Huyi and Xi Bu both fought with grim determination, their eyes focused and their breathing as even as they could make it.

Yet it was a losing battle. She heard Bu gasp with pain as a pointed leg stabbed into his calf.

An Ran was distracted by the sound, and her moment of inattention cost her—one of the larger spiders leapt onto her, forcing her down to the ground. She barely got her arm up as the fangs sank in deep. She bit back a scream—her arm immediately started to burn from the spider's infamous five venoms. Her veins spasmed as the venom took hold.

An Ran contemplated whether this was the end when the spider tore its fangs out, then reared up again, ready to finish its prey.

A small, tanned fist slammed into the center of the beast.

The spider's iron-hard carapace crumpled like paper as it was flung violently off An Ran to slam against a tree and explode, painting the forest glowing green.

"Hello, Smaller Blade of Grass, are you well?" Rou Tigu asked, her face alight with concern. There was another shout as a rough-looking man and a boy entered the clearing, both of them kicking the spiders off Li.

'Of course she isn't well!' a tiny voice chastised, as a small black form leapt from Tigu's shoulder.

An Ran stared as a tiny rat pressed two paws to her arm.

'This one is Ri Zu, please forgive her for not introducing herself earlier,' the rat said, bowing apologetically. She then cocked her head to the side and frowned. An Ran felt green Medicinal Qi dabbing at the wound. *'Does Ri Zu have your permission to help?'*

An Ran nodded, now slightly dizzy. Her arm started to tingle, and she felt faint, muting any shock she was under.

There were several other disgusting splattering noises, but the spiders' assault slowed, recoiling from the sudden interruption.

The rat, strangely, pulled out a waterskin and a piece of chalk. A moment later the treetops started to shake again. Huyi managed to stand, looking disheveled, while Li was dragged over by the rough-looking man, who stared openly at the Spirit Beast.

An Ran's eyes cast about, one hand on her sword. A few other spiders tried their luck, but Tigu simply swatted them out of the air.

'Master's modifications are working well,' the small voice said, intrigued. An Ran glanced back down, then winced. There was a copper wire sticking out of the bite mark and poking into a waterskin, which was surrounded by a small chalk formation. To her surprise, the throbbing lessened. *'Poison may be siphoned like Demonic Qi, but only while fresh, it seems. It did not travel far.'*

A rat knew an advanced medical formation. *What the hells?*

"They are going to be fine?" Tigu asked.

The rat nodded. *'They shall need bandages, and some poultice, but this is well within Ri Zu's medical kit's capabilities!'*

Tigu's worried expression once more melted into a cheerful smile even while the scuttling legs got louder.

"Do you think Mistress would want the venom glands?" she asked, turning around as more and more ruby-eyed spiders approached.

The rat working on An Ran's arm pondered for a moment. *'Ri Zu would recommend you harvest a few, yes!'*

Tigu nodded.

"Loud Boy, Rags. Make sure Ri Zu works in peace," Tigu commanded. Both the men who had come along with Tigu seemed to find the rat just as strange as An Ran did, yet both of them nodded, watching Tigu with clear admiration.

A spider bigger than a horse toppled a tree as it burst into the clearing.

Tigu took a breath.

Yellow eyes sharpened into slits. A snarling tiger rose behind her. Yet An Ran felt no fear. There was no crushing, tyrannical aura.

Instead, she just felt . . . safe.

The enormous spider spasmed as Tigu's intent bore down on it.

Five blades of Qi formed above Tigu's fist.

"Let's have some fun together!" the orange-haired girl said, her smile turning from cheerful to cruel.

An Ran watched the carnage unfold, all while a Spirit Beast carefully tied a bandage around her arm.

"Thank you?" she whispered.

The rat looked around at the people who were staring at her and took a deep breath.

'You are welcome,' the rat said with another bow.

→

"After so long hiding, Ri Zu went and introduced herself properly! She acted, instead of hiding away when our friends were injured, like Mistress said one should!" Tigu reported around a mouthful of spider leg. An Ran wondered how the girl could eat it; it looked disgusting!

The rat squeaked sullenly from atop Tigu's shoulder, partially hiding in her hair again.

It was a shy creature, squeaking with embarrassment when Li had tried to thank it. After the creature had finished tending to them, it had retreated back to Tigu's shirt.

Their walk and explanation had taken them all the way back to the manor, where Tigu began to share some of her "bounty" in the guest room. The other two men who had helped them were there, off to the side, and looking around at the furnishings in curiosity.

An Ran scratched at her bandaged arm again. It was *really* itchy. She forcefully stopped herself from scratching more and making it worse, and instead she raised a bit of leg and took a tentative bite. To her surprise, it did taste quite good. A bit like black-pepper freshwater crab she had once had.

Senior Sister nodded as she took her own bite. "I believe Wa Shi will enjoy this greatly, Tigu," she said before turning to the two others in the room.

"And you, Zang Wei, Dong Chou, have the gratitude of our Verdant Blade Sect. I thank you for your assistance." She stood, then bowed formally to the boy and the man, offering them a warm smile. Both of them flushed crimson at having her attention after they'd awkwardly sat off to the side for most of the time back at the manor.

"A-ha-ha! It's no trouble, no trouble, Miss Cai! Just think of us kindly later on, yeah?" the rough man said, grinning. The boy beside him nodded rapidly. "Besides, I gotta go tell my people I'm back, eh? The conquering hero! We'll get out of your hair, besides, me and Loud Boy here have some things to divide up." He rattled something in his pocket.

The boy, who was looking annoyed at the other man and like he was about to object, suddenly stopped.

"Yes, Lady Cai, we must go. We thank the Verdant Blade Sect for their hospitality!" he shouted.

An Ran winced. He was *very* loud.

"Have a good night, Loud Boy, Rags!" Tigu said, waving.

"Have a good day, Miss Rou!" both men called before they left.

And then there was silence. An Ran looked around at her fellows, all of their eyes downcast. They had a poor showing today against the hordes of spiders. They would have been defeated without timely intervention, and worse, *all* of them were injured. They would surely bring shame to their Sect tomorrow!

An Ran grimaced.

"You did very well today, to face such numbers of Five Venom Spiders, and you must all be tired," Senior Sister said. "I would bid you rest, so you will be fit enough tomorrow."

An Ran nodded. She started trying to get up, but her legs were a bit wobbly. She clenched her hand into a fist, to stop it from itching the wound on her arm.

"Ah, Miss Ri Zu, I do not mean to question your expertise, but is it supposed to be itching this much?" Huyi asked, frowning at his arm.

The rat nodded. *'That means it's almost done,'* she squeaked.

"Almost done?" Huyi asked.

Ri Zu nodded. The little creature seemed to debate something for a moment before she carefully hopped down from Tigu's shoulder and scampered up to Huyi. Small, deft hands untied bandages and scraped away some of the poultice—revealing a wound not even a quarter of the size it once had been.

Li's eyes widened, and he went for his own bandage, eager to see what was underneath. A black blur shot towards him and a tiny tail lashed out like a whip, *cracking* against the back of his hand.

The rat landed from where she had leapt and placed her hands on her hips.

'Leave it on until tomorrow!' Ri Zu scolded. Li recoiled from the rat's glare.

She carefully tied up Huyi's arm again . . . and then seemed to realise everybody was looking at her. She froze, and her eyes flicked back to Tigu, before she coughed, cleared her throat, and went into a short bow.

'It is very nice to meet you all,' the rat whispered tentatively.

An Ran and her companions bowed back, a little awkwardly.

It was very strange, bowing to a rat—but her help meant they would be fully healed for the next bouts tomorrow! An Ran made sure to bow lower than she normally did, to display her gratitude.

CHAPTER 19

THE FIRST ROUNDS

"Are they well?" Xiulan asked Ri Zu the next morning.

'Yes, yes, everything is good to go!' Ri Zu declared from her position on the table, examining the unblemished skin. All of Xiulan's students stared in wonder at their healed injuries. Deep punctures and envenomed bites that had pierced halfway through limbs were gone like mist upon a lake burned off by the rising sun.

"This An Ran . . . thanks you?" the wavering voice began. An Ran glanced at Xiulan, clearly still bewildered at addressing a Spirit Beast. Xiulan nodded. An Ran took a breath, then bowed. "An Ran thanks Ri Zu," she said with more conviction.

Xiulan's students still did not know how to act around the little Spirit Beast, but they were improving, and improving quickly even as they ate their breakfast and prepared for the day. They took their cues from Xiulan, trying to mimic her calm demeanour and easy interactions in the face of the madness that was a friendly Spirit Beast. A Spirit Beast that could *heal.*

As Senior Sister had once said, "You get used to it." Although they had adapted admirably, she didn't think they were yet ready to hear that Tigu herself was a Spirit Beast. *World-shaking revelations should be done one at a time.*

Xiulan finished her meal. She would have liked a bit more cooked spider, but the rest had been packed in salt or was being pickled. A few were left out, just to see if the small amounts of venom would keep them from spoiling too much. Wa Shi would not get fresh limbs, but she had a feeling he would enjoy the surprisingly crablike taste of the preserves.

Ri Zu, her apparent tolerance for interaction reached, swiftly retreated to the confines of Disciple Gou Ren's shirt. Xiulan knew she had been on Tigu's back for the prior matches, but there was no rule against that. Indeed, the tournament organisers would likely be overjoyed if there was some manner of Spirit Beast Tamer in the tournament. Ri Zu was, after all, "just a Spirit Beast." Any who laid eyes upon her during the tournament matches would likely assume she was Tigu's possession. Not that there was danger of that—Ri Zu was quite good at remaining unnoticed.

The Petals were all in a fine mood as they set out once more for the arena. They had not really gotten any real treasures, but they had grown from the combat experience. And they seemed to notice the lingering aftereffects of Senior Sister's medicine, the Wood-aligned Qi from the Lowly Spiritual Herbs invigourating them further.

"Healed by a Spirit Beast!" Li boasted incredulously.

"Lower your voice, you fool," Huyi grunted, his eyes abruptly darting around. "She is shy in the first place, and your voice will attract unnecessary attention. Do you know how rare someone like her is? People will either be clamouring to buy her or attempt to steal her."

Li looked around, chastised, and rapidly nodded. They climbed the stairs, splitting off from the Xong brothers, and stepped once more into the arena.

→

Sitting calmly in the contestants' stands, Xiulan watched the battles unfold. On the second true day of combat, things were still slow. Though half had been weeded out, the contestants were still trying to conserve their strength and not reveal their techniques.

Well. Most were.

"Rags!"

"Loud Boy!"

The two voices boomed as the combatants clashed. Xiulan's eyebrow raised as Dong Chou and Zang Wei—no, Rags and Loud Boy, the two men who had visited last night—met in combat, massive grins on their faces. It reminded her a bit of the times she sparred with Tigu, neither of them holding anything back.

It was quite admirable! They were probably lifelong friends, and it was mere bad luck that they had to face each other so soon.

Yet while their intensity was admirable . . . both had little in the way of technique. They brawled like they were in a pub, Qi turning wild strikes and sloppy haymakers into blows that could shatter rock. The crowd howled with glee at the knock-down, drag-out brawl the rough-looking man and the boy were engaged in. Their Qi was visible around them as they drew on more and more of their strength. One was dark grey, a sluggish aura coming from the ragged man, and the other was bright blue and vibrant, twisting and leaping—and both were streaked through with the occasional jolt of energy that showed that they had not fully refined the medicine they had taken from the Hill of Torment. It was an obvious tell that even mortals in the audience could see.

"They truly had the luck of the heavens with them to find such treasures," Li grumbled from his seat.

"You say that like we found nothing. Be grateful for what we did find," Xi Bu intoned, nodding at his fellow disciple. "Senior Sister Tigu came back empty-handed."

"Sometimes combat experience is worth as much as a midgrade treasure," Xiulan instructed. "Do not discount it. You faced a fearsome foe and returned alive."

The disciples nodded, so Xiulan turned back to the fight. Rags went for a cross, his ragged grey aura coalescing around his fist. Loud Boy's eyes widened at the danger, yet he forged onwards anyway. Xiulan nodded at the attempt. Being shorter, Loud Boy launched his own strike from the inside, attempting to push the blow up and away, his energetic blue Qi swirling. Yet it was all for naught. Rags was stronger, his arms resisting the attempt at deflection. The short boy grimaced, but he pushed forwards, committing wholly to the strike.

Both men's heads rocked back as fists hammered into jaws. For a split second they remained still, glaring around the fists buried in their respective faces, before they went flying backwards. The crowd roared in approval as Rags rolled to his feet, while Loud Boy managed to almost seem graceful as he too regained his footing. She heard Tigu laugh from her own seat, her voice booming across the stands.

"Go on, Rags, Loud Boy!" she hollered like the crowd.

Both men roared again, meeting in a clash that sent a small shock wave through the air. They traded blows—sharp jabs and wild haymakers that had Xiulan's fellow disciples rolling their eyes. It was completely and utterly amateur. Barely any technique, and all instinct, yet the crowd was loving every moment.

Both were panting by the end of it, their auras dying down to flickering sparks. Rags had a split lip and an obviously broken nose, while Loud Boy squinted through a black eye and spat a tooth onto the ground. They sized each other up, smiles slowly crossing their faces.

They both got into their stances, preparing for one final blow.

Xiulan's eyes sharpened. There was something off. Loud Boy's eyes closed for a brief moment, and when he breathed out, his breath released as steam.

Both men exploded into motion, Loud Boy's stance completely different than it was a moment ago. The transition from pub brawler to trained combatant was surprising and instant, and Loud Boy met the oncoming strike. Both of his hands were clasped together in a wedge as he shoved upwards, breaking through the blow and deflecting it wide.

Rags, wholly committed to the strike, could not adjust in time. His body barreled forwards as Loud Boy stomped his foot into the ground, cracking the stone and sending up a shock wave of dust. Living up to his namesake and letting out a booming shout.

[OPEN THE GATES!]

A devastating double palm strike slammed into Rags's chest, a coiling dragon tail forming briefly around Loud Boy. Spit flew from Rags's mouth, and his eyes rolled up back into his head while he was launched through the air.

There was a brief moment of silence.

Then a wall of noise welled up from the crowd as Rags did not get back up. Loud Boy fell to a knee, panting.

"Zang Wei defeats Dong Chou! What an exciting match this was! What power was unleashed by these two men after finding hidden treasures upon the

Hill of Torment!" the man on the dais exclaimed. "What a match—and what's this?"

Loud Boy approached his fallen friend. The man suddenly startled, coming back to consciousness and groaning. Loud Boy offered him an arm. The older man stared at it, his eyes wide . . . and snorted, reaching up to grab the limb. The younger boy helped the ragged-looking man up—and to his surprise, Rags raised the boy's arm high in the air. Loud Boy flushed.

"Ha-ha! Such camaraderie between martial brothers!"

The crowd roared again as the taller man slung an arm around Loud Boy. They glanced briefly at Tigu, who gave them Master Jin's "thumbs-up." Both flushed at her bright smile, offering gestures of their own. Then they limped off the arena together, clearly bickering all the way.

Xiulan watched them go, amused. Steadily, she rose, knowing it was her turn next.

"Next we have Cai Xiulan, the Demon-Slaying Orchid!" the voice boomed, and if possible, the crowd roared louder.

Her opponent was a member of Grand Ravine. For centuries, they had been the measuring stick for the Azure Hills, the mightiest of combatants.

The nervousness on the young man's face was palpable. He was a newer recruit, perhaps some rising star. He carefully set his large straw hat and cloak aside as his sectmates tried to encourage him. Several tattoos crawled up his arms, a legacy from a tribe conquered so long ago none remembered their name. He calmed his breathing and raised his weapon, a hooked sickle with a rope. A tool used for climbing the trees that stuck out of the sides of the Grand Ravine, turned into a devastating weapon. He swallowed thickly. His legs stopped trembling, and when he opened his eyes, they were pure and clear.

Xiulan bowed earnestly in respect for his resolve.

And as the gong sounded, he surged forwards, eyes intent and blade ready. Not reckless, but as measured as he could be.

Xiulan gave his courage the respect it deserved and then struck him once. Not with a gentle push like the first competitor, but a closed fist. The blow landed before he could even react.

The young man toppled, out cold. An inglorious defeat. The crowd's chants of "Demon-Slaying Orchid" were mixed with insulting jeers at the fallen. Her eyes met the Young Master of the Grand Ravine Sect. He was frustrated and angry, but as their eyes met, he offered her a brief nod.

Better bruised pride than a broken body.

Xiulan turned away.

She could feel the eyes of the crowd upon her. The intent of thousands was a palpable thing. Yet she sensed one pair was more . . . focused than the rest. Hungry. Frowning, she turned her eyes to where she felt the gaze coming from. In the box of honour, flying the standard of the Shrouded Mountain, a man lounged upon fine silks. A courtesan was stroking his hair. His fellows were also intent upon her, yet none of them left her with the same skin-crawling sensation his gaze did.

She locked eyes with him.

Ice crawled up her spine.

"And Cai Xiulan administers another swift defeat! Was there any other outcome possible?" The voice boomed across the arena, the sound breaking her out of her impromptu staring contest. She returned to her seat.

"Gan Bijing versus Luo Tai!" the voice of the announcer called out as the next match was to begin.

Xiulan frowned. Zang Li of the Shrouded Mountain. She knew little of the man, save for the fact that he apparently enjoyed his courtesans and was a powerful Young Master. His Sect could single-handedly dominate every Sect of the Azure Hills, should it decide to level its might against them.

Xiulan shook her head a few moments later as the announcer's voice sounded again.

"Rou Tigu versus Jiang Jiang!" he thundered. Xiulan returned her attention to the arena. Tigu was once more seemingly content with trading pointers—until her expression abruptly soured after her opponent shouted something at her.

A tanned fist instantly shattered his guard, sending him from the middle of the arena to slam into the barrier over the stands, which flickered fitfully at the sudden impact.

The girl huffed with annoyance, then returned to her seat without a second glance.

Later that night, Xiulan was listening to Tigu rant about her opponent for the day with a smile on her face.

"And then he said that my tanned skin was ugly! Ugly! He is a man with eyes, yet he cannot see!" Tigu complained, a mouthful of food not impending her angry diatribe. They were seated at a two-person table together in the cramped shop, separated a bit from the others.

Xiulan nodded. "Indeed, he had eyes but could not see," she said with a small smile as she took a bite of her own meat bun from Chao Baozi. These "Contender Buns" were quite good, and they were very invigorating. Xiulan smacked her lips together. The ingredients seemed to have a small amount of Qi in them—enough so that they refilled one's reserves just slightly.

It was less than taking medicine—or for that matter the food served at Master Jin's home—but for those who could not afford reagents, this shop would be absolutely invaluable.

Xiulan swallowed and looked at the small, cramped table where her fellow disciples were seated. Her eyes roved over her students. There had been two victories and two losses among them. An Ran had delivered a terrific strike to her opponent, sending him to his knees, and had come out nearly unscathed. Huyi, on the other hand, had taken a beating until he'd managed to trick his opponent with a feint and knock him out. The black eye and bandages around small cuts stood out starkly. Both of their faces were flushed with victory as they recounted their fights from their perspective to the others. Yun Ren was showing off images he had taken of their battles from the stands while An Ran spoke animatedly with Junior Brother Gou Ren, who was smiling at her.

Xiulan nodded to herself in approval.

Xi Bu was as calm as always. He had given it his best, putting up a fine showing against a superior foe, and seemed content with his defeat. Li, on the other hand, was sitting sullenly and nursing his broken arm. A foolish overextension had cost him—Xiulan hoped this would teach him a lesson on being overeager.

Tigu sighed. "At least the next match should be better. Water Lady is strong, right?" she asked.

Xiulan nodded. "Indeed, Liu Xianghua is a canny and formidable foe who uses—"

"Don't want to know!" Tigu interrupted. "I want to see what she's like, on my own."

The cat-turned-girl popped the last of her food into her mouth and went to join the others, shoving herself in so she could lean over Huyi. She loudly demanded to see the images recorded from her own bout.

Xiulan smirked, then shook her head in amusement.

She closed her eyes taking in the moment, savouring the taste of her food while shouting and laughter echoed from the table nearby.

Such a loud and rowdy bunch they were being. Like the soldiers she'd once known.

An old longing welled in her chest. A desire to sit with her friends and students at their table, damn her status and position.

She looked at them all for a moment, then Xiulan acted on it.

She stood from her own place and approached the other table.

Her hips met An Ran's as she shoved the girl farther along the seat. Her Junior Sister's eyes bugged out as she collapsed entirely onto Gou Ren, and Xiulan took her seat.

Both flushed crimson, and An Ran scrambled back to a sitting position. She was squeezed against his side, though Xiulan could see that she didn't exactly try to push away too fast.

Gou Ren gave Xiulan a look. Xiulan smiled innocently at him, then deliberately pushed slightly more onto the bench. The rest of the table went silent, her students suddenly tongue-tied.

"Ah, Senior Sister, um—" An Ran tried to be polite.

"Yun Ren! Do you have a recording of my opponent's face?" Tigu demanded, completely oblivious to the sudden awkwardness.

"You bet I do. Look at 'im!" Yun Ren shot back. An image formed on the table of a man screaming, his eyes wide with shock.

Xiulan giggled.

The Petals stared at her for a moment in surprise, before Tigu's uproarious laughter got them smiling too.

"He squeaked like a large Ri Zu!" Tigu declared. Ri Zu poked her head out of Tigu's shirt to roll her eyes. Gou Ren handed her some of his meat bun, and the little one disappeared again.

Slowly, her Juniors started to relax as the boisterous Tigu and Xong brothers welcomed her with their usual attitude—until a *spectacularly* drunk man outside started to play a few halting notes on his pipa.

The Xong brothers grinned, recognising the familiar tune.

An Ran looked offended at the vulgar song, while her other students tried to hide their own amusement.

Xiulan bit her lips and very carefully stopped herself from humming along.

The fact that she knew all the words for this song . . . well, she needed to know her students a bit better before she could reveal that, and also be in a more private place.

"The ol' spry whore, and the donkey that came in her backdoOOOoor!" the drunk man shouted cheerily.

CHAPTER 20

METAL AND GLASS

So, everything looks fine with the crystal master?" I asked Noodle, coiled around my arm as he was. Big D and Yin had gone off somewhere today to explore the city, so it was just me and the long green man. All of them had been unconcerned when I came back to the inn in the morning, though they'd gotten an apology anyway. Getting wasted and having to crash somewhere else and then not sending word of it had been a bit rude.

'Yesss, it is as you suggested. I simply asked him, and he answered. He said he knows a Spirit Beast, and that we shall understand when we meet Master Gen.'

"Well, it should be cool to meet somebody else," I mused while we ventured through the streets, heading back to the Azure Jade Trading Company with my cart. They wanted to store it on-site, so I'd gone and gotten it for them.

Guan Bo was organising a team of ten oxen. The man still looked a little ill from last night's celebration. I was surprised he was up already, after how much he had drunk the previous night, but he seemed to be working through it.

The man was directing a flurry of activity and hadn't noticed my arrival. "Yo!" I called out. He turned at my voice, putting on a smile . . . then paled at the sight of me carrying the load.

"Master Jin!" he yelped. He gawped and opened his mouth to say something but seemed to think better of it, closed his mouth, and bowed instead. "Thank you very much, Master Jin. We were just preparing to collect the rest of your goods." The rest of the milling men had stopped to stare as well.

"I was headed in that direction anyway." I shrugged, setting down the cart. "So how's this trip to the Forge District going to work?" I asked.

Guan Bo bowed again as the men who had been staring at me with wide eyes snapped out of their stupor and started arranging the oxen to take the load.

"I will be taking the lead, Master Jin. We will be accompanied by three accountants of our household. As you expressed a desire to inspect the goods at their source, the foremen and forgemasters have been informed of your impending arrival, so we may proceed at your leisure."

It was a little weird to have everyone waiting on me, but I nodded and rolled with it. Guan Bo gestured to his right, and a few waiting bodyguards settled into loose formation around us.

It was still fairly early in the morning, so the streets weren't completely packed yet, but there were still enough people out gawking at the armoured guards. Each of the men wore a thick coat of interlocking plates and carried long spears and swords, but had no helmet, just a cloth headband. The Pale Moon Lake City guards gave us nods as we walked past checkpoints, the buzzers rattling as we got close. We were headed for the outskirts of the city, to where one of the many rivers forked off Pale Moon Lake. There was a giant stone divider and a massive, open gate that indicated the entrance.

I looked around with no small amount of wonder as we entered the Forge District. Yao Che's small forge was impressive enough, as were the ones in Verdant Hill.

But this? This was industry. Great furnaces pumped smoke into the air, and drop hammers—too large and expensive to use near Verdant Hill—swung down with thunderous *booms.*

Hundreds of men toiled, pumping bellows, grinding metal, and feeding the vast furnaces. Even through the wood smog and pollution obscuring the district, it was impressive as hell.

'Thissss is amazing,' Noodle whispered, staring around in wonder. *'The lassst we were here, we gave little attention to this place. I am glad we have this opportunity.'*

Guan Bo spoke up and announced, "The first destination will be Copper Hands. As you said, you are looking primarily for purity, so we have the best of the best arranged for you. Master Hu's family has the purest copper in the entirety of the Azure Hills, with their finest grade being ninety-eight percent pure."

"Lead the way, Guan Bo," I declared. The man nodded and directed us to a large stone building. Guan Bo wasn't joking about having people wait for me. We were received swiftly by a servant, who led us to the meeting room. An old, stern-looking man with a cragged, wrinkled face greeted us, kneeling on a cushion in front of a line of his apprentices. He looked like a stereotypical old master blacksmith.

"This Tong Hu greets the esteemed son of the Azure Jade Trading Company and the Master Cultivator," he said, bowing low.

I returned his greeting, and he waved an apprentice over who was also dressed to the nines in expensive silk. The man carried in a tray of three small copper bars on a lacquered wooden plank. The apprentice presented the bars to us, bowing low.

"Ninety-eight percent pure, on my and my family's honour. Only the finest for the Master Cultivator," Tong Hu said. "May the heavens strike me down if this is a lie, Master Cultivator. This is the finest copper in the city, refined using techniques my family has practised for generations."

It certainly looked right, the warm reddish orange hue. I think that was pretty much good enough, and goddamn fantastic for people using these old tools. Seriously, ninety-nine percent? Cultivators could probably get pure elemental copper fairly easily . . .

I frowned. *Could you put copper through a pill furnace? It would certainly make things easier.* I shook my head, putting the thought aside, and picked up a piece of copper. I currently had no real way of knowing if he was telling the truth—

Ninety-eight point one percent pure popped into my head. I froze at the realisation. Like with the wheat, things had gone a . . . little bit wonky as information flooded my mind. I could feel that there were slight traces of other elements too. Some iron, it seemed like, and a bit of oxides, but there wasn't any lead. I shook my head, looking back up at the forgemaster. His face was pale, and a dribble of sweat ran down his face. I blinked at the sudden tension in the room.

"This should work just fine," I said, and the man let out a breath, the tension abruptly dropping out of him.

"Very good, Master Cultivator. How much of our metal do you require?"

I looked at the bars on the tray before me, then took out my own notebook. Noodle considered the offerings before whispering in my ear. He wasn't the best at metal, but he was definitely better than me. Guan Bo froze in comic horror as Noodle slithered away from me to tap his tail on how much we needed. The rest of the room just stared incredulously.

"About twenty of these," I said simply. Noodle returned to his place and Tong Hu closed his open mouth, then bowed.

"It shall be as you command, Master Cultivator." I turned to Guan Bo, who nodded hesitantly, recovered from his shock.

"Thank you for your time, Master Tong. I, Guan Bo, shall discuss with you the price."

I sat back, content to let the person who knew what he was doing haggle for me.

→

The day went pretty well. Honestly, better than I'd hoped. I tried not to enjoy the privilege of just getting to walk to the front of the line and talk to whoever was in charge *too* much, but yeah, it was nice.

Then I also got to just throw Guan Bo at people. *Behold, my overpowered technique: delegation.*

Guan Bo smiled—he'd just secured another deal, this time for the lead-free flux, the substance that made metals more liquid and let them expel impurities. Then we headed off to our next destination.

With the sudden windfall I had, I'd decided to kind of double-dip on the pipes for the still. I took some of the copper to an artisan, some big-shot guy in the city, and gave him the designs to make the pipes. His eyes gleamed with interest, and he was quite accommodating when I asked if I could watch . . . mostly so I could see what he was doing and try it again with Yao Che at home.

If it worked out, we had two stills and Hong Yaowu got one. If it didn't? Well, at least we tried.

At the glassmakers, however, I got an amusing treat.

'Tch. Look at them. Their technique is all wrong!'

To say Noodle was unimpressed by their showing was an understatement.

'Look at how many hours that polishing will take if you do it like that!' he hissed. *'Oh, if my Master could see these men, he would weep bitter tears for his craft, then jump from joy at the opportunity!'*

I relayed his words to Bo.

"Master Jin, your . . . companion knows of glassmaking?" Guan Bo asked. He looked a bit light-headed and was pinching his finger while staring at the snake.

"Yeah. Noodle is pretty great at this sort of thing."

Noodle? Guan Bo mouthed the name incredulously.

I personally couldn't tell you what skilled glassmaking looked like. They had blown a glass cylinder and then cut it in half, unrolling it and laying it on top of an iron table to cool. It was fairly clear—but I could see distortions forming on it as it cooled. Many others were grinding away at the slightly warped surface, carefully cleaning it and making it as clear as they could, despite the slight ripples in the end product.

It was long, labour-intensive work. And for some reason it seemed *off* to me. Wasn't there something about floating the glass? On liquid metal or something? I think that was how we did it back in the Before—courtesy of one too many late nights watching how things were made. But I had no clue if the idea was even viable here.

I'll bring it up with Noodle later. I shook my head and turned to where the snake was inspecting the sand they were using. While apparently their technique was lacking, their materials weren't. Noodle had only good things to say about the quality of the sand, so we ended up picking up a bunch of it. After that was negotiated, it turned into a tour of the entire area. It was nice, aside from the occasional itching in my back.

Felt a bit like somebody was watching me, but nobody ever came out to say hello.

So I kept a bit of an eye out . . . but nothing out of the ordinary happened.

Well, nothing until I got an invitation to dinner from Chyou, Guan Bo's sister.

Huh, she found those books rather fast.

↔

Two men skulked in an alleyway, their eyes focused on the man as he greeted the beautiful daughter of the Azure Jade Trading Company, Guan Chyou. The woman had spent all day with doctors and scholars, asking about medical books, from what they had gathered.

"Are you sure?" the younger of the two watchers asked his partner. His costume was ragged, as if he was a pauper, but his accent gave him away as being higher class. The older one was dressed just as shabbily in mismatched rags. If you saw them on the street, you wouldn't look twice. Unless of course you looked closely enough to notice a set of matching plum blossom pins hidden in the folds of their rags.

"Did you not see the caravan he pulled up in? He's a cultivator. *And* he matches the description," the elder observer declared, his sharp eyes taking in the two as they conversed briefly.

"When I checked the inn's records, the name was spelled completely differently," the younger said.

"Yes, this is true. However, Master Scribe said he would rather be interrupted with a lead that turns out to be useless than let his search be stymied by something that *we* thought was useless," the elder chastised.

"As you say, Senior Brother."

"Now, let us go. We know where he is going to be—did you see that pearl of a woman? He'll be there all night. Let us leave him to his fun. If he is who we are looking for, Master Scribe decreed he will tolerate no insult to his person."

"Yes, sir."

"Back to the headquarters. We'll make our report."

The two shadowy forms departed.

CHAPTER 21

THE RED FLOWER

Guan Chyou walked beside me as the employees of the establishment led us to a private and well-appointed room. She was a bit less dressed up than yesterday but was still wearing one of those fine and colourful silk dresses with long sleeves. Noodle and I had decided to part ways. He was at the room I had been given, going over a scroll on glasswork while pondering the rough drawing I had done of the metal bath to float the glass on. I knew it needed to be hot, and I think it was either lead or tin that needed to be used. I shook my head and looked around the restaurant. Well, calling it a restaurant wasn't really right.

It was basically a housing complex, with giant, disconnected rooms, surrounded by beautiful gardens and small, koi-filled ponds. Some rooms, I was told, could fit nearly a hundred people. The one we came to was much cozier. It was pretty nice. The sounds of the city were muffled, and it was almost like we were back in the countryside.

"I hope your day was fruitful, Master Jin. Did my brother perform to your standards?" she asked as we sat down at the table. It was a large piece of solid wood, with a hearth in the middle to warm our tea and broth. She poured me a drink while the servants set down plate after plate of food before retreating out of the room. There was a bell we could ring if we wanted them, but this was technically a private meeting, so the staff would be out of earshot.

"Yeah, it was a good day today. We got everything we needed, as well as some other bits. It was nice having a guide, so my compliments."

"I shall inform my superiors of your compliments, Master Jin. Thank you." She smiled, but it wasn't flirty like it was yesterday. *Good. It looks like she's a bit more comfortable now.*

"So, what about you?" I asked. "Everything turn out all right? It was kind of an awkward request, since I was a bit drunk. I was expecting you to take longer."

She shook her head. "Your request was most interesting, Master Jin. I still have several other esteemed gentlemen to meet over the next few days, but I do not believe their voices will add anything noteworthy."

She handed over the piece of parchment.

"I have grouped the ones similar to each other together, and the ones that came recommended by all are in this section." I nodded, looking at the spreadsheet that

Chyou had given me. Authors that were considered the most respected in their field. Price points. Shops that carried specific scrolls, some that could be effectively bulk ordered to save on costs, and ones that were rarer.

"In addition to the medical scrolls, I have also requested the doctors to prepare larger parchments with diagrams of the body, and of energy flows," she informed me. I glanced up as she unrolled a larger piece of cloth parchment to reveal a diagram of a body that looked a bit like a vascular system.

It was something a person could just look up anywhere on the internet in the Before, but here it was handmade and painstakingly labelled. I had seen one kind of like it in Pops's house in Hong Yaowu. A treasure of the family, he had called it.

"The final product would be one hundred eight detailed drawings and diagrams of organs, limbs, bones, and spiritual energy flows. I additionally have a pending request to Chief Doctor Ganji. One of his fellows is in Grass Sea City, a doctor who was once an apprentice of Spiritual Medicine. His cultivation was completely destroyed, but Doctor Ganji is certain he will be able to convince his fellow to part with some of his own knowledge regarding Spiritual Medicine. Of course, if you do not require them, and this Chyou has overstepped her bounds, she humbly apologises."

Her head bowed at this.

I just kept looking over the extensive and detailed list. I really should have thought a bit more on the stuff I needed, but Chyou had covered that. And . . . well, I had the money, and I'd told Meimei I wanted to learn medicine.

"No, these are all fantastic ideas. I appreciate the initiative, Chyou."

She got an odd, calculating look in her eyes for a moment, her eyes flicking over my face, before she abruptly relaxed. She raised both of her sleeves to cover her mouth demurely.

"This Guan Chyou thanks you for your praise, Master Jin," she stated.

"So, what do you normally do for the company?" I asked after a moment. Chyou glanced up from her food and gave me a measured look. Like she hadn't been quite prepared for me to ask her what she did.

"Do you truly wish to know, Master Jin?"

"I wouldn't ask if I weren't interested," I replied. She nodded.

"Normally I work on logistics and acquisitions within the city itself," she started tentatively. "I direct the movements of most of the regular caravans."

I whistled in appreciation. "Sounds like a big job."

I certainly couldn't do that. I was disorganised at the best of times, and planning my own crops was about the limit.

"So, how does that all work, anyway?" I asked.

↔

Ever since her grandmother had taken her under her wing, Guan Chyou had been determined to prove her value to her family—to be as great as her grandmother.

The woman behind the throne, who had taken the Azure Jade Trading Company to unparalleled heights. Grandmother had forged the company into a powerhouse that even the Sects would often step lightly around, else their competitors would find themselves with a sudden windfall. It was not perfect protection. But for these Azure Hills, it was enough. She'd taken lessons in courtly manners. Musical instruments. Logistics.

She was raised to be the flower of the family. A gift to only the most important of men, to whom the Trading Company would tie their fortunes. After the initial embarrassment of her grandmother commanding her to . . . lie with Master Jin had passed, she'd agreed with the decision. It was the right one. Sharing a bed to further a deal was no different than bribing a guard to look the other way. Chyou offered a product of value and in return her family was to gain far more.

They said cultivators were lusty beasts. The three times she had met Young Masters already had proven that right. Their eyes homed in upon her red hair. But with her unavailable, and connected to valuable resources that they needed, most had kept it limited to glances. She was pretty, but not some manner of world-shaking beauty.

Chyou had smiled and flirted with Master Jin, her interest clear. She had been fully prepared for what was to happen that night. She wasn't even dreading it. His form was not unappealing.

Then she was rejected. Politely. Politely, and with another order to allow both her and the company to save face.

There had been no lust in Master Jin's eyes. If anything . . . he seemed to have some strange sympathy for her.

With the rejection, she had immediately changed tracks. He demanded medical scrolls? He would receive medical scrolls. She visited every doctor who was available. And the ones who weren't quickly opened their doors to the name of the Azure Jade Trading Company.

The cultivator, Master Jin, was even *impressed.*

So impressed he had asked her to explain the logistics of her company to him. It had taken over an hour.

"And then it goes into storage and proceeds to distribution," Chyou narrated, just as she finished drawing another part in the chain.

Why is he having her explain mortal supply chains to him?

"It all comes back to this distribution center?" Master Jin asked, scratching at his chin. He considered the paper carefully.

"No, not all of it. We have smaller depots scattered throughout the hills, but these are for common goods and repeat customers," she said, then switched to another, rough map of the Azure Hills, marking out the various substations they used.

He was listening. Listening intently and nodding along. She watched his eyes. Her grandmother had taught her how to read people—how to read the minute facial expressions until she was confident enough that she could deduce what even the Masters of the Azure Hills were thinking.

In this man she saw only genuine interest.

Master Jin spoke the way one would expect of a farmer. Direct, honest.

What does he want?

"Do you enjoy your job?" he asked as he examined the other diagrams. The question was a surprising one. It was something she rarely thought about.

"Enjoy it? I suppose I do. It is the life I've known, though I've largely been confined to the capital." It was a better life than most. She had wealth and power, but . . . occasionally it felt like something was missing. Her brother was the one who got to go out and tell his tales, while the family's flower was protected so she didn't wilt.

It was the intelligent thing to do—at least that was what she told herself. She saw Master Jin look at her. A small flash of sympathy formed on his face.

They lapsed into silence, and Chyou wondered how to proceed. If one door was closed, open another.

Bluntness and honesty? she thought.

"I desire to be useful to my company and my family. My fate has been thrown in with yours, and so I would undertake any task you wish for me to do."

Master Jin's eyebrows rose in surprise at the bluntness before a small smile formed on his face. He snorted. "If only everybody would just say things outright."

He chewed his lip, pondering.

"You said you were confined to the capital most of your life?" he asked her, then took another swig of his drink. "What do you think of travelling?"

Chyou froze.

"Master Jin . . . what are you offering?" she asked tentatively.

"Well, Guan Bo did a good job with the stuff I needed, and so did you. You really went above and beyond. So it's like this: there are some rare mortal fruits that I'm looking into. They'll probably be down south. I would need somebody to go and check it out. If you're up for it."

Chyou kept her face neutral as she processed the words. The images of far-off places flashed in her mind.

"It will be dangerous," Master Jin said after a moment, warning her. She nodded, but there were already facts and figures whirling in her mind. Ship, supplies, and the need to recruit trustworthy guards.

It appeared bluntness and honesty *was* the correct choice.

"It would be my honour and privilege to prepare an expedition, Master Jin," she stated, bowing low. "What would you have me look for?"

The man's gaze sharpened. He took a piece of paper, then began to sketch his own diagrams. sketching out strange-looking fruits, and stranger trees.

"The pods of the cacao tree. The beans of the coffee plant . . ."

She stared at the plants she had never heard of—and some descriptions that tickled the back of her mind with familiarity. Maybe she had read about some of these before? She memorized the detailed descriptions.

And then she turned to Master Jin. She felt a strange thrill as she raised her cup, and they both drank to a fruitful transaction.

He even escorted her home, as a gentleman should, and gave her a warm smile, before they parted ways.

It was almost a pity he was uninterested.

CHAPTER 22

HEARTH AND HOME

Some nights she dreamed. Dreamed about a girl, pacing back and forth. She would occasionally look to the horizon and wring her hands, or fold her arms across her chest.

She always wondered what the dreams meant, because eventually the girl would wander back over to Meiling and curl up on her lap. Her body was tense, and her eyes would flicker. The world underneath them was restless.

Meiling's fingers would trail through short, unruly hair, and the girl would calm.

□

Meiling awoke to a body curled up next to her. It wasn't big and strong, cradling her in an embrace, but it did still feel nice. The bed was just a bit too big by her lonesome. What had woken her up had been a rooster crowing at the sun. It wasn't Bi De but another younger, much-less-skilled rooster. The voice was loud and scratchy as he howled, seemingly trying to make up for lost time, silent as he was when the other rooster was around.

She wished he would take after his sire a bit more. His incessant shouting was annoying, but she supposed she was just a little bit spoiled. Bi De normally only crowed once and then fell silent.

Beside her, her little brother grumbled petulantly, burying his head under the pillow.

She sighed and got up, leaving him for the moment to get dressed. When she was done, she turned back to the bed—Xian still hadn't moved.

"Come on. Time to get up," she cajoled.

Hong Xian the Younger made a muffled noise and rolled away from her, hugging a pillow. Meiling raised an eyebrow, then pulled the pillow out of his grasp. He scrunched up his nose in response and whined.

"If you don't get up, Chun Ke and Wa Shi won't give you any rides," she threatened.

Xian's eyes opened a crack and he levelled a glare at her.

"Meanie," he declared.

But he did get up. He struggled out of the sheets reluctantly, then threw on a set of clothes. Meiling pulled his unruly hair into a braid once he was dressed.

"Right. I'll get started on breakfast," she declared. As she started descending the stairs, a weight pressed against her back as Xian clambered up onto her. She absently caught his legs for support, barely feeling anything.

It was nice to still be able to pick him up with ease. Although her little brother took advantage of it far too often.

As she descended the stairs, her father glanced up at her from his seat, just as he had over the last week since her husband had left for the south. He already had a pad of paper in front of him, his musings on the Spiritual Herbs written down in his formal, exacting detail. It was nice having people around, even after everybody had gone back to Hong Yaowu or departed south. Even if she did have Chun Ke and the rest of their disciples for company . . . it was just nice to live in the same house as her father and younger brother again.

His smile warmed as he saw Xian's head resting on her shoulder, still half asleep. She rolled her eyes, then deposited Xian on top of Chun Ke, the boar snorting a pleased greeting.

She leaned into his embrace as he stood to greet her.

"How's that going?" she whispered, pointing at his pad of paper.

Her father shrugged, stroking his beard. "Qi makes things . . . unpredictable," he admitted. "Especially in such concentrations." He pulled back and stared at her. "I'd like your thoughts on a few things, if you'd give them."

Meiling nodded. "I'll look over it after we're done for today," she agreed.

She then headed off to the kitchen, where Pi Pa and Wa Shi were readying things for breakfast.

The sow perked up as Meiling entered.

'Good morning, Mistress. The fires are lit and ready,' she stated, bowing her head. Wa Shi just slapped his fins on the floor, his head poking out of the river. Already there were vegetables lined up and washed, ready to be cooked. Meiling was impressed. Only a single carrot had its end bitten off.

"Thank you, Pi Pa, Wa Shi." They nodded at her.

Breakfast that morning was something she had made a thousand times before. Rice and eggs. While she did like Jin's strange food, and his bread, there was just something good and comforting about the food of her youth. Doubly so since her father and brother were here.

She went to add more rice to the bowl, but a porcine nose touched her, startling her.

'Too much, Mistress,' Pi Pa gently corrected.

Meiling stared at the scoop, then put it back. She had been about to make the normal amount of rice. It would probably get eaten, but they were missing over half their family.

She shook her head and finished breakfast. How easy was it to slip into a routine again.

A fish in a trough, two pigs, her brother, and her father gathered around the table. Bei Be was still outside. She had made an offer for him to join them, but the ox had politely declined, contenting himself with a meal of grass.

After breakfast they lined up, moving into the morning forms that the family practised—except now it was Meiling leading. She moved slowly, going through the motions Jin had taught her. It was the beginnings of a martial kata, one that left her refreshed and ready for the day. The first times she had done it, her father had raised an eyebrow, though he hadn't commented. Her little brother followed beside her, trying to ape the movements. Her father did his own slow breathing exercise nearby.

Meiling turned around after she was finished. Everybody was waiting for her patiently to begin the day.

She gathered her list and checked tasks off as she handed them out. "Father, could you help us check over the ledgers today? Xian, go around the perimeter and check the fences, please. Chun Ke, could you tell me how things are going upstream?"

There was a chorus of affirmatives.

Meiling set out into the sun and did her own work that day. Milking the cows and moving the sheep to a different pasture. Cleaning the floor and checking in on the apple trees, the fruit swelling on their branches. It was not particularly hard. Most of the chores were simple things, so she ended up spending most of the day looking at Jin's notes. He said she could read them, and if she felt like it, she could test anything that caught her interest.

It was only recently that he'd started including complete instructions on what to do as well.

Meiling considered the recipe. Potato stew? With cream? With a shrug, she wrote it in for dinner, though she got a bit distracted when her brother climbed on top of the balancing poles and repeatedly fell in.

Like all of Jin's recipes, it was a bit strange to cook. A thick broth, rich with cream, and full of vegetables.

It was quite delicious.

□

The girl didn't want to catch frogs. She didn't want to throw mud. She even refused to ride the stone boar that was bigger than Meiling's house.

It was a far cry from the mischievous whelp she knew.

□

Meiling took a breath of the cool forest air. It was much nicer in the shade, rather than the late-summer sun. Meiling hummed to herself as she held on to the straps of the large basket on her back. Her father had looked a little concerned that she was planning on carrying so much weight back, but Meiling wasn't *that* far along yet. The baby bump barely showed!

Xian looked around at the small trail as they walked in the shade of the trees. They were headed upstream today, near the river that ran through the forest.

"Not even a year ago and this was all tangled undergrowth," her father muttered, adjusting the large, empty basket on his back.

And indeed, the forest floor was remarkably clear. Clear like in the sections near Hong Yaowu, where it took painstaking effort to clear the undergrowth regularly and help promote the useful plants and fungus they needed. Meiling herself was no stranger wandering around the forest with an axe and shearing off the vines that grew like weeds, or looking after the pigs as they rooted around, making sure they didn't target anything that was valuable.

Chun Ke, Wa Shi, and Pi Pa had made the forests their foraging ground. In a year, the area had been transformed, now looking like it had been carefully maintained for hundreds.

The massive boar was trotting along, six of the baskets Meiling had on her back strung out over his. Xian had cheerfully taken his place as a rider, looking around at the forest from his lofty perch. Pi Pa trotted beside him, a brush behind her ear, and a ledger tied to Chun Ke's side.

The oddest member of their group was of course Wa Shi, in his dragon form, trotting happily along beside them. His whiskers twitched, and his fishy eyes were locked ahead. A long tongue lolled out, almost like a dog's, and he licked his lips in anticipation.

They came into a clearing. The entire section of forest was blanketed in gentle mist from a small waterfall, pouring continuously onto rocks. Though the occasional tall tree provided cover, it was thin, making room for row upon row of logs, which had been stacked together and leaned up onto small scaffolds.

The sound of flowing water filled the clearing.

Meiling stared at the sight. Her father made an impressed noise.

"That's a *lot* of mushrooms," her little brother said, from on top of Chun Ke. The boar oinked, proud of his observation.

Xianggu, the mushrooms Jin called *shiitake*, absolutely covered the logs.

"It's certainly been an explosion," Meiling muttered. There hadn't been nearly this many the last time she had checked.

And while the black fungus was the most dominant, this entire area was flourishing in the damp and slowly rotting wood. Edible shelf mushrooms. Jadecaps. Other medicinal fungus that her father had given them on their wedding, sprouting like weeds from the trees and the soil.

"I do believe we'll need to make a couple of trips," she said.

□

One night, she asked the girl in her dream what was wrong. The girl pouted fiercely. She looked away and didn't answer for several long minutes.

"I don't like it when he's gone," she muttered petulantly. "It feels weird."

Meiling didn't really know what she was talking about, but she did know the feeling.

"It's better when everybody is home," she agreed, and the little girl held on to her tighter.

"I need him. I don't want to lose him, or you . . . or them," the little one said. "Maybe I should keep them all here?"

The last part was said with an inflection Meiling wasn't sure she liked, as the ground rumbled.

□

They collected the mushrooms from the logs and then wandered the property. She spent time with her father, crushing the Spiritual Herbs into paste and examining their effects.

Even her little brother joined in, though he was mostly just handing them tools.

They did get to spend time together, making medicine. It was something she treasured and cherished. This time, without the worried look on her father's face that had become prevalent with each failed matchmaking. Now his face was at peace. She loved just listening to his calm voice as they worked and seeing her father's proud smile at the carefully organised medicinal plants.

But even he could not stay forever. He had his own duties to attend to.

Another day passed. Her father returned home, carried on Chun Ke's back.

The next day, Hu Li, the Xong brothers' mother, came to visit.

"Ya know, I was a little surprised when you asked me for help with this," the woman admitted, as they worked together.

Meiling squinted at the curdling milk. "Jin likes it," she muttered, her voice nasal from the fabric plugs stuffed up them. "And I want to surprise everybody when they get back home. Make a big feast just like Jin did for me, ya know?"

Hu Li smiled at her. "Making something you hate because somebody else likes it. Oh, I know that. I always swear it's the *last* time I'm going to cook bear, and then my husband comes back with more meat and his dumb hopeful grin . . ."

Meiling nodded, imagining Jin's dopey smile.

"And I see you've been practising." Hu Li pointed to where Chun Ke and Wa Shi were lazing on the riverbank. Wa Shi pushed one of his strangely muscled arms into the basket and pulled out a slightly burned loaf of bread, dipping it in more stew. His entire body shuddered the moment he popped the morsel in his mouth.

"The sourdough stuff bakes strangely," she muttered. "And sometimes Jin uses weird names for spices, but he was super enthusiastic about his 'pizza.'"

Hu Li reached over and ruffled Meiling's hair. "Cute," she declared.

Meiling pointedly ignored her.

Hu Li barked out a laugh as the curds started to separate.

□

She kept stroking the girl's hair. "It's fine, not to want to lose him. But I don't think confining anybody anywhere will work."

The girl turned and buried her face in Meiling's skirt. There was a nod.

"All you have to do is trust that they'll come back. I miss my husband . . . But I've got a family to take care of. Work to do. And I know without a doubt he's coming home.

"And when he gets back, he's going to laugh about the stinky cheese I made him, even though I hate it. He's going to marvel at how nice the house looks, and show me all the cool things he bought in the city.

"And then, when they set off again, you can make sure they have all the supplies they need, and see them off with a smile. Or if you're able, travel with them, and go on that journey together."

The girl mulled over her words as Meiling kept stroking her hair.

She turned, looking up at her with a petulant pout.

She stared out over the river. Her back was resting against a boar, and her fingers played with a dragon's beard as she sipped her tea.

Sometimes, the surrealness still struck her. The small little jolt. When she was scratching a boar who was taller than her at the shoulder under his chin, only for her to blink, and Chun Ke to only be as tall as her waist.

To be minding her own business, then suddenly be wrapped up in the coils of a dragon. Wa Shi's clawed hands on her shoulder as he tried to hide behind her to escape Pi Pa's wrath.

A polite pig, nodding diligently and writing down everything Meiling said. Bringing her ledgers and counting up baskets of mushrooms with her.

Walking to the back, with Bei Be following silently behind her, his plow hanging from his horn. She could almost imagine a stoic swordsman guarding her.

And yet . . . she still appreciated that little jolt. That small feeling of wonder.

Some days felt like a pleasant dream. But it was real, and it was her life.

She put the cup down and continued to write. The proper baking time for the sourdough. Her own idle musings on how to use ingredients, added to pieces of paper.

Her own ideas on how to help their home improve. Maybe they would be good ones. Maybe they wouldn't amount to anything. But she wrote her thoughts down anyway as she sat with the family that had remained behind.

She couldn't wait until everybody got back . . . but for now, she was content.

□

A girl stared at a road made out of gold, leading off into the distance. She poked at it. It was in disrepair. It was broken, and bits leaked golden energy, covered only by the barest of patch jobs.

They were Dragon Veins. *Her* Dragon Veins, broken and shattered.

The road was in dire need of repair. But out there . . . out there was pain. The pain of experiences she had forgotten, scrabbling at the back of her mind. She grimaced as she recalled the crystal her little moonshard had brought back, pulsing with her own agony. She could see more shards out there. Other cracked and broken pieces of herself full of memories and knowledge she wasn't even sure she wanted.

The girl sighed, then got to work. Even if she couldn't travel to him . . . she could make sure he got home safely.

CHAPTER 23

CAUGHT BY A CULTIVATOR

"So what were you two up to last night?" I asked as we walked down the street. Big D and Yin had returned late the previous night. They hadn't exactly snuck in, but I'd decided to wait until the morning to see what had happened. It would have been kind of funny to pull the "stern dad" routine, but I decided against it. Big D wasn't the type to go out and cause trouble.

'We explored!' Yin enthused. *'We found a bunch of abandoned gardens, and then listened to a man play a nice song. Then we went swimming in the lake, and watched the moon rise.'*

The rabbit nodded happily.

"So you guys had a good date, then?" I asked teasingly.

'Yeah, it was great!' the rabbit said guilelessly. *'We should go together next time, Master Jin! With everybody!'*

Teasing denied by a rabbit who really wanted to make friends and share new experiences with them. I rubbed Yin's head affectionately. "Yeah, we'll be with everybody next time and explore the city together. Maybe we'll rent a boat or something, and see if there are any islands we can visit," I said. "So, you just stayed out watching the moon?"

'Indeed we did, Great Master,' Big D declared. *'The full moon, reflected in the lake, was a most pleasing sight. The body of water and the city were both aptly named. It was a pleasant night, but as Yin said, it would be all the better with the rest of the flock.'*

I nodded. "Well, we're going to meet up with everybody else soon. There's one last thing I want to see, then we'll check in with the merchant company, and head out to meet Master Gen for the crystal. After that, we're going to head to the Dueling Peaks. I think we'll get there in time to at least see the finals."

The disciples made noises of interest as I jogged through the city, heading for the thing I'd heard of and wanted to see.

The old "refiner" Pops had mentioned. A device that once concentrated and purified liquids, now standing unused and broken. It really was massive. It looked like something from a modern factory, almost, with just how big it was, taking up an amount of space that could have housed a building. It was mostly made of dark metal, with bronze-gold highlights and designs swirling all over it. There were vents in it, glowing so dully they were hard to see. A tiny puff of steam would occasionally issue forth from the top.

And yet everybody on the street simply passed by this ancient marvel. There was no cordon off from it. There was no guard. It simply sat there, an old machine without a purpose.

I approached and, out of curiosity, pressed my hand to it.

Nothing happened. I didn't get any strange epiphanies. I didn't see anything that would let me fix it.

It was just an old curiosity. It did look amazing, though.

I stared up at it and shook my head, dispelling the desire. I did like the whole steampunk aesthetic it had going on, but really, picking up a building-sized still and carting it away would *probably* get the guards on my ass.

No matter *how* cool it would look next to a big bathhouse or something. I wasn't going to become the guy who hoarded fixer-uppers and had junk everywhere.

I patted the old machine affectionately and left.

↔

Lu Ri moved through the forest, heading north. His pace was measured as he leapt over another hill, his sharp eyes searching for a landing spot.

In retrospect, he should not have gone to the tournament grounds. Jin Rou had seemed scared and defeated. There was the possibility he would wish to strike at those weaker than him, to crush the tournament, but he had not been born in the Azure Hills, so he could not participate.

Lu Ri had scoured the tournament grounds and stayed only for the opening ceremony, then departed. His men were prepared to transmit a message to him on the off chance that Jin Rou did appear at the tournament, but Lu Ri was fairly certain he wouldn't.

A bit more time wasted . . . but it was not too bad. The lead in the north was solid, and he would reach Verdant Hill soon at the pace he had set. Though he kept his hopes quiet. He might have to search far and wide around the empty north, searching for more clues.

He would not be surprised if it took months, the way this hunt was going.

His transmission stone crackled and buzzed. Lu Ri startled, as he had not been expecting any updates today. He considered it for a moment wondering if it truly was important or not. He was so near to his goal, he could almost feel it. But in the end, duty won out. Lu Ri aborted his next jump, landing on top of one of the hills. Moving too quickly disrupted the connection. He brought the crystal up to his mouth, pouring Qi into it to stabilize the spotty connection.

"Pale Moon Lake City, Main Branch reporting, Master Scribe," the voice from the other end stated.

"Is it important?" he asked calmly.

"We believe so, Master Scribe. Members report a man who matches the description given. Tall, freckles, brown hair. Came into Pale Moon Lake City with a large cart only a cultivator could pull, carrying what looked like rice bales. Name given to the inn he stayed at was Rou Jin, though spelled with 'soft' and 'gold,' rather than the characters we were requested to search for."

Lu Ri's mind processed the information. His eyes widened, and he nearly cursed. Neither the north, nor the tournament grounds?

"Is this accurate? Are you absolutely certain?" he demanded. That sounded extremely promising. Was Jin Rou within his grasp? Not just as a rumour, but were his men truly seeing him right this instant?

"Yes, Master Scribe, we have passive observers—" The man suddenly cut off, as there was a voice from the other end. There was a short conversation, and Lu Ri held his tongue, waiting for the men to do their jobs.

"Apologies, Master Scribe. He just met with the Azure Jade Trading Company, and he has a large pack on his back. Our man on the scene says that he may depart the city soon. Orders?"

Lu Ri's mind whirled. He was too far away to get there before Jin Rou left. He would have to order mortals to approach a cultivator and request he stop, which was a thing that was generally not done. It was risky, but it had to be done. His men had already served him well. He could only pray that they would continue to serve him for just a bit longer.

Lu Ri took a breath and made his choice.

"Gentlemen. I commend your work," he said, and meant it. "You have served me well, and now I must ask you to risk yourselves."

Lu Ri did not know how Jin Rou was going to react. The image painted of him, from those he had interacted with on his travels to the hills, was of a virtuous young man.

Yet even virtue may be strained when you are approached by one who had wronged you.

The man on the other end of the recording stone was silent for a moment.

"We serve Master Scribe," he stated formally, and with a determination that Lu Ri could hear.

Lu Ri bowed his head at such loyalty. Truly, the founders were correct when they wrote on the subject. Lu Ri had striven to be a good master, and his work had been rewarded.

Lu Ri gave the command; the man on the other end received his orders.

Then his legs tensed, and the air boomed as he leapt through the air, his passing making the trees shake.

He sped back south as fast as his legs could carry him.

□

The men working on the road, not a hill away, startled at the sudden boom. Many wondered what the great noise was. The ox they were working with, the one who plowed the road, took one of the men back so he could report the disturbance to the Lord Magistrate.

□

"It shall still take a week or two to gather everything you need, and in that time it will be stored here. It shall remain here as long as necessary. Or, should you require it, we can deliver your goods to anywhere in the Azure Hills," Guan Bo informed me, then bowed. We were in his office, with him and his sister.

Chyou was still fanning herself, dealing with the shock of a bunch of animals bowing at her in greeting—the most emotion I had ever seen on her face.

"Thanks. It would be one hell of a pain to carry everything with me," I said, bowing in return. "Thanks for all your hard work. I should be back pretty soon."

Chyou cleared her throat, so I turned to her. She visibly calmed herself before speaking. "It will take at least several months to even start to plan the expedition you wanted, Master Jin. And . . . well, I was quite enthused with the idea last night, yet . . . even the roughest costs I devised will be exorbitant."

Bo looked hesitant when Chyou mentioned the expedition.

"Yeah, I got a bit too excited about that last night too." I scratched at the back of my head sheepishly. The idea had struck me, but I hadn't really thought it through as much as I probably should have. The dangers of the Before were one thing. But the dangers here were . . . Well, was it even worth the risk? Having to run from Earth-Crushing Devil Serpents, and all the Qi-filled horrors of the south?

"We'll talk about it," I settled on. "We'll see what we need, and then we can discuss it in depth."

Chyou gave a small bow.

"As you say, Master Jin," she replied courteously.

"I think that's everything," I said, and Bo nodded.

"May you have good health, Master Jin. Should you wish for anything at the Dueling Peaks, you need only ask. Honoured Grandfather and Honoured Grandmother humbly request to meet you," Guan Bo said.

I nodded. "Definitely. I'll tell them what a good job you two have done."

Both of them blushed at that. Bo looked like Christmas had come early, while Chyou bit her lip and twirled a strand of hair around her finger.

I waved them goodbye, then walked out onto the streets. I'd already given Biyu and Master Fang a heads-up, so all that was left was a leisurely run to the spot on the map.

But it appeared that fate had other plans. Some men started approaching me as we neared the city outskirts.

All of them were immaculately dressed, like noblemen, their hair shiny and in topknots.

But what really kind of worried me was that the street started to clear out of pedestrians.

As one, the line of men bowed to me.

"Master Rou Jin. Forgive these unworthy men for impeding your path," the man said formally, bowing just about as deep as a man could bow to another. "We come bearing a message. Yet if this code is unfamiliar to you, we can only apologise and request that you stay your wrath for this interruption."

I frowned, my eyes narrowed. The Lord Magistrate had warned me that people were looking for Jin Rou, yet these guys had said Rou Jin.

It was times like these that I wished I could properly feel Qi. Were they strong? Or were they just guys who made a mistake in identity?

"What message were you asked to convey?" I asked.

The man rose.

"Your once Senior Brother above the clouds requests a meeting in this city. Failing that, he requests a meeting in the place of your choice."

Above the clouds—Cloudy Sword Sect. Senior Brother Lu Ri? What the hells could the Sect want with me? I had broken ties cleanly, paid their dues—

And made off with quite a few Spiritual Herbs, but that couldn't be it, could it? Could I have screwed up a form somewhere? Just why was the Cloudy Sword Sect looking for me?

I swallowed thickly, as my guts churned.

I could probably run away. Running away from my problems had worked pretty great the first time!

But . . .

I sighed. They'd already found me once—this was something I couldn't run away from. I squared my back.

And I agreed

CHAPTER 24

WORST FEARS

'What is going on? Who were those people? Why are we waiting here?' Yin asked as she scratched at her ear. She glanced towards the window, where the Great Master was sitting at a table, just as he had been for the past few hours.

Bi De sighed. *'I do not know. They spoke cryptically, and what they said was not well received by the Master.'*

Bi De's Great Master was upset.

This was evident to all of them. The Master rested his chin in one hand and absent-mindedly drummed his fingers upon the table. He sat cross-legged on the floor, gazing out the window. The city was shrouded in shadows; the sky had grown dark as the morning sun had faded and given way to churning storm clouds.

His back was not straight. He was slouched, seeming diminished . . . almost small, a far cry from his normal presence. His face was twisted into an expression Bi De did not like either.

Yin's question had been a good one, however. Bi De had no clue who they were, but these men inflicting such a mood upon his Great Master meant they were undoubtedly wicked! He had half a mind to declare them interlopers and strike them down for their words!

Yet his Master had agreed to what the man had requested. He had been shaken by whatever revelation he had received. The Plum Blossom agent, for that much Bi De had gathered from listening, had quickly led them to rooms prepared for their use. The Master had been still and silent since retreating into himself. Bi De could not fathom what troubled him.

Yin, Miantiao, and he had been waiting restlessly in the other part of the room, settled together on the bed's silk sheets, with some of their various belongings packed. Miantiao sighed as the drumming of the Master's fingers on the table intensified. *'We gain nothing by waiting around, do we? A question now may save misery later.'*

Bi De nodded. He was loath to interrupt his Great Master's thoughts, and he hoped his Lord would forgive him, yet he could not wait any longer.

Bi De hopped up onto the table. He knew he looked in a right state, with his feathers puffed out with concern.

'Great Master, you seem unwell. What is it these men said to you, to concern you so?' he asked directly.

His Master jumped in his seat; his eyes went wide at the sudden interruption to his contemplation. He glanced distractedly around the room, at all his disciples, as if just noticing they were there for the first time.

The Master smiled crookedly, then began to scratch at the back of his head. His eyes flicked to each of them, and he gave a pained grimace at their inquisitive faces.

"Ah! Uh . . . sorry for zoning out like that. Just . . . well, just thinking about things." He breathed in deep before he let out another sigh. "But as to your question . . . well, they said they were sent here by the Cloudy Sword Sect to set up a meeting with one of their members, a cultivator named Lu Ri. I . . . knew him once."

Bi De froze at the name. He remembered it. The Cloudy Sword Sect. They had nearly slain his Great Master and forced him to begin the journey that led to Fa Ram.

'The what?' Yin asked, confused. Miantiao and Yin were befuddled as Bi De's Qi surged, his blades of Holy Moonlight begging to be unleashed.

These vile men dared to show their faces? They had the gall, after what they had done, to demand a meeting? They courted death!

Rage surged through Bi De as he opened his mouth to call his friends and companions to arms. They would set out into the city and demand answers from these . . . lackeys.

A warm hand planted itself on Bi De's head, and it quelled all thoughts of vengeance.

"I guess you two wouldn't know about all that," his Master said, looking at Miantiao and Yin. "I'll tell you the story."

Bi De grumbled as his wattles were stroked, allowing his rage to dissipate. His Great Master seemed eager to tell this profound tale, so he let himself be pulled into his Master's lap as the two newest disciples glanced at each other and settled in.

His Great Master's voice was warm and calm as he began the grand tale. His Lord was quite good at telling stories. As he told them of his journey, his distracted tapping on the table stopped, and his slouched demeanour disappeared.

This tale was one that Bi De treasured. It was one that made him feel like he truly understood his Master. He heard his Master once more ask the question:

"What was the point of that life? What was the point of that race to the top?"

And he could tell, it was the same for their newest companions. Miantiao closed his eyes, taking in his Great Master's words. His head nodded slightly, his face full of regret. He understood without prompting.

Yin, on the other wing, simply had her head cocked to the side, listening intently, though she seemed confused. Like Tigu, she still did not fully understand the wisdom of his words.

Yet beneath the wisdom, there was fear. The fact that a person more powerful than the Great Master existed was still something that Bi De had trouble comprehending, even after seeing the flashes of the visions in the crystal.

He listened intently as his Master told him once more of his journey to the Azure Hills.

↔

"And that's why I left," I finished. It was always a bit draining to tell that story . . . but it had taken my mind off things for a moment. I'd felt for a while like I was circling the drain. The questions haunted me. Why here? Why would he want anything to do with me after I left?

"And now . . . this man wishes to meet with you?" Noodle asked after a moment.

I nodded. Noodle hissed with distaste, and I grimaced.

"They're not . . . Well, they're not *all* bad," I began. Xiulan was a cultivator, and she was a good person. There were probably more people out there who weren't assholes.

Before Xiulan, yeah, I would have said they were all bad. That they were terrible people. I had thought all the cultivators must be crazy. But they obviously weren't. Some of them were downright . . . I hesitate to say *nice*, but Lu Ri had done right by me.

"Lu Ri, who I think was the one who sent the message, gave me back my money and let me go. I, well, I didn't think I would ever hear from them again. Why would I? Why would the powerful Cloudy Sword Sect come to the Azure Hills? Why would they be looking for me? I . . . well, I don't really know. It could be for the shoots of the Lowly Spiritual Herbs I took . . . but I don't think it is. Could he have not written down that I paid? Maybe, but I don't think he'd lie about something like that."

My thoughts spilled out to them. I knew I was rambling.

'So . . . what's the plan?' Yin asked.

I paused, and looked at her. *Huh?*

'Do we fight him if he's bad?' Yin asked aggressively. *'I think I should be able to distract him.'*

"What?"

She stood on her hind legs and nodded, suddenly eager. *'If he's bad, we're going to have to defend our home and our friends, right?'*

Big D nodded, while Miantiao snorted.

'You brats.' The snake sighed. *'This Miantiao shall add his strength, meagre though it may be.'*

'Indeed,' Big D agreed. *'We shall support our Master. If he is a friend, we shall give him face, if he is an enemy . . .'*

They all turned to me, staring at me with eager eyes. Ready to stand beside me. Ready to jump to my defence.

They wanted to help me out, just like I had taught them.

I swallowed thickly.

An image flashed through my head. An image of what happened when things went wrong.

There was blood. Blood, and death. Broken. I remembered the feeling of it.

"I will be meeting him alone." I was speaking before I was conscious of it. "And . . . well, you guys have your own stuff to do, don't you?" I asked with the best smile I could put on. "You have Master Gen to see about the crystal."

I couldn't let it happen to them. If the Cloudy Sword Sect was here for a fight, I wanted them out of the city.

"You guys should get that done. Go see the tournament, and make sure Tigu hasn't done anything silly. Maybe see how Xiulan is doing too."

I had sent a rooster off into the wilderness alone.

I had let Tigu go to the tournament.

But only when I knew that they would be stronger than whatever they faced. That they would be safe. Or at least safe enough.

Fear. In the end, all it was, was fear. I wasn't really afraid for myself, I don't think. I could take some lumps. I could bow my head and press my face into the dirt. I could grovel if I had to. But I couldn't stand the thought of them getting hurt.

I wouldn't let them do that. I couldn't stop myself from forcing them away from it.

I swallowed again.

"Go," I commanded, my voice as firm as I could make it.

There was silence. Big D looked like he couldn't believe it. He glanced at the floor before gazing back up at me, his throat working. Yin's eyes were narrow, and she huffed in irritation. Noodle's gaze was just knowing.

The snake knew exactly what I was doing. I couldn't quite look him in the eye. He grimaced, then glanced to the side.

'As you command, Great Master,' Big D whispered finally.

He turned to walk towards where the crystal was, his steps dragging, then began to pack.

I turned away from them and looked out the window again at the churning clouds, trying to stomach my own words.

I had probably lost some respect here. They might even dislike me for it. But it was for the best.

If it would protect them, then that was fine.

↔

He was his Master's loyal servant.

He who was given the spark. He who was nurtured without reservation. Raised above all others.

He would do as he was commanded. Bi De could do no less, even if the action made his heart feel like lead.

Yin's voice whispered harshly in his ears, yet he barely registered the discontent she expressed. She was grumbling and shooting dirty looks back at the Great Master.

His Master wanted the best for them. He wished to protect them as much as he was able.

His Master's eyes were distant and stormy, reflecting the dark clouds above Pale Moon Lake. They looked far too much like Miantiao's when the rooster had first met him.

Words came to him unbidden as he carefully packed his things. *You should help somebody, when they need it,* his Great Master had said with a smile.

His Master's command to leave had pained him, yet he could not disobey. His Master obviously had a reason for sending them away.

Was his potential foe that vile? Were they so useless to him?

Bi De glanced back to his Master, and more words surfaced from his memories.

You don't need to face the heavens alone.

The rations were secured once more. He took out the waterproof covering, then laid it carefully over the items.

It would not take them long to get everything in order. They had been packed and ready to go already.

All that was left was the crystal. Bi De checked it, as he always did. To ensure that the glow was not duller. To make sure that the cracks had not grown deeper.

He remembered his mission. His desire to find out what secrets were hidden in the Azure Hills.

He stared at the dull blue crystal. The fragmented vision of a man stared back from the past.

A man who had shouldered everything alone. Who had tried to fight alone. Who had, in the end, lain broken and alone, mourning his choices as the world was torn asunder.

His Great Master would do the same. He would try to shoulder the weight of the world.

His Great Master who always said he was fallible. That there were times when he would be wrong.

'Everybody needs support, sometimes. Especially the people who seem to want it the least.'

The rooster stared at the fractured crystal.

'I'd rather help somebody and be burned than never have helped anybody at all,' his Great Master had said, resolute.

His Master's teachings were worth more than what his Master thought they were. They had given Bi De his friends and comrades. Sister Ri Zu. Yin, Miantiao, Zhang Fei the Torrent Rider, and even the Blaze Bears. He had applied his lessons, and had always been richer for them.

Maybe if Bi De stayed, this Lu Ri and the Cloudy Sword would slay him. It was not a sure thing.

But he'd rather help out as he could than not help at all.

Bi De made his choice.

'Great Master. You once said the greatest gift we have in our lives is choice,*'* Bi De whispered. His voice was steady as he gazed upon the crystal held in his wings.

He heard the chair creak as his Master turned to him.

He raised the gem, the treasure of his travels. *'Months of journey. Hours of contemplation. Hardship that I dislike to remember,'* Bi De whispered. *'The secrets to a bygone age.'*

He stared at it for a moment, and then cast it aside, negligently. The crystal clinked ominously as it rolled to bump against the wall. He folded his wings before him and bowed deeply.

'Forgive this Bi De. But your humble disciple must choose to disobey your command. I will not leave you.'

Yin yelped, and Miantiao's head whipped around. Bi De saw his Master silhouetted against the dark sky.

'I know. I understand you wish to protect us. But you taught us to help our friends who were in need. And I, your disciple, cannot in good conscience obey your command to leave. Not when I believe you are in need of help.'

Bi De held himself steadily. Proud and unbowed.

'Please, allow us to stand tall at your side, come what may.'

The crystal could wait. It could shatter into a thousand pieces, for all Bi De cared.

For the first time in his life, he purposefully disobeyed his Master.

They stared at each other. One calm, his face set. The other staring back, eyes cloudy and dark, filled with sorrow and pride.

□

I had ended up spending the night at the inn while we waited for Lu Ri. A night, and most of the following day. But eventually, I was summoned. Lu Ri was near.

I walked through the city towards my meeting with my Senior Brother. There was a rooster on my shoulder, a snake curled around my arm, and a rabbit stuffed down my shirt.

I felt really good today. Maybe it was because of that strange recurring dream I had, the one about throwing mud balls at that kid. Before, they'd always made me wake up feeling a bit sad. But today? I was feeling on top of the world.

Maybe it was a bad idea to have these guys come with me to the meeting. Maybe it wasn't. But I had said that they were free to choose.

And to be honest, I was proud of Big D for saying no to me. It was a bit strange to say that, but . . . it was nice to know that someone loved you enough to call you out on your bullshit.

I would respect their choice. For good or ill, I'd face what was to come.

Nah.

We'd face what's to come.

CHAPTER 25

THE RETURN OF SENIOR BROTHER

The land whipped by below Lu Ri in a green blur. Each bounding leap took him over enormous, forested hills and tiny villages.

He had pushed himself hard, moving as fast as he was able. The air had long since stopped screaming in protest. It simply wasn't efficient to travel that fast in this province. The circular breathing of the Clouded Steps was useless when there was no Qi to replenish. Instead, with his tight grip on his power unleashed for haste, the very air that entered his lungs wicked away his energy with every breath.

Far from the more leisurely stroll he'd taken up north, he rushed to his destination this time. His stride was slowed by the Qi-desert, but it was still an acceptable speed. An annoyance, and one that had to be borne. His only regret was that he was still lacking to be struggling like this. There was no flying sword for him, standing calm and unflappable as a cultivator should. Instead, his hair and clothes were tangled and wrinkled, and sweat poured down his body.

Yet his haste was rewarded. A mere day and a half after he'd received the message, Lu Ri could see Pale Moon Lake City at the apex of his jumps.

His transmission stone buzzed.

He drew his Qi inwards after one last jump. It would do no good to shatter all of the detector stones again and rouse the city guards.

"Report," he commanded, as he slowed to a mortal pace and placed his mended hat back upon his head. Joining the crowd moving into the city, he let his pace take him past the carts and masses of people towards the Plum Blossom base. A bath was in order, and he needed to read the final reports his men had made.

While making Jin Rou wait was impolite, it was *doubly* impolite to arrive looking so harried with the filth of the road upon his body. He had an image to maintain as a member of the Cloudy Sword Sect!

"Jin Rou will be at the Pale Moon Pavilion, Master Scribe," the man on the other end of the transmission stone informed Lu Ri. "We have a report prepared and ready to be perused at your leisure." There was a pause as the agent seemed to gather his courage and said, hesitantly, "There is one . . . *complication*."

Lu Ri frowned. "Complication?"

"Yes, Master Scribe. We knew Rou Jin was important to the Azure Jade Trading company. We underestimated just *how* important. They have taken issue with us impeding his path. There are discussions going on between us at this moment. It has been . . . contentious."

"I see." Lu Ri considered this.

The Honoured Founders were conflicted upon the nature of merchants. They decried most as money-grubbers, yet also stated their necessity. The writings on how to deal with them were clear. Courtesy, if no other recourse was available. The grudge of merchants was not something to underestimate. If they were insulted but not destroyed completely, one's enemies might suddenly find themselves *suspiciously* well equipped.

Yet if the Azure Jade Trading Company served Jin Rou as the Plum Blossom served Lu Ri, he would give them face. It was not their place to question Jin Rou or his motives, but doing so out of concern for their master was admirable.

"Convey our apologies for the inconvenience, and arrange reparations. Information is to be invaluable to merchants, is it not?"

"As you say, Master Scribe," the man replied.

Lu Ri nodded. Their mission was soon to be complete, in any case. However, abandoning a man after giving him purpose was to be avoided at all costs—for it produced a desire for revenge that was truly legendary. Lu Ri would likely never return to the Azure Hills, so the men of the organisation he had created had to be given a new purpose.

And if his Junior Brother had close ties to these merchants, in that they were willing to investigate threats to him . . . well, he knew how to manage them.

His path took him to the inner city, to a quaint little walled villa near the tiny Imperial Palace. It was incredibly small for a provincial capital. He entered through one of the side gates, where he was immediately received.

Chan, his most regular aide in this city, greeted him, saying, "A bath has been prepared for you, Master Scribe." He held out to Lu Ri the current findings on Jin Rou.

Lu Ri took the report and leafed through it.

"His temperament?" Lu Ri asked.

Chan seemed amused for a moment before replying, "He is in a fine mood this morning, Master Scribe. He was singing to himself and went to the kitchens to prepare himself a meal. The staff were shocked. Other than that, he stayed within his room."

Lu Ri quirked an eyebrow, nodded, and then walked through the house. Men immediately stepped aside and bowed as Chan led him through the rustic, almost spartan, house.

"The men who participated?" he asked, and immediately another page was produced, detailing the actions each member had undertaken. Lu Ri committed the names to memory.

Merit would be assigned later.

Chan bowed, then gestured in front of the door leading to a bathing chamber. The bath was already prepared, but there was little time to enjoy it. Lu Ri cleaned himself quickly. The dirt and sweat gathered from pushing himself sloughed off quickly, and once that was done he tended to his hair, ridding it of the few tangles. A testament to his speed that it was tangled at all.

A fresh set of clothes was taken from his storage ring, and a replenishing pill took the worst off the dull ache from lightly depleted Qi reserves.

Finally, he looked upon the reports in detail.

Arrived with a large cart that would be impossible for a man to pull. Contents tentatively confirmed to be rice, but the number of guards and the tight-lipped nature of the company suggests something else.

Addendum. Report from Dueling Peaks Auction. Azure Jade Trading Company reports gold-grade rice for sale. Correlation likely, but unknown.

Lu Ri raised an eyebrow at that. Gold-grade rice? Jin Rou had expressed his intention to become a farmer when he had left. *It seems he had used the skills gathered in tending to the Spiritual Herbs to great effect.*

Lu Ri idly wondered what gold-grade rice tasted like. It was considered decadent to consume such a thing, and a waste of money when one could buy cultivation resources instead.

He shook his head and continued reading.

Spent the night with Guan Chyou of the merchant company in a private setting. That she was with him after but a single night indicates extreme favour from the Azure Jade Trading Company.

With Guan Bo, visited or made purchases at the following shops . . .

Lu Ri scanned the list. Copper, glass, sand: all mundane materials, if in high purity, and large amounts.

Temperament seems mild. Was observed getting bumped into on the street, and waved off the culprit. Was polite to all agents. Initially surprised at contact, but accepted easily.

Good news, and confirming what Lu Ri's men had said. There was one last note, however, that gave him pause.

Currently in the company of two or more animals at all times. Rooster, rabbit, snake. Talks to them, and they seem to respond. Tales from the north indicate some manner of rooster that fights against the wicked. Pervasive rumours, from caravaneers. Highly likely they are Spirit Beasts . . .

Lu Ri stoked his chin. Spirit Beasts? That was surprising. But he would take things as they came. Lu Ri centered himself.

Finally, he was nearly at the end of this task.

→

"He is here, Master Scribe," the man beside him whispered.

Lu Ri pulled himself out of his contemplations. Running the scenarios through his head would do him no more good. Jin Rou could be violently angry, meek and cowed, or a hundred other things, yet until he actually met the boy, he wouldn't know. Any of them were acceptable, as long as Lu Ri completed his task.

So he turned his attention to the Pale Moon Pavilion. He had reserved the entirety of it, the other small places empty in the vast garden. It was a calm, quiet place. Ivy climbed the wooden poles, and the last flowers of summer let loose their heady scents into the air. A small river flowed, the gentle trickle of water masking conversations to any attempting to listen from outside. While renting out the entirety of the place was a show of power, hopefully their surroundings would properly convey his peaceful intentions.

It was, after all, rude to damage a mortal's dwellings, unless there was no other recourse. *So spoke the Honoured Founders—*

Lu Ri paused. Had Jin Rou even read their teachings? He hadn't been in the Sect very long, and his time had been consumed with maintenance.

He frowned, considering that the Young Master who'd beaten Jin Rou had deprived him of reading those enlightened texts.

But there was no more time for further introspection. There was power approaching. It felt a bit strange. It was hazy, and it took a moment for him to be able to clearly see it. Second Stage of the Profound Realm, from the Fifth Stage of the Initiate's Realm? A more than acceptable increase, considering he had been here all this time. Lu Ri couldn't imagine gaining a stage, let alone ascending a realm in this deprived province. The fact that he had not neglected his cultivation boded well. Elder Ge would certainly be pleased.

Yet something was amiss. There were two others with him. Two initiates, both of the Third Stage, with one edging on the Fourth.

Lu Ri stood and brushed out his clothes to make sure he was immaculate. He took off his hat, resting it on the back of his chair, and he raised his arm, dismissing his men.

Jin Rou entered the pavilion. He had, as Lu Ri's men had said, a rooster on one shoulder, a rabbit on the other, and a snake curled around his arm. He also had a small box in his hand.

It had been nearly two years since Lu Ri had last laid eyes upon his Junior Brother. An eyeblink, to a cultivator.

Yet Lu Ri wondered if the man before him now was the same boy he remembered.

Jin Rou had always been the odd one out. Poor. Low class. His fellows sometimes said he was barely a cultivator. His tanned skin and freckles had spoken of a lifetime of heavy labour, without the higher realms to prevent them.

He always had an energy about him, however. Always doing something. Filled with fire and a drive that saw him picking up every task he could, and doing the ones forced on him without complaint.

The man before Lu Ri was calm. *Steady.* His eyes met Lu Ri's without fear as his stride took him towards the table.

Jin Rou had always been tall, yet he had, in his absence, grown even taller. His frame had always been unfortunate for a cultivator. Too much bulk, instead of lithe, deadly grace. That feature had only increased, his frame built with thick slabs of working muscle. His freckles had multiplied, and a dark tan deepened the tone of his skin.

Lu Ri's eyes narrowed, flicking to the rooster. It was a magnificent beast, to be true. Its colouration was sublime. It wore a fox-fur vest and was gazing upon him.

Yet *it* was the power. The *rooster* was the Profound Realm cultivator he had felt.

The snake and the rabbit were the initiates. The snake was old and had been damaged by something—it was missing an eye, with odd burn markings on it. The rabbit was a bright silver and was glowering at him. From Jin Rou he felt . . . nothing.

Lu Ri paused as he took the beasts in. Such creatures were not particularly common, but they did appear occasionally.

As harbingers of calamity. If not properly dealt with, they were often an unintentional bane to their owner. The awakened animals attracted other, more powerful Spirit Beasts to feast upon them and often led to the complete destruction of any village they lived in—provided the beasts did not get their own designs of destruction and murder their owner first. If one appeared, it was standard to call a Sect or the government to take the creature or sell it to a noble. In those cases, they were consumed immediately.

But a mere rooster, in the Profound Realm? To think that a rooster is stronger than most of the Elders of this province.

Lu Ri knew not Jin Rou's intentions, and it was not his place to ask.

But the fact that Lu Ri could not feel Jin Rou concerned him. He was clearly a cultivator. He cast out his senses. It was an art to gauge another's cultivation accurately without being intrusive.

There was an inkling of . . . something. But pressing any deeper would be intrusive to the point of offence, so he retracted himself. He was here to make peace, not assuage his curiosity. Was Jin Rou practising some strange art? All things to put in his report to the Elders. Yet that, Lu Ri supposed, was the power of even the lowest disciple of the Cloudy Sword Sect. He could surprise his Senior Brother by disappearing to this backwater and arriving with Spirit Beasts and some strange cultivation technique.

Once more, Lu Ri felt irritation at the Young Master who had beaten Jin Rou. To have pushed away such a talent.

He shoved his thoughts on the matter aside. Jin Rou made to greet Lu Ri first, as their stations demanded.

The situation, however, was different. Lu Ri was to offer Jin Rou face, as it was the Cloudy Sword who had erred.

Lu Ri moved with almost unseemly haste.

"Lu Ri, Disciple of the Cloudy Sword Sect, greets Jin Rou," he intoned, giving the man proper respect.

Jin Rou froze, confusion on his features, as the Spirit Beasts with him hopped down. He was obviously confused about the meeting, and he was guarded. But he too bowed, along with the amusing sight of three Spirit Beasts also offering Lu Ri bows.

"Rou Jin greets Senior Brother Lu Ri," he said, and then Lu Ri was surprised as the Spirit Beasts too spoke.

'Fa Bi De, First Disciple of Fa Ram, greets Lu Ri,' a deep, smooth voice intoned as the rooster lowered his head.

'Liang Yin greets Lu Ri,' the rabbit stated, her voice as smooth and perfect as Senior Sister Yeo Na's.

'Miantiao greets Lu Ri.' The last one was aged and tired sounding. The snake's one good eye examined Lu Ri closely.

"My disciples," Jin Rou said, a wan little smile on his face.

The idea would have been laughable if Lu Ri did not have them before his eyes. *Purposefully training them? Interesting.* The rooster alone was powerful enough to fight in a tournament in Raging Waterfall Gorge. It was enough to make Lu Ri want to examine these creatures in greater detail.

Was this ability to raise Spirit Beasts what had caught his patron's attention? That Jin Rou had brought them was an odd statement.

Lu Ri gave them all brief nods of acknowledgement, as outlined in proper courtesy for lesser disciples, then gestured to the table, offering the odd group seats. The humans sat down, with the . . . disciples taking their places on top of the table. Jin Rou set the box he was carrying atop it as well. Lu Ri set about pouring them both tea. Another technical breach of etiquette, as the Junior was supposed to serve the Senior, but this would be abandoned for this meeting. The tea was a fragrant blend directly from the lower quarters of Crimson Crucible City, where Jin Rou had once lived. Lu Ri noted that Jin Rou's eyes widened in surprise at the scent, his hand spasming briefly against the table.

"It is good to see you again, Jin Rou—or Rou Jin, as it is. It did give me a bit of trouble finding you, I must confess," Lu Ri began. The man flinched at his mention of the deception and laughed nervously.

"Yeah. I wanted a clean break, you know? Just in case that one guy wasn't finished yet," Rou Jin said. Lu Ri winced internally. That was perhaps a good choice, in all honesty. Changing the characters one spelled their name with, as well as the order, had been surprisingly effective.

"Indeed. I see you have been doing well for yourself. That is good."

Jin Rou narrowed his eyes, both confused and suspicious. He tentatively nodded, taking a sip of tea. His breath hitched for a moment before he swallowed thickly. He squared his shoulders.

"Senior Brother. I hope it's not too rude . . . but why are you here?" he asked. "I'm sure it is not for a social call."

Lu Ri nodded. *Straight to the point, then.* He cleared his throat and took out his storage ring.

Jin Rou tensed.

"This Lu Ri is here on official business of the Cloudy Sword Sect, as outlined in the rules and regulations of the Honoured Founders," he intoned. The man across from him folded his arms as Lu Ri pressed his hand to the ring. Jin Rou's eyes narrowed.

Lu Ri pulled out the letter, took it in both hands, and offered it politely.

"Pertaining to the laws of the Cloudy Sword Sect, and the stipulations on Honourable Departure—Jin Rou, your mail."

The envelope was pristine. The seal undamaged. Routed through the imperial army, the name on the front simply was "Grandfather."

Jin Rou stared blankly at it. He looked back up at Lu Ri, a completely dumbfounded expression on his face.

"What?"

YOUR MAIL.

CHAPTER 26

YOU'VE GOT MAIL!

If there was one way I thought my day was going to go, I'll admit it *certainly* wasn't like this.

I had marched into the pavilion as resolved as I could be. Senior Brother Lu Ri was already waiting for me. His dark hair in a topknot. Dressed to the nines in courtly clothes and sitting in the pavilion with moonlight shining on him. It was like something out of a book. If you looked up "severe court scholar," you'd probably get an image of Lu Ri.

Instead of stern, resolute, and scary, my once Senior Brother was polite. *Too* polite. He greeted me first. He nodded to Big D, Noodle, and Yin, which showed a great amount of "face," to use the term. That he even acknowledged their existence meant something, and then *he* poured *my* tea.

Tea from the district Rou was from. Something within me spasmed when I smelled it. A warm flood of nostalgia, remembering the times Rou's parents had made this, mixed with sorrow and grief, threatening to burst out of the dam I had built around my memories.

I was off balance and reeling when he went and delivered the finishing blow.

I'd expected at least a bit of posturing. Of dancing around the issues. But that had gone out the window.

All that, all the fear I'd experienced . . . *was because he wanted to deliver a letter*?

I stared blankly at the envelope that Lu Ri held out to me. I immediately recognised Gramps's handwriting scrawled across the front.

The memories came unbidden. The little shack we lived in, after Gramps pulled me off the streets. Him teaching me the courtly characters. Every morning, running through the katas I *still* ran through. Playing in the river. Throwing dung at his head. Him chasing me down and tying me to a tree in retaliation. Falling asleep against his side, after we ate a slightly burned dinner, because the old man could barely boil water.

Although he wasn't bound to this body by blood, the old man was all the family Rou had ever known. I'd felt . . . *Rou* had felt lost when Gramps had turned his back on him, and sternly stated he had to go away. After the time spent without a word, I'd thought something terrible had happened to him.

I hadn't heard from him for nearly three years. Rou hadn't seen him for nearly three years. Now I find out he'd written me a letter?

What the hell?

With shaking hands, I took it from Lu Ri, the man's face as inscrutable as the Lord Magistrate's. I briefly contemplated tearing it open right then; my friends looked on curiously, and Lu Ri sipped his tea.

"When you looked at how to leave the Sect, did you not also read the sections on Honourable Departure?" he asked curiously.

"Ah . . . no?" I replied.

"In addition to receiving mail, you may rejoin the Sect at any time, and may beg for refuge for your kin in times of peril," Lu Ri stated authoritatively.

I frowned at that. I guess reading ahead on the benefits hadn't really occurred to me. I'd just wanted out fast.

"It's a bit strange that they have those rules," I admitted. Lu Ri looked vaguely amused at the statement.

I toyed with the letter, flipping it back and forth, before sighing.

"Thanks," I whispered. Lu Ri nodded magnanimously.

"It took longer than I expected, but this is a good result," he stated. I glanced at the date on the letter.

It had been sent nearly a year ago.

I leaned back in my chair and looked at his clothes again. They were fresh and well cleaned, but his hat had been mended multiple times and he seemed a bit tired.

"I see your defeat did not crush your spirit entirely, Jin Rou. It speaks well of you. Did you end up becoming a farmer like you said?"

Again, Lu Ri's words were knocking me off balance. Honestly, they shouldn't have. Lu Ri was the man who'd given me back my money when I left the Sect. There was only curiosity in his eyes.

Just small talk over tea. No threats, no sudden fight in the pavilion. Just a mail delivery.

I smiled tentatively.

"Yeah. Yeah, I did. It's been pretty great, actually—here."

I opened up the box I had brought along. I had made it on a whim. Just in case the meeting did turn out to be nothing, and to take my mind off the impending meeting.

Candy making is really easy when you can use a Sun-rabbit as a stove.

Lu Ri raised an eyebrow as the fudge was revealed. He sniffed indecorously. "Maple . . . ?" he ventured, his tone curious, before his eyes widened.

"Oh, you've had some before?" I asked curiously.

"Yes, I have. A delectable offering, but the city contains no more—" He paused, looking up at me, before closing his eyes and chuckling. "It appears the heavens are fickle. To think that I had something produced by your hands months ago. It reinvigorated me during my search."

That was kind of funny, actually.

He took a piece and put it into his mouth. His eyes closed briefly as the taste hit.

"I've been growing rice, wheat, veggies . . ." I decided to take a gamble. "And some of the Lowly Spiritual Herbs."

"You actually managed to grow them here?" he asked. He was surprised, yet unconcerned. He frowned slightly and shook his head. "Remarkable. I am glad that you have had good fortune, Junior Brother, to create things of such quality."

He took another bite of fudge, and a sip of tea, visibly considering how the flavours blended together. He seemed to be mulling something over.

"There is another matter, however," he finally stated.

And just like that, the tension ratcheted back up. His back straightened again, and he held his hands in front of his face, inclining his head.

"Jin Rou. The Cloudy Sword Sect wishes to apologise for the actions one of its Young Masters took against you. The man has been punished. Such an occurrence was not meant to happen, and we accept full responsibility."

I was floored. *The Sects did not apologise.* The Cloudy Sword Sect did *not* go to weak Outer Disciples and say *Sorry for getting you beat up*.

Just what the hell was going on? Why me?

"Additionally I . . . would request that you return to the Sect with me," Lu Ri stated. "You will be reinstated as a disciple, and reparations will be paid for this unfortunate occurrence. Your disciples are of course welcome to come with you, and they will be under my and the Cloudy Sword Sect's protection."

Lu Ri's calm, matter-of-fact voice warred against the impossible things coming out of it. I think I was getting a taste of my own medicine here, with the whole "shocking revelation" thing. My heart thundered in my chest. I felt a bit light-headed.

The Cloudy Sword Sect wanted me back.

"*Why?*" I croaked out finally.

"Because the Elders wish it," Lu Ri stated simply. "Your benefactor is of great importance to the Sect."

Benefactor? Gramps? Just what was this?

Lu Ri looked at my expression and took another sip of tea.

"I have given you much to ponder. I do not need an answer immediately. You may take your time. We shall meet again tomorrow, if it pleases you. If you need me, I am available." He placed a crystal on the table in front of me as I just kind of sat there, chewing my lip.

Lu Ri left the pavilion. I didn't get up.

I stared at the letter.

A letter that had gotten the Cloudy Sword Sect to find me and ask me to return.

I broke the seal.

□

"Little Rou.

"I am alive, if you doubted me, you little brat. And I have not forgotten you.

I apologise for my abrupt departure and lack of contact, but things beyond my control intervened. If you can avoid it, never owe another man a favour. They tend to call them in at the worst times!

"I am well! This duty is merely tedious, and not actively threatening, though it is taking longer than I would like. And yes, it is a duty, boy, even though I cannot say much about it. I know you like to call me a drunkard, but this is not a mere social call to some beauties and a fine bottle of wine!

"Even though I wish it were. It would be much more enjoyable. You're finally a man now, aren't you? The women were quite enamoured with me in my youth. Kowtow a hundred times for me, and I may just teach you my secrets!

"Perhaps on the road. When this is all over, I'll take you with me for a little excursion. The world is too large to stay in one city all your life!

"Yet this is not about me. How are you enjoying yourself in my old Sect? I know you passed, boy. A friend told me. But don't get a big head now, even if passing the entrance exam of the Cloudy Sword Sect is a feat to be acknowledged!

"Perform your duties there well, even if they must be easy compared to all the work you used to do. I'm sure you have plenty of time to meditate and grow your strength.

"But I, your grandfather, am feeling generous and will give you some pointers.

"First, the best place to read in the library is the south corner. Take your time and examine the texts there thoroughly.

"Second, when you can, I would suggest you take a walk through the Cloudy Forest. There are the occasional caves there that are most effective for one's meditation.

"Third, ask your Seniors for pointers when you can. It may be a bit painful, because of your lack of skill, but it's the best way to learn quickly!

"Lastly, a gift. I know you were frustrated I would not allow you to hold a sword, but do you see the seal at the bottom of this letter? When you hit the Second Stage of the Profound Realm, it will unlock. Take it, and learn what you can.

"I look forward to seeing what you do with it—provided you can even hit the Profound Realm with your talent! A challenge. If you show sufficient mastery of the technique, I may even allow you to ask a boon of me.

"Rou. When you can, send me a reply. This old man worries sometimes about your health. I know you are in good hands, for the Cloudy Sword is righteous, but I do wish to hear of your time firsthand.

"Though only if you refrain from stuffing this letter full of dung.

"My contacts in the Imperial Army will ensure its delivery."

□

Jin Rou dropped the letter on the table and rubbed at his eyes. The pale moon cast its glow across the pavilion, staining the leaves and the flowers silver.

He looked up at the sky, leaned back in his chair, and sighed. Remembering.

CHAPTER 27

ROU AND GRAMPS

Hey, brat. Where did you learn to shovel like that?" The voice startled him. Jin Rou paused in his work and turned, wiping his sweaty face on his sleeve. There was an old vagabond sitting on the stone steps where he was working. The man wore a threadbare tunic and had a ragged straw hat that was hanging down his back.

The boy frowned at the old man and his relaxed posture. His face was creased and he seemed lethargic, but his eyes had a small spark of interest. The boy considered him and saw no harm in answering.

"I watched the older guys, but they were too tall. So I figured things out myself," he said simply, then turned back to shoveling. He twisted his hips to heave the load over his shoulder. It was easier on his back. The other street cleaners were often amazed that he managed to finish his assignments so fast. But all he had to do was be efficient. His father had always said one should find a way to do things better.

The boy grimaced while he continued shoveling. The old man watched him for a while, until the boy left, grabbing his waste cart, and heaving it up. It was almost too much to handle, but he was good at judging the weight.

"Why do you struggle so hard, boy?" the old man asked.

Rou paused at the question. He turned to glare at the old man.

"To live," he stated simply. The old man raised a brow at his answer but said no more.

He put the old man out of his mind and continued on his day. He worked until the sun set, counted his earnings carefully, ate as much as he could, and then saved a bit so he could afford to take a day off at some point. Food was more important than a roof right now; with the heat of summer, sleeping in the streets wasn't too awful, as long as you knew which street corners a boy could sleep on.

→

And so it continued. The week of work, leading to his day off. The day he'd scrimped and saved for. Rou bathed thoroughly, washing the stinking of waste off his body, then travelled to his destination.

The Archive.

There he met another man, a student who was aiming to be a scribe. The price was steep for a boy like him, but the one day a week was cheaper than an actual school. He had to work. He couldn't afford to learn full time.

Reading is important, his father had said. *Better jobs come to those who can read.*

So the older boy put him through the courtly characters. He was overly fond of cuffing Rou for any mistake he made, but Rou was learning. Those were annoying, but some strikes from the foppish boy were nothing compared to the time he accidentally crossed the gang. He hadn't been able to walk right for weeks, and the hunger pangs had been . . . difficult.

Rou worked diligently. He practised on the slate. He noticed an old man glancing at him from the corner of his eye. He looked a bit familiar, but once more Rou put him out of his mind and redoubled his efforts.

→

The next day the waste collectors didn't want him. That was unfortunate, but Rou was just a boy. They wanted the stronger men. So he went to the next job, asking for work.

Then the next one. Then the next one. Nobody would take him.

Until an old man who looked very familiar offered him some food to sweep the street in front of his old house.

Rou was surprised he even had one.

It was a good job. He practised his brushstrokes of the characters as he swept, the old man having gone inside. It was a balancing act between getting the job done in time and squeezing in some practice.

"Do you know the character for 'sword,' boy?" the old man asked. Rou nearly jumped out of his skin at the voice—the old man was right behind him, looking down at the sweep marks.

But he didn't seem mad. In fact, he seemed to approve.

"I don't," Rou replied.

The old man took the broom from him. It swirled almost hypnotically along the ground, leaving a single character.

The old man smirked as Rou took back the broom. His body twisted, trying to ape the old man's movements.

The character for "sword" rested beside the first. It wasn't a perfect replica, but it was passable.

The old man grinned and pulled the broom back.

"This one is 'cultivate,'" he decreed.

The broom spun, and Rou watched intently.

Rou spent the rest of the day sweeping characters into the ground.

And for the first time since his parents had died, he smiled.

The old man even bought him dinner. His stomach grumbled.

"If I had not offered you a job, where would you have gone next, boy?" the old man asked.

Rou shrugged. "The night soil collectors and corpse disposal crew start recruiting at night. Either that or the rat catchers."

The old man raised an eyebrow. "All that, to learn a few letters and get some food in your belly," he mused.

"It doesn't matter if the job is dirty or disgusting. I'm going to get out of this place." Rou turned his hungry gaze to the old man.

The old man smiled.

"You can sleep here tonight," the old man decided.

Rou grinned. "Thanks, Gramps," he said.

The old man's jaw dropped. For a moment he seemed utterly confused by the term of endearment before letting out a great belly laugh.

→

The boy and the old man became companions. The drunken lout would laze around while Rou worked, occasionally offering comments on what to do or quizzing the boy on characters he'd just learned.

He was better than Rou's previous teacher, at least. Gramps didn't cuff him as much.

He still did get a smack when he called the man an old bastard, though, or threw dung at his head.

The old man tolerated it for some reason. He'd act mad, but other than a few light smacks, he let it go.

It was kind of fun.

They prowled the city together. Gramps occasionally bought him food or made him do weird breathing exercises.

They slept in the same tiny shack together. When it was cold, Rou would shove his feet into Gramps's side. The old man never complained about that.

It was almost like having a family again.

Rou ran through the streets, terror in his heart. The flesh traders were out and in force, scooping up the refuse of the city, and had their sights set on him.

Three were hot on his tail, and one was gaining on him.

Rou ran for all he was worth, but the day's work had taken its toll. He was just a boy, and the grown man was faster. Much faster.

Desperation burned in his breast as the man closed. Jin Rou searched for something, *anything* to aid him.

He found nothing but a broom.

With strength born of desperation, he lunged for it. His hands fixed around the handle, and he swung it with all his might.

Something snapped inside him.

The broom moved far faster than it should have, clubbing into the man's skull with the ugly crack of breaking bone.

The man fell and didn't get back up. Rou sank to one knee, panting.

The other two didn't pause, lunging for him. Rou's legs shook. His vision blurred.

But he stood up anyway, ready to fight to the death—

Both of the flesh traders hit the ground, their necks bent at awkward angles, and Gramps appeared in the space between heartbeats. Rou hadn't even seen him move. Rou blinked to clear his vision and looked up at the old man.

He was smiling. Gramps was smiling, a massive, pride-filled grin as he stared at the man Rou had killed.

"The streets aren't safe this late, brat," the old man said after a moment, his gaze on Rou.

"No shit," Rou said, then collapsed. Gramps caught him before he hit the ground, laughing all the while.

→

Jin Rou didn't need to work anymore. Gramps said that cultivation was much more important. There was a kind of hunger in his eyes that Rou strived to meet. He cultivated as hard as he could to achieve power like in the stories.

So he could make the old man proud.

"Rou, you're not done yet?!" the old bastard demanded. "This should be simple!"

Rou's eye twitched. That night, he replaced the old turd's wine with horse piss.

Gramps almost seemed impressed, even as he hung Rou upside down from a tree.

→

But all things come to an end.

Rou watched anxiously as the old man packed. Gramps's eyes were cold and hard, like he had never seen them before.

"Go to the Cloudy Sword Sect," he commanded. "I have things to attend to."

And then Jin Rou was alone again.

CHAPTER 28

TOGETHER, TO THE FUTURE

Rou stared up at the night sky, which was filled in with a thousand cracks of gold, and the glimmering points of stars. It was warm here, like a late-summer evening. The deck he was sitting on felt comfortable and worn, as if it had seen a thousand nights just like this. The area they were in seemed both endless and tiny at the same time. The grass stopped not far off the deck, fading into darkness, yet little golden trails continued onwards, far, far away until Rou couldn't see them anymore.

Rou contemplated his surroundings, absent-mindedly tapping his leg. After all this time, a letter.

Gramps . . .

So the old bastard was fine. That was good! Better than good. Rou was glad he was okay. Glad it wasn't something Rou had done that caused the old man to leave. Gramps had been angry at somebody else—that was why he had been so short. It had been about some other guy calling in a favour. He'd even apologised in the letter.

That meant something. It had to. Gramps hadn't just abandoned him.

Rou was still angry. Really, Gramps just said it was a mission, then didn't explain, the bastard. He dumped him off at the Sect, where Rou had worked like a dog—

And then he died . . . or would have died.

Rou sighed and glanced at the leg he was tapping. It terminated at the ankle, turning hazy and indistinct, before transitioning to the other guy's leg.

There was silence. For once, at least, the other guy was quiet. He wasn't saying something stupid or inane, shoving memories down their shared . . . whatever, like an annoying asshole. He quietly sipped the tea from home as he sat beside Rou. The flavour and smell dredged up bittersweet memories.

The asshole had let Rou take over for a while. It might not have been intentional, but the other guy hadn't fought it. *Something* had happened. When he was reading that letter, it had been Rou alone.

For a brief moment, he'd felt a flash of exhilaration. This was his chance. Perhaps he could be the one to take command permanently! But as quickly as it came, it faded.

The only reason he was alive in the first place was because of the shattered remains of the other man propping him up. A hand that had reached out and kept him around when he'd been fading away into the darkness. Picking up the pieces and putting them back together, even when he barely had enough will for it himself. Now he felt more and more alive. More like he was living again, despite the walls between them. Able to see and taste and experience outside of this waking dream, rather than simply watching from afar and longing.

Jin had a thousand chances to snuff him out. A thousand chances to destroy what was left of the man once called Rou.

Yet he hadn't. He hadn't even once considered it.

Rou sighed and looked to his side at the other guy.

"Hey," he whispered. Jin perked up, his good eye opened, glancing at him—the other was a ruined mess, covered completely in gold.

"Thanks."

There were no real words needed other than that. Jin nodded to him, not bringing any more attention to it. He understood. They were kind of similar, like that.

There was silence, as they sat together.

"So. What do we do about the Cloudy Sword Sect?" Jin asked. Rou rolled his eyes.

"See how sorry they really are, take them for whatever reparations they're gonna give, then tell them to screw off," Rou declared instantly.

The other guy looked surprised.

"*Huh*. I thought you would have wanted to go back. Go and get that heavenly ascension power," he muttered.

Rou stared at the idiot.

"Our Qi don't work right using traditional techniques. We might have to destroy our current cultivation to *start* practising normally again."

A farm. Something he had never even seen before, being from a city. He had scoffed at the other man's memories, thinking them worthless and idealized. But the more he'd worked on it, the more he'd grown to love it. He finally had something that was his. No corpses in the streets. No gangs to demand protection money. Lazy days by the river. Seeing it grow and change. Knowing that it was *his* work that made wonders.

"We'd have to leave the farm. We'd have to give up every single thing we have now to go back—" Rou started.

Meiling pulling up her shirt and exposing her stomach, grinning at him as she turned, showing him the small bump. A child. *His* child.

Bi De bowing to him, and following him around like he was something worth respecting. Staring at him and defiantly choosing to stand with him until the end.

Tigu jumping onto his back, like that little girl next door used to before her skin turned pale and grey from the Demon's Black Hate.

A happy boar. A proper pig. A clever little rat. A stoic ox. A gluttonous carp, a kind old snake, and a naïvely powerful rabbit. Gou Ren helped him build the drop hammer. Yun Ren laughed as he pranked somebody. Xiulan's soft smile, Pops nodding to him like his own father used to.

To Rou, it was like the heavens on earth. But that was what the other guy wanted to create, wasn't it?

Rou gritted his teeth. "And if you think I'm leaving my family, you got another thing comin'," he snarled.

Jin's eyes widened.

They might not have liked Rou. They might not have liked a street rat full of piss and vinegar. But the life was his, just as much as it was Jin's. The affection he felt for them wasn't imagined.

"The Cloudy Sword Sect fucked me up once; I'm not gonna let them fuck us up again, and I'm *sure* as hell not letting them fuck up what we have now."

Jin smiled. Rou turned away, glaring at the darkness around them.

"Like you would have gone anyway," he muttered, before shaking his head. "The bigger question is what do we do now? The Cloudy Sword Sect knows about us. We're dumping gold-grade rice onto the market. We even asked that Chyou woman to put together an expedition to the south. We can't stay a secret anymore. Somebody has already come knocking. This time it was just mail, but next time?"

Jin sighed, looking down into his tea. "Yeah. I know. The world ain't sunshine and daisies, and I've gotten a bit complacent. It's the Azure Hills. I thought we were strong enough to handle anything that came towards us. Who would look twice at this weak place? But now we got the Cloudy Sword Sect interested in us; Gramps is apparently influential enough that the Cloudy Sword mobilized a Senior Disciple to deliver mail," he said, then lapsed into silence.

Rou frowned. He never had known how strong Gramps was. Never really tried to see. But weren't strong guys supposed to have all sorts of special cultivation resources? Rou hadn't gotten any from Gramps, not as far as he remembered.

"We protect what's ours," Rou finally said. "If the Cloudy Sword Sect really is looking to make amends, well, they can help us out when we need it."

Jin rolled his eyes. Then he smiled and asked, "Does that mean we can start asking people if they dare oppose the Cloudy Sword Sect?"

Rou barked out a laugh.

The two half men stared at each other. At the web of gold, and the points of connection between them.

"We protect what's ours," Jin said, holding out his arm in a fist.

Rou tentatively reached his arm out and punched Jin's fist with his own.

The two ruined, mirrored halves pulled together.

"Remember to write a letter to Gramps, would ya?" Rou asked.

Jin nodded. "I'll let him know we're okay. If he wants to see us again, he can come and visit."

Rou felt his eyes start to close. But then he realised he did have one more question.

"Hey . . . do you think Yin would be willing to crap in an envelope for us?"

"She might actually do it," his other half mused. "But come on. Asking a lady to do that is just *rude*. We can go and fill the letter with horse shit, like *normal* people."

Rou's eyes closed, a little smirk on both sides of their face.

□

My eyes opened. I stared at the ceiling of the inn. My hand absently came down to stroke the rabbit sleeping on my chest. A rooster was sitting beside my head, and a snake was coiled tight around my arm.

It wasn't quite like waking up to Meimei, but it was the next best thing.

I gently scooped Yin off my chest. The rabbit grumbled, then curled tighter into Big D as I laid her down. Noodle woke up from the movement, staring at me a moment, before nodding his head and slithering off to coil up near the others.

I stood up and padded over to the desk, where there was already a brush and paper prepared.

A letter, huh?

What to write?

I pondered the message and reached out, grabbing Gramps's letter so I could look at the seal on the bottom.

I pressed my Qi into it.

The seal shuddered, then disintegrated. With a muffled *pop*, a sword and a scroll appeared out of thin air.

Both were simple and unadorned. But the sword was high-quality steel, and the scroll had another seal upon it.

I stared at the gifts.

Gramps's gifts.

I pondered them. A sword on my mantelpiece, perhaps. Or I would train with it. I didn't know quite yet. Carefully, I packed both away for the journey ahead, then turned back to the desk.

I grabbed the brush, dabbed it in some ink, and started.

"Hey, you drunken old bastard . . ."

↔

The next day, Lu Ri beheld Jin Rou once more. He no longer seemed to be unsettled. His back was straight, and his stride was self-assured.

There was no trace of any confusion or worry that Lu Ri could detect.

Their meeting took place once more in the pavilion. The streams bubbled pleasantly, and the last flowers of summer filled the air with a heady scent.

Lu Ri greeted him, standing to receive his guest and the man's Spirit Beast disciples.

"Senior Brother," Jin Rou said, after the pleasantries had been dealt with. "I will not be returning as a disciple to the Sect. Too much here requires my attention." Jin Rou's voice was calm. His voice had a firm strength behind it as he met Lu Ri's gaze.

Lu Ri frowned internally. For a brief moment, he desired nothing more than to take Jin Rou back to the Sect by force and finally put this chapter behind him. Elder Ge had said not to force the issue, however, so he pushed aside the impulse.

"Your decision is unfortunate," Lu Ri admitted, "but understandable at this time."

"However, if the Cloudy Sword Sect wishes to make amends . . . I *can* think of a few ways." He smirked, a sly note entering his voice. "And I have this, if you need us to speak again."

He held up the transmission stone Lu Ri had given him yesterday.

Lu Ri nodded. "I shall convey your wishes back to the Sect," he said. He did need to report his success in person, after all. "Since you are not coming back, you may have this, by order of Elder Ge." Lu Ri handed over a piece of parchment, emblazoned with the symbol of the Cloudy Sword Sect. "Should you require assistance, present this to any person of merit; they will know you have our favour and shall be honour-bound to aid you."

It was not something given lightly . . . but amends had to be made.

The man took the cloth delicately. "Let's hope I never have to use this, eh?" he asked, and Lu Ri agreed. "But . . . uh, I do have a request. Could you ensure this reaches the right place at the Imperial Army Headquarters in Crimson Crucible City for me? It's my reply to Gramps." Jin Rou brought out a scroll case, one that was firmly sealed.

Lu Ri stared at the letter, his entire journey flashing before his eyes. *Deliver another letter.* Every moment of frustration and searching. There was the brief urge to smack it out of Jin Rou's hand.

We are to make amends, Elder Ge had said.

Lu Ri plastered a stiff smile onto his face. "I shall convey your letter, Jin Rou. Though I must ask . . ." He glanced at the Spirit Beasts and considered the man's well-hidden power. "Are you certain of this course of action? The Cloudy Sword Sect's protection and backing is no small thing."

Jin Rou considered the question for a moment, before smiling.

Something arrived. Or rather, it was revealed to Lu Ri.

It blanketed the entire pavilion with a gentle touch, then slowly expanded over the entire city. It grew until it went past what Lu Ri's senses could detect. Feather light and hard to distinguish. It was all around him.

It was vast in its size, yet quiet in its intent. It was the land under his feet, it was the air in his lungs, it was the sky above his head.

Yet it did not seek to crush him. It did not shout its power, or its intent. It was simply *there*, silent and unmovable. Diffuse and hard to grasp. For a moment, Jin Rou was the land, and the land was Jin Rou.

Lu Ri's eyes widened. He still could not feel *what* Jin Rou's level was. It was shrouded to him. Yet this was utterly beyond anything he could have expected.

"I think I'll be okay," Jin Rou said, then smiled. The roses were straighter. The stream's water seemed to clear. The grass deepened in its colour and stood taller.

Lu Ri had lived for longer than most mortals. He had seen many tournaments, with wondrous techniques.

Yet it was his first time witnessing a power so subtle yet so vast. He longed to ask. To question. To know just what, exactly, Jin Rou was doing.

Yet he could not. Jin Rou's intention was clear, and he had a mission to fulfill.

"I shall go for now, Jin Rou. May the heavens favour you," he intoned.

Jin Rou stood, along with the Spirit Beasts. All bowed their heads.

"May the heavens favour you, Senior Brother. And here." He brought out another package.

A large jar of maple syrup.

"Something for the road," Jin Rou said, flashing a boyish smile.

CHAPTER 29

THINGS HEAT UP

"Man, this thing is *so* cool," Gou Ren said to his brother as they rose into the air. They were standing on a large platform alongside an entire crowd of people. The chains attached to it rattled and clanked as the platform moved, dragging it up the mountain.

"It is pretty neat," Yun replied, before glancing back down at the scroll in his hands. It was an explanation of the tournament, along with the matchups and a bit of commentary. They were sold at each street corner; lots of people seemed to be buying them, eagerly discussing what would happen in each. "Looks like An Ran is opening today."

"Yeah. She's a bit nervous, but she thinks she can win it."

"Oh? She talked to you about it, huh?" Yun Ren jabbed, a grin spreading across his face. "Speaking of that, I didn't see you after we got back from the restaurant. Do you have anything to say to your big brother?"

Gou Ren flushed. "Shaddup. Like I told the other vultures, we were just sitting on the roof talking. Nothin' happened."

He was half thankful—and half frustrated—at Xiulan pushing An Ran to sit with him. She wasn't being subtle at all. Sure, the night had been pleasant, sitting on the roof and just talking with the woman. She was nice. A bit less high strung when she wasn't dealing with her fellow Petals and hounding after them like Meimei hounded after him and his brother. She had a lovely singing voice, and a quick wit—he'd learned that after the two of them had started rattling off increasingly nonsensical poems. And they might have fallen asleep together on the roof, staring at the stars. And she *might* have snuggled up to him during the night. But that was all!

He shook his head to get rid of the images, his face flushed.

Yun Ren arched an eyebrow, but then he seemed to let it go, turning back to the tournament bracket scroll. "Huyi is near the middle along with Xiulan, and Tigu is last. Then it's two more rounds before the final. They have another day's break after this round, and then they have a full five days before the last match."

The lift ground to a halt, and they joined the crowd.

Gou Ren frowned. "Seems a bit awkward."

"Probably for rest reasons? Don't want the final fight to be two people absolutely exhausted and injured."

"Probably," he said, shaking his head and starting up the flight of stairs to the seats, but he paused when something caught his eye.

The brothers noticed somebody leaning against the wall, panting as people passed him by.

"Isn't that the guy we sold one of the images to?" Yun Ren asked, struggling to place the boy's face.

"Yeah. I helped him get back home afterwards." Gou Ren explained. "But he lived in one of the manors. Ain't important guests supposed to have their own boxes?"

His brother shrugged.

Somebody knocked into the boy, and he scowled, nearly losing his balance, but managed to recover his footing.

Gou Ren pushed his way forwards, his brother trailing behind, a frown firmly on his face.

"Hey," he greeted the boy. "Surprised to see you here, Young Master." He leaned against the wall below the kid. Somebody bumped into Gou Ren's back and cursed, before going around him.

Bowu's face ran through a number of emotions before he settled on something neutral.

"Is it truly so surprising?" he asked, quickly looking away.

"Yeah, I thought you'd be up in a box or something, but you've decided on the true way to experience a tournament!" he said, parroting Tao the Traveller.

The boy smirked, some of his grimace fading.

"Indeed. It is as you said, Gou Ren, Image Master. I wished to get the 'real experience,'" he said, shaking his head.

Gou Ren glanced at his brother. Yun Ren shrugged, then nodded.

"Hey, if you're on your own, you feel like sitting with us?" Gou Ren asked.

Slowly, the kid's face morphed into a tentative smile. He stood up straighter.

"I suppose I can grace you with my company," he allowed.

Yun Ren snorted, amused at the kid's arrogance. "Well, lead on, *Young Master*." It was lightly teasing, yet the kid seemed inordinately happy about it. Determination suddenly overcame his face, and with his crutches, he started stumping his way up the stairs again. The brothers walked slightly behind him, in case somebody bumped the kid again.

It was slow going, but they managed to finish climbing the stairs and get into the seating proper. It was pretty easy to find a spot to sit, and the kid settled in, looking around with interest.

He seemed a bit amused at the crowd.

"You get to see what happened yesterday?" Yun Ren asked.

Bowu shook his head.

The recording crystal came out, showing Bowu the highlights of the previous day.

Slowly, the stadium filled, and the booming echo of the announcer's voice resounded as he welcomed everybody back.

An Ran stepped into the arena. The girl glanced up at the stands and offered Gou Ren a small smile.

↔

The trick to avoiding boredom with these matches, Tigu found, was to act like the crowds above.

They shouted and ranted, and it was *quite* fun to copy them. Especially as she could shout the loudest out of any of them. Her Qi enhanced her voice and sent it booming off the stands. The people watching listened intently to her shouts and echoed her sentiments. Even Ri Zu was getting into it as she poked her nose out, chittering excitedly.

"Go on, Smaller Blade of Grass! *Fight!*" she demanded, her voice booming off the stands. Her opponent, Zeitao Mao of the Lone Tree Sect, was pressing her hard, using his greater size and strength to try to keep her off balance with fierce thrusts of his guandao.

Finally, Tigu got to watch something mildly exciting. An Ran looked far more composed now than she had that morning. During breakfast the Petals had questioned Gou Ren and An Ran as to their whereabouts after the meal—both had turned a shade of red and let out frantic denials that they hadn't done anything the previous night.

The rest of the Petals had found this most amusing, and Xiulan had been smug about it for some reason.

All Tigu had heard the previous evening was the two of them talking about growing crops. Or at least Gou Ren had talked, while the Smaller Blade of Grass had listened. Then they started making increasingly nonsensical poems before they fell asleep on the roof, the fools; Tigu had needed to get them a blanket after Ri Zu had insisted they might catch a cold.

Now the Smaller Blade of Grass's eyes were focused and narrow, even as she was pressed. Minor cuts appeared across her arms, and one small gash tore open her cheek.

Her eyes glanced at Tigu, then the Blade of Grass, before she refocused on the heavy blade heading for her throat.

The next strike she blocked fully, throwing herself backwards and grasping her sword tightly with both hands. With a flip, she landed on her feet and took a breath. Her hair waved in the wind as her eyes scrunched closed.

An Ran pulled her arms apart. The blade separated into two. The second sword was ghostly, and smaller by half. Near-ethereal, its form was not quite solid.

"And An Ran shows the main technique of the Verdant Blade Sect, the Blades of Grass!" the announcer boomed. "What an accomplishment!"

Xiulan was on her feet, and Tigu leaned forwards, interested. Xiulan's swords always felt the same. As solid and dependable as the original; the Smaller Blade of Grass's, however, was only half grown and incomplete. More a dagger than a blade.

Mao seemed surprised by the sudden shift, so An Ran abruptly went on the offensive, trying to capitalise. It was inexpert, and she'd clearly never used the weapon in a real battle before, but it was the tipping point. The Smaller Blade of Grass managed to block the man's strike with her dagger, the blade shattering from the force, yet the strike diverted enough that she got in a clean blow. It was a cut down the side that sent the man sprawling, before she followed up, her sword tickling her opponent's throat.

Tigu shouted with the rest of the crowd as the announcer proclaimed An Ran's victory.

An Ran managed to stagger out of the arena under her own power, and the next contestants took their place.

Tigu smiled at who it was.

"Go and win, Handsome Man!" she shouted, her voice echoing. The crowd roared its approval, and a few began to laugh.

Handsome Man's face turned bright red at Tigu's shout. He tentatively raised his hand, waving at her. Tigu smiled brightly at him and waved back. The man's face somehow got even *redder*. His entire body coiled as he turned to face his opponent. His shoulder muscles bunched up, and his arms flexed most pleasingly.

The match was called to begin.

Handsome Man simply charged his opponent. His large, superior frame slammed into the smaller man like Chun Ke. The spearman tried to put up a fight, yet his weapon simply skittered off the Handsome Man's skin.

"The Hermetic Iron Body!" the announcer roared, as the twitching spearman failed to stand.

The Handsome Man looked back at Tigu, who clapped at his victory. He would be fun to fight!

↔

The day progressed, and the fights accelerated in speed and violence. This . . . this was something more like what Gou Ren had expected from a cultivator fight. Fire started to swirl, the earth heaved, and the arena's floor was scarred by blades and hammers.

"The Rumbling Earth's Wrecker Stance," Bowu narrated as the entire arena shook. Dulou Gan rocketed forwards like the guy Tigu called "Handsome Man" before leaping into the air. "Said to be derived from studying the ancient Wrecker Balls. They still live within an ancient one's shell, said to be two li in length—and surrounded by thousands of other, smaller shells that give the Bonepile its name."

The man slammed into his opponent and hit him so hard he rebounded off the barrier. The crowd roared, and Gou Ren winced—he'd heard bones crack even from up where he was.

The next match got just as wild. Tian Huo spun almost like a top through the air, his sword a mad flurry of colour as his opponent desperately tried to block or parry the powerful strikes.

"The Dervish Dance of the Azure Horizon Sect. Said to be the technique that Sun Ken derived his own Whirling Demon Blade from," Bowu said, continuing his narration.

Blood splattered into the air. The kid was excited as he explained, noting the techniques and history behind every move. It was kind of interesting, yet Gou Ren was uncomfortable seeing the sword hack downwards and cut into another contestant's chest, sending him sprawling. The crowd's glee was palpable.

Yun Ren chewed his lip as he glanced at the arena through his crystal, and Gou Ren could tell that his brother was feeling the same as he was with what was going on. It was a dizzying array of techniques and powerful strikes, and it definitely *looked* amazing . . . but Gou Ren winced every time he saw something leave a body that was supposed to stay inside. Maybe he had spent too long with Meimei, learning the consequences of all that damage. At least he could see people rather casually walking back to their seats after getting hurt so badly. One guy just shoved his intestines back into his stomach, took a pill, then staggered off to the stands to meditate.

"Cao Ci versus Guo Daxian, Young Master of the Grand Ravine!"

Guo Daxian had his face fixed in a vicious glare as he stood with his arms crossed, blue tattoos bright on his arms.

And then he exploded into motion, far, far faster than anyone other than Xiulan had moved.

"The Grand Ravine's Canyon Spanning Strikes," Bowu stated as the strange rope-blade lashed out from Guo Daxian.

The weapon seemed to have a life of its own—it snaked and slithered through the air, striking so fast it seemed to be in five places at once.

Daxian's opponent was a man who looked familiar; he was in blue silks and carrying a spear. He desperately backpedaled, defending as best he could, until he suddenly grinned, slamming the rope-blade down and into the ground. With an explosive leap, he launched himself at the Young Master of the Grand Ravine. The man suddenly seemed to get yanked off his feet, travelling towards the point stuck in the ground at incredible speed.

The spearman ran face first into the other man's fist, his eyes wide in surprise.

"Traversing the Grand Ravine. One of the few movement techniques that exist in the Azure Hills, so it ensures their dominance," Bowu muttered.

Cao Ci went flying, yet managed to stabilize himself. The rope-blade was already waiting for him—he raised an arm to block it, instead of it cutting into his chest.

And then Guo Daxian was *there*, pulled to the point on his bladed rope. He tore it free and struck three more times. The arm broke, then the ribs. Then finally, he delivered a brutal strike to the jaw. That put his opponent down.

The Guo Daxian snorted and walked off.

Gou Ren grimaced. *He'd certainly hate to be down there against him.*

↔

The rest of the day proceeded most pleasingly to Tigu. The fights were getting so much better! Well, aside from Xiulan's fight—*that* had ended as soon as it had begun, again—but Loud Boy's bout made up for it! The boy had managed a victory that had seemed certain to end in his defeat. The sudden reversal in fortune had been interesting.

"And our final match for today! Rou Tigu versus Liu Xianghua!" the fat announcer man boomed.

It was finally her turn! Ri Zu sighed and exited her shirt—she would wait for Tigu in the stands. Tigu bounced from foot to foot, her blood pumping merrily in her veins. This Misty Lady was supposed to be strong! This is what she'd come here for! *This* was what it was all about!

She was going to face a worthy opponent!

Hopefully.

She managed to prevent herself from skipping into the arena out of sheer excitement. It was a close thing, but she managed to calm herself and focused her intent. She expected to see her opponent in a similar state: ready for battle, as they tuned out all the unnecessary distractions.

The other woman was tall and lithe. Black hair hung in a loose cut down her shoulders. She wore the colours of her Sect and stood proudly, an expression of calm focus on her face. A strange contraption was on her back, and there was a large pipe sticking out of it so it rose just slightly above her head. A gauntlet was strapped to her left arm. It looked like a recent addition, and her sword was strapped to her waist.

But the Misty Lake Lady was distracted. Her eyes were searching the stands, almost frantically, until they alighted on something. Her gaze abruptly softened, and a small smile appeared.

Tigu glanced at where she was looking. *Her gaze is directed to her fellow disciples—? No, a small boy sitting with them.* The boy had a pair of crutches leaned against his shoulder, and he was staring directly at the Misty Lady, a complicated expression on his face.

Tigu's eyes snapped back to her opponent.

The Misty Lady's soft smile morphed into a grin as she planted her hands on her hips. She took a deep breath.

Then she began to laugh, her hands on her hips.

"Rou Tigu! I, Liu Xianghua, acknowledge your cultivation!" she boomed, pointing directly at her. "But be warned! Even your power, a stage above my own, will not be enough! The Techniques of the Misty Lake Sect shall defeat you!"

Tigu cocked her head to the side.

"Kowtow before this Young Mistress, and I shall take it easy on you!" the Misty Lady declared.

Tigu frowned, annoyed that this woman would dare insinuate that. But the woman's full attention was not on Tigu. Her eyes strayed to the stands, and there was a sparkle deep within them. Tigu glanced back to the stands, where the boy with crutches was. He was chuckling, clearly amused at Xianghua's words.

She was doing it because the boy in the stands found it amusing?

Some of the ire faded. Tigu snorted and smirked, then she rose up haughtily.

"Oh, *you* dare? This Young Mistress shall surely defeat you. Kowtow before me a hundred times, and *I* shall take it easy on *you*!"

The Misty Lady's eyes snapped to Tigu and her smirk.

"Hmph! A peasant raising her fangs at the heavens," she declared.

Tigu picked at her ear with her pinky. "Did you say something, Damp Pond?" she asked, feigning boredom.

The Misty Lady recoiled, her eyes narrowing, but a small smile tugged at her lips.

"You court death with your words! Very well, I shall crush you with all I have!" She flipped her hair out of the way and leaned back slightly, so she was purposefully looking down on Tigu.

Her eyes flicked once more away, this time to a box seat, high above. She locked eyes with a man who looked around Xiulan's father's age. There was a flash of irritation before she rolled her eyes.

They suddenly focused, going cold and hard. Tigu had her undivided attention.

Mist began to swirl on the ground, getting thicker and thicker, as the Misty Lady's Qi formed around her.

For the first time in the tournament, Tigu formed a Qi blade.

Tigu glanced at the announcer man, who for some reason hadn't called for the fight to start yet. He had a massive grin on his face and was rubbing his hands together. He raised his hands dramatically.

"Begin!" he boomed out finally.

Tigu attacked. A relatively gentle, probing strike. To be on the offensive was her place. It felt right—natural. While her instincts to hunt might have faded, this had remained. In her previous two disappointing matches, her opponents could not even react to her.

For a brief moment, Tigu thought this would be the case for the Misty Lady too.

Until she moved with grace, stepping out of the way. Tigu's blades missed by a hairsbreadth. The Misty Lady drew her sword. Its blade was a metallic blue colour, mixed through with swirls of white, with the tip completely white and slightly transparent, making the sword look slightly shorter than it actually was. If Tigu hadn't been paying attention, she never would have noticed.

For the first time in the tournament, an opponent truly challenged her. The sword lashed out for Tigu's head and she jerked herself away, a single strand of orange hair falling to the earth.

Tigu bounced away, creating some distance.

"Hmph. Is that it?" the Misty Lady demanded haughtily. She had a bit of a smirk on. "I suppose it is the natural way of things for lessers to scurry away from their betters after a single exchange!"

Tigu stared at the fallen strand of hair. She considered her opponent, and her reactions.

Then she grinned.

One Qi blade multiplied to six. Three for each hand. The smirk vanished from the Misty Lady's face.

Tigu absently heard the crowd's gasp as she poured on the speed and closed the distance, her claws ready. The Misty Lady's eyes widened briefly a moment before Tigu unleashed herself on the woman.

A relentless barrage of strikes, coupled with her own bouncing movements—attacks that had given the Blade of Grass pause.

The Misty Lady proved why she had named herself Xiulan's rival. Six blades tried to break through her guard, and six blades failed.

The Misty Lady's sword slid through the air like a swan through a lake. She moved across the battlefield, silent and deceptively calm. It reminded Tigu a bit of Bi De. A kind of serenity radiated from her in the heat of battle. The Misty Lady's eyes shot from side to side, missing nothing as she catalogued every threat and responded accordingly.

Two more Qi blades formed above Tigu's hands.

Tigu pressed harder. Little cuts appeared in the woman's clothes. A strand of black hair, tinted blue, drifted free—only to be torn to pieces by a storm of flashing blades.

And still, the Misty Lady held. Her breathing grew heavier. Tigu could feel the grin stretching at the corners of her mouth as she pushed harder on Misty Lady's defences.

The mist started to gather around the lady. Her form became indistinct, and her sword wavered as it seemed to disappear and reappear.

But whatever trick it was, it couldn't defeat Tigu's eyes. She ignored the illusion and let her fist pass through a hazy mirage of the Misty Lady's head. The woman grunted as she was forced to twist unnaturally to avoid the blow that blew past her illusory double.

The hazy outline disappeared.

"To—defeat the Misty Shrouded Swan is no—*hmph*—mean feat!" the woman shouted at Tigu, trying to project her voice.

Tigu responded by slamming a kick into the woman's side—which she blocked with her gauntleted arm. The woman grimaced at the force of the blow.

The Misty Lady let out a breath, then stepped into the next strike. Her sword deflected the claws made of Qi as she tried to counterattack.

Tigu flipped away, the bold counter striking only air. She landed gently. Silently. Tigu approved of the aggression.

Her opponent was breathing heavily, but with a single huff that ceased as well. She clicked her tongue. The woman reached behind her back and pulled on something on the contraption.

It coughed once, then hissed. The entire device squealed loudly as the vents on it lit up from dull red to bright orange.

Tigu paused as the air seemed to shudder and a burst of Qi washed over her.

"I see! You will not be defeated so easily, Rou Tigu. Loath as I am to use this against you, it seems I must employ all of my skills!" she boomed out.

The pipe sticking above her back puffed, a great billowing cloud of steam pouring out; instead of travelling up into the sky, however, it lingered, completely obscuring the Misty Lady from view.

"Behold the technique that will defeat the Demon-Slaying Orchid!"

↔

"Blazing Breath, First Form. Heron's Beak," Bowu muttered. His eyes were locked on the contraption on Xianghua's back. "Steam generation is good. The gauntlet and seals are holding. The control formation is . . . working?"

Gou Ren raised an eyebrow at the whispers. The kid had been quiet the entire bout so far, flinching at every hit Tigu landed, and clenching his fist every time she dodged.

"You know what that is?" Gou Ren asked. The kid's eyes were locked on the fight.

"A converted pill furnace, burning Smokewater root, and filled with the Misty Lake's Qi-infused water. Attack and defence all in one. A trump card able to be used against Cai Xiulan, or any of the Young Masters of the Azure Hills . . . our masterpiece."

↔

Tigu bounced up and down, her eyes searching the mist. Her Qi Blades increased once again, going from eight to ten.

The mist was foul-smelling. Like the city, or a forge.

Something hissed again. Tigu could hear something that sounded like Chun

Ke when he started to run. The steady *puff puff puff* as he got faster and faster, gathering his speed.

Tigu's eyes widened as she remembered one of her Master's sayings, about what Chun Ke did.

Building up steam.

The cloud abruptly sucked inwards, pulled into the gauntlet the Misty Lady wore. Her skin was flushed pink, and her eyes were the same orange colour as the fires within her contraption.

She opened her mouth, and steam poured out in time with her breath.

CHAPTER 30

LIU XIANGHUA RISES

The repurposed pill furnace closed with a soft *clunk*, its long smokestack properly affixed. "It's as ready as it'll ever be," Xianghua's brother said with a sigh as he wiped his hands of soot and grease. "Be careful with it, okay? You can't push it too hard."

Xianghua smiled at him, her hair tied back and her hands similarly greasy, as she checked the fuel one last time. "Indeed. Three may have exploded from my might, but this one shall last!" she declared.

Normally, the response would have him laughing at her over-the-top boast, but instead Bowu turned to face his sister with a worried look on his face. "Please be careful?" he asked, rubbing at his crippled leg.

Her eyes softened. She reached out and pulled him into a hug, inside the small shack on the outer courtyard that was their workshop. It was cramped, but neither of them minded.

"Yes. I'll be careful," she whispered.

The boy sighed, then pulled back from the hug, staring at her with a gimlet eye.

"I'm sure you will be. Just like you're careful with your actions and words," Bowu muttered.

"Indeed, I am a paragon of temperance. Thank you for noticing, little brother." She puffed out her chest, her hands still on his shoulders.

"Like when you challenged Miss Cai?" he deadpanned. "She seemed pretty annoyed with you."

Xianghua frowned as she remembered the last encounter she had had with Xiulan.

She'd stared at those hungry, desperate eyes. Xiulan's movements were off. She was unsettled, with an almost manic energy about her.

"You're courting death," Xianghua told her rival bluntly.

Cai Xiulan's eyes had narrowed, and her face twisted.

"I knew exactly what I was doing," she stated primly.

"And the fact that you tweak Father's nose every chance you get?" he whispered.

She shrugged again.

"I want to live my life without any regrets," she said. "If Father wants me to leave you alone, he can try. I seem to recall he failed the last time."

"You threatened to destroy your own cultivation."

Xianghua waved her hand negligently. "He hasn't had any luck with his concubines. I'm all he has."

Her brother sighed again. "So what do you plan to do, anyway?"

"I'll go as far as I can. I'll defeat this Rou Tigu and have my rematch with Xiulan. I may have fallen behind . . . but I'll surely rise, just like she has." Her voice was firm and proud. "Maybe this year, I'll convince the Blade of Grass to come drink with me. Or perhaps I'll hunt down her friend. He hasn't visited yet, and this Young Mistress finds herself most insulted!"

Her brother rolled his eyes. "What did you say his name was again?"

"Gou Ren. A handsome and upstanding gentleman. He has a cute smile."

Bowu paused. "A cute smile—You already remember his face?" he asked her, his eyes wide, and she nodded. "Tall guy, looks a bit like a monkey?"

"A monkey? No, he looks like the depictions of the Great Sage Wukong!" Xianghua refuted. Indeed, it had shocked her too that he was so easy to remember. Normally it took weeks, but he shone clearly in her mind's eye.

"Who is a monkey," Bowu sniped, before he smiled, pleased at her progress. "Gou Ren? He's a good guy. He helped me out."

"You met him?" she asked excitedly, shoving her face into his personal space and nearly bowling him off his chair.

□

Her opponent was strong. Her opponent was fast. Her opponent required absolutely everything she could give, or else she would lose.

It truly was a shame to reveal this so early, but there was no point holding back her strength if it meant she lost.

Liu Xianghua absolutely refused to be anything less than her best.

The air screamed. Her furnace pumped, reacting with the reagents within, and spewing out clouds of steam.

Xianghua brought her arm back, coating her weapon in Qi and steam. Her sword thrust forwards.

Rou Tigu, her eyes wide, barely managed to interpose her blades made of Qi, reminiscent of claws. There was a ringing *clang*, and hairline fractures snaked up the blue blades of energy.

Tigu was thrown from her feet from the force of the strike, flipping through the air. She barely managed to get her feet under her before Xianghua was on her again, driving her to the ground.

The modified pill furnace on her back was heavy, but it did not truly slow her down. The gauntlet on her arm whirred and hummed as the formation sucked in the steam. It was working, just like they had envisioned it.

←

"It's your brother, Xianghua," Sei Fen said, turning to show her daughter the small swaddled bundle of pink skin.

Curious, her little one took the bundle, staring at the pink face.

"He is very ugly," she opined, and Fen sighed at the blunt statement.

They'd have to fix that at some point. Her daughter was a strange child. She never smiled, or really had any sort of emotion at all besides the occasional fit of anger. She played strange games, pretending not to recognise her cousins, or other servants. She was far too blunt and literal. And *disturbingly* obedient.

Her husband saw no problem with it. He commanded, and she obeyed without question or hesitation, cultivating until told to stop. Once, that had been until she collapsed, because she hadn't received the order to stop.

There were whispers from the servants about her strangeness. That she was broken in the head.

Liu Xiang chuckled as the girl held the small bundle.

"Xianghua, make sure to protect him," the man declared pompously, so happy to have a male heir.

Xianghua stared at the bundle. A small pink face, eyes barely open. Tiny and fragile. He blinked, his eyes focusing on his sister. A little hand pulled from the swaddling, grasping for Xianghua's face.

Interest flashed in the girl's eye, and her own hand came up instinctively to grasp the finger that reached out for her.

Her daughter's lips quivered. Like she didn't quite know what was happening. Slowly, a smile spread across her face—the first one that Fen had ever recalled seeing on her daughter.

"Understood," she said, in that blunt way of hers. Fen smiled at the seriousness in her eyes, relief flooding her as her daughter finally did something *normal*.

It was rather cute. The two siblings were inseparable from that day forwards.

→

Xianghua's blade, Shrouded Intent, snapped forwards as if it was a heron's beak, spearing a fish out of the water before it had time to react. Her arm protested as the blade struck down, again and again. Tigu managed to dodge, her movements tight and controlled even as she frantically rolled across the ground. For the first time in the tournament, little nicks and scratches marred her body.

Speed and power.

That was the method of victory Liu Xianghua had decided upon to fight against Cai Xiulan. When faced with an absolute defence of floating blades, she had to be fast. Disrupt her opponent's concentration. Force the normally aggressive Xiulan onto the back foot and break through.

It was no movement technique, but hopefully it would be enough. It would have been good enough . . . if Xiulan hadn't gone and surpassed her again.

Ah, such frustration.

But there was no sense dwelling on such things. While that strategy had originally been for the Blade of Grass, speed and power were universal in their application.

Rou Tigu was good. The short girl managed to regain her feet, even through the brutal strikes. She deflected where she could and dodged when she couldn't. But she was off balance and reeling from the sudden assault.

A gauntleted fist hammered into the girl's stomach. Tigu folded over the brutal strike, coughing as spit flew out of her mouth. She was thrown across the arena, slamming into the ground and rolling.

Something inside Xianghua winced, wondering if she had overdone it.

"Hmph. Is that all you have?" Xianghua demanded, even as she felt her skin start to burn. Her furnace hissed angrily, so Xianghua modified the amount of her Qi feeding the alchemical reaction within.

She kept her face impassive. She had pushed just a little too hard, but surely she had dealt a blow Tigu could not recover from.

←

She practised within sight of his bed. She followed the maids around whenever they took care of him. She marched around like a little Imperial Guard, always looking for threats to her diminutive charge.

And when he finally started to walk and started to train, she was there with him every step of the way. Liu Xiang praised his daughter's devotion. She patched up her little brother's wounds. She stayed with him for hours, aiding his attempts at cultivation.

In return, he helped Xianghua with her troubles. He spent hours devising ways to help her remember people. Telling her to look at clothes and gait rather than the *blank* that was most people's faces.

But there was something wrong. A shadow, over their little lives.

"Still not ready?" Xianghua asked her little brother bluntly, her head cocked to the side.

Bowu frowned, yet wasn't bothered by her question, as he stopped his frantic sword practice.

"Not . . . not yet. But! I'm sure to ignite my dantian any day now!" the boy said, his eyes determined.

Xianghua smiled at his determination. "You're right, I'm sure things will be fine. The Spiritual Doctor will clear out the block, you'll see. Everything will be fine tomorrow."

The doctor came. Xianghua held Bowu's hand throughout the entire proceeding, as the bearded man poked and prodded before he finally rose, shaking his head.

The bottom dropped out from Xianghua's stomach. Her father's face twisted as he rounded on her mother. Her mother's eyes flashed as she crossed her arms.

That night, the shouting started.

That night, everything went *wrong.*

→

Laughter.

The girl on the ground was *laughing.*

Tigu pulled herself to her feet and planted her hands on her hips. Her shirt had fallen open, exposing her stomach and the slight bruise on her skin from the blow.

And that was it.

A bead of sweat dripped down Xianghua's forehead as a massive tiger formed in the mist, its eyes burning with as much glee as its mistress.

Deadly. Domineering. Playful.

"*This* is what I've been waiting for," Rou Tigu declared, her cheeks splitting into a wide, happy smile, full of teeth. Her yellow eyes had turned to slits. Every muscle flexed, eliminating what little hints of feminine softness Tigu possessed and leaving only cold, predatory power.

The sheer joy on her face after she'd been struck by a blow that would splatter a mortal across the entire hill was infuriating; the only evidence of the damage done was the light bruise and slight hitch to her voice.

Standing there unfazed, Tigu seemed unbeatable.

But Xianghua stepped forwards anyway. She threw herself back into the fray without reservation.

She'd never been very good at giving up.

←

Her mother and father forbade her from seeing her brother. Her Bowu.

It did not make sense. She was supposed to protect him, was she not? She liked protecting him. He never looked at her strangely, like the maids sometimes did, and was always glad whenever she was there.

But he was gone now. Gone, and Mother and Father hated each other. They shouted and snarled, as Xianghua sat in the corner trying to tune out the words.

"Cripple."

"Broken meridians."

"Never be a cultivator."

They blamed each other.

She searched high and low for him but couldn't find him in the Sect.

Until one day there was a great commotion in the Sect. Xianghua wondered what it was. There were shouts, and there was screaming.

She pushed her way through the crowd and came upon a scene. Her little brother, grabbing his leg and sobbing.

Xianghua's blade was out before she realised what she was doing, throwing herself at the one who dared to do this—

Her father's sword blocked her own, knocking the blade from Xianghua's grasp. He grabbed her arm and wrenched her away from the other disciple, who looked terrified.

"Bowu. As our deal stated earlier, you have lost. Now begone from my sight."

Her brother was carried away, clutching at his leg.

Protect your brother. The command rang in her head. She made to move forwards. She would strike down the little bastards who dared to—

Her father kept his hold on her wrist. His eyes were dispassionate.

"You need not concern yourself with the cripple. He takes up too much of your thoughts, when you should be focusing on your own cultivation."

He turned and pulled her away.

Something inside her snapped.

→

The air rang with impacts.

One, ten, a hundred in the space of a second.

The heron's beak clashed with savage claws. They were even. Their blows matched perfectly. The world narrowed to the gap between heartbeats.

A gauntleted fist caught Qi claws and forced them up, Shadowed Intent drawing a shallow line across Qi-hardened skin. Like a Spirit Beast's flesh, it was tough beyond measure. In retaliation, a knee planted itself into Xianghua's side, driving the air from her lungs and disrupting her breathing.

The steam flowing into her gauntlet destabilized, and she let it. *Then she forced it to go further.* With half a shriek and half an explosion, her fist rocketed forwards again, hammering into Tigu's face.

Both women were sent flying away from each other by one another.

Once she landed, Xianghua sank to her knees, greedily sucking in air. Tigu kicked out, spinning her legs and landing in a crouch, her knuckles on the ground, watching intently.

Waiting for Xianghua to get back up.

Xianghua huffed out a laugh and decided not to test the strange girl's patience. Almost in response, however, her furnace spluttered. She grimaced, rising to her feet again.

←

Bowu lay on his bed, clutching at his leg. The break was a bad one. It had damaged his knee, and even a week later he could tell it was healing poorly.

"You are my blood. Be thankful for this," his father said before banishing him to the edges of the Sect for being a worthless cripple, and for failing their bargain—if he had won that bout, he could continue to train. But he had lost. "You are a mortal. If you walk this path you will die. So know your place, boy."

Bowu gritted his teeth at the memory of his father's voice.

His mother's eyes had ghosted over him; she'd said nothing—like he wasn't even worth the words.

Even his sister was—

"Bowu."

He flailed, scrambling, looking for the interloper.

Xianghua was there. Her normal blank expression on her face. Or at least on half of her face. The other half was bruised, with her eye swollen shut.

"Xianghua—your face?" he gasped, shocked to see her. He had thought she had abandoned him too, after not seeing her for a week.

She smiled at him—something she only ever *genuinely* did for him—then pulled him into a hug.

"It's fine. Father was just a bit rough today," she whispered into his ear, hugging him tight. "Don't worry. I'll be here for you. *I promised.*"

Tears formed in Bowu's eyes, as he held on to the only person who cared.

↔

"She's not gonna last," Bowu muttered, staring down at the fight. He could see the rattle in the furnace. Its glow was bright, meaning it was dangerously close to overloading. It was nearing its limits, and Xianghua seemed to notice it too. Her face was slick with sweat and blood.

But her opponent was slowing down too. Tigu was getting more cautious, even while the grin on her face was growing wider.

"Man, they're really goin' at it, eh?" Gou Ren muttered. Unlike the other bouts, where he had looked mildly concerned, now he just seemed amused.

The Image Master snorted. "Just like with Xiulan. I thought they were gonna kill each other the first time, but she was smilin' then too."

The women below clashed again.

Xianghua took a breath and let it out, a jet of steam erupting from her mouth and forcing Tigu to dodge away.

Xianghua seized the opportunity. She reached back, pulling again on the furnace.

Every vent opened, spewing great gouts of steam and shrouding the entire arena. He saw his sister wince as the burns she had received from the furnace on her back made themselves known.

The crowd howled and booed—they could no longer see anything.

[Blazing Breath, Second Form], he heard his sister's voice echo. [Keelbreaker's Bite].

"Prepare yourself!" Xianghua shouted.

□

His sister met with him every day she could. She made him his cane. She brought him the healing herbs, though they didn't seem to do much.

When Father was gone, she smuggled Bowu into the library. They played on the lake. And she complained about her teachers.

"The etiquette teachers are being annoying. They keep saying their faces are meant to convey something, but I don't get it," she muttered, staring at the ceiling of his shack. "The only person I *understand* is you."

Bowu frowned. Most people reacted strangely to his big sister's blunt monotone and it messed her up, never knowing how to parse the subtle expressions people made. Their confusion about her mannerisms in turn confused her.

"I dunno—but if you don't get them, maybe you can lower the range of emotion, and force people to be more obvious about it? Maybe you can just act like one of those arrogant Young Mistresses? That way you'll always know what they're thinking. Big emotions make for big responses, don't they?" he asked, and then took a sip of his tea.

Her blank stare lingered on him for a moment before she shifted. Her posture straightened and her head tilted up—like she was looking down on him.

"Oh, you *dare* approach this Young Mistress?" she demanded, her personality as far from what she was normally like as possible.

Bowu spat out his drink.

"Ha? *You're courting death!*" she shouted, one hand on her hip, and her finger pointed straight at him.

Bowu howled with laughter and missed the gleam in his sister's eye.

He was in the crowd the first time she said that to the visiting Sect's Young Master. He just nodded along, like her behaviour was expected.

And for some reason, the man seemed to take less offence to the insults when she shouted them, instead of when she spoke in her usual blank monotone.

The Young Mistress act became more and more common. Like Bowu had thought, it *did* make things easier for his big sister. To think it had started as a joke. He never could stop himself from smiling when she did it.

Their lives diverged as they grew up. But she was always with him. She told him about the friend she had made, this Xiulan, and how the girl was *far* too boring for her own good.

He had even met the woman once. Xiulan. She was nice. A bit too obsessed with duty and honour, but she had chased off the bastards who popped up occasionally when Xianghua wasn't there to drive them off.

But his sister always, always came back, with a new tale, or with a present, and a smile just for him.

□

Neither of them could see. She heard Tigu start to sneeze when Xianghua's Qi invaded her nostrils.

Xianghua took off her furnace, quickly pulling on it and resetting some of its functions, as well as pouring one of her waterskins that was under the furnace into the depleted chamber. Leaving the hissing contraption on the ground, she stepped away from it.

She could feel through the steam. The feather-light touches that told her where her opponent was, stalking cautiously towards the hissing steam furnace.

She kept her breathing shallow so she wouldn't give away her position. She couldn't be *completely* sure the other girl's senses would be fooled. Tigu had seen through her illusion the first time.

She could feel the smaller girl stalking forwards, heading towards the hissing furnace and walking right by Xianghua. Perhaps it was cowardly to attack her from behind. But Tigu was far too great an opponent to not try to take every advantage Xianghua could.

With her Qi all around Tigu, her intent was masked completely. It was a silent whisper, aiming for a debilitating strike to the shoulder. With this element of surprise, she would hopefully end the fight immediately.

Rou Tigu *dodged.*

Even Tigu seemed confused as she moved exactly out of the way, dodging an attack with no Qi signature from outside her line of sight.

Tigu blinked. "Mud Balls are truly profound," she stated, sounding impressed.

Xianghua had no idea what the girl meant, though she didn't stop to think about it—she pulled the steam around her, hazy outlines of steam swimming into focus and attacking.

She made a dash back to her furnace, grabbing it even as Tigu followed in her wake, yelping when the ghostly figures mobbed her and burned her skin with superheated steam.

□

Bowu was largely stuck between worlds. A cripple living at the outskirts of the Sect. He did odd jobs and worked with numbers when his mortal employers allowed, while his sister fought in grand battles she brought back stories of or grabbed him scrolls that looked interesting from the library.

He had been looking through some ancestors' notes on mist. Some kind of channeling array. It was old and out of use, but it was kind of interesting. He was fiddling with the pinwheel his sister had brought him back and leaning back in his seat when his water for tea came to a boil. In the cramped shack, when he leaned back, his hand was nearly over the firepit.

And the pinwheel was over the pot. He stared idly at it as it spun, faster and faster, over the boiling pot.

Steam turned into force. Force was *power.*

He looked back to the channeling array. Mist was gentle and quiet. It whispered. Steam was harsh, violent almost . . . and both were water, suspended in air.

He could not channel Qi himself. But the steam, combined with the channeling array . . . ?

He looked at his leg, sighed, and put the thoughts away.

But not before sketching out a prototype.

□

The furnace had cooled down. Its vents were duller, and it would be able to start pumping out steam again.

Tigu snarled as she chased down yet another shadow, rending it to pieces before sneezing again.

"Come on, Misty Lady! Stop hiding!" Tigu demanded, her voice echoing from off to the right.

Xianghua tapped at her gauntlet, opening it up and checking the formation inside it, but then she felt Tigu suddenly crouch down.

There was a clatter—she seemed to be taking off something and dropping it? *What is she—?*

[Pounce of the Tiger]

The air cracked and screamed, and suddenly there was a hole through her mist. Buffeting winds ripped and tore at her defence as she tried desperately to keep the steam in place.

Then it happened again. Xianghua threw herself to the ground as a bolt of orange thundered overhead.

And again. Tigu rebounded throughout the arena, slamming into the ground and breaking it nearly half a dozen times.

The steam was being forcefully blown away by the wind that was generated from Tigu's passing. Xianghua saw great divots form in the ground as Tigu shattered the earth with each leap.

Until with one last jump and howl of wind, the arena was once more visible. Tigu panted harshly as she turned, her eyes alighting on Xianghua.

"Found you!" she declared, her smile all sharp teeth.

Xianghua pulled on the starter on the furnace. It spluttered, coughed, and then started up.

□

His sister was distraught. Her rival had bested her. Ascended past her. She even went so far as to say she had lost her way.

Whatever the case was, Xianghua had been furious over what had happened in Grass Sea City. She cultivated the best she could. She even went to Father, demanding cultivation resources, and he allowed it. Some expensive reagent, imported from the Howling Fang Mountains.

Bowu chewed his lip, then pulled out the old drawing she had made. His father had been able to help . . . so maybe he could too? Perhaps, if he tweaked the formation there—

He showed the steam furnace design to her. It had originally been for himself, to ape cultivation, but . . . he didn't know if he would ever be able to use it properly.

Xianghua had set her mind on something—and what kind of brother would he be, if he didn't give her every advantage she could get?

Xianghua seemed a bit confused by the logistics and the math, but she sat down with her single-minded focus, learning what he was doing so she could help.

She believed in his work.

And there was no way he would let her down.

Both of them were spent. Tigu was finally running out of energy. Her strikes were slower. Her Qi-blade claws had dipped in number, yet there was a look of contentment on her face as they battered away at each other.

Xianhua's furnace hissed. It was the only thing that had kept her in the fight.

It was breaking down. It was cracking, as she poured everything she had left into it.

They both staggered back from each other's strikes. They both fell to a knee.

Tigu *roared.* Her claws multiplied again as her shirt fell around her waist. Her muscles bulged bright red, and her eyes turned completely yellow. A snarling demonic tiger appeared behind her, its eyes full of joy.

Xianghua reached back and pulled on the starter. Her furnace screamed—it began to overload, fire tearing out from the smokestack. The last of her steam coiled around her—a fierce heron glared back at the tiger.

[Blazing Breath, Third Form—!]

[Claw Arts—!]

Both of them threw themselves forwards in one last clash, howling battle cries.

[Spearing the Dragon!]

[Ten-Fold Reaper!]

The heron's beak met a tiger's claws for the last time.

□

His sister stared around her at the devastated training arena. The shattered stone walls and the steam-boiled dummies.

She cradled the furnace like it was the most precious thing she had ever received.

"I'll take it with me to the heavens," she swore, then reached out her hand to him.

Bowu took it.

CHAPTER 31

THE TIGER AND THE HERON

She awoke to a dull roar. It was like a physical weight. She could feel the rumble deep in her chest from the sheer power of it all. An all-consuming buzz of a hundred thousand voices, screaming and hollering. Stamping feet, thunderous applause. The members of the Hermetic Iron Sect striking their hammers against anvils. The howls of the Grand Ravine, and the slamming bargepoles of the Misty Lake.

"What a battle! What an *extraordinary* battle! I swear upon my honour that this bout will be spoken of for the next thousand years!"

The announcer was beside himself, voice hoarse as he shouted into his artifact. His aides were hollering and hooting, forgetting all decorum as they too joined in the roar of the crowd.

She could feel the dirt on her face from where her cheek lay. The sun was beating down onto her back.

"In all my years! In every tournament I have ever witnessed! *Never* have I seen such a bout!"

She got one of her arms underneath her and tried to push herself up. She failed. Groaning, she rolled over onto her back, wincing at the aggravation to her injuries.

She opened her bleary eyes.

The first thing she saw was her furnace. Its ports were dull. There was a crack from its impact into the ground, and its ripped straps hung loose.

Xianghua raised a shaking hand and brought the back of it across her eyes, shielding them from the sun.

"All hail the victor! All hail Rou Tigu! The Tiger in the Grass, who has pounced into the tournament. Conqueror of the Mists!"

Xianghua bit her lip—her shoulders were shaking from bottled-up emotion.

She wanted to scream. She wanted to cry. First Xiulan and her miraculous ascension, and now this one. In any other year, in any other time . . . She would have won.

The heavens were a fickle mistress. They spat upon her and her brother's efforts.

She glanced out of the corner of her eye at her opponent. Tigu's shirt was around her waist, with only her chest wraps preserving her modesty. She had bruises all over her stomach, burns across her shoulders, and Xianghua could hear a wheeze in her breath.

Tigu's eyes were closed, and her face was directed at the sun, a look of absolute peace on her face.

She pulled her shirt back up around her shoulders. Yellow eyes locked onto Xianghua's grey.

Her hands raised in the gesture of respect, her head bowing the lowest acceptable to any who were not her Master.

"Thank you," Rou Tigu intoned. Her head came up, eyes still closed, a grateful smile beaming at Xianghua.

There was absolutely no mistaking that look on her face besides being one of praise and admiration. Even Xianghua could tell that she wasn't patronizing her.

"Xianghua! Xianghua!" She heard her brother's panicked voice calling her name. He was at the edges of the arena, both hands braced on the stone divider. Idly, she wondered how he'd managed to get down there so fast, until she noticed Gou Ren, his hand on her brother's shoulder, brows furrowed in concern.

She held up a hand, weakly waving at him, and she saw her brother sigh with relief.

She catalogued the injuries she could feel. There were some burns, and likely broken bones, but besides that Xianghua felt fine. Well, she would hesitate to say *fine*. She felt like she had been run over by a Wrecker Ball. Tigu had been remarkably restrained. Xianghua didn't know if it was insulting or not that Tigu had sheathed her Qi blades at the last moment.

Xianghua breathed deep and centered herself. It was time to get up. She pushed herself up, wincing at the pain. Her legs were shaking. Her eyes were still a bit blurry, but she managed to stagger to her feet.

The wall of noise redoubled in its intensity.

"And still she can stand! Such resilience! Such fortitude! My friends, can you believe this? The Mist over the Lake is eternal!"

Xianghua turned to face her brother, who had collapsed backwards onto Gou Ren, the man holding him up without complaint. He nodded firmly to Xianghua.

The small feeling in her gut when she looked at him intensified. She turned away so she could bow to her opponent, as tradition dictated, yet Tigu was already moving.

Tigu darted around the arena, bending down to pick up . . . *parts of Xianghua's furnace*? She took them up with obvious care and placed them in a cloth she had pulled from her shirt, packing everything together.

"This is an amazing artifact!" Tigu called out as she reached the furnace. Her eyes were bright with interest as she walked around it twice before gently picking it up as well as bringing it over to Xianghua. "Make sure it gets fixed for our next bout!"

Xianghua stared at Tigu. She didn't exactly know how to react to such aggressive . . . *cheerfulness.* It wasn't even contentment with victory, but from the fight itself.

"I like you!" Tigu declared bluntly. "Fight with me again, okay?"

Such a strange girl.

Almost absently, she nodded her head. The offer of a powerful sparring partner was not something to turn down lightly. The fight had been a good stress test for the furnace. She had discovered a hundred different tweaks to improve it, which she'd need to share with Bowu.

Xianghua took a breath and straightened herself out. Finally, she bowed to Tigu.

"I thank you for the match, Rou Tigu. I have learned much from it."

"Have dinner with me tonight!" the girl demanded.

Really, who is so friendly after such a bout? Xianghua chuckled—which forced her into a coughing fit.

"Though I'm afraid you shall have to wait at least a week," Xianghua muttered once the coughing fit passed. "The only thing in my future right now is rest. Tell your handsome brother to visit this fair maiden, won't you?"

Tigu frowned. She cocked her head to the side before reaching into her pocket and pulling out a small packet.

"A week is too long," she decreed petulantly. "Take this, it will speed your recovery."

"Oh, you dare insult me by giving me medicine?" she asked, but really, her heart wasn't in it. Xianghua could feel the Qi pulsing outwards despite the wrappings. Just what was this child giving her?

"Yes. Become angry with me, get stronger, and challenge me again!" Tigu demanded, pressing the packet of herbs into Xianghua's hand. "But do not get too angry to eat with us later!"

Xianghua shook her head in exasperation before once more taking the haughty stance of a Young Mistress.

"Ha! You may have beaten me this day, but I'll return. Watch yourself, Rou Tigu!" she declared, snatching the medicine from the girl's hand. "You'll regret giving me more power."

She got a bright smile in return.

Xianghua picked up her furnace and its broken parts, then began to limp out of the arena. She paused, the chanting from the arena finally registering.

"Xianghua! Xianghua! Xianghua!" the crowd roared.

They were chanting *her* name.

Xianghua, Young Mistress of the Misty Lake, looked up into the crowd as the people from the Misty Lake slammed their poles into the ground, their eyes full of proud tears.

"A peerless competitor! The wielder of a powerful, heavens-shaking artifact! Liu Xianghua! We, His Imperial Majesty's Tournament Commission, salute your might!" the announcer roared.

She managed to get out of the arena before she had to lean against the wall.

A loss. A frustrating loss. But there was a smile on her face.

A heavens-shaking artifact, hm?

They were absolutely correct.

→

Xianghua stared at the ceiling from the bed a few hours later, the afternoon sun filtering through her windows casting the world in gold. Lifting the platform in the Earthly Arena had been a difficult task, but at least she'd had help. It was not too often that she worked together with so many others—especially while they were all lifting an enormous arena up a mountain.

A loss. Another loss, and even earlier than the last time. Though the last time she hadn't gotten as injured; instead, she'd spent the rest of the tournament trying to goad Xiulan into sneaking out and enjoying the festival with her, rather than just cultivating.

She rolled the small ball of medicine Tigu had given her between her fingers. It was potent, absolutely filled to bursting with Qi. A treasure that even an Elder would hoard.

And she had been given it without a second thought.

She idly wondered if it would help with her brother's leg, but the injury was years old by now. Even an ocean of Qi couldn't cure that. Nor could any doctor she'd come across.

She had paid a lot of money over the years, and each time they returned shaking their heads.

She sighed.

The world lapsed into silence again.

There were footsteps outside her door. "Leave us," a familiar voice commanded, and there were several whispers of acceptance. Xianghua slid the medicine under the covers.

The door to her room opened, and her father strode in. His blue robes were immaculate, and his hard eyes locked onto her as he stepped through the doorway.

There was silence while he took in her condition.

"You lost," her father said.

"I did," she replied with a shrug, not bothering to sit up.

The man stared at her. Something crossed over his face. She had no real idea what exactly he was thinking. She never cared to learn his expressions. It wasn't worth the time.

She wondered when he would leave.

"Strength, however, forgives all. And we are . . . pleased with your performance."

The words were said haltingly, as he loomed over the bed. His hand extended, and she glared at him when the offending appendage grabbed onto her shoulder hard enough to hurt.

It lasted a brief moment before he pulled away.

The man turned, glancing at the furnace. He considered it. He opened his mouth to say something. But in the end, he didn't comment on it, instead turning his eyes back to Xianghua.

"I will not be seeing you for quite some time. I have things to attend to out of the province. In my absence, Elder Bingwen shall be in charge," he stated matter-of-factly.

Xianghua was confused. He was leaving? Why? What could be so important? Yet the man did not elaborate.

"Take care of the Sect." He clenched his fists. He stared at her with a piercing gaze before turning on his heels to leave.

He opened the door and paused at another two people just outside it. Elder Bingwen stood with a smile, waiting outside the door. Elder Bingwen, who had his hand on Bowu's shoulder. Bowu seemed a bit confused but shrank back from their father, glancing at the ground. Her father's face was stone. He glanced at Bowu once before continuing to walk away.

"Go on, Young Master," the Elder said, releasing her brother's shoulder.

Bowu hobbled forwards as fast as his legs could carry him.

Xianghua rose up and opened her arms when he clambered onto her bed, but her eyes were locked on the Elder. He walked into her room, a gleam in his eyes.

"A fine show today, Young Mistress, a fine show," the old man said, stroking his beard. "But now is not the time to speak on it. Please rest until your wounds are healed, and then enjoy yourself for the rest of the tournament."

He was . . . happy? Inordinately happy, from what she could tell.

He stared at the furnace, and his face broke into a wide smile.

"We look forward to both your future growth." He glanced for a moment at the pair before departing.

Xianghua frowned after him.

"What happened?" she asked her brother.

He shrugged. "The Elders all came and said that I needed a bigger room," he whispered back. "They were all . . . well, they were a bit weird, and polite. They said . . . well, they said there was going to be a lot of changes. And that I could come into the main compound whenever I wanted."

Xianghua pondered the new development.

"Are . . . are you all right? Gou Ren and the Image Master said that Tigu never hurts people she likes too bad, but . . ." He trailed off, wincing at her wounds.

She smiled at his concern.

"They are right. I'm mostly just tired, and out of Qi," she confirmed. "A few breaks, but nothing too concerning. I could even get up right now if I wanted!"

Her brother chewed his lips as he stared at her. Eventually he nodded.

"Then . . . do you want to go and get dinner together?" he asked shyly. "Gou Ren said they were going to have a bit of a party . . ."

To be able to openly have food with her brother . . .

Well, that was no choice at all, was it?

But he had called her bluff.

"Just give me a moment to take my medicine," she said. "I need some strength."

She reached back into her hiding place and retrieved the pill. She considered it for a second again, but after one more glance at the hopeful look on her brother's face, she bit down on it.

It's probably going to take a bit for it to activate, but perhaps we'll be able to catch the tail end—

Her eyes widened as the Qi within surged.

□

The dumpling house was awash with noise. Loud Boy was covered in bruises but was still triumphant as he raised a cup with Rags and the rest of Rags's friends.

Fish Eyes and the Smaller Blade of Grass were both slumped over, sighing at the thought of their next matches. The Smaller Blade of Grass was against the rope man from the ravine, and Fish Eyes had the misfortune to be against Handsome Man.

Both were complaining, though Huyi more than An Ran, who was again seated beside Gou Ren.

Tigu was content as she stared around. She felt relaxed—she would sleep very well tonight.

"Oh? You dare start without me?" a voice boomed. Tigu perked up.

Xianghua unceremoniously shoved a chair in between An Ran and Gou Ren, knocking the other girl aside and sitting down beside him. The Smaller Blade of Grass's eyes were wide in shock—especially when Xianghua leaned on Gou Ren, smiling brightly at him.

Gou Ren froze as Xianghua leaned in. Two fingers walked their way up his chest. The boy with the crutches was sitting beside Yun Ren, both with intense looks of interest on their faces.

"But I *suppose* I can find it in me to forgive you," she said, before glancing out the corner of her eye at Xiulan and smirking.

Tigu saw the Blade of Grass's eye twitch at the blatant invasion.

CHAPTER 32

RECONCILIATION

Xiulan's eyebrows rose at the tall, solidly built Young Master of the Hermetic Iron Sect. His face was flushed, and he nervously glanced back at his Junior Disciple, who was nodding rapidly. He took a breath and then held out a necklace with an intricately carved pendant.

"Rou Tigu! I—I, uh, made this for you."

The night had started rather innocently enough at a Chao Baozi, aside from Xianghua's interruption. The restaurant was crowded at this time of night. Rags's and Loud Boy's mortal friends had gone to get more drinks. Even Xianghua's sudden arrival had been but a splash in the pond. As the ripples settled from her arrival, her Junior Brother, having swiftly retreated from the overtly flirty woman, had taken a seat with the boy Xianghua had brought with her. Xiulan felt a certain measure of satisfaction that her Junior Brother recognised trouble when he saw it.

It had taken her a second to place this Bowu, though. A half-forgotten memory had risen of coming to the aid of a crippled boy when she had visited the Misty Lake Sect. Xiulan had intervened when she'd seen a Junior Disciple mistreating him. After sending the disgraceful Junior on his way with a warning, she had then aided the boy in getting back to his home. She hadn't even known Xianghua had a sibling at the time; the familial resemblance was obvious, though, once you saw them together.

Xianghua had let Gou Ren go without much complaint, simply smiling when Gou Ren started his conversation with her brother—she was accosted by Tigu a moment later.

An Ran had seemed to not really know what to do at the stronger cultivator's sudden intrusion and had retreated to speak with the rest of the Petals.

That was when Rags's mortal friends had returned, each one carrying an entire tray of wine bottles.

Xiulan had understood that there were no fights the next day, but really, the fact that those boys were so loose about things was astonishing.

She had joined in, although in moderation, but then something unexpected had happened.

She had noticed the Young Master of the Hermetic Iron Sect, Tie Delun, entering the establishment, which was a bit strange. None of the other Sects were here, and he seemed nervous and uncertain.

After Tigu had spotted him, she'd eagerly waved him over to join them.

"Handsome Man! Come eat with us!" she had shouted merrily, hanging off Xianghua's shoulder.

The man's face had flushed at the attention from Tigu. He'd squared his shoulders, glanced at his Junior for a moment, then marched over to Tigu to present the necklace.

Tigu cocked her head to the side. Her eyes shone as she looked over the piece and its intricate detailing.

"Why did you make this for me?" she asked.

The man blushed deeper. "Ah . . . A token of my appreciation, for your support during my match, Miss Rou. Your words . . . er, inspired my strikes."

Tigu actually coloured, and she scratched the back of her head. Xiulan raised an eyebrow. Was she about to see Tigu try to run off and inform Master Jin of a suitor?

"Ah, it truly helped you? Ah, then—" She stood and performed a proper bow. "Thank you for this gift."

She took it, her fingers ghosting over the carvings. Tie Delun grinned and breathed a sigh of relief. He nodded happily, oblivious to Loud Boy and Rags, who were staring daggers at the man.

Tie Delun bowed his head to Tigu. "I'm pleased that you accept this token. I shall leave you to—"

Tigu grabbed his arm, stopping him, then pulled him into the seat next to her.

"How did you make it?" Tigu asked, her eyes shining. "Do the carvings mean anything? What material is it?"

The man seemed taken aback at the rapid-fire questions; Yun Ren leaned in, staring at the pendant curiously. "Ah, it is made of silver, from the mines near the Silver Shore," Tie Delun began.

Two of her fellow disciples, Huyi and Li, decided that the table had gotten a bit too cramped for their tastes and rose, dragging another table over so they could sit elsewhere. They nodded to Delun's Junior Brother who, after a glance at his Young Master, tentatively came over and sat with them.

Tigu calling out to Tie Delun seemed to be some sort of breaking point.

Another cultivator, wearing a blue tunic, approached the full table, curious at the sudden gathering. "What is going on here?" he asked, looking around at the strange group that had formed.

"A good time!" Rags declared. He took a sip of wine, tilted his head to the side, and then offered up a bottle to the newcomer.

"This is pig swill," the cultivator in blue stated primly, brushing down his expensive clothes. He brought out a bottle that had been tied around his waist. "*This* is what a man should have."

Rags took a swig of the proffered bottle. He nodded at the taste. "Smooth. Have a taste, Brother."

He handed it to Loud Boy, who indulged—then promptly started coughing.

Uproarious laughter followed. Rags offered a seat at the table to the cultivator, and the man in blue sat down.

Xiulan drifted off to the side, simply observing. She sat at the bar and watched as the others interacted, Tigu somehow managing to pull in more and more people with her boisterous attitude. It was amusing to witness how happy she was. There were some intense stares that some of the men sent her way, but so far none had tried their luck with her, for which Xiulan was grateful. Being seen as aloof and untouchable had some benefits after all. She watched the gathering in peace.

It was like the soldiers she'd once known. Rowdy and growing rowdier. The thought invited a dull ache, but it did not hurt as much as it once had. She idly sipped her drink, remembering the names.

More and more people came to see what was going on as the table grew louder. Two disciples from the Misty Lake Sect, who Xianghua waved at, joined the Petals. A nervous-looking woman wearing a beautiful brooch, who Tigu seemed to know, was waved over. The orange-haired girl slung an arm around the woman's shoulder, declaring them friends.

Members of the Framed Sun Sect, their forces entirely defeated and looking tired, noticed the commotion and wandered in. They saw the mix of three different Sects and independents. Several scoffed, and Xiulan thought they had a mind to start trouble, until they saw an image projected on the wall. Yun Ren had brought up the image he'd taken of the Dueling Peaks' sunset, the inspiration for their Sect's techniques.

The Young Master of the Framed Sun Sect marched over immediately, his eyes focused on the image.

And another group joined the party.

The crowd grew rowdier, gathering even more stares from the curious. Cultivators wandered in from the outside, happily joining the group in their celebration. Disciples went back to their Sects to spread the word of the gathering, which brought yet more to the establishment.

There was some commotion as Tigu started arguing with someone about art, clearly getting frustrated.

"Oh, so it's like that? Well, allow me to show you!" Tigu suddenly boomed, pointing at another person. She raised her hands, a single Qi blade forming over each. They were quite small, Tigu clearly being too tired from the competition to summon her full strength.

It was enough for her desires, though, and Tigu's Qi blades rent into the table.

"Hey!" the owner of this branch of Chao Baozi shouted, who until this point had merely been watching them warily. He was fat around the middle with massive arms and a bright-red nose. His face was a cross of fear and indignation, and an older gentleman, who had been leaning against the bar all night, straightened up. He was some manner of cultivator, that was clear to Xiulan, the Fifth Stage of the Initiate's Realm from what she could gather from careful examination of his Qi. She had not seen him in the tournament, however.

Tigu flushed, seeming to realise what she had done, and stood, bowing her head to the owner.

"Rou Tigu apologises for the damage to your property!" she said contritely. "I shall acquire another table for you!"

The man seemed surprised at her display of remorse.

"Ah . . . uh . . . if it can be repaired, we'll do that instead," he offered. "How bad is the damage?"

Tigu nodded, and several people lifted up their plates, bowls, and cups so she could pick it up and show the owner.

A carving of Tie Delun stared back, his muscles bulging as he and his hammer, in midmotion, delivered a strike to an opponent. So lifelike it seemed that the hammer was ready to whirl out of the carving and strike down whoever was facing it.

There were gasps of shock and whistles of appreciation from the crowd.

The owner stared at the carving in his table for a moment. He licked his lips. A mercenary smile stretched across his face.

"I'll forgive you if you do the rest of the tables like that. A different one for each," he offered.

Tigu brightened.

"Handsome Man, I challenge you!" she shouted. "I shall finish more tables, and at a higher quality than you!"

Tie Delun seemed utterly confused as Tigu gave her terms to her fellow carver, but he squared his shoulders and nodded.

"As you say, Miss Rou. I apologise, but I'll be challenging your might."

Tigu laughed. "I welcome every challenge! Never apologise for it!"

The pair spread out and began to work. Ragged cheers rose up from the crowd as splinters of wood started to fly.

"Hmmm? Sitting off to the side like always, how *boring*." Xianghua sprawled into the seat next to Xiulan. She had a wide smile on her face as she took a swig of her own wine. "Though I'm surprised you're here at all. I try for years, and nothing. Tell me, who succeeded in making Cai Xiulan come to a bar? Who stole this accomplishment from me?"

Xiulan let the needling comment slide off her back. Even after nearly a decade of *tolerating* Xianghua, Xiulan didn't know what to make of the woman. They didn't see each other often, and Xianghua was everything Xiulan wasn't, or so she had thought. Arrogant and boastful. Free with her words and rebellious. Constantly needling Xiulan, or demanding that she go out and do something not related to cultivation . . .

And Xiulan had refused her every time, claiming that the time was better spent cultivating.

She could admit now that Xianghua had tried to be her friend and she had rejected her. Xiulan looked at Xianghua, whose eyes were on Bowu. The boy was deep in discussion with Gou Ren. The look on Xianghua's face was a sister's smile. Her shoulders were not tense. She looked like Xiulan herself had felt when she left Fa Ram.

"I wish I had done so sooner. Back when you offered," Xiulan replied, words tinged with regret. Memories of a friendship that could have been, if not for her own thoughts on duty. Xianghua had put in the effort, and Xiulan had refused her . . . but it wasn't too late to rectify things. "It is an enjoyable experience. As are the songs. Have you heard of the one with the Whore and the Donkey?"

Xianghua made a show of glancing into her cup curiously, then looked back at Xiulan.

"Are you *sure* you're the Cai Xiulan I knew?" she asked with a raised eyebrow.

"No. I don't think I am," the Blade of Grass admitted after a moment.

Xianghua's face went blank as she examined Xiulan's expression before scoffing.

"Don't change so much, fool. It makes things difficult for me," she declared, turning back to the party. Several shirts had come off at some point, as people whooped and cheered. Yun Ren had stopped his images, instead setting up a collection of cups and a ball, a game he had learned from Master Jin. Despite Xianghua's words, Xiulan realised there had almost been a fondness in the other woman's voice.

Xiulan closed her eyes. They sat together, both watching as the carvings got more and more intricate and the game became quite competitive.

Xiulan poured Xianghua a drink.

"*Hmph.* Took you long enough," Xianghua said.

She held up her cup.

Xiulan hooked her arm around Xianghua's.

They drank, their arms linked.

Xianghua seemed inordinately pleased with herself.

"Before the semifinals, will you have another drink with me?" Xiulan asked.

The answer was immediate.

"Of course not," Xianghua replied bluntly, sticking her nose in the air. "I have to take care of that handsome brother over there."

"Do not toy with him or his heart," Xiulan said, focusing her intent on Xianghua. The other woman paused and raised an eyebrow. "And don't interfere with my Juniors."

"She certainly let me monopolize his time easily enough." Xianghua smirked.

Xiulan frowned.

"You are infuriating sometimes."

"This Young Mistress can only be infuriating to her lessers. Do work on your composure, Blade of Grass." She smirked again, before her eyes turned serious. "It is not my intention to toy with him."

"What about your father?" Xiulan asked.

"What about him?" Xianghua replied derisively. "If he thinks to choose my future, he is a fool. I choose my own destiny. Is that not what a cultivator does?"

Xiulan went quiet, digesting her words—and suddenly, there was a commotion. Two men stood and started snarling at each other. Tigu for a brief moment perked up, looking both happy and excited. It seemed that Master Jin's statement about cultivators and restaurants was about to come true—before Tigu slumped, clearly remembering the tournament rules. *No fighting outside designated areas.* She considered the two men before her eyes widened with an idea.

Things were getting heated in the argument when Tigu came back with a barrel. She went to the arguing pair with it.

"This doesn't count as fighting, right?" Tigu asked as she slammed a barrel down in between the two angry men. She looked over at the owner of the restaurant for confirmation.

He blinked, seeming confused for a moment, before he realised that Tigu meant arm wrestling. The fat man nodded tentatively.

"Go on, then!" Tigu demanded. The men seemed utterly confused . . . but complied with her demand. The two angry cultivators rammed their elbows onto the barrel and clasped hands.

The entire restaurant's attention turned to the pair.

"The next round on the one in yellow," Xiulan stated to her friend.

"A fool's bet, but I shall oblige you. Be thankful for my charity, Cai," Xianghua replied.

Both women snorted.

There was a roar as the yellow-clad man toppled his opponent. Xianghua waved for the bottle as they watched another man walk up to challenge the man in yellow.

→

Eventually, the night wound down. Xianghua collected her sleeping brother from Gou Ren. The groups of cultivators broke off, or some simply fell asleep across tables, much to the owner's exasperation.

Even hours later, one thing stuck with Xiulan.

Xianghua's statement of choosing her own destiny.

It invaded her thoughts as she tried to get to sleep, Tigu curling into Xiulan's side.

She thought of it on the day of rest while Tigu slept, recovering her strength.

She thought on it up to the last minute before her match, the first of the day.

Duty warred with desire. She pushed down the intrusive thoughts and tried to focus—which was a struggle when she saw Xianghua cheerfully leaning up against Gou Ren. Junior Brother looked mildly concerned at the aggressive tactics and seemed to be trying to use Bowu as a shield against his sister. Yun Ren just kept taking pictures.

"The Beautiful and Graceful Demon-Slaying Orchid versus—"

Xianghua caught Xiulan's gaze and winked.

The match started. Xiulan's opponent took advantage of her lapse in concentration, throwing himself forwards. *Her own destiny.* What *was* her own destiny? It was still something she was figuring out.

She thought about it as her body moved of its own accord.

What happened next was neither beautiful nor graceful.

There was an ugly *crack* as Xiulan stepped forwards.

Two foreheads connected. Her opponent was sent sprawling to the ground.

The shocked silence afterwards was broken by Tigu's laughter.

CHAPTER 33

THE MASTER OF CEREMONIES AND MERCHANDISE

"The Azure Blade goes in, Huo Jian tries to counter—no, the blade strikes true! And there it is, the winner is the Young Master of the Azure Horizon Sect! Raise your voices for his victory!" Bai Huizong, His Imperial Majesty's Director of Spiritual Ascension Affairs for the Azure Hills, shouted into his Resounding Crystal Dais.

There was some polite clapping and cheers from the spectators. The fight had been quite good, in Huizong's own humble opinion, but the crowd had gotten a taste for grander fare in the preceding days. He once more cursed the fact that Xianghua and Tigu were placed so close together in the brackets—one of the newer aides had entered the data wrong into the Dueling Peaks' systems when they had assigned the brackets, and by the time anybody caught it, it was too late to change things. The Imperial Government didn't make mistakes, after all—though he was likely going to get some pointed questions from the Misty Lake Sect later. The aide responsible was currently cleaning out the *very* full waste cisterns deep in the mountain.

Huizong sighed. That had been a semifinal match *at least.* Hells, if it were within his power he would have torn out one of the other competitors instead, just to bring her back! Xianghua was a *serious* moneymaker.

Huizong's eyes scanned the crowd as the groups settled into idle chatter. It was quite low energy today, the crowds watching out of the corners of their eyes while chatting about Xianghua versus Tigu. They seemed to feel like there was nothing else to look forward to, even after the amusing defeat Cai Xiulan had handed her opponent. Really, that was most unexpected! It took until the next competitors were in the arena for the shock to wear off.

Though it did present Huizong with a problem when writing out his narrative account of the tournament. What manner of upstanding Young Mistress would *headbutt* her opponent?

He considered his choices. He could either turn it into just a punch, omit the fight . . . or say that it was retaliation against some manner of unwanted advance. That one was probably the best, and it wasn't like On Gang's Rumbling Earth Sect could retaliate, even if they did take offence. Huizong vaguely remembered that they had interacted once before. Young Mistress Cai had rebuked him then as well. Huizong nodded. That would definitely work.

The next match was also met with polite clapping.

An Ran versus the Young Master of the Grand Ravine Sect.

According to the rumours going around, she had recently gained the moniker "Smaller Blade of Grass," *which is quite apt*, he thought with a smirk. She certainly was *smaller*, especially where it counted. Against her was Guo Daxian, the favoured son of his Sect. From what Huizong knew of the place, Daxian was some kind of revered name granted to the leaders of the Sect and their direct line.

It was another mismatch, but it was notable for the Verdant Blade Sect to get so many disciples so far into the tournament. He had assumed that after the devastation Sun Ken had visited upon them, they would have lost some strength, yet their newer recruits and the Young Mistress seemed to have shored up that weakness.

"An Ran, the Smaller Blade of Grass, versus the Mighty, Unflinching Young Master of the Grand Ravine Sect, Guuuuuoooooo Daxian!"

There was no talk between the combatants this time, to Huizong's disappointment. Prefight banter always got the crowd more invested. Instead, all An Ran did was take deep, calming breaths while her opponent studied her. Daxian's face was a stony mask.

"Begin!" Huizong commanded.

Guo Daxian moved immediately. His rope-sword lashed out, stabbing into the ground near An Ran. In an eyeblink, he was right next to the younger woman.

An Ran barely got her sword up to block the attack, the blade skittering off her own, but then Daxian hammered a fist into her gut, folding the woman in half from the force of the blow.

"A fiery beginning!" Huizong shouted out. Guo Daxian seemed to have tried to take her out quickly, so as to not lose too much face in battling an opponent weaker than him. Cai Xiulan had instantly defeated one of his own sectmates, so the Young Master would match her deed. A bold strategy, and the fast-paced nature of the attack had clearly caught the crowd's attention.

Daxian continued his combo, hammering into his younger opponent.

"A strike to the side of the head—An Ran manages to deflect—oh, not entirely!" Huizong belted out as fast as he could, the cultivators practically blurs. An Ran's arm had been opened up, and blood sprayed into the air. It was looking like her defeat was assured as Daxian closed to end it. The rope part of his weapon went to wrap around and snare her arm, while the blade was in Daxian's hand, ready to end the fight.

An Ran's sword split in two, a smaller dagger allowing her to parry the blade, and a second blow making Daxian retreat.

"A magnificent escape! But is it enough?" Huizong shouted, and the crowds roared in response.

An Ran staggered, regaining her balance from the vicious assault, then took a breath, returning to her stance.

Daxian's frown grew heavier at his still-standing opponent, his eyes narrowing with wrath.

But the distance she created was not to her advantage—the Young Master from the Grand Ravine Sect switched tactics.

The attacks came absolutely relentlessly. The weapon Daxian used was a strange one, his blade attached to a long rope, apparently something traditional to the ravine. The rope snared his opponents, while the blade danced about in unpredictable patterns. Attempt to deal with the blade, and the rope would suddenly be tangling a foot. Strike the rope, and the blade would whip around like a snake, biting from an unexpected angle.

An Ran desperately parried, her eyes darting about and attempting to keep track of everything while still trying to close the distance. Daxian's weapon snaked and slithered like it was a living thing, foiling her plans. Against Cai Xiulan, or any core disciple of the Verdant Blade Sect, this would not be so nearly a devastating advantage. Their floating blades would turn the distance back into an even fight. An Ran, however, could not make her blades float, locking her into one range. She had no recourse but to charge forwards, into the space Daxian controlled.

Daxian denied her charge. He was carefully keeping An Ran away while whittling her down. Some might have called it cowardly, but the Grand Ravine's people were notorious for their hit-and-run style of combat. Huizong didn't care either way. It certainly made for a tense show.

"Another strike! Even with her two Blades of Grass, An Ran can't close the distance!" Huizong's voice boomed as he narrated, trying to further rouse the crowd's spirits. Tigu was certainly loud enough, shouting and heckling both combatants, for which Huizong was thankful.

He might even do something nice for the girl. She was already making his wallet much heavier.

An Ran charged, purposefully ramming into the rope and trying to unbalance her opponent. She threw her short, ghostly blade through the gap; it seemed to curve of its own accord, almost flying through the air, and headed right for her opponent.

Daxian backhanded it out of the air, unconcerned. The blade exploded into wisps of Qi. His rope curled, wrapping around the woman's body, its blade coming to bear, ready to punch deep and end the fight. There was a gasp from the crowd.

Guo Daxian grimaced and pulled his strike. The blade on the end of the rope, instead of striking home, curved at the last moment, wrapping around An Ran's chest and neck, binding her tight. The blade kept up its momentum, landing back in its Master's hand. Guo Daxian pulled on the rope, part of it wrapped around his arm, and the other attached to the blade in his hand. An Ran was yanked off her feet and towards the Young Master of the Grand Ravine Sect.

Daxian caught her out of the air and pinned her with one arm, the other pushing his blade against An Ran's throat.

Immobilized and unable to struggle free, the girl went limp, surrendering.

The gong sounded.

"And victory for the Young Master of the Grand Ravine Sect!" Huizong shouted.

There was some grumbling from the crowd, but it was mostly drowned out by polite clapping. They always appreciated when a beautiful woman walked away relatively unharmed. *She's a cute little thing. It's almost a shame she's a cultivator, but alas, that's what she is.*

Though Guo Daxian's concerns were likely of a more practical nature, if Huizong's guess was right. The young man rarely restrained himself so much, and cared little for the sex of his opponent. No, his concern was honour, as well as something more immediate. The Demon-Slaying Orchid had restrained herself when facing one of his own Sect members, handing him a polite defeat without even injuring him. A bit of an insult, but that was preferable to being absolutely brutalized.

The Young Master of the Grand Ravine Sect turned to the Verdant Blade's competitor section and nodded his head. Cai Xiulan inclined hers in return.

It was only intelligent that Daxian did the same. The girl seemed close to her Young Mistress . . . and Daxian was going to have to face the Demon-Slaying Orchid in the semifinals.

The Demon-Slaying Orchid, who so far had not shown a single technique. Who had defeated most competitors in a single blow in a display of absolute dominance.

Yes, the smart thing to do was to repay her kindness, and none had ever accused the Grand Ravine Sect of being foolish. *Barbaric Tribals*, perhaps, whispered behind their backs, but never foolish.

Huyi versus Tie Delun was another swift defeat. Huyi gave a surprisingly good showing, managing to get close and hammer his blade into places that were generally weak points . . . only for those strikes to skitter off Delun's skin and a massive hand to close around Huyi's throat, lifting the Verdant Blade Sect disciple completely off the ground. One last strike to the elbow failed to accomplish anything, and Huyi promptly surrendered.

The next fight was another odd one. It started out as expected, with Zang Wei getting the hells kicked out of him by his more-experienced opponent. Each strike was perfect, laying the little independent out on his arse in short order. Huizong had blinked when Zang Wei landed on his back, his opponent going for the finishing blow, but in that space there was the sound of shattering masonry and Zang Wei was standing again, the beaten boy grinning through his swollen face. His opponent collapsed on the ground, eyes rolled up into his head—he was unconscious.

Chants of "Loud Boy! Loud Boy!" filled the arena as he basked in his victory.

The last fight of the day was, for the second time in a row, Tigu, and once again she delivered. It was a knock-down, drag-out slugging match against Dulou

Gan, though it was more due to the man's resilience than anything else. He got the worst of it as Tigu pummeled him. To be fair, it was less exciting than the charged match against Liu Xianghua but acceptable for a final bout.

Huizong took a swig of his water as the Earthly Arena was raised again, then closed his eyes as the cool breeze whispered across his balding head.

Rising higher into the sky never truly got old.

An odd tournament this year. Full of upsets, and with a twisting, turning story.

A small smile spread across his face.

Now it was time for his *other* job.

→

"No, no, not *that* one. The muscles are too big, soften her out a bit. Fix her eyes too, they're too narrow. Too predatory." Huizong shook his head at the artist as he continued to draw out his newest article.

The artist frowned, considering his work. "Dangerous, but not entirely villainous? Play up the young girl angle, rather than the fighter angle?"

"Exactly!" Huizong nodded. "She is your cheeky daughter. A bit different than we were going for at the start, but it's fine this way too. Cocky and impertinent, but not some beast that will ambush you on the side of the road. Like a beloved youngest daughter."

"Yes, sir, I'll get it done." The artist bowed.

"Good man!" Bai Huizong set down his brush and handed the scroll off to one of his aides. He was seated at his desk on a small balcony, overlooking the workshop below. Hammers pounded and needles flashed as his workers below crafted the designs for the dolls that he would be selling.

"Get that over to the transmission stone. If we work fast, we'll still manage to get it out today." His aide nodded, scurrying off. "Hu! How was the previous report received?"

Another aide stepped up and bowed.

"Very well, sir. The scribes put on a rush order, as you said, and they got the banners up. Reception for Liu Xianghua and Rou Tigu has been excellent in Grass Sea City, and we'll know by tomorrow how things pan out in Pale Moon Lake."

"Sales figures?" Huizong asked.

"In line with expectations, sir. Though the scribes had to pull a second shift—they sold out of the first copies."

"Excellent! Add a bonus for whoever completes the most copies," Huizong declared.

"As you say, sir."

Huizong smiled, stretching and plucking another honey candy from the bowl on his desk. The honey helped soothe his throat after a long day. He certainly wasn't getting any younger, and his voice tended to start to blow out at the end of an event.

"How are the designs going?" he asked the head of the workshop, Hei Cho, who had been working for him for over two decades. She knew exactly what he wanted to see.

A tray of dolls was presented to him.

"Simple but effective," Huizong stated as he picked up the one of Rou Tigu. It was quite well designed, the markings on her face being prominent, with yellow-painted eyes and orange-yarn hair. Easy to produce.

"Yes, sir. Overhead on Liu Xianghua will be higher if we include her furnace, however," Cho warned.

Huizong scratched his chin as he picked up the other doll. The green furnace and smokestack, made out of carved wood, was strapped to the doll's back. "Include the furnace, but keep the price the same. We'll make up for lower profits with more sales. I have a good feeling about this one. Are we still in line with the timetable?"

"We can probably get one more out, and keep the main release in line with the end of the tournament," Cho informed him.

Huizong pondered for a moment before shaking his head.

"No, these are good enough. Get them and the designs to the runner, and start production as soon as you can."

"Yes, sir," Cho said with an elegant bow.

Huizong kept his eyes on her rear as he watched her go. The woman still had it. He smiled at the hypnotic sight.

Until he heard her chuckle.

He coughed, shaking his head, and turned to the rest of his men.

"Anything else to report?" he asked.

Hu nodded, stepping forwards again. "There are whispers of another party that is going to happen on the first day of the break before the finals. We missed the last one, but this one seems like it's going to be significantly larger."

"Is there a main organiser?"

"Chen Yang of the Framed Sun Sect . . . and Liu Xianghua. There are invitations. From the rumours? Every person who has taken part in the tournament is invited."

Huizong hummed.

"Interesting. Get some men into the crowd and inform the merchants. The brave can get their reward—with our cut, of course. And if things turn sour with a bunch of drunken youngsters, make it clear it's not our problem."

"Indeed." Hu chuckled at the statement.

"Anything else?" Huizong asked.

"The owner of Chao Baozi is refusing to sell to us. He wants to keep the carved tables in the restaurant."

"Change tack, see if he'll let us take charcoal reliefs of them, and if he says no to that . . . just do it anyway."

"As you say, sir."

Huizong nodded. "Then I'll get started on tomorrow's paperwork. Get the lads down there something special—they've worked hard these past days."

Hu clasped his hands together and bowed, accepting the dismissal.

Huizong reached into the tray his aides had organised for him, grabbing the one right at the front. He frowned at the piece of parchment before him: authorizing another set of barrels for the delegation from the Shrouded Mountain Sect. *How much can these bastards drink?!*

With an irritated sigh, he signed it.

CHAPTER 34

TO THE FINALS

Another day, another short fight. Xiulan was starting to understand where Tigu was coming from. It was unbearably boring just sitting in her seat with nobody to talk to. She had given leave for the Petals to sit in the crowd with the Xong brothers and watch the tournament from there. Because she was alone, she couldn't congratulate her Juniors for making it so far, or speak about their fights.

The rest of them were up in the stands. Gou Ren and Yun Ren were in their usual seats, along with Bowu, and a strange-looking man with a bunch of patches on his clothes. Gou Ren's look of panic when An Ran had sat beside him on the opposite side of Xianghua had been rather amusing. As had Ri Zu's flight. Xiulan caught sight of the small black streak as she transferred from Gou Ren to Yun Ren, fleeing from the line of fire.

An Ran had found her courage, it seemed.

Gou Ren was sandwiched between two flowers who were both glaring at each other, though Xianghua seemed more amused than annoyed. Xiulan had given him a thumbs-up when she felt his eyes, begging for aid.

She left him to his fate.

The most exciting match of all had been when Loud Boy had taken to the field against Tie Delun. The scrappy young man had held out admirably, managing to strike Delun's massive hammer so hard it broke, shattering into a thousand pieces . . . yet Tie Delun dealt him a grievous blow in retaliation.

Xiulan thought that was the end of Loud Boy's defiance, yet he'd dug deep, stomping forwards.

A second strike hammered home, managing to *barely* break through the Hermetic Iron Body. An ethereal dragon's tail writhed around Loud Boy as he sought to end the fight in a sudden reversal, like he had in each fight before.

Delun staggered back. His skin was cracked and his eyes had gone wide as he received the devastating strike. For a moment, he faltered.

Until Tigu started cheering. Immediately, Delun's eyes had sparked and fire had steamed out of his mouth like an active forge, his cracked skin hardening once more. He dug in his feet and managed to force his way through the dragon's tail, landing a powerful uppercut and taking Loud Boy out of the fight with a broken jaw.

Loud Boy's face twisted from where he lay on the ground, his eyes narrowing with something ugly—until Delun offered him a hand, nodding at his accomplishments.

The crowd echoed this sentiment, shouting the name Loud Boy as he departed.

Loud Boy had seemed very surprised, and rather contemplative, as he left the arena.

And then there were four.

Cai Xiulan of the Verdant Blade Sect. Guo Daxian of the Grand Ravine Sect. Tie Delun of the Hermetic Iron Sect. And the independent, Rou Tigu.

□

The day of the quarterfinals was charged; Xiulan could feel the electrifying atmosphere in her bones.

The thunderous beat of the drums and the howling of the crowds was deafening.

They once more entered to pomp and ceremony. It was a play on the opening ceremony, where the contestants had entered and lined up in the hundreds.

Now they had been greatly reduced. There were no disciples beside them. Each entered alone. Xiulan, with the banner of the Verdant Blade Sect. Guo Daxian, with the Grand Ravine's. Tie Delun, to the ringing of iron.

And the last, Rou Tigu, carrying the flag of the sectless. She seemed a bit amused to be carrying it, and as she placed it below the phoenix banner she flipped her hair, exposing the symbol on the back of her shirt. While the others had their Sects cheering for them, and people who were invested in their cause, Tigu had the majority of the crowd.

Loud Boy led the call, his jaw having been healed by Ri Zu. The crowd was ill-organised but full of spirit as they shouted her name. Even if she wasn't truly the underdog, she was a manifestation of their spirit. A girl who had come out of nowhere, without the backing of one of the established powers.

The first match was hers. Her opponent, Tie Delun.

He shuffled uncomfortably.

"I'm looking forward to this, Handsome Man!" Tigu shouted. "Come, show me all your strength!"

Tie Delun gritted his teeth, took a deep breath, and steeled himself.

Tanned skin turned to grey, like iron.

His skin was inviolate, even against Tigu's mighty blows. Her claws scraped off him without finding purchase.

But Tigu had trained with Xiulan, and against Bi De. Tie Delun's hammer, a new one, was fast . . . but not fast enough. His smaller opponent danced circles around him.

He even once left himself open, purposefully taking a punch in order to land a devastating hammer strike on the smaller girl. The blow shook the entire arena.

An explosion of dust rose up as Tigu was driven into the ground with all of his considerable might.

Tie Delun staggered back, panting. He looked worried that he had done Tigu harm. Such a strike likely would have killed another contestant.

The small, orange-haired girl staggered to her feet. Some of her ribs were obviously broken.

She flashed her brilliant smile.

"A fine blow!" she praised him, kicking off her sandals. "My turn."

She crouched down and dug her toes into the solid stone of the arena.

[Pounce of the Tiger]

A meteor struck Tie Delun, moving too fast for his eyes to catch.

His iron skin broke.

The fight ended with Tigu sitting atop his chest like a cat, smiling down at him.

The crowd roared her victory even as she helped her opponent up. The master of the Resounding Crystal Dais was yelling himself hoarse.

And then it was Xiulan's turn. She was facing Guo Daxian, the Young Master of the Grand Ravine Sect. A man who had laid her low once before, at a previous tournament.

The cheers were deafening, but inconsequential.

Daxian, in contrast to Delun, was calm. His eyes were focused as he took Xiulan in.

"Thank you for your consideration for my Junior, earlier in the tournament," Xiulan whispered.

The man's voice was deadly calm. "I would be a fool not to return your favour, woman. But now, are you going to disrespect me as well? Strike me with that open hand of yours?"

Xiulan considered him. He was a prideful man. One who would take her being kind to him as an offence. He would bear a grudge for not seeing her might.

He was a bit like Tigu in that way.

"No, I will not. Out of consideration for the Young Master of the Grand Ravine Sect's talent."

Daxian nodded.

"Show me," he commanded. "Show me the power of a cultivator in the Profound Realm."

The gong sounded.

Xiulan obliged him—and for the first time, she let loose her power.

[Verdant Blade Sword Arts: Thirty-Two Blades of Grass]

The roaring crowds went silent. A halo of jade-green swords surrounded Xiulan, pointing upwards like grass growing towards the heavens.

Slowly, they grew. They orbited her in the first steps of her dance, a green procession of Qi-infused metal.

Until they all froze and shifted. Each and every blade turned like a living thing and pointed directly at her opponent.

Guo Daxian uncoiled his weapon, the rope and blade sliding down from his arm to rest in his palm.

He faced the storm with a straight back, even as Xiulan's swords descended on him like a pack of ravenous wolves.

He was a testament to his line as he began a charge that was heroic, almost noble. A dive straight into the jaws of death.

There was no denying his skill. There was no denying his ability. He deflected and parried her blades. He chained his movement technique so often he was a blur across the arena.

And yet . . . he could not get closer. Xiulan had long since realised the reason why Tigu was so successful. She was in the end, a Spirit Beast, and they were naturally more durable, *tougher*, than men. Blades that Tigu would deflect with her body instead cut deep lines into Daxian.

Xiulan's assault was overwhelming.

She did not move a single step.

Daxian roared, and his tattoos glowed blue. He called upon the strength and protection of his ancestors, doubling his already impressive speed and shielding him from her blade's bite.

Xiulan stepped to the side as her opponent's weapon reached out desperately to score a hit. A few strands of her brown hair fell from her head.

Daxian shot past her, ready to swing around for another attempt . . . but too late he realised it had been a trap. His missed strike had brought him directly into a cage of blades, all of them pointing at him. This time, there would be no room for him to dodge.

He looked almost resigned as the jade swords descended. But he still turned, intent on launching one last attack.

There was a *thud* as he was driven to the floor, looking for all the world like there were blades of grass growing from his body.

The crowd was silent as they stared at Xiulan. Even Xianghua had ceased her games, gaping at the execution that had just taken place.

Xiulan's copied blades disappeared, combining together until only two were left.

Xiulan bowed to her defeated opponent.

□

Xiulan and Tigu stood across from each other. Ten paces behind them stood their opponents and the rest of the defeated.

Both Delun and Daxian looked dead on their feet, covered in bandages but still standing as tall as they could.

Out of the corner of her eye Xiulan saw the tournament organiser look at them all with a pleased smile. "What a lineup! What a magnificent set of contestants, do you not agree?" the man boomed into the Resounding Crystal Dais. The crowd roared their approval. "The strength! The passion! I have no doubt this Dueling Peaks Tournament is one for the ages! One that will resound throughout our Azure Hills! Even the defeated are of a quality that we rarely see! In any other year, I can think of many of these combatants who would rise to be champions themselves! The quality of this tournament shall be spoken of for generations!"

More roars as the people shouted names, Xianghua and Loud Boy prominent among them.

"Now we commence another break, so that the contestants may fight at their full strength during the coming final bout! But do not fear for lack of entertainment! We have the Amateur Pill Maker Contest in the Stone Pavilion, an event that's sure to be . . . *explosive*!"

There was some laughter at that. Xiulan had never been, but there was a reason that one was held in a fortress of stone, with nothing flammable near the contestants.

"For the Mortals that wish to catch a Sect's eye with your skill and strength, the Mortals' Contest shall be held in the lesser arena on the south side. It's sure to be an interesting set of bouts! And finally, we have the lesser events. A performance every day from the legendary Skytree Troupe! The Hero of the Ravine, the Demon-Slaying Orchid, the Song of the Framed Sun, the First Emperor, and of course, the always entertaining Ballad of the Drunkard! Standing is free, courtesy of our tournament!"

Xiulan watched Bai Huizong bask in the adulation of the crowd, raising his hands high.

"Contestants! You are all dismissed for today. Remember to return for the final ceremony, and don't get *too* wild during your time off," he finished with a chuckle.

Done for the day and a weeklong break to look forward to. Normally, she would have spent the time cultivating, but . . .

She glanced at the crowd as the majority filed out.

Xianghua caught her eye, waving her hands and making a drinking motion, and Xiulan rolled her eyes . . . then nodded.

Yes, she'd remembered the party that night. Yes, she would be going. Xianghua really didn't need to keep annoying her about it—she wasn't going to change her mind and bow out. The last couple of times had been fun.

She idly wondered who would be there today.

→

"Haha! *Behold*, the benevolence of this Young Mistress!" Xianghua roared, her voice echoing across the street as she stood with Chen Yang of the Framed Sun Sect, the man grinning at all the eyes on the two of them. They were on a small, raised platform in the street's square, addressing the crowd. Streamers of cloth and paper lanterns lit up the area, somewhere musicians plied their trade, and this street in particular was jam-packed with bodies, raising their cups to the two figures standing on an impromptu stage.

There was a roar of approval, some laughter, and some jeers at Xianghua's words.

As it turned out, *everybody* showed up. Or nearly everybody. The Grand Ravine Sect was nowhere to be seen, but it seemed like every other person who had participated in the tournament was in attendance.

Xiulan, quite frankly, had no idea how Xianghua had managed it. Although the promise of free drinks on her was likely the deciding factor for many who were present. There were many here who could be classified as the Misty Lake Sect's enemies, like the Azure Horizon Sect. Yet there the Young Master of the Sect was, raising his cup.

Xiulan supposed that even being Xianghua's enemy didn't stop him from taking advantage of her generosity . . . or the Young Master just didn't particularly care.

Honestly, most didn't seem to care. There were some groups that formed, sticking together, but for the large part, they mingled. Oh, how a party changed things. Or at least this party had. Perhaps it was the youthfulness of the attendees, but Xiulan had once imagined these kinds of parties to be . . . tenser affairs. The few she'd been to in Grass Sea City had been. She'd had to watch herself closely, and there were veiled words and pointed questions from rivals. The pageantry of the palace had been mind-numbing. That, in addition to the questing eyes, had made her write them off. To her, parties had just seemed a waste of time.

Instead, there was little propriety. The vaunted Young Masters and Mistresses . . . *were acting like mortals.*

It was an amusing thought.

Xiulan hummed to herself and tapped her feet to the music as she wandered around the venue. Some made room for her. A few she absently dodged as they gesticulated wildly.

Somewhat surprisingly, very few eyes were directed her way, as most seemed to be looking at the wall Yun Ren had commandeered to display his highlights of the fights.

There was even a small corner, off to the side, where several people were setting up a mahjong table. Xiulan turned to where the person who'd invited her to the entire affair was.

Xianghua was still belting out how she was an untouchable, generous goddess. *She might be at it for a while*, Xiulan thought.

She took a moment to consider whether it was worth going anywhere near Xianghua, and then she turned back to the table setting up for the mahjong game. They noticed her approach.

"Ah . . . Miss Cai, do you wish to join us?" one of them tentatively asked, gesturing to the table.

"If you'll have me," she replied.

Their game began. The rest of the players were intensely nervous, shooting her glances, but slowly they seemed to calm down as the game progressed.

Her opponents were quite skilled. Much better than Master Jin, though she'd never been able to tell whether he was *actually* bad at the games they played or just didn't care about winning them.

And her new opponents were actually rather pleasant. They snuck their glances but seemed content to merely discuss the game and didn't ask any awkward questions.

The eventual winner was the largest of them, a thickset and thuggish-looking Qiao Dan, who was the son of an official from Grass Sea City. He had chewed his lip for a full minute after Xiulan played her hand before finally playing his.

"Nine Gates of Heaven," he intoned as he revealed a play that bested her own. He seemed a bit nervous.

Xiulan inclined her head. "A fine game. Another?" she asked.

The men looked around at the table. They shrugged and started again . . . and Xiulan did even worse than the first time.

"Ah! There you are, Cai. Huddled off and playing over here!" Xianghua said in the middle of their game, leaning on Xiulan's shoulder. With no regard for what Xiulan was doing, the other woman started to rearrange her tiles.

Xiulan slapped her hand away and put them back how she had them.

"Begone, Damp Pond," she stated, irritated, but took the cup of wine that was shoved into her hand.

Xianghua scoffed. "You're terrible at this, Xiulan. Really, I'm doing you a favour."

"Haa? Get over to that side, then, and see if you win," Xiulan demanded, glaring at Xianghua. Her other opponents just sat by, watching meekly as the two argued.

Xiulan dealt her into the next game.

It turned out to be a mistake.

"All Green Imperial Jade," Xianghua announced smugly.

Xiulan tossed her tiles aside in disgust as Xianghua got up, laughing all the while.

Xiulan reshuffled the tiles and found herself facing off against a fresh set of people. Inevitably, Gou Ren and Tigu got involved.

Gou Ren proved a challenging opponent.

"Here! The Great Pillars of Fa Ram!" Tigu exclaimed as she revealed her hand.

Gou Ren stared blankly at her.

"*That isn't even a hand*, Tigu."

"But it is the best-looking of the arrangements!" she argued.

"You don't get any points for how pretty it is!"

"The largest picture, then?"

"No! You're as bad at this as Jin is!"

Xiulan hopped from table to table, game to game. Occasionally playing with somebody she knew, but most of the time with people she didn't.

She even indulged in the game of dice she saw the soldiers start up, in the time they made camp while hunting for Sun Ken.

And swiftly realised why they were so addicted to it.

She probably lost more money than she should have, but she had gotten *most* of it back. She managed to get in games and was in the middle of the sixth when there was a small commotion near the edges of the party as the Grand Ravine Sect arrived.

It spoiled her throw. Instead of the dice landing properly, they turned to damnation.

The man running the game smiled beatifically even as Xiulan cursed, turning to the tardy arrivals.

"Hmph. So these bastards *can* throw a party," she heard a loud voice call. Some of the talk went quiet. Guo Daxian and the Grand Ravine Sect members stood, their arms folded across their chests.

Xiulan rolled her eyes at his aggression and stood up straighter. If he wanted to ruin Xianghua's party . . .

Guo Daxian made a great show of looking around, a smirk coming across his face. He didn't look like he had good intentions. "I think we should—"

"Ah! Blue Man! I have been meaning to speak with you!" Tigu called out, accidentally interrupting him. She marched straight up to Guo Daxian. The Disciples of the Grand Ravine Sect seemed taken aback by the sudden accosting.

The eyes of the Young Master of the Grand Ravine Sect narrowed as Tigu approached him. The smaller girl stood before the hard man. His hair was covered by his bandana, and his bright tattoos stood out on his arms.

"What is this art upon your skin? I like it!"

Guo Daxian looked directly at Tigu, an eyebrow raised.

"Aren't you the brat who carved my face into a table?" he drawled.

"Yes! Your tattoo was hard to get right! I had to look at Yun Ren's recordings many times to capture the intricate detail!" Tigu replied. "To cover your body in art! I think I like it! Though too much might ruin the aesthetic of one's muscles . . ."

Gua Daxian paused, his face still locked in his frown, but seemingly a bit confused. "Yun Ren? Recording?" he asked, and Tigu pointed to her fellow disciple.

Yun Ren perked up when he saw her pointing, wandering over.

"What's going on?" he asked, putting a hand on Tigu's shoulder and leaning towards Guo Daxian in a manner that suggested he was backing Tigu up.

Daxian glanced at Yun Ren, and his eyes became thoughtful as they landed on his scarf.

He started intently at Yun Ren's manner of dress. Now that Xiulan was looking at it more, the tattoos on Guo Daxian's arms were *quite* similar to the design on Yun Ren's scarf. He glanced over to Tigu and then back to Yun Ren.

"Which tribe do you hail from?" he asked, his eyes narrow.

"From up north aways, yanno?" Yun Ren replied, putting on a thick accent that Xiulan had heard his mother use and dodging the question.

Daxian barked out a laugh before replying with an odd accent of his own. "That be fair enough."

He looked at Tigu, considering her . . . before dropping his arm and pulling at his shirt, better allowing Tigu to see the ink upon his skin.

"It is the legacy of our ancestors. Only the mighty may bear these marks, following after the great warriors of old."

Tigu's eyes sparkled as she looked at the ink.

"A needle, imbued with my father's Qi. Ink, infused with my own blood. The process is painful. Only the greatest of warriors can withstand it, and a true man must receive his ancestors' blessings without making a sound."

Tigu made an impressed noise.

"I bet I could do it," she said, her gaze challenging.

"Feisty little brat, you are," Guo Daxian muttered, before shaking his head and gesturing to one of his comrades. "Oi, Little Brother, what manner of style do you think would work on this one here?"

One of the Disciples of the Grand Ravine Sect looked closely at her.

"Perhaps Ancestor Daxian the Ninth?"

The conversation continued as the notoriously standoffish Grand Ravine Sect claimed a table and started talking to Tigu, who listened intently.

Another cup of wine was shoved into Xiulan's hand—Xianghua had found her again.

"Drinking contest is starting!" she shouted into Xiulan's face, and started dragging her off.

It was a whirlwind. A sometimes chaotic, confusing mess, as Xiulan slammed back the drinks that were put in front of her.

She didn't realise she had won until Chen Yang held out both arms, presenting her to the crowd; Xianghua doubled over and looked like she was about to—

Xiulan grimaced and patted her back as . . . liquid splattered to the ground. She then staggered to her feet, pleasantly buzzed, and brought her friend to Gou Ren's care. He was sharing drinks with her Petals.

She was so proud of them, performing so well! They were quite reliable! She smiled brilliantly at them all and patted An Ran's head, much to the girl's confusion, before dumping Xianghua into Gou Ren's lap.

She had cleaned up Xianghua's face; *it was fine*.

Xiulan wandered around again; the lights were very floaty and pleasant.

Stalls had popped up around the outskirts. People selling food and drink, with the bold even wading into the gathering of cultivators. Xiulan, with a craving for something greasy, wandered over to one food stand, picking up a large order of . . . meat? *Something* that was rotating on a spit. It smelled heavenly, whatever it was.

She wandered back to the table where she'd left Gou Ren and the Petals, her arms laden with food.

Tigu was shouting excitedly. Yun Ren had his hand on her arm as a blue tattoo scrawled across her shoulder, formed out of an illusion. Several people looked on with amusement as what looked like a mustache formed on her face swiftly afterwards. Xiulan handed Yun and Tigu some food before continuing back towards the table.

She bumped into a very drunk man and they both staggered slightly.

He squinted at her through his bleary eyes and red face.

"Marry me, oh otherworldly and beautiful fairy," he asked dreamily.

Xiulan stared at him.

"Terribly sorry, Miss Cai!" one of the men with him said, pulling at the drunk man's arm.

"Yes, Miss Cai, we'll get him out of your way!"

His friends grabbed the drunk's shoulders and pulled him out of her path.

Such nice fellows.

Xiulan returned to her seat and began distributing the food.

An Ran, her face flushed bright red and her eyes hazy from drink, stared at her. "Marry me, oh otherworldly and beautiful fairy," she slurred.

Xiulan stared at her and shoved a bite of food into An Ran's mouth. Disappointed by the response, An Ran turned to Gou Ren next.

"Marry me, handsome brother," she demanded. Gou Ren grimaced at her sour breath even as his face flushed.

"She's been like this for a while," Huyi muttered, shoving a glass of water into An Ran's hand.

An Ran blinked and turned to him.

"Mar-*hic*-ry me, handsome fish," she hiccuped. Huyi's dead-fish-looking eyes twitched.

Xi Bu, the only one of them who hadn't drunk anything, let out a heavy sigh then picked An Ran up.

"Marry me, cute little one," An Ran muttered, as Xi Bu started walking in the direction of their Sect's manor.

→

The moon was very high in the sky as the world trailed mostly back into focus. A large space had been cleared in the square, free of obstructions. The outskirts were full of clapping revelers, while inside, people danced with abandon. Most looked quite drunk. Xiulan stomped her foot and clapped her hands in time with the music.

She saw Tie Delun boldly approach Tigu, who was on the other side of the circle, still with Yun Ren. Face red, he whispered something in her ear.

Tigu grinned and grabbed the large man's arm.

Xiulan laughed as Tigu jumped into the circle, dragging Tie Delun along with her. The man looked panicked when she started to move, bouncing around with abandon.

Some people pointed and jeered, but most seemed content to watch or chat.

The song petered out, and then an older gentleman took the stage. Wrinkled and toothless, with only a pipa to his name. He grinned through his gums and started to play.

An old song. Old, familiar—nostalgic. It stirred something deep in Xiulan's soul hearing it.

Tigu's dance changed, now looking like she was copying Bi De's dance. The one that Senior Sister had said was from her village.

Tie Delun danced with Tigu. Awkwardly at first, for it was clear they had been taught two different movements to the same song. While Tigu's movements were sharper, more like a flickering flame . . . Delun's was slower. More solid. Halfway between earth and metal.

Xiulan watched the dance fondly, but there was something itching in the back of her mind.

It was rough. It was imperfect. But there was something . . . *magnetic* about it.

Something that drew her in.

Xiulan's feet moved of their own accord. Moving to a dance she knew.

Moving to the dance that the Earth Spirit had taught her.

Wood joined the movements. Slower than fire, but more vigorous than stone. It was a dance she knew by heart. She slotted into the movements perfectly. Like it was made for three.

No . . . this was made for five. Xiulan knew.

Xiulan's focus was on the three of them.

Xianghua joined. Drunk as she was, it wasn't perfect. She was staggering a bit as she danced. It was something Xiulan had seen before, in the villages around the Grass Sea. It flowed and surged like water.

Each step was different, yet in perfect synchrony. Occasionally, their movements would intersect.

The music faded out until the only thing left was the beat.

The world compressed as Xianghua's movements became more sure. Tigu's eyes went blank. Tie Delun's dance smoothed out.

Fire. Earth. Water. Wood.

They moved together in a circle.

Some of the movements were wrong. Some of them were not what they should be. And they were missing metal—

The pounding reached a climax. Their movements synchronised.

There was *something* there.

Their feet slammed into the ground as one.

The song ended.

The spell broke.

The world swam back into focus, and the breaths of all four dancers came out in great gasps.

It had been a spark, a brief connection.

And then it was gone, yet Xiulan herself still felt energised. The old man, however, was just getting started. His fingers began to pluck out a new tune.

Her feet continued their tapping. Her arms moved as she started to flow through the movements.

People joined the circle. People left it—but no trace of metal was to be found.

Xiulan danced until the sun came up, breaking through the sky and appearing framed in between the peaks.

CHAPTER 35

PLUM BLOSSOM CONTEMPLATIONS

Chen Lianji, of the Plum Blossom's Shadow, was nervous. Master Scribe had called a full assembly for the first time in months. Had they failed somehow? Was their lord displeased?

They had found this "Jin Rou." Their Lord had spoken with him, and then he had been spotted leaving the city. Had the meeting gone well? Had something unfortunate happened? They were all questions that had no answers.

There were soft murmurs as they all stood at attention in the hall of the building that had once served as the main base of operation for the Long Knives. It had been taken over, cleaned, and repurposed after the fools had attempted to assassinate Master Scribe. Lianji still remembered the lack of change in their Master's expression as the attack began. A poison smoke bomb had been sealed up with a flick of a finger. Fires extinguished by him merely breathing out through his nose. Knives and darts had been plucked out of the air as soon as they left their owners' hands.

At the end of it, *not a hair was out of place*. Master Scribe only seemed *mildly disappointed* at the men for "acting out" after they had tried to kill him. The best killers and assassins in Pale Moon Lake City were unruly children before Master Scribe.

Lianji shook his head, ridding himself of the image while Master Scribe walked onto the dais, his feet absolutely soundless as always. His aides and top members were with him and all looked pleased.

"We pay our respects to Master Scribe!" the assembled members of the Plum Blossom's Shadow shouted as one, bowing their heads.

Their Lord nodded his head, gazing out over his assembled men. He was stern and proud. Handsome, like he was carved from stone. Yet his eyes were what *truly* set him apart. They were heavy with a weight that sent a thrill through Lianji when he gazed into their resolute depths.

The eyes of a leader. Of a man already looking beyond the horizon.

"Members of the Plum Blossom's Shadow, allow me to begin the meeting with praise." His voice was calm. There were a few breaths of relief, and a few pointed glares at their leaders, who had kept the reason for the meeting a secret. He could see the amused smiles on their faces, at causing their subordinates some grief.

"Performance in this task has been exemplary. Above my expectations. Your loyalty, initiative, and ability deserves reward. Today, we are gathered for those among you who have done the most to receive merit."

Men stood even straighter at that.

One by one men were called up from the ranks to stand in front of their peers, to be praised and given accolades.

Men who had stepped up to speak with an unknown cultivator, who might have objected to their presence. Men of courage. Men who'd had the initiative to contact and include every piece of information, no matter if they thought it was irrelevant.

And then it was Lianji's turn. He had written the main report that his Master had read, organising all the information. An administrative role.

"For the works of Chen Lianji, I award him a first-tier merit and promote him two ranks. His initiative and thoughtfulness should serve as an inspiration to every man in this organisation," Master Scribe declared. Chen Lianji bowed his head, accepting the pouch of money as well as the scroll that detailed his new position.

Not for the first time did Lianji thank his stars that Master Scribe had taken over. He was achieving real rewards. *Actual merit.* True respect.

He finally had a chance to rise, rather than being forced to run drugs or shake down people for protection money.

He was still light-headed as he walked back to his position.

Master Scribe nodded.

"This concludes the awards for merit," he stated, his timeless eyes gazing upon them. All felt their backs straighten.

Their Lord considered them for a moment.

"Now, on to the next step. This mission is accomplished. However, there is much speculation about the man you were tasked to find. And while it is not truly necessary for you to know, curiosity can drive men to foolish endeavours. I believe it best to end such speculative endeavours; there are some facts I will share with you."

A few men shuffled uncomfortably.

No one had actually expected to get answers. That just *didn't happen*. That the Master Scribe was willing to let them see even a fraction of what was going on was a measure of trust few of their number had experienced.

"Jin Rou is an important Junior Brother of mine. It is for this reason he is not to be accosted and the area of Verdant Hill is to be designated as priority. If any undesirables attempt to take root, pluck them out, but otherwise do not delve into his business."

"Yes, Master Scribe!" voices called. *A Junior to Master Scribe?* Murmurs broke out in the crowd as they discussed this development. Their mission had been more important than they'd thought. Any Junior to their Lord would be powerful in his own right—and he was. Did not the Azure Jade Trading Company start asking questions when they involved Master Jin?

Lianji didn't know why the man would have been in hiding, however, to the point where Master Scribe had needed to forge their organisation. Perhaps there was some enemy of Master Scribe afoot? Lianji scowled. An enemy that could force one of Master Scribe's compatriots into hiding would be a powerful foe. Perhaps that was why he'd chosen them? They were certainly more discreet than most of the cultivators Lianji had seen. It opened up more questions than it answered, but Master Scribe's orders were clear. His curiosity would be set aside. Perhaps they were not ready to hear the whole truth yet, but Lianji was satisfied for now.

Master Scribe nodded as the murmuring fell of its own accord. "Excellent. I shall allow your heads to say a few words as well," Master Scribe stated, and stepped back.

Xun Huang, the head of merchant information, stepped forwards.

What followed was more praise and more distribution of merit. The difference was stark. He knew that his previous bosses took them for granted—outside of the few leg-breakers, who were royally rewarded. That they, the ranks, were receiving such attention . . . it made Lianji's heart sing with joy.

Bing Yan of the Underside, his twitchy eyes rolling around, came up next. He was the man who rubbed shoulders with the criminals and who rebuked those who would dare resist their Master's will.

Zhen of the Palace. The plain, unassuming woman with no surname who could intercept transmission stone messages.

And finally, Aiguo Han of the Beggars. The man who had sent his subordinates to be the eyes and ears in the streets. The beggars in particular owed their loyalty to Master Scribe and the Plum Blossoms. Master Scribe had seen a gold mine of information in the poor and destitute, and now the slums and secret places were dyed in the Plum Blossom's colour.

Each boss stepped up. Each boss handed out a reward. Each boss elevated the talents of those beneath them. All the while, Master Scribe looked on in approval.

Until Huang stepped up again.

"Finally we, the Plum Blossom's Shadow, would like to thank our Master Scribe for this test of our abilities. However, we have a burning question: what is the next step that we need to take?" Boss Huang asked, his eyes focused.

"Indeed, Master Scribe, we thank you for this opportunity, but we are eager to receive your orders. We request our next assignment so that we may further your designs!" Zhen implored him.

There were murmurs and nods. That was the consensus among the men. That this mission was a test, or the first of many. For who would craft an entire organisation to find a single man? Master Scribe obviously had some grand design, and they, his instrument, were quite eager to see his will done.

Their Lord considered his underlings. His face was stone as always.

He nodded his head.

"The Azure Jade Trading Company is of importance to my Junior Brother. For now, the goal shall be to integrate yourselves with them and aid their operations."

There were whispers. The Azure Jade Trading Company had been one of the first to use their services, as Master Scribe had defined them. The merchants had been very pleased with their work, driving out the other gangs and making the streets safer for them to conduct their business. A profitable relationship.

After they held up Master Jin, however, their private guards had started stalking around the alleyways, and the leadership of the organisation was asking *very* pointed questions about why they had accosted "Master Jin."

It was good that their interests would align.

Information and trade. Their organisations together would have a grasp upon the entire province.

Their Lord truly was an ambitious man.

"As you command, Master Scribe."

What followed was a grand feast. They ate, they drank, and they were merry, the Master's reward for their service. But he had one more announcement before the end of the night.

"I shall once more be out of the province, as I have some business to attend to," Master Scribe informed them. "It likely will not be for very long, and I shall return soon. Huang will be in charge in the interim. Continue operations here for now. I'll be expecting good news when I return."

"Yes, Master Scribe!" the roar once more went out.

The Plum Blossom's Shadow had its new orders. The Azure Jade Trading Company would come to serve Master Scribe. And from there, the Plum Blossom's Shadow would have the whole of the Azure Hills in their palms.

Lianji basked in the glow, the feeling of being worth something. He spoke with his fellows as they enjoyed themselves. Master Scribe eventually excused himself, leaving his subordinates to it.

But it was still the height of summer, and the room was getting a bit hot. Face flushed with alcohol, he padded out of the big hall and into the courtyard. To his surprise, there was another here.

"Master Scribe?" he asked the man, staring up at the sky in contemplation.

"Yes, Chen Lianji?" his Lord asked, turning from the moonrise. Lianji's eyes widened—Master Scribe remembered his name.

"Uh . . . sorry for interrupting you, Master Scribe. I was just surprised to see you, sir."

Master Scribe considered him for a moment. "I see," he stated simply.

Lianji shuffled uncomfortably under his Lord's gaze, but his mouth got the better of him.

"Ah, Master Scribe, if you do not mind me asking . . . what is it that you were thinking about?"

Master Scribe seemed a bit surprised by Lianji's question. A small, indulgent smile crossed his Lord's face. Like he was entertaining the question of a child.

"Contemplating a task. A long, frustrating, and tedious task," he said before raising an eyebrow. "How would you seek to accomplish a long, difficult task, Chen Lianji?" the man asked.

"Uh . . . my ma always said to start small. Chip away at the base, day by day?" Lianji returned uncertainly. "It'll get finished eventually."

His Master considered him for a moment longer.

"As fine an answer as any, I suppose," he replied, turning once more to the moon. It was a dismissal that even Lianji's tipsy mind could comprehend. But there was one last thing he felt obligated to say.

"And, um, Master Scribe? May you have good fortune on your journey."

His Lord's lip twitched slightly upwards.

↔

Lu Ri's face was fixed in a small smile as he sped across the land, heading back to the Cloudy Sword Sect. Each leap took him across another hill, and each moment brought him closer to the mountain. There were some things that were frustrating, true. Jin Rou having refused to return to the Sect, for one. That Lu Ri was once more a messenger, another.

But he *had* completed his mission. He was not returning empty-handed. He would be able to give his findings to the Masters, and then he might be able to put this frustrating business behind himself.

He took a deep breath as he departed the Azure Hills and traveled into the Howling Fang Mountains. It was the fastest route back to Raging Waterfall Gorge. Qi once more filled his lungs as it ought to the moment he entered the mountain peaks, invigorating and strengthening him—washing away some of the fatigue and bleeding out the tension from his body. He felt as light as a feather. Like he finally could breathe again, after his chest had been crushed by a mountain. That Jin Rou had managed to form his odd cultivation in that place was perplexing, to say the least, but it was not Lu Ri's place to push the issue.

The deprived land of the Azure Hills was . . . a complex issue in his heart. On one hand, he hated the place. On the other . . .

What he had created in the Plum Blossom's Shadow was quite fascinating.

Truly, the Honoured Founders' teachings were sublime. Such loyalty! Such passion! If only his own subordinates at the Sect were half as driven as these mortals, the Cloudy Sword Sect would have never been brought so low in the Elders' eyes!

But it was also shameful that he had hesitated on seeing their passion. He had meant to hand over control of the organisation entirely. Or at least to begin to wean them off his influence.

Yet instead, he'd only half gone through with the plan. With Jin Rou still in the province, Lu Ri might have a need for their abilities in the future.

And . . . he was loath to give them up so easily. They had aided him greatly in finding Jin Rou. To leave them without giving them further guidance sat ill with him. A part of him wanted to see just how far they could go. What could these mortals accomplish, if he continued to give them the Honoured Founders' wisdom?

He pondered what to do as the day wore on. His return was not quite as urgent. Elder Ran had received his message, and Elder Ge was still upon his own quest. Elder Ran had been pleased the subject had been found . . . but still wished for Lu Ri to report in person. Transmission stones were hardly secure.

Still, his mission was currently complete. He knew where Jin Rou was; he had received news that Jin Rou was not coming back to the Sect. Everything else was up to the Elders . . . but he had a feeling his own involvement was not yet finished.

He sighed when he stopped for the night. The stars were brilliant in this section of the Howling Fang Mountains, complementing the cold mountain air perfectly. There was no snow here, yet the vegetation was pale with frost. The hardy trees and plants withstood the conditions, the proud evergreens uncaring of the cold.

Lu Ri settled down to meditate for his rest and took out the gift he had received from his Junior Brother.

An entire jar of maple syrup. It made up for *quite* a bit of the frustration he had felt.

He carefully ladled some out onto the small pieces of bread he had. The almost smoky, savoury-sweet flavour assaulted his tongue. He could put as much as he desired upon his meal, instead of the bare drizzle that was served at the restaurant. And the best part was that it was not even too much of an indulgence. It was not a base luxury, to be avoided, it was also a cultivation aid. There was a quantity of Qi within the syrup. It was noticeable, especially now that he had a greater volume than the tiny amount he had been served in the tea shop.

Enough so that even a cultivator in the Profound Realm could likely derive some use from it. Enough that Lu Ri could benefit eventually, though it would likely take gallons of the stuff before it had any true effect . . . not that he would mind consuming that much. Perhaps he could make a pill out of it? That it was made in the Azure Hills was astounding. And that it was Jin Rou who had made it . . . It was not quite as good as a Lowly Spiritual Herb, but it was still *far* beyond what one could expect in those hills.

He finished his consumption and returned to the lotus position. Then he closed his eyes underneath the stars and took deep breaths of Qi-rich air.

His thoughts wandered back to the scroll he was delivering. His entire mission up until this point.

He, a cultivator of the Cloudy Sword Sect, had been used as a messenger. It should not have been necessary. There should have been another, better way.

Yes, there was the Imperial Army, and there were Imperial Messengers. But both had their own inefficiencies. Sending a message out of the province, especially to a place that wasn't an Imperial Palace, tended to be a bit of a game of chance on whether it would arrive or not—and hellishly expensive besides.

Spirit Beasts. Qi-powered weather. The normal moving and shifting of the world. There were many things that could stop a message from being delivered. There were many improvements that could be made, and many challenges that would have to be overcome. But largely, as long as the palaces remained open to communication and the Sects could be found, there was little initiative to fix or change anything. The system had held together for thousands of years.

Even transmission stones had their problems, with their connection issues. Good messengers were few and far between. It was an inefficiency of the Empire as a whole—spotty transmission stone connections and the slow speed of letters led to vast inefficiencies.

Lu Ri frowned. How could he fix such a thing? Fix it so he wouldn't have to constantly be sent back and forth.

A set of trusted messengers who would be able to deliver things anywhere. But that was a monumental task. To fully create a different system, and test it out . . .

My ma always said to start small. Chip away at the base, day by day.

Lu Ri paused on that thought. He had an organisation eager to prove itself, and a place to test some ideas . . .

A place where he could chip away, day by day, at his leisure.

He considered the merits. It might never amount to anything, and it would require a bit of research, but the idea was intriguing.

He wondered how he was going to create a new postal system.

CHAPTER 36

THE MONKEY'S BUSINESS

I have to admit, I had a bit of a spring in my step as I set off in the direction that Master Fang of the Crystal Emporium had laid out for me. We moved at a decent clip without the cart, eating the distance once more.

I just . . . felt good.

Relaxed, I suppose.

I hadn't had to fight anyone, and while the fact that the Cloudy Sword Sect still had business with me was a bit bothersome, Senior Brother Lu Ri seemed content to let things lie.

There were no threats. There was no face-slapping or grudges to last a thousand years. Just a dude delivering mail.

There was the revelation that Gramps, the old drunkard, was somebody *important*, but I'd cross that bridge when I got to it.

The hills and forests of Pale Moon Lake transitioned to the Grass Sea. Oh, there were still plenty of hills, but they were flatter and smoother, more rolling rather than the enormous mountains in all but name in the north and by Pale Moon Lake.

I'll be honest, I was a sucker for the scenery. The gentle, green rolling hills, the soft grass; it looked near Photoshopped as the grass waved gently in the wind. The prairie back in the Before was the closest thing I could think of to it. There were herds of wild horses running across the hills and towns every five minutes, it seemed. The north was definitely sparser in population.

We were moving at a pretty steady clip. Yin was hopping along, Big D was taking his bounding leaps, and Noodle was curled up with me. It was quite the relief not to haul around the cart. All of them were in good spirits, racing along with me.

I smiled at them.

And maybe I was looking at things with rose-tinted glasses right now, but the three places we had stopped in for the night had all been agreeable. The people were all kind and welcoming, eager to hear stories of the stranger from Pale Moon Lake, or just have a drink with him. The fare was slightly different as well. A lot more beans than I'd been expecting, and even some kind of dish that tasted a lot like chili.

Needless to say, I had picked up some beans for later, as well as their recipe. It was damn tasty for what it was.

Honestly, though? Right now, with the sun on my back and good food in my belly, it felt a bit like I was on vacation. *I'm definitely going to take Meiling down here, even if just to visit.*

I felt an itch in my back and I started slowing down, glancing round at the road we were on and noticing the landmarks.

It was another one of those . . . *things*. I had never been the greatest at reading maps. I had nearly taken a couple of wrong turns getting to the Azure Hills in the first place, and that had been on the main thoroughfares. Here? We were running through oftentimes-unmarked country roads, searching for a spot in a valley to turn off.

But bringing out the map and looking at the hills around us . . . I was certain this was the right place.

Three enormous hills, at the edge of the Northern Grass Sea.

"What do you guys think?" I asked my companions. Noodle squinted at the map, and Big D hopped up onto my shoulder.

'I do believe this is the place, Great Master,' Big D said, and Noodle gave his assent too.

I nodded, and we turned off the road. Our giant strides slowed as we got into the hills. The third one on the left. The one with the ghost of a path leading higher into it.

Master Gen *certainly* lived off the beaten path—not that I could really talk.

If we were not cultivators it would have been a rather arduous climb. Instead, it was a mostly pleasant walk while in the shade of the trees. There was no real sign of human habitation.

It was partway up the hill when things started to change. The hill became rockier and formed into a passageway. A ravine, really.

A ravine that felt a bit . . . *strange*. We stepped forwards, between the two rocks and up the obvious path. For the briefest moment I felt something, like there was cool water on my skin, teasing the edges of my senses, before it faded away.

And then there was colour.

On either side were two giant rocks, perhaps about thirty feet tall. They had a swirling, multicoloured design upon them. It looked, for all the world, like strange ivy, or a thousand types of flowers, but the way it had been "painted" was the interesting part.

There were no brushstrokes. Instead each line, each part of the design, was created by a handprint. Layered on top of each other a hundred, a thousand times.

And not *human* hands either, if I was right. The palm was too long. It was just slightly uncanny, and with the way the fingers looked? *It's probably a monkey's handprint. Or several* hundred *monkeys' handprints.*

'A bit like what Senior Sister Tigu makes,' Yin opined from where she was studying the wall.

"She'd probably like to see this, yeah," I agreed. It did look kind of neat, and it led up into the rocks.

We continued up the hill, the sides of the pathway similarly covered in the whirling designs. I started to get a sense for them. They looked like stylized caves. Stalactites, mushrooms, and waterfalls.

We reached the top of the incline and the passageway seemed to open, revealing a fence. It was much like mine back at home, yet this was absolutely covered in fragments of crystal, hanging from strings.

On that fence was a monkey.

Another golden snub-nosed monkey, like the one Crystal Master Fang had. It was seated on one of the fence posts, scratching at its side, and was wearing a necklace, also made of crystal. It cocked its head to the side curiously when it noticed us staring at it.

It blinked languidly as we approached.

"Good afternoon?" I greeted it, wondering if it was a Spirit Beast. The monkey's eyes held no spark, but neither did Babe's.

The monkey considered us for a moment longer before hopping off the fence. It worked for a second at the other side, and then the gate swung open, letting us in.

If I weren't so used to this kind of stuff, it would have seemed strange. *A monkey butler, welcoming us in.* I snorted with amusement.

Familiar sights and smells welcomed us as we entered the gate. Loamy soil and growing crops.

Beyond the gate was a small farm on top of the hill. It had a small, single-person shack. It reminded me very much of my first house. There were small gardens but no rice paddies. Just the stuff you would need to have fresh greens.

But the house was where the familiarity stopped. There was a large, warehouse-looking building—and a whole lot of crystals.

Water poured out of crystal fragments, flowing like a spring out of the glowing blue pile into small irrigation canals by the gardens. Light was cast by others, like lamps. The trees around the fence and property must have had thousands of small crystal fragments, whether for decorations or something else, I didn't know.

And, of course, the multitude of monkeys hanging out on the roofs, or in some cases, doing the gardening.

The little one who had let us in dashed ahead before stopping at the porch and chittering at a man who was smoking a pipe. He had large sideburns and almost an Afro with how bushy his orange-gold hair was. He was wearing several necklaces and bracelets with small chunks of crystal in them.

"Oh? Visitors?" he asked, turning to face us. He raised a large eyebrow, smiling almost mischievously. "So, are you the ones old Fang sent our way?"

"Unless you were warned to meet anybody else from him," I said. "Rou Jin greets you."

Big D hopped forwards and bowed.

'We pay our respects to Master Gen,' he intoned, with Yin and Noodle also bowing their heads.

The man stared at them, his eyes curious.

"Huh. Well I'll be," he muttered, before shaking his head. "Ah, you've mistaken me, my friends. I am not Master Gen. I am Song Ten, his assistant."

Slowly, the older man got up.

"However, most are not allowed to meet with the Master, so I deal with them. But with Master Fang vouching for you and your companions . . . I do believe an exception can be made. Come, follow me," he said with a bow. A monkey clambered on top of his back.

He entered the house, holding open the door for us . . . and then removed one of the floorboards, revealing a ladder.

With an ease that spoke of doing this hundreds of times before, the spryer-than-expected old man planted his hands and feet on either side of the sturdy metal device and just slid down.

"This way please!" his voice echoed up. With a shrug I followed, sliding down the ladder after him. We emerged into a small hallway, which was glowing bright with crystal and pleasantly cool. But it was kind of a warren. There were holes all over the ceiling and in the walls. Too small for a human . . . *But probably just big enough for one of those monkeys.*

Soon enough we reached a heavy wooden door, which Song opened.

We walked into a cacophony.

Monkeys chattering away as they sorted rocks and crystals. Monkeys chirping as they worked grinding stones. Monkeys letting out loud *whoops* as they pounded at geodes with hammers.

And what looked like monkeys praying to a sarcophagus set into the far wall. Others brought up carts loaded down with dirt or presented picks and hammers to the carved casket, then bowed their heads.

I stopped walking and stared. I often compared my own life to a storybook, with all the talking animals, but this was nuts. They had an entire secret monkey society down here! Monkey miners! Monkey crystal polishers! Monkey blacksmiths.

'Are they all Spirit Beasssssts?' I heard Noodle whisper in confusion.

"No idea . . ." I whispered back.

It was an entire underground workshop, with tunnels leading deeper into the earth.

My eyes landed on one monkey in particular, who had a vest on and a pickaxe over his shoulder, standing on a small dais overlooking the work. His eyes were cold and stern, like a no-nonsense foreman, but he seemed pleased.

'A good haul, brothers and sisters, a good haul!' he shouted. His voice was gruff.

Song politely cleared his throat.

The monkey's gaze levelled upon us. He glanced at me once, then turned his attention to the Spirit Beast companions with me.

He huffed.

"May I present Master Xang Gen Ten, Lord of the Xang Clan," Song declared. The monkey tapped at his throat twice, where there was a small shard of crystal.

"You. You are Jin? Friend of Mengde's Crystal Emporium?" he asked. Not in the odd kind of Qi-speech most Spirit Beasts had, but true, actual speech emanating from the crystal at his throat.

I raised my hands in greeting and bowed. "Yes, Master Gen. This one is Rou Jin," I greeted him politely.

'This one is Fa Bi De,' Big D said, as he bowed his head.

'Liang Yin!'

'Miantiao.'

Master Gen considered us all.

"I see now why he trusted you with our secret. I greet you all, friends of Mengde's Crystal Emporium," he stated, bowing back to us. "Come. Join me. I am not one for ceremony."

He turned and beckoned us up to a second room, where there were a couple of cushions for us to sit on.

"Now, show me this crystal you wish to transfer," he grunted as soon as we were seated. Blunt and to the point. "I have a selection that might be able to aid in this endeavour, but I shall need to see the piece first."

Big D glanced at me, then brought out the crystal, taking it from where it was tied on his back.

Gen's eyes widened. "So, it was no lie. I have seen a crystal of this design only once before." He carefully took it from Big D's wings, staring at it reverently.

He paused as his face shifted into a frown. "Friend Fang did not convey just how *bad* the state of this is, however. Heavens, has it been dropped?"

Big D looked stoically ahead, even as his feet shuffled uncomfortably.

→

Once again, we sat around for several hours while somebody else examined the crystal.

"I can see confusion in your eyes. Speak," the monkey stated as he examined the crystal, glancing up at us.

'Are all out there Spirit Beasts?' Noodle asked, then took a cup of tea from a monkey.

"Not quite," Gen stated. "It is my own cultivation. Near all these crystals, in our ancestor's home, they are nearly aware. About as smart as a human babe, or a bit smarter."

"How did you get involved with the Crystal Emporium?" was my question. It was a bit odd to me. Mining monkeys.

"It was before my time. My own Master was the one who set the deal in place. Both we and the Crystal Emporium just continue it, as we have for a thousand years. Now we supply the majority of the crystals they use, and in return we are defended and left alone."

"Does the barrier have anything to do with that?" I asked, remembering the strange feeling that had washed over me, and the sudden burst of colour in the ravine.

The monkey sighed. "If you have already experienced it, there is no point hiding it. Their founder was the one that crafted the barrier around this place. Any with ill intent are lost, unable to find our home."

In truth, I had no idea if it was strong enough to send off a determined person. I suppose for the Azure Hills it was powerful enough.

"Mengde sends their most promising and loyal students to us. These hills, specifically this hill, have an abundance of crystals. Most are near unusable. Fragments and malformed things, yet there are a lot of them. And for every hundred broken, there is perhaps one suitable to be used. However, that was before this Biyu found out how to use the broken ones. I should like to meet that girl sometime in the future."

We lapsed into silence. Big D pulled out his own map and tapped at where we were, considering it.

We were quite close to the center of this giant formation. Big D quickly marked out several other places, equidistant from this one, around the formation.

He frowned at it. He looked up at Master Gen and seemed to come to a decision.

'There may be more crystals in these locations,' Big D said, sliding the map over to the monkey.

Master Gen paused in his work and picked up the map. His eyes widened when he caught sight of the spiraling formation.

"This . . ." he whispered, before he suddenly stood. He swiftly moved over to a portion of the wall and grabbed a crystal out of the pocket on his vest. Then he pressed it onto the wall, and after a moment, it slid open. After a moment of rummaging around, the monkey turned back to us with an absolutely ancient-looking piece of cloth. Carefully, he spread it out on the table, beside the map.

Upon the piece of cloth was the same spiraling design. Both rooster and monkey stared at the pieces.

"This crystal. It contains the secrets of this formation?" Master Gen asked gruffly.

'We believe so,' Big D said.

The monkey chewed his lip for a moment.

"A trade. If there is any knowledge in this crystal of my Master, that shall be our payment," the monkey demanded.

Bi De considered the bargain. I was keeping out of it, since it was his choice in the end. He glanced back at me once before he nodded.

Master Gen returned to his work with almost feverish energy, his eyes shining.

Eventually, after a small lunch brought to us by another set of monkeys, Gen nodded.

"It can be done. We shall use one of the ancients, from Master's tomb," the monkey said reverently. "However, there are some issues. The transfer may be risky. One of the large issues will be Qi. We shall need a lot of it to complete the transfer. The second . . . Once this starts, there is no going back. We cannot stop halfway through. The choice you must make— The slower route has a higher success rate, I do believe . . . But it is not guaranteed."

'How long would it take if we did it this way, the faster way?' Bi De asked.

"Three days," the monkey replied.

I looked to Big D and shrugged. Three days? We should still be able to make the tournament, and with plenty of time too. If I had my distances right, it would only take a day or two of running to get to the Dueling Peaks . . . less if I really pushed it.

"Your choice," I said to him. A faster, but more dangerous route? Or a slower, steadier one?

Big D considered the crystal.

'I do not know if I will be alive, if it takes the time Master Fang said,' Big D said quietly. *'I, who have lived but two years. The time Master Fang asked for is still unthinkable to me. It may be youthful recklessness . . . but I choose the fast way.'*

CHAPTER 37

THE OLD AND THE NEW

Bi De and Miantiao were silent as they walked together—the usual state of affairs between them. Miantiao was the silent sort, and Bi De just appreciated the snake's company. Miantiao chuckled as Yin provoked the monkeys into play. She bounced up around the trees and onto the roof, much to the creatures' shrieking laughter. Bi De's own Master was deep in conversation with Master Gen, the old monkey gesturing around while he groomed one of the little ones and occasionally reached out to take a puff of his pipe.

It was slightly surreal, Bi De thought, to wander a place that was so similar yet so different from Fa Ram. The ambient Qi here was higher. Spirit Beasts, or at least near-to Spirit Beasts, went about their chores, aiding the human Song Ten.

The monkeys were smart. Yet, like his own offspring, the majority seemed to possess no *true* spark of their own. A duller, quieter thing. Like Chow Ji's minions.

Bi De felt a mild sense of distaste at the servant creatures, yet there was little similarity to those rats so far. The monkeys seemed well cared for, though their personalities were less mischievous than Bi De thought they should be. Another one of the things Bi De *knew*, without ever having to learn it. The beasts here, however, were relatively serious and industrious, tending to the mines and even communicating by signing with their hands in addition to their usual calls and body language.

The ones beneath the ground universally wore helmets and had trinkets of crystal upon them, crafted lovingly by other monkeys.

He had now encountered three beasts that had power over their own kin: Chow Ji, the wolf who had terrorized his student's village, and now Master Gen. Bi De wondered if he had the same ability—to command the lesser chickens.

He did not know. He had never actually tried giving them orders like he witnessed. Could he infuse them more with his strength? An interesting question to explore later.

Bi De and Miantiao wandered the outskirts of this place, this Crystal Hill, as Master Gen named it. The day was nearing its end and they were all resting. Master Gen had started crafting the formation, poring over scrolls so old they nearly were dust, then copying out the arcane runes that made Bi De's head hurt just looking at them. He also required them to infuse their Qi into the array.

It was a task that was boring and draining in equal measure. But that was the trade-off, time for risk.

In the end, it was not a choice at all.

Thirty changings of the season. Thirty winters. Thirty years. Bi De . . . Bi De could not comprehend it. He knew of cycles. He knew of time. Yet so much had changed in but two years. He could not imagine the transformation in thirty. He remembered the burnt-out villages he had seen. Miantiao's own decade of vengeance. Would Bi De still be around in ten years? He dearly hoped so.

And then, if something went wrong, and the repair did not work . . . he would have waited thirty years for failure anyway.

He wanted to know what this formation was all about. What had caused the calamity.

At first, it had merely been about the dances. Curiosity. What did they do? He saw only a small portion of the formation and assumed it whole. His whole journey had been intended to be a short pursuit to learn and grow. But now . . . that was no longer the case. The dances and formation were connected to those past visions. The calamity that had burned the province to cinders.

He would learn what had happened. And after that, he had one goal: *to never let it happen again.*

If it did occur, then it might swallow up Fa Ram, or Hong Yaowu, or the Correct Location Eight.

The array was dead and mouldering. It had been for thousands of years. Reclaimed by nature. Taken over by Spirit Beasts.

But the images he had seen were too vivid. They were too painful to ignore.

So he would learn this crystal's secrets. He would study them and not allow the mistakes of the past to come forth once more. Even if he had to uproot every single stone and change the dances that had been taught for longer than there was memory.

He stopped at the edge of the small farm, at their own Great Pillars, which were covered in old ropes and pieces of crystal.

Some form of protection. Bi De could feel little from it. He hadn't truly noticed it. There had been a slight tingle on the edge of his senses, but nothing that had made him stop and take notice.

'An interesting construction. Ussseful to keep those unwanted out,' Miantiao whispered from beside Bi De, staring at the crystals. Bi De knew his regrets—and his interest—well. If Miantiao's village had had this, then Sun Ken never would have slaughtered the inhabitants or ended Miantiao's Master.

Bi De was interested but skeptical. It seemed too good to be true.

"It's quite something, isn't it?" Song Ten asked as he approached them. A small blue face poked up over his shoulder. The man and the monkey looked at them with interest.

'Indeed. How does one make such a formation?' Miantiao asked.

Song Ten puffed at his pipe. He looked at the formation, considering it.

"I have no idea," he stated simply.

Miantiao blinked. *'What?'* the snake asked, confused.

"We maintain it the best we can. But if there is a record on how it was created, such a thing was never left for us. Or Master Gen. We know not all the materials, or the basis for the ritual, or the full requirements for the alignment of the crystals . . ." Song Ten sighed and shrugged.

'But could you not try to re-create this place, using what you do know?' Bi De asked.

Song Ten shook his head. "I've tried a hundred times. Nothing. It kept failing. It's what brought me here in the first place, to swear my oaths to Master Gen, yet I'm no closer now after forty years than I was at the beginning."

Both Bi De and Miantiao considered the man's words.

"In my time with Master Gen, one thing has become clear. *Time degrades all things.* The wonder of the past is never to be remade. All we can do is study their work and hope to ape a fraction of their glory." He flashed a sardonic little smirk. "The crystals of the past were larger. They were better, with fewer defects. You know it yourself. The recording crystal that you brought is far beyond the quality these hills produce nowadays."

Was that true? Bi De frowned. The great formation had spanned the entirety of the hills. The powerful crystals had been abundant. The visions that he had from the crystal they were trying to fix had been of an Empire rich in treasures and Qi. Song Ten's words were not entirely false, were they? They were lesser than the past.

Song Ten looked at Bi De's considering expression. "There used to be hundreds of Spirit Beasts here, or so the tales say. They could even transform into humans. Many left, to either travel outside the province or live among the people. Yet now . . . all that's left is this."

He gestured forwards out into the lands. The wind blew through the trees. Like so many places in the Azure Hills, it was a remnant of what had come before.

Song Ten looked melancholic. "I do hope you find some value in that crystal of yours. The profound wisdom of the ancients always does surpass ours."

Bi De frowned at the ancient formation. Some of Song Ten's words were true. Yet . . . they had one flaw. He turned back to his Great Master—who had a monkey on his back going through his hair while he himself picked through the fur of another. Several were hanging off his arms, and two were using his feet for seats.

Song Ten snorted at the view as Master Gen watched over them and puffed away on his pipe.

'With respect, Master Song Ten, I do not believe the past is always the pinnacle. I think that they may have grown to a lofty height . . . But in time we may be able to surpass it. After all, I know a Spirit Beast who has turned into a human, and that took less than a year.'

Song Ten puffed at his pipe, considering Bi De's words.

"I'll believe it when I see it," he finally said, shaking his head.

There was a call for dinner as a monkey wearing an apron walked awkwardly out of the house, much to the Great Master's amusement.

Bi De let out a breath and looked up at the sky. Tomorrow was another full day of work upon the formation before the transfer could begin.

Hopefully it would end well. Hopefully he would have his answers and then he would see his companions again. His Great Master had said that after this they would be travelling to the Dueling Peaks.

A tournament. A place to battle. Tigu was likely enjoying herself greatly, surrounded by others who wished to fight.

↔

Tigu was on the edge of her seat as she watched the arena below her. Qi swirled around the combatants. Their faces were masks of concentration as they gave it their all, battling their enemy.

Yet one of them had a lapse in concentration.

The young man's eyes bugged out as the Qi surged out of control and the pill furnace started to shake and rattle.

He shoved it off the bench and dove to the side behind the wall. The pill furnace hit the bottom of the ditch constructed for this purpose—yet instead of simply cracking and setting off a muffled *whump* like what had happened to the previous contestant, its bottom blew off and sent the tumbling furnace straight up into the air, where it then exploded in a flash of red light.

"He tried to speed up the process and took a calculated risk! But I do declare he needs to study his math formations more!" the Announcer Man cackled as the crowd howled with laughter. "I think that's the best one we've had yet!"

"This is great," Gou Ren said excitedly, as he shoved more food into his mouth. He wasn't as bothered by the presence of Damp Pond . . . and neither was the Smaller Blade of Grass. But that was mostly because the woman looked like death had walked over her grave—she was wincing at every explosion. The rest of the Petals were back at the house and looking terribly defeated. Tigu had seen their expressions before, when the guests had come for her Master's wedding. It was a "hangover," an ailment that Ri Zu had said there was no cure for—a truly debilitating and insidious affliction!

"I think they saw that one in Pale Moon Lake City!" the Announcer Man shouted as yet another furnace exploded.

Tigu laughed and cheered along with the Xong brothers. This was spectacularly exciting, and the Announcer Man's commentary was making it even better. There was Qi and explosions. It was no real fight, but it was fun.

Ri Zu didn't seem to think so, though. She had found out there were pill furnaces involved and refused to come, instead staying at the house with the rest of the groaning Petals so she could look over her medical scrolls. From what Tigu had seen, she was looking at the structure of legs and making notes.

Ri Zu had said she would be introducing herself to Damp Pond and her little brother soon. Tigu was quite proud of her!

But there was one small blemish on things.

"I wish the Master were here," Tigu shouted above the crowd to Xiulan. "He would enjoy this a lot."

Xiulan chuckled as the top of a pill furnace burst open, belching out even more smoke than Damp Pond's steam furnace. "Yes, I think Master Jin would like this very much," she agreed.

They settled in for the rest of the day. They met up with Loud Boy again, as well as Rags and Handsome Man, to go see the performance that was on that night.

The Tale of the First Emperor was *way* cooler than Tigu had thought it would be. The sets were fantastic! They had carved and painted backgrounds that the performers could spin, to make the background appear like different places. The clothes were quite appealing too!

↔

A man watched a recording. His eyes were focused on it completely. The movements. The positions of her arms.

The feral eyes. The look of glee on her face as she battered her opponent into submission. Lu Ban smiled. Yes, she was perfect. Well, not *perfect.* She would need some work first, to properly cultivate that violence. But she had potential. The way her eyes narrowed into slits and her body contorted. And she was in the category of the sectless. She was sure to jump at his offer.

Rou Tigu was, as far as Lu Ban was concerned, even better than Cai Xiulan. This trip had not been wasted after all.

Lu Ban smiled, even when there came a knock on his door.

"Young Master, the report you asked for." Chang's voice carried through the wall.

"You may enter," he stated, resetting the recording to the beginning. "Anything?" he asked, affecting boredom—like he wasn't eager to know more about his future acquisitions. Cai Xiulan he would have his fun with, then consume, while Rou Tigu would make a fine attack dog with a bit of coaxing. Truly the heavens were smiling upon him.

"They did not seem aware of my observance, Young Master. There was little of note. She is from the north of the province. However, Rou Tigu did mention a Master during my observation. Cai Xiulan referred to him as Master Jin," Chang said, bowing his head.

Lu Ban's hand spasmed. "Master Jin?" he asked, his good mood immediately dying.

From the north. North, where he had been humiliated. Humiliated by a *Jin.*

"Yes, Young Master."

Lu Ban's hand started shaking as he clenched his fists.

"I see. Leave."

Master Jin.

"Do you know a Jin Rou?" the man in his room had demanded several weeks back, intent flooding out of his body. His eyes were cold and resolute, like the face of a mountain that rose above the clouds.

Rou Tigu. Master Jin. Master Jin Rou? Rou Jin?

He clenched his fists until the shaking stopped.

Blood dripped to the floor, where his fingernails had cut the skin.

CHAPTER 38

THE TALLEST BLADE OF GRASS

Cai Xi Kong, Grandmaster of the Verdant Blade Sect, had almost completely calmed his beating heart. Beside him, his cousin's breath was heavy. Yi's stern face was hard as he collected himself, seated to Xi Kong's right. Lifting the Earthly Arena was always difficult. Managing the enormous chains, locking in the support pillars . . . In truth, the defeated contestants did little. Lifting hundreds of thousands of tons of stone as well as a hundred thousand people was *quite* beyond the younger generation, especially when after their fights they were usually injured and out of Qi. Instead, it was the Elders who did the majority of the lifting—Elders from every Sect, allowing the younger generation to stand upon their shoulders and benefit from their abilities.

Or at least that was how Xi Kong saw it. He glanced around at the closed eyes of his fellows while he tried to project an air of serenity—every person sitting around this table acted as if they felt nothing from raising the arena.

Though this place always put him a bit on edge. The Dueling Peaks' Grand Hall was an ancient place. Its air was still and quiet, oppressive with the weight of eons. Tapestries thousands of years old hung on the walls. Some had long since degraded to the point of illegibility, while others remained as vibrant as if they had been crafted yesterday. The enormous stone table had evidence that it had once been painted, but that had long since disappeared.

One wall was completely made of crystal. It was a device that recorded every single fight that took place here, a repository of knowledge . . . or it would be. It only worked some of the time nowadays; the recordings were grainy and tended to cut out.

Xi Kong much preferred the Azure Sky Summit. The mountain was cold and the ruins old, but somehow they felt less unnerving, less dead than this place, deep in the Dueling Peaks' heart.

The majority of his contemporaries were deep in thought. Two contestants were left. At the start of the year, Guo Daxian had been the clear favourite to win—the Grand Ravine Sect usually won. It was just a matter of who took second place. Yet now, every other power had been defeated. Only his own Verdant Blade Sect, and a girl who had entered as an independent but obviously had a backer of some sort from the symbol on her shirt, were all that were left.

It had been the topic of much discussion, that much Xi Kong knew. Discussion and furtive glances, as Rou Tigu was staying at the Verdant Blade Sect's manor.

While the younger generation honed their strength, the Elders meditated and engaged in politics. Such things were frustrating at the best of times. Long meetings were spent drinking tea and talking. And about such mundane things too. The trade agreements and territory disputes were generally settled at the Azure Sky Summit, while the talks in the Dueling Peaks were generally of gossip and the occasional marriage alliance.

Finally, there was a sigh from the head of the table. The strongest Sect claimed that right, and Guo Daxian the Sixteenth was one of the strongest. Or at least his father was, the only Elder who was at the cusp of the Spiritual Realm . . . and had been there for over three hundred years.

It was time for the meeting to truly begin.

"Onto the suggestions put forwards by the Tournament Commission, we shall take a tally. His Imperial Majesty's Director for Spiritual Ascension Affairs has raised concerns about the presence of a disciple in the Profound Realm in the tournament. He states that the prize is useless to them, so they had no need to enter, skewing the fights and unfairly suppressing others. He politely suggests that we consider those in the Profound Realm be banned from competing, to preserve the integrity of the tournament," Guo Daxian stated with a slight smirk.

There were immediate whispers from all around. It was a good point, Xi Kong mused, from a mortal point of view. To a cultivator, however?

There was a contemptuous snort from Elder Sheng of the Azure Horizon Sect. "How foolish. Who has ever heard of a tournament with a cutoff for one whose strength was too *great*?" Sheng asked, his eyes narrow.

"None. There is no precedent for such a thing. Tradition is tradition, as Kongzi the Wise holds true. The wisdom of the ancestors should prevail," another elder said simply.

"Why would we chastise a promising disciple for growing too strong?" another Elder, of the Rumbling Earth Sect, said while stroking his beard. "It is true that Cai Xiulan, or any in the Profound Realm, would derive little use from the prize . . . but the prestige of winning the tournament and ascending so high is great indeed."

"Most tournaments are self-regulating. Who would join a tournament for a prize worthless to them? It is a rare case when such things happen. And even then, one usually uses this opportunity to crush their enemies, but such a thing is foolish and invites retaliation. Even the courtesy of Elders may be strained by such an event," Chen Tai of the Framed Sun Sect stated, referencing the generally accepted courtesy that Elders did not involve themselves in the disputes of the younger generation.

"He asks for fairness, yet the world is inherently unfair," another added.

Guo Daxian snorted. "All in favour of this measure?"

No hands rose. Why would they, when next time it could be their Sect's time in the heavens?

"It is rejected, then. On to the next matter . . ." Daxian stated. He raised a hand, lazing as he was in the stone chair, and an image formed of the rows that their Sects would stand in. "Speak now if anyone has an objection to the final arrangement for the closing ceremony."

There was a brief discussion before the arrangement was accepted.

That was how the hours went. A matter was brought up, a matter was decided upon. Minutiae, proposals, rarely was the decision of anything of worth—yet it was something they all participated in anyway.

→

After their discussion ended, they entered a different hall, adjacent to the main one. The atmosphere was a bit more relaxed, and they settled into separate tables to mingle and discuss things. There was a recording playing of Xiulan and Guo Daxian the Junior's battle. Xiulan's serene expression warmed Xi Kong's heart, and he couldn't help but smile when his contemporaries searched for weakness. They found none. His daughter had grown magnificently, rising up like one of their ancestors.

"The heavens have truly smiled upon the Verdant Blade Sect," Elder Bingwen of the Misty Lake Sect intoned, lowering his head in acknowledgement with a soft smile on his face. Xi Kong nodded back at his ally. There had been a small stir when Bingwen had appeared instead of Liu Xiang. It was not something Xi Kong had expected. Liu Xiang had always been an honourable man when they worked together.

He wondered about the relationship between their Sects . . . but Bingwen had been quick to assure him nothing had changed. In fact, the man was quite eager to strengthen ties and had proposed some joint exercises between their disciples.

The Verdant Blade and the Misty Lake Sects sat with each other, and all eyes were upon them.

The Verdant Blade was ascendant—and their allies as well, if they could make more of those strange pill furnaces. Calculation and envy gleamed in the other's eyes.

And marriage offers for his daughter. The answer had been the same three times.

"She is at a critical stage in her cultivation and needs no distractions."

Yi had complained, but that was one thing Xi Kong would not budge on. Even if the Grand Ravine Sect itself were to make him an offer.

"Indeed, it would seem they have. We are blessed with a dutiful daughter and skilled initiates to our Sect."

"Indeed, indeed," Bingwen mused. "And an ally as well in Rou Tigu. Do you think she would be amenable to visiting the Misty Lake Sect in the future?" he asked casually.

Xi Kong held back a sigh of irritation at Bingwen's inquiry. Though they were allies, that was a tricky question.

"I shall see if she is amenable . . ." he said, but had little desire to push the issue with the girl. "However, she—"

He was interrupted by a small commotion. A disciple of the Grand Ravine Sect, one of the older ones, stepped into the room and whispered something to his Master.

Guo Daxian's eyebrow rose.

Another disciple entered, this time of the Framed Sun Sect, and whispered in *his* Master's ear.

Now Xi Kong was intrigued.

Which was when a member of his own Sect, Bolin, entered. He seemed quite amused.

"In the central square, Master. I think it is something you should see," he whispered in Xi Kong's ear.

It was evidently nothing urgent, yet as more older disciples entered some Elders started to rise.

They ventured into the city, following the shouts and pounding music.

The Elders descended onto the rooftops and alighted on lantern poles. They gazed imperiously down at the younger generation.

What he beheld sent a surge of shock through the all the Elders present.

Guo Daxian was chatting almost amicably with Rou Tigu, reaching out to ruffle her hair while his cheeks were flushed red from how deep in his cups he was.

Chen Yang of the Framed Sun Sect was singing badly to the Young Mistress of Raging River Sect, while two young cultivators had their arms on a barrel, wrestling for control.

It was organised chaos. It was a mishmash of every Sect colour and disciple. Quite frankly, it was a miracle a fight hadn't broken out yet.

"The hells?" Xi Kong heard one Elder mutter, a bewildered expression on his face. Even Xi Kong was quite bemused by the whole thing.

It was . . . Well, it was the passion of youth, to do the unexpected. The reaction from the other Elders was mixed. Some frowned at how loose their disciples had gotten. Some looked on, amused at the folly of the youth. Most . . . most either shook their heads with exasperation or stared in contemplation at the party below.

But none interrupted. It was not the Elders' place to interrupt them. Just as they rarely interfered in fights, this was part of the unwritten rules.

Even if two Elders' eyes twitched as they stared at two disciples from different Sects competing to see how far down each other's throats their tongues could go.

His own Elders were mostly neutral, though Yi had a disapproving frown. Which was normal—his sworn brother disliked most things that people enjoyed. He was morose by nature, paranoid at times, and Xi Kong had to admit, kind of an asshole—but Yi had stuck by his side, watching his back for decades, even through the worst things they had experienced. Xi Kong shook his head and turned back to the disciples.

Something had happened here. The normal groups of alliances had broken down. Enemies sat together, drinking and cheering.

Xi Kong's eyes were drawn to the center of the crowd . . . the center of the crowd, where a ring had formed, centered around his daughter.

Xiulan was smiling.

Genuinely smiling as she danced.

He drank the image in. The look of absolute peace on his daughter's face melted his heart.

Few—if any—below noticed them.

Slowly, the Elders turned to leave. There would either be scolding or praise in the morning, for most of them.

CHAPTER 39

STEPS CLAD IN GOLD

There was a *click*. Then, once more, connection. A girl wearing a yellow helmet panted with exertion, yet smiled at the little pristine golden pathway she had made. She was getting better at this.

This part of the road . . . it was bad. Terrible. It was some of the worst she had seen. Well, that wasn't quite true. There was a patch near where the Connected One, her Connected One, had gone, near that cursed lake, where there was just nothing left at all. There, the road was so torn and shattered there was no trace, save for where the web abruptly ended.

Here? Well, there were at least bits left.

Lots and lots of little bits.

And farther in . . . broken roads. Roads like the ones near her home, shattered into a thousand pieces and torn to shreds, barely leaking drops of energy they were supposed to be full of.

A part of herself. A part that she had only the most tenuous of connections to, but she knew if she went any farther with her road, the pieces would connect.

And a part of herself would slot into place.

She reached out a hand.

Painterrorscaredbetrayedwhywhywhy

She clenched her fist and grimaced, pulling back. She staggered backwards, then bumped up against a massive body.

The enormous boar made of earth chuffed with concern, a yellow helm also covering his head.

The girl grumbled and pressed her face into the boar's flank, drawing comfort from it. Her trusty steed rumbled comfortingly, nuzzling at her.

The girl climbed onto his snout and Chun Ke lifted his head obligingly, allowing her to roll onto his back.

She curled up into a ball and pulled the helmet off her head. It was kind of uncomfortable, with its odd brim and bright colours.

'Hardhat protect Big Little Sister's melon. Big Little Sister is building, needs hat,' the boar had declared authoritatively. So, she had made them. Made them of bits of herself, and of her Qi. "Boss," the character on the front said.

An amusing distraction.

The girl sighed with frustration, dropping the yellow thing onto her face.

'Is scary and painful?' the boar rumbled beneath her.

"Yeah," the girl whispered to him. "It's scary. But . . . I should . . . I should get this over with. I need to . . ."

The boar shook his head. *'Is fine. Take slow. Big Little Sister go at her own pace. And when ready . . . family and friends go help as we can.'*

Her fists clenched the rust-red grass that made up his coat, and she bit her lip.

'Besides, Chun Ke bonk head like what you did to Pretty Flower and Tigu'er if you go too fast. Not good to not follow one's own words.'

The girl laughed despite herself. "Oh? You seek to challenge my skull?"

'Chun Ke head like rock. Will win!' The boar chuckled merrily.

The little girl slapped the boar's stone back and rolled, laughing with him until their merriment petered out.

'Big Little Sister is with Big Brother now . . . how about we go ahead a bit? Meet with Tigu'er, Rizzu, Little Brother Gou, Pretty Flower, and Yun. Make path for Big Brother this time, instead of the other way around?' Chun Ke asked her.

The girl mulled over the question. They weren't her Connected Ones, but . . . well . . .

Gou Ren ruffling her hair and giving her piggyback rides . . . before throwing her in a mud pit.

The dreams of a boy haunted by a fox spirit and a sword he didn't notice. They watched over him with fond eyes, as he showed her his latest masterpiece.

A silly cat, with the same wish she had once had.

A dancer, who didn't know how to dance properly.

Her people.

The girl hopped off the boar's back and shoved her helmet back on her head. The boar sniffed the air.

"That way," he declared, pointing with his snout.

The little girl nodded and took a step forwards, into the darkness.

Each step was traced in gold.

□

The night spent on Crystal Hill was pretty peaceful, save for the fact that a bunch of monkeys decided I looked very pillow-shaped.

It probably would have been unbearably hot—if that stuff didn't bother me anymore unless I really thought about it. The heat, the humidity, even the cold . . . I could feel it, and feel when things were nice, but I didn't really sweat or experience the heat unless I was *really* working.

Then again, I could also reach straight into ovens or swim in frozen lakes with no trouble, so it wasn't *that* surprising.

And in the morning, I got treated to a little bit of a childhood dream of mine.

Monkey butlers.

Well, not *really* monkey butlers, but a pack of monkeys starting cooking fires and chopping ingredients under the watchful eye of Song Ten. It was like Xiulan's blade symphony in the mornings, or Wa Shi setting out all the ingredients.

I tried to help . . . but I got waved back to the table, as I was a guest.

Instead, Noodle, Big D, and I went over the formation with Master Gen. He had completed the rough part of it overnight. Apparently, it had mostly been done already, so he was just using a tweaked version of one of his Master's designs.

"So, do we agree on this design?" Master Gen asked.

I looked at it closely. There wasn't anything obvious that I could see that was off. Rou didn't have a particularly strong grounding in formations, and neither did I, but racking his memories let us understand a bit of it. Gramps had mostly taught him how to recognise things that would hurt him and how to break certain points on them, rather than how they worked and how to put them together. And all of Rou's knowledge on it was *theoretical* at best.

I nodded. "You know, I was expecting you to be a bit more cagey with this information," I said to the boss monkey as a couple of the babies combed through my hair. The little brats had decided I was a jungle gym, though I didn't really mind. The gruff Master Gen seemed to be warming up to me, at least a little bit. He snorted as Yin dashed across the room, chased by a small horde of monkeys, hooting and hollering.

Cute little things.

Master Gen looked at the scroll. "Master was adamant that all formations that take as much Qi as this will be checked over by both parties. He said it was too easy to slip something in if a person was unscrupulous."

Well, that was the paranoid cultivator mindset, but . . . I mean, I couldn't really blame that. It was a good idea, and seeing as I was going to be hooked into it, I would have to make sure it wasn't doing anything bad.

It looked like I was gonna be a battery again.

"Then we shall begin the construction of the array," the gruff, no-nonsense monkey declared. He took a drag on his pipe, and then his eyes changed subtly.

'I ask for my kin. Who will hear this call?' he "said," reverting to the Qi-speech. His voice echoed oddly.

The monkeys around us perked up, like they had been jolted by lightning. They seemed to oscillate wildly between being . . . well, monkeys, and being as coordinated as a human. A spark of *something* bled into the eyes of a few of them.

His call was answered. Swiftly, ten monkeys lined up, carrying picks and chisels.

'Hai Ten, Feng Ten, Po Ten, Li Ten . . .' The old monkey whispered the names fondly as he got up, walking over to them and clapping each on the shoulder in turn. *'Thank you.'*

'This ability . . . I must confess my ignorance of how it works,' Big D observed.

Master Gen looked upon the monkeys, which were *almost* Spirit Beasts. "It is a stirring of the soul. It may be used for control . . . but I am no emperor. They are my family. To control them, to sacrifice them on a whim? It would be an unforgivable sin."

Big D stared at the monkey for a moment before bowing his head and raising his wings in respect.

'I appreciate you enlightening me, Master Gen,' the rooster intoned.

Master Gen coughed, seeming slightly embarrassed. "Now, enough of this. This ritual must be performed in a specific place. We must go to the underground."

Big D winced.

→

It was a long way down.

We entered the workshop again, and then into one of the tunnels beyond that.

The tunnels that had largely been built for creatures barely three feet tall.

I was six foot two and . . . well, *bulky*.

At least I wasn't alone in my claustrophobia. Big D didn't look particularly enthusiastic about being down here either, though Yin and Noodle were unconcerned.

Some parts I got to stand up in when the ceiling expanded.

Most of the tunnels down this way were lit by crystals, though there were long stretches of darkness and those were illuminated by mushrooms of all things.

Glowing mushrooms ran the colours of the rainbow, growing from the walls and floor. They had an almost neon hue, like a synthwave album cover, or those glow-in-the-dark mini golf places. Absently, I tapped one of them and a shimmer of spores came off, glowing in the darkness and coating my finger.

"Are these edible?" I asked curiously, hoping to distract myself.

Master Gen paused in his forward march and plucked one off the wall. "They are not poisonous . . . but they do not taste particularly good." With a shrug he bit into it and drops of glowing purple, almost inklike ichor, splattered on the ground.

He chewed and swallowed before opening his mouth and revealing that it was glowing.

I chuckled and pulled the mushroom off the wall.

It tasted a bit like . . . well, kind of like chewing on leather. Slimy leather. With an undertone of that goop toy that used to be super popular—yes, to my shame, I know *exactly* what that tastes like.

Yeah . . . definitely not eating these too often. But now I have a glowing green mouth, so I was obviously the winner here.

And then Yin started purposefully rubbing against them so her fur was streaked neon. I grinned at the rabbit and she giggled, then started painting on Big D's feathers. He was distracted enough not to really notice.

"Just a bit farther," Master Gen said, smiling with neon teeth shining in the dark.

We just had a couple more squeezes until we were through.

Naturally, that was when I got a bit stuck.

Panic surged in my throat, and I took a breath at the sudden tight feeling around my chest—the stone cracked and crumbled, bedrock crumbling into dust from me *breathing in.*

Luckily, without collapsing the tunnel.

I swallowed thickly.

"Everything all right back there?" Master Gen asked.

I glanced back down at Noodle, who raised his good eyebrow.

"Great! Everything's good!" I called back while I went around the last bend, then took in the area.

My jaw dropped.

There was a *jungle* underground.

I saw massive ferns with fronds so big they could be used as blankets. Carpets of moss covered the ground, forming a soft and springy carpet under our feet. Waterfalls spilled down the walls, kicking up clouds of mist and making the air so humid that water would condense on your skin.

The ceiling was dominated by a set of enormous light crystals, so bright and shiny that you might think you were outside under the sun.

Finally, there was a space in the center of the rivers, directly underneath the center of the crystals in the roughly circular room.

I let out a whistle. Master Gen was frowning at the ceiling.

"A bit brighter than usual . . ." he muttered before shaking his head. "This is where we shall perform the transfer."

Master Gen pulled out his scroll, concentrated on the formation on the page, and then closed his eyes.

The monkeys perked up, just like they had when Master Gen called them.

'This is what needs to be done, my brothers and sisters.'

Picks were unlimbered from their straps. Chisels prepared. Master Gen pulled his helmet onto his head.

The monkeys began their work.

□

The restaurant was once more crowded and busy when they sat down for their evening meal. Xiulan passed some of the wine to An Ran.

"Have you never seen that play?" Huyi asked Yun Ren, who was looking at his recording crystal.

"Nah. We live too far away from the cities. We only get puppet shows, if that," he said. "Those costumes were great, though."

"Yes, the colours were commendable! Bright Smile, that was the founding of your Sect?" Tigu shouted across the hall.

"It was! Quite the tale, wasn't it? My Honoured Ancestor had quite a wonderful way with words!" Chen Yang of the Framed Sun Sect shouted from his own table.

"Didn't he also write 'The Wind Blows'?" Guo Daxian heckled. Xiulan snorted at the mention of the crude poem.

"Lies and slander!" Chen Yang roared.

"'I have two mouths and two voices, one speaks willingly, the other without my consent . . .'" Daxian started, earning him several chuckles.

"It has no name on it! How can anybody think that the venerable wordsmith would be so crude?!" Chen Yang whined.

Yun Ren shook his head, a grin on his face. "We could try our own production at some point. My images would make for fantastic sets."

"Maybe we could do a production of the Demon-Slaying Orchid," Gou Ren said, needling Xiulan. She glared at the cheeky grin on his face.

Tigu perked up. "Ah, I can portray her perfectly!" She shouted before grabbing several of the baozi on the table and stuffing them down her shirt. "Behold! I am the Demon-Slaying Orchid!"

Xiulan stared at Tigu's suddenly bulging chest and haughty expression. It worked . . . surprisingly well on her.

"You need a few more in there," Xianghua said, her lips twitching as she shot a glance at Xiulan's chest.

Xiulan palmed her face.

She enjoyed these fools . . . *most* of the time.

Tie Delun and Loud Boy came over to talk to Tigu. Guo Daxian kept the argument running with Chen Yang for far too long. Gou Ren finally gave up and opened his mouth, about to accept an offering from a triumphant Xianghua . . . when Xiulan beat her to the punch, shoving one of her dumplings into his mouth and making him choke.

"So, what are we doing tomorrow?" Tigu asked excitedly as they walked back to the manor. Xianghua and her brother had walked away, leaving only the members of the Verdant Blade Sect and companions. "Rags and Loud Boy want to go gambling!"

"You're *not* going gambling!" Yun Ren and Huyi both yelped.

Xiulan rolled her eyes as Tigu started complaining, then caught a glimpse of Gou Ren, who was walking slightly slower than everybody else. He appeared contemplative.

"A coin for your thoughts, Junior Brother?" Xiulan asked.

Gou Ren startled, glancing over at Xiulan, before looking at the backs of everybody else. A soft smile stole across his face.

"They aren't worth much. I was just thinkin' about the tournament. It's been fun. I'm glad I came."

Xiulan smiled at his words. "I'm glad you are here too. Yun Ren, Ri Zu . . . even Tigu," she jabbed.

Gou Ren chuckled.

→

The manor was quiet when they arrived after the evening drew to a close and everyone returned to their Sects. Quiet, save for Bolin, her father's man, who waved Xiulan over.

"The Elders wish to speak with you, Young Mistress," he whispered in her ear.

Xiulan sighed and nodded.

She waved her companions good night, then entered the main building.

CHAPTER 40

SOWING SEEDS

Xiulan walked into the meeting room and bowed to her Elders. They were arranged as they always were, her father at the head of the room and the other Elders flanking him. But there was something subtly off about their demeanour. Her father especially almost seemed annoyed, before his face smoothed out and he acknowledged her.

"Forgive us old men for calling you so late in the day, Daughter," he stared off, "but there are things that need to be addressed."

"As the Elders will," she stated formally.

"First, we wish to congratulate you, Disciple. Reaching the final round of the tournament is no easy feat, and we applaud your strength." Her father's voice was formal and full of warmth at her accomplishment. He gazed upon her with pride . . . before he glanced out of the sides of his eyes at the other Elders. They nodded along at his words, then Cai Xi Kong straightened his back and looked directly at Xiulan.

"The hour of the final bout draws near, Disciple, and though we have no doubt about your ability . . . our Honoured Elders have a few questions about . . . decorum." His voice was stern and firm.

Xiulan sat up a tiny bit straighter in surprise and opened her mouth to answer, but then Elder Yi interjected.

"We have observed you, these past days. It does a warrior no good to be lax. Especially for one to be getting drunk and gallivanting off with other Sects. This is not the way the Verdant Blade Sect does things."

Xiulan's face flushed red in anger at Yi's words. But with that rage came a twinge of guilt at an Elder stating it so openly. She had been drinking and relaxing instead of cultivating. Was it that obvious? Was it that worthy of rebuke?

"I am fully confident in my abilities," she had managed. "I have sparred with Tigu many times, and this is no different. We both know the outcome of this bout."

Tigu would fight anyway, of course, and try her hardest to win. But neither considered this match much. It was almost routine.

Elder Yi looked like he wanted to press the issue, but her father intervened.

"We were all young, once," Cai Xi Kong stated, glaring at Elder Yi. "But . . . take care that you do not overindulge. We merely wished to hear your thoughts upon the final match. And isn't it good that she is so confident that she does not need to train at the moment? You all know our dutiful Young Mistress's nature. Do you think she would change it so easily?"

There were a couple more nods, while her father turned to look directly at Yi. They engaged in a silent battle of wills before Elder Yi turned away.

"I am merely concerned for her well-being," Yi stated stiffly, then turned to Xiulan. "Beware you do not fall off a virtuous path. If you are to be an Elder, you must hold yourself to a higher standard."

"Thank you for your concern, Elders," she said, bowing before turning away. She barely restrained herself from storming out of the meeting room. Her back was ramrod straight.

Yet as much as she hated the question, and as much as she was angry . . . Elder Yi's words did cut deep.

She had done absolutely no training since she'd returned. She hadn't even meditated.

Xiulan grimaced and paused. Instead of heading back to her quarters, her feet took her to the rooftop. Once there, she leaned back against the roof and sighed. One leg was pulled up to her chest, while the other dangled off the edge of the roof and out into open air.

How quickly a mood can be ruined, she thought bitterly.

She had thought she had been prepared. Prepared to stand atop the Azure Hills. But as the tournament progressed, the feeling of fire and assurance had faded. She respected her opponents. She fought and rose higher.

She was likely going to win the Dueling Peaks Tournament, the greatest tournament for her generation in the Azure Hills. The biggest event in eight years . . . and . . . and she didn't *care*. The pride was gone. The drive was gone. The finals evoked no special emotion in her. It was just another fight with Tigu, just this time in front of an audience.

It was not the culmination of her journey. A bright spot upon her path. It was not everything that she once wanted.

It was something she was doing because she thought she had to. It was a chore.

She was more concerned with seeing plays and drinking with her companions; she wanted to make up for lost time interacting with others.

Instead of wishing for triumph . . . she was just wishing that the tournament were over already, so she could go and give Tigu a tour of the Grass Sea.

She was practically shirking every single one of her duties.

In some ways . . . it felt like a betrayal. A betrayal of her ideals, and a betrayal of the people who relied on her Sect.

Winning the tournament would help her Sect. It would help the mortals who relied upon them for protection. It would increase their prestige and might.

Xiulan bit her lip. Loyalty. Duty. Ideals she had tried to live her life by. The tales of virtuous warriors had enthralled her as a child. The deeds of stalwart protectors drove her onwards, making her wish she could have perhaps a fraction of their nobility and virtue.

Had she betrayed those ideals? *Was* she merely gallivanting around? Hearing one of her Elders say it had been a blow to her heart.

She had to be better, because she was to be in a position of authority. Her Sect was going to make her an Elder.

Yet they still treated her like a slip of a girl who didn't know any better.

Too far in one direction was the life of Sun Ken, doing as she pleased and taking what she wanted. Yet too far in the other was barely a life at all.

She was pulled. Pulled in two directions. Duty. Happiness. The Verdant Blade Sect. The Azure Hills.

She had gotten strong. Yet her strength was aimless.

Choose your own destiny, Xianghua had scolded.

What *did* she want to do? What was this strength of hers *for*?

It was a question that more and more needed an answer.

She tapped her fingers against her leg. She stared up at the moon and started muttering the names of the soldiers that had fallen in the valley. She had started doing that less and less recently. Some nights she didn't do it at all, as her dreams grew more peaceful.

But it was part of why she had trained so hard. Her strength was to protect. Protect not just her Sect but those who could not protect themselves. That was her original reason for getting stronger.

Do it for yourself, Master Jin had said as he slung an arm around her shoulder with a smile.

Her father had agreed with Yi: she had been a bit too lax. The weight of responsibility was heavy.

The mortals smiled as they marched with her.

The valley filled with screams.

Never again.

Xiulan sighed.

Part of the reason why Sun Ken had been so successful was the fact that he knew these hills. He knew of the petty Sect rivalries and had fled in between their territories. When an Elder tried to hunt him down, they would often be intercepted by another Sect asking pointed questions about what they were doing on their land.

And the Elders thought that he was too weak. Too beneath them. A prize for the younger generation, as he only preyed upon mortals.

It was disgusting. Even she hadn't acted until her own people were threatened.

Rivalries and petty squabbles had prolonged the suffering of others for decades—

"Blade of Grass, there you are!" Tigu shouted as she clambered onto the roof. "We were wondering why you didn't come back!"

Xiulan, startled out of her introspection, nearly fell off the roof.

"Ah . . . I'm fine, Tigu. Just thinking," Xiulan replied.

"Eh. You think too much," Tigu decided. "Always with that look on your face, too. C'mon, Rags and Loud Boy are back, and they found a tasty food stall!"

Tigu pulled, and Xiulan allowed herself to be dragged to her feet.

You don't need to face the heavens alone, Senior Sister had said as she cradled Xiulan's head in her lap and ran her fingers through Xiulan's hair.

Guo Daxian, Tie Delun, and the Young Masters and Mistresses of the Sects all in a room together. Talking and laughing, instead of staring down at each other with domineering sneers.

Something had happened that night during their frivolous party. Maybe it was a one-off thing. Maybe those feelings would fade in time.

But Xiulan . . . Xiulan got an idea.

What if . . . what if she could keep those feelings going? What if she could make that brief connection into something more permanent?

It was a thought that held her as she descended from the rooftop, pulled along by Tigu.

Perhaps . . . perhaps this gallivanting around is not so frivolous . . . ?

↔

"Ha! We're on top of the world!" Loud Boy shouted, his voice echoing off the mountain and down into the valley below.

Tigu grinned wildly, up in the cold air. They stared together from the top of the Dueling Peaks. The Earthly Arena was directly below them on one side, and the other stretched off into the distance at a field of verdant green that rolled into the horizon.

"Hello!" Tigu shouted, her voice echoing down. She giggled.

Rags rolled his eyes beside her. "You brats," he muttered.

"So? How you feeling about your match tomorrow?" Loud Boy asked her. "Gonna be tough going up against Miss Cai, yeah?"

Tigu shrugged. "It's just another fight against the Blade of Grass."

"*Just another fight against the Blade of Grass*," Rags mocked, shaking his head.

"Hey! I've beaten her once!" she retaliated . . . before frowning. "But it didn't *really* count because she was being stupid."

Both of her friends stared at her with raised brows.

"What? She hadn't slept for a week, the fool. Master and Mistress had to fix her before she hurt herself."

"Master, huh?" Loud Boy mused. "What kind of man is he, if you don't mind me asking?"

"The best and the strongest." Tigu said immediately. "Mistress is amazing too."

"Oh? Was he that confident you were going to win the prize?" Rags asked.

"Prize? I just wanted to fight." Tigu declared.

The boys looked at each other. "That . . . well, that explains a lot," Loud Boy said.

Tigu shrugged again, staring out at the horizon. "I wish he was here. He said he *might* come . . . but he doesn't like this kind of stuff. Or other cultivators at all really. He said the sect he was from was—" she cut herself off and pouted.

"Well, Master does what Master wants to do. Besides, the First Disciple needed his help more. *I* am entirely self-sufficient! He may be stronger than me, but he always needs me to look after his mistakes!" she declared pompously.

"Wait, *stronger than you?!*" Loud Boy's shout of shock lived up to his name.

"Mmm. For now, at least." She shook her head. She took in one last breath of the air, then slashed her claws down into the snow. "Well, I'm good to go!"

Both the boys stared at her.

"Wait, that's it? I thought you got us up here to get in some last-minute training." Loud Boy admitted.

"Eh? No, I just wanted to carve my name into the top of the mountain. Besides, Handsome Man wants to meet us for tea!"

"He wants to meet *you* for tea." Loud Boy muttered.

Rags just laughed as they started back down the mountain. Down the severe slope at the top, clear of trees. Down the side, where there was the occasional stone entrance hacked into the side of the peaks. Some were ancient and caved in, while others still lead into empty chambers. Slowly, the mountain transitioned into town. Into the massive manors of the sects, and from there, into the crowded streets beyond. Loud Boy and Rags heckled each other constantly while Tigu skipped along, humming to herself as she went to visit another friend.

Which is when her back began to itch.

She felt like she was being watched. A tingle on the back of her neck. Something that set her instincts ablaze—

"You alright, Tigu?" Loud Boy asked.

Tigu shook off the feeling, her heart hammering in her chest.

She frowned, but the feeling was gone.

"Ah, Tigu!" Handsome Man called her, his face bright with a smile. He strode forwards, happily . . . before he noticed her other companions. His face fell.

"Handsome Man!"

↔

Little hands worked, writing things down on a small pad of paper. Acupuncture points, hypotheses on damage locations, a treatment plan.

A distraction for her own nervousness. Which was a bit foolish considering Ri Zu had asked for introductions to be made.

"Ah! There you are!" Ri Zu heard Tigu proclaim as she entered the small storage room where she had been deep in contemplation. "They shall be here soon!"

Ri Zu nodded her head as the cat-turned-girl sat down in front of her with a smile. She took a breath trying to calm herself.

The feeling in her stomach just wouldn't go away. There was always that tiny voice in the back of her head, making her shy away from those she did not know. It was just part of who she was. An instinct that couldn't be ignored, like Tigu's own predatory behavior. It had saved her life when Chow Ji was in charge . . . but it proved to be an impediment now.

She had needed a kick in the rear to meet people last time, only intervening when it was life or potentially death for the Petals.

'*Yes. I am preparing things. Ri Zu needs to do a closer inspection of his leg, but she does not think it should be as damaged as it is.*'

Tigu nodded her head, grinning. "Hopefully everything will go as well as when Loud Boy and Rags asked you for help! They fell down at your feet in praise!"

'*It was just some of Master's acupuncture.*' Ri Zu deflected. The two of them had asked for her assistance after Loud Boy had been injured in the battle against Tie Delun. The fool boy's jaw had needed setting, but Rags had to *drag him* to Ri Zu. He seemed quite surprised that she helped him.

"I don't have any money," he whispered in shame.

'You may pay Ri Zu back later then,' she replied to the dejected man. It wasn't like she particularly needed it.

The number of times his head hit the floor as he kowtowed had been quite embarrassing.

'*Rag's liver was in truly deplorable condition, and Loud Boy had some strange snarl in his Qi. Ri Zu thinks it was from all the times he blocked hits with his face.*'

Tigu started laughing.

"Ah, hard to believe it's almost over. One more match against the Blade of Grass!" She had a giant grin on her face, and Ri Zu offered her a small smile in return. "We shall have to come here again! Or visit Handsome Man or Loud Boy and Rags!"

'*Perhaps . . .*' Ri Zu said noncommittally. *'Ri Zu is sure you will at least have made some friends here.'*

Tigu frowned slightly at the awkward pause in the conversation. She bit her lip and stood up, walking over to the small window.

". . .This hasn't been enjoyable for you, has it?" Tigu asked. "And . . . well, I have been doing things and paying you little mind, haven't I?"

Ri Zu's eyebrow raised as Tigu carefully looked out the window. It still struck her how much Tigu had changed. Tigu, who mere months ago, never would have even considered the words that now came out of her mouth. Apologizing to the "prey" would have only happened over her corpse.

But . . . there was truth to Tigu's words. Tigu came back each day with a smile, talking rapidly about how fun things were. Ri Zu listened, but it was hard not to feel a bit left out. But at the same time, she often didn't know what to say. All she knew was medicine. And when she spoke of her passion to An Ran, the Smaller Blade of Grass's eyes started to glaze over and she couldn't keep up. It was simultaneously frustrating and scary. She was frustrated with herself every time she decided not to join in, and whenever she did start to talk to people, it got awkward. To think that she, the one who learned to truly speak first, was the worst at conversation.

Ri Zu shrugged. '*Some parts have been quite fun. Looking for herbs. Preserving the spider legs. Ri Zu thought she would be more fine with simply observing . . . but she thinks she knows how you felt now. Ri Zu appreciates your concern, Tigu.*'

The cat crossed her arms and grumbled. "I feel kind of bad now, though," Tigu muttered.

Indeed, this entire adventure was not quite what Ri Zu had imagined it to be. All the fighting, meeting with the Petals, Rags paying her in bottles of wine that she still had no idea what to do with.

It was . . . well, an interesting experience to say the least. She flipped the scroll over and looked at the notes on transformation she had made.

'*Well, Ri Zu will simply make you carry her things when she visits these places again.*'

Tigu perked up and grinned. "Or we could find some place you want to go. There's supposed to be a big herb auction in Grass Sea City—I asked Xiulan about it. We could go over there?"

Ri Zu chuckled and shook her head. '*Ri Zu would like that. Just the two of us, a trip for us girls?*'

Tigu cocked her head to the side, "But why wouldn't we want Master and Mistress and our other disciples?"

Tigu didn't seem to get the same exhaustion Ri Zu got when talking to multiple people . . . but it was a good idea. All of them together. '*Ah, yes, a trip with the Master and Mistress sounds grand.*'

Tigu's grin spread across her face. "Of course, my idea is good— Ah! They're here!"

Tigu held out her arm.

Ri Zu steeled herself, scampered up Tigu's arm, and settled into the back of her shirt.

Underneath Tigu's collar was warm and safe, Ri Zu reflected. Almost as warm and safe as underneath Bi De's coat.

It was warm and comfortable. Safe, riding on the back of a cat. How strange.

Ri Zu could feel Tigu's steps were bouncy as she entered the main meeting hall. There was a clink of teacups as their guests were served.

"You said a great doctor wished to speak with us, Cai Xiulan?" The voice of Xianghua was domineering and demanding, but there was an undercurrent of worry and hope.

Ri Zu steeled herself and slid out of Tigu's shirt. She alighted on the table before them. Xianghua flinched at the sudden movement and aborted shoving herself in front of her brother.

'*Good Day, this one is Hong Ri Zu. She greets you, Liu Bowu, Liu Xianghua.*' Her greeting was clear and enunciated properly. Her accent and speech was under control. It was a perfect introduction!

Still, the stares always made her squirm. Bowu, the small boy with the limp, seemed curious, but his elder sister was kind of amusing. Her jaw dropped, her eyes went wide, and she looked absolutely flabbergasted.

She pointed a finger at Ri Zu and turned to Xiulan, a look of utter bafflement on her face.

→

'*The damage to the knee is less severe than Ri Zu thought. The scarring is there, yes, but it is spread out along these sections,*' Ri Zu muttered as she worked, tracing her paw lined with medical Qi down the boy's leg.

He was laid out on a cushion with his head in his sister's lap. Xianghua's eyes were sharp as daggers as Ri Zu worked. Her body was coiled tense and Ri Zu could *feel* Xianghua's intent on the back of her head. It was almost predatory, but she ignored it. This was her duty.

Bowu, on the other hand, just seemed fascinated, and slightly hopeful. He kept pinching his arm whenever he looked down at Ri Zu's small form.

Xiulan was seated at the table along with Yun Ren and Gou Ren. The Petals had vacated the area, giving them some privacy.

Xianghua frowned. "I have gotten many doctors to look at his leg. All have said that it was unsalvageable with their techniques . . ."

Her voice was hard as she delivered the statement.

'*Ri Zu knows this, but . . .*' She brought out a sprig of Spiritual Herb. Xianghua's eyes widened.

She chewed her lip. "Some of the same that Tigu gave me?"

'*Yes. This may not be enough, but Ri Zu's Master is trying to find ways to fix another patient, one whose injuries far eclipse yours. Ri Zu cannot cure this now . . . but she thinks she can lessen the limp you have.*'

Xianghua's face was carefully blank.

"What sort of payment would your Master require for such a boon?" she asked.

'*You have many plants in the Misty Lake, yes? She would ask you to grant her seeds, saplings, and mushrooms from your home.*'

The woman's eyebrow raised. "That's it?" she asked, glancing to Xiulan.

Xiulan nodded her head and glanced to Ri Zu.

'*Master's hobby is . . . well . . . She would prefer things that cause debilitating, but not lethal side effects.*'

Xianghua raised an eyebrow.

"Your Master sounds terrifying," she stated blandly.

"She is," Xiulan and Gou Ren muttered in unison.

Xianghua considered it for a moment. She looked to her brother.

"If you think this will help . . ." Bowu said. "Then please, do whatever you think needs to be done."

Ri Zu nodded. She would make her Master proud.

And after several hours of work, with needles and herbs . . . It was quite the treat to see the boy take a single, halting step, *without* his crutch.

Ri Zu wiped some sweat off her forehead. '*Now, the Heavenly Herbs—er Lowly Spiritual Herbs, have an extremely potent regenerative effect. This, placed directly in drops into the muscle, promotes healing of the affected area. However, for this to be completed, it is likely the scar tissue will have to be scraped out and the bones realigned internally.*'

Xianghua just stared at her brother. She stared as he took another step forward and stumbled. She rose to catch him, but Gou Ren was already there, smirking as he stopped the boy from hitting the ground.

"You require herbs from the Misty Lake, Sister Ri Zu?" Xianghua's voice was intense. As intense as Xiulan's had been when she swore her debt to Master Jin and Master Meiling.

Ri Zu felt her face heat up at the polite speech.

Xianghua stood up.

"This Young Mistress will repay these herbs a thousand fold!" She roared. "She will dig up the entirety of the swamp around the lake and carry it on her back to wherever you desire!"

'*Eh?! Ah, no, we just need a few specimens—*' Ri Zu squeaked, but Xianghua's eyes were shining now.

A hand plucked her off the table and planted a kiss onto Ri Zu's forehead.

And then a second.

Ri Zu barely managed to escape, scrambling up into Tigu's shirt as the girl laughed at Ri Zu's misfortune.

She had to hide in Tigu's shirt again to escape the affection suddenly leveled at her by Damp Pond.

CHAPTER 41

THE CAVE AND THE CRYSTAL

It had been many long hours underground, yet this time Bi De did not find it quite so oppressive. The large, vaulted ceiling and the light probably helped.

And the fact that he had something to focus upon.

Bi De felt his soul stir as Master Gen finished the formation. His own blood dripped into key points. A spiraling formation was carved into the floor. The symbols of the elements stood out clearly, arranged around a stone pillar that jutted up from the ground. On either side of the pillar, the crystals would be placed in the gaps formed by the carving of the taijitu, the symbols for yin and yang arrayed precisely in the center.

Master Gen's brow was heavy with exhaustion, but he held himself well. With his kin around him, he could work like he had twelve additional pairs of hands.

It seemed it was a more willing exchange, and one that appeared to cost Gen greatly, rather than taxing his followers.

"It is time," the old monkey declared. His voice carried out along the cavern. There was a nod from more of Master Gen's kin. They had slowly trickled down during the day, bringing with them food and water as well as items for the ritual.

The crystals in the ceilings dimmed.

Drums thundered in the deep.

Shrieks and cries echoed off the vaulted ceiling.

Picks hammered in unison onto the ground.

There must have been nearly a hundred monkeys gathered around them. Their faces were covered by masks. Their crystal jewelry rattled and chimed.

Ten of them carried with them a funerary urn. Another, a sealed case.

"Great and Honoured Ancestor, please watch over your unworthy sons and daughters . . ." Master Gen whispered.

The funerary urn was placed with great reverence on the ground while Master Gen approached the sealed case.

From within he withdrew a crystal. It was obviously ancient. It had some of the same carvings upon it like Bi De's crystal had, but it was also . . . lesser. The facets not quite the equal to the one Bi De had. But it was also in pristine condition. It had no extra pieces coming off it. No crystals had been fused to it.

Master Gen nodded to Bi De, and then to the Great Master.

Bi De approached the dais in unison with Master Gen.

The drumming reached a fever pitch.

Both placed their crystals upon the platforms and retreated. The monkey nodded to the human.

The drumming stopped.

Bi De's Great Master grumbled, just barely loud enough to hear.

"*I* love *battery duty.*"

He took a breath—

And the formation lit up. A beam of light connected the two crystals together, and the empty one started to glow.

Master Gen recoiled, his eyes widening, before he mastered himself.

'Is it working?' Bi De asked.

The old monkey nodded.

"It is. Now . . . all we can do is wait."

→

Indeed, they did have to wait.

It had been ten hours already.

Bi De took some of that time to clean the fluorescent mushrooms off himself and Yin in a nearby river. He hadn't noticed that Yin had painted on him until the drying liquid started to itch.

Miantiao had promised Bi De to keep watch over his Master, the snake still a bit suspicious, but Bi De thought the monkeys would not attempt to betray them. Their wonder at the crystal was too honest for that.

Yin heated the water with the power of the sun, as Bi De's beak combed through her fur. The mushroom sap was sticky and difficult to remove. He grew increasingly frustrated until one of the monkeys who had brought them food handed them a sweet-smelling clump of herbs. Once crushed, the liquid within foamed and fizzed as it touched the fluorescent gunk, and after that, it left them both pristine. They exited the water, and Yin's heat dried both of them off.

'You should take better care of your fur,' Bi De tutted, staring at the beautiful silver coat.

The rabbit just shrugged. *'It's fur. It's supposed to get dirty,'* she said matter-of-factly. *'A weapon doesn't need to be pretty. It needs to do its job.'*

Miantiao flinched at the words as they settled in beside him again. They turned back to watch the monkeys and Bi De's Master as he conducted the transference. A slightly awkward silence ensued.

Bands of light connected Bi De's Master and the two crystals. He was perfectly still as he provided the precise amount of energy to the formation. Bi De couldn't tear his eyes away. All he could think was *This is a Master Cultivator.*

Yet even as he looked on with reverent pride, he was . . . *vexed.* It galled him that he was not the one seated there and that his Master had to be the one to complete the ritual.

Bi De had started this quest to find the secret to the formation, but it was not he who would complete the final step.

His Great Master, with his limitless wellspring of strength, was the only one who could shoulder such a burden. Bi De looked on in awe as his Master bestowed the precise amount of power required to the formation, his Qi as unwavering as the solid earth.

Bi De had a long way to go.

While his Master was silent and still save for his steady breathing, the monkeys and Master Gen were whirlwinds of activity.

Some of the monkeys stood in a circle around the formation at regular intervals, each holding crystal instruments and closely observing them. Meanwhile, others hurried from one point to another, taking readings with their own instruments and hooting. Master Gen sat at the center of it all, receiving his kin's reports and recording them. Occasionally, he would venture to a point in the formation and, with a careful hand, he would remove the barest pieces of stone from the array.

With each precise action, the brightness of the beam connecting the crystals would subtly intensify, and the crystals' slight fluctuations would settle. Every movement refined the array, showcasing the extraordinary skill possessed by Master Gen, who could enhance the formation even while it was in use.

It was certainly going to be a long wait. Bi De looked up at the ceiling and shuddered. Although being underground remained as disagreeable as it had been during his initial experience, at least they weren't as far down this time. It was only mildly uncomfortable instead of *completely* unbearable.

Bi De shook his head. No sense dwelling on it.

'How goes the transfer, Master Gen?' he called out when the monkey paused. Things seemed stable for the moment, and the monkeys had stopped rushing around so much.

Gen Ten startled and looked up from his work. He seemed to have forgotten their presence.

"It is *remarkably* stable," Master Gen observed, his gravelly voice coming from the crystal at his throat. "Normally, there are fluctuations, but this is . . . solid. Like stone rather than water, yet still flowing. I dare say this will be completed sooner than I thought."

Bi De nodded proudly. Of course his Great Master would accomplish this task with ease. *'My Master's Qi is a stable, nurturing force. It is as the earth below our feet.'*

The monkey nodded, looking on as the transfer continued. "If he weren't so big, he'd make a good miner. Slow and steady, like my lot."

'It's kinda weird he's so quiet,' Yin said, after a moment longer. She was used to his Lord constantly moving or cracking jokes. *'I wonder what he's thinking about?'*

'He is *quite different like thissss,'* Miantiao noted. *'Normally, he isss much more animated.'*

"Most likely something profound. These cultivators have their sutras and mantras. He must be in a state of perfect peace to have such calm Qi," Master Gen said.

'Maybe he's thinking about training with whoever taught him?' Yin pondered. *'That always makes me focus.'*

'Perhaps he thinks of his projectssss?' Miantiao mused. *'Or maybe his focussss is sso complete he thinks of nothing at all?'*

'I say he thinks of Fa Ram and his wife, of the pleasant rivers and beautiful sun,' Bi De said. It was what he thought of when he wished for perfect peace.

↔

One thousand one hundred ninety-eight bottles of beer on the wall; one thousand one hundred ninety-eight bottles of beer. Take one down, pass it around; one thousand one hundred ninety-nine bottles of beer . . .

↔

For thirty hours, there was little change in the proceedings. The Qi connecting the two crystals simply got thicker, more pronounced and opaque.

Several monkeys relieved their kin, starting up a new shift, and food was brought from the surface.

They kept up their silent vigil. There was no sun to mark the passing of time. The enormous crystal in the ceiling shone down on them with a constant brightness.

→

It happened abruptly, in the thirty-fourth hour.

The first disruption since the transfer had started.

One of the monkeys at the edge of the circle suddenly hooted, holding up his crystal instrument. It was buzzing.

Master Gen frowned but did not seem overly concerned as he walked over to the creature. He took the instrument and peered at it. Then he nodded.

Bi De had risen to his feet and was watching. Master Gen smiled at him as the crystal slowly stopped buzzing.

"A small spike. Nothing to worry about—"

Bi De had began to sit back down at Master Gen's words when a second monkey hooted and raised his crystal instrument.

Then a third.

Then a fourth.

Then Master Gen's crystal started buzzing again.

The hooting spread until every monkey had joined. Their concerned cries mixed with the buzzing of their crystal instruments, creating a cacophony that reverberated and intensified within the stone walls. Before long, the entire room vibrated with the calls of worry.

Master Gen's head whipped back and forth as Bi De alighted beside him along with Yin and Miantiao.

'What. Is. Happening,' Bi De demanded.

There was a pulse of Qi from the monkey, and all of his kin stopped their wailing, leaving only the buzzing of the crystal.

"I don't know quite yet. Everything just suddenly started spiking, but—" The monkey stopped abruptly as he glanced up, his eyes locking on the large crystal. The band of Qi was thickening rapidly, and the crystals, floating low over the dais, began to rise into the air.

"What?" Master Gen snapped. "The calculations of our Great Ancestor are perfect! I triple-checked them. This . . . this . . ." The monkey trailed off. The thick band of Qi began to froth, strands of energy sloughing off it as the connection got thicker and thicker. It looked like liquid as it churned and bubbled, multicoloured light refracting off the crystal above.

Bi De glanced at his Master, but he was fine. In fact, he didn't seem to have even noticed.

Master Gen swung into action, removing another crystal. It was a flat pane of bright-green swirling bands of black and pink across the front of it.

Master Gen's fingers flew across the device. Bi De restrained himself from commenting as he watched him work. The concern in the monkey's expression was evident. His eyes were narrowed in concentration. Bi De checked on his Lord again. A single bead of sweat had formed upon his brow, but his eyes were still closed as he fueled the formation.

The crystal in Master Gen's hands chimed. He nearly dropped the piece.

"Honoured Ancestor preserve us," the monkey breathed out. The tone that prayer was said in was exactly what Bi De *didn't* want to hear. "I thought it was part of the crystal. Part of the recordings," Master Gen murmured, his deep voice calm as it came through the crystal on his neck. "But"—he swallowed thickly—"there's something *alive* in there."

The crystal shuddered. The band of energy thickened to be wider than the crystals, churning ominously.

The giant light crystal in the ceiling flickered again. The monkeys' buzzing crystals reached a painful pitch—and then, all of a sudden, every single one of them shattered with a loud crack and went deathly silent.

The monkeys screeched in shock and fear, the hooting starting up again. Things were getting out of control too fast for Bi De's liking.

At that moment, he felt a resolute calm come over him as the Qi in the air began to writhe.

'Master Gen, how do we abort the transfer?' he asked.

The monkey stared at him uncomprehendingly for a second, then shook his head. He hooted, then froze, his fingers coming up to the cracked crystal around his neck.

'Your Master must stop the transfer of his Qi. Failing that, we can break the formation, but the backlash for doing that would be . . . not ideal,' he said in Qi-speech.

Bi De nodded and turned to alert his Master, but Yin was already there at his side, staring up at the unmoving man with worry.

'Uh . . . Bi De? There's something wrong with him!' Yin shouted, staring worriedly at the Great Master. He remained unmoving, even as the crystal shuddered again and sucked more of his Qi into its ravenous depths.

The sloughing tendrils slithered and expanded, filling the room with light. It seemed malevolent now, writhing and *pulling*.

Bi De was beside his Great Master in an instant, who was like a statue as he sat there, completely oblivious to the rumbling and flickering.

'Master! Great Master!' Bi De tried, but it was for naught. His Lord was in some kind of trance. Yin slammed her feet into the Great Master's side. A blow that could reduce a tree to splinters in an instant struck home . . . and did nothing.

The great formation that shone down on the cavern from above flickered and died, while the sinister glow from the memory crystal intensified.

'Gen! Break the Formation!' Be De commanded.

The monkey, to his credit, nodded solemnly. He raised his hand high, the limb covered with radiant Qi, and brought it down upon the formation. It was a strike strong enough to disrupt it and cut off the energy.

The monkey's fingers slammed home on the precise point that *should* have ended the ritual. Instead, it bounced off with a snap as one of his fingers broke, ricocheting off the Great Master's energy as it saturated the ground.

'Shit,' Yin commented.

'Shit,' Bi De and Miantiao agreed.

The light from the crystals burned, becoming too bright to look at directly.

And then tendrils of light lashed out from the connection, enveloping each and every one of them.

CHAPTER 42

LOST IN MEMORY

Bi De was walking along a churned dirt road, a ribbon that stretched haphazardly over the hills, just wide enough for two carts to pass side by side. The breeze held the sweet scent of flowers and wild grass that grew along the roadside. At the end of the road was his destination. He anticipated no problems and was rather enjoying himself on his jaunt out of the office. It was about time he got away from all the paperwork.

Looking down at the tilled soil he was walking on, the highway of the realm, he smiled in satisfaction. For a moment Bi De paused to feel the warmth of the sun, high in the sky, and the gentle wind on his face.

Wait. Sun?

Bi De kept walking, letting his worries melt away. He knew his friend had to be around here somewhere—

Ah. Near here. Bi De smiled as he stepped forwards, his foot pressing down on the road.

The churned earth gave away, revealing a pit trap. Bi De fell, landing on his feet easily. Those little rascals. *They dare?* he thought with amusement.

Immediately, a child and a small Roadspinner burst from some bushes and poked their heads down into the pit. The armadillo-like creature looked as eager as the child, hopping up and down with glee. The little wild-looking boy was grinning widely, but his blank, milky eyes were looking too far to the left. The blind boy was not *really* seeing him.

Roadspinner? Not Wrecker Ball? This felt odd. Familiar.

"Ha! I told you we'd get him!" the child, Dulou, gushed. His companion, Dizhou, tapped his thick claws on the side of the pit in agreement.

Bi De chuckled at the enthusiastic children.

"Yes, yes, you got me. A very good pit! I give it an eight out of ten!"

Dulou laughed happily and held out his fist for his companion to bump . . . pointing it in the complete wrong direction. Dizhou scrambled over himself to get to the other side of the boy and headbutted his hand.

"Mission successful!" the boy boasted.

"You do realise that I must retaliate now, no?" Bi De said. With a single leap, he was out of the pit, landing in front of the two.

The boy and the Roadspinner fell back on their butts in surprise. Then they looked at each other and nodded. The Roadspinner curled up into a ball and shot off in one direction, the boy racing along after him, looking entirely too coordinated and sure of himself for a blind boy.

Bi De rolled his eyes and gave chase, happy to play with the children.

That was . . . not right at all. Children were . . . strange. He wasn't good with children.

Things suddenly snapped into clarity. Bi De metaphorically shook his head as the images, *the memory*, fuzzed and frayed slightly. All of a sudden, he wasn't in the man's body anymore.

He had felt this before. He had been this man before, when he first touched the crystal.

He was inside a memory.

Unlike last time, the memory didn't eject him once he recognised it for what it was. Instead, he became an observer. The man, not Bi De, chased down the child and the Spirit Beast, and captured them both, laughing and joking with them like old friends.

There was a spike of unpleasant worry. Bi De had no clue what to do, but the feeling of being this man was . . . intense. If he hadn't felt it before, he probably wouldn't have been able to tell for hours. Hours he did not know if he had.

His concern deepened as something within him twinged, the crystal drawing out some of his Qi. It was subtle, *very* subtle, but the small drain was there.

His thoughts and concerns were not for himself, but for his Great Master, Miantiao, Yin, and the monkeys. His Master was in some manner of trance, while his companions were weaker than him. He could only pray that their lives were not snuffed out by this crystal.

If they were hurt in any way, he would have his vengeance upon this wicked crystal and the witch who had given him its location.

Assuming he survived, of course.

He had no body, just a mass of Qi trapped in a memory. He took a metaphorical breath and spread his awareness out. The memory blurred slightly. It distorted as his Qi quested through it, the colours melting like wax and running. The recording itself began to skip, stuttering back and forth. Bi De caught a glimpse of a giant, curled-up Roadspinner, its shell big enough to house most of a village within, before the memory stuttered again, leaping back in time, and replaying what Bi De had just seen.

Bi De hit the confining edges of the memory. His Qi reached forwards carefully.

It was like a bubble. A thin film surrounding the memory.

He pressed up against it, probing for a weakness, searching for anything that would let him escape.

The walls of the bubble resisted, pressing back, but Bi De would not be denied. The walls of the memory shuddered and rumbled as he bore down on it.

For a moment, it felt as if he would not succeed, but his will was stronger than the walls of this prison. A breach formed, and Bi De pushed free.

Immediately, he was assaulted.

Colours speared into his eyes, a hundred thousand voices and the clash of weapons ringing in his ears. An array of scents assailed his nose, causing him to grimace. One moment, the sweet smell of flowers; another, a scent of death so powerful it made his eyes water. Tastes, from delicious foods like the ones found in blessed Fa Ram, to things so foul that they had no description and made him want to empty his stomach. Even his own feelings were not spared as the crystal forced him to feel the heights of triumph and the depths of despair.

Bi De's questing Qi recoiled from the sundered wall in the bubble of memories. He was slammed back to the bottom as the entire thing warped and twisted like a nightmare. The sheer, raw emotion from the void outside rushed towards him through the tear.

The First Disciple of Fa Ram would not be defeated. Bi De charged back into it, gathering his will, and pushed against the encroaching darkness that was attempting to tear the memory bubble apart. His silver Qi grew like a net and captured it, holding it at bay. He knew not what to do, only that he had to hold it still. The rent in the sky, exposing the howling darkness, pressed against him . . . then started to close.

Inch by inch, it sealed shut.

Bi De managed a sigh of relief as the memory stabilized and restarted, this time, deep into the night.

→

Bi De pondered his failure. Brute force had not worked, but he was undeterred. He would experiment.

The Great Master was clear in regard to experimentation. One must study the world carefully, then form a hypothesis.

He might be able to leap into the maelstrom of memories, but if he did that, he would not be able to find his companions. Or if he could find them, what would he do? Plunge into their memory bubbles and then leap back into the void with them? No, that wouldn't do. He could attempt to find his Great Master, but he, too, was being held in some sort of trance. Bi De doubted his ability to wake his Lord if whatever was happening was strong enough to affect him.

Bi De pondered his predicament as he turned his contemplations to the contents of the bubble. The man drew what looked like a rough map in the dirt, and the blind boy nodded happily as he pointed something out.

The slight twinge in his Qi occurred again.

He had to escape. But how to collect everybody? As he brooded over this, he observed the man accepting some herbs from the Roadspinner. The little creature's nose twitched in a way that reminded Bi De of Sister Ri Zu.

Bi De paused. *Ri Zu.*

Sister Ri Zu used a needle as her tool of choice. A needle that could pierce, that was hardened and durable. It was designed to be precise.

Inspired, Bi De once more gathered his Qi. He compressed it like his blades, but concentrating it to a point instead of a line, forging silver light into a needle. Slowly, he approached the walls of the memory yet again. A tiny needle of silver Qi pressed into the edges. With great care, Bi De pressed against the walls. A tiny part of himself, attached to a thread.

He pierced the side of the bubble. Immediately, he was struck by the void, but his will was strong and he was prepared for it this time. The little silver needle ventured into the darkness.

→

He found Yin first. Or rather, it would have been harder to *not* find Yin. The memory bubble she was in was thrashing and writhing with the golden light of the sun, nearing destabilization.

Bi De entered it carefully, wary not to destroy it.

A man wearing robes stood above another—the one who was writhing with sunlight, the man through whom Yin was seeing this.

"You should have known your place, peasant," the robed man declared as he stepped on Yin's chest. "I, your grandfather, will show you your place."

Bi De saw the defeated look on the fallen man's face. Yin's Qi spiked around him, trying to get up, trying to fight.

"I'm not going to give up. Not now, not ever," the man snarled. His voice sounded more like Yin's than his own.

The memory shuddered as the man clenched his hand into such a tight fist that it looked like the bones might collapse inward from the pressure.

'Yin. Please stop. It is only a memory,' Bi De said.

His simple words stopped her from destroying the memory and sending herself adrift into the maelstrom. Instead, everything froze as Yin restrained herself from launching her attack, then rewound to a scene of a man sweeping the street.

Bi De's Qi pressed against her own, sharing what he had discovered.

Yin blinked at Bi De, or at least at the part of him that was there. The world stopped breaking, and the older version of Wu faded away, leaving her staring at an unfamiliar ceiling.

'It is only a memory. Hold fast. I will find the others,' Bi De's voice said, and she could hear its intent as it was transmitted to her.

She let his memories explain what he had done, the link he had forged. Yin understood he could not take her with him. Not without tearing a massive hole and disturbing every memory within this place.

But a needle and thread, tying each separate memory together? Slowly pulling them together until they touched? And then extracting everybody into one place?

'Let's do this!' she exclaimed, thumping her feet against the floor.

Sun and moon touched, holding fast. Their Qi threaded together. One band of silver light connected two memories.

Bi De set off again.

→

The next to catch Bi De's eye was a steady thrum of Qi that felt like glass. Bi De descended into the memory and, to his surprise, found that Miantiao was already free.

Bi De glanced at the memory's contents and raised an eyebrow.

'Glass? I would have thought that this would have consumed your attention, yet you broke out?'

'The method they use is inferior to my Master'ssss,' Miantiao said dismissively, his eyes tired. *'That . . . and I felt happy.'*

Bi De closed his eyes at the snake's admission. Miantiao relaxed as he felt Yin's Qi aiding Bi De.

'Are we to attempt to leave together, then?' Miantiao asked. *'Us three have found each other.'*

'No. Not yet. I will not leave anyone behind,' Bi De replied.

For a brief moment, it looked like Miantiao was about to argue against saving the others.

But then the old snake sighed, and his eye became filled with resolve.

'No one gets left behind,' Miantiao agreed.

→

Back into the maelstrom Bi De went. A single silver needle, backed up by the sun, and magnified with glass.

Bi De pushed his Qi further still, struggling through the jumbled chaos of assorted memories. Things weren't as clear now. He could not feel either the monkeys' or his companions' Qi.

But he would not give up on them. Not one.

It was a difficult, painstaking search.

But as his Great Master said: one step at a time.

He did not rush or panic, which could make him miss something. Careful observation and a calm demeanour were what was required of him, and Bi De rose to the task. Even battered by the torrent of emotions, the silver needle did not waver for a moment; its body was pure, clean, and without flaw. He searched through a hundred little stable bubbles of memory. Each one pulled him into a different vision. Once he completed his search within, he exited the memory. Every time he went back into the void, he had to center himself fully, lest he be washed away.

And then, he found one that was different.

It was a minuscule difference, but his sharp senses, honed by his hard work, picked out the slight tremor within the bubble.

Hopefully, it would be Master Gen. With his Qi and his connection to his kin, he could help Bi De find the others with greater ease. Yet even as he pierced the bubble to land in a massive ravine, he could tell that whoever this was, it was not Master Gen.

The Qi was different. Unfamiliar. Bi De could feel the confusion as people swung like monkeys from long ropes. The massive ravine had trees growing from its walls, growing horizontal to the ground for the lengths of two people before arching towards the sky.

He touched the unfamiliar Qi. It was unrefined. Fluctuating. *New.*

The monkey startled at the intrusion, taken aback by the sudden realisation that they were trapped within a memory.

'Wha—? What's going—?' the monkey asked, waking from the dream. His voice was rough and gravelly. *'What? I'm . . . I'm . . . I'm me . . . ?'*

He had *awakened.*

What a poor place to do such a thing. He was already remarkably coherent, though. His thoughts were fully formed, his mind functional. His spark must have been powerful indeed.

Yet Bi De did not have time to explain things.

Bi De's Qi touched him, calming the panic and fear with his conviction, his absolute confidence.

'There was an incident, young one. All will be well, do you understand me? But right now, we must escape this place, and for that, I need your assistance in finding your brothers and sisters.'

The monkey's Qi, full of fear, strengthened at Bi De's words.

'The Clan is in danger . . . ?' the monkey asked. *'Ah, like a cave-in. How do we dig ourselves out?'*

Bi De was pleasantly surprised at his immediate grasping of the situation.

'I need you merely to grasp tight to this thread. Do not let go for anything.'

'Aye. I can do that,' the monkey said tentatively.

'Do you have a name?' Bi De asked him.

'Huo Ten,' the monkey answered. *'That's what Master called me.'*

'Then, Huo Ten, calm your breathing. We shall be out soon.'

The monkey's Qi and resolve grew stronger, enveloping him in a sensation akin to being encased in solid stone.

And then the silver needle was off again.

→

One monkey. Then two. Then three. The connections came faster and faster as Bi De refined his search. The web of silver light expanded, weaving together the memories.

Bi De looked at each of them.

They took place in a myriad of places: In deep valleys. In grassland watering holes. In great stone quarries and enormous mountains. In little towns and ring-shaped cities.

These were the memories of a man, achingly familiar yet eerily not.

After the tenth found monkey, there was still no sign of Master Gen.

Until Bi De realised something.

Most had been confused or actively trying to escape the bubbles. Their little eddies of Qi had had knock-on effects.

But what if one knew that what was happening was a memory, yet did not want to leave?

→

He found the Old Master staring with teary eyes at an entire village of Spirit Beasts. Men and monkeys mined crystals together, while others danced and played. All of them paid their respects to the maker of the crystal, greeting him as their Lord.

They talked, played, and laughed together. It was an entire society.

Bi De stayed silent for a moment longer.

'I am sorry if you were looking for me,' Gen whispered to Bi De. *'It's beautiful, isn't it?'*

'You may examine it at your leisure later, Master Gen,' the rooster stated, not a hint of reproach in his voice.

'Thank you,' the monkey stated simply. *'Whatever you need, our resources are yours to command.'*

Silver light met the monkey.

'Let us discuss such matters later. For now, we must escape.'

→

Bi De's eyes snapped open as the last of the threads connected to a monkey. Eighteen had been in the cavern with them. The needle wove off the last end.

The rooster took a metaphorical breath and slowly began to pull.

The threads tightened, and the bubbles, stitched through with silver light and stabilized by Bi De's Qi, slowly began to move. It was like tugging on a mountain. Each moment was a strain against the nature of this world as emotion battered against him.

Yet he was not alone. Miantiao. Yin. Master Gen.

They fortified his spirit, shoring up the fragile bubbles.

And they moved, ever so slowly, pulling the memory bubbles together.

A massive Wrecker Ball, the size of an entire village, squinted down at the crystal bearer. His armour was covered in a thousand scars, and his face had laugh lines all over it.

He let out a booming laugh, then said, "Leave it to me! This Rumblin' Yao'll get it done, Little Lord!" the massive creature roared, as he guzzled a barrel of wine. "Rumbling Earth Gang! Let's roll!"

The humans and the Roadspinners roared with laughter, rough and tumble, one and all.

And then, as the spheres touched, the orb went blank. The bundles of memory fused.

Bi De was suddenly within a white void, together with Yin.

The change was abrupt, but there was no time to celebrate.

Both blinked in surprise at each other, but Yin immediately brightened up. She moved to latch onto one of the threads, helping to pull it in.

Huo Ten joined them next, hooting nervously at his sudden induction.

Then came Miantiao.

However, Bi De noticed something starting to go wrong as they pulled on the next orb. They started shifting, for lack of a better term. The bubbles were being pulled down by a force. They began to "fall" deeper into the crystal.

The orbs that had yet to be merged that were farther away pulled on the silver threads Bi De had bound them with. As they fell, and as more memory bubbles were added, things began to change. Bi De clenched his beak as his form solidified, gradually becoming more himself.

He would not relinquish a single one.

Of course, that was when the dense ball of memories impacted a more chaotic one. They merged and then a feeling of wrongness took over. The white orb began to bleed black fluid.

And from that fluid came the beasts of hell. They were horrifying, clad in black armour and white faceplates. Their forms were a mockery of humans, twisted images in a mirror. Bi De's very soul was repulsed by their presence.

Demons. Even the memory of their Qi was corrosive. They moved and shambled about without purpose, but their presence made Bi De's Qi begin to steam, holy moonlight battling against the corruption.

Alone, he might have fallen.

But the Sun was with him.

Yin abandoned the strings of silver and exploded into motion. Her solar Qi was tinged with Bi De's own moonlight-blessed silver as she smashed into the creatures, the shades shrieking and flailing as they burned. Her body was armoured with sunlight—pure, clean and bright, blazing in the defence of others.

The demon memories screamed as they beheld her, their ethereal flesh bursting into flames.

Those who survived the devastation caused by Yin's armoured form were then subjected to shattering blasts of glass from Miantiao. The manifestation of the snake's rage tore through them like paper.

Those who were left faced Master Gen.

Master Gen was no warrior. He was an artisan, a craftsman. Bi De knew that the monkey had very likely never fought in his life, safe behind his protective formations.

Yet his family was in danger. Master Gen's face was a mask of silent fury. The caustic Demonic Qi burned his hands and his fur, yet the golden figure rent them asunder. Fingers that could crush rock shattered demonic scale. Fists that excavated mountains struck out and skulls exploded off the bodies they were once attached to.

The furious Spirit Beasts brought enough time for Bi De to reel the last of the memory orbs in. Able to focus, Bi De reinforced the bubble with his silver threads as it fell and fell until it slowly came to a stop.

As suddenly as they had appeared, the demons disappeared.

The memory bubble shuddered.

"Interlopers."

The voice was a raspy growl. A snarl that nearly sent Bi De to his knees as the most magnificent creature Bi De had ever seen stepped into their little bubble. The monkeys dropped to their knees upon merely catching sight of it.

A proud and noble animal, unequaled in heaven and earth. Bi De knew this beast's name simply by laying eyes upon it, a primal part of his soul whispering the creature's name directly into his mind, demanding his respect and veneration.

Temple Dog.

Defender of the righteous, a Heavenly Beast.

Bi De had seen this creature's corpse. It had lain in the room before the crystal, dead for thousands of years.

This was not the original beast that had remained loyal. It was a mere shade, only a memory of it, an image that bore not even a fraction of the original's power. But it was still a great foe, even weakened. Bi De was not sure he could best it.

But still: among chickens, he was Bi De.

He would have to try, if only for his Great Master's sake.

'Yin. Reinforce this place, please,' he asked the rabbit as he strode forwards to meet the shade.

Then, out of the blue, both the rooster and the Heavenly Beast exploded into motion at the same moment. Bi De could tell that the blow from the beast was formidable as it came for him. It was a strike that would kill him instantly if it connected.

So the only way to defeat the beast would be to not let it hit him.

It was almost nostalgic, to be so utterly outclassed again. It reminded Bi De of fighting Basi Bu Shi, the fox that had once been his greatest nemesis.

The Temple Dog struck out with its mighty paws, moving with a speed and skill that were incomparable to a mere fox that had barely awakened. But they were movements Bi De still knew.

To move in this place was simple. There was no up or down, no pull of gravity, as his Great Master had named the invisible force. Only Qi. Only thought.

Bi De was a silver needle, and then he was a rooster again.

The memory's eyes were focused solely upon him, as he, the First Disciple of his Great Master, Guardian of Fa Ram, fought the shadow of the Heavenly Guardian of ancient memory.

The air pressure of the dodged blows hammered into his body. The beast's teeth grazed him in near misses, ripping feathers from his form. Despite the peril, Bi De could see that the guardian construct was fading.

When it had been recovered, the crystal had been near destruction in the first place. The energy within it was nearly nonexistent, and the beast was drawing from those meagre reserves. It could not last.

Both the power of the moon and the sun burned away the darkness.

[Rising of the Crescent Moon]

Basi Bu Shi. Chow Ji.

And now, the Heavenly Beast, Guardian of the Temple Doors.

The moon rose, and Bi De with it. His legs struck the dissipating construct's face, dealing it a mortal blow.

He felt no satisfaction as it faded, white giving way to gold, the memory descending further.

→

It was then that Bi De beheld the true form of the Temple Dog. Not the guardian construct he had faced, but the creature that was nominally alive.

The beast's eyes were milky white, completely blind, and its skin had festering tears in it, exposing tendons and organs. Bi De could see the places where its muscles were now reduced to skin and bone. Both of its horns were cracked and splintered, and its tusks had long since fallen out. It was pitiful and broken.

Its sightless eyes were locked on a golden orb that it was cradling in its massive hands, its claws bare nubs.

Within the orb, a man was seated, eyes closed, a troubled look upon his face.

Bi De's Great Master.

He swallowed as the Temple Dog breathed in. The golden orb quivered, releasing a mist that was immediately sucked into the beast's shattered nose. Bi De felt his own Qi quiver, separating from his body and being drawn into the suction.

"Master. Master," the Great Guardian whispered, its voice raw with pain. "Master, I knew you would return!"

Love. Loyalty. Devotion.

There was no grand battle that needed to be fought here.

Bi De bowed his head as his Great Master opened his eyes. He seemed dazed. Confused.

And yet, as he opened his eyes and focused, he took one look at the whimpering broken creature before him and extended his hand.

The guardian beast's blind eyes shed tears. Great droplets streamed down its muzzle as it leaned into the touch with desperation.

"It hurts, Master. It *hurts*. But I never doubted you!" it moaned. It gave a great, racking cough. "Even though you told me I should go if you did not return, I stayed! I knew you would return to me if I waited but one more day!"

The madness and despair in its voice were evident. Bi De couldn't help but feel a certain sense of kinship with the creature. He knew these creature's feelings like they were his own. For what was Bi De without his Great Master?

If his Master died, would he be able to give up? Would he be able to move on? Or would he guard his Lord's resting site for all eternity?

It was a question he knew not the answer to.

"I'm sorry. You waited a long time, didn't you?" he heard his Great Master whisper. The enormous beast whimpered.

Its body was rent and ruined. Its mind was in shambles. Yet it persisted. It persisted through thousands of years.

It persisted through death.

The golden light touched the incredible beast. Bi De's Great Master gently took its ruined paw and touched its decaying flesh. He took the creature's enormous head into his lap and stroked its soiled and ruined mane.

"Master. Oh, Master, it hurts so," the beast that could challenge the heavens rasped. "For so long, it has hurt."

"You did your job. You did it so *well.*"

Golden light seeped into the great Temple Dog. The light steadily turned to earth brown and grass green as it was drained. The world around them stabilized.

"Yes. Yes, I did my duty. Master, may I rest now, Master?"

"Yeah. Yeah, you can sleep, now."

The Temple Dog heaved a great sigh, relief and sorrow mingled in it. The broken and ruined body of the creature faded, leaving only faint motes of light behind.

Bi De watched as a golden core of energy materialized in his Great Master's hand. It contained power so potent that Bi De felt energised just from being near it.

His Great Master cradled the core in his palm.

"It's okay, boy," his Master murmured, his gaze distant and lost within the depths of his own memories. The golden core crackled and turned to dust in the darkness. "You sleep well now."

□

I was feeling utterly exhausted, and my eyes were crusty with tears. It felt like somebody had scooped my insides out. The formation had stopped taking in my Qi, and I had a pounding headache. It felt like a really bad hangover.

I was also lying on my back instead of sitting.

'Master?' Big D asked, his voice full of worry.

Groaning, I opened my eyes, then immediately closed them again at the sheer brightness from the crystals in the ceiling.

I rolled on my side and tried again.

My fingers curled into soft moss as I pushed myself up and looked around. Everybody looked like they had been awake for weeks. Their postures were droopy.

The monkeys looked positively shell-shocked. Some were nursing bruised hands; others were bleeding, with little bits of crystal and stone poking out of their skin. Small pieces of stone medallion and all of Master Gen's instruments lay strewn around the ground, shattered and broken.

If the cave was a jungle before . . . Well, now it was nearly impenetrable. The ferns had grown massively, almost touching the ceiling. Mushrooms sprouted out of every inch of wall. Green moss had crawled across the floor, leaving not a scrap of bare stone.

I opened my mouth to ask if everybody was all right—and vomited.

→

As it turned out, everybody *did* seem to be okay, once I got up. The monkeys were quick to reassure me, Master Gen bowing low, and said that everything was in order. We stayed down in the tunnels just long enough for Master Gen to confirm that the memories had been transferred perfectly to the crystal before climbing out back into the surface. I felt like shit, though, and wasn't really in any mood to be genuinely happy about it, so I just nodded.

Mission accomplished, I guess.

Having to trek out of a cave and a tunnel system when you have a pounding headache sucks. I was pretty nauseated, and having to squeeze through narrow passageways that were already too small for me really didn't help matters. I ended up hurling a second time on the way back up. Of course, all this was compounded by the fact that I was feeling something I hadn't felt in a very, *very* long time.

Qi exhaustion. *Real* Qi exhaustion.

I might have dumped my Qi into the earth every day to the point of tiredness, but a good night's sleep fixed that right up.

This? This was the day after running a marathon with no training while somehow managing to have an eighteen-wheeler run over every single one of my organs. *Everything* hurt. My muscles, my bones, my guts and even my *soul* were bruised. I could feel the mystical ache every time I focused.

I barely managed to drag myself to the bed that was provided for me and collapsed onto it, grimacing as some of the flashes of memory invaded my mind. They were indistinct things. Bits and pieces. A murky mess that only renewed my resolve to stay away from all this crap.

One of the memories was clear, though. A vivid one of a dog.

Hell, it was an odd-looking thing. Definitely something native to this world, with horns and tusks. It almost looked familiar, like a carving from the outside of a temple come to life. But it was a dog, there was no doubt about that. I knew those eager eyes by heart, and the feelings that came to me from the crystal. The amusement. The love and the fondness.

I did sympathise with those memories.

I remembered my own dog, in the Before, long since passed. The good boy I had grown up with. The same one who had been by my side and gone on adventures with me until his old bones had finally failed him.

Until he finally had to go to that final sleep.

So, when the vision, the memory, had shifted to the pitiful thing—the broken, old dog, whimpering and nuzzling into my hand—there was only one thing I could do.

Maybe it had been the lingering feelings that had prompted me to comfort it, or maybe my own, but it didn't matter. Nothing so loyal deserved to die like that, alone and in the dark.

Exhausted, I closed my eyes and fell asleep.

CHAPTER 43

TIGER AGAINST THE GRASS

The day was bright and sunny. Tigu stood on the roof, her eyes peeled as she watched the horizon.

"Still watching for Jin?" Gou Ren asked as he clambered up onto the roof beside her.

"Yeah," she said, before sitting down and sighing. "I . . . don't think Master is gonna be here."

Gou Ren looked to the horizon too, before he reached over and ruffled her hair. "He must've gotten stuck in the city, or held up by something. Maybe Bi De ran into a bunch of bandits again and he had to take care of them."

"Like bandits could stop Master," Tigu scoffed.

"Even if he's not here, Yun has plenty of pictures. You can show off your fights and tell him everything that happened," Gou Ren said.

Tigu leaned into him and nodded before springing up. "You're right! I shall tell him a tale that far eclipses Wa Shi's! Of my battles with strong opponents, and the greatest feat of all: finding a woman worthy of you!"

Gou Ren coughed. "You hardly found her . . ."

"I have already defeated the Blade of Grass in this battle once before, so today is merely a formality! Damp Pond may ask Master and Mistress for your hand when she gathers her courage—I shall allow it!"

"Shouldn't she be asking *my* parents—wait, only guys are supposed to do that!"

"Really?" she asked before shrugging. "Huh."

"Shaddup and come down. Food is done," he grumbled.

Tigu smirked and skipped after him. The house was pretty empty save for Ri Zu and Yun Ren. Ri Zu was making notes, while Yun was carefully polishing his recording crystal. He even had some expensive oil he had brought, using the money he'd earned from selling his images. It made the piece of blue crystal almost glow.

The Blade of Grass was in the main manor with the Petals. They claimed there was a "conflict of interest" to sleep under the same roof that night, which was a bit of a shame. Something about some people poisoning each other or something—like either of them would do something so *rude*. Tigu had to content herself with sleeping with Yun Ren, even though Xiulan was a far better pillow.

She would have gone with Gou Ren, her second choice, but Damp Pond had stayed quite late, forcing his head into her lap. Though it was less forced this time. Gou Ren appeared to have given up resisting.

She ate her meal and went back up to the roof.

The time until the last fight passed unbearably slowly. She kept an eye on the paths into town, but nobody showed up. The rest of the time, she stared out at the crowds and at the peak.

The waiting itself was worse than what was waiting for her. She knew what fighting Xiulan was like. This? This was just *annoying*. So she distracted herself. She played games with Gou Ren, and listened to Ri Zu talk about Misty Boy's leg, as the sun rose higher in the sky.

Finally, it was time. She had been instructed to go to the east side of town . . . where a surprise was waiting for her.

She knew that the Blade of Grass would be escorted by her Sect to the mountain for the last time, but she had expected to go there alone.

Instead, those that had been sectless at the beginning of the tournament were arranged as an honour guard for her. Several clapped her on the back. Others nodded firmly at her. They closed their ranks, forming a circle of nineteen. A mix of rough clothes and silk. Blues, browns, and violets, with every colour represented.

"The first independent in the finals in one thousand twenty-four years," the man wearing the tournament organiser uniform whispered to her. "We had to dig through the archives for the proper protocols."

Loud Boy smirked as he hefted the flag, which had the symbol for Azure Hills upon it.

Tigu kept her head held high as she walked through the streets. People howled and cheered her on, and she waved occasionally at them with a smile on her face. It was fun, and it drove them wild when she did it.

She was paraded through the streets to the mountain itself. The sun was at its zenith as she entered the yawning cavern and proceeded to the lift.

It was silent initially, save for the clanking of the chains as they rose higher and higher before Tigu stepped out of the lift—

—and walked into a cacophony just as loud as the entrance ceremony.

There were people in the stands shouting her name. Blue Man's tattooed people stomped their feet. Handsome Man's friends slammed their hammers into their anvils; Handsome Man himself pounded out a truly thunderous beat on three separate pieces of metal.

Rags's hooligans and ruffians let out howling whoops, somehow managing to make themselves heard.

Tigu's head twisted from side to side as she waved at everybody, provoking more laughter and cheers.

This was fun!

In contrast to Tigu, Xiulan was doing that boring "head held high" thing she did sometimes. Her eyes were focused solely on Tigu.

Both groups came to a pause. The Petals in their uniforms stood across from the sectless. It was a contrasting image. The single unified block against the wild styles of the independents.

They stared each other down across the arena. Tigu might have been their adversary at one point, but to many she was suddenly proof that they, despite their lack of backing, could rise up as high as she had.

Tigu stopped waving, staring only at the Blade of Grass.

A hint of a challenging smile appeared on her face.

Tigu grinned back.

The flags were once more planted under the banner of the Empire.

Announcer Man, Bai Huizong, stepped onto the dais. His grin stretched across his entire face. One of his men had a recording crystal out, staring intently at them.

Tigu waved to that too.

"Honoured guests. Honoured combatants. Thank you for coming. Before the final bout, we do have some last rituals to take care of . . ."

↔

"Sorry," Gou Ren called as he bumped into somebody. He kept a firm grip on his prizes.

"Sorry," the other guy apologised, his hands out and ready to catch any of Gou Ren's stuff should it fall. Gou Ren jerked his head down the stairs, and the other guy nodded, scooting back a bit and letting him pass, before walking towards the vendor himself.

Gou Ren squeezed past another person and headed back to his seat. After the flags had been planted, there was a brief intermission as the rest of the people filed out of the arena and went to their seats, and Tigu and Xiulan had been sent to meditate, giving them one last chance to prepare themselves. Gou Ren had used that to get a bit more food and drink—mostly because their collection of seatmates had steadily grown . . . and they might not be able to get anything later.

If the stands had been crowded previously, they were absolutely packed today. It was a sea of people. More people than Gou Ren had ever seen at one time in the city. The talking and shouting was even more intense than at the opening ceremony, and the constant roar echoed out over the arena.

After a few more awkward dodges, he reached the section where his group was seated.

He handed over drinks to Bowu and Rags's friends, who were teaching the kid several words that probably shouldn't be used in polite company. He took his seat beside Xianghua, who had claimed the spot beside him. She smiled warmly at him and entwined their arms. He felt his face flush at her closeness.

He still didn't know *quite* how he felt about Xianghua. She was a bit strange, and a little intimidating, but anybody who loved their brother that much couldn't be a *bad* person.

So he just "went with the flow," as Jin had suggested once.

And the flow had a pretty girl smiling at him, asking him earnestly about his home, and listening intently about how to grow rice.

For all that she shouted and boasted, she was surprisingly good at listening. Though she did get a rather intense expression on her face quite often, like she was committing what he said completely to memory.

Gou Ren glanced at the top of the arena, where what looked to be a bunch of the fights were replaying themselves in midair. And not just the fights from this tournament. There were people who Gou Ren had never seen before smashing into each other. Were they fights from previous tournaments? As he watched, the strange illusion fuzzed out and stopped, to angry boos from the crowd.

His brother, on the other side of Xianghua, clicked his tongue in annoyance.

Gou Ren's attention wandered around the arena. Massive braziers had been lit, and he was rather glad they were up so high, because otherwise the summer heat combined with the flames would have been unbearable. Instead, it provided just enough warmth to keep away the chill.

Gou Ren noticed movement from the corner of his eye, so he looked over at the approaching people. He scooted over, pressing into Xianghua as Rags, Loud Boy, and a few other people who had been with Tigu finished making their way up into the stands. An Ran and the rest of the Petals would be up in the Verdant Blade box for this one. Loud Boy grinned appreciatively when Gou Ren handed him over a baozi.

"Thanks, Brother," the kid said, before shoving his food into his mouth and chewing loudly. He stared excitedly down at the arena. "Who do you think will win?" Loud Boy suddenly asked, as he forced himself into the seat beside Gou Ren.

Gou Ren paused and considered. "I think Xiulan? I've never really seen them go all out on each other, but I know Tigu has won a couple of times before she managed to transfor—er, complete one of her moves."

"So . . . she has a chance?" Loud Boy asked.

"Maybe? I've certainly seen her shove Xiulan's head into the pond enough times . . ."

Abruptly, there was a hiss, as Bai Huizong stepped onto the crystal dais and tapped on it. The talking started to peter out.

"My friends, my friends. Honoured guests. Warriors who gave it their all. It is time. Our final combatants are now prepared."

The crowd grew quiet.

"What a tournament it has been! A tournament that will be spoken of for generations. A battle for the ages. And now . . ."

The man clapped his hands together. The sound thundered out.

"Onnnnn the east side! Don't let her small size fool you—this girl is a fierce tiger! Were it any other tournament, she would have already won! The independent who came from nowhere, taking the tournament by storm! The relentless, the unyielding Roooooouuuu Tiguuuuuuu!"

The crowd erupted, and Gou Ren added his voice to the shouts—he was cheering both of them, so it wasn't like he was playing favourites!

Tigu sprang to her feet, seeming to be glad the meditation was over. Her body practically vibrated with energy.

"Onnnnn the west side! You know her name! You know her deeds, written in song and play! The Demon-Slaying Orchid! The Young Mistress of the Verdant Blade Sect! The beautiful, the virtuous Cai Xiulaaaaaaaaaan!"

The roar from the crowd equaled the shouts for Tigu. People held up posters of Xiulan from plays, dolls of her likeness, and one section even had an effigy of Sun Ken that people were gleefully smashing around with clubs.

Xiulan's steps were more measured, moving with a grace Gou Ren hadn't known was possible before he met her.

They approached each other in the center of the ring—

And bowed without prompting from Huizong, who nodded.

"We can expect an honourable fight from these two, there is no question about that! But that is enough from me. The Elders are prepared. The stage is set. Combatants, to your positions!"

Both girls walked a few paces from each other and stood across from each other. Xiulan's swords floated up behind her.

"Look at your rival! Your fated opponent! Let them know your strength!"

Xiulan's lips quirked into a smirk, and she said something to Tigu that Gou Ren couldn't make out, but it got Tigu rolling her eyes so hard he could see it from here. Xiulan took an obvious breath, then closed her eyes.

Qi poured from her. It flowed around her, saturating the air and becoming almost solid. With the blades pointing towards the heavens, and the light of the sun above her, it looked like a gateway to a small field. The Azure Hills in high summer, containing healthy, verdant grass that stretched for thousands of li. For a brief moment, the grass and blades waved in the breeze, seeming almost peaceful.

Until Xiulan opened her eyes and the grass stilled. Each blade of grass was ready for what was to come. She was no longer just a person, but a landscape, ready for battle.

A tiger formed behind Tigu. It slunk into view. Instead of the mass of furious, dominating Qi that had characterized her spirit in other matches, the tiger was silent. Hazy and shrouded. Its blazing eyes were intent, focused solely on Xiulan. Its haunches coiled and tense, embodying a predator on the hunt.

There was silence as the crowd held its breath. The man on the crystal podium looked up to the top of the arena, where the massive gong sat, and raised his hand.

Gou Ren looked up with him.

Instead of a couple hundred men with chains, now there were barely thirty. Gou Ren recognised one of them—Xiulan's father. The Master of the Verdant Blade Sect. The rest were unknown to Gou Ren, but they were mostly old men. Yet instead of the gasping, grunting masses who normally pulled back the giant piece, the men who stood atop the arena moved with ease and grace. Thirty pulled back with only one hand apiece on their burden.

"Let the final match of the Dueling Peaks Tournament," Bai Huizong thundered while throwing his raised hand down, "*begin!*"

The elders thrust the striker forwards. It swung, a battering ram that would surely shatter any castle's walls in a single blow.

For a brief moment Gou Ren was worried that the gong would break as it was struck.

The thunderous peal made the entire arena shake. It was a perfect, clear note. The sound roared down from the peak into the hills beyond. And as the note held, the barriers around the arena flickered, becoming visible for a brief moment as the peal of the gong reverberated and doubled back on itself until it felt like the entire world was drowned out. It made Gou Ren's heart thunder in his chest, and he could feel it in his bones. Beside him, his brother had lowered his recording crystal, amazement plain on his face. Loud Boy and Rags were gaping with open mouths. Others had their hands on their chests, the gong clearly resonating within each and every one of them.

Slowly, the long, drawn-out tone faded into silence. And in the last fading note, the battle began.

[Verdant Blade Sword Arts: Thirty-Two Blades of Grass]

[Claw Arts: Tenfold Reaping Blades]

Xiulan's swords shot forwards like arrows loosed from a bow. A forest of blades aiming to end the fight instantly.

Tigu dropped to all fours.

Her sandals had already been kicked off. Her fingers and toes dug into stone.

Tigu exploded into motion. She threw herself into a storm made of blurs of green.

Gou Ren remembered the care with which Guo Daxian had to navigate the blades of grass, and the cuts that had formed on him at the slightest touch. The crowd gasped as Tigu slammed into the blades attempting to impede her path.

Tigu caught some of the blades on her flesh. Most skittered off, drawing lines on her skin, while others penetrated deeper and drew blood. Her assault, however, carried her through.

Xiulan was forced to block. Qi blades clanged into Xiulan's jade-green ones, a shriek of metal on metal that sent Xiulan skidding backwards slightly. Gou Ren realised that clashing had never been Tigu's intent. She scythed past Xiulan, keeping ahead of some of the blades that had wheeled around to follow her, then attempted to strike her opponent from behind.

That was her plan, or at least the one Tigu had told him. She got talkative when she was bored, and now Gou Ren knew more about Xiulan's fighting style than he'd ever expected to know. Tigu was faster than Xiulan's swords—albeit barely. She had to keep moving. She had to burn energy, to stay one step ahead of defeat.

Tigu landed, then immediately jumped again. The air screamed in protest, breaking under her speed. She spun around too fast to see, closing from another angle, and smashed into Xiulan's defence like Chun Ke. A living battering ram of Qi blades and muscle.

She slashed past Xiulan once, twice, three times, cratering the ground wherever she landed and ricocheting off, searching for an opening.

"And for the first time, somebody manages to press the Demon-Slaying Orchid!" the announcer called to the cheers of the crowd. "A realm behind, yet still putting up a fight!"

Xiulan was as calm as ever. Each pass, she adjusted. Each time Tigu slammed into her, she blocked. Her eyes were calculating. She seemed to press a bit more at each pass.

Until on the fourth pass, she stepped into the strike. Blades deflected Tigu's assault, and a fist hammered into Tigu's stomach. The smaller girl gagged and slammed into the arena floor. She bounced from the impact before flipping to her feet.

Both women paused for a moment, assessing their opponent. Xiulan raised a delicate eyebrow.

Tigu's face split into a savage smile. Xiulan smiled back, amusement dancing in her eyes.

"And this set of rapid exchanges is just the warm-up!" Bai Huizong shouted. "My friends, we are in for a treat!"

The markings on Tigu's face seemed to feather and turn jagged. Her muscles flexed and hardened. Gou Ren grimaced. It almost made her look like she had been skinned alive when she did that. No fat. No softness. Just muscle. A predator through and through. The look in her yellow eyes as she focused on Xiulan made his spine tingle.

Tigu moved. Xiulan met her.

And Gou Ren stopped being able to fully follow the fight.

Tigu's Qi blades met Xiulan's swords in clashes that sounded like peals of rolling thunder. Her hands blurred as she thrust forwards, trying to get inside Xiulan's guard while the taller woman deflected the blows. Jade blades crept up behind Tigu, laying a trap. They surged forwards from Tigu's blind spots, and Gou Ren thought that was the end—

[Claw Arts: Crescent Hunter!]

This time, the blades formed on Tigu's heels like a rooster's spurs as she threw herself into a flipping kick. A ring of energy surrounded her, blasting the swords away. Xiulan was clearly surprised—and even more surprised at the foot that hammered into her jaw, snapping her head backwards.

"And the Demon-Slaying Orchid takes a solid blow! A powerful hit! The first time in the tournament she has truly been touched! Rou Tigu does the impossible!" Huizong shouted, spurring the crowd into an even deeper frenzy.

"Ha! You dare try that one on me?" Tigu shouted gleefully, loud enough to be heard over the roar of the crowd, then threw herself forwards again, intent on capitalising on Xiulan's surprise.

"It worked enough times before, *Little Sister*," Xiulan retorted while backpedaling, spitting out some blood from her split lip. "Taking lessons from the First Disciple? I thought you said it was beneath you!"

Tigu laughed just before she tackled Xiulan, managing to grab onto her arm. The orange-haired girl pulled her downwards and attempted to headbutt the taller woman.

Xiulan obliged her. There was a nasty *crack* as both of them connected. Gou Ren winced in sympathy at the sound. They were thrown back—but Tigu seemed to get the worst of it. Xiulan merely skidded backwards, while Tigu hit the floor of the arena, rolling three times before springing to her feet and rubbing at her forehead.

Xiulan made no move to follow up as her swords once more formed up around her.

"Unfair!" Gou Ren heard Loud Boy shout—Tigu once more had to push herself through the storm of blades to close the distance with Xiulan. The kid seemed angry at Xiulan retreating rather than closing in again.

"Unfair?" Xianghua demanded, glaring at Loud Boy. "She's taking Tigu seriously. What sort of fool closes the distance so readily with that little monster? Look at her, she's already healed some of the cuts from the beginning!"

Xianghua was right. The blood that had been leaking out from the deeper wounds had stopped. All that was left on Tigu's shoulders, arms, and legs were little white lines, standing out starkly on tanned skin.

Tigu braced herself for the arrival of the blades. She pulled her arms up and tightened her guard. Her hands lashed out, tipped with Qi claws. She began her charge again, smashing some of the swords into the ground so hard they stuck there—Gou Ren saw Xiulan grimace as instead of the blades pulling themselves out to continue the chase, they jerked and rattled, stuck fast. Tigu closed the gap—Xiulan's swords, the originals and not the copies, met Tigu. Claws met the blades again, as Xiulan artfully deflected each and every strike, flowing through and into Tigu's savage blows. With a gentle tap and a feint, Tigu's arms were thrown open. Xiulan's blade descended. Tigu barely managed to interpose one of her Qi blades, yet the force of the strike still threw her to the side, slamming her into the dirt.

Xiulan descended on her.

Tigu managed to shove off the ground, rolling away from the follow-up blow. She twisted and contorted like she didn't have any bones, slipping through the strikes with only scratches. With a kick, she managed to both knock a blade away and create distance, rolling up to her feet.

But her stance was low and crouched. She was panting.

Tigu was tiring. And while Gou Ren spotted a bit of sweat beading down Xiulan's face . . . her breathing was far more even.

Tigu laughed and stood up, bursting into a sprint. She assaulted Xiulan's fortress of blades again and again. Each time she was rebuffed. Xiulan calmly and methodically surrounded her opponent under a relentless, grinding advance of blades and counterattacks.

"Tough little brat," Gou Ren heard somebody mutter.

"Go on, Tigu!" Loud Boy thundered. His voice rose well above the crowd. "Tigu!"

The crowd took up the chant. First Rags, then Tie Delun. Then the random people of their section as Tigu got slammed into the dirt once more, yet again managing to avoid defeat by the skin of her teeth.

And again, she closed the distance, relentless. It was not a mindless effort. She varied her approach. She tried to trick her opponent. With strength and skill, she held on.

"The tenacity! The drive! Rou Tigu strikes forwards again!" the announcer roared.

But the small, orange-haired hellion couldn't keep it up forever. She snarled happily, her hair growing wilder, and her body contorting, and her flesh seeming to boil as if there were something trying to claw its way out of her skin—

Tigu gasped, and flinched. The almost grotesque cut of her muscles started to fade into something more natural. Her feral features began to even out.

A blade she didn't manage to deflect sliced into her biceps; the deepest one had managed to penetrate her skin.

Xiulan advanced. Every sword was arranged behind her, a flowing field of grass that surrounded her head in a circular formation. She flowed into what looked like the start of a dance. Her hands crossed and thrust forwards.

What rushed towards Tigu was a wall of swords.

Tigu took a deep breath. She clasped both of her hands together, pointing them in front of her and directly at her opponent. The Qi blades at her hands thickened and lengthened, touching to form a pointed shield in front of her. It almost looked like Loud Boy's technique.

[Claw Arts: Thunderous Breakthrough!]

The air protested as Tigu launched herself forwards one last time.

Xiulan charged to meet her, pulling back her fist.

Ten blades, then twenty, spiraled around her arm. Points touched, forming what looked like a drill.

[Verdant Blade Sword Arts: Lotus Blossom—]

Blades met claws. A sound like the gong rang throughout the arena, making the barrier flare with the force. Tigu, for a valiant moment, held out. She took one step forwards. Then another. She opened her mouth and roared.

Her shield cracked.

[—Bloom]

Then shattered. The blades struck home. The small, orange-haired girl was thrown backwards, slammed into the side of the arena, and went still.

Her shirt had been blasted open, showing off the cuts from the final attack, resembling flower petals carved into skin.

Tigu grimaced and tried to push herself up. Tried to get back into the fight. Blades floated above her in warning.

Groaning, she slumped in defeat.

The crowd exploded.

"What an ending! An explosive match! I must admit, I had my doubts that this could be as exciting as Tigu versus Xianghua, but Rou Tigu held on valiantly! She truly showed the power of one at the cusp of the Profound Realm! Though she failed to bridge the gap this day, she showed what even a cultivator in the Initiate's Realm is capable of!"

Xiulan held her hand out to Tigu.

The cat-turned-girl took it, pulling herself to her feet—then continued to pull, bringing herself and Xiulan into an embrace.

There were several noises of appreciation as Xiulan with obvious affection brushed some of Tigu's hair from her face. And then raised an eyebrow. Tigu's legs were still shaky. But she shifted, managing to slip around Xiulan and duck down to scoop the taller woman onto her shoulders.

"Ha! You love to see it, my friends. A bond undiminished by defeat! Truly, this tournament has been something special."

There was an answering cheer from the words. Gou Ren added his voice to it.

His brother, Loud Boy, Rags, and the rest of the people sitting with them howled and stomped their feet.

Xiulan's and Tigu's eyes found their section, and both of the women waved.

Gou Ren, unable to help the smile on his face, waved back.

↔

Xiulan was alone. Alone in the center of the arena.

Her eyes wandered through the crowd. To the approving smile on her father's face, before he disappeared, to hoist the arena one final time.

The crowd was deafening. The sun was warm, and the breeze was cold. Xiulan closed her eyes.

A victory. One she had actually earned this time. She sighed as some of the tension in her shoulders bled out.

She was satisfied with this.

The great gong sounded.

And then the Earthly Arena moved.

One last rise. The highest one out of them all. From their position, it rose smoothly. Higher and higher, until they were at the very peak of the mountain—and then above the mountain.

The afternoon sun was dipping low in the horizon. The sky was turning to night, and she could see every bright speck, every star above starting to shine.

There was a soft shudder as the outside of the arena came to a halt. The stands and the stage remained in place, but the floor of the arena continued to ascend.

Like giant steps, each concentric ring rose to a certain point before slowing and stopping. Until the center of it, the part that she was standing on, was the last part left. Until the peak that had been split in two once more resembled a single mountain, connected by the Arena. Xiulan was at the highest point. Higher than the gong.

The wind flowed around her body as she stood at the peak. How often had she dreamed it would be her up here?

There was a blur of movement. Around the edges of the arena, the Elders leapt into place. To mortals, it was likely that they just seemed to appear, materializing out of thin air.

The Elders, as one, raised their hands into the gesture of respect, then turned to the gong. They pulled back its striker one last time and heaved it forwards.

It echoed clear and pure across the entire hills.

The ancient characters on the arena floor burned blue and scrawled up the rings before bursting into the air. They flowed around her. Other victors had said that they did nothing. But as Xiulan looked at them, she felt closure and a certain kind of peace.

Normally, the victor was supposed to simply look towards the heavens. Xiulan . . . looked down. She stared at the crowds—as they cheered and applauded for her.

This was the end of one chapter of her life and the start of a new one. Xiulan felt her conviction firm. She looked down the mountain to the people below. The smiles they gave her. The trust her friends had in her. The untold masses, with smiles, instead of villagers sobbing in burned-out homes.

Her power was to protect. And she would try her hardest to make sure no one down there would experience something like Sun Ken again.

Maybe she was arrogant. Perhaps it wouldn't work. Perhaps trying to break down the barriers between Sects would prove more than she alone could handle.

The rest of the contestants climbed up. From the bottom of the arena to the rungs below her, in the order that they had been defeated.

Tigu grinned up at Xiulan and waved. Xianghua smirked at her. Her Petals smiled up at her with pride and admiration.

But . . . she knew that she would not have to do it alone.

Xiulan stared at the prizes. Three Profound Breakthrough Pills. A princely reward . . . for anyone *other* than her. The eight Spirit Beast Cores were similarly of little use, though the sprigs of Spiritual Grass would at least be useful for Master Jin—hopefully.

The party was in full swing—though it was a bit more subdued than the last two. It was more a formality than anything, especially with several Elders actively in attendance.

There would be little acting up with them around.

"I can't believe people are already packing up. I would have thought that they would have been here longer," Gou Ren said as he looked over the other tables. Indeed, for while many were drinking, quite a few were saying their goodbyes or speaking with servants.

"The Sects are, largely. They have to return to their territories. The mortals, however, will stay for another week at least," Xiulan said.

"Huh, what's the plan for us, then?" he asked.

"We'll stay as long as you please. Tigu wants to wait for Master Jin," Xiulan said.

"Where is Tigu, anyway?" Yun Ren asked, looking around at the knots of people, clearly expecting to see her there.

"With Loud Boy and Rags; they said they found a good spot to look over the city," Gou Ren replied.

Xiulan nodded, then paused when she saw Bolin approach.

"Mistress." His voice was apologetic.

Xiulan sighed. "Another meeting?"

Bolin nodded. "I'm sorry, Mistress. An important guest requested your presence."

Xiulan got up, shaking her head.

"Well, Tigu will turn up sooner or later," Gou Ren said with a sigh. "See you later, Lanlan."

She smiled at her companions and nodded, then followed after the disciple.

"Who is this guest, anyway?" she asked.

"The Shrouded Mountain Sect, Mistress."

CHAPTER 44

UNEXPECTED VISITOR

What would the Shrouded Mountain Sect want with me? Xiulan pondered the development as Bolin led her back to the manor. The question whirled in her mind.

The Shrouded Mountain Sect had called on her personally. Such a thing was not done. Sects from out of province rarely, if ever, ventured into the Azure Hills—they disregarded them completely as beneath their notice. A Young Master or Mistress her age in those provinces would be nearing, or within, the Spiritual Realm, not barely breaching the Profound.

The Azure Hills, for all intents and purposes, were cut off from the rest of the world. They were too weak and too Qi-deprived to produce anything of value.

It protected and sheltered them from the greater machinations of the powerful. But . . . it also hindered them. Few of those who tried to leave lived long.

Even with an outside backer, it was well known that most from the Azure Hills simply grew more slowly than people of other provinces, even when they were given equivalent resources. Some did get stronger . . . but either way, those who left rarely returned.

Xiulan imagined that the other reason was far more simple. The Azure Hills was their home. The Sects stayed out of obligation for the millennia that their ancestors had spent building their homes. She knew that every Sect Master of the Verdant Blade Sect swore to guard the heartgrass that grew in the center of the Sect until their deaths, and had done so for thousands of years. Ancient oaths bound them.

"Formal attire, Young Mistress," Bolin whispered to her, and Xiulan nodded.

The first thing Xiulan had to do was change. She sighed as she got out the box filled with layer upon layer of silk, in pinks and purples. Her finest clothes. Despite her current dress being perfectly acceptable for most occasions, for greeting the Shrouded Mountain Sect she could only wear her best. So she changed into her finest garment. It was many-layered, in an imported style, and a bit hard to move in—if only because she might tear it if she shifted too quickly.

Xiulan disliked the garment and the design philosophy within it. It was said that cultivators of other provinces used the most fragile and rare fabrics imaginable—that a single errant breeze would render the clothes to dust, so it was proof of mastery that they could move with ease in them.

The Azure Hills only really had some particularly thin silks, and the entire thing was normally an exercise in frustration and concentration. The outfit's only redeeming quality was that it did look rather nice, like a many-layered orchid . . . but it would probably look better on someone else. Xiulan preferred things with more movement. Xiulan did her hair up in a more formal style as well, placing the headdress only reserved for very formal occasions on her head.

Xiulan idly imagined Senior Sister in the garment, and smirked as she visualized the look of disgust—Senior Sister's nose would scrunch up and her eyes would narrow into slits. Yes, Senior Sister would probably hate this piece. Her own and Master Jin's styles were much more appealing, but arriving in front of the Shrouded Mountain Sect wearing flannel and pants was likely asking for trouble.

The garment was easier to walk in than she remembered—her cultivation advancing had at least made it a bit less annoying.

Bolin led her to the meeting room. She felt the other cultivator before she saw him. He was leaking power like a river. There was the tang of recently struck lightning that pressed down on Xiulan, as well as the charred smell of ash.

Fire, and enough Qi to make any amount of grass burn . . . but it felt a little strange.

Her father and the three Elders were already within when she arrived, entertaining their guest. Xiulan knocked twice on the door and was admitted.

"May I present my daughter, and the pride of our Sect, Cai Xiulan," her father proclaimed.

Xiulan bowed low, hiding her lower face behind the voluminous sleeves instead of giving a more standard gesture of martial respect between Sects.

The bowing and scraping one must do, when the disciples of a Sect could handily defeat the Elders of another. Especially when the disciple was leaking Fire Qi in such great amounts.

"This one is Cai Xiulan, of the Verdant Blade Sect. She greets the Disciple of the Shrouded Mountain Sect," Xiulan intoned formally, keeping her eyes low. She had a brief glance of him as the door opened, holding out his cup so that Elder Yi could pour him a drink.

"Hmm, a fast reception and hospitality," the man stated. "You may be of the Azure Hills, but you understand yourselves well."

Xiulan kept her head bowed as she smelled a waft of maple. The man shifted slightly in his lounging position.

"This one is Zang Li, Young Master of the Shrouded Mountain Sect," he stated, and Xiulan was a bit surprised at the polite and formal language that flowed from his mouth. He was giving them quite a lot of face to speak with them like this. Yet Xiulan could feel the intent upon her as the Disciple of the Shrouded Mountain Sect weighed her worth. She looked up, raising her eyes to meet the man who had requested her.

He was stunningly handsome, in the traditional style. Long silky hair done in a topknot. A soft, pale, and flawless face with just a bit of hardness underneath. He had a haughty, domineering expression, and there was a flame-burst symbol painted in red on his forehead. His face was timeless—though he still appeared rather young to her eyes. She'd heard he was eighteen, several years younger than herself.

He was also the one who had been staring at her from the box seating—and undressing her with his eyes. But there was no rebuke she could offer the Shrouded Mountain Sect, so she had to stay quiet.

Even as she began to feel uncomfortable from the steady lapping of his fiery Qi touching her.

He suddenly smiled, a charming, boyish thing, and nodded to her.

"This Young Master shall get right to business, then. I am here on behalf of the Shrouded Mountain Sect. The purpose of our visit is to scout new talent. Indeed, I would like to think it is fate or the heavens smiling upon us. For the first time in the centuries we've sent an envoy to this tiny well, we have found a small gem among the inhabitants."

The bottom dropped out of Xiulan's stomach at the implication.

"I have seen enough from your daughter. I would give her the gift of being able to join my retinue and see the Shrouded Mountain." His voice was commanding and imperious, as he all but demanded her. "Of course, our Sect would look kindly upon such a thing."

The entire room was silent at his words, save for the small fire being used to boil tea. The crystal hummed softly and the flame burned as the water started to boil.

"It is a fantastically generous offer, Young Master," her father stated. She could see the tenseness in his shoulders. "May we have a moment to discuss such a . . . wonderful opportunity?"

"Oh? You need to discuss my offer?" he asked blandly. He gazed at them all with a touch of amusement at the collective pause. "Very well. Bring me some more of this." He waved a cup that smelled of maple. Her father winced slightly. "Speak quickly, for I shall be leaving soon. Your daughter can show me your hospitality."

"Of course, Young Master," her father agreed. The Elders bowed and exited the room, leaving Xiulan alone with Zang Li.

↔

Ri Zu smiled up at the moon as she hopped across the rooftops. She leapt higher and higher, jumping through the air just like Bi De did. Nobody was looking up at the rooftops, and her paws didn't make a sound when she landed. The night air was pleasant on her fur, especially since she was out of the confines of Gou Ren's shirt. He was quite comfortable, but Ri Zu had decided enough was enough when he'd offered to walk Xianghua home.

So she had bid everybody goodbye and gone out into the night. She had debated going to find the cat, but she was out with Loud Boy and Rags, so that was right out. The little annoying one hurt her ears.

So back to the manor it was. Ri Zu had scrolls to read and she was a bit curious about why Miss Lanlan had to leave. A meeting with the Something Mountain. She had heard that much, and for some reason the name sounded vaguely . . . familiar.

It bothered her, though she was having a bit of trouble recalling why.

She shook her head and hopped the wall, alighting on the guesthouse. The little courtyard was quite aesthetically pleasing. A wonderful collection of trees and a pond, where there were some busy-looking people packing things away. Ri Zu glanced down. The guesthouse was cold, dark, and still, with nobody in it.

Ri Zu didn't like silence, despite her love of reading. She normally went to find a room with somebody else. So she considered her options but then paused when a conversation caught her ear.

"Yes, he said the Shrouded Mountain," one of the servants muttered to another as they walked past the building with loads of laundry.

"Really? Shrouded Mountain Sect? Here?" the smaller servant girl said, excited. "The heavens smile on our Sect to have such auspicious guests."

"Don't be too happy. There's . . . well, I talked to a girl from the, you know. The one with the lip who cleans the girls' clothes. She said he goes through women like a scythe through rice."

Shrouded Mountain?

A memory surfaced. *Hadn't the Mistress told her of a man who'd claimed to come from there?*

Ri Zu frowned.

"Yeah, finger marks on their necks. Qiqi is kind of a freak, though, she . . . actually *volunteered* for a second round."

Ri Zu flushed as one of the other girls let out a scandalized gasp.

Eavesdropping was quite rude . . .

But the memory was making her worry. There was somebody from Shrouded Mountain here. Ri Zu rubbed her hands together as she glanced at the main house.

She could sit and wait . . . or she could go and take a look.

She mentally apologised to her hosts.

Ri Zu hopped to the main manor and entered through one of the open windows. Her heart slowed and her Qi pulled into herself, just as it always did when she wanted to hide. When she actually made an effort to conceal her presence, even Tigu couldn't find her.

"Oh? You need to discuss my offer? Very well. Bring me some more of this. Speak quickly, for I shall be leaving soon. Your daughter can show me your hospitality."

The voice was haughty and arrogant and made Ri Zu immediately dislike the speaker.

"Of course, Young Master," the voice of Xiulan's father called. A door opened and shut, not too far from where Ri Zu was. She followed the noise. She hadn't actually been in this section of the house, so finding where things were with sound and without being able to know which room was where was a bit of a problem.

If there was one thing Ri Zu both liked and hated about herself, it was just how good she was at sneaking and remaining unnoticed. Tigu always spoke of the amount of effort needed to place each paw just so, yet Ri Zu could move quite quickly—her light body and lighter steps did not disturb anything, even the dust in the roof.

Silence and darkness. The things that Chow Ji had liked, once upon a time. A sneaking, slinking rat.

"No, I will not even consider it—" she heard Xiulan's father snarl, and she paused as they passed right under her.

"Your emotions get the best of you, Sect Master," another voice stated. "Calm yourself, you look like you're about to spit blood."

"Indeed," she heard another voice rumble. "We will consider this offer in its entirety, and its use to the Sect. We would not wish to give up an advantage when it dangles itself in front of our faces."

"And what do you think of this offer, Yi? It's a very good one, I do imagine . . ." Xiulan's father's voice was still angry, but a bit more in control.

"It is indeed . . ." Yi said calmly, his voice fading as they passed underneath her and into another room.

Ri Zu debated going after the old men . . . but instead sniffed the air.

Maple, ash, and Xiulan.

She set off in that direction, carefully moving along the beams, until she could poke her head out into the room where Xiulan was, her needle clutched tightly in her paw, just in case.

She frowned at the scene she witnessed.

Xiulan was seated beside a thin, pale man with long hair who had so much Fire Qi that Ri Zu could *smell it.* She calmly poured him a drink—a cup of maple syrup.

An entire cup? How greedy. Who is he, Wa Shi?

"Another little gem in this place, this stuff. Quite the find. Perhaps I shall ask your Elders for some more, hmm?" the man asked.

"If you wish, Young Master," Xiulan replied demurely. Her face was a soft mask of a smile. The one she used when she was *really* angry.

The man only seemed to find it amusing, or perhaps he just liked the sound of his voice. He was smirking and acting like he was an Emperor, lounging and lazing arrogantly.

Ri Zu's distaste for the man only grew.

"And my congratulations at standing atop this whole pile. A small feat, but quite worthy of praise for your humble origins."

"My thanks for your kind words, Young Master."

"More of this dish," the man commanded.

Xiulan served him. He ate a mouthful, his eyes upon her, and drank the syrup out of the cup.

Who was this man, to treat Miss Lanlan like a servant?

"I disliked this place at first. But the more time I spend in this province, the more palatable it becomes. Tea," he demanded. Xiulan glanced at the pot and leaned slightly across the table—

He caught her chin between two of his fingers and pulled her face to meet his. "Truly a beautiful gem."

Ri Zu felt her blood boil, and her grip tightened on her needle. But she could feel the man's power. She remembered her Master's lessons. Patience. She couldn't do anything. Yet. And Tigu had pounded into her head how *not* to approach a being that eclipsed her.

He leaned forwards, like he was about to bring his lips to meet Xiulan's. The woman's eyes narrowed, and Ri Zu felt the spike of intent from her, murderous fury wafting off her.

The man drew back instead, releasing her chin. He smirked.

"My apologies, Cai Xiulan. Merely a joke." His grin was that of a child ripping the wings off an insect.

"A wonderful joke, Young Master," Xiulan stated. "Truly, Zang Li of the Shrouded Mountain Sect has wit beyond measure."

Zang Li.

Hearing the name was like Brother Chun Ke accidentally stepping on her that one time. Her breath wheezed out.

Zang Li.

She knew that name. Her Master had told her that name.

"The weedy bastard walked around the corner and just demanded Meihua sleep with him," her Master had said with a snarl, scorn lacing every word. "'This Young Master is Zang Li, you shall have the honour of sharing my bed tonight.' Of course, Jin was having none of that. The stupid bastard broke his fingers on Jin's chest. I can only imagine what kind of torment he's going through for daring to impersonate the Shrouded Mountain Sect." Her face had split into a vicious grin. "I wonder what cultivators do to people like that. I wouldn't mind learning."

Her Master's grin in that moment had been vindictive and cruel, something that scared Ri Zu whenever it crossed her face.

Ri Zu shook her head, startled, as she realised somebody had started speaking again.

"Hmmm. A bit feisty. I do enjoy women like yourself. Like your companion, Rou Tigu. She reminds me of somebody. Tell me, is she of any relation to a man named Rou Jin?"

Zang Li's eyes suddenly focused as for a brief moment; Xiulan's mask cracked, confusion overcoming her features.

Then he smiled.

"My apologies. Rou *Jun*. I do tend to forget insignificant men's names."

Xiulan started to answer, her mask slamming back into place. "I do not believe I know a man by that name."

The door opened, and Ri Zu nearly jumped out of her skin as Xiulan's father and the other old men walked in.

As one, they bowed. "We thank the Young Master of the Shrouded Mountain Sect for his offer, and the face it gives us. It truly is most generous, and something we would be honoured to accept. To have our daughter accompany you would be a boon."

Ri Zu gaped. *Just what the hells is going on here? They're going to just give Miss Lanlan to Zang Li?! They were going to—*

Ri Zu nearly pounced from her hiding spot. She had to warn Xiulan!

"Unfortunately, our Young Mistress has too many duties, diplomatic and martial, for her to be spared," Xiulan's father continued, and Ri Zu scrambled to return to her hiding spot. "The drink you so enjoy is the result of her efforts with a Hidden Master to whom the Verdant Blade Sect is connected. We dare not insult him by taking away his point of contact—or the Shrouded Mountain Sect by requesting greater compensation than what they were prepared to offer our lowly Sect. This is the decision of the Sect Master of the Verdant Blade Sect, in unison with all his Elders. We will of course be discreet; none will breathe a word of this . . . disagreement."

Zang Li's eyes darkened for a moment before he shrugged.

"Hmm, a *Hidden Master*. A Hidden Master in these hills! How interesting. Truly, you are blessed by the heavens to have so many eyes upon you, Cai Xiulan." Zang Li looked amused before nodding to her father. "Ah, it matters little. Very well, I shall allow it. This meeting never happened. I merely wished to be served by your daughter and show my appreciation. You may thank me for my generosity."

The older men bowed their heads. "Thank you, Young Master," they chorused.

"'Tis a pity. I might have even deigned to marry her," Zang Li said, clearly as a parting jab, rising to his feet. "But I have a busy night ahead of me. I thank you for your hospitality and your time."

Xiulan's father nodded. "Please, allow me to escort you to the door."

"But of course. It is likely the last time we shall see each other."

Ri Zu's eyes flicked from side to side, first to Xiulan, then to the man who was leaving. She saw Xiulan slump in relief as the old, strong men surrounded her. She was safe for now.

Ri Zu scrambled after the two men who were leaving.

He had asked about Master Jin and Tigu.

Ri Zu scribbled out a note. She couldn't get Xiulan's attention without alerting everyone else at the moment, so she took a detour, throwing the small pad of paper with her writing on it to the guesthouse's door, where Xiulan would be able to see it later.

She managed to do it and turn back just in time to see Xiulan's father bow to Zang Li. The boy didn't bother to return the bow.

Ri Zu shadowed his movements as he walked past the manors, until he came to the corner of the street . . . and jumped.

He'd moved faster than Ri Zu could track.

Ri Zu swore.

↔

Xiulan sighed, slumping.

Elder Yi's eyes narrowed at her, and she straightened up again. He looked away.

"Did he touch you?" Elder Sheng asked, his brow wrinkled with concern.

Xiulan shrugged. "Only a small amount."

Sheng began to grumble, his Qi spiking for a moment before he calmed himself.

Xiulan smiled at his outrage. Really, it wasn't that bad. But there was one thing that was surprising.

Xiulan turned to Elder Yi, whose face was a mask of calm.

He turned to her, his eyes judging.

"Disciple, explain to me why our decision was unanimous," he demanded.

"Guaranteed resources from the Hidden Master are more useful than some 'maybes' from the Shrouded Mountain Sect," Xiulan answered immediately, thinking of the likely answer.

"Correct. The Hidden Master has already helped us and is poised to help us in the future. Second, I know that man's type. He had no virtue. He wished for a pretty flower to warm his bed, and would likely go back on any promise he did make. Unacceptable." Elder Yi was obviously angry. "*And* he gave up too easily."

Xiulan nodded. "He did."

Yi considered her.

"You are released back to the festivities, if you can maintain your bearing, Disciple," Yi decided. "I do not believe even he is brazen enough to make trouble tonight. I shall be leaving presently to scout the road ahead, and Elder Sheng is going to the Misty Lake Sect with Elder Bingwen. Tomorrow, you shall be in command of the servants for the final preparations."

"I obey, Elder Yi," Xiulan said. Elder Yi waved her away. *Permission from Elder Yi? How rare.*

She changed out of her clothes, a chore that she eventually called in the servants to help her with, specifically for folding all the silk and getting it back into the box.

That piece truly was a pain.

After that, she scrubbed her face until it felt a bit raw. She was a little unsettled. The man's sudden question about Master Jin, even if he'd "corrected" himself, was a bit . . . concerning.

The man was a dark spot on an otherwise wonderful night.

But the night was still young, and there was still plenty of time to have some fun.

And find Tigu just in case.

Xiulan nodded, her course set—until a panicked, squeaking rat impacted her stomach.

CHAPTER 45

INTO DARKNESS

Xiulan's heart pounded in her ears as she raced across the town around the Dueling Peaks, towards a small, forested hill just out of town.

"Yeah, they said they were headed for Little Pimple. A bit far for us to get to tonight, but they should be back soon," the mortal friend of Rags had said.

She sped onwards to the hill, focused on the objective. A little creature hung on in her shirt, shaking slightly.

"Where are the brothers?" Xiulan asked her. She hadn't had time to check but assumed they were still in the town.

'Gou Ren is with Xianghua. Yun Ren went with the Petal-grasses, still at the party.'

Xiulan breathed a small sigh of relief.

Most likely safe, then. A strike in full view of everybody won't go over well—But . . . will that stop them?

Ri Zu's story had sent chills down her spine. Xiulan's swords floated behind her as she sprinted, but she didn't know the first place to start looking. She couldn't just bash down the doors to the Shrouded Mountain Sect's quarters—she didn't even know if they had her. Could he have even gotten Tigu in the time he was in their Sect? Had he sent others?

Xiulan didn't know. All she knew was that Tigu was with two sectless companions and likely isolated.

Xiulan poured on the speed. She raced to the mountain, her eyes searching for clearings.

Please, please, let this all be nothing—

Ri Zu let out a mournful squeak. Xiulan's heart fell, as she came to a gap in the trees.

A shattered bottle of wine. Cuts in the trees. Disturbances in a savaged clearing, evidence of a short and brutal fight.

Blood.

Xiulan skidded to her knees. Rags was flat on his back. His chest had been torn open, red pooling into the dirt around him.

'Heart Beating. Barely. His Qi is . . .' Ri Zu cut herself off with a grimace. Her little hands moved to her pouch of medicine and she pulled out a pill. A pill made of the Spiritual Herbs.

But she hesitated. Her eyes flicked to the ball of medicine.

'Only one more left after this,' she whispered. *'And it might not be enough.'*

Xiulan closed her eyes. "Do your best."

Ri Zu nodded.

Xiulan stood, looking around. There was Rags, but where was—Xiulan saw a path leading down the side of the peaks.

Pushed-over grass and a trail of blood.

Xiulan followed it as Ri Zu tended to Rags, mashing up the medicine pill and mixing it with some water, to be able to get it down Rags's throat.

The trail got quite far down the mountain before she saw who made it.

Loud Boy was slumped against a tree. His eyes were cloudy and he was muttering to himself. Tear tracks stained his face. His shirt had been blown open, revealing a conspicuous mark near his navel. An impact mark where his dantian would be.

"Gotta warn them, gotta warn them, gotta warn them . . ." he whispered repeatedly, even as sobs cut through his words. Blood splattered to the ground from his mouth when he coughed a second later.

Xiulan was beside him in an instant. The boy startled and flailed at her, his eyes going wild.

Xiulan gently caught the blow and cupped his face with a hand.

"Loud—Zang Wei. Zang Wei, it's Xiulan," she whispered to him.

The boy paused in his flailing. His face twisted as more hot tears stained his face. He tried to look away from her.

Xiulan pulled him into a hug. The boy stiffened in shock before collapsing onto her.

"What happened?" she whispered to him, even as sobs racked his body.

He couldn't be more than fifteen at most.

"I don't know. I don't know. The men . . . they came out of the trees. They said they were Shrouded Mountain Sect, and that Tigu had to go with them," he choked into her dress.

"She said . . . she said that she couldn't go with strangers without telling other people first. They said she had to go with them now. We tried to fight—we tried, but Tigu was still tired from her battle, and they . . . they killed Rags and . . . and . . ." The boy hiccuped. One hand went from where he was holding Xiulan to his stomach.

They had destroyed his cultivation.

Xiulan's breath was a sharp intake and she felt her own stomach clench. She took a deep, steadying breath, then pulled back.

"Zang Wei. Zang Wei, listen to me. Rags is still alive," Xiulan said in what she hoped was a reassuring voice.

The boy spasmed as hope blossomed on his face.

"Ri Zu is taking care of him. He might be in bad shape, but she thinks he might be able to make it through the night."

"But . . . but what about Tigu? Th-they took her away," he said, though his voice wobbled.

Blood. The Valley. Sun Ken. Xiulan grimaced at the memories.

"I'll take care of it. I'll make sure nothing bad happens," Xiulan said with a forced smile.

Loud Boy's grip on her hands was weak. But for a brief moment, it firmed.

"Don't let them take her."

"I won't."

Never again.

↔

Ri Zu's heart pounded in her chest. Her breath came in little gasps. Her nose tasted the air, picking up the faint scent of blood in the wind. There was a small commotion behind this place. The sounds of movement.

She stared up at the imposing walls of the manor. Xiulan had said that this was the most likely place for them to be.

Xiulan had taken over tending to Loud Boy and Rags. The look on her face had been calm, yet Ri Zu could see the pain and fury within her crystal-blue eyes.

The same pain and fury Ri Zu felt.

But they needed information. They needed to know if Tigu was actually in the guest building or somewhere else entirely—so Ri Zu had volunteered to scout.

Ri Zu swallowed. She closed her eyes. Her thundering heart quieted.

Now ready, Ri Zu ascended the wall. Her steps were soft and silent, a wraith in the dark.

She poked her head up over the top, her nose sniffing rapidly.

"Stack that one over there," said a man carrying a crate. "They want to be gone by sunrise." Ri Zu stopped herself from flinching.

Clambering down from the wall, she skirted along the outside of it, avoiding the men packing bags. She followed the light taste of blood and what was unmistakably Tigu's scent.

She paused for a moment when she got to the house. Then she clambered up the side, and into the rafters.

Tigu was here. Ri Zu was fairly certain of that. But where exactly? She had the scent, though it was still a bit muddled with blood and sweat.

"I can't wait to be rid of this hellhole. This entire province is like a pig shitting into my soul," a voice grumbled, to the laughter of others nearby.

"This sits ill with me," a calm, exacting voice stated. "For what purpose was this carried out?"

There was the sound of rustling, and a heavy body shifting.

"Come off it, Yingwen. The Young Master said the girl challenged the Sect, then spat in his face when he tried to offer her a place with us. Such insults can't be borne, you know."

Yingwen clicked his tongue. "You ape your better, Fenxian. I was the one who said that yesterday, fool. Indeed, a firm chastisement is only right and proper. But to take her? That is beneath the might of our Sect. Bordering on uncouth, I might even say. It could be tolerated, but he even wants us to collect her companions."

Ri Zu paused at the statement, then drew closer. She poked her head into the room, seeing two men. The one lounging on the floor was nearly as big as Master Jin, large and muscled. The other was thin and morose-looking, leaning against the wall, his brow furrowed. Both had long, sleek hair in topknots . . . and were surrounded by copious amounts of bottles lining the floor. Even as she watched, the thin one drained another, then glared at it.

"Uncouth is allowing one to tarnish the name of the Shrouded Mountain. Let her hang, or be remoulded into something useful," a third voice intoned, as a man opened the door and sat down. He had grey hair and eyes.

Yingwen scoffed.

"Brother, how was guard duty?" Fenxian said, tossing him a bottle.

The man caught it. "Boring. She's still unconscious, but she's a tough little beast—some of her bruises are fading already. Or you're getting weak. Six strikes to take her down, Fenxian? For shame."

Ri Zu felt her face twisting as fury filled her.

Yingwen's head snapped up, his eyes searching.

Ri Zu froze. Her heart slowed to nearly a stop, and her Qi dissipated into nothing. She pushed herself carefully back into the slight hole in the wall that let her poke her head out.

"What's the matter, Yingwen?" Fenxian asked.

Ri Zu heard the whisper of movement, so she stilled again; a moment later, the man's hand caught the ceiling beam and he pulled himself up. Ri Zu could feel him. She could sense him, as his Qi tingled her body, passing over her.

Silent.

Invisible.

She heard the man move towards the wall—

Then drop down.

"Nothing. Though this building may have a pest infestation."

"Wait, really? Don't they have seals or something to keep them out? Even when I think they can't be any *more* useless, they surprise me!"

Ri Zu caught the scent of the man who had just come from "guard duty." She followed it back through the manor, and then down.

Down, into a basement. Where the construction turned to heavy stone.

Down she slunk, in the shadows of the stairs. There was no noise, save for breathing coming from the bottom. Breathing from two sources. One heavier and one lighter.

Ri Zu swallowed as she finished the descent, peeking around the doorframe.

A man reclined on a seat, in front of a cage. Its front held no keyhole; instead, a piece of paper was pressed over the edge where it would open, filed with arcane symbols.

Ri Zu put it out of her mind.

Because there was Tigu. Lying on her front, with her arms clamped by steel and several more pieces of paper behind her back.

Tigu's face was bruised. Some blood had pooled out of her mouth to stain the floor. The happy, cheerful grin was nowhere to be seen.

Ri Zu committed the man's face to memory. She committed the taste and tang of Tigu's blood to her mind.

The people who had done this to Tigu would *pay*. Icy-cold fingers crawled up Ri Zu's spine as she imagined the man writhing with Reaper fungus toxin, or vomiting out his insides.

Medicine turned to poison. Some of the recipes for Chow Ji's pills danced tantalizingly in her mind's eye.

Those pills were made out of people. But being made into a pill might be too good for this scum.

Her fingers itched for the needle she had left behind, as well as her Master's final gift.

"If you're ever in any trouble, mix these two together, and add ground riverwort," her Master had said. Her eyes were cold. Ri Zu sniffed the bottles, and her eyes widened.

'Master, this is—'

"Hong Family recipe. It doesn't have a name. But . . . it's supposed to be bad. I've never used it before. And I pray that you don't have to either."

Yes. That was perfect. She could go back right now, get the needle, and strike like Tigu had taught her. A blow to the neck would spread the poison the fastest, and then—

There was a sudden sound from the top of the stairs.

Footsteps. Ri Zu twitched, her eyes searching for a hiding place. No holes in the walls she could use, and the sound was too close for her to have the time to climb up to the ceiling—

She whipped around and shoved her body into one of the stairs. It had a slight overhang. Just barely enough to shield her from view.

The stomping feet resolved themselves into a woman, who looked rather nervous.

She walked right past Ri Zu's hiding spot, carrying a tray.

"Master, the meal you requested," the woman said demurely, taking great pains to not look at where Tigu was lying.

The man grunted, then grabbed his food.

Ri Zu's beating heart slowed. She took a breath.

To go and attempt this alone was foolish. There were too many variables.

Ri Zu scurried back up the stairs, heading back towards Xiulan.

↔

Xiulan tapped her fingers impatiently as she waited for Ri Zu to return. She knew she wasn't particularly quiet or stealthy, so Ri Zu had volunteered to see where Tigu was being kept.

It did not make the waiting any easier, however.

Rags and Loud Boy were lying side by side on bedrolls, Xiulan watching over them.

The others still weren't back. Not that she could blame them. They had been expecting a night of fun.

Xiulan bit the nail on her thumb.

What could she do? What could she do?

Xiulan closed her eyes. Elders Yi and Sheng had already left and would be hours away by now. Her father and Elder Zei would be with the other Elders of the Azure Hills. She could find them, and tell them . . . and then what?

The problem was blatantly obvious.

If they went for Tigu while the Shrouded Mountain Sect already had her, they would be opposing the Shrouded Mountain Sect—and that was suicide.

They had no demands that they could make. They had nothing to bargain with to get the Shrouded Mountain to return her friend.

Zang Li was stronger than her father. Her father, who was at the Second Stage of the Profound Realm and near the Third.

Against Zang Li's blazing Qi and the secrets of the Shrouded Mountain Sect? It would be like throwing a handful of grass into a bonfire.

They did not face Zang Li alone either—he had an entire retinue of other cultivators with him. An entire retinue that could be in the Profound Realm as well—at minimum, they were at either the Fourth or Fifth Stage of the Initiate's Realm, and for the Shrouded Mountain that would be considered weak.

Even if every Verdant Blade Elder were here, the Shrouded Mountain Sect could duel the entirety of their Sect and crush them with ease.

She could possibly rally other Sects to their cause, which would have been a daunting task even before telling them who they would be fighting. Who would dare be willing to impede the Shrouded Mountain Sect's path? Who would dare to make demands of a Young Master who could crush even Elders beneath his heel, all for a sectless girl that held no value to them?

Even if they did succeed in delaying them, or managed to fight and win, if Zang Li, or any member of the Shrouded Mountain Sect, escaped, or even if they capitulated and handed over Tigu . . . the remaining members would tell their Elders of what happened here, *especially* if her own father got involved.

And then . . . it would be over. The Shrouded Mountain Sect would brook no insult, especially not one of that magnitude. Mere insects assaulting their majestic falcon? The very idea would have men in the Spiritual Realm striding down from the Shrouded Mountain in force.

What could she do? A man who had been insulted and defeated by Master Jin now sought revenge against him through his student and family.

What can I do? Xiulan took a breath, and then a black form appeared in the window.

Ri Zu had returned.

'They're packing—preparing to leave. They will be gone by morning.'

No time. No time. We have no time.

Xiulan bit her lip.

She had made a promise to Master Jin to protect them.

Her Sect would likely survive. She could throw herself at Master Jin's feet and say that they hadn't been able to stand against them. He would be angry. He would be furious . . . And he would likely go against the Shrouded Mountain Sect alone.

He had said to value her life more. That she shouldn't be so willing to run headfirst to her death.

But that was not the kind of woman she was. She would not sit back and let others die for her.

Xiulan let out a breath and opened her eyes. *She was out of time.* They had to go before the Shrouded Mountain Sect left, and Master Jin wasn't here.

"My plan is foolish and dangerous. I do not know the chances of success, but it is better than doing nothing. Ri Zu, will you help me?" she asked.

The little rat nodded.

"Are you sure? Are you sure you can do this?" she asked.

Ri Zu glared at her. The rat's eyes were full of a kind of vicious malice that equaled Senior Sister's, as well as a grim resolve.

'Ri Zu . . . will be brave.'

□

The brothel girl had been easy to convince to turn away and let Xiulan take over for her. A bit of coin in her purse, and she was on her way—a much better alternative to accidentally getting caught in the crossfire.

Xiulan approached the manor and its pristine, tasteful stone walls from an alley. She seemed to appear from nowhere. She had a pack on her back and a wide-brimmed traveling hat for noble ladies upon her head. A pink silk strap kept it in place as her swords floated gently behind her. She had changed out of her soiled clothes into another dress. It was a bit looser in the top than she normally wore it.

There were no guards outside the door. The street was empty.

Xiulan knocked on the gate.

She had to wait for but a moment for the gate to be opened by a member of the Shrouded Mountain Sect, looking annoyed.

"Who dares call upon us at this hou . . . er . . ." He trailed off as Xiulan tipped her hat up, leaning forward slightly and giving the man a warm smile.

His face flushed.

"Pray, forgive this one's interruption, Expert of the Shrouded Mountain. This humble one calls upon your Young Master, as he requested earlier."

"Ah—um—" The man coughed, composing himself. "Yes, the Young Master mentioned meeting somebody earlier. This way, please, miss."

Xiulan bowed appropriately to him, lowering her head. The man flushed yet again.

He let her into the compound. His eyes kept flicking to her as she pushed her hat back, letting the lantern light shine and catch her hair and skin. His steps were lurching when he led her to the main house.

He turned completely, and she gave him another smile.

The man stared, before coughing and opening the door for her.

"Miss, forgive me, but before you meet the Young Master, you must surrender your weapons," he stated as formally as he could.

Xiulan nodded agreeably. "A wise course of action. Please, by all means."

Xiulan handed over her swords. The man took them, placing them on a rack. Xiulan leaned on the counter as she watched him work. "Do you need to search me as well?" she asked, though it was stilted. She cursed internally. It hadn't come out as flirty as she'd wanted it to, yet the man didn't seem to notice. He nearly dropped her swords as his head whipped around to stare at her. She fixed her smile—before realising he wasn't staring at her face.

"Ah . . . no, you are surely an honourable woman, to agree to our terms, Miss Cai."

She let out a pleasant chuckle. "Ah, a man of your power and skill remembered this one's name? My thanks, sir."

The man looked away.

"This way, please."

He led her through the manor, through the intricately panelled halls that some said used to have defensive wards on them. The building was very, very old, but still in good repair. *Only the best for honoured guests to the Azure Hills . . .* Xiulan glanced to the side as they passed a set of stairs that led downwards. Eventually, they reached the door to the main room, which her guide knocked upon.

"Young Master. Miss Cai is here to see you."

There was a noise of interest from the other side.

"Let her in," Zang Li said, amusement clear in his voice.

The disciple of the Shrouded Mountain Sect opened the door for her. Zang Li was seated in the center of the room, reclining on silks and pillows. A woman sat behind him. Her eyes were tired and mournful-looking, but she dutifully ran her fingers through Zang Li's hair. His shirt was slightly open, exposing his chest, and the room smelled of perfumes and food.

"Oh, what's this? The Young Mistress of the Verdant Blade Sect coming into my home on her lonesome, defying the decision of her Elders?" Zang Li asked. He laughed as he sat up straighter.

Xiulan bowed her head.

"Yes, Young Master. I do not believe they had my best interests in mind. I would take you up on your most generous offer. Traveling with you would be an honour beyond compare."

The man who had let her in glanced at his smiling Young Master with a look of admiration.

He nodded to the man. "You can go, Huang. Same to you, girl. I have some . . . business to attend to."

"Of course, Young Master. Have a pleasant time," Huang replied, bowing low. The woman behind Zang Li stood. As she rose, Xiulan noticed a scar on her throat. She said not a word, merely bowing and exiting with Huang.

Zang Li leaned forwards as the doors closed and the footsteps receded.

"You're certainly audacious, woman," Zang Li said, his voice abruptly becoming less refined. "Let me guess, you're here to beg for my forgiveness or ask me to reconsider taking you on?"

"I have come to bargain for Rou Tigu," Xiulan stated simply.

"I beg your pardon? Miss Cai, this Young Master has no idea what you're talking about."

"She is here."

Zang Li leaned back in his seat and sighed. "You seem certain she's here. Why, it's insulting to suspect a member of the righteous Shrouded Mountain Sect of a base deed like . . . *kidnapping*."

Xiulan stared at the man. His smile widened and he started to chuckle.

"Kowtow before me and perhaps I may hear what you have to say."

Xiulan took a breath, got on her knees, and bowed her head. There was a noise of mild surprise from him.

"Cai Xiulan begs the Young Master of the Shrouded Mountain Sect for his benevolence and generosity."

Zang Li laughed.

"Ah, that's good! That's good. *That's* how things should be."

In an instant, he was on his feet and he grabbed her hair, jerking her face up to look him in the eyes. Xiulan hissed in pain.

"Unfortunately, this Young Master must decline your request." He threw her into his seat, the mound of blankets and silks. "After all, I would have to recall my best men. They're quite busy at the moment."

Xiulan's eyes widened.

↔

Yingwen's eyes catalogued the two below him.

A man and a woman, their lips pressed together. One of them had the target symbol on his back. The other was from the Misty Lake Sect. It was unfortunate that there were bystanders, but not unanticipated. Hopefully the woman would not interfere.

His face was stone as he dropped down, his hands behind his back.

↔

Ah, there the bastard was. Fenxian smiled as he saw the man through the window, laughing at something another person had said. That was the symbol, right there.

Fenxian grinned as he slammed open the door. "Quite the party you've got here!" he thundered.

The entire room was silenced as they stared at him, awe and shock on their faces. Ah, that never gets old.

↔

Zang Li smiled at her, shaking his head. "Really, what was your plan, anyway? Come in, seduce me, then hopefully make off with the girl? I'll again say you are audacious, but foolish. Did you really think I would fall for that?"

"You seem like the kind of man who would."

Zang Li laughed. "How rude! Though I will thank you for coming to see me. I had almost given up hope of being able to sample you before I had to leave. A pity, but there are always sacrifices we make for our goals." He stroked her cheek. "It would have been a shame to lose such a prize."

Xiulan glared at him.

"You court death. Master Jin will destroy you utterly for this insult."

Zang Li's face flashed with fury, his fiery Qi spiking. Xiulan flinched, but as soon as his power came, it faded, and the man shrugged. "Oh, I'm sure he could. But he's not here right now, is he? And when he finds out . . . well. Elders don't get involved in the struggles of the younger generation. But they would get involved when a Master attacks their home, wouldn't they?"

Xiulan snarled and swung at him—he caught the blow and laughed. His other hand jumped up, fixing around her neck.

He overpowered her in an instant, pushing up against her.

"I do like them feisty . . . let's make a deal, you and I. For real now. Be a good girl for me and I'll let you be the one to tell him about Tigu. I'll even spare your Sect. Otherwise . . ."

The fire surged and Xiulan hissed as her skin grew hot.

"So tell me, *do you dare oppose the Shrouded Mountain Sect*?"

Xiulan's breath caught. She looked away. Zang Li smiled indulgently.

He pressed his lips to hers, claiming his victory.

Xiulan felt overwhelming revulsion—and also a surge of victory, for he was now distracted.

She looked above to the rafters and saw a slight figure cloaked in shadows. Ri Zu was glaring at the man from the ceiling. A tiny green blade, infused with Xiulan's Qi and something far more insidious, was strapped to her back.

It was the broken, incomplete version of her Sect's technique that every initiate struggled with. The small blade that was too fragile, too weak, and above all, too small to actually accomplish anything. It would have faded to nothingness already . . . if Ri Zu hadn't kept close enough for Xiulan to be able to maintain the tiny, almost unnoticeable strand of Qi that fed it and allowed it to exist.

Ri Zu nodded and let the blade fall. She then turned around, leaving to begin the second phase of their plan.

Xiulan's Qi plucked the tiny blade out of the air. It was coated with both Ri Zu's energy and Senior Sister's poison.

If Xiulan had not spent so much time practising with knives, chopsticks, and other small things, this plan would never have had a prayer of working. She wouldn't have had control fine enough.

Her opponent was distracted. He was trying to deepen the kiss.

Xiulan struck. The tiny, jade-green blade penetrated the soft skin behind his ear.

It went barely halfway in. A cut that wasn't life threatening in the slightest.

Zang Li jerked backwards, his hand coming up even as her blade disassembled itself into Qi, dumping any remaining poison on it into the tiny wound.

The man's eyes widened as he pulled back, shoving her away from him. His face twisted with surprise and fury. His Qi burned her wrist where he was holding it.

"Poison? You *whore*—"

Xiulan smashed her forehead into his nose, forcing him away from her, then spat on the ground to get his taste out of her mouth.

Fire exploded from the wall Zang Li had been thrown into. Xiulan moved, dodging past the flames. She then smashed through the door and raced down the hallway, bursting back into the entrance. The disciple of the Shrouded Mountain Sect—Huang, she recalled—looked dumbfounded as she hammered a knee into his gut and sent a palm into his nose. Her Jade Grass Blades leapt to her command, slashing open his back.

Xiulan grabbed the hammer on the desk and slammed it into the warning gong. Shouts of surprise and alarm echoed through the building.

A moment later, she exploded out into the night, tumbling past eruptions of flame and the snarling, crackling hiss of lightning.

CHAPTER 46

THE WORLD OF CULTIVATION

The night was beautiful and pure. Almost as beautiful and pure as the sound of clinking coins entering his money purse. It was a busy night as his customers drank and celebrated. The inn, his Jolly Fatty, was jampacked with people.

Ming Mao was in his element. He poured drinks into cups and slid them down the bar into eager hands. He took orders and carefully wrote them down, checking them off when complete. Three of his employees cooked in the back and delicately plated the food to be brought to the many hungry mouths. It was handed off to his wife or his daughter. They danced through the tables, setting them down in front of satisfied patrons. The silver flowed freely, as people shouted over the din to be heard.

The back room door opened. His son marched in, the rack on his shoulders carrying a bundle of forty ducks.

"That's the last of them, Father," he called as he set about washing his hands again, ready to begin work.

"How did the sale go?" he asked. "They give you trouble this time?"

"No, sir. I did what you taught me. Not a coin more than we were willing to give."

Ming Mao smiled proudly at his boy. He was doing well. The greatest and largest inn in Rolling Green would be in good hands. All the boy needed was a good woman, and then he would be set for life.

Ming Mao and his wife were very carefully making that match. His boy deserved only the best!

He smiled out at his domain. The forty tables on the floor and the forty rooms for weary travelers above.

It was nearly booked out.

Thank the Heavens for the Dueling Peaks Tournament. They were a week and a half away by foot from the place, but lots of people passed through the town on the way.

Ming Mao finished pouring another drink, tipping the barrel to get the last of it out. He hummed to himself as he hefted the empty vessel and put it to the side, grabbed another from beneath the counter, and replaced the empty one. A new spigot, a quick swing of a hammer, and he was ready to pour again. He nodded to some of his regulars, who raised a toast in his direction.

Happy customers, happy coin purse.

His father had said that food and lodging in the same place was the best, and his wisdom was vindicated year after year. What man wanted to walk so far for his meals when there was food right there?

And when there were no travelers? Well, every night there were people here to eat, offsetting the costs.

The door to the inn opened again, and Ming Mao turned to greet his new customer, rubbing his hands together. His guest had to duck down slightly to get in through the door. He was a huge lad, with rippling muscles and freckles strewn across his face. Probably a farmhand from one of the villages nearby. Ming Mao paused. He also had a silver rabbit stuffed down his shirt and the most magnificent rooster on his shoulder.

Ming Mao frowned. The only animals allowed in his inn were the cats! The Magistrate Fluffy and his kin were friends of the Jolly Fatty, and they had learned to do their business in designated areas. Other animals needed too much cleaning to be allowed.

But he did not speak up, for the rooster was strange. It wore a fox-fur vest and a silver necklace. The man held the door open and a monkey toddled in after him.

What? What sort of menagerie does this man have?

Ming Mao was so distracted he wasn't able to approach the man and ask him politely to leave the animals outside before the man came up to the counter.

Now that he was closer, Ming Mao realised the man looked a bit worse for wear. He had bags under his eyes and his skin seemed a bit pale. He appeared exhausted, or as if he was just recovering from a bout of illness. Ming Mao hoped he wasn't still sick, but he wasn't coughing or sneezing, so it was probably fine.

The farmhand with the animals opened his mouth to speak before his stomach growled so loudly Ming Mao heard it over the din of the restaurant.

The man flushed.

Ming Mao regained his wits and cleared his throat. "I must apologise, sir. The animals will have to be taken outside."

The man paused and his brow furrowed as he processed what Ming Mao told him. Ming Mao could practically see the man's thoughts ponderously moving through his mind.

Was he a dullard or something?

The dullard frowned and turned to rummage in his pocket.

Ming Mao sighed. Just what was he going to bring out? A copper coin to ask him to let the beasts stay, or perhaps some "family treasure" that was nothing more than junk?

The man put a jade token on the counter. A jade token, with the symbol of the Azure Jade Trading Company upon it.

"That change your mind?" he asked politely.

Ming Mao stared blankly at it. *That couldn't be real, could it?*

"One moment, sir." He picked up the token and walked into the back room to his office, where he kept his papers. Ming Mao rummaged around for a moment, taking out a document from the Azure Jade Trading Company. He compared the seal to the official one the Azure Jade Trading Company had given him.

It was a perfect match.

The man and his animals were swiftly seated.

"Terribly sorry for my rudeness, honoured customer," Ming Mao simpered. He gestured wildly to his wife and daughter, who immediately approached. "How may we serve you this evening?"

"What's the special today?" the man asked, his baggy eyes skimming over his wife and daughter without any thought before looking at Ming Mao again.

The honourable member of the Trading Company, who was surely tired from a long day conducting business, let his eyes droop and he shook his head. The rabbit in his shirt was fully asleep.

"Roast duck, on account of the tournament," Ming Mao replied automatically, bowing his head. "My son will be preparing them personally."

"Great . . . great. I'll take three of those," the man said before frowning at the sleeping rabbit. "And . . . also a bunch of vegetables. Some roasted, some raw. You want anything special, Bi De, Huo Ten?"

The rooster and the monkey both shook their heads.

Ming Mao swallowed as his wife and daughter both stared in shock at the animals. The rooster bowed to them both.

They all beat a hasty retreat.

"Hao," Ming Mao called for his son. "Only the best," he commanded. "Look over each leaf individually if you have to. Nothing wilted or even *slightly* misshapen, do you hear me?"

"You got it, dad," his son said seriously.

Ming Mao kept an eye on the man as he went back to getting more drinks for his customers, but the stranger just had his head in his hands and his eyes closed.

The rooster too seemed to be dozing while the small monkey was looking around excitedly, seated on the chair and kicking its legs like a toddler.

Soon enough, the spread was finished. Ming Mao and his daughter brought the plates over. The man perked up at their approach, then smiled tiredly at him. He fished the rabbit out of his shirt, the little beast squirming and rousing to wakefulness.

The ducks were placed in front of the man. He gestured at the animals for the rest of the plates.

Ming Mao bowed back awkwardly to the rooster as it accepted his offering. Cultivator. This man was definitely a cultivator.

"Might this unworthy one know your name, honoured customer, and those of your er . . . companions?"

The man looked up in surprise before pointing to himself.

"Rou Jin . . ." His finger flicked to the rest of the animals in order. "Bi De, Yin, Huo Ten, Miantiao."

The rooster bowed. The rabbit cocked her head to the side. The monkey waved. And then he tapped his armband—which was not an armband at all, but a *snake*, who lifted his head and gave him a nod.

Ming Mao bowed back.

Master Jin, his eyes still drooping, picked up an entire leg of duck. He stuck it in his mouth, bit down, and pulled it out.

All the flesh was gone.

Ming Mao swallowed nervously.

"Can . . . can I get you anything else, Master Jin?" he asked.

The man jerked to attention, paused midbite. His teeth sheared through the duck bone. He considered Ming Mao for a moment as he absently chewed.

"Yeah, actually. I've been on a pretty straight road to get to the tournament and I wasn't sure of the exact time . . . Can you tell me when it ends?"

Ming Mao grimaced at being the bearer of bad news.

"It ended today, honoured customer. In fact, we are just waiting for the announcement of the victor—"

The door to the inn burst open.

"Cai Xiulan defeated Rou Tigu! The match of the century!" the boy shouted, waving around a piece of paper. "Transcribed straight from the transmission stones! News directly from Lord Bai Huizong!"

The customers of the inn cheered, and eager patrons surged forwards, ready to buy a copy.

Master Jin sighed and slumped. "Damn it."

The rooster clucked forlornly, as if sad to hear the news, and the man rubbed its head. "That's what we get for messing with ancient portents of doom. Three days. Of *course* it wasn't only three days to fix the crystal . . ." His voice was light, but Ming Mao could hear the underlying strain. It wasn't particularly well hidden.

The man sighed again. The monkey hooted and gestured at the man selling the copies.

Master Jin looked for a brief moment like he was going to stand himself, before collapsing back into his chair. He nodded at the monkey and tossed it a coin.

It eagerly got up and trundled over to the crowd, pushing its way through. The rest of the customers seemed amused at the creature, letting it pass. It held out its coin to the boy.

The rest of the patrons laughed as it received its copy and marched back.

The monkey placed the paper in between the man and the rooster. Several of his customers were looking over curiously, but Ming Mao made a hand gesture.

Cultivator.

Their eyes widened, and they quickly went back to minding their own business.

The rabbit, Yin, prodded at the snake, which slithered off his arm to sit with the rest of the animals.

Master Jin's face was half a frown, half a smile as he read the paper. He closed his eyes and sighed.

A warm summer breeze flowed into the shop as the door was blown open slightly. The night outside suddenly seemed even nicer. The perfect temperature. The stars even seemed slightly brighter.

The cultivator absently placed the last of the food into his mouth, then nodded and stood up, holding out an arm so the monkey could climb onto his back while the other beasts took their places upon him as well.

"You don't need a room for the night?" Ming Mao asked.

"Nah. Got a bit of a run ahead of me. Thanks for the food, by the way, it was good. I'm feeling a *lot* better."

Indeed, the odd cultivator did look invigorated from his meal.

"We may have missed the final match, but let's see if we can make it to that party," he muttered as he exited the inn and broke into a loping jog.

↔

Yingwen alighted gently on the ground behind the couple and waited for them to notice. It was the least he could do: allow them one final show of affection before separating them. It was a stroke of luck that the scouts had found them leaving the confines of the Sect manor, so he and Fenxian had been dispatched early.

The surroundings had been catalogued. A pond, in a pavilion. Remote. Out of the way. Surrounded by a high stone wall that made it peaceful and private. Near the couple were the remains of a meal and an open box, displaying one of the Qi furnaces the woman, Liu Xianghua, had used to interesting effect.

Personally, Yingwen thought it an unacceptable crutch, but she was a cultivator far below the Shrouded Mountain Sect, so he could not begrudge her inferiority too much.

He waited a moment longer, hoping that they would stop, and he would not have to interrupt—

Liu Xianghua pulled open his quarry's shirt and pressed him harder against the wall.

Yingwen cleared his throat politely before things progressed any further.

He stayed still when the woman jerked and threw a knife at him. It whistled past his cheek and stuck into the wall. A polite warning.

"Who dares?" the woman demanded, turning around. Her eyebrows scrunched into a truly furious frown. The man he was looking for simply appeared dazed, an idiotic smile on his face.

"Forgive my interruption. This one is Zhou Yingwen, Disciple of the Shrouded Mountain Sect. I have business with the man accompanying you, Young Mistress. Would you be so kind as to hand him over?"

The furious woman paused, her posture becoming more cautious. The boy shook his head, his eyes widening before filling with anger.

"What sort of business do you have with my Gou Ren?" the woman asked.

"I am afraid I cannot discuss this. No blood needs to be shed tonight if you do not defy the Shrouded Mountain Sect. He shall come with me, and that shall be the end of it."

The woman stared at Yingwen. Then she looked at the boy she had been kissing. The boy bit his lip as his eyes stayed focused on Yingwen.

Liu Xianghua's face went absolutely blank. She turned and kissed the boy on the cheek . . . then started marching off.

Yingwen raised his eyebrow as she stepped right past him with absolutely no emotion on her blank face. She passed within an arm's reach of him and did nothing. She marched behind him, did not turn, and simply continued towards her belongings. She bent down and grabbed something from under the seat, then set about collecting her possessions.

"Wise decision," he said, his gaze still on the boy, who swallowed.

How unfortunate to be abandoned.

"Will you be as wise?" he asked calmly. The boy's eyes darted around until they alighted on some bamboo poles, ones that had been left behind by construction workers. He dashed over and kicked one into the air, grabbed it, and levelled it at Yingwen.

It wavered uncertainly in the boy's hands.

Yingwen nodded and drew his sword.

"I see," he said. "Unfortunate."

Yingwen moved. The boy started in surprise and swung his makeshift staff. The Young Master desired this man alive, so Yingwen would endeavour not to kill him. Yingwen raised his sword, intending to cut through the wood and follow up the attack with a strike to the stomach. Nonlethal, though rather painful.

His sword met bamboo. It bit into the wood, but to Yingwen's surprise it did not simply slide through it with ease. In fact, it got stuck. The jarring impact sent vibrations up Yingwen's arm, and he leapt backwards in shock pulling his sword free of the wood before landing near the pond.

He studied his opponent. Such a powerful and quick reinforcement was surprising, but that was it. Merely surprising. The boy held his ground, seeming to not know how to capitalise on the brief opening. Slow, and clearly unused to truly fighting—

There was a loud *clank* from behind and the sound of a cord being pulled. Something flew towards him.

Yingwen spun and cut the approaching object in half.

The bulging bundle unfurled into a bedroll—one that had been freshly washed and perfumed, with nice blankets.

[Breath of Steam: Heron's Beak]

He barely managed to get his sword in the way in time as a blow from behind him screamed for his throat. Xianghua smashed into his guard, his blade screeching with the sound of metal on metal.

The impact was equal to that of his Brother Disciples. Xianghua, unlike the boy, had no trouble trying to push the advantage. They clashed three times with strikes that had his arms tingling from the force of the blows.

Yingwen's own blade cracked with lightning. Xianghua grimaced when their swords connected again, then staggered backwards.

"A powerful artifact for these hills, to be able to bridge the gap between realms," he said conversationally. "But that was foolish."

"This night was going as planned," she said calmly and matter-of-factly. "Things were just getting good. You have *ruined* it."

Yingwen glanced at the bedroll. The young man looked at it too, and his face went crimson.

The steam billowed up and out of Xianghua's mouth, a fierce heron glaring at him. Yingwen sighed. His own Qi formed a snarling hound whose growl sounded like rolling thunder—

"Young Mistress!" a voice called out. "Young Mistress, I'm terribly sorry for interrupting, but there's an urgent message from Cai Xiulan!"

A servant rounded the corner, and his eyes widened as he beheld the scene before him. He glanced nervously at their postures. "Uh—"

Yingwen considered the man. Xianghua kept her eyes on him. Feeling a bit of mercy, Yingwen nodded, allowing her to take the man's report.

The woman grudgingly acknowledged his benevolence.

"I give you permission to read it," Xianghua stated. Her eyes remained focused on Yingwen. The servant stared at the trio for a moment before fumbling with the seal. He opened the letter and paled.

"'The Shrouded Mountain Sect took Tigu. Either stay in manor or get out of town. Attempting rescue,'" he read out.

A sudden noise permeated the clearing—a far-off explosion, and a roar of fury that sounded suspiciously like Yingwen's Young Master's voice.

A second, slightly closer shout of outrage sounded. Fenxian's.

Yingwen's left eye twitched.

He briefly debated disengaging, but he was committed now. He was a disciple of the Shrouded Mountain Sect. He could handle an Initiate and this woman with her crutch of an artifact.

And . . . he didn't think she would let him run, judging by the murderous aura coming off her. "So, the Shrouded Mountain Sect dares target the friends of Xianghua?" she demanded.

Yingwen wished it hadn't. The Young Master's plan was foolhardy. Improper. But . . . orders were orders. He owed everything to the Shrouded Mountain Sect.

"Indeed it does," he replied, inwardly resigned.

He raced forwards. His sword met Xianghua's. The furnace on her back shrieked with Qi and steam.

"Gou, get out of here. I'll handle this, and then I will collect my reward later! I shall defeat him shortly," she declared. Her words were full of insulting bravado even as she winced from the aftereffects of Yingwen's lightning.

But the boy had frozen up.

"You took Tigu?" he asked, his voice a whisper.

His face twisted with rage. His knuckles turned white as he gripped his bamboo staff, a dull grinding sound emanating from the action, like stone on stone.

"You hurt my friends?" He took a step forwards.

Yingwen's eyes darted to the boy, and his stance adjusted as Gou Ren's Qi manifested around him. The Qi of most cultivators was a liquid, or a gas, swirling and ever changing.

This felt like an array of stones . . . The sturdy wall of a castle, dense and compressed.

Heavy.

The boy who was not a threat suddenly became one.

Gou Ren's Qi wrapped around him like armour. It spread as it covered both his arms and the bamboo pole, churning and solidifying into a heavy armour of stone-grey Qi.

The walls around them suddenly seemed firmer. Taller.

With a roar, Gou Ren launched himself at Yingwen. There was no real form or style. He was a pure brawler who simply wound up and tried to hit Yingwen as hard as he could.

Yingwen observed the energy gathering at the end of his staff—and then a split second later made a decision. A cultivator in the Profound Realm was forced to dodge the attack of an Initiate.

He did not negligently deflect it. He did not try to block it.

He moved out of the way, because it was dangerous.

[Raze]

The ground shattered. Cracks and rents radiated out from the impact point, crawling up the nearby walls like he had manifested a small earthquake.

The pond water rushed in to fill the new hole. One of the walls crumbled.

Gou Ren's eyes burned through the dust and the steam, locking onto Yingwen.

↔

Fenxian smiled around the bar. Their laughter had died down, and now the entire pub was staring at him in shock.

"Ah, what's the matter? I know it's a true privilege for a Disciple of the Shrouded Mountain to grace your halls, but really, don't be such bores!"

There was a sharp intake of breath. The owner of the pub ducked down behind his counter.

"I am Gen Fenxian, disciple of the Shrouded Mountain Sect. I am looking for a man wearing a shirt with that symbol upon it," he said to the—

To the woman.

Fenxian blinked.

He was looking for a man, wasn't he? The woman was gaping at him from where her foot was still planted on the table, her arm outstretched. Her shirt was open a bit, like it didn't entirely fit. Or as if she had just put it on.

She had a face that was rather fetching, he had to admit. Her eyes were sharp and narrow, with a hit of red colour framing them. Almost like a fox. Their ancestral enemies were nothing if not attractive, the foul, tempting, soul-eating wenches. But this wasn't a member of the Howling Fangs. This was just a pretty woman.

"Was there a man wearing that shirt here?"

"I'm sorry, he just left," the woman said demurely. Her voice was deep for a woman, but she had no bulge in her throat, and her shirt was open enough that he could see her . . . assets. A nice size, like a perfect baozi. "I won this off him in a game of dice and he left to go get more money and get his clothes back."

Fenxian frowned heavily, glancing at the group sitting with the woman. They were members of the . . . Green Blade Sect? The one that the woman with the enormous chest was a part of? They were the little ants who scurried around her heels.

They all nodded.

"Yeah, he left not too long ago," another person from a nearby table chimed in. He had a shirt with a rising sun on it. "Went east, you should be able to catch up to him."

Fenxian considered this.

"Or I could just wait here until he returns," he stated, his eyes landing on the open seat near the fox-woman.

The pretty girl shrugged, sitting back down. "If he even comes back. The bastard owes me some money. Not a lot, but you *know* how some men get." She waved her hand.

The woman had a point. Fenxian sighed. Here he was, hoping for a fight, and the target wasn't even here.

Well, this is boring, Fenxian thought.

"East, you said?" he demanded

There were several nods.

Fenxian turned around, frustrated, and left the bar.

The Young Master wanted his prize quickly, and Gen Fenxian never disappointed!

↔

"What was that about?" An Ran asked curiously.

The woman wiped her hand over her face and brought it down to her exposed cleavage. Her features became decidedly more masculine and the smooth flesh shifted back into dumplings. Yun Ren pulled the meat bun out of his shirt. The skit had been going so *well* too.

"I have no idea," he muttered. "But I don't think he was here for a good time. Thanks for the cover, Yang," he said to the Young Master of the Framed Sun Sect.

"Anything for the Image Master," Yang replied cheerily. "Shrouded Mountain Sect bastards throwing their weight around . . ." he muttered.

Yun Ren shook his head. There was something fishy about this. Alarm bells were blaring in his head. *Somebody was looking for people with this kind of shirt?* "This doesn't sit right with me. I'm going to go find Gou and Tigu."

He paused before deciding on a course of action. Gou first. Tigu could take care of herself.

He turned and headed towards the window.

The door to the pub suddenly opened again. The man, Fenxian, swaggered back in, with what he probably assumed was a dashing smile on his face.

"Actually, pretty sister, you should come with me. This brother will ensure he returns your money—"

The smile fell off his face. The man gaped at Yun Ren, his finger pointing directly at him.

Yun Ren clapped his hands together. A searing flash of light burst from his hands and sent the man recoiling. As Fenxian staggered about blindly, Yun Ren dove out the window.

Fenxian roared with fury. The streets suddenly shook with the peal of thunder that blew out the side of the tavern.

↔

Xiulan had five people chasing her. Five disciples of the Shrouded Mountain Sect, who either were at the Fifth Stage of the Initiate's Realm or had entered into the Profound. From what Ri Zu had reported earlier, and with the number of people present, it seemed like the dungeon guard had abandoned his post. Her swords spun around and fired backwards, providing distractions and forcing her opponents to block or dodge. Each blow goaded them to chase her all the more—they wanted to repay her for the cuts they'd received as she managed to break past their guards.

Through it all, she never moved in a fully straight line. She used the roofs and alleyways of the empty manors to block their vision and then had swords strike up from wherever she landed, harrying her pursuers.

Some of the blades were blasted out of the air with lightning, or were swept up in Zang Li's blazing aura. Those swords turned into blazing comets as they ignited, slipping from her control as they attempted to harm Xiulan's foes even in the midst of their own funeral pyres.

Her opponents were fast. Zang Li was in the middle of the pack, but his breathing was hard and he seemed to be having trouble controlling his Qi. Ri Zu had done something to the poison Senior Sister had given her. She said it would act faster and be harder to remove—Xiulan risked a glance backwards. Zang Li threw something into his mouth and bit down on it in frustration, but that didn't seem to provide any relief.

The fact that he was still after her was testament to his Profound constitution. Ri Zu could paralyze Tigu with a few drops in a cup of tea. Whatever was going on in Zang Li's body had slowed him, but he was nowhere near out of the fight. A poison that would lead to the death of a mortal in seconds was a mere inconvenience to a Cultivator in the Profound Realm.

"Cut her off!" She heard the shout from Zang Li ring out.

[Thunderous Steps]

With a *crack-boom* of displaced air, one man leapt forwards like a bolt of lightning, his body transitioning to golden light—for all of twenty steps. His eyes widened as he stopped *much* earlier than he'd obviously meant to over an alley. His momentum carried him forwards, but he started to drop. His foot caught on the roof and he went spiraling off, slamming into the ground. To his credit, he immediately kicked to his feet, scrambling to resume the chase.

"The air here is interfering with our technique's Qi-propagation," the man yelled out as he leapt up onto the roof nearby.

"This *fucking* province" came the response from another.

Xiulan kicked up a roof tile and threw it backwards. It shattered when one of her pursuers punched it out of the air.

Thirty more tiles shot her pursuers' way in less than a second, and then with a mighty leap Xiulan launched herself out of the main town.

She angled herself down into an old, abandoned set of stone buildings. It was a small village just outside the town—an ancient warren of stone and collapsed buildings, underground passages, and dead ends. Decrepit, crumbling, and abandoned.

The perfect spot to drag in and slow down her pursuers.

They were lost in their hunt, baying like hounds and just rushing headlong after her. Exactly as she intended. They were running directly into an ambush.

Her plan was simple. Cause a big enough distraction, do enough injury to get people chasing her, and *run*.

Xiulan had spent three months in a brutal guerrilla conflict with Sun Ken before she'd finally managed to corner him and force him into open battle.

She had learned those lessons well. It might have been dishonourable to ambush and retreat, but Xiulan had little care for honour today.

Xiulan had no intention of dying or being taken.

She raced around the twists and turns, her swords flying off in a dizzying array of patterns. She sacrificed ten of them, feeling the drain on her Qi as Zang Li burned them all, but the brief moment they blocked her pursuers' vision was all she needed.

Xiulan reached into her pack, pulling out one of the bottles Ri Zu had given her. The rat had kept the last of Senior Sister's family recipe, just in case. None of her other concoctions were as powerful or debilitating, but they did act quickly.

Ri Zu had given her three vials. She grabbed the first one she laid hands on and emptied it onto her sword.

Several of her pursuers went in the complete wrong direction, chasing her floating swords. Another, however, was so close she could feel the crackle of lightning.

He turned the corner, and his eyes widened as he found her waiting for him.

Swords stabbed down from every direction, but unlike Huang he was not caught entirely off guard—he started throwing his punch as soon as he rounded the corner.

[Fulmination of the Mountain]

Lightning struck as she parried with her sword, the familiar tingle racing up her arms and into her spine. It was weaker than one of Wa Shi's full-power blasts but still enough to sting. Xiulan's muscles spasmed, but she managed to power through the strike and punched her opponent in the throat even as blades cut across his torso and the back of his legs.

The man howled in pain and backpedaled, raising his arms to guard—

But Xiulan had already disengaged. She made it around the corner before the grey-haired man regained his wits.

"Gah! *Coward!* She's over here!" he shouted, before snarling in pain.

Xiulan shot around another corner, and then she hid, watching the disciples from the shadows. Several more of her swords burst into flames when Zang Li smashed through a wall.

She felt where they had been destroyed, and nodded. He was far enough away.

"Are you all right?" one of her pursuers asked, slowing down to check on the wounded man.

She just had to keep them busy, keep them off center—she couldn't stay still for long.

Xiulan slid through a small opening in a wall and ran through an ancient, abandoned shop. Her father had taken her here to look at the old architecture, years ago, and it hadn't changed.

She nearly slammed into the next member of the Shrouded Mountain Sect. His eyes widened as her swords cut deeply into his thighs, and then he fled down a side passage.

"Over there! Cut her off!"

Xiulan was gone again, running for the outskirts. Some of the walls around her shattered. Indiscriminate lightning techniques erupted the stone.

"Jump" came the simple command from Zang Li, terse and clipped. Xiulan saw the Shrouded Mountain Sect disciples immediately obey, and she realised what was about to happen. She poured on the speed. She couldn't quite move as fast as Tigu—

[Descent of the Southern Star]

CHAPTER 47

DESPERATE HOUR

The streets filled with fire.

The ends of Xiulan's hair caught alight as she raced ahead of the wall of flame coming towards her, until eventually she could outrun it no more. She jumped. The blastwave threw her out of the town and sent her tumbling into the grass.

She landed on her back, wheezing as she hit the ground. Her eyes immediately sought out her enemies. Zang Li was down on one knee, shaking his head. Three of her pursuers had paused to survey the damage.

The last, the one she had only managed to score a few cuts on, was racing towards her, his eyes full of murder. He raised his sword—before suddenly doubling over, clutching at his stomach.

His eyes went wide and a whining groan escaped his lips.

He glared at her, tears in his eyes. "What did you do to me, you—" His words were cut off by his screams.

Just what did Ri Zu give her?

There was an unpleasant sound and an equally unpleasant smell. The man's face flushed crimson in absolute mortification.

Oh. Senior Sister's favourite. But when had they made it injectable?

Xiulan flipped to her feet and kicked him in the jaw. A couple more cuts to his legs and he was down and out.

Zang Li rose again. His eyes were locked onto her. He made to move after her again, when he paused and glanced back at the town.

Realisation shone in his eyes. "She's baiting us! The rest of you, back to the manor," he commanded.

Xiulan grimaced. She dumped the other two vials onto her swords before smearing the blades against each other.

Then she picked up her downed opponent. The rest of the disciples flinched, glaring at her.

Zang Li's eyes narrowed. He took a breath, his eyes shining.

[Thunderous Steps]

Zang Li disappeared in a bolt of golden light. Xiulan jumped backwards, dodging as his sword simply sheared through six of Xiulan's blades and a torrent of fire erupted out of his own.

Zang Li, to her surprise, grabbed her captive's leg. Xiulan let him be dragged out of her grip. He threw her defeated opponent backwards, and another disciple caught him.

Zang Li coughed and shook his head. He stood up straighter, though his face twisted. For a brief instant, his grey eyes flashed bloody red.

"Back to the town. Even poisoned, I'm more than enough here."

His men nodded.

Xiulan swallowed, her eyes flicking to the men who raced back to town. Xiulan's swords tried to pursue, but a wall of fire intercepted them.

"Now. *No witnesses*," Zang Li snarled.

Another jet of fire, this time looking slick and oily, burst out of the puncture wound Xiulan had made.

She took a deep breath and moved into her stance.

A warm summer breeze flowed through the grasslands.

□

It was dark.

Loud Boy screamed. A high keening that set Tigu's teeth on edge.

This wasn't supposed to happen.

The men had approached them. They had ordered Tigu to come with them.

Tigu had refused and challenged them. It had gone well at first. They were powerful opponents. Nearly as powerful as Bi De. She could tell they were pulling their punches, but it was still a fun fight. They were like Wa Shi—though electrified men, instead of electrified fishes. She wondered if they were gluttons too.

It had been fun, even though she was exhausted. It had been fun, until Rags had made that awful choking sound. It had been fun, until Loud Boy *screamed.*

Tigu had stopped playing around after that. Her claws went for eyes. Her blades tried to gouge out arteries.

A vicious and brutal fight to the death.

A part of Tigu enjoyed that too. She had felt the joy. Her bloodthirst had risen to the surface, and her teeth had sharpened.

And then one of the men had held up Rags, his sword to her friend's throat. Some part of her demanded that she disregard him, that he wasn't worth it. That *she* was the only thing that mattered. That only *her* victory was important. An old, cold part of herself that didn't care that Rags would die.

It disgusted her to feel that.

Tigu had frozen.

A fist had hammered into her jaw. She staggered. A second blow rocked her head to the side.

Then a third hit.

Rags smiling and ruffling her hair. Rags, falling over, his eyes dull.

A fourth hit.

Loud Boy's cheeky grin. His screams and tears.

A fifth hit spun her around completely, blood flying out of her mouth.

"I hated them," her Master had whispered. "I hated them all."

She hadn't known what he had meant back then. Fighting was so glorious. So fun.

But she had never *really* lost before, had she? She had never been the mouse.

At the sixth hit, there was only darkness. Darkness, and the smell of Rags's blood. Loud Boy's scream was the last thing she heard.

At the sixth hit, she understood.

"Tigu!" Loud Boy shouted, for her. *"Tigu!"*

The screams haunted the darkness. Even now, she could hear them. *'Tigu!'*

'Tigu!'

'Tigu! Tigu, wake-rouse yourself!' a little voice demanded. Something foul managed to make its way through Tigu's blood-clogged nose. Her face was sore and wet from the blood dribbling down her cheek.

She gagged and spat. A broken tooth clattered to the bottom of the cage.

"Ri Zu?" she asked, blearily looking around. She was in a small stone room, bars just before her hazy vision. She tried to move her arms, but they were stuck fast, clamped behind her.

'Praise the sky-heavens,' she heard the rat's voice say, clearly relieved.

"Where am I?" Tigu groaned, getting her knees under her body and trying to move. The room was dark. She ached all over and her arms would not move.

'You were captured-taken. Ri Zu does not have time for a full explanation—'

There was a cracking, shattering peal of thunder. Tigu couldn't help but flinch.

'We need to get out of here, and Ri Zu needs your help.' The rat paused. *'Tigu, Ri Zu needs you to transform. Ri Zu removed the Qi binders, but she can't get the shackles off your arms. And the door to the cage isn't opening.'*

Her voice was as calm as it could be, but Tigu could hear the undercurrent of tension.

A spike of fear pierced Tigu's gut. "I can't. You know I can't—"

'You can. Ri Zu knows-thinks that Tigu can do this,' Ri Zu said encouragingly. Tigu swallowed thickly.

She gathered her Qi, just as Wa Shi had said.

Tigu *tried.* She really did. She pictured the form in her head. The little cat. The little failure. The beast that was merely tolerated instead of loved. The form that she had so often boasted about, yet even now detested. Things were *so* much better for her as a human. She loved the feelings, the sensations, the camaraderie, and above all the lack of urge to eat her little friend sitting on her back. It had been a constant battle to not just pounce upon her. Tigu the cat was a bitter, arrogant creature.

Tigu the human was loved.

Her Qi fizzled.

"I can't!" Tigu snarled, panic overtaking her.

Ri Zu hopped from her back, where she had been working on Tigu's shackles. Her little paws touched Tigu's face.

'Ri Zu knows it scares you. She knows you don't want to turn back. But you must. Master Jin still loves you, whatever form you take; Mistress Meiling does too—and Ri Zu loves Tigu. No matter what you are, you are Tigu. Always Tigu.'

Tigu clenched her teeth as the hot tears dripped onto the cold metal.

'For Xiulan's sake. For the brothers' sake . . . For Loud Boy and Rags's sake. You must.'

"I don't . . . I couldn't . . . They got hurt. They died," she whispered.

'Rags and Loud Boy still draw breath. And this Ri Zu will not let them perish,' Ri Zu insisted. *'Just like Ri Zu will not give up on you. We will get out of here.'*

Tigu bit her lip. The knowledge that they were still alive sent a warm surge through her. She cared about them. They were not of Fa Ram . . . but they were her friends. She needed to get out and help them. Help everybody—

Her Qi gathered and spluttered again. More hot tears splashed from her eyes. Her heart thundered in her chest.

There were voices outside. Men were shouting, and the sounds of battle broke through to the prison.

Ri Zu tensed.

"You should go. They don't know you're here," Tigu whispered.

Ri Zu flinched. Her eyes went wide, then rolled in her head, as the fear made the little rat twitch. Except instead of running, Ri Zu shook her head. *'Ri Zu is staying right here until Tigu is ready. She is not leaving without you. What would Fa Ram do without its Young Mistress?'*

Ri Zu's honest words were painful and relieving in equal measure. The one who hated that body the most was fine with it. Tigu groaned. Her form shook with the strain.

She tried to visualize the cat.

It was still a part of her. It was still *her*. It was still something that she could be. Something that right now, she *had* to be.

She bit her lip. Her mind filled with memories.

Master's warm hand on her head.

Loud Boy, Rags, Handsome Man, Blue Man with his cool drawings on his body.

Did it really matter what she was? Cat or human? Xiulan and everyone else were fighting for her. Even little Ri Zu, her eyes wide and terrified, was fighting for her.

The least she could do was return the favour.

Something in her chest cracked.

Lightning sparked around her body; her heart seized in her chest.

Her Qi guttered and fizzled.

Tigu screamed.

↔

Yun Ren's flight took him to the alleyways. The strange Shrouded Mountain man had been distracted for a moment when a few people threw drinks at him. The Petals and Chen Yang had tried to intervene, but Yun Ren only saw the aftermath. There was a crack of lightning and several screams as the asshole simply slammed his way through five other cultivators, then went through the bar's wall.

"Where are you, you bastard?" the man, Fenxian, roared.

Yun Ren didn't answer him. He simply pressed his hands over his body, dragging them along his face and his clothes, changing the colours. His skin lightened as he undid his ponytail, and his hair went from black to light brown. The technique was a thin skin over his body, originally developed to make people laugh.

He's too fast. I can't run. What should I—

Yun Ren's sword rattled.

'Left alleyway. Poor visibility from above.'

Yun Ren startled at the quiet voice but obeyed it, darting into the alleyway. He picked up a discarded bottle and slumped against a nearby wall like he was a passed-out drunk.

His heart thundered in his chest as there was a rustle of air. The man passed overhead.

"You can't have gone far, damn it, you worthless fox bastard!"

There was another crack of thunder, followed by several screams.

What can I do? What should *I do?* His thoughts whirled. His Qi churned.

Something in his pouch started to rattle, followed by a certain familiar warmth as his bag suddenly expanded—

And a tiny white fox head poked out.

"Looks like you're in a spot of trouble, Nephew," the familiar face declared.

Yun Ren stared at it; it was ghostly and like it was barely here. He could see through it to the cracked gemstone he had gotten from—

"Nezan?!"

"In the flesh, or I suppose in spirit," the fox said, tittering to himself. "Well, *part* of me. I couldn't leave you all on your lonesome—especially when I felt this foul lightning," the little beast stated primly.

Yun Ren's sword rattled again.

"Of course, dear, you're here too," the fox said indulgently. He glanced up as Fenxian shot overhead again. "That man is not going to stop until he finds you."

There was an explosion of Qi as the man lit up an entire alleyway with lightning.

"What the fuck can I do against *that*?" Yun Ren hissed.

The little beast grinned. Its face stretched into a cruel, toothy, vulpine smile.

"Why, fight him, of course. My dear friend's sword chose you. Us against the Den Stealers, just like old times!"

A rattle came from Yun Ren's belt.

'Draw me,' the voice commanded.

Yun Ren's hand moved on its own. There was a scraping sound as he withdrew the sword Yao Che had made for him. Simple steel bled into a beautiful white blade as the illusion on it melted away. The darkness of the night seemed to ebb, like the dawn was coming.

Summer's Sky, the inscription on the blade read.

"I'll handle the defence. If you please, my dear?" the fox asked.

'Summer's Sky greets the Eighth Master,' a voice in his head whispered. *'Request. After battle, tea and show images.'*

Yun Ren stared blankly at the sword—he was in way over his head. He had a magical, ancient, talking sword, and a fox spirit had crawled up onto his shoulder. For one hysterical moment, Yun Ren remembered that time Jin had ranted about magical girls and talking dolls.

Irrationally, Yun Ren had the sudden image of himself in a frilly dress.

Then there came the sound of more people shouting. Cracks of thunder to the west, and there was a blazing fire staining the sky orange.

"Wait, if you swapped out my sword, and you can talk, why didn't you say anything beforehand? I used you to chop wood and as a skewer for meat!"

'Interesting experience. Approval.'

He felt Fenxian approaching again as he dropped his disguise.

Yun Ren stood up and swallowed thickly. His legs wobbled.

Welp, first time I've ever used a sword to actually fight somebody.

Nezan's eyes glowed.

"There you are!" Fenxian roared as he slammed into the alley.

Facing the entirely wrong direction.

Yun Ren reflexively stuck him in the ass.

The man shrieked and whipped around, his blade aiming for Yun Ren's head even as he swung blindly.

'Thunderblade Sword Arts. Effective, especially against other sword wielders. Ineffective against Summer's Sky. Phoenix Guard high, deflect.'

"What the fuck is a Phoenix Guard?" Yun Ren shouted hysterically as he dove aside instead. Fenxian's eyes were hazy as he continued to strike at empty air. Nezan grunted, and the sword rattled.

'Ah. Eighth Wielder's abilities are low. Challenging. Interesting. Approval.'

Yun Ren swore yet again.

↔

'Against the wall. Against the wall. Hurry-quick,' Ri Zu instructed her companion. Her eyes were full of worry as they finished getting out of the compound.

Tigu was hyperventilating. Her eyes were wild and rolling; she was stumbling and staggering on her four legs. She wasn't used to moving like that anymore.

The cat retched. Ri Zu barely recognised Tigu in this form. She was different. Her fur was a brighter orange. Her stripes were a deeper black. Like a little tiger, even more than she once had been.

Ri Zu could hear the men of the Shrouded Mountain Sect entering the building. And they immediately started swearing at the empty cage. The empty, *unopened* cage.

'Tigu. Stay with Ri Zu, Tigu,' the rat begged. Tigu grimaced. She took a deep breath. Some of her shakes settled.

"Go out. Search the town, and if you can, aid in our brothers' fights!" one shouted.

Ri Zu kept her hands on the shuddering cat, murmuring encouragement as she tried to keep her moving.

The cat slumped against her side. There was a *pop* and a young woman took her place. The smell of half-eaten food filled the alley as she vomited.

Ri Zu sighed in relief.

Tigu looked frantically at her hands before she let out a shaky breath. She clenched them into fists.

'Are you okay to fight?' Ri Zu asked.

Tigu nodded.

"They're going for Gou Ren, Yun Ren, and the Blade of Grass," she said, her voice slightly deeper than usual. Slightly deeper. More guttural. Filled with fury. "I have more reach like this. More power."

She gagged again and spat a mouthful of bile to the side.

She held out a hand for Ri Zu.

The rat clambered on as Tigu brought her up to her face. Their foreheads touched.

Tigu transferred Ri Zu to her shoulder. To her normal spot, under her shirt.

Tigu's Qi blades formed. Her teeth sharpened into points. The marks on her cheeks spiked as they turned more bestial and savage.

↔

Tie Delun of the Hermetic Iron Sect was *bored*. He'd had to pack away most of his Sect's forging gear, so he had missed the opportunity to ask Miss Rou to accompany him on a walk. Loud Boy and Rags had beaten him to it.

Unfortunate. He was leaving in the morning and would have liked to see her one last time. Or at least hear her call him "Handsome Man" again.

So instead, he was walking by himself. Away from the sounds of fighting. He had no desire to engage in whatever was going on. After everybody was freed from tournament restrictions, things tended to get a bit out of hand, and it looked like this year was especially bad.

Which was a shame. Things had seemed so good for a while.

There was a shout and a peal of thunder close by. His eyes widened as an orange missile hurtled towards him

He caught it out of the air.

"Tigu?" he asked. She was smoking and injured, but even as he looked at her, some of those cuts healed. His eyes widened at the feel of her energy. Tigu was looking back at him, pain in her eyes.

"Miss Rou, what's—"

Three pursuers slammed down in front of him.

They were all of the Shrouded Mountain Sect.

All of them were sporting blade wounds. One smelled rather foul, his face a crimson rictus of rage and humiliation as he struggled to remain standing.

"Hand her over, in the name of the Shrouded Mountain Sect."

Tie Delun looked down as Tigu staggered to her feet. She gave him a shaky little smile.

"You should go," she whispered.

Tie Delun saw the pain in her eyes.

He had always had a temper. He knew that much. It was often a struggle to control.

But right now, as Tigu stood in defiance against the Shrouded Mountain Sect . . . he let it flow.

[Hermetic Iron Body]

A hammer was drawn.

"Like hell."

↔

Yingwen's face was stretched into a grimace. With her engine, Liu Xianghua was the near equal of himself. It would have been no contest if they were not in the Azure Hills, yet here, the draining properties of this place were messing with his control.

His Thunderous Steps were unavailable to him.

And had he been facing just her, he would have been able to prevail, even without his technique.

But the boy, Gou Ren, was proving intensely irritating. He was wild and unrestrained, letting loose enormous, wide, swinging hits that were easy to exploit and would have gotten him killed had his flesh not been harder than steel—and if Yingwen's orders were not to take him alive.

The times Yingwen's blade connected with him had little effect. It was like hitting an unbreakable wall. The boy didn't even budge while his feet were planted upon the earth, and he'd lash out with his makeshift staff in return every time.

Each hit was wide in its impact, shattering the stone around him and shaking the foundations of the street.

But Yingwen could see he was tiring. Slowly. The rage in his eyes still burned, but his strength was dimming.

Yingwen, however, was still being forced back.

Thankfully it was not all in his opponents' favour. Liu Xianghua had an enormous number of electrical burns sliding up her arms, and her furnace was starting to cough and splutter.

Yingwen leapt backwards. A measured fighting retreat to tire them out would suffice. He could feel the discharges of his fellow disciples nearby.

His sword lashed out again as Liu Xianghua closed the distance, scoring a shallow cut on her that made her flinch as electricity poured into her body. He followed it with a strike to the stomach, but Gou Ren was there to attempt a full-body tackle.

He clicked his tongue and leapt backwards into another plaza—

—which was nearly full of members from the Sects of the Azure Hills. Bystanders who had gravitated towards this fight.

Yingwen sighed when he spotted his sectmates fighting an escaped Rou Tigu. She and another man were staggering under the assault, barely able to keep their arms up.

His Brother Disciples nodded at his presence, and they formed a defensive circle.

Xianghua landed straight after him, then paused. Her eyes flicked to the number of Shrouded Mountain Sect disciples.

All of his brothers had wounds upon them, but even now, victory could be claimed. Rou Tigu was on her knees, and the other man slumped forwards in exhaustion, his armour shattered and smoking.

Yingwen paused, considering the predicament the Young Master had landed them in. He glanced around at the crowd of witnesses. Perhaps he would be able to salvage the situation.

"Enough!" Yingwen shouted loudly to everyone. "Do not make this rebellion worse on yourselves. Cease attacking us, and we shall be generous, allowing you to live."

The crowd was muttering. Murmuring. *"They attacked the Shrouded Mountain?"* was the refrain, staring at his enemies like the fools they were for defying him.

Both Gou Ren and Xianghua were hesitating. *Good. Good, this is working,* Yingwen thought, relieved.

Then there was a shout from the top of a building. It was a raw and powerful voice.

"Rou Tigu was taken for no reason by the Shrouded Mountain Sect! When Xiulan went to bargain for her safety, they attacked her too!" Every eye turned towards him. "They broke my cultivation and nearly killed Rags! These honourless bastards are nothing but scum!"

For a brief moment, there was silence.

Guo Daxian, the Young Master of the Grand Ravine Sect, stepped forwards.

He pulled his weapon from around his arm, the vicious blade attached to a rope. Several more cultivators stepped forwards, including a couple of scorched-looking members of the Verdant Blade Sect.

"Are you all going to assault these members of the Shrouded Mountain Sect?" Yingwen asked.

Guo Daxian spat to the side and smiled at them.

"It's just a little scuffle between disciples, isn't it?" he asked blandly. "Or did something worse happen?"

Yingwen swore, a split second before a rope dart sliced towards him.

↔

There was pandemonium on the streets. Walls crumbled and thunder resounded.

Steam and Qi screamed.

Yet the Elders of the Azure Hills saw little of this, trapped inside the vast halls of the Dueling Peaks.

Ancient mechanisms whirred to life. Gold flashed across every crystal, a stringing web that connected the entire mountain.

The barriers hummed and shimmered, as every rune in the Earthly Arena turned burned gold.

"What the hell's going on?" Guo Daxian the Elder asked.

□

"You're *really* bad at this," Nezan stated as Yun Ren ducked again.

His opponent was beguiled in illusions, lashing out randomly . . . and Yun Ren still couldn't finish it.

"I'm an artist, not a fighter!" he yelped back before dodging another wild swipe from the angry cultivator.

It was . . . well, it was a bit embarrassing. Chen Yang, who had caught up to them, had tried to help again, but he had gotten electrocuted by an omnidirectional blast.

Yun Ren was barely in the fight himself. Only the fact that any lightning that headed towards him was instead sucked up by Summer's Sky and thrown back had kept him standing.

And for some reason . . . he felt pretty fine. His panic had long since died down, and he felt . . . warm. Kinda like he was safe, despite the fact that he was facing down a massive brute who was shrugging off multiple stab wounds.

Finally, Fenxian paused. He lifted a hand to his head.

There was a crackle of lightning that suffused his hand, and then he touched his temple.

He had electrocuted himself. Yun Ren swallowed. His opponent's eyes cleared.

"*Fox*," his voice boomed; he was completely focused on Yun Ren.

[Thunderous Steps]

He moved too fast to see. Too fast to block.

Yun Ren stared his death in the face.

↔

Fire roared. Grass blades burned, only for a fresh set to take their place.

The woman was annoyingly persistent. The sheer amount of Qi she was throwing around was honestly enviable. He had no idea how she hadn't collapsed from exhaustion yet.

She was only in the First Stage of the Profound Realm, and yet she was managing to hold her own against one three Stages higher. Each moment they dueled, she stayed one step ahead of death.

Each swing of his sword ignited ten or more of her blades. Her own Sect treasures were cracking, and pieces of green jade were flaking off. Her clothes had mostly burned away, barely sparing her modesty. Her body was littered with cauterized wounds.

Each breath sent a new wave of swords at him, trying their hardest to cut him down—but she had reached her limit.

And Lu Ban had surpassed his.

Oil, Fire, and Blood purged whatever poison she had afflicted him with. His body was adapting, was recognising the subtle, insidious Qi in the poison that kept it lingering, damaging his body and spirit.

In a few more moments, he would be free of it.

But now . . . now it was time to end things. His opponent had been clever with her initial trap. But she was not the only one who could perform such maneuvers. She hadn't noticed the flames carving a formation in the ground around her.

[Phoenix Hell Inferno]

She could not flee anymore. Flames burning white hot erupted in a cage around her, cutting off all retreat. The only open path was through Lu Ban himself.

There was delicious fear reflected in her blue eyes, yet she did not back down. She did not flinch, nor did she hesitate.

Lu Ban *hated* her. He hated the look of disgust in her eyes, as this weaker cultivator *looked down on him*, like people had looked down on him all his life.

He rose up into the air. An orb of flame formed in his hand, the size of a pea, so hot it burned white.

"I would have liked to keep you alive, but that will not be happening." His voice was conversational. His blood-red eyes intent.

There would be nothing left of this woman. Not even ashes would remain for her crimes.

The ball of heat in his hand pulsed.

[Descent of the Southern Star]

The orb dropped.

Cai Xiulan stared her death in the eyes.

[Aegis of the Full Moon]

A silver shield sprang up between his target and the descending orb. It was a full, perfect circle of celestial light whose brilliance blinded him for a moment.

His soul shuddered as his flames bore down upon the face of the moon. The hellish heat was enough to scorch its surface, burn the blinding light, and darken it for a moment. But it did not break. The flames dissipated under the cold, lonely light of the moon.

The smoke cleared.

Standing before Cai Xiulan was . . . a chicken. Its feathers shone a brilliant red. Its tail, a perfect jade green. Its fox-fur vest was absurd.

Lu Ban stared blankly at the creature, unsure if the heavens were playing a trick on him.

"It seems you have had fun playing with my Junior," the beast said in a deep, smooth voice. "But she has had enough for one day. Do you mind trading pointers with me?"

Lu Ban gaped at the Spirit Beast.

"You stand before Fa Bi De, First Disciple of Fa Ram," the rooster continued, before stroking his wattles with a wing. *"Student of Rou Jin."*

Lu Ban's hand spasmed. The one that had been broken.

A warm summer wind caressed his face and made shivers crawl their way down his spine. He looked at the ground. At a field of ash.

Little shoots of grass had begun poking out of the devastation.

CHAPTER 48

FEAR NOT THIS NIGHT

The first sense that something was wrong was the itching down my back.

I had been in fairly good spirits when I departed the town. My belly was full of good food, and there was the possibility of making at least the party so I could congratulate Xiulan and Tigu. I could finally experience something nice, instead of days I'd spent sitting still and feeding energy to a crystal.

At least I wasn't feeling nauseous anymore. Each step had made me more energised. Each moment had washed away some of the exhaustion. But . . . it had also started to seem *urgent.* My excitement transitioned to nervousness.

My stride ate the ground beneath me. It was said that the Dueling Peaks was a week and a half away from that village for a normal person, but I must have poured on more speed than I thought, because after not too long I saw two mountains rising up into the sky.

Or maybe I hadn't really been paying attention—because the sky was glowing with the light of the dawn.

That isn't the light of the dawn.

It was smoke. Smoke and fire, an enormous amount of it, to the west of the town.

I heard the noise. What had at first seemed to just be shouts of partying and the *pops* of firecrackers turned out to be roll of thunder and screams of the populace.

I skidded to a halt.

The sounds of combat.

A waft of air flowed from the town. The smell hit me, immediately making my gorge rise in the back of my throat. Blood. Sweat. Ash. Screams. The tournament was over. But there was still fighting. *Unorganised* fighting.

My first thought was incredulous and hysterical; *of course the tournament arc always goes to shit.*

There was another rumble, from deeper in the town. The snarling roll of thunder. The screams got louder.

The sounds of battle filled my ears. They made my heart spasm in my chest.

A real cultivator fight. Real stakes. Blood and death and crippling—

There came a memory of a fist pounding into my face. Another strike to the solar plexus.

The world shuddered as another peal of thunder *boomed* out. I flinched.

One to my chest, right over my heart. The ugly feeling of something stopping. The feeling of my blood sloshing and settling in my veins. The sudden lack of a familiar rhythm in my chest.

I swallowed thickly. I could feel the sweat bead on my forehead. My foot lifted involuntarily as I started to take a step backwards.

I remembered the darkness starting to overtake my vision. The feeling of being torn to pieces. I didn't want to go, I didn't want to go, I didn't want to die—

My foot stomped down, a little harder than I'd meant it to. A step not backwards, but towards the town. I bit my lip. For a brief moment, the thought of running overtook me. But my friends were in there. Yun Ren. Gou Ren. Tigu. Xiulan. Ri Zu.

"Great Master, what would we do?" Big D asked through the small piece of crystal behind his silver necklace.

His eyes were focused on the town in front of us, stern and uncompromising.

I had promised myself, no more running away. I straightened my back. I took a breath and drew on my Qi.

Yin and Noodle gasped. Huo Ten chittered, the monkey sliding off my back. I considered the situation as Yin leapt out of my shirt and Noodle slithered off to join her. The fire in the distance was concerning, but it was ultimately outside the town. I didn't know if it was important yet, but there was one guy who could check it out then come back quickly.

"Big D, investigate the fire, then come back and get me if it's a fight and somebody we know. Yin, go with Noodle and find Tigu, Ri Zu, and the Xong brothers. If they're in trouble, come get me. Huo Ten . . . find someplace to hide. This battle is not for you."

My voice was short and sharp—much more commanding than I normally was. I can't say I liked my tone, but the disciples perked up to attention.

"Yes, Master!" the animals chorused, bowing as one.

"Go."

We burst into motion. Beyond running fast, I never really used much "cultivator" movement. No standing on stalks of grass or ninja-leaping through the trees.

This time, I *jumped.*

A single leap took me above the houses and onto a rooftop. My landing was a bit gentler than I'd envisioned. I'd half expected to shatter roof tiles, but instead they didn't make a sound as I alighted on them. As I stood on the roof and gazed out over the town, I could see the flashes of techniques, the fires, the smoke, the yells, everything seeming to expand before me. I could hear it. I could taste it. My eyes were immediately drawn to the closest sounds of battle.

"Fox!" a voice boomed. A giant of a man lifted his sword high, pointing it at—

I accidentally kicked the roof off the house when I jumped towards the voice. The entire structure crumbled beneath my feet. I slammed into the road and grabbed the asshole out of the air.

He looked surprised for a brief moment, eyes widening in shock.

I immediately punched him in the jaw. A part of me said that cultivators should be slightly harder to knock out than a tap to the chin.

I felt vaguely disappointed when the big guy's eyes rolled up into his head after the first punch and he went completely limp.

As his sword clattered to the ground, I turned to Yun Ren, who was gaping at me.

"Hey, Brother," I said as calmly as I could. "Sorry I'm late."

His face, streaked with grime, sweat, and splattered bits of blood, lit up. Amber eyes, wide with terror and desperation, froze as he looked at me. Relief. Assurance. His face faded back to his normal cheeky grin.

"Hey, Brother," Yun Ren gasped out in return as he collapsed to a knee, giggling hysterically. "Well, better late than never."

I eyed the magical-girl mascot-looking fox-thing on his shoulder and the shining, pure-white sword in his hand. The fox was staring at me, its mouth open.

I put it out of my mind and crouched down, putting my hand on Yun Ren's shoulder.

"What's going on?" I asked. "Why was this guy attacking you?"

He shook his head. "I've got no fucking clue. This guy just started going after me! He spouted something off about the Shrouded Mountain Sect, then just started swinging!" He glared viciously at the downed guy before his amber eyes widened. "And somebody shouted earlier that they took Tigu!"

Yun Ren winced as my grip unintentionally tightened on his shoulder.

I took a deep breath. *The Shrouded Mountain Sect? Hadn't I dealt with their imposter?* I shoved the thought away. That was irrelevant now.

"Find some place to lay low. I'll take care of everything," I promised him.

Amber eyes stared into my own. We were in the middle of a busted-up alleyway. He looked at the defeated cultivator, then shook his head.

"I'm coming," he stated simply.

I closed my eyes and nodded. I . . . I wanted him somewhere safer, but . . . just like Big D, Yun Ren had the right to make his own decisions.

"Then let's go."

I let go of his shoulder and stood. There was a rapid *tap tap tap* and a silver rabbit landed near us. She looked frustrated.

'Master, Sister Tigu, and Gou Ren are this way!' Yin shouted down at me from a nearby rooftop. *'They're fighting, but Shifu always said I gotta obey orders in a fight, and you said come back and tell ya, and can I kick the bastards who are attacking them's asses?'*

I took a breath and stared down at the cultivator. "We'll see, Yin. We may not have to fight at all, but if we do . . . well."

The rabbit thumped her food in anticipation. I nodded and picked up the downed guy. First an imposter, now the actual Shrouded Mountain Sect. The same guys both times. The Sect was supposed to be pretty strong. Enough so that Rou had heard a few stories about them in their youth, so why was this kind of stuff happening?

I threw the asshole over my shoulder like a sack of potatoes and followed after Yin.

↔

Bi De stood proud before the interloper. He gazed imperiously at this foul creature who had dared to assault his Junior.

He kept his breathing calm even as his Qi roiled. This creature's blow had been beyond anything he had ever received before. The full strength of the Aegis of the Moon had been brought to bear, yet even then it had almost not been enough. The holy light had been scorched and blackened by the beast's mighty blow.

He had originally meant to merely observe, as his Master had ordered. Observe, and return to his Lord so that he might render judgement. But upon discovering it was Xiulan locked in mortal combat and about to perish, he *had* to intervene. His Great Master would surely forgive him.

He was lucky his Great Master's name seemed to be a talisman against this creature. He had merely meant to stall for a few moments longer, to collect himself, but the utterance of his Great Master's name had sent the wicked thing recoiling. His eyes widened and his body spasmed.

"Really? Really? The heavens mock me with this!" the man snarled as he glanced back at the town. His eyes flicked to the ground, where the little shoots of grass grew.

Bi De took the moment of reprieve to glance out the corner of his eye at Xiulan. She had collapsed to one knee, panting.

It was only by her Qi that he recognised her. Her clothes had been mostly burned off her body. Her skin was flushed red from the heat, and cauterized wounds littered her arms and legs.

"He took Tigu," she whispered, "He is a man who was defeated by Master Jin—" She cut off with a racking cough. Little sparks of fiery Qi and flecks of blood drifted out of her mouth. Her cultivation seemed to be under fiery deviation.

But her eyes were still defiant.

Xiulan would have to be seen by Ri Zu as soon as possible. Bi De returned his attention to his enemy. This wicked foe would not give them the opportunity to seek aid.

The man paused as he glared at the town. "Perhaps this may yet still be salvaged," he mused. His eyes locked onto Xiulan, full of murderous intent. "I will finish things here. Alas, my compatriots were made martyrs by this vicious and unprovoked attack upon the Shrouded Mountain Sect. Only Zang Li managed to escape."

He fingered a talisman he pulled out from his robes and glanced at it. Bi De could tell the man was nervous. His eyes flicked to the ground again before he took a deep breath.

The fires around him exploded in intensity. The whites of his eyes turned pitch black.

"That was a good trick, Fa Bi De. Let us see if you can replicate it." His words were laced with absolute contempt. "A chicken. You are an ant, challenging the heavens."

Bi De stepped forwards, his blades of moonlight forming. Six Swords of Grass rose in support. Zang Li took a breath.

[Thunderous Steps]

And then their opponent was upon them.

A blade of fire swung for Xiulan. This interloper seemed intent upon her death, and Bi De could not abide that.

His holy spurs interposed themselves, halting the blow just long enough for Disciple Xiulan to move out of the way.

The blow was mighty. Just as mighty as the fires that had scorched his shining aegis.

Even through his exhaustion, this man was more powerful than any foe Bi De had come across. A single blow from him would have slain Sun Ken. A single blast of fire would have burned the flesh from his bones and ended the bandit.

Over the last year, Bi De had not been idle. He was not the same as when he battled Sun Ken. He had ascended past his limits with understanding and skill, rather than brute force like this one.

Bi De took a breath and focused his gaze on the assailant. Copying Sister Yin's style of Qi manifestation, Bi De clad himself in silver moonlight instead of the gold of the sun.

"Your breathing is off," Bi De informed the wretch, keeping the strain out of his own voice. "A paltry blow."

[Wheel of the Crescent Moon]

The man's eyes widened as Bi De threw himself into a flip. The ring of silver light lashed for his throat but struck an arm instead when the man barely moved out of the way in time.

Silver cut lightly into the man's arm. The interloper screamed. The flesh hissed, and silver veins immediately began to spread from the small injury.

The man stared at his arm in shock—and then two blades from Xiulan slashed against him, throwing him forwards.

But Xiulan was flagging, so the blows hadn't had the energy behind them to properly cause damage. The man turned to strike her, but Bi De shot forwards, foiling the assault.

"Inattention in a fight is lethal," Bi De mused instead, attracting the man's attention once more.

His face twisted, and his body shuddered.

A return strike nearly took Bi De's leg. The man screamed as the fires erupted around him and his sword started to vibrate.

"You're right. It is," he snarled, turning his eyes back to Xiulan.

His opponent was committed now. He was stronger and faster than Bi De. His blows were mighty. While normally Bi De would attempt to dance around his opponent's blows, this fiend took every opportunity he could to strike at Disciple Xiulan. She was weakened by her previous efforts and could barely dodge his hungry, burning blade.

Holy spurs clashed with a blade made of an inferno. The impacts rattled up Bi De's legs. He made the mistake of jumping, and the meteoric impact smashed him aside. The beast grinned, then dove for Xiulan, trying to end her life . . . but even as damaged as she was, she fought on. Her swords cracked even more, and no more blades floated around her, yet she held him for just long enough for Bi De to reenter the fray.

"Poor posture," Bi De declared, his spurs raking across the man's back. A small chunk of flesh flipped off the man's body.

The man howled.

Fire exploded off the interloper, filling the sky and singeing Bi De's feathers. It hurt, it burned, and yet Bi De acted unaffected as he landed and stroked his wattles once again.

"Hmph, your power is far below that of my Master," Bi De snorted contemptuously. "You are beneath his notice. Look at you, struggling so greatly against just his *chicken*."

The words made his opponent flinch, and the fires around him flared all the hotter. Zang Li's eyes focused fully on Bi De, finally giving his undivided attention. The interloper's eyes started to weep oil.

"I'm going to stuff you into a soup pot!" the man howled, his voice becoming oddly two-toned, as if another man were speaking just under the surface.

Yet Bi De's opponent's rage blinded him and distracted him.

He did not notice the small streak of black and silver rushing back to the town.

[Split Faces of the Half Moon]

Bi De was, after all, a diligent disciple. His Great Master had commanded he be alerted. And alerted he would be.

CHAPTER 49

BREAK THE ROCKS

Yingwen sucked in a deep breath as he deflected three rapid spear thrusts and struck his opponent in the arm. The other man snarled in pain and retreated. His fellows struck back. The plaza was shrouded in smoke and covered in scorch marks. There was blood splattered across the ground. The cultivators of the Azure Hills, roused to righteous anger just a few minutes earlier, were finally starting to falter.

The difference in power was telling. Even surrounded and outnumbered, the quality of the Shrouded Mountain was far beyond what the Azure Hills could muster. The Qi-less air, interfering with their techniques, had been steadily overcome. As the disciples of the Shrouded Mountain Sect battled, they refined their techniques and perfected their breathing. It almost seemed like the ambient Qi rose the longer they fought, making their abilities easier to control—Qi flowed around him on a gentle summer breeze.

That was not to say their side were unscathed. Two of five were on their knees and had been pulled into the defensive circle. His brother disciples were wounded and suffering, but the number of wounds and damage that they had inflicted in return was disproportionate.

Still, they were on the knife's edge. Yingwen caught his breath and glared at the disciples surrounding him. Those of the Azure Hills that remained standing prowled like wolves, searching for any weakness. However, their numbers had been cut drastically by the repeated assaults.

Everyone was flagging. They could possibly yet achieve victory—or more likely, escape this encirclement and flee . . . Shameful, absolutely shameful.

Yingwen mentally cursed his Young Master. Elder Chongyun and Elder Shenhe had been right in their suspicions of him. There would be a reckoning when they got back to the Sect.

There was a small commotion.

Liu Xianghua had refilled her engine. It was cool again, its vents ready for another bout. Gou Ren staggered back to his feet from where he had been slumped against the wall. Rou Tigu looked even more feral than normal, her eyes full of hate and her teeth bared in a snarl.

Yingwen grimaced. It was time to take a gamble. There was no more lightning coming from Fenxian's direction—that area had gone silent. He would never have just defeated his opponent, then returned to the manor. That he was not already heading in this direction meant . . .

It did not bear thinking about.

"Great Heavenly Breakthrough Formation," Yingwen commanded. His Brother Disciples nodded, their eyes hard and laced with exhaustion. "I will retrieve Fenxian. The rest of you retreat to a more defensible location." Their bodies flowed immediately into their positions, ready for the signal.

The disciples of the Shrouded Mountain readied themselves, their faces twisted into snarls. The air became charged with their thunderous Qi, blazing like miniature stars. It was the wrath of the heavens made manifest. The disparate Qi signatures of the Azure Hills rose to meet them, every element and ability twisting, the ants readying themselves to tackle the heavens. He could feel Rou Tigu's eyes especially, the burning yellow slits full of wrath—

The summer wind blew.

"*Enough,*" a voice said. In truth, it was a command. A command that cut through the ranks of the disciples.

Techniques spluttered and died. Cultivators flinched. Yingwen lost control of his lightning, because all of a sudden there was a *mountain standing in the square.*

It had been invisible. It hadn't existed at all. Yet all this time, he had been in its shadow—

Rou Tigu, ready to strike, seemed to collapse in on herself. Her slitted eyes faded back to something more human. Her firm composure melted.

And a bright, hopeful smile spread across her face.

"Master?" she whispered.

"Jin," his original target, Gou Ren, said, then promptly collapsed onto Xianghua with relief. The woman stared at him with concern.

A hand landed on Tigu's head. Large and tanned, it ruffled gently through orange hair. Tears gathered in the corners of Tigu's eyes as she looked up at the person touching her.

He was an unassuming man, tall as Fenxian. He wore rough, simple clothes that were a copy of Rou Tigu's own. Tanned, freckled skin, the same tone as Tigu's. A slight familial resemblance.

He looked like a farmhand.

Save for the fact that Fenxian was currently slung over his shoulder. There was another one of the Young Master's targets with the newcomer, but Yingwen's attention was entirely consumed by the man before him.

He could not properly feel the man's power. He could only deduce that it was vast, impossibly vast. It extended past his senses, seeming to become one with the very mountains around them.

The man's eyes softened as he looked upon Rou Tigu. She threw herself forwards, latching onto his side. He patted her back while he nodded at Gou Ren.

"It's gonna be okay now," he whispered to her. The small woman nodded in return and rubbed at her eyes, stepping back with a tired smile on her face. She had gone from fighting to the death to utterly relaxed. Like she was sure there was nothing in the world that could harm her at that moment.

The man looked at her body. At the bruises and the blood. His face became stone, and he looked back up. His eyes focused directly on Yingwen.

And then, so too did his intent.

It was like the Dueling Peaks had decided to lean in from their positions—like the entire mountain was directly over his head, looking down upon him and finding him wanting.

Yingwen felt the blood drain from his face. One of his Brother Disciples slammed down to his knees, sweat pouring down his forehead.

The man took a step towards them.

Yingwen swallowed and stepped back.

The man took another, closing the distance.

Yingwen tried to take another step . . . and then realised he couldn't lift his feet. It was as if there was a great weight upon his shoulders.

Each step from this man-shaped mountain was quiet, yet in the sudden silence it felt like an avalanche approaching their defensive formation.

A defensive formation that suddenly felt like it provided no defence at all. Instead, the Shrouded Mountain Sect had all conveniently grouped up so this man could squish all of them like insects without having to expend more energy.

And then he was in front of Yingwen. He was merely head and shoulders taller, yet it felt like if Yingwen wished to look at the man's face, he would have to crane his neck to look up at the heavens.

He was not so foolish. He kept his head lowered deferentially.

"This one greets the Great Expert. This one is Zhou Yingwen," he said instead, politely greeting his Senior first.

The man tossed Fenxian into their circle, apathy filling the movement. The large disciple lay unmoving, but alive. That he was not dead yet was either a good sign . . . or it meant they were all about to be brutally tortured for several years before being allowed to perish. The latter was more likely.

"You may call me Rou," the powerful expert stated.

Rou. Rou Tigu. Yingwen closed his eyes. Family. She was this powerful expert's daughter, most likely. They were all going to die this night, weren't they?

"You tried to take Tigu'er," Expert Rou said. His voice was calm. Dangerously so. "You hurt Gou Ren and Yun Ren too."

It was a statement, laced with fury. It left no space for a lie. If Yingwen tried, he would be destroyed utterly. Experts could tell if one told falsehood in their presence.

"Yes, Great Expert," he confirmed it.

Expert Rou looked at him, considered him, and sighed. He appeared fed up, tired, and confused.

"Why?" he demanded. "Did you even have a reason?"

Yingwen glanced up. His mind worked. Loyalty warred with a desire to live. A desire to report back to the Elders of just how far this had spiraled out of control. The Shrouded Mountain Sect needed to know of this shame and this reckless foolishness now more than ever.

In that moment, he made his choice.

Bowing deeply and showing supplication, Yingwen laid down the truth. "Upon the orders of our Young Master. He claimed Rou Tigu greatly shamed our Sect and that she needed to be punished. I objected to this course of action, yet he was insistent."

"Just following orders, huh?" he asked. The pressure increased. Yingwen didn't understand why that was the wrong thing to have said. Following the orders of one's Master was a high virtue. But the man before him clearly did not think much of his response. "And who is your 'Young Master'?"

"Zang Li," Yingwen replied. The pressure, for a brief moment, released.

"Zang Li?" Expert Rou asked, his fury turning to confusion. "Zang Li . . . I know that name—the imposter?"

Yingwen's eyes widened. "Imposter?" he ventured, a new avenue of . . . not victory, but something that could salvage the situation.

Expert Rou glared at him. "I encountered him attempting to rape a friend. I objected to this and defeated him. At the time, I was of the opinion that the Shrouded Mountain Sect could not have had a man that weak and wicked within their ranks. I thought the Shrouded Mountain Sect would take care of him. It seems I was . . . *mistaken*."

The entire world seemed to tense. Yingwen's knees bent from the pressure.

Yingwen's mind worked. Zang Li had been defeated in the Azure Hills. He'd claimed the attack had come out of nowhere. All thought this was the case. But . . . to hear it from this man, that Zang Li had been defeated for assaulting Expert Rou's ally, and that Rou had trusted the Shrouded Mountain Sect to take care of things . . .

It was cowardly what Yingwen was about to do. Most scrolls said he should stand by his Young Master until the end.

But if he did that, he would be dragging the Shrouded Mountain Sect into open conflict with this expert. There would be resources pushed into the Azure Hills. There was no doubt as to the outcome—the Shrouded Mountain Sect would win and crush the petty Sects here. It would not even require too many resources if an Elder was deployed. A single cultivator in the Earth Realm could defeat every cultivator here single-handedly, save for the man before him.

However, their reputation would certainly suffer. It would be known that the Shrouded Mountain Sect had been insulted by the Azure Hills. That they had done something so unforgivable even the weak Sects had had no choice but to object to them.

The Azure Hills were not the problem, but the reaction from the other Sects—the ones that mattered—*would be.*

"An imposter? You are likely correct, Great Expert," Yingwen stated, having weighed both paths and decided to discard the Young Master. Expert Rou froze, unsure of Yingwen's angle. "A member of the righteous Shrouded Mountain Sect, doing these things? Unlikely. A foul demon, or worse, a fox, a wicked beast, is attempting to bring the Shrouded Mountain Sect into conflict with an expert of your caliber. His technique is powerful and managed to deceive our eyes, but you have shown us the path." Yingwen lowered his voice to say, "The Elders were suspicious and bid me keep an eye upon him. It seems their suspicions were correct."

Expert Rou's frown deepened. "And this fight?"

"As Guo Daxian said earlier, it was merely a small scuffle—a drunken brawl," he confirmed, before pitching his voice slightly louder, so others could listen in. "Should we be slain, the Shrouded Mountain Sect shall come looking for us. Especially with your involvement, it would no longer be a battle between disciples. The Shrouded Mountain Sect was not challenged today." A Master had gotten involved now, and things had escalated, but . . . perhaps Yingwen could still save his Juniors.

"Just a drunken brawl?" Rou turned to the other members of the Azure Hills.

Several of them looked nervous at the prospect of the conflict escalating.

Tigu's face twisted. She looked like she wanted to say something, but Guo Daxian's hand landed on her shoulder.

"Yes, sir. Just a drunken brawl," the foreign Young Master said, not looking at Expert Rou but instead glaring at Yingwen.

Tigu looked outraged. "He crippled Loud Boy—"

"And if the Shrouded Mountain Sect comes here, people are going to get a lot more than hurt," Daxian muttered, his voice pitching lower.

Tigu's eyes shot up to a roof, where the Loud Boy was. He looked around at the scorched and destroyed square. He grimaced, then nodded to Tigu, agreeing with Daxian. The Young Mistress scowled, crossing her arms.

"As you can see, Great Expert"—Yingwen bowed once more, not quite begging—"there was no quarrel between the Shrouded Mountain Sect here and the . . . esteemed cultivators of the Azure Hills."

Expert Rou frowned, but his attention was not on them. Instead, it was upon a silvery projection, a rooster, beckoning him.

The man shook his head.

"I don't like this outcome. But I will accept it for now. Go back to your manor. We'll talk more in the morning," he commanded.

"We thank you for your consideration, Great Expert," Yingwen stated, bowing for a *third* time that night.

But the man was already gone.

Standing up straight, Yingwen gazed warily at his once-enemies, but they made no move to stop him from leaving.

"Should we make a break for it?" one of his Juniors asked nervously.

"So that we may die tired?" Yingwen asked. "We shall await him at the mansion, where we may be able to escape from this with our lives."

↔

Why were the heavens like this? Why did they give him things, only to snatch them away at the last moment? For every lucky break he encountered, he received a heaping dose of misfortune that canceled it all out . . .

Lu Ban's sword rapidly parried the silver blades of moonlight. He had learned early on to not get hit by them.

It's not fair.

He clenched and unclenched his fist. A small nick on his arm was glowing silver, with luminescent veins trailing up his arm. The bird's Qi acted like poison. It burned, and it disrupted his Qi, but it still wasn't enough to stop him.

His parents, his Master, every time things started to get better, something took it away from him.

Poisoned twice over. Antidotes not working properly. Attacked by two Profound-level cultivators. A jade sword, still on fire, stabbed into his back.

He reached deep and burned some of his Vital Qi, some of his *life*. Years would be lost.

But it didn't matter. All that mattered was victory.

Oil and blood erupted in a tide as his opponents recoiled.

Nothing was enough. Nothing could stop him. Nothing could keep him suppressed. He was *Lu Ban*.

And he would rise to the heavens of this worthless world.

[Blood Arts: Strength of the Feast]

Both Cai Xiulan and the rooster screamed as the wounds on their bodies ripped open further and their blood started to flow towards Lu Ban. The grass around him withered.

He felt the flesh of his face melt slightly as his Blood Art interfered with the body's natural lightning alignment. Something he would have to fix later—he just needed a bit more time. The shouting had stopped from the square. He had to move quickly.

Lu Ban's Qi coalesced.

And his enemy's doom descended.

↔

Was it the right choice? To leave the Shrouded Mountain guys?

I wasn't sure.

They were exhausted and defeated already. Maybe I had been too soft. But when I saw them and they just folded over . . . well . . . some of the fire faded.

I'd hesitated. I didn't want to kill them. I didn't want to kill *anybody*. Maybe some of this could be resolved with words still. Maybe not everybody had to die.

I didn't like the deal I had made. I didn't want to just let this go. But what could I do right then? If I forced the issue, there would be a war. A war the Azure Hills would lose.

What could I have done? I wasn't some sort of master negotiator. Nobody was happy with the outcome, but I couldn't really think about it right now.

I followed the spectral chicken, one of Big D's techniques, to the blazing fire and the man screaming with rage and hate. His eyes were wild. He had small silver cuts trailing around his body.

But he looked familiar . . . Even with his black sclera and red eyes. Even when coated by a miasma of blood and oil.

This was the bastard who had tried to take Meihua, a year ago.

When I had taken him to jail . . . Well, I'd had no real expectation of him living. The Sects really didn't like people impersonating them. I knew, when I'd delivered him to that jail cell, I would never see him again.

But I'd been wrong.

Fire rained down around him as he tried to kill my friends.

He was the kind of man that *couldn't* be reasoned with.

[Blood Arts: Strength of the Feast]

I felt the pulse from the man. A split second later, Big D and Xiulan both screamed. I felt the grass wither. I felt the ugly, gaping void that he spawned.

And then came an eruption of fire that threatened to consume both of them.

He was nothing but a rabid beast, wasn't he? And every farmer knows what to do with rabid beasts.

Even though no farmer ever enjoys it.

I took a breath.

'Do you want me to do it?' Rou asked. Like he wanted to spare me from doing what needed to be done. I had never killed anybody before.

No. We'll do it together.

Zang Li was everything I had ever run away from. Every piece of cultivator bullshit, all in one person. Attacking my friends, my family. All of it was right here, culminating in this fucking asshole.

I clenched my fist and felt something like approval. Small arms around my neck. Lips pressed to my forehead.

I stepped into the flames.

↔

Lu Ban's attack was to be the end of it.

Instead, oil, blood, and fire were dispersed like water droplets being shaken from a leaf, as a man walked through the flames like he was taking a casual stroll.

It was a man whose face had haunted Lu Ban's nightmares for the past year.

Lu Ban's fingers spasmed. The rooster and the woman turned, looking up at the man as he walked between them, snuffing out the fire with each step. Behind him, in the ashes, grass grew out of the blighted soil, and flowers bloomed.

Rou Jin.

His eyes were cold and hard.

Throughout this fight, Lu Ban had known he was racing against time. He'd had to defeat them before their Master arrived. He'd failed.

He swallowed as the summer breeze, once so gentle, became unbearably hot.

"One chance to surrender," Rou Jin stated simply.

Lu Ban's face twisted. At the confidence. At the *assurance*. At a man with power looking down at him once again.

Lu Ban snarled as he concentrated. His defences were prepared. He could possibly escape. He couldn't fight him now, but—

Rou Jin brought back his fist and the world shuddered with anticipation. The earth stilled, even as the heavens churned.

Thin, golden cracks appeared. First, they formed from his knuckles, branching out up his arm like a virulent weed and traveling all the way to his shoulder. They were breaks in his skin, fractures that made it look like his arm was more stone than flesh.

It was something shattered and broken, repaired with gold.

The cracks flowed from his shoulder, across his chest, and up his face. His eyes were clear and pure, full of resolve.

Crushing. Suffocating. The very land itself was staring at Lu Ban with disgust.

Rou Jin brought back his fist.

It was a simple punch. The simplest of punches. The foundation of all cultivators, the first thing all warriors learned. His stance was wide and stable. His fist chambered like it was from a training manual.

A technique to be practised and refined. Diligently studied and then abandoned, as a cultivator learned better and more powerful techniques.

Lu Ban did not pause to see what would happen.

He threw himself backwards as fast as his body could carry him.

But there was a whisper on the wind, a chanting sutra from ages long past filling his ears. A five-element-formation grew and shimmered behind him. The golden cracks spread to the very air around him, cracking the sky like glass.

'And so the Great Ancestor Shennong commanded his disciple in the ways of preparing the fields. Till the land. Fell the trees. Divert the waters—'

[BREAK THE ROCKS]

His feet drew power from the Earth. His hips twisted to refine it in the core. His core stabilized and channeled energy to the shoulder. His shoulder pulled back the arm to condense Qi. The arm lengthened to send forwards a fist.

The fist became a blow.

With all the weight of the world behind it.

Lu Ban was away. Far away, beyond the man's reach—but the fist did not have to hit him to strike him.

All five of Lu Ban's talismans activated. Treasures that each could survive a blow from the power of one in the Earth Realm.

There was a sound like breaking glass as all the talismans attempted to save Lu Ban.

Attempted.

The earth did not heave. The heavens did not shatter. There was no devastation at all.

One moment, Lu Ban was a form in the air, and the next . . .

He was gone.

□

The birds chirped cheerily, the little devils. They were always far too happy this early in the morning.

Ganshi examined the heads of rice growing from his field. The harsh, rocky soil and altitude weren't the best for growing the crop, but this year things seemed to be different.

They were much larger than he'd been expecting. How had they grown so tall since he'd last examined them? He had only looked at them last week!

Well, at least this was something good. The entire village had been in an uproar over the earthquake last night. The chickens wouldn't stop crowing, the fence around the cows had toppled, and the only reason the beasts didn't escape was that they were clearly too terrified to.

"Love, have you seen the size of these earth apples!" his wife asked, her eyes shining. "This is amazing!"

"I have," Ganshi replied with a laugh, loving and sharing the joy his wife found in an unexpected bumper crop.

Indeed, as he walked around his farm, he noticed that everything was huge. He must have twice the yield as last year! All of his crops were heavy, fat, and delicious-looking, almost glowing with vitality.

Even he felt better. Like he was energised.

And it was not just him. When he went to talk to his neighbors, they too raved about their increased yields. Later that day when he went into town, it was the same thing. Even the little balcony gardens were seeing yields that far surpassed what they normally gave.

It got to the point where the Magistrate had sent a transmission to the next town over . . . whose Magistrate reported the same thing—as did the next town, and the town after that.

It was as if the entirety of Yellow Rock Plateau had suddenly been blessed by the god of agriculture! Shennong was truly with them this year!

But there was a bit of a concerning story as well. Apparently, there had been a rockslide on Tianliyu Heights, a few hundred li to the south, after a great *something* had impacted there.

There were whispers of a Spirit Beast or some other thing having destroyed half the mountain, but it was quite far away, so Ganshi put it out of his mind. Instead, he moseyed on home—back to the edge of the plateau.

It was always his favourite spot. He could see down across the Azure Hills from here, and on a good day, without any mist, sometimes he could even spot the barest tip of the Dueling Peaks, a thousand li to the distant north.

CHAPTER 50

VICTORY?

The previous day, moments after Jin left with Bi De's shadow . . .

There was silence in the square as the Shrouded Mountain Sect disciples left to follow Jin's orders. Yun Ren watched them go with mixed feelings. Part of him wanted to chase after the bastards and stab them all, but that would obviously be a bad idea. He could barely fight one of the guys with the support of a super artifact and a spirit fox. Charging into the rest of them? Stupid.

After all his resolve, he hadn't needed to do anything.

Kind of anticlimactic, really. He glanced around at the broken-up square and the unconscious and bleeding people. He winced, turning away from them and to Nezan.

The fox was still staring blankly in the direction Jin had headed.

Yun Ren left him to his gaping and immediately searched for his brother. Tigu looked pretty fine, but Gou Ren had slumped against the wall and was grimacing. His arms had bloody red lines all over them.

Xianghua gave one last look towards where Jin had left before immediately ripping off the sleeve of her nice silk robe and turning it into a bandage. Yun Ren was about to walk over, but then something broke the silence.

"Yin!" He heard a shout as Tigu raised her arms to the air and caught a white blur. "Miantiao!" The rabbit slammed into her, a snake coiled around the mid-section, and Tigu staggered from the force. She snuggled the rabbit to her chest, rubbing her cheek against the little creature, before she gasped.

The rabbit had a satchel—one of the bags Meimei had given out, full of medicine. Tigu immediately shot over to Tie Delun, the "Handsome Man" groggily waking up after being blasted by lightning. He immediately took Tigu to the chest as she hugged him. "Loud Boy! Come here! We've got more medicine for you!"

The spell broke. Murmuring filled the crowd. Fearful, hushed murmuring.

"By the blood of Da Ji," Nezan whispered, startling Yun Ren when the voice came from his shoulder. "What the hells?"

'New arrival's Qi is subtle. Unable to sense. Infusion Earth-Wood? No, just Wood? Earth from somewhere else? Unknown. Unable to determine. New experience. Interest. Approval.' The sword was back to its grey colouration, looking for all the world like a normal blade once again.

"I see that *now*, darling. I would have come out to say hello if I could have felt that before. *He's* the one who taught you how to use Qi, Nephew?"

"Yeah," Yun Ren whispered. He made eye contact with his brother and jerked his head over to Tigu. Gou Ren nodded and pushed himself off the wall.

"I did tell you he was strong, but like . . . that's the first time I've seen him like . . . *ya know*?" Yun Ren said.

Nezan nodded. "Well. Something interesting to tell myself when you come back and visit me later."

Yun Ren peered closely at the fox. "Tell *yourself* later?"

"Hm? Ah, of course." The fox's body faded slightly, revealing the glimmering gem Nezan had given him. "A technique we can do. I would not recommend it, as it does weaken the main body, but one can split off small parts of their core and allow them to take form. I'll be integrated back when you visit later. I gave you the perfect gift: myself! You may praise me now, Nephew."

Yun Ren sighed and ignored the bastard, making his way over to Tigu.

The girl was fussing over Tie Delun and Loud Boy, circling around both of them like . . . Well, like a protective cat. Gou Ren walked up, wincing. And he was immediately pushed down too. Tigu rubbed her cheek against his before switching to Xianghua.

Ri Zu and Yin were both just staring at her with amusement.

"That's her . . . Master? Father?" Guo Daxian asked. The man was staring at one of Meimei's medicine balls like it had all the secrets of the universe within it.

"Bit of both, honestly," Yun Ren said.

Daxian nodded before his frown deepened. "Where are our Elders, though? Things were hardly quiet—"

The world pulsed. Something broke. *Everyone* flinched.

There was a sudden hum as the Earthly Arena of the Dueling Peaks shot halfway up the mountain . . . before slowly dropping back down with a groan and settling.

"I thought its floating mechanism was broken ages ago?" Yun Ren ventured.

"It was." Daxian swallowed thickly. "Tell me, how do we stay on Master Rou's good side?" he asked immediately.

"Well, ya helped out Tigu, so you're prolly there already. Jin's the kind of guy who pays his debts, yeah?" Yun Ren replied.

Daxian let out a tentative breath.

It wasn't long until Jin came back. He was half carrying Xiulan—Yun Ren couldn't help but wince when he saw her. She had burns all over her body as well as some cuts that looked like the ones Sun Ken had given her, or at least the brief glance Yun Ren had seen of them. Her skin was flushed red, and she was shaking and sweating like she had a fever.

The other hand was carrying a sword. A stained red blade. Jin's frown was heavy, and it didn't look natural on him at all.

He looked better smiling.

The square snapped to attention at his return.

"Tigu. Get everybody to a place to rest, okay? I've got one last thing to do tonight," Jin said.

Tigu nodded, Yin on her shoulder. Jin looked at her and offered her a small smile. The girl's grin turned bright, and she set about getting everybody ready to leave. Jin turned his eyes to the square.

He glanced at the red sword and grimaced.

"What a *mess*," he said with a sigh.

↔

The air was tense in the Shrouded Mountain Sect's manor.

Yingwen sat in the lotus position and tried to meditate, waiting for Expert Rou to return. The rest of his fellow disciples were not as calm. They were walking around nervously. Fenxian had woken up, though in a foul mood. The normally loud man had been suppressed swiftly and brutally; he'd been defeated in a single blow, his jaw broken.

None spoke as they waited. None spoke after the summer breeze had turned sharp for an instant, like it was flaying them to their souls.

They felt the mountain turn its gaze towards them once more. The man entered, a chicken on his shoulder. It was a bit worse for wear and singed-looking, but it was still a magnificent animal.

"Expert Rou." Yingwen greeted the man as he walked in with Young Master Zang Li's sword, a bit surprised. The man had said they would talk in the morning, but he had obviously changed his mind. There was a sharp intake of breath from those around him, as well as several curses. Zang Li, for all his faults, had at least been free with his coin purse and with lesser cultivation aides. He just hadn't inspired much loyalty.

And now he was gone.

Expert Rou was carrying the sword by the blade, negligently. Like it was something disgusting. It was disrespectful for such a fine sword—but there was something off about it.

The blade had been blackened. Tainted. Its once pure lines were now pulsing with ugly, corrupted Qi.

"Wha—" Fenxian slurred through his healing jaw. "Tha hells?"

"Is this not normal for the Shrouded Mountain Sect?" Expert Rou asked, handing over the blade.

Black, acidic blood that smelled of rot covered it. There was the taint of something demonic and corrupt.

"No, Expert Rou. No, it is not," Yingwen stated. His Brother Disciples were staring in concern.

"Who was with him last? He was alone when I found him," Rou asked, voice calm.

"He ordered us all away," Brother Maohai said. "He was poisoned quite badly, but he demanded that we all retreat and that she was his alone."

"Come with me," Rou said. All followed him from the manor—even the ones who really should have stayed back at the manor resting. Brother Huang still looked like he would fall over from a slight breeze.

He took them to a field outside the town, and all of them followed behind, absolutely silent. Yingwen thought for a moment they were simply being taken out to be buried, but that was not likely.

They were brought to a field that had husks of withered plants pushed aside by new growth. There were many patches of blood on the ground.

Yingwen examined the blood thoroughly. His fellows marched around the field as well, collecting some of the remains. There was a piece of tainted flesh with silver veins running through it—Pure Qi battled with corrupted and Demonic Qi. There was the remnants of fire . . . as well as drops of bloody oil.

This . . . this was unbelievable. The first thought in Yingwen's mind was that this was planted evidence. But he had felt this powerful expert's Qi; it could not possibly be tainted.

Yingwen had simply imagined the expert had been trying to allow them to save face. The story of Zang Li being an imposter would let them overlook his involvement, but . . . had Rou been telling the truth the entire time? Was there some deeper force at play here? Was the man the expert claimed to be an imposter truly some manner of insidious creature?

No member of the Shrouded Mountain Sect should have tainted blood like this. They were examined for fox illusions after they were deployed to high-risk areas, their hated enemies skilled at entrapping minds—

—and the Young Master had not been. He had been in the fort for most of his time up north and had refused or been barred from the expedition to attempt to find Summer's Sky. He had *not* been looked at in great depth. Merely cursory examinations. To be able to hide beneath the purifying Qi of lightning the Zang Clan of the mountain was known for . . .

There was something foul afoot here. Something that had Fenxian staring at Yingwen with as much concern as he had ever seen in the large man's eyes.

"Sir, are there any more remains?" he asked carefully as he stood. "If we could retrieve his corpse, we would be better able to confirm this."

Expert Rou grimaced. "Maybe," he admitted as his eyes grew distant. "Over that way, somewhere. Not in the Azure Hills. I think in Yellow Rock Plateau."

That was a thousand li distant—Yingwen, however, once more kept his face carefully blank. Possibly there could be a corpse. *Possibly.* Yet even without it . . . the evidence was beginning to look damning to Yingwen's eyes.

Zang Li had either been corrupted . . . or truly was an imposter.

"Expert Rou. This has escalated far beyond expectations. We would leave to pursue this, with your blessing."

"Not all of you are going," he said bluntly.

"Of course," Yingwen replied. "I shall select several of our men, and I shall remain under your care, if it pleases you. Or you may select any of the others."

The expert stared at him with cold eyes before sighing at the urgency in Yingwen's voice. He turned to look up at the sky.

"I still don't like this. You attack my family and go and waltz off into the sunset? You hurt people. Destroyed one's cultivation."

"We shall leave all the medicine and resources we brought with us behind. Compared to the pills of the Azure Hills, they are far more potent. Any damage is likely to be healable. But the crippling . . ." Yingwen took a breath. "I will submit to your judgement. The cultivation of one in the Profound Realm could be said to be at least ten times the value of one in the Initiate's Realm. I would only beg that you spare my Brother Disciples your wrath."

The man sighed. His fingers twitched, like he wanted to run them through his hair, yet refrained.

"Fine. Get your men ready. I'll let you retrieve the body."

"You are most benevolent, Expert—"

"*But this ends here.* No retaliation. No offence to being challenged." His eyes turned back to Yingwen and the rest of the Shrouded Mountain Disciples, who were still combing the grounds. He considered them at length, his presence an ever-present sensation that made Yingwen sick to his stomach. Rou reached into his pack. "I recently had a meeting with my Senior Brother. He said that if I needed aid, all I would need to do is ask. I told him that I would be all right and that he didn't need to worry about me. And he left me this."

A small piece of parchment unfurled. A small piece of parchment with a symbol on it. A symbol every son and daughter of the Empire knew.

A proud mountain, jutting above the clouds, with the symbol for "sword" etched into its face.

Yingwen felt as if every single one of his ancestors had just coughed blood all at once; he nearly fell on his ass.

The greatest of martyrs and heroes. The Masters of the Raging Cloudy Sword Formation. A Sect who stood at the pinnacle, whose name resounded throughout the world.

The Cloudy Sword Sect.

"I would really rather avoid having to get him involved, wouldn't you?" Rou's voice was calm and matter-of-fact.

Yingwen struggled for a moment before swallowing down the ball of spit in his throat. He slammed his hands together in the gesture of respect with unseemly haste.

"Lord Rou, your temperance and manly virtue humbles this Zhou Yingwen. He thanks you for your benevolence and restraint."

If Rou was this strong, then his Senior Brother would easily have the power of an Elder.

Going against the Cloudy Sword Sect would be like the Verdant Blade Sect challenging the Shrouded Mountain Sect.

Dishonourable defeat was the only outcome. If Master Rou were any more a vengeful man, the entirety of the Shrouded Mountain could burn—or worse, be labeled as a demonic Sect by the Imperial Authorities.

An Imperial Decree that the Shrouded Mountain Sect were Demonic Cultivators would be like having the entire world declaring war on them.

"By your leave, Master Rou. We shall have the truth of this matter posthaste. I swear it upon all of my ancestors—and though you may not value the name, the name of the Shrouded Mountain Sect."

The man's gaze was inscrutable.

"Three stay. The most wounded."

"As you say." Yingwen whirled around. "Make preparations for departure. *Now.* Brother Huang, prepare the carriage. I am declaring: *The Fangs Come for the Mountain, Yet the Heavens are Silent.*"

Every man straightened like a bolt of lightning had struck his body at the urgent code.

"By necessity I remain behind. The rest of you will take the carriage south. Resupply at Tall Rock, and stop for nothing until we have the body. Silence and haste are paramount. Accomplish this mission or die trying."

"Yes, Brother Yingwen!" They exploded into motion, Yingwen in the lead.

"How deep is the shit we're in?" Fenxian asked quietly.

"Deep enough to cover the peak of our mountain."

Fenxian stared at Yingwen and rubbed his jaw. "*Fuck*," he declared.

Yingwen disliked cursing. It was the vocabulary of one without wits. He looked Fenxian in the eye.

"Fuck," he agreed.

The sun peeked over the horizon. A carriage, pulled by yoked spirits, headed towards the south.

CHAPTER 51

DAWN

Xianghua felt hollow.

She always did after a fight. Like her insides had been scooped out and her emotions were more muted than normal. This time, she couldn't even muster the energy for her usual act. She hadn't raised her voice once since Master Rou had arrived.

So she worked.

Xiulan had been in poor condition when Tigu's Master had brought her back. She'd had a horrible fever, and her body was littered with angry burns along with a thousand other wounds.

She looked like she was about to die.

Xianghua had been frozen in place, staring at the enormity of the damage . . . until the little doctor Ri Zu began squeaking angry orders that had them all racing off the street and into the Verdant Blade Sect's manor. Ri Zu had recruited both Xianghua and An Ran to assist her, while Gou Ren and his brother aided Tie Delun. They both swung into action at Ri Zu's squeak, immediately cataloguing wounds—but they had been taught differently than Xianghua had. They focused on more minor injuries that cultivators were largely taught to ignore since their bodies could handle the strain.

Xiulan, at Ri Zu's command, was placed into a water bath, so as to begin cooling some of the heat raging in her body. The water had immediately warmed to the temperature of a hot bath, and so An Ran, despite her arm being in a sling, was sent to fetch more.

Poultices of herbs were produced from the bag that Master Rou had given to Ri Zu, the same kind that had completely healed Xianghua . . . except they used four of them, further revealing the extent of the damage.

Ri Zu delegated this task to Xianghua, her larger hands able to spread the mashed Spiritual Herbs more easily, while the rat brought out a piece of chalk and referenced a tiny notebook.

'Reverse here for inject instead of siphon. This one will be water, this one will be to reduce, this one to intensify,' Ri Zu muttered as she drew out a circle. *'Miss Xianghua, may Ri Zu use your water to attempt to help douse the fire within Xiulan?'*

Xianghua nodded. It was only right. So her hands were placed on Xiulan's stomach and little Ri Zu guided her Qi while An Ran hovered nervously nearby, her eyes upon her Young Mistress.

It was rather amazing how swiftly Xiulan's face went from an angry red colour to its normal one. Really, this rat was better at medicine than every Spiritual Doctor Xianghua had ever paid for! *What sort of master was powerful enough to teach a rat such powerful formations and healing techniques?* Senior Sister Meiling was truly a woman worthy of awe and fear—a mountain, like Master Rou.

Xianghua imagined there being another one of those mountains, and shuddered. Then her lips quirked in pleasure as she imagined what was happening to the Shrouded Mountain Sect at that moment.

Xianghua and An Ran waited in silence while Ri Zu worked. The occasional groan drifted into the room from one of the other men as they too were administered to. There was a knock on the door. A female Sect servant entered with a basket and gasped upon seeing the Young Mistress. Xianghua took the towels and bandages from the woman.

"Get some bedding ready for the wounded. They will need space to recover. Inform any messengers that the Sect is closed for the evening. I want no rumours, understand? Have the uninjured disciples take the watch. The Elders will sort it out," she commanded. They were orders she had no authority to give, but the shaken woman bowed her head and departed immediately.

It was around an hour later when Ri Zu paused and placed her fingers on Xiulan's pulse. She was standing on the edge of the tub, her fur wet from when she'd dove into the tub to check on the other wounds.

'Things have improved, but . . . there is damage. Damage Ri Zu does not know how to fix. Xiulan's Qi caught alight.'

An Ran's face fell and tears gathered in the corners of the young woman's eyes. Indeed, the ignition of a member of the Verdant Blade Sect's cultivation was the thing they feared the most. It would burn and burn and burn until all of their power was ash—crippled and unable to cultivate again. A normal cultivator in the Azure Hills had no real hope of accomplishing the feat. But one from the Shrouded Mountain, in the higher ranks of the Profound Realm, could manage it.

Xianghua grimaced.

"Young Mistress—*Xiulan*," An Ran whispered. Her eyes unfocused and her face twisted. Xianghua carefully studied the expression, the . . . grief? Rage? A tricky, twisty thing overtook An Ran's face. "Those Shrouded Mountain bastards. I'll kill them all—"

Little paws clapped together, and An Ran jolted as if she had been slapped. Her eyes refocused on Ri Zu, who was at her feet.

'Miss An. Please help Ri Zu get friend Xiulan to bed and make her comfortable, yes?' Her voice was soft and full of gentle prodding.

"Ah . . . um. Yes," An Ran said, placing a hand on her chest to calm her racing heart. Her snarl was gone and replaced with something small and lost, as she stared at her teacher. She hesitated for a moment, then started to carefully tend to Xiulan.

Her arm was still in a sling, though, so her ability to assist the rat was limited.

Xianghua sighed and picked up the slack. Never in her life had she expected she would have to help Cai Xiulan into her robes.

After she was dressed, they carried her up the stairs into the room that had been set aside for her. Xianghua looked around it, curious, after they pulled the covers over the woman. She was fast asleep. Her pained grimace had smoothed out to gentle breaths.

The room was largely empty. There was a bed and a pack in the corner of the room. But one thing stood out. One of Yun Ren's images cast onto a piece of rock. Xiulan smiling with Gou Ren, Yun Ren, Master Rou, and a woman Xianghua didn't recognise. All of them making stupid, childish faces.

She looked so blindingly happy and unguarded. Xianghua smiled at the image, and after An Ran finished brushing a few errant strands of hair out of Xiulan's face, Ri Zu spoke.

'Ri Zu will stay with Xiulan. Go, and rest. Ri Zu will call if she needs help.'

An Ran looked like she was about to protest and just stay. She glanced at the floor, as if considering sleeping at the foot of her Young Mistress's bed.

Xianghua rolled her eyes, then caught An Ran's arm, pulling the girl out of the room. They marched back down the stairs. The sky was slowly lightening, dispelling the darkness. It would be dawn soon, and Xianghua needed at least *some* sleep.

They entered the main room of the manor. The servants had done her bidding, bringing in blankets and bedding for them to rest on. It was a large room and could easily accommodate them all spreading out with their own space . . . but instead, everybody seemed to collect into little piles, cramming themselves together. Tie Delun, Rags, and Loud Boy, the most injured of them, were in a neat row off to the side.

Tigu had slumped over in between Gou Ren and Yun Ren, clinging to the rabbit and snake that had arrived with her.

It looked like quite a comfortable position.

An Ran stared at Gou Ren, flushed slightly, and went instead to rest with her fellow disciples.

Xianghua felt no such hesitation. The heavens provided to the bold. It was foolish to give up an opportunity such as this. She marched over to where her Gou Ren was lying down, gently pulled his bandaged arm up and away, careful not to aggravate any wounds, and planted herself beside him.

An eye cracked open, and she smirked at him. He snorted and put an arm around her back, pulling her closer. Her eyes soon drifted shut.

She slept contentedly, waking only once when the door opened and a servant came in to check on them. They paused in the doorway and remained as quiet as they could so as not to disturb them unduly.

A warm summer breeze came in from the open door.

There was no feeling of threat. Surprisingly . . . she felt oddly safe.

→

Xianghua awoke to Gou Ren shuffling around and the sounds of chopping from outside the room.

She cracked open an eye. She was lying on Gou Ren's chest. He had shifted to lie on his back. He looked peaceful while he slept, his features calm, instead of twisted with anger.

Xianghua sat up. The room was bright, the sun long since risen. She directed a bit of Qi around her hair—it was always frizzy in the morning. Her power took hold of the moisture in the air and collected it. She ran her fingers through her hair, flattening it back out. She glanced down at Gou Ren. His eyes were screwed up and he was stirring. His brother was awake and leaning against the wall with a cup of tea in his hands, his eyes closed tight and a sword in his lap, clearly meditating early in the morning as all cultivators should. Tigu was gone, and she could hear the sound of someone moving outside the room. There was the scent of some kind of unfamiliar tea in the air.

Gou Ren shuffled slightly, turning again, and buried his face in her thigh. He groaned and pulled at the bandages on his arm, revealing unblemished flesh. The angry red lines and scars from last night were gone.

She returned to her study of his face.

Xianghua absently reached out and brushed a finger through his hair. The man was only roused to violence and anger when those he loved were in danger. He was, like she had said in the beginning, such a fool.

And her heart was beating faster again. His eyes cracked open and he leaned into her touch. They stared at each other, smiling in the morning light. The moment was broken when the door opened again to admit someone; she heard soft shuffling footsteps.

There was a *hoot* from beside her. Xianghua turned her head to the servant interrupting and paused.

It was a short, toddler-sized creature. Its face was bright, pale blue, and its fur was muted gold. It had a necklace with a crystal on a string around its neck and a cup of tea in each hand.

A monkey.

Xianghua closed her eyes, rubbed them, and opened them again.

The monkey was still there. It hooted again, cocking its head to the side.

Gou reached around from behind her and took one of the cups.

"Thanks," he said, nodding his head. Xianghua tentatively took the other cup. Not so much different than a medical rat, she supposed. "What's your name, buddy? I'm Gou Ren."

The creature nodded its head and chattered.

"Nice to meetcha, Huo Ten. Thanks for the tea," he said with a smile, raising his cup to the monkey. The monkey bowed and retreated.

Xianghua stared after it.

She heard Gou take a drink from behind her and make an appreciative noise.

She absently raised her cup and took a sip as well.

It was like nothing she had ever tasted before. Oddly earthy, with the undercurrent of lemongrass. It wasn't bad, but she was more used to finer teas.

Xianghua took another sip, then turned to Gou Ren.

"You understood that?" she asked curiously.

Gou Ren nodded. "He's got a bit of a strange accent, but yeah. You didn't?"

She shook her head.

"Wonder why . . ." he muttered, trailing off.

"It's just 'cause they're both monkeys," Yun Ren croaked out from beside them, cracking open his eyes to smirk at them.

Gou rolled his eyes, while Xianghua's face went blank at the insult. She couldn't measure the severity of the words yet. The brothers seemed to like each other . . . But she hadn't figured out the fox-faced boy well enough to tell yet.

"And you've got a fox, so we're even," Gou said bluntly. "Where is that . . . spirit, anyway?"

"Said he would need to rest and recover his strength," Yun Ren replied. His sword rattled. Yun Ren glared at it and grumbled. "Shaddup. It *still* makes no sense when you explain it. I'll have to go out and practise."

"You speak sword now too?" Gou Ren asked. Yun Ren shrugged and drew the weapon. The pale grey of iron turned to purest white, the sword vibrating with Qi.

"It followed me home," he snarked. The sword rattled a second time.

Gou Ren stared at the sword, then turned to his own hands. He sighed and leaned back.

"You holding up okay?" he asked, his voice full of concern for his brother. Yun Ren sheathed the sword and seemed to consider the question. Xianghua kept silent. A moment between siblings was to be respected. So instead, she just closed her eyes and enjoyed the feeling of Gou Ren's arm around her waist.

Gou Ren's brother sighed. "Dunno. But I think Jin and Meimei were on to something about this cultivation stuff. Bastards."

They lapsed into silence at his declaration.

"Not *everything* about cultivation is bad," Gou Ren muttered. Xianghua opened her eyes to catch Gou Ren staring at her.

"Oh, this Xianghua is just *not bad*, is she?" she asked.

Gou Ren's eyes went from lidded to panicked—before he realised she was teasing him. He pulled her closer to him, then turned her so that she was leaning against him. She allowed it, for she was a kind and generous Young Mistress . . . and his blush was quite fetching.

"Where is Tigu?" Gou Ren asked, searching the room for the orange-haired young woman.

"Outside with Jin, Miantiao, and Yin. Dunno where Bi De is, though," Yun Ren replied.

Gou Ren nodded. They all lapsed into silence, simply sitting together in the stillness of the late morning.

Some of the hollowness in Xianghua's chest faded as she sipped her tea.

Slowly, the room roused to wakefulness. Xiulan's students stirred one at a time, with An Ran in the lead. The smaller woman pulled off her sling and flexed her arm. Satisfied the break was healed, she immediately stood, marching up the stairs to check on Xiulan. The rest of the Petals followed one at a time. They nodded to Xianghua and the brothers, but their distraction was clear as they rid themselves of bandages and slings—and, in the green-haired one's case, an eyepatch.

Loud Boy woke soon after, grumbling and groaning before suddenly shooting bolt upright and clutching at his stomach.

His face fell and his eyes teared up—but he shook it away and went to check on Rags and Tie Delun.

For a brief moment, her brother's face etched itself over the young, crippled cultivator's. Xianghua closed her eyes. If Master Rou did not take him, Xianghua would offer the child a place in the Misty Lake Sect. Such loyalty and dedication should always be rewarded.

But there was still one problem. Just where *were* all the Elders? They had all, according to the snippets Xianghua had heard last night, departed for the Dueling Peaks and stayed inside the entire time. Had something gone wrong? Was the Earthly Arena rising into the air the omen of something worse?

Xianghua kept her thoughts to herself and finished her tea, enjoying the moment of peace. The servants came in and cleared most of the bedding. The wounded were checked over at the edge of the room. They put in a large table and set down plates and chopsticks. The Petals soon returned with Ri Zu.

'Xiulan is improving. The fires have completely gone. Her temperature is normal, and her external wounds have fully healed,' the rat reported. Xiulan's students brightened, and Xianghua herself sighed in relief.

The smell of food from outside got stronger. It would probably be ready soon.

They seated themselves around the table. The Petals grouped up, while Gou Ren sat with Loud Boy, clapping him on the shoulder. Xianghua set herself beside Gou, while Yun Ren put away his sword. The monkey, Huo Ten, handed out more tea.

The back door opened and the smell of herbs, eggs, and meat intensified. Xianghua turned her head, her stomach rumbling, and froze.

For it was no servant bringing in the food, but Master Rou.

His face was calm. His terrifying Qi was absent, and such was his power that she could not feel a scrap of his strength. His control had to be something extraordinary to manage such a thing. He held a large wok full to the brim in one hand and a pot of rice in the other.

He was wearing a servant's apron.

Completing the image was an orange mop of hair resting on his shoulder. Tigu was riding upon her Master's back, her arms and legs locked to keep her in place. Her eyes were closed in contentment.

"Good morning, everybody," he said as he strode over to the table and set down the food. There was—realisation?—on An Ran's face, while Loud Boy just stared, his jaw open.

Xianghua breathed in and put the absurdity of such a powerful Master cooking them food out of her mind to observe the proper protocols.

Xianghua's hands came together in a salute as she rose, bowing her head. "This Xianghua pays her respects to Master Rou," she declared as gracefully as she could. Gou's Master raised an eyebrow, as the others chimed in after her, scrambling up to greet the man. He shuffled in place.

"Oh, right. Sorry for not introducing myself properly last night, but you all needed your rest." He cleared his throat and returned their respect. "This one is Rou Jin. It is a pleasure to meet you all. Just call me Jin, okay?"

'I'm Liang Yin! I helped make the food!' A silver rabbit hopped up onto the table and nodded to the room. She looked at them all with what seemed to be curiosity. Now that Master Rou's power was no longer overwhelming everything, Xianghua reached out, trying to truly feel the rabbit's strength for the first time. It was not trying to hide. It blazed forth like the sun above, firmly within the Fourth Stage of the Initiate's Realm.

Xianghua took a deep breath. A medical rat was one thing. But the way Tigu smiled and scooped the little beast up to snuggle made it look like Tigu's pet had the same cultivation as Xianghua did.

She raised an eyebrow at Miantiao the snake bowing politely. Xianghua returned it, of course. While the rabbit burned, the snake was reflective. She had a hard time feeling its power, but it was weaker than the rabbit, of that she was sure.

The table was silent after the introductions finished. Master Jin took a seat at the head of the table, which had remained vacant.

"Jin . . . uh, what's going on, with . . . everything?" Gou Ren ended lamely, breaking the silence.

Master Rou—Jin—sighed. "After everybody finishes eating, we'll get to the heavy stuff, okay?"

The rest of the table agreed with the Master's proclamation.

It was surreal. Like Tigu, the man was a tiger among men. But this tiger had tucked in his claws and was pretending to be a housecat. A tiger that was serving them all food and pouring their drinks like he was their *Junior*. All of them began to eat, not wanting to offend him by refusing his generosity.

He was an *excellent* cook, though. She supposed every old monster had to have some pastime.

"Are you the one from whom the Young Mistress learned to cook?" one of the Petals, Huyi, asked.

"Lanlan? Yeah. She got good fast. The only thing she could make when she first joined us was trail rations," Master Jin replied with a chuckle. The diminutive nickname rolled off the man's tongue. An Ran mouthed it in shock.

So *this* was the man who had changed Xiulan so, and the man who was Tigu's Master.

Xianghua could definitely see the resemblance between Tigu and Master Jin. The skin tone, a bit of the eye shape, and the bridge of her nose. Tucked in beside the powerful expert she looked more like a farmer's daughter.

"Did the city hold you up?" Yun Ren asked as he shoved food into his mouth.

"A bit of the city, and a bit of a miscalculation, we'll say. You know that crystal Bi De had?" Yun Ren nodded. "Well, we were doing stuff with it and the crystal Master said it would take three days, but it took longer. Wiped me the hell out. And there was some stuff inside it, apparently."

'*Yup!*' the rabbit chimed in. *'The cave went all wobbly, then I fought somebody but not really, and then there was a bunch of memory demon things, and I beat the shit out of them,'* the rabbit said, her voice refined like a court lady . . . save for her choice of words. The snake hissed *'Language'* at her scoldingly, but the rabbit forged on. *'Then Brother Bi De kicked a Temple Dog in the face. It was pretty great!'*

The table went quiet again.

"I'll explain it later," Master Jin said, shaking his head and turning to look at the nearly empty wok. "I was right, you guys were starving. The clay pot rice is almost done, I'll—"

"I'll get it," Tigu said, looking up at him. The man nodded and ruffled her hair. Tigu hopped to her feet and skipped out of the room, the rabbit following after her.

An Ran seemed to be ready to ask a question, but then there came a long groan from a bedroll tucked in the corner of the room. The occupant was awake.

"Aww fuck," a rough voice muttered.

"Rags!" Loud Boy shouted with glee, scrambling to his feet to check on the man.

Rags pushed himself up, squinting at the source of the noise before his own face lit up. "Loud Boy! You little bastard!"

They clasped arms and Rags grinned brightly. "You little shit, I *knew* you would survive!" he said gleefully. He pulled the smaller boy into his arms and thumped him on the back. After they parted, he looked down at his chest and peeled back his bandages. His grin got brighter at the scarring.

"Praise Ri Zu! Ah, I feel good as new! Even the Shrouded Mountain Sect couldn't keep the heavens-defying Rags down! *HAHAHA!*" he boomed with laughter, his hands on his hips. Yun Ren let out a cheerful whistle, and Gou Ren nodded at the man.

"Well, I'm glad you're feeling better," Master Jin said, smiling at Rags. The man jumped and squinted at Master Rou.

"Whoa, you're a *big* fucker, ain'tcha?" Rags said, looking Master Rou up and down.

An Ran choked on her drink; Huyi slipped off the arm he was leaning on, bashing his chin on the table; Xianghua made a sign of prayer. *Really, saying that to a man that powerful straight to his face—*

Master Rou laughed at Rags's words. "Yeah, I guess I am pretty tall, aren't I?"

"Yeah, you are. As big as this bastard." He gestured to Tie Delun, who groaned and also began stirring. Rags ruffled Loud Boy's hair and looked at the rest of them, still staring with shock. His body tensed. "We won, right?" he demanded. "Where's Tigu?"

"Out back, getting the rice," Master Rou said, smiling at the man's question.

Rags burst into more laughter and walked over to the table. Tie Delun sat up and ran his fingers through his hair.

"Ha, of course we won! And all thanks to the overwhelming tenacity of this 'Rags' Dong Chou! I got a good hit in on one of those Shrouded Mountain bastards. Pop! Right to the gut, he flinched, that's right, he did!" Rags slammed himself down and immediately helped himself to some of the food, stuffing some of the vegetables into his mouth, and hummed happily. "This is the good stuff! What about you, big guy? You manage to lay the hurt on those assholes? You look like you'd be pretty good in a scrap. Whaddaya say about joining my crew? You get to join forces with the man who defied the Shrouded Mountain Sect!"

Xianghua just stared in awe at the fool as he ran his mouth. Rags didn't see Loud Boy rapidly shaking his head, nor any of the Petals making "stop" motions. Tie Delun grunted, looking a bit confused by all the reactions.

Master Rou just looked incredibly amused.

"Sorry. Don't have time to join a gang. The missus would have my head," he said with a smile. "Thanks for the offer, though."

Rags sighed dramatically. "A shame, a shame. Ah, I guess it's fine. You're missin' out, but a man gotta provide, or he ain't no man, huh?"

Master Rou nodded sagely.

"So, what's your name, big guy?" Rags asked. Xianghua's face hit her palms. *He hadn't even asked the man his name before asking him to join his gang!*

Master Jin opened his mouth to speak but closed it when the door opened and Tigu came in carrying an enormous pot of rice.

"That's the last of it— Rags! Handsome Man!" she shouted. She slammed the rice bowl onto the table and launched herself over it, tackling Rags, who laughed and ruffled her hair. Her hands ghosted over his chest where the bandages were, but the man didn't wince. Satisfied, she switched targets, ramming into Tie Delun and holding him tight.

"'Handsome Man'?" Master Jin asked, raising an eyebrow.

Tigu turned from where she was rubbing her cheek against Tie Delun's.

"Yes, Master! Look, he is very pleasing!" she said, pulling up one of Delun's sleeves, exposing his muscles, then pointing to his face.

Rags choked on the food he had put in his mouth. Tie Delun's face, once happy, transitioned to pale, as he turned to look at Master Rou.

"M-Master?" Rags asked, sounding like he wanted to curl up in a corner and die.

"Yeah. Rou Jin. Nice to meet you, Rags . . . *Handsome Man*." A smile spread across his face.

Tie Delun suddenly looked as if he was about to head into battle unarmed and unarmoured.

Tigu rubbed her cheek against his again.

The Master just laughed and shook his head.

→

Eventually the food was finished. Rags was not struck down for his disrespect and went the longest without swearing Xianghua had ever heard him go.

The table was cleared away, and they all seated themselves before Master Rou. The scene should have been a comical one. Tigu was in his lap. Miantiao had curled around his arm. Yin the rabbit was down Tigu's shirt. And Huo Ten was sitting beside them, on his knees with his hands placed upon them, like a retainer.

Master Jin took a deep breath. He looked at them all. His face serious. The sunny demeanour gone.

"Please. Tell me what happened last night," he asked gently.

Loud Boy was first.

He spoke of their adventure to the hill Little Pimple. Of the men who'd tried to take Tigu, and of them tearing open Rags's chest. His eyes filled with tears at recounting the strike to his stomach that shattered his cultivation. The strike had shattered his foundation, the Shrouded Mountain Sect's superior cultivation transforming a negligent blow into one that broke him. Xianghua knew the scrolls said it was fixable . . . but it would be an arduous process.

To his credit, the churning, oppressive power that had shrouded Master Jin the previous night, like a mountain rising up and going to war, did not flare up again.

But it was still there, lurking beneath the surface; instead of glaring down at them, though, it felt . . . warm. Like lying on a grassy hill in the middle of the summer.

Xianghua was next. She told her story with a minimum of embellishment. There was no need to boast to a man who eclipsed her like an elephant eclipsed an ant. It was certainly an amusing and good thing to imagine—her father, staring up at a giant and weeping blood.

It was too bad he wasn't here so she could actually see the expression of despair on his face as he beheld Master Jin, lowering himself to make them a meal and attending to them. Offering his lessers face and clasping Loud Boy on his shoulder to comfort him, his eyes full of compassion.

Oh yes. She would like this man and her father to meet.

It was in the back of her mind as she recounted her tale. Luckily, her story was not as brutal as Loud Boy's had been.

Master Rou had even let out a huff of amusement.

"You threw your bedroll at him?" he asked, a little smile on his face. Rags and Loud Boy both barked out laughs. An Ran looked scandalized. Yun Ren pulled Gou to him and ruffled his hair.

"Indeed. The heavens will never forgive Zhou Yingwen for interrupting a maiden so rudely," she stated seriously.

"Absolutely unforgivable," Master Rou agreed, his smile wide. His eyes flicked to Gou Ren and he nodded.

"You approve?" she ventured.

"It's not my place to approve," the man said with a shrug. "But you fought for him, so that's enough for me."

He was a strange Master. But . . . well. Her recounting got a *bit* more boisterous after that. It cut some of the tension. She noticed little smiles appearing on people's faces.

Then it was Ri Zu's and Tigu's turn, and the mood blackened. Tigu rose from her place in his lap and took a seat in front of Master Jin to recount her part. Ri Zu interjected at times and told her tale as well, her voice strong and largely devoid of emotion. And then it was done.

Master Rou's eyes closed. He took a breath. When he opened his eyes, they had a hint of sadness in their depths. He rose from his seated position, onto his knees—

The powerful Master pressed his head to the floor, kowtowing before them all.

Xianghua took in a sharp breath. Loud Boy gaped.

"Thank you. Thank you all."

This kind of event only happened in stories. A powerful Master thanking those whom he was so above. In those tales, foolish heroes bested the odds and managed to win, simply because of their virtue.

He raised his head, conviction burning in his eyes.

"I swear, I'll do my best to make all this right," he declared. "I owe all of you a debt for this."

Xianghua couldn't find it in herself to doubt his words.

The man returned to his seat, allowing them a moment. None of them knew what to do. None of them knew what to say to such an oath.

And yet Master Jin continued on.

"Now . . . the Shrouded Mountain Sect . . . well. They have a lot to deal with right now. They shouldn't have any grounds for retaliation at the moment . . . but that's something your Elders also need a say in."

"Where are all the old bastards anyway?" Rags asked.

"The mountain is shut. I checked it last night, but the whole place was crawling with officials and the inner vaults are completely sealed," Master Rou stated. "Bi De is keeping an eye on things for me."

Xianghua nodded, then noticed a pensive expression on Tie Delun's face. Something truly must be urgent for the mountain to still be closed off, and it confirmed the rumours. Both would have to return to their Sects soon, as they were currently without orders.

"Um . . . Master Jin? What should we do?" An Ran asked.

Master Jin considered for a moment before he shrugged. "That's for you to decide. But while I'm waiting for your Elders, I have to go to the Azure Jade Trading Company."

"Are they holding some manner of treasure for you?" Loud Boy asked, looking interested.

"Nah . . . I need to buy some wood. I kinda . . . exploded a house on the way here. I need to fix that," he stated as if it were the most natural thing in the world.

Beside her, Gou tensed up.

"Uh . . . Jin? You wanna add some paving stones and stuff to that? I'll pay you back, but I kinda . . . smashed a couple walls and stuff . . ." He trailed off.

Master Jin nodded. "Yeah, let's go assess the damage and wait for the old men to come out from their secret vault."

CHAPTER 52

THE OLD MEN, LOST IN THE MOUNTAIN

The previous night . . .

Bao Wen sighed as he jabbed the maintenance rod at another crystal. The ancient stone rod, inlaid with crystal, pointed directly towards the black, lifeless gem, and once again it did nothing. It was part of his duties, his superiors said. It was an ancient and necessary tradition!

He was sure it was. The crystals sometimes flickered and hummed, but did the little dance they had to do have to look so silly? It was embarrassing.

Bao Wen grumbled, irritated.

He was new in this job, as one of the members of the Affairs for Spiritual Ascension. His father had pushed him into it. He had thought it would be an interesting, exciting job. Instead, he was just a manual worker. He had to do weird body movements and breathe correctly while jabbing the maintenance rod at things. Nobody even really knew how it worked, other than that it was essential to prevent the Dueling Peaks and Earthly Arena from degrading further.

The crystal he pointed at stayed dark. He sighed and took a breath, rubbing at his arms. It was kind of cold down here in the vaulted stone hallways, with no heating crystal system in place. And creepy.

But even this would have been tolerable . . . if he had been assigned any place useful.

Instead, he was in the "Dead Wing." Surrounding him were rooms and corridors that hadn't been used in centuries, everything within cold and lifeless. No crystals recorded. Nothing floated. Even the lights had died ages ago, necessitating a lantern.

At least the rod opened some of the doors. You pointed your rod at them, and they opened! The ones that still worked, anyway.

Still, six months of studying movements, only to go around performing maintenance on things that had broken millennia ago, which he couldn't fix. It was a complete waste of time.

He jabbed the maintenance rod at the dead crystal again.

He considered just . . . not doing it. It wasn't like anything in here worked anyway, and his Senior had gone to take a piss.

He could just say he had done the entire wall. Spare the asshole from smirking at him as he "supervised his Junior's work."

Bao Wen sighed again. His anger warmed him like a summer breeze. He looked up and glared at the ceiling, jabbing the maintenance rod at it in frustration.

The rod lit up, signaling a successful activation. Every light in the room turned on with a blaze of yellow. The crystals hummed and chimed as the entire mountain shuddered.

The area on the ceiling he was pointing at burned with gold light as weakened locks broke. The hidden compartment opened up, and a crystal gently floated down.

Bao Wen fell on his ass.

↔

The night had seen Cai Xi Kong experience a roiling storm of emotion. Joy and pride in his daughter's victory had been dampened by a most unwelcome visitor, plunging his mood into black fury and making the sting all the more bitter from how joyous he had been just a few hours prior.

The Shrouded Mountain bastard lusting over his daughter and throwing his weight around. It was a bitter pill that one so young held such power over Xi Kong and his Sect. At least the other Elders were in agreement. He had taken satisfaction in refusing the shit, and to his relief the little bastard had accepted the refusal. He could have pushed the issue, but Zang Li's own youth stymied some of his authority. If it had been an actual Elder asking for Xiulan, he and the other Elders would have had to swallow their objections, bow their heads, and thank them for giving his Xiulan the opportunity.

The thought stoked fresh rage in his heart.

Still, the man had left in the end, and the night had seemed to be looking better. Xi Kong had taken his leave of the Sect's manor to go attend to the last part of the ceremonies. In the depths of the Dueling Peaks, each Elder still present would kowtow to an ancient banner and swear that the event would continue as long as the peaks stood.

A final bit of tradition, continued unbroken as long for as they had records. A promise to continue to raise up the younger generation. His body felt warm, like he was standing in a summer breeze, and he let the last of the rage fade away.

Bai Huizong, of Spiritual Ascension Affairs, was present, making a record of their oath.

"That is all for this year, Honoured Elders. We thank you for your—"

The entire mountain shuddered.

"What in the blazes was that?" Bai Huizong demanded, sitting bolt upright in his seat. Several of his aides were looking around in shock, while the Elders snapped to attention, casting their senses out.

A woman's panicked scream echoed down the hallways.

Xi Kong was out of his chair and heading towards the disturbance, several of his fellows in his wake. They shot through the darkened corridors, moving at speed.

They did not have to travel far.

It was one of the recording crystal rooms. One of the dead ones . . . yet every light was on.

A rather terrified-looking young man had landed on his rear, his eyes wide as he stared at a floating crystal in the center of a room in shock. The maintenance rod he was holding had fallen to the wayside.

Xi Kong stared in wonder, seeing the same thing the boy was staring at.

The crystal floated serenely above them, like most recording crystals, but it was of a style Xi Kong had never before laid eyes upon. Its facets were reminiscent of what the Mengde Crystal Emporium used, but the cut was far, far more complex. The facets had facets within them, and they were glittering with characters, rather than the regular flat cuts of the Crystal Emporium.

Xi Kong glanced at Elder Daxian, who was staring at the room with a frown. This was one of the dead rooms. So why had it now awakened?

"Boy! What, by all that is good under these heavens, did you do?" Bai roared as he arrived behind them. The man was portly, but surprisingly fast for a mortal, and he skidded to a stop in front of the gaping young man, huffing and puffing.

"Lord Director! I was following the manual! It said to perform this rite here, and . . . and . . ." The boy pointed helplessly to the ceiling and the shining crystal that had descended from it.

Bai Huizong's face twisted, but he visibly calmed himself. "It happened after you used the maintenance rod?"

"Yes, Lord Director! I swear, Lord Director! How can a maintenance rod make the mountain tremble?"

Daxian picked up the rod. He glanced at it, then at the mortal boy.

"One way to see," he declared, holding the rod out for the young man to take. "Boy. Perform the rite again. Try to turn this crystal on."

The young man looked at the rod as if it was going to bite him but did as the Master of the Grand Ravine demanded. Taking the rod from Daxian's hand, he stood still, drawing a breath to center himself . . . He then went through a series of movements that looked like a basic martial kata. The movements were largely useless, Xi Kong had deduced long ago, but they did aid one's focus and breathing.

The rod pointed to the crystal and it flashed. The floating crystal flickered to life, then fuzzed and hissed before the image cleared up.

Xi Kong sucked in a breath, as did his fellows.

An image of a mountain split in two appeared in the air. A deep pit had been carved into the earth, and men were heaving huge blocks of stone around.

"By the heavens . . ." Xi Kong heard somebody muttering.

It was the Dueling Peaks. *The Dueling Peaks under construction.* They barely had records of that time, faded passages carved into stone, but *nothing* like this. This recording was thousands of years old—from the Age of Darkness, before they had any reliable records.

A piece of the past, locked in time and preserved forever.

The recording crystal moved. The image was silent, but the focal point floated through the arena. Workers turned and waved at the person recording or made silly faces. The crystal got closer to one of the workers. The man waved the crystal over and pointed to a carving. He looked back up to whoever had the crystal, nodded, and got out a large sheet of paper—a blueprint—then pointed to the symbol on a formation that travelled all across the arena.

"Get the others," somebody ordered as they all stood transfixed at the images. Bai Huizong collapsed into a nearby chair, while the mortal worker stood, shuffling around nervously.

The rest of the Elders filed in just as the recording suddenly stuttered. The image was now outside the Dueling Peaks, resting upon a giant tree. It was so large that ten men lying head to foot would barely be its diameter. Xi Kong recognised the wood of the massive tree; it was one of the strikers of the gong.

Another grainy blueprint was revealed to the crystal, as the man spoke to whoever was controlling it. Elder Shu of the Reed River Sect had brought out a brush and was frantically glancing back up at the scroll, copying down the formation blueprint.

The crystal started moving again. Guo Daxian the Elder took a sharp breath as it revealed a man with blue tattoos, dressed in the style of the ravine folk. He clasped his hands together in the gesture of respect to whoever had the crystal, before he caught a jug of wine thrown at him from behind their field of view.

He burst out into silent laughter. The recording continued on, heading back towards the arena, but suddenly the person walking stopped.

The crystal shook, like it was being poked.

The recording cut, then turned back on. The view was different now, the inside of a well-furnished room.

"—Wait, it's doing it properly now—or is it?" a voice without a face asked.

"It wasn't recording sound this *entire time*?" a female voice exclaimed, incredulous.

"I—uh, maybe?" the male voice stuttered.

"Ha! The great and powerful—" The recording stuttered again. "Doesn't know how to use a recording crystal properly!" the woman cackled.

"*Shut up*, Tianlan," the male voice demanded, sounding annoyed. The crystal rolled over. A woman was lying against a cushion, howling with laughter. She was dressed like a princess in a fine blue-and-green dress, her silky brown hair tied in an elaborate knot. The only blemish on her porcelain skin was the brace of freckles across her cheeks.

She grinned at whoever was not in view. "Recordings are forever," she sang.

The recording cut off abruptly; the crystal went dark. Xi Kong just stared in stunned silence, as did the rest of his fellows.

"Boy. What is your name?" Daxian asked, his eyes boring into the young man.

"B-B-Bao Wen, Master Cultivator," the young man stuttered.

"Bao Wen," Daxian's voice commanded, his eyes returning hungrily to the crystal after witnessing one of his ancestors within it. "Perform the rite again." The boy complied, yet the crystal remained dark.

Daxian grimaced. "This one, then," he said, pointing to another.

The crystal fuzzed to life, though this time showing an empty hallway. It was completely silent, until two men walked past, rolling a cart.

"That's Fang and Yu," Bai Huizong muttered. "They're on the other side of the mountain."

Wen performed the rite for a third time, this time on the largest crystal, the one that took up the entire wall.

It hummed and flickered to life. It immediately began playing the match between his daughter and Rou Tigu, the fight captured perfectly. Then the crystal beside it lit up. Xi Kong's eyes widened. It took him a moment to place it, but the person in the recording was himself, when he was young. He was doing battle against a member of the Azure Horizon Sect. Another crystal lit. Another member of the Verdant Blade Sect, showing who Xi Kong guessed was his father.

One by one the crystals lit up, spreading out and across from each other. Each one showed a member of the Verdant Blade Sect, until finally the ancient, floating crystal also awoke for the second time. This time it showed the image of a woman. She was dressed in a flowing dress with long sleeves. Fans floated behind her as she danced with elegance and grace. There were gasps as the Elders were struck dumb by her beauty. She could have been the sister of his own daughter—

Then suddenly, golden cracks appeared across the image. They took over the crystal and it went dark. The cracks spread like vines over every crystal in the room, moving in a wave from the crystal in the center, and with them each recording cut out.

The mountain shuddered again. Something in the walls began to whir.

"The *hells* is going on?" Daxian demanded.

The heavens seemed to give him an answer. A section of the wall hummed and lit up. It had the same symbol upon it as the maintenance rod.

The Elders turned to Bao Wen expectantly. The boy swallowed. His maintenance rod moved.

With a *hiss*, the previously completely nondescript section of the wall pulled inward and slid to the side. It was a thick, solid piece of stone, and yet it moved like it had no weight at all.

It revealed a flight of stairs.

"There aren't any records of a false wall here," Bai Huizong muttered.

The Elders glanced at each other before coming to the same conclusion: a previously unexplored section of the Dueling Peaks. Ancient treasures could lie within, or relics of their ancestors.

"We shall be going. Director," Guo Daxian said. "It may be dangerous, so why don't you remain behind?"

"Ah . . . uh . . . Wonderful idea!" the chubby man said. "I also have a meeting with the Azure Jade Trading Company I must attend to . . ."

He trailed off when he realised nobody was listening to him—they were all looking at the new doorway. The man sighed and turned to leave.

They descended the stairs. Guo Daxian seized the lead, to grumbling from the others, his body tense and ready for anything. Xi Kong was next, his blades floating down the stairs, taking the position by dint of his Sect's rise. The rest squabbled for a moment, but no fights broke out. The stairway was wide and well lit. They kept Wen in the middle of them, ready to protect this boy who had the luck of the heavens on his side. Best to keep that luck with them.

They plunged into the bowels of the earth. The walls were sanded smooth and rounded, grey stone, but completely undecorated. They advanced slowly. After a few minutes the flight of stairs ended, transitioning to a curving hallway with branches leading off to the side. Most of the branches were caved in. Occasionally, an Elder would break off down one of the side passages to search for anything of note. Most returned empty-handed. But one came back with an entire box of maintenance rods.

They only had one path forwards.

"It seems to curve underneath most of the mountain," Elder Shen mused as they advanced.

"East for five hundred twenty-three paces, with the curve. We're under the seating section, beneath the arena," Elder Chen said. Xi Kong did the math in his head and found no fault with the man's conclusion.

They were on guard for anything. The traps of the ancients would surely be deadly . . . yet there did not seem to be any.

They came to a locked door, which had the rite of maintenance symbol upon it. The Elder with the box of rods, Elder Hai, drew one and performed the same movements, attempting to open it.

The door didn't budge. No flash happened.

Daxian the Elder chuckled. "Bao Wen, we request you give this old man some pointers," he jabbed. Elder Hai flushed red with anger, glaring at Daxian, before he huffed, stepping aside for the mortal boy.

He moved to do the rite, and the door opened.

"What manner of training did you undergo, mortal?" one of the Elders asked.

"Uh . . . a month of technique and breathing training after signing the contract?" the boy answered nervously.

"An attunement, then," Elder Hai muttered. "It just needs some time."

They entered the vaulted room. It was dark at first, the crystals within flickering fitfully, but the light grew in strength each moment, revealing a squat, hulking thing in the side of the room.

It was an arcane thing. All pipes and pieces of crystal that were embedded in the walls, and this ancient piece had not emerged unscathed either. Several of its pipes were broken by fallen rocks or had been torn loose from the walls. In a better time, the room would have been dominated by the creation of the ancients. Now it was a husk.

Obviously, none present knew what it was. They stared at the silent machine even as a soft golden glow began to rise off its vents, strengthening within the crystals.

Pulsing like the beat of a heart.

One of the Elders licked his lips, then forged ahead towards it. His body was tightly wound, ready to spring away at a moment's notice. He wove around the larger rocks to the machine's bulbous core. There were cracked formations and levers upon it.

He studied it tensely, examining the side of the machine for a maker's mark or some description as to its use. "Most of it is gone, but this is the character for 'cycle.'"

The machine vibrated. Everyone in the room tensed, and the Elder hurled himself away as fast as he could. The machine coughed and spluttered as the golden glow grew stronger.

It was activating on its own.

"Bao Wen, see if you can shut it down," Daxian began. A sound plan. They did not know exactly what it did.

The boy swallowed. "I—I don't really know what I'm doing, Master Cultivator—" the boy said with complete honesty, his eyes fearful as something within the construct engaged. The whirring sound intensified, something within the mechanism began to grind.

"Attempt it," Daxian commanded. "I shall be with you." The Elder placed his hand on the boy's shoulder, a rope-blade uncoiling from his arm.

The boy swallowed thickly and raised the maintenance rod, beginning to walk forwards. Elder Daxian was at his back, clearly ready to whisk him to safety should the machine explode.

Yet before he could do anything, the construct of the ancestors heaved and shuddered. Qi within it pulsed. The earth rumbled again.

The machine screamed, the gold turning to red.

There was another *click* and then a grinding sound.

The doors slammed closed and the room pulsed with Qi, barriers springing up around both the crystal and the walls.

Wen paled, turning to the Elders with panic in his eyes.

Daxian stared at him, then at the walls. The machine continued to wail.

"Unexpected," Daxian declared.

□

Bai Huizong, Director of Spiritual Ascension Affairs, sat in the crystal room, staring at the secret passage. The Elders had left to explore its inner reaches not long ago, delving into ancient depths in search of secrets.

Of course, Bai Huizong wouldn't be caught dead going down some strange, unknown tunnel in the Dueling Peaks, no matter how many Elders went along with him. He had too much common sense. Better to profit off whatever they dragged up later, rather than risk his neck.

He did feel a bit bad for the lad, though. Having the direct attention of so many cultivators wasn't really worth the trouble most of the time. Oh, it was fine when you were the funny little mortal who organised things for them and announced their fights, but anything else? No, you wanted to avoid being interesting.

There was a knock on the door and one of his aides entered and approached him, then knelt down to whisper in his ear.

"Sir, your meeting with the Azure Jade Trading Company."

Huizong jumped. "Ah, right, I've got that tonight, don't I?"

Quite frankly, he didn't even know why the Masters of the Azure Jade Trading Company had requested a meeting to "discuss the sale of Rou Tigu dolls." It had never happened before. They had always been good customers, and he even preferred shipping with them!

The letter requesting the meeting had been worded politely. And politely usually meant problems.

The meeting room was a lovely little villa sticking out of the side of the mountain. It was well furnished and with a commanding view of the entire south side of the town out into the hills.

When Bai Huizong entered the room, he was met with two faces with whom he was intimately familiar. The first was Guan Ping, Master of the Azure Jade Trading Company, who had a calm, grandfatherly smile on his visage. Huizong's elder by several years, he was always slow and deliberate in his dealings.

Lady Daiyu, on the other hand, was still an absolutely stunning woman. She seemed untouched by time, aging as fine wine did. She had a few wrinkles, but her scarlet hair was brilliant, and she was still a peerless beauty.

She smiled at him, showing her perfect white teeth, and Huizong wished he could appreciate her smile . . . but he knew better. Behind the beautiful mask was a tiger, a woman as ruthless as any cultivator.

They exchanged pleasantries as he took his seat across from the pair. Lady Daiyu accepted a fan from her servant, ostensibly so she could smile at Huizong from behind it. The fan had a painting of a dragon surrounded by billowing clouds. *So, she's a bit upset, but not truly angry. Good news.*

"So . . . to what do I owe the pleasure, Lady Daiyu?" Huizong asked leadingly. He knew whom to address here. "Your letter was . . . vague."

"Our apologies," the woman said, snapping her fan closed, its message having been delivered. "There are just some concerns about the Rou Tigu doll. You see, we have . . . suspicions that Rou Tigu is related to an extremely valuable customer. We would wish to ask him about it before you went ahead in distributing his symbol, no?"

Huizong raised an eyebrow. "That's never been a problem before . . ." he ventured. The Sects . . . well, the Sects didn't care really as long as the use was respectful enough. He knew the cultivators had seen the dolls he made. It wasn't not like they were a secret. But a mortal's toy and a simple likeness? They allowed it. It was best to be seen as a hero by the mortals and have their children recognise your symbol by heart.

"It . . . has the possibility to become one. If Rou Tigu is unrelated, then you may continue. If she is related . . . well. We wished to speak with you about it in advance. We would see our honoured customer's daughter get her fair share if you are using her, no?" she asked, her cold eyes never once leaving his face.

Huizong grimaced. The Azure Jade Trading Company was going all in for this customer. But it wasn't like he could refuse.

"May I know why this customer is so important?"

"Eighty thousand silver coins in a single transaction. With two hundred thousand more in the future."

Bai Huizong stared blankly at them. *Two hundred thousand—*

"And we will of course keep the Honoured Lord Director in our thoughts," Lady Daiyu finished. "It does no good to alienate a powerful man such as yourself."

This . . . this was big. If the Azure Jade Trading Company was talking those numbers, then it was massive. And from one man?

The Azure Jade Trading Company would occasionally crack the heads of men who reneged on deals. This? These were the numbers that got the Azure Jade Trading Company to start hiring cultivators. *From outside the province.*

"Of course, I'll inform all of my business associates that there may be a delay while we sort this out," Huizong said.

And then there came a loud explosion. It echoed out over the hills and all talking ceased.

Huizong sighed. *Things had been going so well this year too.*

"If that's everything—" he started, but then there was a pounding alarm gong and a rapid-fire roll of thunder. It sounded quite a bit louder and harsher than he was used to hearing.

Lady Daiyu frowned heavily. "Lord Director, do you mind?" the woman asked, pulling out a minor transmission stone.

"Ah, no, please, Lady Daiyu."

She turned to take the transmission. Bai Huizong stared enviously at the little stone. Well, after this year he might be able to get a few more for himself. The damn things cost an arm and a leg.

The woman walked to the window, so Huizong could only make out parts of what she said.

"Thank you. Guan Shi. Yes, Nephew. Yes, you have permission. Pack up and get to the safe house."

There were more crashes and shouts.

"Yes, I've got a feeling about this one. Fast as you can, my dear. Ah, Shiling and Liuhua are staying? Good. Remember their hazard pay, please."

The woman handed the transmission stone back to her servant.

"Will we be safe here, Director?" Master Guan asked lightly.

"Of course we will. It's likely just a little scrap—" Huizong started to respond.

Another explosion tore through the night, lighting the town up with a false dawn. Huizong nearly fell out of his chair.

"On second thought, let's retreat a bit farther into the mountain," he corrected. They swiftly stood and exited the meeting room, his aides rapidly coming towards him from where they had been stationed in the hall.

"See if you can get the Elders; their children have gotten *far* too rowdy," he commanded, and the men nodded before rushing off. Huizong was in his element now, striding forwards and in command. They managed to make it to his main office in record time. Lady Daiyu could move surprisingly quickly for a woman her age.

"Do not fear. Everything is absolutely under—" The crystal lights turned red and everything started to wail.

"—under con—"

The doors slammed shut behind them.

"—trol."

There was an ominous *click* as the doors locked.

Lady Daiyu turned to Huizong and raised a single eyebrow in response.

□

Fists slammed into the door. The Earth Wrecker Stance, wielded by an Elder, could shatter stone as easily as a hammer could shatter glass.

The Elder bounced off the barrier, the thing shimmering for a moment and the entire room shuddering.

Several of their number glanced at the ceiling as dust collected on the blue shield above their heads.

The strike failed, just as the maintenance rod had. They were, for the moment, trapped down here. The best the Azure Hills had to offer. Nearly every Elder. Trapped by curiosity.

"We might be able to break it down . . . but it might also bring down the ceiling. Digging our way out would be . . . annoying," Daxian concluded, raising his voice slightly over the wail the machine was still emitting. Xi Kong agreed. They would likely survive such an event—though it was not guaranteed with this much stone, especially if they got trapped and couldn't move.

Elder Chen of the Framed Sun Sect returned to the group, having gone to examine the perimeter of the vault. "One of the barriers to the east is damaged. All along the wall it flickers for two seconds, before restarting. It leads to another tunnel. Let us see if it yields answers before resorting to force."

The Elder of the Rumbling Earth Sect glared at the doorway before nodding.

Xi Kong glanced at the mortal Wen, who still looked like he was about to be ill.

"It's hardly your fault, lad. If we didn't know what would happen, you cannot be blamed for it."

Some, of course, would blame the mortal boy anyway.

"Now, can you walk?" he asked the boy. "We'll have to go a bit longer."

The maintenance worker swallowed thickly. True to Chen's words, the barrier would drop, the blue colour cutting out, before it would restart with a hiss at a regular interval.

It was a simple matter to pass through it and continue on to the hallway beyond.

They all set off to the east. The tunnel they were travelling down was surprisingly well lit, with glowing crystals running along it at roughly head height. They were wary of traps, but privately, Xi Kong did not think they would encounter any. If his hunch was right, this was just a maintenance tunnel.

His fellows seemed to think the same, as their stances became less guarded.

Still, the mortal was flagging, his steps starting to stumble. It certainly was a great distance to walk for a mortal, and they had increased their pace.

The boy looked nervous, twitchy, and close to breaking, surrounded as he was by Elders.

"Tell me, Bao Wen. How did you become a maintenance worker?" Xi Kong asked.

The boy jumped at the question. His eyes locked onto Xi Kong, who kept his expression warm. Sweat poured down the mortal boy's face.

"Uh . . . well, my father talked to Lord Bai . . ."

Then the dam broke. The boy just started talking. His tale went quickly from how his father was friends with Bai Huizong, to his childhood in Grass Sea City, to his worries about attending the first of his matchmaking meetings.

"And I have *no idea* what to do. She's beautiful and elegant, but how do I . . . How do I even . . . *Girls*, you know?"

Xi Kong and several other Elders nodded sagely.

"Remember to order a small selection of the pastries and take note of which ones she eats. If there is a second meeting, then bring more of the ones she likes, yes?"

"Ah . . . yes, Master Cai," Wen said with a nod, taking his advice with a bewildered expression. The mortal was flagging from the walk but trudged along admirably. "This Bao Wen thanks you humbly for your wisdom, Master Cai."

"Indeed. Cai speaks true. Brush up upon your poetry or your ability to play an instrument. A man must have a broad selection of skills to attract a wife," Chen said.

"This Bao Wen humbly thanks you for your wisdom, Master Chen," the boy repeated.

Several others chimed in.

"You may not be able to take down a Spirit Beast, boy, but a woman needs to know her man can protect her. Get a spear and take out a boar! Women love that—or hunt her a rack of horns from a big buck," Elder Gang of the Bonepile demanded.

"Your father is friends with Bai Huizong? You have connections, boy. Use them. Show your wealth and power. Perhaps even I might pitch something in. You have aided us this night and we should be generous, no?" Elder Xinling of the White Water Sect added, the woman looking at the boy with amusement.

The maintenance worker blushed at her words . . . but their conversation had succeeded in distracting the boy for the better part of an hour.

"Another door ahead. Bao Wen," Daxian stated bluntly.

The boy swallowed and dashed head, scrambling over debris from the partial cave-in before the door.

The door chimed when he pointed the rod at it, then opened, much to the boy's obvious relief.

Another vault. But instead of housing a crystal, this one contained tables and shelves.

Row upon row upon row of neatly organised shelves. There were also bright chandeliers from which light crystals would hang. Chairs and lecterns were arranged at regular intervals.

A massive library or archive, filled to the brim with scrolls. Twice the size of Xi Kong's own Sect's archive.

However, the wonder had obviously seen better days. While the room was largely intact, it was still dusty and dirty, shattered crystals lay in pieces on the floor, and several of the light fixtures were broken.

They approached a table, the one closest to them. It was covered in dust, but they could still see the outline of three scrolls upon it, knowledge undisturbed for thousands of years.

Guo Daxian approached, reverently lifting a scroll. He brushed some of the dust off and read the title aloud.

"*Functions and Maintenance of the Arena Stage Shifting Mechanism, Scroll 22 . . .*"

He hummed, interested, and opened it.

It was an instruction manual. It showed platforms of floating stone, another with lakes and waterfalls, and a third with buildings covering the floor of the Earthly Arena.

No one alive had seen the arena with anything but a bare stone floor.

"I have seen some of these symbols. But how could such a thing . . . No, this part has been broken for thousands of years," Daxian muttered.

"It would *generate* it? How would it generate the earth and the water?" Elder Gang grunted.

"To think the Earthly Arena is capable of this . . ." Elder Xinling breathed.

The other scrolls were Scroll 21 and 23, each with their own revelation.

"Truly, the wisdom of the ancestors is unsurpassed," Guo Daxian declared.

None cared to disagree.

"Perhaps we may find a way to turn off the barriers within the scrolls?" Xi Kong suggested.

"Good idea, Elder Cai," Daxian said. "We should attempt to find the mechanism. To have to free ourselves by breaking this place would be a sin and would dishonour our ancestors. No harm shall come to these works."

There was a chorus of agreement.

Several Elders split off to explore to the sides, but Xi Kong simply kept walking, heading straight for the back. The place was neatly organised. The lanes between shelves had arrows, upon which side a person should walk when they were going in a certain direction. There were a few broken carts clearly meant to hold scrolls.

Yet there were no bodies. It seemed to Cai Xi Kong that every person within had just . . . *disappeared*. He took a moment to pull another scroll off the shelf. A maintenance log on one of the floating mechanisms, along with what they had done to fix it. They would have to remove this entire archive and set it somewhere else. Or keep it secret.

He set the scroll back in its place and looked at the room. A treasure trove of lost knowledge. Each scroll he pulled off revealed more manuals on mechanisms, or more maintenance logs. There was even a pay stub for one of the workers, but Xi Kong didn't understand the currency that was being used.

The vault . . . contained the complete knowledge on how to build and maintain the Earthly Arena. Written by the ancestors themselves, whole and undamaged, instead of pieced together from carvings in the walls or oral histories.

But all this was useless if they didn't find a way out.

Xi Kong made a circuit of the vault.

The rest of the entrances were blocked with rubble. They would have to either find the answers in here . . . or dig their way out. And digging their way out risked damaging this archive.

Xi Kong took in a breath and started looking for a scroll with the word *cycle* upon it.

→

It was several hours later when one of them found what they'd been looking for.

"It's one of the regulators for the floating mechanisms. It says here if it detects damage . . . it also acts as one of the security mechanisms. With so much of it destroyed, it thought it was under attack, and so it activated every defensive measure it could," the Elder of the Azure Horizon Sect stated.

"Thus locking the doors and activating the barriers. Is there any way to remove this?" Daxian asked.

"Yes. But we'll need the mortal's assistance, and to dig out some of the components. Or simply wait until it runs out of energy again," the Azure Horizon Elder replied.

Several started arguing the merits between attempting a repair and simply waiting it out, for it likely didn't have much energy left—it was a derelict wreck at the moment.

Somebody started brewing tea. Bao Wen had taken off his outer layers and bunched them up like a pillow, now attempting to get some sleep.

Smart lad. We could be here for a while, Xi Kong thought. He chuckled as the arguments started between the Elders. At least the priceless scrolls surrounding everyone prevented them from exchanging blows.

Xi Kong sighed. All he could feel was the humming of the Qi from the machine and the resonating barriers.

It had been rather a long time since he had gone on an adventure.

CHAPTER 53

IF IT'S BROKEN . . .

I checked in on Xiulan while everybody else was getting ready to head out. She was lying in a bed, looking for all the world like she was just sleeping in for a bit.

She didn't move a muscle when I entered, save for the steady rise and fall of her breath.

A memory of an off-white room came to me. Of another lying unmoving, back in the Before. But here, unlike Before, there was the smell of Meimei's herbs instead of a harsh, antiseptic tang like if she were in a hospital. Xiulan's cheeks were still full instead of gaunt and pallid. At least there weren't any tubes sticking out of her.

Xiulan will be fine, I told myself. *Cultivators are tougher than normal people. She'll get through this.*

I knelt beside her bed, hesitated, then took her hand. Her grip reflexively tightened on mine for a moment. It was still strong.

I hadn't even known her for a full year, yet she had thrown herself at the Shrouded Mountain Sect without hesitation in order to save Tigu. She'd mourned for those that could be considered her lessers. She constantly looked forwards and did what she thought was right without hesitation.

I was glad I had met her.

I sighed and put my forehead against the back of her hand.

The argument could be made that if it weren't for her, I'd be back at home without any cultivator problems at all . . . Nobody would have come to the tournament. Nobody would have been kidnapped.

But it had happened.

As I had learned with Lu Ri, I couldn't hide forever.

Now all I could do was my best.

I had responsibilities. Right now there were things to do, no matter how much I didn't want to do them.

I gently placed her hand back on the bed and patted it twice.

I rose from my position and straightened out some of the covers.

"Wake up soon, okay?" I whispered.

And . . . I don't care if it's improper, I'm hugging the hell out of you after I get done with this world's "proper" actions.

Speaking of hugs, while Tigu was accounted for, Gou Ren and Yun Ren hadn't received their allotment yet. It would of course be manly, with lots of back thumping, but they were totally getting it later.

I opened the door and heard a squeak. I looked down and smiled at Ri Zu, her bag on her back and ready to knock on the door. She bowed in thanks, then immediately set about her business, scampering up to Xiulan and taking her pulse.

I left the door open a bit as I exited, so she could get out later.

Everybody else was ready and waiting for me when I came downstairs, lined up by the doors. The members of Xiulan's Sect, my friends and disciples, Rags and Loud Boy, Xianghua, and Handsome Man. He was grinning at Tigu . . . and then he noticed me and flinched, shuffling a bit so he wasn't as close to her. Well, I didn't know how exactly to deal with that, but I wasn't the kind of guy to go around giving people the shovel talk.

We'd probably have a sit down to chat later if things like that kept up, but for now it wasn't anything to worry about.

Obviously he hadn't tried anything, because Tigu definitely would have told me already if he had . . .

Everyone waited for me to make the first move.

I guess I walk in front, huh?

I pushed open the doors and exited the Sect compound into the streets, the heavy doors moving without a sound.

There were two people waiting outside for us. They froze upon seeing me. Their eyes flicked from me to the escort behind me. I paused, then nodded in greeting to them.

They needed nothing else.

"Young Master!"

"Sister!"

Two voices shouted out. There was a beaten-up, lanky guy wearing armour, and a kid who hobbled towards us with a limp.

Xianghua's eyes lit up as the kid tackle-hugged her, while the young man skidded to a stop to bow respectfully in front of Handsome Man.

The boy started prodding and looking over his sister, his face flushed with worry.

"Haha! As if they could lay a hand on this Young Mistress! I slapped them across their faces until they begged me for mercy!" Xianghua let out a laugh as she posed with her hands on her hips.

She began immediately boasting about how she was "the perfect, untouchable Young Mistress." Her language fit her stereotype perfectly. She spouted off how "they met with the wrath of the heavens," with a completely straight face, while continuing to raise her nose higher and higher until she was looking directly up at the sky.

The woman was nuttier than a box of acorns.

She had a little smirk as her brother started laughing and Gou Ren was shaking his head with amusement. She caught me watching and froze, but I just smiled and nodded at her.

But hell, she was good people.

I smiled at them as they had their reunion and the kid scrambled onto Gou Ren's back.

Already at that stage, huh? I thought with a smirk . . . though I couldn't exactly talk. I was the guy who'd asked a girl to marry me after only a couple of months of knowing her.

I led the way through the streets towards the local branch of the Azure Jade Trading Company . . . and the amused atmosphere started to fade.

When we got into the town proper and not the Sect mansions, the damage started to show.

The streets had rubble strewn about them. Walls had been caved in. Fragments of stone had shattered roof tiles and broken windows.

Gou Ren slowed when he saw the full extent of it. His eyes were wide as he stared around. The buildings destroyed was one thing.

But the other thing was the *people*.

The noncultivators were huddled together. They were hesitant and scared even as they started the arduous process of cleaning up. Their movements were slow from lack of sleep, and a lot of them were just standing around looking miserable. A little boy was sobbing over a destroyed street stand. His father stood away from it, despondent. A woman chucked splinters of wood out of the hole in her wall.

It was like all those newscasts back in the Before. Like the history textbooks, showing the Battle of Britain. Shelled-out houses. Destroyed livelihoods.

They were walking through a war zone.

"Gou, could you guys go and assess the damage while I pick all of the materials up?" I asked. "We'll meet back up in the square in a bit."

There were several nods from the cultivators behind me as they dispersed. I continued on my way until I got to the local Azure Jade Trading Company. There was a bit of superficial damage to the building, but when I knocked on the door it was promptly opened.

However . . .

There was only one guy. And he seemed a bit shocked to see me, after I pulled out the Azure Jade Trading Company token.

"Forgive us, Master Jin, but the esteemed Master of our company evacuated the majority of our staff to the mountain when the fighting broke out. We only have myself and one other. We volunteered to stay," the frazzled man said. Which was honestly smart. I don't know why I'd assumed this place would still be open. "I'm afraid all of our treasures are gone, so all that's left is the mortal goods. And with the mountain closed . . ."

I frowned. *Will I have to pull open a door or something? If the lockdown lasts any longer I might have to.*

"That's perfectly fine. It's actually what I wanted anyway. I need tools. Tools, wood, and some paving stones."

The man seemed bewildered but complied with my order.

Soon enough, I had my building materials and emerged into the streets, heading towards the square.

A square now full of cultivators who were sitting around or milling about uncertainly.

The guy with blue tattoos from yesterday was there, idly flipping his rope-knife around and sitting on the edge of a mostly demolished fountain.

There was nobody cleaning up here.

He stood, and the rest of the square went silent.

"Guo Daxian pays his respects to Master Rou," the tattoo guy said.

The rest of the assembled cultivators did the same, all bowing.

"Master Rou. Forgive this Daxian's impertinence . . . but with our Elders still lost to us, trapped in the mountain, I would humbly beg your advice and wisdom."

I glanced at the assembled, uncertain cultivators, then looked around at the street. The destruction and the people who weren't helping. The cultivators who were just wandering around like headless chickens without their Elders, unsure of what to do and looking to me for advice.

I picked up one of the hammers I had and tossed it to Guo Daxian.

He caught it and stared at it.

"If you break something, *fix it*," I stated simply.

□

Xianghua rose up from putting a rock in the wheelbarrow and stared at the path leading away from the pond and clearing. Three walls had been entirely destroyed. They would have to rebuild them completely.

They had with them Rags's mortal friends, Tigu, Yun Ren, and Loud Boy. The rabbit Yin was with them as well. Tie Delun had gone off to hew the raw stone into something that could actually be used, and Xiulan's Petals were the next street over.

It was an odd thing, to be rebuilding mortal houses and fixing walls. But Gou Ren, at first in a foul mood as he stared at the destruction, seemed to be getting better as he worked. He was even explaining things, his voice full of enthusiasm as he talked about the design of the walls. She committed every word to memory, naturally, just as she did when her brother spoke about the steam furnaces.

It was just as odd to see the cultivators of the Azure Hills labouring like mortals, tools in hand. None had disregarded Master Jin's calm statement. The powerful expert commanded the town to be healed, and so it would be.

The mortals seemed bewildered and flabbergasted as cultivators took to the streets, helping with the repairs. They worked, the sun hot as they toiled.

"Hey, Tigu. You said you escaped . . . But *how* did you escape, exactly?" Loud Boy asked, as he tried to lift a large rock . . . only to have it not budge. He jerked backwards with the motion of attempting to lift it and turned to stare incredulously at the stone—he was obviously used to being able to lift heavier things than he could now.

Tigu glanced at him. She grimaced, her face twisted.

"I transformed," she said, picking up another bit of broken masonry.

"Transformed?" Rags asked, jerking his head at one of his mortal friends, who nodded. She looked at the stone the former cultivator was struggling to lift, then walked over a larger stone.

"Hey, Loud Boy, can you help me with this?" the woman asked. Loud Boy startled again, but nodded, determined. He marched over and together they heaved the piece up.

"Transformed," Tigu stated again.

"Is it some kind of technique that turns you into a powerful monster?" Loud Boy asked as he puffed.

The young woman sighed. She looked around the street, flinched, and screwed up her face.

With a *pop* of displacing air, there was a cat sitting where Tigu had once stood.

Or rather . . . a small tiger.

Everybody paused to look at her.

"Hey, you finally managed that!" Gou Ren said, sounding impressed.

There was another *pop* and Tigu reappeared, looking dizzy.

"Don't like that," she muttered, shaking her head.

"Oh, the Path of the Tiger? A legendary cultivation technique that lets you draw on the power of the Tiger of the West?" Loud Boy enthused.

Tigu shrugged, amused at Loud Boy's enthusiasm, but Rags seemed more contemplative.

Xianghua glanced at the Spirit Beasts with them.

She made eye contact with Rags. The man's face was pensive . . . but eventually he shrugged.

Well, she supposed it was Tigu's secret to tell. If she even originally was a cat. The distaste for the form of the tiger, how quickly she turned back, and her resemblance to Master Jin meant it *could* just be a transformation technique.

"So . . . how many Spirit Beasts does Master Jin have, anyway?" Rags asked instead, looking on as Yin shoved another piece of rubble to the side.

"Hmmm, there's my Junior Sister Yin, Miantiao, Ri Zu, that blue monkey, and Bi De here in the Dueling Peaks," Tigu counted off. "Then back home there's two pigs, Chun Ke and Pi Pa, an ox, Bei Be, and a . . ." Tigu's nose wrinkled in distaste. "A dragon, Wa Shi."

"A dragon?! Master Jin tamed a *dragon*?" Loud Boy asked incredulously. Xianghua too had paused at the mention of the powerful creature. "What does he do? Guard your master's treasure? Command the heavens for him?"

Tigu looked at him, confused.

"He washes the dishes."

Loud Boy's face fell. "What?"

"He washes the dishes, and sometimes waters the crops."

"Come off it, Tigu, you're having us on—" Rags started.

There was a crystal chime as Yun Ren held up his recording crystal. An image formed. A flood dragon appeared, holding a wok and a washcloth while grinning at a massive boar who had a stack of bowls balanced on his nose.

Rags gave up, raising his arms into the air in confusion.

Xianghua chuckled.

"Indeed. Brother Wa Shi is a valued pupil of the Great Master. Though he may be gluttonous, his role is unique and appreciated," a deep, booming voice echoed out. The power of a Profound-level cultivator, more powerful than Xiulan, more powerful than Xianghua's father, filled the alleyway.

She turned, ready to pay her respects, and froze. A proud, resplendent cock was perched above them on a nearby wall.

"Fa Bi De, First Disciple of Fa Ram, greets you all, and thanks you for taking care of his Juniors," the Spirit Beast declared, smiling warmly at them.

The rabbit she could take. The dragon she could take.

A *chicken*, more powerful than the Sect Elders of the Azure Hills?

Xianghua raised both hands in the air in a gesture of defeated confusion as the rooster hopped down off the wall to stride regally towards Yun Ren.

Gou Ren looked at her and patted her on the back consolingly.

"You get used to it," he said.

CHAPTER 54

FIX IT

Tigu shifted her hips and twisted, sending the piece of rubble into the wheelbarrow. It landed with a *thunk*. Absently, her eyes travelled back to where Loud Boy and Rags were working with the rest of her friends. Bi De was helping as well. Master had relieved him from his watch over the mountain, so he was spending his time talking to Xianghua, Loud Boy, and Rags. She could hear him asking them about where they had come from.

Loud Boy, after his initial shock, seemed to be the most animated while speaking to the rooster. He was smiling again, at least.

They all seemed to have it well in hand, so Tigu turned and looked back down the street at the shattered walls and broken homes.

When she was smashing people into buildings and tearing off roof tiles to throw at people last night, she hadn't exactly been considering just how much damage she had been causing—though somehow Gou Ren had managed to eclipse her. The streets had been outright destroyed by his strikes, shattered like he had taken a massive hammer to them. Her fellow disciple was enthusiastic at repairing things, but she caught him wincing every so often when he looked at just how much damage he had done.

The battle had lasted but a couple of hours, and yet this was the result. Destruction, in addition to the harm visited on her friends. She looked up and around the street. There was a lot of it. Too much.

Another act by the Shrouded Mountain Sect. All the damage they had done. Loud Boy, Rags, Xiulan, the town . . . It made her furious.

And what was going to happen to those bastards, even more so. She had asked her Master about it, and his answer had made her angrier still.

"The ringleader is dead. There will be reparations, but other than that . . . I do not know. We'll take care of our own and pay back everyone who helped us," her Master had murmured into her hair as he'd stirred the eggs in the wok that morning.

He had said that . . . and yet he had spoken nothing of vengeance.

Why would her Master be so lenient on them? They had hurt her. Hurt Xiulan. Nearly killed Rags and Loud Boy. Caused so much destruction—

She snarled and her shovel came down, smashing a rock.

Why would they still live? Surely her Master was strong enough to destroy them, wasn't he? Why were they not being punished to the harshest extent?

The questions ate at her.

Tigu sighed and leaned on her shovel, dark thoughts churning in her mind.

↔

Chaoxiang felt ill. His daughter's sobs echoed through the streets. Ning clutched the broken sign to her chest, her stuffed doll fallen to the side.

All he could do was stare at his destroyed shop.

The thunder last night had been terrifying. His family had all hid under their table in their house on the outskirts of town and waited desperately for the sounds of fighting to stop.

The first thing in the morning he had gone out to survey what had been done to his shop. At first, he had been optimistic that the damage would be minor. It wasn't even that bad on this street. A few errant stones out of place, but every other building in the row was fine.

Every other building but his.

His shop was a pile of rubble. Like something massive had just decided to squash it. He was glad he didn't live in his shop, like so many others.

Chaoxiang forlornly pulled at a piece of wood. It didn't budge.

His neighbors shared commiserating looks with him, and a couple had approached him to help out . . . but . . . well. It was pretty much a wash. The roof had been half torn off, and the other half had caved in. Most of his stock of iron was buried beneath it all, and it would take weeks to dig it all out and do inventory.

Well, that was the price of doing business with cultivators.

Chaoxiang sighed again. It was such a monumental task that he felt his motivation shrivel up and die. He even considered just leaving and coming back tomorrow.

"Huh? Why are they all here?" somebody muttered.

"Bastards. Haven't they done enough?"

Chaoxiang turned from his destroyed shop and looked in the direction most people were looking. There was a tall, muscular, freckled man wearing simple clothes walking down the street towards them. He had a symbol on his shirt that Chaoxiang vaguely recognised, and he was pulling a cart loaded down with what looked like stone and tile, building materials. He had deeply tanned skin and looked a lot like a farmhand.

But strangely, he was being followed by cultivators. Cultivators who were following at a respectful distance, save for four who looked a bit worse for wear. It was comical; they were trying to seem nonchalant, but you could tell they were focused on the farmhand, all eyes warily watching his progress. Chaoxiang idly wondered what that was about—when the farmhand suddenly stopped, directly in front of Chaoxiang.

"Excuse me, sir. Can I lend you a hand?" the freckled farmhand asked. He gestured to the destroyed building.

Chaoxiang recoiled in shock. Yes, he needed all the help he could get, but he didn't know the man. Had never seen him before.

"Thank you for the offer, lad, but . . . why my place? We're pretty far on the outskirts," he said instead. Chaoxiang had heard that the heaviest fighting had been in the square. Surely, they must be worse off than him?

The farmhand bowed at a full ninety-degree angle to Chaoxiang, and the watching cultivators took in sharp breaths of shock.

"Because I was the one who destroyed it," the man said. His neighbors then went dead silent. The farmhand was a *cultivator*. Chaoxiang felt his face go white and his bowels clenched up in fear. Chaoxiang's mind raced and it clicked why the other cultivators were following him.

"My name is Rou Jin. I apologise for my actions. I would like to pay for any damages I have incurred on you and aid in your rebuilding. If you don't want me here, I'll leave, but only after I pay for the damage."

The man stayed bowed—nobody moved or dared to breathe.

Except one.

"You destroyed our shop?" Little Ning shouted with all the indignance a child could muster. She stomped up to the cultivator, tears still in her eyes and hands on her hips, the sign left back where she had been standing.

Panic surged in Chaoxiang's throat as the cultivator rose out of his bow to crouch down before Ning. His neighbors remained silent, terrified, and bewildered, unwilling to get involved.

"Yes. I've done a very bad thing," the cultivator said gently, looking at Chaoxiang's daughter. "So I've come to beg your forgiveness and make amends."

Ning's glare softened at the genuine contrition in the cultivator's warm voice and his serious expression. She then puffed up and nodded imperiously.

"I'll forgive you, but only if you fix it," his daughter decided.

"Thank you." The cultivator bowed his head to Ning, accepting chastisement from a mortal child. He rose and turned to Chaoxiang. Chaoxiang tried to swallow the lump in his throat and hastily bowed.

"Ah . . . thank you for your benevolence in noticing this lowly one, Master Cultivator. Your generosity knows no bounds." He stumbled over his words, practically cowering.

The cultivator let out a little sigh, looking at him, then placed a hand on Chaoxiang's shoulder.

"I'll make it right," he declared, turning to assess the damage. "Now. Let's see if we can get this done today."

Today?!

The cultivator turned back to the men who had followed him; Chaoxiang noticed most of the other cultivators had disappeared, all except the four. "Yingwen. Either sit there and don't move, or lend a hand," he said to them.

The cultivators looked at each other before this "Yingwen," who was the least injured out of all of them, stepped forwards.

The rest followed.

□

All around the Dueling Town, as the locals called it, people worked with heavy hearts.

Many did not know the cause of the fight last night. Some whispered of a kidnapping, others a drunken brawl.

None knew for certain. All they had were rumours. The officials were still busy with the closed mountain. It was both worrying and confusing, why the incident had been going on for so long.

So they did the only thing they could do: they went to work. They repaired the damage done as best they could.

Like they always did. It had been the worst fight outside the arena in centuries . . . but they had gotten off lightly, all told. Only two deaths that he knew of. Luckily, the worst of it seemed to have happened outside the town. The old stone village was completely destroyed.

Shu, the owner of a pottery house, sighed. His old hands shook with exhaustion, and it wasn't even noon. His kiln had caved in, a hit from an errant piece of masonry. He was definitely going to be in the red this year, and his apprentices would go hungry—

"You there!" a haughty voice called.

Shu turned—and immediately recoiled at the sight of a cultivator glaring at him.

"Me, Mistress?" Shu asked, clutching at his shirt, head bowed.

"This one is Yinxia Qiao. Be grateful, for I have decided to assist you. What needs to be done?" she demanded.

Every worker had gone silent. All movement ceased.

"Well? I do not have all day!" she commanded. "I am the equal of any task that could be required!"

Shu, bewildered and in shock at the cultivator's fierce eyes, gestured to the mass of stones that had been his kiln and said the first thing that came to mind.

"This needs to be removed and broken down by the masons' guild." As soon as the words were out of his mouth, he regretted them. Surely, the cultivator would be angry? Why was she offering in the first place? He expected her to explode.

"Hmph." The cultivator woman clicked her tongue, then stared at the rubble in disdain.

She rolled up her immaculate silk sleeves and picked up a chunk of kiln bigger than Shu.

One of his men turned to Shu, pure confusion on his face.

Shu shook his head, just as bewildered as his apprentice. The woman had lifted hundreds of pounds of stone like they weighed nothing—and then she suddenly paused and set her burden back down. She rummaged on the ground for a moment before coming back up with a broken plate.

"Ah, this one is quite a fine design!" the woman declared. "I shall allow you to have my business when this is over!"

Shu pinched himself. Maybe a piece of the rubble had hit him, not the kiln.

↔

"Truly? It needs to be destroyed?" Chen Yang of the Framed Sun Sect asked. He stared at the building. It seemed serviceable enough to him, but he knew barely anything of carpentry or the building of houses. Many cultivators had "chosen" to do basic manual labour so as not to make fools of themselves, rather than admit that they had no idea how to help.

Really, the only useful member of his Sect was his Junior, Ai, as her father had been a carpenter. Something he hadn't known before she volunteered.

"Yes, Master Cultivator," the mortal foreman said. "That wall is load-bearing. We can't work with it like it is. Too much pressure. The wall will collapse."

Ai whispered in his ear, "We could just lift it up? That would take the pressure off . . ."

Chen Yang nodded. He walked under the rubble and the half-collapsed building. The beams were still fairly solid. He placed his hands on them, got a good grip—and lifted the roof off the building.

"Ai. Do what you need to," Yang commanded.

She nodded, and the Framed Sun Sect got to work.

Yang considered Ai. She worked with speed and grace, while a bunch of the mortal men stared at her in awe.

Perhaps I should learn something like that? he thought.

↔

"Dumplings, get your dumplings!" a man shouted, pushing along a cart.

Shan pulled out his pockets and grimaced at the number of coins he had. He could get one. *Maybe* two . . .

"Give food and drink to all of them," Luo Shi, the cultivator who had inserted himself into their work group, commanded. "Will eight silver coins suffice?"

The dumpling seller did a double take as the cultivator strode towards him.

"Eight silver coins," the man demanded again. Shan knew that all the dumplings would not cost anywhere near that much.

"Ah . . . uh. You are too kind, Master Cultivator, but . . . that is too much—" the dumpling man tried to get out, but the cultivator ignored him. A coin pouch was thrust into the man's hand and the dumplings collected.

"You may praise me for my generosity, mortals," Luo Shi declared.

The men cheered.

↔

"What ails you, Sister?" Bi De asked from atop her wheelbarrow. Tigu startled on hearing the rooster's voice out loud rather than in his normal Qi-speech. His words had always been full of strength, but as they reverberated through the air, they seemed somehow . . . *more.* She could even admit in the hidden parts of herself that he was almost regal.

No matter how much another part of her rebelled against ever thinking of Bi De as regal.

She looked at him. The honest concern on his avian face.

The bastard . . . no, no, he had never really been a bastard to her, had he? *She* had always been the one instigating things. Tigu remembered the feelings of contempt every time she'd looked at Bi De. Her mocking laughter as she'd insulted him over and over again.

And yet . . . he had never really taken her bait. He had always called her his Sister Disciple and respected her.

The reflexive reaction to tell him to mind his own business faded.

He had gone on his own journey. He had delved into the secrets of this world. Perhaps he had some wisdom for her?

She crushed the feeling of shame at having to ask for help down again. Instead, she just stared out at the streets.

"Have you ever seen any place like this?" she took a breath and asked finally.

The rooster looked over the broken buildings, his eyes taking in everything. "Yes. I have witnessed many, many destroyed villages. Most were utterly devoid of people. They were . . . wrong. I did not like finding them. Those cold and dead places were the majority. But I have seen such destruction in the direct aftermath only twice. The first was our own home, after Chow Ji," Bi De said.

Tigu searched her memories. They were a little bit fuzzy. She had been mostly awake then but still had flashes of darkness. Looking back on it . . . it had been pretty bad, hadn't it? She'd had no frame of reference before. The wounds inflicted on Bi De, Chun Ke, and Pi Pa had been marks of shame in her eyes. Failures. Now all those memories elicited were concern. "The other was Correct Location Eight."

Tigu chewed at her lip. "The place with the wolves? The one you talked about in your letter? What happened there afterwards?"

The rooster turned to her.

"The town was repaired. The people mourned the fallen . . . and then life went on," the rooster said simply.

Tigu paused at the bluntness of the statement. "Did they hunt the wolves to the end?" she asked. The beasts had visited such destruction upon the town from Bi De's tale. Surely they must have retaliated.

The rooster shook his head. "No, they did not. After that night . . . it ended."

A story of blood, vengeance, and hate . . . just petering out.

"Why?" Tigu asked.

The rooster pondered the question. "Allow me to ask you a question instead. What would they gain from such a thing?"

"Their enemies would be destroyed," Tigu stated simply. "They could never again bother them."

The rooster nodded. "Now . . . what would they lose?"

Tigu froze at the question. *What would they lose?*

Bi De nodded at her silence and the thoughtfulness on her face. She had never really thought about the price . . .

"Indeed, they could have chased the wolves forever. They could have hunted every last wolf down and exterminated them. But . . . what would they lose in doing so? Who would guard the sheep? Who would take care of the children? Who would perform the tasks around the village? And finally . . . what if those actions spawned another wolf with Qi? A wolf with Qi that hated them just as much as they hated it? Before they slew the wolf pups. Before they embarked upon the first campaign of extermination . . . the wolf that was once called the Terror was just a wolf with the spark." Bi De brought his wing to his wattles and stroked them, while Tigu took a moment to think on what he said.

"Now, in some cases such an extermination may be the correct answer; this Bi De lacks the knowledge to know when one's spurs must be wielded in such a way until the bloody business is done. But first, one must always ask themself: *What am I willing to lose for it?*"

Tigu turned to Loud Boy and Rags. To the Misty Lady and Gou Ren. She thought about Xiulan, who was still lying in her bed.

How much were her feelings worth, really? How much was hurting the Shrouded Mountain Sect worth?

What *was* she willing to lose? Her Master had destroyed the man who had ordered the assault. What would she gain from striking down every man involved?

That was probably what her Master was thinking of. What he had to lose if things escalated. If a fight between *disciples* could produce this much damage . . .

Tigu had things she wasn't willing to lose either.

Tigu pondered the rooster's words as she scooped up another piece of rubble.

"Bi De?"

"Yes, Sister Tigu?"

"Thank you."

The rooster seemed taken aback by her honest words for a moment, before his eyes softened.

"If my words have aided you, then it is all worth it," he said. "The Great Master and the Healing Sage say knowledge unshared is worthless! We give to each other and are repaid in kind, no?"

We give to the Land and the Land gives back. Master was quite fond of that saying.

Tigu felt a small smile cross her face.

"So you're extorting your Junior Sister for knowledge now?" she asked coyly.

Bi De looked offended. "I merely wished to know of your adventures—"

He cut off at Tigu's mocking smile, leapt up to her shoulder, and cuffed her gently on the ear with his wing. Tigu giggled at the fond amusement emanating off him.

"Very well, I shall regale you with my exploits!" Tigu declared. The rooster shook his head but settled in for a tale. His beak preened her hair as she told him all about the tournament, and of the friends she had made.

Bi De listened to her, nodding along to her story. Eventually she wandered back over to everybody else, Loud Boy occasionally chiming in to expand on her already boastful recounting. Gou Ren ruffled her hair, and Yun Ren brought up another image.

Tigu didn't feel entirely better, as she laughed and joked with her friends. Things were too raw, too fresh still.

But as the street cleared from devastated ruin to something that could be repaired, and as Handsome Man walked over to have lunch with them . . .

Tigu thought perhaps things could get better.

CHAPTER 55

COMING CLEAN

The previous night . . .

[Break the Rocks]

The words echoed in the air. The world shuddered. And then, it was over.

Master Jin turned to Xiulan and Bi De. His eyes were calm and serene.

Xiulan coughed. Fire erupted out of her mouth. The burning in her chest tore the breath from her lungs, and she collapsed. Master Jin's eyes widened—he hurried forwards to catch her.

He slung one of her arms over his shoulder and carried her with him. Then she felt him move, speeding back to the town. Xiulan could barely breathe; the burning was getting worse by the moment. The firebreaks, the cracks she had made in her own cultivation to stop the spread of the flames, were overwhelmed.

The last thing she saw before everything went dark was Tigu's face, safe and sound. *It was worth it.*

The darkness claimed her.

→

It was almost abstract, watching the destruction of herself.

To stand on that grassy field and observe the flames rage, drawing closer and closer.

There was a sort of resignation to the inevitability of it all—a sort of grief, as everything she had ever worked for in her life was consumed by the ravenous, orange maws of fire.

It was, however, mixed with righteous conviction. This was the price she had to pay. The cost of challenging a cultivator in the Fourth Stage of the Profound Realm and fighting him to a standstill. *This* was what it took to uphold her oath to Master Jin and rescue Tigu. If this was what it had cost, so be it, she would pay it.

The fires were getting ever closer to her dantian. She could barely breathe for all the acrid smoke; the sky looked like the maw of some angry hellbeast. She was barely upright, forced to lean against a rock in a field of grass littered with gold cracks.

Until, suddenly, her salvation came. From the heavens came a torrential downpour, a crush of water and mist that swept across the plains. It was Qi, Qi that felt . . . familiar. Half-concerned, half-boasting that the fire was nothing, even as the water disappeared into gouts of steam from the force of the raging inferno. It didn't let up, relentless in its headlong drive to the core of the fire.

The fire tried to burn her. It tried to drag more of her Qi from her, but she was so spent, all it could do now was gutter and die.

And then she was alone. Alone, in a field of desolation. The only things remaining were ash and puddles of water.

Her cultivation had been reduced to the Third Stage of the Initiate's Realm. She knew that such a thing would be irreversible. The grass was dead. Her cultivation had been mostly destroyed. Before Master Jin, it had been a lifetime of spending every waking moment pursuing cultivation to arrive at the Third Stage of the Initiate's Realm. She was back. Back to what she had been before meeting Master Jin.

A bitter victory, but a worthy sacrifice.

She crouched down and placed her hand against the ash and heated earth. She took a handful and let it fall down through her fingers. A memory rose up, whispering in her ear. The scent of rain, as she sat beside Master Jin.

After the fire burns through, the grass comes back, stronger than ever.

Xiulan froze.

Could this be fixed? Could she fix it? Could the grass grow again?

Or could she accept this? To be forever stuck at this level, a permanent scar from Zang Li?

No. No, she would *not* abide it. Not when she'd finally found purpose. Not when she finally had a real goal to strive towards.

The dregs of Xiulan's Qi churned. She staggered to her feet. She raised her hands, clapping them together just as the Earth Spirit had taught her.

Shoulders set. Eyes forwards. Plant that lead foot.

Xiulan's feet moved into position.

She felt the extent of the damage. The ravaged destruction of her cultivation.

But for all the fire's ferocity, it had not been able to reach beneath the earth. It had not the power to burn out everything. It hadn't destroyed her completely.

Her first steps were halting. Slow and not at all sturdy. But as she moved, she picked up speed. She picked up strength. The uncertain stumbling became graceful. The sound of drums thundered in her head, pulling up the memories of a life she had fallen in love with.

An Earth Spirit's lessons. A farm full of warmth.

Her feet tapped out the rhythm. Her body moved with a dance that was ancient beyond all reckoning.

A goal. Purpose. Something to strive for, to achieve, to have as her own, borne from her own ideals. Those in the Azure Hills were all just tiny blades of grass. Alone, they were nothing. Alone, atrocities festered and mortals lived in fear of them.

No more.

Now it was time for the future. Xiulan kept her eyes closed as she completed the first act. Her feet moved into position for the second set, a loud stomp in time with the drums—

And a second foot planted itself into the ground, *thumping* loudly.

Xiulan didn't dare open her eyes. She didn't dare falter as her Qi spun and surged.

Fire from Zang Li, burning away impurities to birth earth.

Earth from Master Jin, setting foundation for new growth, hardening into Metal.

Metal from a soft, whispering touch, condensed and formed to collect Water.

Water from Xianghua, cooling and nourishing, all helping to give rise . . .

To Wood.

The acrid smell of corrupted ash faded. A warm summer breeze flowed through her soul.

Xiulan opened her eyes. There was a little girl beside her. Around her was now a bright, sunny summer's day, and a pure breeze flowed through her core. Her feet no longer stomped into acid dust, alight with foul Qi, but instead, soft, loamy soil and green shoots.

Xiulan's body moved through the final forms. Her partner did the same, mirroring her movements. They flowed as one, in perfect harmony. There were no corrections, there was no mocking laughter.

The final beat sounded. They both stopped in the position Xiulan had started in. Her hands were clasped together like she was praying.

Xiulan bowed to her partner, signaling the end of the song, and the Earth Spirit did the same.

They rose as one, and Xiulan finally beheld the spirit.

She was in both better and worse shape than Xiulan had seen her last. The gold plate that once covered a full third of her face was much more healed-looking than it had been.

But while that piece of damage had been repaired, the gold itself was . . . dull. As if it had been drained of vitality. The Earth Spirit was drooping and had bags under her eyes. She seemed completely and utterly exhausted.

"Are you well, little one?" Xiulan asked the Earth Spirit.

The spirit startled at her question. Her eyes narrowed with anger and fear . . . before that drained away.

The little one beckoned Xiulan over.

Xiulan complied, kneeling down to be at eye level with the Earth Spirit. Her exhaustion could not be from the dance. It looked bone deep, and painful. Xiulan wondered how she could aid the little one—

The Earth Spirit grasped either side of Xiulan's face and brought her down. Xiulan reflexively flinched, expecting a headbutt.

A pair of lips pressed against her forehead instead.

Xiulan woke up.

Ri Zu, whose paws had been on her neck, jumped a foot in the air.

→

Ri Zu's paw was on Xiulan's wrist, checking her pulse. The little rat tapped out a rhythm and nodded in satisfaction.

'Qi is . . . stable. Heartbeat normal,' Ri Zu recited as Xiulan spooned some cold broth into her mouth. She could have asked for something freshly made from the kitchens, but Master Jin's food was just better, even if it was cold. Ri Zu sighed, finished with her examination. *'You gave Ri Zu a scare when your Qi started doing that!'* the rat scolded. *'And when you started sweating out that filth!'*

Ri Zu gestured to the dark spots on Xiulan's covers. Impurities. They smelled disgusting; the dark, sludgy spots had ruined both the covers and the sleeping robe.

"My apologies," Xiulan whispered. Her voice was a bit raw, but she could feel her strength returning. "Do I have a clean bill of health?"

Ri Zu glared at her. *'No. Your Qi is still diminished. Your nerves are damaged in your hands. Your muscles will be sore . . . However, you can get out of bed if you do not overexert yourself! Understood?'* Ri Zu sternly commanded.

Xiulan nodded. She had awoken restless, and on learning that everybody was already out and working to restore the town from the damage done . . . Well, she couldn't be absent from everything that was happening!

"I shall be careful, Ri Zu," she said, only to get a glare in return—before Ri Zu sighed.

'Take care of yourself, Xiulan. None of us wish for you to be hurt further,' she said before scampering out of the room to give her some privacy.

One of the maids had drawn her a bath, but Xiulan declined her offer of assistance in bathing. The woman looked ill from the stench of the impurities in the room, and Xiulan had no desire to inflict that misery upon the poor woman.

Xiulan changed out of the stinking, sweat-stained sleeping clothes she had been changed into while she recovered, then rolled them up and put them on top of a wooden tray. They would have to be burned.

After washing her body, some of the sweat disgustingly sludgy, she intended to get dressed.

Only to realise her normal dress was completely beyond repair. It was torched and torn to pieces, just as ruined as her body had been, before Ri Zu had worked her potent healing arts. So she chose another one. Slightly less flowy than her previous garment. Less embellishment. A simpler robe, with wider sleeves and a belt, in light hues of green. She briefly considered wearing the clothes Senior Sister had made for her . . . but eventually decided against it. She would be going out into a destroyed town, and hopefully helping to clean up a bit. It wouldn't be in defiance of Ri Zu's orders. A bit of lifting wasn't stressful.

Xiulan looked in the mirror. She ran her finger down the small crack of gold in the center of her chest. A crack in her porcelain skin, which had been filled in with metal.

One of the blows Zang Li had dealt her. An imperfect blemish on her otherwise perfect skin.

Xiulan instantly liked it, that tiny blemish, even as she bound her chest—it was proof of what she had chosen to sacrifice. Little white lines, already fading, crisscrossed her arms and legs. They were hidden by her dress.

The burns on her face had peeled off, with only slightly pinker patches to show where they had been. A brief brush of makeup and they disappeared completely. Her hair ties had been burned and her normal hairpieces had been damaged beyond repair: one melted and the other shattered.

So she tied her hair into her customary braids.

She looked at herself in the mirror. Besides the mark on her chest, not a single trace of the damage looked to remain from that night. It was just her. It was just Cai Xiulan.

Satisfied, she closed her eyes and reached within herself. Her Qi rose to meet her.

Xiulan was at the Third Stage of the Initiate's Realm. Her cultivation had been burned straight out of her . . . but it had not been destroyed.

She felt those eager tendrils, excited to grow, and smiled. It would be hard . . . but she would return to her former strength one day, and then beyond it as well, her grass growing stronger after the flame.

She met Ri Zu outside her door when she was ready. The rat sighed and raised an eyebrow at her.

'Really?' she asked. Xiulan bent down so that Ri Zu could climb onto her shoulder. Ri Zu, recognising that Xiulan probably wouldn't listen to any command to rest, scampered up her arm and cuffed her ear.

Xiulan smiled as she descended the stairs. At the bottom, the mortal servants were all waiting for her. She knew each one by name. Xiping was wringing his hands, nervous. Liuan was brewing them tea.

"Young Mistress . . . are you sure you are well?" Xiping asked as she approached them, full of concern.

"Yes. I'm all right, Xiping. Thank you, all of you, for your concern," she replied.

The tension dropped at her smile, the servants smiling with relief.

"That's our Young Mistress!" one of the old grandmothers said approvingly.

"I—it was our pleasure, Young Mistress," Xiping said, his face flushed as he looked at her smile. He shook his head, then rapidly made the gesture of respect, the rest of them following through. "Do you require anything else . . . ?"

"If you can, see about aiding the rest of the town, and be sure to pick up extra food. Everybody will be hungry tonight."

"Yes, Young Mistress!"

Xiulan nodded to them all and walked out into the courtyard to the gates. She took a breath, then opened the gates, stepping out onto the street.

She only made it a block before she paused.

A mortal foreman was directing the Young Master of the Rumbling Earth Sect, who was placing cobble into the roads. The young man nodded at the old mortal's words. The foreman rapidly filled in a section of the road, the Young Master looking almost impressed at the skill born of age.

Xiulan forced herself to stop staring and kept walking. As she passed by more streets, she needed an iron will to keep her mouth from opening in astonishment.

Cultivators were repairing roofs. Cultivators were hauling water. Cultivators were having a contest to see who could split logs the fastest.

The mortals with them appeared bemused, or at least slightly less fearful.

A smile tugged at the corner of her mouth. She was fairly certain she knew who had prompted all this.

Ri Zu just nodded approvingly at the sights, as if this were something normal. Xiulan supposed that for Ri Zu, it was.

She walked on, observing the work being done all the while. Ri Zu sniffed at the air and pointed the way to their true destination.

Those who noticed her paused in their duties. The cultivators began to whisper while the mortals just stopped and stared.

"Fought a man in the Fourth Stage of the Profound Realm . . ."

"Fought off ten disciples of the Shrouded Mountain Sect . . ."

"Barely even injured . . ."

The whispers followed her, carried on the wind.

She paid them little mind, simply continuing forwards to her destination. She passed by Guo Daxian, who was weaving together ropes. He paused and gave her a nod, a measure of respect in the normally surly man's eyes. Xiulan nodded in turn to the man, a little confused by how friendly he was being.

She continued on until she found her destination.

A group of familiar friends sitting together. Xianghua was hanging off Gou Ren's shoulder while she smirked at An Ran. In turn, Xiulan's Junior Sister was rolling her eyes at whatever Xianghua was saying. Xiulan noticed Huyi, Xi Bu, and Li cheering on a dancing rabbit, while Yun Ren stood nearby with hands pressed to a wall, a mural of Yin's dance flowing out from him.

Xianghua's little brother, his eyes wide and shining, was pointing at a scroll and eagerly explaining something on it to Master Jin. The man looked intensely interested, and he said something to the boy, who flushed and bounced excitedly. Tigu was curled up in Master Jin's lap while Bi De was beside them both. Tigu's fingers wove through his feathers as the rooster rested, his eyes closed.

Xiulan paused to admire it all for a moment. *It was all worth it.*

Tigu was the one to notice her first. The girl's yellow eyes widened.

"Lanlan!" the girl shouted, bursting up from her seat. "Ri Zu!"

"Young Mistress?" An Ran responded in shock.

Tigu's dash sent her rocketing towards Xiulan, but instead of a tackling hug that Xiulan had been braced for, the girl skidded to a stop before her a split second after Ri Zu squeaked out a warning. Tigu's wide eyes searched her up and down, checking her over for injuries.

Xiulan opened her arms.

Tigu jumped the last part of the distance, clamping on to her and sniffling loudly, trying to hold back tears.

The rest of them followed soon after.

"Young Mistress!" Li wailed, looking like he wanted to join in on Tigu's hug.

"Up already? Our Young Mistress is the best!" Huyi declared, his regular cynicism on hold as he grinned. Even his eyes were less fishlike.

"Ha! As if even *twenty* Young Masters could keep Cai Xiulan down! I shall have to challenge *thirty* cultivators superior in cultivation to me this year and defeat them!" Xianghua bellowed.

"Please don't do that," Gou Ren and her little brother said in unison.

"Junior Sister, your exploits were most magnificent!" Bi De praised, and Ri Zu squealed happily.

'She beat the shit outta them!' Yin enthused, bouncing up and down.

Xiulan felt the last of the tension drain away as she was welcomed back. As she was clapped on the back and hugged. As her friends swarmed around her.

All but one.

Master Jin watched on with a smile, waiting patiently for them to finish greeting her.

He made a gesture that he wanted to talk privately.

Xiulan basked in the glory for a moment longer before she excused herself to hear what Master Jin had to say.

→

"I'm getting a lot of practice doing these," Master Jin said with amusement, then kowtowed before her, even as Xiulan held her head in her hands.

"Master Jin, please," Xiulan muttered, her face flushed. "You didn't need to lower your head so far to me. I only did as my oaths demanded—"

"And I appreciate that, so now I owe you a debt," Master Jin cut in, firm. "Thank you, Xiulan," he said with conviction.

Xiulan took in a breath as the words struck her: earnest thanks from Master Jin.

He rose from his bow to take the seat next to her. They were seated together in a quiet spot of the town, a space with a bench that looked over the plains to the south. It was quiet and few people came here.

She stared out at the plains, still a bit embarrassed after Master Jin had kowtowed to her.

It was horrifying that such an expert would lower himself so far to her—all she'd done was fulfill her expected duties . . .

Especially after what had happened.

Xiulan let out a breath she hadn't realised she was holding. "What happens now?" she asked.

Master Jin turned to her and raised an eyebrow.

Xiulan chewed her lip. "I attacked the Shrouded Mountain Sect. I could not stand by and do nothing. There will be consequences . . ."

Master Jin turned away from her to look out at the plains as well.

After a moment, he spoke in a tone that brooked no argument. "I don't know exactly what will happen, but I'm not going to let them take you. Besides, I don't think the Shrouded Mountain Sect will be too keen on trying to force the issue," he said as he reached into his pack and pulled out a scroll.

Xiulan was stunned. She knew Master Jin was powerful, but what threat could he offer to deter the Shrouded Mountain Sect—!

Xiulan was confused as he handed over the scroll to her. It was a rather simple, unadorned document. She glanced at him for permission before unrolling it, and he nodded. Curious, Xiulan opened it up.

She stared at the impossible symbol emblazoned on it.

For a full minute, she just stared at it, her mind frozen.

As calmly as she could, she rolled it back up again. With a slight tremor in her hands, she handed it back.

Master Jin took back the scroll and stared at the sky before sighing and turning to her.

"I don't know if this is the best time for it . . . but . . . you deserve to know this story. To be fair, I probably should have told you sooner, really." His face twisted into a sad, crooked smile.

"There once was a man who joined the Cloudy Sword Sect . . ." Master Jin began.

→

When Master Jin finished his story, Xiulan remained silent.

She stared at him.

Here was a man who had abandoned the great Cloudy Sword Sect. Left it all behind to come to the pitiful Azure Hills. Not for any cultivation gain. Not to defy the heavens, or for any kind of secret method. But to farm. And in the end, he'd grown stronger for it.

All of that was beyond her ability to absorb in this moment. All she could focus on was one little fact.

"You're *younger* than I am?" she eventually said, disbelief colouring her words.

"Yeah," he said, smirking at her. "Maybe I should start calling you Senior Sister, eh?"

He sighed. The smile faded from his face. "I feel like I've led you on."

Really, it was obvious now. But she had just *assumed*, like an idiot. No wonder he kept just telling her to call him just by his name. If anything, it was beyond impressive. In any Sect he would be an unparalleled genius. A man who would forge a new age.

And he had given all of it up, disregarding power. Or, if his words were true . . . He'd become powerful *because* he had given it all up.

Xiulan's mind whirled. She leaned back in her seat and looked to the sky.

His story was absurd. And yet it made so much sense.

In the past, she would have scoffed. To give up on the path of defiance, to choose to be mortal? Was not their goal in life to ascend? To strive for the heavens?

And yet . . .

What was the point of striving to reach the heavens when you could make one upon the earth?

His words . . . they resonated with her. They were the catalyst that consolidated her own thoughts on her experiences. She wanted to prevent another Sun Ken from ever existing. She wanted to live her life to the fullest, like she did at Fa Ram. She wanted to make a better world, for every person in the Azure Hills.

What was the point of bettering a world you would leave behind? What was the point of life, if not to become immortal? In the end that was the question: *What was the purpose of it all?*

Did it really change the respect she had for him? Master Jin and Senior Sister Meiling had saved her life. They had saved her soul by helping her lay her demons to rest. Fa Ram and its people had given to her without restraint, aided her because they could.

She was better now in ways she hadn't even known she could become better in.

And he had done it all not out of a desire for anything from her, and not as a Master training her for his own amusement or pride.

But simply because he thought it was the right thing to do.

Create his own heaven.

Xiulan felt her heart beat faster. She closed her eyes, remembering his look of conviction.

It was a goal that she could only declare as something worthy—A goal that she hadn't truly realised she was already following. That already the Sects were following: cleaning up a shattered town, coming to each other's defence.

Something gentler. Something kinder than this brutal world.

Xiulan turned to look at him. He appeared nervous. Young. Even knowing it now, it didn't seem real.

She took a breath and stood up, walking so that she was in front of him. She clasped her hands together in a gesture of respect.

"I do not regret a moment I have spent with you and Senior Sister Meiling," she said, looking him directly in the eyes. "You do not wish for it, but what Bi De calls you, what I call you . . . I think you deserve that title. I would be honoured if you would allow me to call you my Master." His face flushed crimson with embarrassment and he looked away, scratching at his chin. "And I would be twice as honoured to call you my friend, Jin." She bowed to him.

His face screwed up—she could see him flashing through several emotions—before he sighed. "Is what I've done truly that worthy of respect?" he asked, uncertain.

"Yes," she stated simply, rising up from her bow and looking at him.

He took a breath and stood, then bowed back to her. "Then . . . I swear this on the trust you have for me. On my family that you've saved. I would be honoured to call you my friend, and sworn sister."

He offered her his arm in the traditional warrior's clasp.

Xiulan took it without hesitation.

"Please take care of me, *Senior Sister*." His voice had a hint of teasing in it.

"Please take care of me, *Master*," she returned, playing their game.

He glared at her. "So. We're as good as family now, right?" he asked.

Xiulan nodded firmly.

The grip on her wrist tightened. She was pulled into his chest as his arms wrapped around her shoulders and held her tight.

Her own arms were frozen in shock for a moment.

And then she relaxed, leaning into his embrace.

"Thank you, Xiulan, for everything," he whispered to her.

He pulled back slightly so she could see his warm smile.

In the end . . . it was all worth it.

He sighed. "Thanks for listening, Lanlan. I'm gonna go get back to work. The houses won't build themselves."

She nodded, stepping back. "I'll join you soon. I just . . . need a moment."

Jin nodded to her. He turned and left, walking back to the street where the rest of her friends waited.

Xiulan hummed to herself as she watched him go. A man who cared nothing for defying the heavens . . . There was probably a song there. A legend that in time would be told for a thousand years. She sat back down on the bench.

He thought he was a farmer. She thought he was a Hidden Master.

Both of them were right.

In the end . . . she couldn't help but think it fitting. It was so . . . *Jin*. Xiulan's shoulders began to shake. A little giggle slipped out of her throat.

She hugged herself, clutching at her sides, then laughed until she started crying, the tears of mirth sliding down her cheeks.

CHAPTER 56

MASTER ROU

Cai Xi Kong watched as Bao Wen performed the maintenance rites in front of the humming machine. The boy's eyes were screwed up in concentration.

They had been down there for over a day already. Their first activation of the machine had shut off part of the barrier. The upper floors, judging by the diagram on the machine. He could tell that Bao Wen was obviously tiring. After the endless debate had concluded, they had decided upon this measure simply because there was no food in the depths. The Elders could afford to wait for weeks or months, but the mortal could not.

Xi Kong turned back to the ongoing discussion between the various Elders about the future use of their collective discovery . . . and naturally who should get first priority of its use.

"Open the vault to one Elder every year?" Elder Xinling asked.

"But who should have priority on the texts?" Elder Shen questioned.

"Your Sect can't *possibly* make as much use of this knowledge—" Elder Shu commented.

"And yours can, you bastard? You could study the ancestors for a thousand years and gain nothing!" Elder Gang snorted.

The squabbling was hushed so Bao Wen couldn't hear them; it would not do to expose the mortal boy to the Elders bickering over minutiae like merchants.

This wouldn't end anytime soon. Xi Kong himself was aware of the dilemma. How to disseminate the information. Sects wanted priority, special considerations . . .

Xi Kong remembered something his daughter had told him, or rather confided in him, on how these mortal archives worked.

"No scrolls leave the archive itself. A single copy per person may be made every month," he said, adding his own thoughts to the discussion.

His point was considered.

"Is that not too generous?" Elder Shen asked. "Once a month . . ."

"I agree, no scroll should leave the confines . . . but what about jurisdiction? Even if a copy is made, if the knowledge is worth enough I can see things . . . going missing," Daxian returned.

There were several shrugs. They all knew that would happen. Something going missing was inevitable, and he wouldn't put it past his fellows to attempt something later down the line. Xi Kong himself was tempted to see if he could sneak some of the ancient manuals away.

"Is this place not already under the control of the commission? The Sects agreed that this palace is neutral ground. Could we not keep it that way?" Xi Kong asked.

"We could, but the knowledge is worth too much. We would need to create a separate group to protect the archive. It would require a competent and trustworthy person to head such a division. Few would even be able to know . . ." Elder Xinling returned.

The Elders trailed off.

Guo Daxian the Elder looked at Bao Wen. Several other heads also turned in his direction.

"It's a big promotion, for such a young lad," Xinling murmured.

"He will have to be impressed with the need for secrecy . . . but I suppose he's an acceptable neutral party," Elder Gang mused.

"He does require a reward for discovering this place," Elder Shu muttered.

Xi Kong held back a sigh. He could see the calculating gleam in the eyes of his fellows, no doubt already thinking of offering bribes to "cut the queue," as it was.

Bao Wen . . . well, he was lucky, but there were always those who wished for that sort of luck.

The mortal flipped to another scroll and nodded, as he looked at the diagram he had to follow. He shifted his body.

A moment later, the barriers hummed and died, and the machine snapped off with a hiss.

Every Elder heaved a sigh of relief.

"Excellent work, Bao Wen," Guo Daxian stated. The boy flushed as several Elders nodded in praise. "A fine show, child. Rest now. The Elders of the Azure Hills will pay their debts."

↔

Huizong was in a *terrible* mood. First, he had been trapped in his office for nearly eight hours. Eight hours with an increasingly skeptical Master and irate Lady of the Azure Jade Trading Company. The entire mountain had rattled and shook, and each time it had set his heart pounding.

At least they were somewhere comfortable and nothing bad had happened . . . save for when water suddenly started pumping through long-unused pipes and into basins that had been used as extra storage. He'd had to scramble to get everything out.

All he could do was wait. He'd managed to catch some sleep, fortunately, but it was in his chair. The couch was surrendered to Lady Daiyu . . . who then surrendered it to her husband, citing his bad back. She ended up in another chair. The woman simply worked through the night, on a little travel desk she had brought with her, steadily finishing documents one at a time as if nothing at all were the matter.

When Huizong woke in the morning, Master Guan was already going over the papers his wife had worked on, nodding and occasionally writing something beside them, checking over sums and figures.

Huizong was just starting to get really hungry when the doors finally opened.

A deluge of servants immediately poured in.

His entire day, needless to say, was ruined. He was angry, hungry, and sleep deprived. He ushered Lady Daiyu and her husband out, then sat down to report after report of the unfolding disaster outside. Damages to the town unseen in decades, whispers of an assault on the Shrouded Mountain Sect and their manor, the entire Earthly Arena levitating—

And the Elders were *still* nowhere to be found.

It was enough to drive a man to drink.

One of his men dashed into the room as the afternoon sun beat down. "Sir, the other sections of the mountain have reopened," he said. "The Elders are on their way."

Huizong breathed out in relief at the news and prepared himself. True to his man's word, the cultivators entered moments later, already deep in discussion.

"Master Cultivators! Esteemed Elders of the Azure Hills!" Huizong called out, standing to greet them from his table with a smile. "It's good to see you again, after . . . well. The entire mountain is in an uproar, and I dare say you have a tale to tell, so . . ." He trailed off leadingly. He hoped it wasn't anything serious.

"They may cease their uproar. The mountain has been quieted, and Guo Daxian of the Grand Ravine Sect guarantees there is nothing dangerous," Guo Daxian declared.

"As does the Verdant Blade Sect. An old formation was activated, but it has been safely disabled," Cai Xi Kong said from beside him. Huizong noted the power shift. Normally it was Azure Horizon who spoke next.

"There is nothing to worry about, then? No threat to the mountain?"

"None at all," Daxian reiterated.

"Excellent! Excellent! There is just . . . one other thing," Huizong said. The Elder raised an eyebrow and gestured for Huizong to continue.

"There . . . there was a battle yesterday. A large one that shook the streets of the town. I have seen the damage myself and it is severe, but we're getting conflicting reports as to the nature of it. As His Majesty's humble servant, I would politely request if the esteemed Elders of the Azure Hills could aid him in shedding light on the situation," Huizong said, folding his hands together.

"Conflicting reports?" Daxian asked.

"Yes, ah . . . They say that it involved the Shrouded Mountain Sect."

That got *all* of their attention.

"As you say, Lord Director. We shall see what this is all about." The cultivators looked at each other.

And then the Elders left as abruptly as they had arrived.

Huizong sighed and leaned back in his chair. The entire situation was a nightmare.

The one bright spot was that the bastard cultivators had decided to actually help repair the town. He had questioned the report, yet his men swore that it was true. Cultivators, taking responsibility for their actions and doing mortal work!

Actually . . . he could work with that . . . That might make a good story. Cultivators have a fight, then repair the damage!

Huizong snorted. A most fantastical story indeed.

↔

The march down from the mountain was conducted in silence. They headed out, exited from the main entrance, and strode down the streets, past the Sect manors. There were bits of rubble, but it was probably nothing. Mortals often mistook the severity of a cultivator's fights. It was more likely to be a minor drunken brawl, but the fact that the Shrouded Mountain Sect was involved was very concerning—

Naturally, none of them were prepared for what they saw when they came to the main square.

The cultivators of the Azure Hills, the Young Masters and Mistresses were . . . cleaning up.

They were repairing the damage to a square that looked like a Spiritual-Level technique had gone off in it. The damage was partially repaired, but the telltale signs of heavy combat remained. Stones had been shattered. The street had collapsed in one location. Several buildings had holes in them, and there was a fountain that had been completely demolished. It clearly was not just a mere drunken brawl.

Much heavier combat than any of them had been expecting.

Needless to say, it surprised all of them.

Several of their disciples were sitting around, laughing and joking with mortals as they worked. An independent cultivator shoved a brush through a gutter, cleaning it of garbage and filth, to the disgust and disapproval of the Elders.

"They dare lower themselves to this?" Elder Shu demanded. He looked like he wanted to stomp over and pluck his boy up by the ear for doing mortal's work. "The other provinces already call us almost mortals, and now here they are, acting like them!"

Xi Kong could feel the disapproval among the gathered Elders rise.

The mood had turned sour. A couple of the boys closest to them, hailing from the Rumbling Earth Sect, were laughing—until they felt the intent of their Elders.

Just what happened last night?

The boys froze midtask and seemed to realise who was watching them. The mortals sensed the change and they too paled. The Masters of the Sects had arrived.

The square slowly became silent as the Elders took everything in.

The disciples of the Azure Horizon, Rumbling Earth, and White Water Sects looked at the ground.

"What is going on here?" the Elder of the Azure Horizon Sect asked, spearing his son with a look. The boy dropped his chisel.

"We are . . . fixing the street, Fath—Sect Master," the boy stuttered out.

"And why does the street need to be fixed, Disciple?" the man asked again.

The boy swallowed and looked at the ground.

"There was a drunken brawl, Father," a voice called out. Guo Daxian the Younger approached, his shirt obviously hastily put back on.

"A brawl?" Elder Gang asked skeptically. He looked down an alleyway and at a destroyed shop within.

The boy licked his lips.

"Yes. A brawl. Officially."

Murmurs broke out at the boy's words among the Elders. They glanced around at the other disciples, who were all nodding. All of them stood ramrod straight and were most certainly lying. The Elder of the Grand Ravine Sect raised an eyebrow.

"Officially?"

"Yes, Father," he replied, remaining stoic.

Guo Daxian the Elder stared at his son.

"Then how about these sons and daughters of ours come inside and explain to us this . . . 'drunken brawl.'"

→

Behind closed doors, the Elders of the Azure Hills were politely informed by several of the younger generation what had happened. The Elders sat at a curved table, with the disciples placed between them, surrounded on all sides. Daxian the Younger had taken the lead.

"They what?" Cai Xi Kong demanded. Thirty-two blades grew into existence behind him. Blood leaked out of the corner of his mouth and every vein in his head bulged out. He knew he must have looked grotesque at that moment.

They'd attacked his guests, they'd assaulted his daughter—his teeth ground against each other.

Xi Kong had half a mind to go out and get her, but he bit his tongue.

The rest of the hall was silent.

"What happened next?" Daxian the Elder demanded.

"Rou Tigu escaped with the aid of Cai Xiulan and happened upon Tie Delun—who joined the fray. The fight continued into the square, where the rest of us were gathered. The last enemy arrived, fleeing Liu Xianghua. Zhou Yingwen attempted to threaten us against interfering."

Daxian the Elder placed his hand over his eyes and massaged them.

"You interfered."

"Yes, Father."

"You interfered with the Shrouded Mountain Sect."

The boy swallowed. "I did, Father."

Guo Daxian the Elder simply kept massaging his temples.

"Who else joined in?" Elder Gang of the Rumbling Earth Sect asked, though he looked resigned to the answer. The boy stayed staring straight ahead.

"Everybody."

"Everybody?"

"*Every* cultivator in the square, every Sect in the Azure Hills intervened on Rou Tigu's behalf. From the Verdant Blade, to the Framed Sun Sect, and the Rumbling Earth Sect. *Everybody.*"

The hall was silent as the grave. Xi Kong's gut churned at the glares sent to the younger generation. The entirety of the Azure Hills rising against the Shrouded Mountain Sect was an unforgivable insult. There would likely be war for this.

What was worse, nobody could throw anybody else under the weight of the mountain coming towards them. If all of their disciples had intervened . . .

"You said . . . it was officially 'just a drunken brawl.' I take it you mean that the Shrouded Mountain Sect agreed to this?" another Elder asked, clearly skeptical.

It was a good point. If the Shrouded Mountain considered this a brawl and not an affront . . . it would at least keep the Elders away. *The younger generation, though.*

Guo Daxian the Younger shuffled uncertainly. "Yes. Rou Tigu's Master arrived last night. He put a stop to everything, and, well . . ." The boy swallowed. "It would be better to ask Master Rou yourself, Father."

"He just showed up and commanded the Shrouded Mountain Sect to stop?" he confirmed.

Daxian the Younger looked incredulous. The other disciples glanced up at the Elders, looking similarly baffled. "You did not feel his strength?" Daxian asked. "You did not feel the world shudder with his passing?"

The Elders went silent.

"We were deep within the mountain, seeing to a separate matter at the time," Daxian the Elder explained. The boy shuffled again, uncomfortable.

"Father, did our ancestors not say to listen when the Land speaks?" the boy said, making a strange sign with his hands. The focus of the Master of the Grand Ravine sharpened.

"They did," Daxian the Elder said, watching his son carefully.

"Last night, the Land spoke. I would have been a fool not to listen."

The strongest Elder in the meeting considered his son's words before making the same sign.

"Is there any way we can meet this man?" he asked.

Daxian the Younger nodded.

→

Xi Kong followed the boy into the streets.

"Where is this Master?" Elder Gang asked, frowning around the street.

Guo Daxian pointed.

A large, tanned man had a child on his shoulders, the girl eagerly hammering a nail into a new construction.

"That's it. You got it, Ning," he said encouragingly; she threw her body into each blow, grinning.

He had tanned skin, instead of pale purity. He had freckled blemishes adorning his cheeks. His body was built like a thug, instead of for lithe grace. The man looked nothing like a cultivator at all.

And yet . . . there he was.

Men wearing Shrouded Mountain Sect robes swept the street behind him.

There were no guards. They were not tied up. They were sweeping the roads diligently, and without complaint.

This was the Hidden Master that his daughter had spoken of.

The three Elders were frozen as Daxian the Younger shifted uncomfortably.

The little girl finished hammering in her nail.

"Great job, Ning. But you gotta get down for a minute, okay?"

The girl on top of his shoulders pouted as the man gently set her onto the ground.

"I'll be back later, though. I promise, 'kay?" He held his pinky out to the child, who with all seriousness took it.

"You'd better!" she commanded impetuously. The man laughed.

Then he rose and waved her off. The expert took a breath and glanced at the Elders. There was a gentle summer breeze—

And then all of them froze.

One moment, the man was nothing. The next . . . they all felt very, *very* small.

They all realised exactly what Guo Daxian the Younger had been talking about.

As the farmer looked at them, so too did something that encompassed the entire town.

"Yingwen, with me, please," the man said. One of the Shrouded Mountain Sect disciples—presumably Yingwen—dropped everything he had and bowed his head to the man.

The man, this Master Rou, turned to them.

"Let's talk," he stated simply.

CHAPTER 57

SUDDEN POSITION OF AUTHORITY

Let's talk. Let's talk?! Really, that was the best I could come up with?

I kept my face as calm as I could. There was a gross feeling in the back of my throat, but I forced it down. I really wasn't cut out for acting stern, and I might have overdone it. Mostly because I had no real clue what I was doing.

I had rehearsed the conversation in my head while working on the demolished shop. I'd have to watch where I stepped next time. What was I thinking? Next time? I couldn't stop my mind from racing through it all again. What I wanted, what I planned on doing . . . and all that went out the window as the Sect Elders approached.

For all that I could probably punch my way out of a fight if push came to shove, that was one thing I wasn't prepared to do. I had to politick! With men who had been doing it for longer than I'd been alive—even if I stacked my age and Rou's age on top of each other. Forty wasn't exactly old for a cultivator.

I tugged at my Qi a bit. It was bubbling like when Meimei had talked to me nearly a year ago, after I had sent that Blaze Bear packing.

The three Elders who had come to meet me now led the way, walking in front of me. The one on the left was obviously Xiulan's father. He had the prettiest eyes I'd ever seen on a dude. It's kind of a stereotype that girls get their looks from their moms, and I'd thought that too, to be honest. But, well, Xiulan's dad was pretty. He was still obviously masculine, with his topknot and small beard, but he definitely looked like Lanlan. This wasn't how I wanted to meet the man, frowning at him and being led into the Dueling Peaks.

The other guy, Guo Daxian the Elder . . . well, he looked like a biker. He had his arms all tatted up, dark hair and eyes, and a bandana holding his hair back. His build was different than most people I'd seen in the Azure Hills, kinda like the guy who I'd handed the hammer to earlier. Something about the frame and the eye shape.

The third guy looked stereotypical in comparison. Elder Gang had hard eyes, a long beard, and fine robes.

The Shrouded Mountains guy, Yingwen, was behind all of us, walking in my shadow.

"We shall convene in the Grand Hall, if it pleases you, Master Rou," Xiulan's dad, Cai Xi Kong, asked politely, turning back to me. The question startled me, especially since it was strange seeing those eyes on somebody else. "Is there any refreshment in particular you would prefer?"

"I'm fine with anything," I said simply. He nodded at my statement, going quiet. He seemed to realise I didn't want to talk too much.

"Cleaning up the town . . . you tasked our disciples with this?" Elder Gang asked lightly.

"They were aimless without you, and their hands were idle. I set them a task. It's really rather rude not to clean up after yourself," I replied.

I was a bit surprised when Gang nodded. "A wise course of action, Master Rou," he said, before we lapsed into silence again.

I did feel some of my tension fade as we got closer and closer to the mountain. Fear was replaced by awe at the Dueling Peaks.

"It's quite a sight," I couldn't help but say to the Elders, pausing for a moment. The guys leading stutter-stepped before smiles broke out on their faces.

The Dueling Peaks were stunning. I imagined this must be what people felt when they saw the Colosseum or the pyramids of Giza. I'd never been to either, but even the pictures contained a bit of their grandeur. Ancient constructs of stone that made you question how humans could ever possibly build something this vast. Sure, they were cultivators . . . but it was still impressive. I hadn't really been in the right state of mind as I left Raging Waterfall Gorge to appreciate any of the things I had passed by. *Maybe I should take Mei on a tour sometime.*

A mountain reached into the sky, looking like it had been split in two by a sword, with the largest stadium I had ever seen cradled between the two peaks. The colourful pennants and flags that crisscrossed the gap added to the appeal.

It was beautiful, even if it did look a bit like something out of a video game.

The entrance to the inner complex was an absolutely massive gate, which was already open. Statues flanked us on either side on the path leading to the gates; some of them had clearly been broken long ago, weathered and ruined.

Then we were beneath the mountain. There were wide, vaulted ceilings and ancient-looking murals covering the entire place. Light crystals burned in the walls, throwing everything into sharp relief under the orange light.

A mighty urge to just go exploring down the corridors came over me. I had been a bit of a history buff, or at least I liked reading about it. I loved the tales of ancient heroes and had spent hours looking at the monuments the ancient people had built. This place felt like a living museum. Except with no barriers or velvet rope preventing you from getting as close as you'd like . . . it was tempting.

But would I ever be able to? I couldn't exactly go tourist mode in a place like this anymore. All of a sudden I was somebody. A somebody who was being escorted to speak with the most powerful people in the province.

That thought brought me crashing back down to earth. I fiddled with my Qi again, trying to stop the annoying, bubbling, and irritated feeling that it produced.

We eventually arrived at a large set of double doors. Glowing runes on them flared as they opened of their own accord. Beyond them was a massive room. Ancient banners hung on the walls. A large stone table dominated the room, long and rectangular. And there sat the Elders on stone . . . well, they almost looked like thrones, all of them facing towards the door as I entered. Twenty people stared directly at me.

I looked over them and their placid expressions. A couple of them even looked away as I met their eyes. It was a bit weird having so many older people be, well . . . intimidated by me.

To be honest, I was kind of upset with everybody in this room, the Elders. They either hadn't noticed the fight last night or had been too consumed with whatever they were doing in here to care.

They all stood up as we entered.

There was an obvious spot free at the very end of the table. I took a breath to calm myself and walked towards it as Xiulan's dad, Biker-dude, and Elder Gang went to their own seats. Soon, everybody was standing around the table.

Biker-dude took the lead. "We, the Elders of the Azure Hills, pay our respects to Master Rou," he intoned, bowing lower than I had been expecting him to.

"We pay our respects to Master Rou," the rest of the room chorused, bowing as one.

I kind of didn't know what to do here, so I just raised my hands and inclined my head.

"I wish that we could have met under better circumstances," I said, trying to put on a friendly smile. I think it failed spectacularly—I felt the corners of my lips twitch.

With the pleasantries done, we all sat down on the ancient and uncomfortable-looking chairs. There were five dark lines in a strange design on each of them.

To my surprise, mine lit up. The dark lines thrummed. Green, red, a dull brown-orange, gold, and blue, converging on a spot above the backrest's head. It looked . . . well it looked like it had a bunch of LEDs in it. The rest of the chairs, where the Elders were sitting, lit up too. Although every other one of theirs only had one colour each. Xiulan's dad's chair lit up green.

They had frigging gamer chairs. The thought was absurd, but that was what it looked like.

The room was uncomfortably silent after that. Biker-dude was staring wide-eyed at me.

I took a breath, putting it out of my mind while I tried to compose myself. I nearly tugged at my Qi again, but instead I pushed it away.

The silence stretched on. I felt my mouth go dry as they all stared at me expectedly until finally I cleared my throat.

"I hope that none of your disciples are in too much trouble for helping out Tigu? I know they all took a big risk doing that," I asked. I wouldn't say that all the cultivators in the streets were good people quite yet . . . but they had helped me out quite a bit. I wouldn't forget it.

"No, Master Rou, they are not," one of the Elders declared, bowing. "They showed honour and virtue in interfering on her behalf."

There were several more nods from the long table. The actions looked a bit too rapid to me.

Well . . . that was easy.

I nodded, and everybody lapsed into silence again. They were waiting for me to take charge, apparently, so I turned to Yingwen, signaling for him to start speaking.

"We, the Disciples of the Shrouded Mountain, have surrendered ourselves to Lord Rou's care because of . . . extenuating circumstances . . ."

I stayed mostly quiet as Yingwen explained the situation, or at least the story that the Shrouded Mountain Sect wanted to go with. The drunken brawl was started by the Shrouded Mountain Sect disciples. That much . . . well, that much I could agree on, even if I didn't like it.

I saw Xiulan's dad looking kind of annoyed at the story. Yingwen was speaking like a politician, carefully considering his words so that it *almost* sounded like it wasn't his fault.

For some reason, I had expected a bunch of shouting, "You dares?!" and spitting blood, but they all just ended up listening quietly to Yingwen's statement, digesting and considering his words.

They looked thoughtful once Yingwen fell silent. And . . . well, a bit more like people than I'd expected, instead of featureless automatons. They muttered to each other. Some appeared pleased, while others didn't particularly seem to like the direction this was going.

"Such a mess."

"Hmph. If it weren't the Shrouded Mountain Sect . . ."

"It's quite the stretch . . ."

I could make out the voices, the snippets of nearly silent muttering, though it was interrupted when one of the Elders, Biker-dude at the end, cleared his throat.

"What about your Young Master?" Biker-dude asked after Yingwen finished.

Yingwen looked directly at him. "It is a matter between the Shrouded Mountain Sect and Lord Rou," he said bluntly. "Though . . . I believe that Lord Rou will soon have the utmost gratitude of our Sect."

At this he turned and bowed to me.

"Why?" one of the women asked. Her face was half-hidden by a veil, a wide-brimmed hat on the table in front of her. "Why would the Shrouded Mountain Sect be willing to accept these terms? Why would they be willing to forgive all of this?"

The other Elders all seemed to agree with the woman's skepticism.

Yingwen looked at me, and I couldn't help but sigh. *Guess we aren't going to get out of this without me pulling out the scroll.*

As I took the scroll out, I finally understood why all those Young Masters liked saying, "You dare oppose my Sect?!" It was really, *really* nice to have a get-out-of-jail-free card.

I still felt kind of shitty for using it, though. Especially after saying to Lu Ri that I was fine and could handle everything for myself—I'd ended up leaning on the reputation of a place I hated.

This all would have been infinitely harder without a piece of paper from a powerful Sect. I knew it was lucky as hell I had it, and I knew relying on it *too* much was a bad idea, but for today it was what I needed to do.

I slapped my metaphorical dick on the table, opening the piece of parchment.

"Because *nobody* wants this to escalate," I said.

There were exhales of shock. Several people recoiled. One guy's mouth actually started leaking blood . . . which was concerning. I hadn't known that people actually did that. I'd thought it was just an expression.

Finally, Biker-dude, who I guess was the leader, spoke.

"I see. This explains much. But Master Rou . . . whatever do you need us for?" he asked.

"It's your home. Some of your students were hurt. It would be irresponsible to leave you in the dark . . . and I would also ask your opinion on the matter of reparations."

"Reparations?" Elder Gang asked. He suddenly looked eager, leaning forwards like he was about to get an early Christmas present. A kind of greedy gleam shone in his eyes that I instantly disliked.

Well, if they think I'm going to squeeze the Shrouded Mountain for resources, they're about to be disappointed.

I didn't exactly know what to ask for. So I asked for the things I thought made sense.

"To pay for the rebuilding of the town. Reparations to the families of the two mortals who died. As for the rest . . . I've had my justice." My stomach twisted as I remembered killing a man. Then I levelled my gaze at the Elders.

This was over. The guy who'd ordered it was dead as a doornail. Honestly, I probably could have asked for more. Squeezed the Shrouded Mountain Sect. Would it be seen as a weakness that I hadn't? I didn't know, and I'm not sure I cared to even if it did. All I knew was that I wanted nothing to do with the Shrouded Mountain Sect. They had apparently missed a Demonic Cultivator in their midst—

I paused. Had they missed him, or was he allowed to do what he did? Yingwen seemed pretty shocked about it, so at least the rank and file thought it was bad news . . . but the Elders . . . ?

Maybe I would need to ask Lu Ri for a favour after all.

I shook my head. That was for the future. For today, I had a simpler goal. The people who had been hurt . . . I'd help them. They were my people now. If I had to go out and do cultivator things to help, I'd do it.

I wasn't going to risk them by relying on people who probably didn't like me for something like that. If they poisoned the things they gave us or something . . . Meimei was good, but her area of expertise was mortal poisons, not the bioweapons cultivators could make.

I wanted them gone. Yesterday. Maybe I could go around acting big and taking things . . . but I had less than zero intent to start that fight. Some people might have needed to die for what happened the previous night, but at the same time an eye for an eye made the whole world blind. The cycle of vengeance stopped here. If anybody took issue with it, I'd fight back . . . but I hoped it wouldn't come to that.

Or the very earth would rise up and go to war.

I looked up at the Elders again, who were waiting for me to finish. "I was wondering what the . . . *Esteemed Elders* of the Azure Hills think would be right for such an . . . event," I said, hoping they'd at least have some ideas.

Everybody paused.

The cultivators started discussing things among themselves in low voices.

I bit back a sigh. *This is gonna take hours. Dealing with cultivators is so damn stressful.*

□

Two thousand li north, a certain Lord Magistrate paused while doing his paperwork.

He felt oddly peaceful. Like some kindred spirit had finally grasped his woes.

He smiled and took a sip of his tea.

□

The conversation was subdued as they retired to discuss things over some tea. Master Rou was seated at a table. Beside him, the Shrouded Mountain Sect disciple was on his knees, making the man tea like he was a servant. Every Elder in the room was having trouble concentrating—they all kept sneaking glances at Master Rou.

The Elders had thought they'd been prepared to meet a powerful Master. Yet Rou Jin had caught them off guard from the moment he had appeared. First was his appearance.

Master Rou's simple clothes were covered in dust. His face was spotted with freckles. He had a tanned brown skin one saw on labourers.

All things that showcased a lack of mastery to cultivators. A lack of control and ability. A life of proper cultivation should have prevented them. Body refinement would have excised the imperfections entirely.

Jadelike skin and a body free of defects were what was desirable.

Yet his appearance belied the feeling that silenced all who gazed upon him.

He sat in the stone chair like it was a throne, greeted by the Dueling Peaks. None of the Elders had even known the chairs to ignite in such a way, forming a five-coloured halo of light above the man's chair. It was like the mountain itself was welcoming the Emperor, not a dirty labourer off the streets. It would likely lead to years-long discussions on the true nature of this ancient arena, and countless hours spent poring over the old manuals just to see what it all meant.

And then the power stopped, vanishing into thin air like it never existed. Master Rou had displayed a mastery of Qi control those in the Azure Hills had only ever read about.

All of a sudden, it was a mere mortal sitting at the head of the table.

"What a monster," Elder Shu muttered.

None of the gathered Elders cared to disagree with him.

"Yes . . . yes, he is a monster," Elder Daxian said. He was the most distracted of them all, tapping his fingers against his leg and thinking deeply on the matter. "He gives us much face by even consulting us."

"We could see how hard we can bleed those bastards for this. The man is *strong*. The resources we could ask for would be but a drop in the bucket for the Shrouded Mountain. Would he even care for their pitiful value?" Elder Gang asked.

"You're a fool for wanting to press the Shrouded Mountain," Elder Xinling snarled, a voice of caution. "He has restrained himself; we should also restrain ourselves. The Cloudy Sword Sect is said to value etiquette and temperance. If we reach beyond our grasp, his mood may turn."

Xi Kong sighed and looked towards the ceiling. He loathed politicking. His instinct as a father wanted him to demand a vast price for those bastards harming his daughter . . . but she was under the powerful expert's protection. There was more to be found for Xiulan there than petty revenge against the Shrouded Mountain Sect. What reparations could he demand that were not already being given by this man?

"Elder Cai, Rou Tigu was under your roof. Did you know about him?" Daxian asked after shaking his head.

Xi Kong shook his head. "My daughter was healed by the powerful expert after slaying Sun Ken. When she came back to us then, she told us he was impressed with her abilities and so he gifted her training. After that, she returned to him . . . and he trusted her enough to send his disciples to stay with us at our Sect's manor for the tournament."

The other movers and shakers of the Azure Hills considered his statement.

"He remained quiet for a reason, then," Daxian concluded. "But why the Azure Hills? Most cultivators of power say they feel uncomfortable in this land, yet he doesn't seem perturbed at all."

They lapsed into silence.

"Then we must find a happy medium and not overreach. Exercise caution . . . and make sure those mortals get their repayment," Xi Kong said.

"Director Huizong will be happy, at least," Elder Gang grumbled.

"Are we in agreement?" Daxian asked. There was a pause as the Elders considered the question.

"What else could we be, save for in agreement?" Elder Gang muttered.

The Elders stood as one and approached the man. He looked up from his tea and raised his eyebrow.

"We, the Elders of the Azure Hills, have finished our discussions, Master Rou. We shall create for you a document to peruse at your leisure."

The man raised an eyebrow at their words.

"Already? Well, that's good. We'll wait for news from the Shrouded Mountain Sect Disciples . . . and with luck, this will all end without any issue."

He spoke with calm optimism.

"Yes. We would request Zhou Yingwen stay, so we may make sure the details of this tale are accurate. No harm shall come to him; you have our word," Daxian said.

The Master nodded. "Thank you for taking the time to speak with this Rou Jin," he said, rising from his seat and bowing slightly. The Elders scrambled to emulate him, but no one else spoke a word.

They simply bowed. All except Cai Xi Kong.

"Forgive me, Master Rou, but . . . why here? Why the Azure Hills?" he asked carefully.

The man seemed surprised at the question. He considered it and responded.

"Because it's relatively peaceful and quiet here. I . . . didn't want to be bothered," the man stated. "Though that may no longer be possible. I'll figure out some way that you can contact me, if there's an emergency, but I would *appreciate* it if you respected the boundaries of my home."

As the words finished, an inkling of his power came back. The ground under their feet seemed to writhe with displeasure at the mere thought of them visiting.

"Of course, Master Rou. We would not dream of trespassing," Daxian responded immediately. Xi Kong saw some of the Elders wince slightly. They had likely been imagining sending their students to negotiate with him . . . but breaching a Master's requested privacy with such petty concerns was just not done.

Rou Jin nodded. The feeling of being judged faded.

"We'll keep in touch, then, and make sure this all goes smoothly," he declared. "If you'll excuse me . . . I have a house to finish."

The lights in the room darkened as he exited, leaving the Elders of the Azure Hills to contemplate the words and deeds of this peerless master.

↔

I marched right out of the room and down the hall. I didn't make it very far, though, as I chose a nearby door and went for it. It glowed briefly and then opened automatically.

I stepped in and the door closed behind me. It was another beautiful stone room, carved with reliefs and richly adorned.

I managed to keep from hyperventilating until it shut with a *click*.

I had no fucking clue what I had just done. Had it gone well? Had I done poorly? I could only guess.

Fuck me, I hated being the guy in charge.

I slumped against the wall. I had come in, said my piece, and everybody had just . . . agreed to it. No arguments. No nothing. Just "Yes, sir."

There was no way everything was that easy, was it? Was this how things were supposed to go? I had no idea.

I ran my hand through my hair. Meimei was getting lessons from Lady Wu . . . maybe I could ask the Lord Magistrate for some help with this whole high-society-and-negotiations thing. He seemed pretty good at it . . .

Slowly, I stopped jittering. I took deep, calming breaths. It had turned out fine. Everything would work out. All I had was a hope and a prayer. But with luck . . . Well, with luck I wouldn't be dragged any further into this mess than I already was.

Just because I didn't hide didn't mean I wanted to deal with people or . . . kill anyone. I wanted my charming, slow, pastoral life, damn it. Go away, xianxia!

Ugh, and I have to meet with the Azure Jade Trading company too . . .

Was it bad that I was just as nervous about that as I had been about stepping into a room full of cultivators? The Elders had been . . . well, less extra than I had been expecting, but that was a good thing. They were people, not characters. They almost seemed reasonable.

Or maybe they'd just been shitting their pants too hard.

Man, how did these people act so grim and serious for so long?!

CHAPTER 58

SMALL CHANGES

"Your characters are amazing!" the mortal, Guizhong, exclaimed in praise to Chen Yang. He stared in wonder at the sign, proudly proclaiming *Guizhong Bakery*. Chen Yang grinned. He had practised for years to refine his writing, dabbling in poetry in the hopes of one day penning a work as enlightened as his ancestor's. *The Ballad of the Framed Sun* was something he read at least once a month, internalizing its lessons and practising the brushstrokes. It was amusing to think after all the years of practice, his first true work was a sign for a bakery. Still, it looked quite good, if he did say so himself!

The sun was getting lower in the sky, which was reflecting the colours of dusk. Chen Yang rose, looking around at the streets. They were certainly less messy now. A lot of the debris had been cleaned up, though the roads were still in pretty bad shape. They looked ripped up with piles of stone beside them.

He grimaced at the amount of work that still needed to be done. Last night, in the heat of the moment, it hadn't seemed too bad. But in the light of day after it was all over . . . He had seen how fast the mortals could work—this would have taken them months to clean everything up.

He turned away from the road and looked back at his sign. Yes, the mortal was right. His calligraphy *was* great. Ai had cut the piece of wood he had written on for him, and now all who looked upon this sign would surely be drawn into the bakery!

The man could boast for generations that the Young Master of the Framed Sun Sect had painted the sign above his door! Maybe Yang would do more. The Framed Sun Sect's main compound was perhaps a day's journey away, on another hill, so that they could see the entirety of the mountain. There was a little village quite close, and he did enjoy eating at the one noodle shop. Madame Fang's was delicious. Maybe he'd do a sign there too, just to show his appreciation—

"So *this* is what you all have been up to. Hmm. Acceptable characters, Disciple. You've been practising."

Yang flinched as his father's voice echoed from behind him. He'd been so engrossed in his work that he hadn't noticed the Elders once more stalking the streets, their faces severe.

Yang swallowed as his father gazed at him. His fellow disciples shuffled their feet, pausing in their sawing and hammering. One carefully put down a mortal he had been holding up. His father examined the house they had rebuilt. Yang clearly remembered his father once telling him to *never* lower himself to a mortal's level. That their Sect was weak enough as it was, without the ridicule from other Sects. Yang glanced anywhere but his father's eyes. He could see others waiting for the rebuke.

Instead, there was a simple command.

"Continue," his father decreed.

"Wha—?" Chen Yang asked, mouth open in shock.

"You have been given a task, continue it," his father repeated, walking closer to their building material. "In fact, what wood is this?"

His father picked up one of the planks, flipping it over in his hands like it was something he had never seen before. He looked to the startled mortal, who had been stacking the planks.

"It's . . . uh, well, what we used before, Master Cultivator." The mortal trailed off.

Yang's father pushed his Qi into it and looked at it from all sides. "It's warped. There are defects, and it wasn't dried properly," his father said after he finished examining it. The man winced.

"Good wood is expensive, Master Cultivator," the mortal ventured.

"Expensive, you say?" the Master of the Framed Sun Sect asked. He pondered the wood, then smiled brilliantly. "Well, that's fine. Son! Get only the best for this mortal! Price is no object!"

His command echoed through the streets. Yang saw several other Elders now stroking their beards, more than a few nodding heads.

Guizhong's jaw dropped.

"Yes, indeed. We shall rebuild it *better*, not merely as it was. And we shall repair the most, out of any Sect in the city. The tournament was lost to us, but now we have another prize!" his father declared.

"Thank you, Master Cultivator!" the mortal shouted, immediately bowing. "You're too kind, Master Cultivator!"

Orders were given and, clearly surprised, several more mortals stopped what they were doing to watch. They pulled down some of the other pieces of wood and set about examining the stone while his father looked on.

Yang, confused, leaned in. "Father . . . why?" he asked.

The man's smile widened a bit and he winked at Yang. "We aren't paying for it. The Shrouded Mountain Sect is. It's a bit petty to demand recompense in such a way, but mortal building materials aren't *that* expensive."

Yang's eyes widened at his father's wink. The man looked back down at the street, where Master Rou was accepting a drink of water from a mortal girl. She was tiny, with brown hair and eyes. The most average mortal one could see, really. Master Rou accepted the drink with a grin, thanking her for her generosity.

The Master of the Framed Sun Sect considered Master Rou, then turned to the pile of logs.

He picked up one of the hammers and tested its weight before turning his gaze to the house consideringly, almost like he was about to join them . . . before he put down the hammer again and instead went to check on what his other disciples were doing.

The day passed, dusk turning to night as they toiled.

On Yang's last trip of the day to get some wood, he passed by Master Rou. Yang stopped and watched the strange expert. He was crouched beside the same little girl from earlier, holding up a single nail. The girl had a hammer in her hands, though with how small she was it looked like she was trying to wield one of the Hermetic Iron Sect's war-hammers.

"The last one, and then I've kept my promise. A shop in a day," he said to her with a grin.

The little girl smiled up at him. "And I can hammer the last nail in?" she said eagerly.

"'Course you can, kiddo. Remember what I showed you!"

The little girl climbed a ladder. Her father watched, a bit worried, while Master Rou held on to one end.

Yang watched, a slight smile on his face, as she carefully worked her way into position. She took up her hammer and aimed carefully, tongue stuck out from between her teeth. She swung . . . and missed. She dropped the nail. Master Rou just handed her up another. It took twenty strikes. Twenty tiny strikes to hammer it in while Master Rou waited patiently.

When she had finally succeeded at her task, Master Rou raised the girl upon his shoulders and praised her. She giggled before running with abandon to her waiting mother. Her mortal father grinned and bowed to Master Jin.

"Good practice. My own is going to be coming soon," Master Jin confided in the mortal with a little smile.

The man, who Yang recalled had been so lost and despondent in the morning, laughed and offered congratulations.

Yang took it all in before he shook himself, darting off to finish his own project. If a man like Master Rou was doing that . . . well. Was it really lowering yourself?

And so the first day passed.

They returned bright and early the next day and toiled all through it.

□

The sun had set. Lanterns twinkled with light, shining like flame beetles. The smells of food and drink were fading, a supper freshly finished. Voices carried on the wind. The day was finally winding down, a gasp of tension released after the terror of the night and the sudden labours of the day.

Cai Xi Kong sat upon the roof of his manor, observing the stars. It was a habit of his, to climb up on something tall whenever he needed to find peace. A habit his daughter shared. He took a sip of tea, which was a fine blend from Yellow Rock Plateau, and glanced down at the guesthouse. He heard laughter and bright noise rising up from within. Master Rou had joined Xiulan and the other students in the guesthouse. A great honour, yet one he didn't know how to approach. Xi Kong had, of course, welcomed the man, making available for him the finest rooms as the most honoured guest he had ever received. If Master Rou had demanded Xi Kong's own bed, it would have been given over without hesitation.

Instead, the man had simply said he would sleep in the guest room on the floor.

Who was Xi Kong to deny the man? He had no clue what to make of Master Rou. Peerless expert one moment, mortal man the next. Stern commander one instant . . .

Xi Kong glanced down at the sound of a loud, joyous laugh from the guesthouse. He looked in through the open window.

A bright happy smile adorned Master Rou's face—he was howling with laughter at something the man known as Rags and Yun Ren were doing.

Master Rou clapped Loud Boy on the back, nodding encouragingly at the unfortunate and whispering something in his ear.

Xi Kong observed Liu Xianghua, daughter of the Misty Lake Sect, approaching him with her brother at her side. Both made to bow.

Master Rou placed his hand on Liu Xianghua's shoulder midbow and pushed her upright, shaking his head. Gou Ren waggled his finger at her, and Xi Kong heard him say, "I *told* you he'd say that!"

The woman appeared stunned . . . and then tears gathered at the corners of her eyes as she this time completed the bow. "This Liu Xianghua will repay Master Jin and Senior Sister a hundred—no, a *thousandfold*!" she thundered, her eyes blazing as she brought her fist up to the sky.

The man just smiled at her as Tigu draped herself over his shoulders.

Xi Kong carefully kept his gaze away from the Profound-level chicken—no, Spirit Beast. He had nearly spat blood when the creature had introduced itself as Master Rou's disciple. The fact that his daughter called him Senior Brother had required a stiff drink.

Xi Kong shook his head. He would have to talk to the Spirit Beast soon and take its measure.

His thoughts tonight returned to focus not on the cultivator below or his strange family but on his daughter's smile.

He'd had no idea his daughter could smile like that.

How *could* she smile after what had happened to her? He had called her to him earlier. His daughter had sat in front of him, a look of serenity on her face. She'd sipped her tea even as Xi Kong paced throughout the room, agitation pouring off him.

"It was a worthy sacrifice," she'd said simply.

The Third Stage of the Initiate's Realm. He felt his heart ache to know she had been reduced so far. He wanted to rage. To scream. But he did not. He could not. Not when his daughter stared up at him with that expression.

She looked at peace. Like her mother before she'd gone on her journey. Before Liusei had left and never returned.

That soft little smile.

There was another shout, and Xi Kong came back to the present.

Master Rou slung an arm around Xiulan's shoulder and pulled her into a half hug as she laughed, looking more at peace than he had seen her in years.

Pride warred with shame. Xi Kong's shoulders slumped slightly. How fast she'd grown without him and the Sect. How fast she had grown, listening to the teachings of another. He wished he had been of more help to her. And right now . . . he didn't think she needed his aid at all.

A cultivator faced the heavens alone. That was the mantra that had been pounded into his head by his father.

He looked down again at the laughter of the younger generation and pondered the wisdom of those words before he sighed and downed the rest of his tea.

It was cold.

□

"Thank you for taking the time to meet with us, Master Jin," Shan Daiyu, the Mistress of the Azure Jade Trading Company, said with a graceful bow, hiding her face behind a fan with bowing willows on it. The design signified, in the language of the courts, peace and contentment.

Two things she was *certainly* not feeling right now, but the game had to be played.

The cultivator smiled at them and nodded. "Sorry about the circumstances, and for postponing the meeting," the man said, sounding genuinely apologetic.

The thing that had struck her the most as she walked into the meeting was how young Rou Jin looked. With his freckled face and tanned skin he looked like one of the boys who did the heavy lifting on caravans. His smile reminded her not so much of the cultivators she knew but of her grandson, boyish and embarrassed after making a mess she'd inevitably have to clean up.

Yet this boy was taking responsibility for everything that had happened.

It was hard to reconcile that with the man who could bring to heel every Elder in the province. A man who could bring to heel the Shrouded Mountain Sect. He had a disciple of that very Sect who could walk the breadth of the Azure Hills with impunity, bowing his head and acting like a loyal dog at his command. He should be nothing less than a cunning power, yet he stared back at her with honest sincerity in his eyes.

"Think nothing of it, Master Jin," her husband said. "We are at your disposal."

Any other man, even a cultivator, would have at least gotten some small manner of rebuke for wasting their time.

The cultivator nodded and sipped his tea. "Still, it was rude of me," he said, giving them face.

"How is the reconstruction going, Master Jin?" her husband asked. "We've had some reports, but I would be honoured to hear your opinion on it."

Her husband easily distracted him, smiling attentively and nodding along as Master Rou spoke eagerly of a shop he had finished repairing that day.

Shan Daiyu carefully studied the new variable in front of her.

For fifty years she and her husband had toiled, building the power and influence of the Azure Jade Trading Company.

She had braved Wrecker Balls like the legendary Road Emperor, Blaze Bears that torched entire caravans, and had once survived Two Venom Serpents spewing their toxic mist into the air. Hail, landslides, and scorching heat. Cantankerous cultivators, greedy nobles, the corrupt, and the banal. She had risen above it all.

She was the one who'd begun the great auction. Drawing from every corner of the Azure Hills those who could afford the rare goods she braved danger to bring. For fifty years she had hosted those auctions and events, carefully and politely managing to navigate the twists and turns of being a beautiful morsel in a den full of tigers. She had learned to read the currents and shifts in the powers that walked the Azure Hills. To walk with nobles, cultivators, and mortals alike.

She had built an Empire. A small one, perhaps, but it was hers.

Both she and her husband were getting old and weak. Yet she would not go without leaving a legacy that would last for generations beyond her. Shan Daiyu sought out something to put a stamp on the world. One last hurrah. And now, one last chance to forge a legacy was sitting on her shoulders. One last opportunity to provide for her family, to boost the Azure Jade Trading Company to heights unseen before the inevitable end to a mortal's life.

And then finally, like a gift from the heavens, little Bo had come down from the north with that syrup of his. A passing novelty at first. Until the man who'd sold him the syrup came down to Pale Moon Lake City with *three hundred bags* of gold-grade rice.

Master Jin was the answer. The answer to the company's biggest hurdle: breaking out of the Azure Hills and into the wider world. It was a goal Daiyu had worked for decades to accomplish. They need enormous capital and a surge of new connections to accomplish such a feat. They had already done price analysis, and it would have taken at least eight more years to get the finances they needed to embark on the plan Daiyu had wanted to pursue. Eight years that could be condensed into less than eight months with this bounty of rice.

Offering him their flower, Chyou, had been admittedly a bit of a long shot. But her granddaughter was intelligent, and men were men, even if they cultivated. The marriage would have borne fruit quickly. Her granddaughter would have taken over all that pesky mortal business for the man and left him to cultivate in peace. He would have all he needed, and Daiyu's Empire would have been secure for generations.

But he had rejected Chyou's advances; instead, he'd leveraged her *actual* skills. To the point where Daiyu's dear granddaughter was singing the man's praises, eager to help him, especially on that expedition to the south he had put in her head.

Which was why Daiyu was cautious.

As she sat with him today and listened to him talk, he sounded more like a nervous farm boy, but she could not forget. For this man to immediately realise her Chyou's worth . . . it spoke of great insight. Even now, he vacillated between agitation and absolute calm. It was nearly impossible to get a read on him.

"This Guan Ping is honoured that our Azure Jade Trading Company was so helpful to you. We strive for our members to be the best," her husband said. The cultivator nodded appreciatively.

Daiyu frowned behind her fan. This was going nowhere.

She closed her fan and glanced at her husband, tapping her finger twice on her knee. Her husband didn't nod, though she did see the two taps he made back.

Daiyu interjected herself smoothly. "Speaking of assistance, my dear granddaughter spoke at length about some manner of expedition to the south . . . ?" she asked pleasantly. It was foolish, in her opinion. Such an expedition would take years. But if Master Rou wanted specific, mortal plants . . . then the payoff had the potential to be legendary.

"Ah, yes. I'm sorry about that. I got a bit ahead of myself when I was talking to Chyou," the man apologised. "I'm uncertain if it's even feasible. If it doesn't work, please don't worry about it. I'd rather have accurate bad news than a pleasant lie."

Daiyu hummed, considering his words. At the very least, the man seemed impossibly reasonable. That was how he had acted with little Bo and Chyou, so she felt certain that she could conclude that he wasn't the mercurial sort. It wouldn't do any good to see if she could push that reasonable nature. He had, after all, reportedly destroyed Zang Li of the Shrouded Mountain in a single punch.

"We'll endeavour to keep you informed, Master Jin," she said, smiling vacuously at him.

Their talk started to meander again. Small talk was the basis for relationships, after all. Master Jin was quite the boisterous and chatty fellow. Enthusiastic, driven men were a treat, rather than the humourless boors she had to deal with regularly. As soon as they finished their tea, Master Jin announced he had to go.

"Thank you, Master Rou. If there's anything we can do to aid the reconstruction, please don't hesitate to contact us," her husband said.

The cultivator nodded.

"Thank you. And it was good to meet you both. I only wish it were under better circumstances."

"We are ever at your service, Master Jin," she said. "Although . . . there is one more minor matter. There appear to be dolls in the likeness of Mistress Tigu being sold in markets by a merchant house. We wished to make sure that you were aware of this. Of course, as a favour to you, we could put a stop to it . . ." she ventured. At once, the man's gaze sharpened.

He considered her words before he sighed. "I'll ask Tigu what she thinks about it . . . but if she agrees, that means she'll be getting royalties, yes?" Master Rou said casually.

Daiyu almost lost a grip on her expression in shock.

Royalties. A cultivator who knows about that sort of thing, instead of deriding mortal merchant work beneath them. "But *of course*, Master Rou. You are an honoured customer of our Azure Jade Trading Company. We always have our due, and as our generous friend, so shall you."

The cultivator grinned at them, a bright and toothy thing.

They waved him off with a smile as he went back to work, leaving her and her husband in the sitting room. Daiyu waved her hand, and the servants exited, drawing the shutters and leaving the elderly pair in privacy.

"What do you think?" her husband asked after a moment.

Daiyu considered the meeting.

"In all honesty, I do not believe our original assessments have changed," she said finally. "It's just that our new client is an order of magnitude more powerful than anticipated."

"We shall be the most loyal of servants, then. And feast upon the scraps falling off his plate?" Guan Ping mused.

"Yes," Daiyu agreed. "My dear, could you start on cost analysis for an expedition to the southlands? It should be feasible . . . I'll speak with Chyou and get the numbers she thinks will work. The damn fool girl was so giddy about it when I heard her on the transmission crystal . . ."

↔

Fenxian glanced backwards at his Brother Disciples. Five cultivators from the Shrouded Mountain Sect stared at the section of collapsed rock. Their faces were lined with stress, and their eyes were baggy from three days of searching without rest.

They stood on the side of Mount Tianliyu, about halfway up it, in the heart of Yellow Rock Plateau. Their yoked spirits pulling the carriage had carried them two thousand li in a day, up the side of the massive plateau, and high into the air. They had stopped for not even an hour to resupply and gather information, but had then chanced upon the lead of something impacting the mountain.

And so a grand search had been conducted, scouring the mountain.

"This is the place the mortals meant?" one of them asked. "Will there even *be* a body?"

"The hell if I know," another answered. "I'm just glad we found it."

Fenxian grimaced at the mound of rocks, covered in dead plants. If their mortal guide hadn't been adamant the rocks had fallen recently, they would have missed it—the formation looked like it had been there for years.

The hairs on the back of Fenxian's neck rose up at the proximity. His stomach felt like it was going to drop through his knees.

Because he could feel the ominous wind that came from the rocks.

They started digging.

The rocks fell away as they tore into the collapsed earth. Their fists shattered the ground easily, tearing into tons of stone. And then the stench hit them.

One of their number gagged, doubling over, and Fenxian grimaced. He looked down into the crater.

There was a corpse with its chest caved in. It looked like it had been rotting for weeks, rather than just a couple days. The skin was drooping, and it appeared like the body had been consumed from the inside, decomposing for months instead of days. A disgusting slurry of oil and blood pooled in the crater, swirling and stinking.

Fenxian turned away from the body of Zang Li, the cadaver's face twisted in horror.

Deep enough shit to cover the Shrouded Mountain indeed.

"Come on. Let's get this over with," he commanded.

They ended up using a spiked pole to retrieve the body—none of them were willing to touch the foul concoction that filled the hollow. After packing the body into a barrel, the weary Disciples of the Shrouded Mountain Sect sealed it tight with a preservation talisman.

"The illusion repelled, the truth laid bare," Fenxian spoke into the transmission stone. "It was, in the end, the enemy."

His Brother Disciples bowed their heads, shame shrouding their auras.

Fenxian turned to the pool of filth, rage burning in his gut. This bastard . . . He had spat on the heroes of the Shrouded Mountain Sect. He had made mockeries of their power and dragged all of them to hell with him. Lighting crackled across his fingers.

There was a thunderous *boom* as he vented his rage, lightning arcing into the pool. The oil within recoiled from the strike burning and twisting like it was alive.

The disgusting liquid could not stand against the light of the righteous.

Fenxian fired again, and again, and again, until there was nothing left of the blood and oil.

"Rot in the hells, you bastard," he snarled, spitting on the ground.

CHAPTER 59

THE TRAVELLER'S TALE

When it was all said and done, when the thunder and Qi faded, this humble traveller emerged to a town that had suffered the ravages of battle.

Sixty-three buildings had been heavily damaged, five had collapsed completely, and the roads had been shattered and torn.

Upon witnessing the destruction wrought upon the fair town, the cultivators of the Azure Hills, being of high virtue despite their low ability, did descend upon it. Not with blades and techniques, but with mason's hammers and carpenter's saws.

They set themselves the task of making whole what was broken.

□

Bai Huizong, Lord Director of Spiritual Ascension Affairs, sighed heavily. He was seated in his office with his two most trusted employees.

"Are you all right, sir?" he heard his top aide, Hu, ask as he placed a drink in Huizong's outstretched hand. Huizong had his feet up in a chair as Cho massaged his shoulders. A damp cloth lay across his face, soothing his headache and preventing him from seeing the mess that was his desk. So much damn paperwork.

"I'll live. Lower, my dear, lower—oh." The fingers moved and Huizong sighed with relief. "That's the ticket." He heard the snort of amusement from the woman.

Huizong took a deep quaff of the wine and sighed in satisfaction.

The day had started out well enough. A talk with his suppliers, organising his aides, and commanding the staff of the mountain. Paperwork was last. He had sent out the usual polite request to the cultivators to be informed about what had happened, as a representative of His Imperial Majesty, fully expecting to be ignored.

He was entirely surprised when he'd gotten a message back with an apology for not speaking with him sooner.

That . . . that didn't happen. Huizong held the title of Director, true, but it was just that. A title. A grand one for a man who organised tournaments. He had as much power as the Sects let him have. And those in his position that overstepped their power . . . well, they weren't Lord Director for long.

His aide and the mistress of the workshop stayed silent as they waited for him to gather his thoughts.

"Things . . . well, things need a reevaluation, to say the least. That new cultivator? The rumours were true. Master Rou is in charge now. He led the procession in, took command of it. Then he explained what was going on with the rebuilding and assured me I wouldn't have to pay for any of it," Huizong said.

Hu hummed, then asked, "I know he managed to conscript the disciples into helping with the town . . . but how deferential were the other Elders?"

"Elder Xinling brought a guzheng along and played it for him as we took tea," Huizong said wryly. He felt the fingers on his shoulders pause.

"Didn't she stab Elder Gang a few years ago when he asked her to play for him, saying it wasn't for his crude ears?" Cho asked from behind his chair.

"Yes. *And* she wasn't wearing her veil." Huizong shook his head. "Well, if she wanted him to look, Master Rou didn't care. He complimented her playing, and then poured me tea . . . after Elder Daxian poured *him* tea." Huizong grunted. He sat up in his chair, pulling the cloth from his eyes, and focused on Hu. "Anything on him?"

Hu shook his head immediately. "No, sir. The information brokers refuse to divulge anything. Not even when I offered ten times the usual rates. They just kept saying they didn't know, and it was probably a good idea to stop asking."

Huizong grimaced. Those Plum Blossom bastards had run everybody else out of town, or taken them over. They were incredibly skilled, and their prices were great compared to the mess before. To have them suddenly go silent was . . . concerning.

"The Azure Jade Trading Company?"

"We only got a message from Lady Daiyu saying things can proceed, provided we agree to Master Jin's terms."

"She calls him Master Jin? Not Master Rou?" Huizong asked before taking a swig of wine and handing it off to Cho. There was a *glug, glug, glug* sound as the woman standing behind him took a seat and drained the bottle.

"Yes, sir. She said he was a *very* important customer."

Huizong grunted and grabbed the new bottle Hu passed him, considering the outcomes. Shake-ups to the hierarchy were normally chaotic. But this cultivator seemed determined to minimize the chaos. And he had politely requested that his name be omitted from any report, though he understood if Huizong had to talk to the authorities.

Huizong wasn't stupid. If the information brokers wanted to keep mum about the man, Huizong certainly wouldn't say anything. "Well, I'll say this about him. He works fast, and for that, I salute him."

Or rather, he planned to stay far out of his way, and reap the rewards as he always did with cultivators. He grinned as he got an idea. He could apply for emergency funds because of cultivator damage from Grass Sea City—and then pocket the whole lot.

The Shrouded Mountain Sect was going to be paying for everything . . . but the officials in the city didn't know that. The trick to embezzling was always to have some deniability.

And besides. His employees' bonuses had to come from *somewhere*. Better somebody else's pockets than his.

"On to the next subject. The catacombs. Did you get anything from Bao Wen, Hu?" Huizong asked. The man nodded, pausing in the middle of getting out an inkstone.

"Bao Wen was reluctant . . . but I managed to persuade him," Hu said simply. "The boy can't hold his drink. Though that is another matter that I would advise discretion on. Bao Wen says there's an entire archive down there. A complete library on the mountain and the Earthly Arena . . . and how to repair it."

Huizong froze.

"They can repair the floating mechanisms?" he asked.

"Bao Wen thought so, as did the Elders."

If they could repair the Dueling Peaks to their former glory . . .

Huizong grinned. He could feel the silver coins clinking already.

"Well, now that is some good news," he said lightly. "Excellent work, you two. This . . . well, it's turning out much better than I expected."

"No cultivator war?" Cho asked, making sure.

"No cultivator war," Huizong said. "Or at least I don't think there's going to be one today."

"Thank the heavens for that," Hu muttered before shaking his head. "I'll do the rounds and collect all the reports, sir. Your brush is ready for the report you have to send."

"What would I do without you, Hu?" Huizong asked with a chuckle.

"Flounder helplessly?" the man replied cheekily without any bite, setting off to do as commanded.

Cho sighed and got up too, starting to walk away. He gave her shapely rear a swat and the woman yelped, shooting a glare at him.

Then she reached out and stole his last two bottles of wine. Fair trade. He chuckled and turned to his parchment.

Just what to pen to his superiors, though . . . ? And how? He'd toe the line with the drunken brawl story. He wasn't stupid enough to air the Shrouded Mountain Sect's dirty laundry. Eventually, Huizong shrugged and simply wrote down what he thought would fly. *Drunken brawl, town repaired, old vaults found, no danger to the mountain. Requesting additional supplies.* Keep it as simple and dry as possible.

The heavens knew being at the epicenter of these events didn't make anything less confusing.

He finished writing, then read it over again. There, it sounded perfect. If significantly more polite and flattering in the courtly characters they used. It'd probably just be filed away like all the others, never seeing the light of day again.

He rang a small gong next to his desk, and a junior aide entered. He handed the letter off to the boy, then turned his attention to Master Rou's request for a feast to celebrate the reconstruction effort. It was a good idea, if he was being honest.

Imagine that. A cultivator with a good, practical idea.

□

The cultivators took to the crafts of the mortals with great speed and skill, never faltering for a moment. This humble traveller was amazed to see what would have taken mere mortals years to accomplish, the cultivators finished in three days.

The rubble was cleared in hours. The necessary supplies were procured out of their own coin purses, for it was commanded by one of the Elders that the common folk should not have to pay for their suffering.

Guo Daxian of the Grand Ravine did weave ropes in the style of the ravine tribes; Chen Yang of the Framed Sun Sect did craft new signs, his calligraphy enticing all that witnessed it; Tie Delun of the Hermetic Iron Sect did craft paving stones for the road, strong and enduring as iron. All that the cultivators touched was elevated by the touch of those striving for the heavens.

Indeed, each Sect competed to lay claim to which among their number was the most adroit at rebuilding. The Grand Ravine Sect in the end proved the champion, followed by the Framed Sun Sect—though there were arguments from the Rumbling Earth Sect that their repairing of the roadworks should have been valued more highly . . .

□

If anybody had told Cai Xi Kong he would at some point in his life sit down for tea with a rooster, he would have considered them mad. If they had said the rooster might be able to match him in battle . . . Xi Kong would have been forced to ensure that the one who uttered that grave insult never spoke again.

Now he was looking across the table at a Spirit Beast well into the Profound Realm. The rooster was the pinnacle of his kind, a creature out of an idealized painting. Each feather looked impossibly soft, yet chiseled from stone. His wattle and comb had not a single defect nor blemish. His beak and spurs shone in the light, like they had been freshly polished.

And he had just finished tying a cloth around his neck, and now settled in on the cushions stacked high so he could reach the table.

"Fa Bi De pays his respects to Cai Xi Kong," the rooster intoned, sweeping into an elegant and regal bow. His fox-fur vest was resplendent in the light of the sun. A necklace glinted with silver light, hanging down to the rooster's breast. Intelligence and refinement shone from the Spirit Beast's eyes.

"Cai Xi Kong pays his respects to Fa Bi De," Xi Kong returned. He poured tea from the pot between them. They were together on the balcony of a teahouse that overlooked the town. He had wished to speak with the creature about Xiulan and her time spent at "Fa Ram." It was necessary for Xi Kong to take measure of the expert tied to his daughter. Master Jin was a mystery. Opaque. Xi Kong could not understand the man.

And so, he had sought out the one who claimed to be his First Disciple. It was a Spirit Beast. Surely it could be outwitted and led into revealing what Xi Kong sought. "I thank you for your time. Your Master is busy, and I would not bother him with the mere concerns of a father."

The rooster cocked his head to the side, examining Xi Kong. "The Great Master is not one to feel bothered over such questions. Nay, I would dare say my Lord welcomes them. He enjoys such conversations," the rooster immediately replied. He bent his head down and sipped his tea with impeccable manners.

The rooster's words were light, but as Xi Kong took a sip of his tea he considered the implications.

Perhaps Xi Kong had been arrogant, but he had never met a Spirit Beast willing to sit down and talk. Those that could speak either just raged . . . or were horribly arrogant creatures sounding remarkably like some of the Young Masters Xi Kong knew. They were full of entitled arrogance. They thought the destruction they wrought was not just good, but *right*.

Still, he had some caution to him. In addition to the fact that the rooster was dear to Master Rou, he knew of Ri Zu the healer, who was, according to Liu Xianghua, beyond compare.

Xi Kong hummed and then decided upon bluntness. "Indeed. Master Rou is a man of virtue, and I dare not cast doubt upon his name. However . . . I would hear it not from the Master nor the student, but one . . . not as embroiled. One sees more of the mountain from an adjacent hill, no?"

The rooster considered Xi Kong for a moment—to his surprise it felt as if a seasoned warrior was taking his measure—before nodding.

"That is indeed a good point, Elder Xi Kong. What do you wish to know?" the rooster asked.

"Your thoughts upon her growth," Xi Kong began.

"Her growth, hm?" the rooster asked. Xi Kong raised his own cup to take another drink. "She was suffering greatly when she returned to us," the rooster stated.

Xi Kong froze, his cup halfway to his lips. *Suffering greatly?*

"Her sleep was disturbed. Her concentration wavered. It was my understanding that for several months she had struggled with the deaths of the soldiers she commanded," the rooster continued. "Their faces haunted her memories, and her battle with Sun Ken and the pressures placed upon her contributed."

His daughter hadn't spoken a word of it to him. But . . . wasn't that the way? Who among them would admit any sort of weakness? Xi Kong grimaced.

"She was aided in this . . . tribulation of the heart?" Xi Kong asked.

"She overcame it. With the aid of the Healing Sage and the Great Master, she was guided to recover. I believe her time within Fa Ram helped her make peace with the past."

"You face the heavens alone," his father had said, after striking Xi Kong across the face.

That was the last day any tears had come from his eyes.

Xi Kong shook off the memory.

"She received aid, and in return has aided us greatly. This is one of the pillars of my Master's knowledge: One who cheats the earth shall be cheated by it. One who gives to the earth shall surely be rewarded."

It sounded so simple, despite coming out of a rooster's mouth. Give and receive.

"And after . . . ?"

"Afterwards, she received the honour of being trained personally by the Great Master," the rooster stated simply. "Along with myself and Tigu."

"What manner of training does your Master command?" Xi Kong was intrigued by the man's methods. To raise even a rooster up so high must require great feats and meditation.

Bi De nodded, then told Xi Kong of the activities Xiulan partook in.

Looking after mortal children. Dodging balls of mud. Cooking, with ten levitating knives.

Individually, they sounded like childish games.

And yet . . . the control of her blades was exemplary. Her reactions and speed were enough that Xi Kong could not state with full confidence that he could win a battle against his own daughter.

Xi Kong looked away from the rooster to gaze down to the square. His eyes found his daughter. She was speaking with Guo Daxian the Younger, who was nodding in agreement. His daughter was smiling. Xi Kong had kept an eye on his still-healing daughter. He had watched as she approached the other Young Masters and Mistresses, joining in on their work and speaking to them. He had not stooped to eavesdropping . . . yet. Whatever was said seemed to have positive reception from most of them.

She was undiminished, confident. Her head was held high. She was . . . quite different from the girl he remembered. Before coming back from Fa Ram, his daughter had been closed off, standoffish. She'd had a mask in place between herself and the world at large. A tool to keep the unwanted away. It insulated her from danger and isolated her from everyone in turn. Xi Kong could not blame her for that choice. The looks and words she had received even at twelve had been appalling. Xi Kong had slain one man over it, a man who he'd thought was a friend.

And yet here she was. Willingly engaging with others, taking charge, being . . . open.

She was making and securing alliances instead of just being his obedient daughter. A single year had changed her so *much*.

He turned away from the scene below, back to the rooster. Bi De's talon shot out, cutting a pastry into bite-sized pieces. He then wiped the digit on a provided napkin.

Xi Kong leaned back in his chair, looking to the rooster. "Tell me, Bi De. Where do most of your contemplations lie? I, as my daughter, have contemplated deeply on the mysteries of a simple blade of grass."

The rooster perked up. "The majority of my meditations are spent upon the glory of the moon and its holy luster."

"The moon? Truly?" Xi Kong asked.

"Indeed. The holy aegis is the most perfect celestial object—"

The rooster was suddenly cut off by loud, obnoxious humming. Xi Kong glanced down at the street again, where the young disciple Gou Ren was stacking bricks, looking entirely too cheerful, a massive, idiotic smile on his face that Xi Kong could see from there.

Xi Kong raised an eyebrow. "Your Junior Disciple is certainly in a fine mood," Xi Kong observed.

"Ah. He disappeared for a few hours last night with Liu Xianghua," the rooster decreed, a knowing gleam in the Spirit Beast's eyes. "They've both been like that all day."

Oh my, Xi Kong thought.

That girl was entirely too rebellious. One should be wed before such things happened. But the passion of youth oft raged uncontained. And the daughter of his ally could have certainly picked a worse candidate.

The boy was going to be there for a while, though, and his voice was irritating.

Xi Kong paid for their tea. "Will you walk with me, Fa Bi De? I would continue our discussion, and would appreciate a change of scenery."

They spoke at great length about the grass, and the moon above; it was one of the best conversations Xi Kong had ever had.

□

For three days and three nights, the cultivators toiled. The roads became pristine. The houses of the mortals looked as palaces.

On the third day, the streets were swept for the last time; the one known as Master Rou proclaimed their duty finished, to the clamour of the crowds.

Thus was the town around the Dueling Peaks returned to glory.

Master Rou commanded that a feast be made; and so, according to his will it was. He honoured both the mortals and all who had aided in the reconstruction.

All those who knew how to cook went into his service. From the victor of the tournament, the Demon-Slaying Orchid, to his own disciples. From the

Demon-Slaying Orchid sprang forth sixteen knives, each one wielded with elegance and grace.

Rou Tigu, who took second place in the tournament, and her pet, a monkey of some manner that had fur of gold and a face as blue as the frosts, attended to the tables. She served mortals and cultivators alike without reservation.

The Lord Director and the Azure Jade Trading Company both added their considerable wealth to the festivities.

An accounting of the feast is as follows: three thousand baskets of pork baozi. Two thousand servings of dandanmian. Some three thousand fish and ten thousand pots of rice . . .

□

Xiulan sat with her father in the tearoom. The scent of tea was heavy in the air. There were noises of amusement from the guesthouse. Her father seemed . . . unsettled. He was silent, deep in thought, so Xiulan let him think. It was good to have a moment to gather one's thoughts, especially after such a feast, and it was nice to once more have tea with the Honoured Father. He had arranged some lotus mooncakes, their favourite dessert.

"You've been speaking at great length to the other Young Masters and Mistresses, Daughter," Xiulan's father observed quietly, finally breaking the silence.

"Yes, Father. I have," she stated. Internally she sighed. Xiulan wasn't sure she was prepared yet to speak to her father of her plans for the future. It was all . . . tentative. Approaching all the others, weakened as she was, had been a gamble. But in their minds, she was still the woman who had slain Sun Ken, won the tournament, and fought against the Shrouded Mountain Sect. The respect was there. It had earned her enough credit to be heard. Tigu had volunteered to come with her when she told the girl of her intentions, which had further heightened her legitimacy.

So when she had spoken to them of the possibility of a summit of the younger generation, most were receptive to it.

A step forwards. A step towards her own path.

Her father studied her, but he did not immediately press for answers on why she was meeting with the others, like Elder Yi had. Instead, there was simply trust.

"I see . . . well, enough about that. What are your plans for the future? Though your strength may be diminished for now, if you are certain it will return, you may still be made an Elder," he ventured.

Xiulan pondered the offer. It ought to have been an honour. She had earned it. But . . . Xiulan didn't feel quite ready to take the title. To take that step. She had things she wanted to do, and being an Elder . . . the responsibilities would hinder that. Xiulan was not ready to settle quite yet.

"With my injury, I cannot accept the title of Elder at the moment," Xiulan stated. "With your permission, father, I would rest and recover my strength for a few months before returning—and then I will depart upon my Dao," she said with conviction.

Her father's gaze was intent for a moment, before he sighed, seeming almost sad. "He has truly helped you greatly," he said quietly. "This man . . . who is he to you?"

Xiulan smiled at the question. Hidden Master. Strange farmer. Younger than her. A good friend.

"He is . . . Jin."

Her father met her words with silence. He took a breath at the look on her face and sighed. "Very well. You have my permission and my blessing," her father said, bowing his head.

Xiulan bowed deeply in return. "Thank you, Father."

She would stay several months, if they would have her. She did want to see that dance Bi De talked about. Perhaps . . . to the new year? Yes. To the new year. And then . . . in the spring, she would set off again—

"Though I would request an invitation to the wedding," her father said.

It took her a moment to process her father's words. Xiulan jerked her head up, her eyes going wide. She gaped at her father, feeling her face burn red with embarrassment.

"Ah, wha—?! No, Father, there will not be a wedding!" Xiulan spluttered.

Her father's face fell. "No marriage? I see. Unfortunate . . ." her father replied, a seemingly troubled look on his face. "Will I meet the children of your union?"

Xiulan felt like Zang Li had lit her face on fire all over again.

"Father, no, our relationship is not like that! We are not . . . *He is my sworn brother!*" she insisted. Her father raised an eyebrow, and she could not tell whether he was teasing her or not.

"Hmmm. Pity."

"Father!"

□

Thus, the feast and the rebuilding ended. This traveller began his next path, heading to Yellow Rock Plateau—

"That's bullshit," a man said, throwing down the scroll in disbelief.

"What?" Tao the Traveller demanded.

"It's bullshit. What kind of Young Mistress cooks mortals food? I think you were drinking too deep, Tao."

"Tall-tale Tao," another man in the pub heckled.

"You bastards! When have I ever told a lie?!" Tao demanded.

CHAPTER 60

INSIDE A SHROUDED MOUNTAIN

The good mood after our little celebration was short-lived. Early the following morning, the Shrouded Mountain Sect's chariot came back.

The disciples of the Shrouded Mountain Sect looked like death warmed over as they showed me the barrel that they had collected. The corpse inside was disgusting, but they'd found the body and that was the important part. After that, they requested we exchange Yingwen for two more of their number. Yingwen was apparently the most familiar with the Elders, and the most senior of their group, so he would be the one to give their report.

It had taken some negotiation to settle on the official story—about an hour of me standing with my arms crossed and either nodding or shaking my head. Zang Li, tired of the Azure Hills, had wandered off without an escort to Yellow Rock Plateau, where he was slain by a Demonic Cultivator. A wandering cultivator witnessed this atrocity and slew the Demonic Cultivator in retaliation. Originally they wanted to say it was the noble Cloudy Sword Sect who had done it, but the fewer things that could get them involved, the better.

It was a cover-up, a blatant one that only worked if *everybody* agreed to it, but what could we do? Shouting to the world that the Shrouded Mountain Sect had completely missed a Demonic Cultivator after being warned about it once already? It would completely trash their reputation and credibility.

Easy to see why Yingwen wanted to avoid that. But why would *I* want to avoid that? Blackmail.

Or at least the threat of blackmail. To a Sect, reputation was all-consuming. Anything that could damage the aura of righteousness built up around the Shrouded Mountain Sect was a threat. It was like a gun to the head.

They were cultivators, so their first reaction would probably be to try to kill whatever threatened them. A peasant who knew a dirty secret would quickly become a dead peasant.

But I wasn't a peasant.

I didn't know if a Shrouded Mountain Sect Elder could kill me. I knew I was strong; I didn't know how strong. But people in the Profound Realm don't immediately capitulate and start serving you tea unless you have the power to splatter them across the landscape.

If they couldn't remove the threat . . . well, then they would have to play nice. My presence would force them to the table. They would honour their agreements, lest something unpleasant leaked out.

It was a dangerous game.

All I could do was wait as the carriage pulled by blue swirling spirits in the shape of six-legged horses sped away. Wait and hope.

□

"This is a mess, is it not?" Jian Chongyun, Elder of the Shrouded Mountain Sect, asked pleasantly. His companion did not answer aloud. He absently raised his hand as a lightning bolt lashed out, deflecting it and shaking out the charge. He raised an eyebrow at the woman beside him, a murderous aura around her body so intense that poor disciple Yingwen had fallen unconscious after delivering his report.

Zang Shenhe's face was completely steady, even as lightning sparked and crackled around her. Her blond hair rose like a halo around her head, and her storm-grey eyes were burning with rage. She wore intricate dark robes punctuated by electric-blue sashes and trimmed with fox-fur collars, the regalia of an Elder, untouched by the raging lightning. A testament to her control.

Chongyun flattened some of his hair, which was rising up through the static fury pouring off his fellow Elder. Though she had not been especially close to Zang Li, she had cared for the boy in her own way. She saw in Zang Li's struggles with his cultivation and the injury that had stunted his growth a parallel journey to her own troubles. The blood of the Arch-Traitor Wen flowed in her veins, and she had had to prove herself a hundred times more than any other just to show that she was not like the one who had betrayed them all to the foxes.

There was a soft cough from one of their servants. An inquisitor, one who examined the mind and body for the foxes' corruption, shuffled forwards. His body was encased in black clothing and his face covered completely by black cloth. The man stepped away from the barrel that contained their once-disciple's remains and held his hands raised in front of him, bowing his head.

"Report," Shenhe ground out, her normally soft and musical voice rumbling like thunder.

"It has been hollowed out for quite some time, Honoured Elders," the aged man stated immediately. "This one has not seen this manner of possession before, though it bears some resemblance to the body-eater techniques told of in the restricted scrolls. Such things were supposedly rendered extinct thousands of years ago during the Blood Arts Purge."

Chongyun frowned. That was *most* concerning. "So it was an imposter the whole time?" he asked, clarifying.

The Inquisitor bowed again. "As far as this one can tell, yes. The formations speak true. Young Master Zang Li was lost to us near a year ago, his soul tortured, and his body devoured."

There was silence. Abruptly, the sparks around Shenhe stilled. The scent of blood filled the room as she bit down on her lip, forcefully calming herself.

"From the beginning, Inquisitor. Everything you and your fellows have found," Shenhe commanded, blood dripping down her lip. The Inquisitor had been part of the flurry of activity that had taken place ever since the first emergency transmission. Thus, he would be well placed to report the details to the two Elders.

The Inquisitor bowed a third time and cleared his throat.

"Zang Li. Youngest Son of the Zang Clan. Inheritor of the Fulmination Meridians and Fulmination Bloodline. Noticeably slow cultivation growth. Two years ago, he finally broke into the Profound Realm. After this accomplishment he requested a leave of absence, ostensibly to gather resources for his continued advancement. It was granted as par for the course," the Inquisitor recited. "He travelled northeast towards Blackfire Fang City. He was there for several days, then left north towards the Sea of Snow."

"Why was he in the Azure Hills, then? Did no one find that element worthy of investigation?" Elder Shenhe asked.

"Verdant Hill, the town where he was found, is northernmost in the Hills . . ." the Inquisitor said lightly. Chongyun knew what he was implying.

"He was taken by a Howl?" The fearsome windstorms generated by the Northern Tempest could easily carry a cultivator away.

"Yes, Elder. While most aren't blown quite that far, there are those who are sent into the milder climes near the Azure Hills. Most attempt to return immediately once the snows and winds die down, but they are usually on missions and thus bound to leave. It was plausible that one on personal leave simply decided to explore, which was this imposter's story when we asked him about it, thinking he was Zang Li."

Elder Shenhe said nothing, though Chongyun could feel her seething rage.

"In this town, as the Elders know, he was defeated by an unknown cultivator and deemed an imposter for being too weak. Zang Li claimed to have been attacked without provocation . . . though this was not examined too closely. The boy lost and shamed the Sect, and thus he was confined and ridiculed by the Inner Disciples. There is a report that there were two others with him during his defeat, but Outrider Jian had them disposed of for shaming the Sect," the Inquisitor continued.

Chongyun just sighed, inwardly cursing their most accomplished scout and executor. Normally his swift judgement was considered a necessity, but now . . . Chongyun thought that the man was getting a bit too hasty with consigning those who displeased him to death. The sentence should have been confinement and corporal punishment.

"How did we not notice?" Elder Shenhe finally asked aloud.

"There were three light examinations of the Young Master, and a deeper one to check for illusions of the Enemy upon his mind. All said the same thing: It was

Young Master Zang Li's body and there was no influence upon his mind," the Inquisitor reported, voice quavering a bit.

Chongyun knew that such examinations were difficult to fool. They'd had thousands of years to perfect those studies, and to have them all come up clean was proof of the power of the Demonic Cultivator's technique.

"We asked others who knew him if they had noticed any changes. They reported that Zang Li was more vindictive and had acquired a sudden taste for the finer sex, but this one speculates that such things could have been dismissed as emerging because of the ridicule he'd received from the Inner Disciples. By all accounts he was an exemplary, if aggressive, member of the Shrouded Mountain Sect. A true son of the Shrouded Mountain."

The last remark was chilling. Silence filled the room, only punctuated by breathing.

"Leave us," Shenhe commanded after a moment. The Inquisitor bowed immediately and departed after resealing the barrel.

Chongyun sighed, pondering the words of the Inquisitor. Chongyun himself had become suspicious of the boy because of his sudden and unnatural growth. Zang Li had struggled all his life. He was quieter than most. He rarely offered insult. Then all of a sudden he'd begun lashing out at all who opposed him. In truth it had seemed . . . *off* to Chongyun.

"How did Zeng not notice?" Chongyun muttered in exasperation.

Shenhe snorted. "Cousin Zeng cared little for his youngest. The weakest and slowest of his offspring received little of his attention. I would have been more surprised if he *did* notice." She idly ran her fingers along the sheath of her sword, glaring hatefully at the barrel. "His eyes were too greedy. I knew little Li's eyes. They were purer than that. His was an honest desire for strength, to prove himself to his father and his Sect." Her own words sounded wistful to her ears. "And now he's dead, eaten by a parasite, and we can't do anything about it," she finished. Shenhe turned her eyes to the scroll sitting open on the table beside them.

The other problem in the room. The one that had to be handled most delicately.

"The Cloudy Sword Sect . . . Out of everything in this tale, that is the most unbelievable," Chongyun mused.

"He shames us with these demands. He equates the might and worth of the Shrouded Mountain Sect to that of mortals," Shenhe bit out.

"Yet that proves it is the Cloudy Sword Sect making these demands. Only they would be so . . . *arrogant*. I do not doubt Disciple Yingwen's assessment that this Jin Rou was powerful. But to completely disregard what we would give for this? No, that, more than any show of force, is a sign of his strength." Upon the offending scroll that Yingwen had presented was written a list of demands, demands that were very light by most standards. Insultingly light. Whoever had penned this scroll had such little regard for the Shrouded Mountain Sect that Chongyun believed he could feel the disdain wafting up from the page. "Yet at the same time he is lenient. He has allowed us to keep our honour. This set of demands keeps us upon our mountain with the majority of our strength intact. Why?"

Shenhe froze at the question, her scowl deepening. Chongyun had an inkling. An inkling of what this was about, and he wasn't sure he liked it.

Chongyun's eyes narrowed. "Think. For what reason would a member of the Cloudy Sword be in the Azure Hills, even stooping to raising his daughter within their Qi-starved confines?"

"He would not be. Not unless there was *something* there that attracted him," Shenhe whispered, her lightning fizzling out. "At first, he specifically called us instead of destroying the creature himself. It was young and weak, and he did not remain in one place, according to the mortals. He immediately left—you think he could have been on the trail of another such creature?"

It was a bit of a jump, but it was plausible. Could this be a precursor to invasion? The Lost Blood Arts coming from the Sea of Snow and the Northern Tempest? That Shenhe had so quickly reached the same conclusion he had made his blood turn to ice in his veins.

"We are famed for our ability to peel back the lies of tricksters and thieves and reveal them for what they truly are. If this line of thinking is correct . . . he gave the beast to us in confidence. The Cloudy Sword Sect had expectations for us, and we failed to meet them." Chongyun grimaced. "Now he has given us enough rope to hang ourselves with."

"I suppose we go and meet him in person to properly bow our heads for the favours he has done us," Shenhe said finally.

"I would recommend caution. The last demand on the scroll is that no member of the Shrouded Mountain Sect may set foot in the Azure Hills without permission. Only Yingwen is listed as being able to bring back the reparations. Besides, what would you do if your daughter was abducted by a Demonic Cultivator that you had trusted another to deal with?"

Shenhe's silence was an answer in itself.

"I shall inform the Patriarch," Shenhe finally said.

"I shall prepare our recompense," Chongyun stated.

The Elders stood, nodding at each other. Then Shenhe disappeared in a flash of light.

□

The days passed. I got my tour of the Dueling Peaks. I had tea with a couple of the Elders, a tense experience I had no desire to repeat again, especially when they started politely asking about cultivation advice. Luckily, I'd been able to spend most of my time hanging out with the rest of the crew.

I tried to enjoy myself, but in the end I kind of failed. Things were just too tense. I needed something to occupy my mind.

So I started wandering around town, thinking things over. Looking for something, though I wasn't sure what . . . until I found somebody familiar working at a forge.

"So, what do you think of something like this?" I asked "Handsome Man" with a little smile. I'd brought my designs with me, so I decided to show him, figuring he might be able to help. The guy was stiff as a board, his eyes fixed entirely on the pipe drawing.

I had thought teasing the guy would be a bit of fun, but I was already regretting it. He looked like he wanted to crap his pants.

"It is not my expertise, Master Jin, but this Tie Delun will do his best or die trying," he replied, projecting his voice, determination in his eyes. "I will prove myself to you!"

I sighed. Really, the guy was so fixated on Tigu. Most people seemed to like her, but "Handsome Man" here gave her mushy eyes every time they met. He seemed to be a good kid. He had jumped in to help protect her; I didn't want either him or Tigu to get hurt.

But what could I say? I watched the guy for a second, and he seemed to shrink into himself.

"Listen, Tie Delun . . . you don't need to prove yourself to me," I said, and the guy immediately perked up. "But! I don't think Tigu thinks about things that way."

He paused, confused.

"She's still immature. Young. She sees you as her friend. Perhaps, in a few years, she might consider it, but right now . . . right now she just needs a friend, do you understand?"

The boy swallowed and nodded.

"You can come visit if you want. We'll go fishing, and I may have some commission work—your Sect does metalworking, right? Does that sound good to you?"

Tentatively, Tie Delun nodded.

'Good man—" I started, but I was cut off.

"Master Rou! Master Rou, the Shrouded Mountain Sect's carriage is approaching!" a voice shouted.

I took in a breath. *Showtime.*

CHAPTER 61

AN END TO THINGS

The air was tense in the stone room, buried deep within the mountain. I was in another one of the thronelike seats. Honestly, they were less uncomfortable than they looked. Either that, or since I was a cultivator I just didn't feel discomfort as easily.

Guo Daxian was seated to my right and Xiulan's dad, Xi Kong, was to my left. Daxian had pushed part of his robe off his shoulder, exposing the mass of tattoos that ran down his arm and chest like he was some kind of yakuza. Xi Kong had his hands linked in front of him in the robes of his sleeves, looking like a much more traditional figure.

The rest of the Elders were seated behind us; some of them were even leaning on walls. The Shrouded Mountain Sect disciples had been grabbed and were sitting on their knees before us. They looked as uncomfortable as I felt.

And me? I was front and center with my arms crossed and a chicken on my shoulder. I felt a bit underdressed in my normal outfit, all rougher linens rather than the silks everybody else was wearing. But it had the symbol Meiling had designed over my heart and on my back. I liked this uniform. It felt right. And maybe, just maybe, remembering her with her tongue stuck out as she sewed the design on helped me calm down a bit.

Still, it made me feel just like a mafia boss or something, about to give the Shrouded Mountain Sect an offer they couldn't refuse. *Or had I already given them that?*

It was a funny image, yeah, but right now I was seriously questioning where things went wonky. How did I go from running away from the Cloudy Sword Sect to being the guy in charge of the cultivators of the entire Azure Hills?

Just what has my life become?

There was no time to dwell on it, though. One of the cultivators outside the door slammed three times on it and declared, "Zhou Yingwen of the Shrouded Mountain Sect!"

I sensed everybody else tensing up even more as the young man entered the room. I could feel the Qi pouring off the people behind me. They were nervous, and I felt my Qi burble unpleasantly in response.

I heard a hum of irritation from Daxian when nobody else came in after him.

"No Elders, they insult Master Rou," I heard another snarl as Yingwen entered, unarmed and wearing his Sect's robes. He walked forwards until he was in front of me and dropped to one knee. *Huh, they had actually listened when I said only Yingwen was allowed back.* I honestly hadn't been expecting that.

"Zhou Yingwen pays his respects to Lord Rou," he intoned. His head was bowed completely. Nobody else spoke, waiting for me to start.

"Are you it?" I asked.

"I beg your indulgence, Great Lord. I have brought with me the words of the mighty Elders of the Shrouded Mountain. They have agreed to do as you have ordered, Lord Rou: no member of the Shrouded Mountain Sect has stepped foot into the Azure Hills without your permission, save for myself," the young man stated immediately. "I am sent to relay their communication. If you feel this one is unfit to bear the words of the Elders and would prefer to directly communicate with them, Elder Chongyun of the Shrouded Mountain Sect has agreed to meet with you at a place of your choosing."

I raised an eyebrow at the statement. Honestly . . . I had kind of been expecting an Elder to come around anyway. Counting on it, even. But was this really them preemptively doing what I asked them to, or something more nefarious? I had no idea. This. *This* was why I hated politics. I had no doubt that the Shrouded Mountain Sect Elders could probably run circles around me. They were actual people rather than the incompetent old men who grabbed the idiot ball and ran with it, so common in stories.

The cultivators of the Azure Hills seemed pragmatic and practical, without much arrogance, but I didn't know if that was because they were all scared of me or not. People tended to act differently when you walked into the room carrying a loaded gun and told them to get along. They were all still trying to kiss my ass.

What's more, they were all still waiting for my response. I simply nodded.

"So, what do the Masters of the Shrouded Mountain Sect have to say?" I ventured.

"Elders Shenhe and Chongyun thank the wandering cultivator Rou Jin for his virtue and benevolence, avenging the death of the Young Master. Should he require anything, the Shrouded Mountain Sect will do their utmost to aid the man who avenged Young Master Zang Li," Yingwen said, his eyes still on the ground.

"What about the damage inflicted on the town?" I asked.

Yingwen grimaced. "The Elders apologise for the deplorable conduct of their disciples. It was disgraceful to become so intoxicated and cause such a disturbance. However, it was the foolishness of youth that drove them to such a state, and in that spirit the Elders ask for understanding from you, Great Lord. The Elders wish to show gratitude to the Great Sects of the Azure hills for their forbearance in this matter. They have heard your virtuous suggestion that recompense is needed. I have brought with me that recompense."

Was that it? Really, was this the end of things?

I hummed and gestured for Yingwen to continue. Yingwen stood and took a couple of steps back. He reached into a pouch on his hip and pulled out a ring. For an instant, I was confused. Then I remembered that spatial rings existed. They were basically bags of holding, from what I remembered.

There was a flash of light and a burst of Qi.

And then there was a table in front of us. Piled high with pills and giant pouches with the symbol of what this world used for currency on them. It looked like a fortune in goods.

I heard a strangled gasp as the feeling of tension ratcheted up again. Every eye was on the new table, or more specifically, the rows and rows of pills on it.

"Spiritual-Level Refining Pills?"

"Thousand-Year ginseng—!"

"Iridescent Soulflower?"

The whispers and mutters raked across the room. Every Elder was staring greedily at what the Shrouded Mountain Sect had produced.

"The Shrouded Mountain gives these small treasures in recompense and asks you, Lord Rou, to disseminate them as you please."

I guess they couldn't resist giving the Azure Hills at least *some* nose tweaking. Nothing on that table was small to the folk of the Azure Hills. I looked around at the shock and greed in their eyes and couldn't help the rather loud sigh that escaped my lips.

Surprisingly, the action immediately shut everybody up, the press of bodies craning to look at the resources on the table snapping back into position. Xiulan's father and Guo Daxian looked almost embarrassed at their exclamations.

But I just had one last question.

"And what about you?" I asked.

Yingwen stared directly at me. He seemed resigned. "That . . . is for you to decide, Lord Rou. The Elders have decreed that I have brought shame on the Shrouded Mountain. They ask that you determine my fate."

The silence was deafening. Yingwen walked forwards and once again dropped to a knee, bowing his head.

It was an odd feeling hearing somebody casually give you permission to kill somebody else as if their life was just . . . *nothing*.

I pitied him, at that moment. He was probably wondering if he was going to die, and yet he'd walked forwards and bowed his head with dignity. I hated it. I hated the fact that Tigu, Xiulan, and everybody else had been hurt. I hated the fact that this world was like this.

It all weighed down on me.

I just felt exhausted.

For a moment, I closed my eyes and let myself breathe. Who was I?

I had already killed one man.

Maybe I was weak . . . but I couldn't stomach the thought of more killing. Not by my hands.

"Go." I opened my eyes and stared steadily at the kneeling man. "Take the others with you. Go, and never return."

The Disciples of the Shrouded Mountain Sect stared up at me with wide eyes. A moment later, Yingwen rose from his bow and looked back to me, his relief obvious.

"We are unworthy of the mercy you show us, Great Lord. Know that this Yingwen will never forget your generosity," Yingwen said before bowing once more and leaving with the rest of the Shrouded Mountain disciples trailing behind.

And that was that.

The whole altercation with the Shrouded Mountain Sect was finished. All I would have to show for the entire meeting was a scroll written from the Elders of the Shrouded Mountain Sect, and a whole load of stress.

Being the guy in charge *sucked.*

→

The rest of the day was spent handing things out for the most part. I got the Lord Director money for the reparations. I had to oversee a bunch of old people squabbling over the stuff the Shrouded Mountain had given like birds fought over a berry, while other people quickly took care of all the cash.

I kept my arms crossed and my face stern, speaking little, even as my Qi occasionally bubbled unpleasantly. Best to let them work it out so they didn't start thinking of me as the guy to go to whenever they fought.

With the immediate threat of the Shrouded Mountain Sect out of the way . . . things got a lot more hectic.

It took a day of meetings to get everything settled. Starting with Loud Boy . . . well, the kid was really loud, especially when he started bawling his eyes out after I gave him the stuff that could possibly help restore his cultivation. I still don't know if I trusted the Shrouded Mountain Sect's resources, but a primer on ways to repair broken cultivation had been added. The rest of the cultivators were all pretty hyped about the pills and stuff, once they were divided up. The normal people had just stared blankly at the "compensation" they were getting, and had then gone nuts at the sheer amount of money that was being pumped into the town. After all that, the messages started pouring in.

Invitations for dinners. Invitations to visit people's Sects or their manors. One from the guzheng-playing lady, Xinling, who requested a private, late-night dinner. *Everyone* seemed to want to meet with the Great Master Rou Jin. It was a massive pain in the ass. I could have stayed for weeks, just dealing with everything and answering all the invitations.

Thankfully, there was one big benefit of being in charge that I did like.

You can tell everybody you didn't want to deal with to *sod off.*

"You can contact me through the Azure Jade Trading Company if there is an emergency," I said pleasantly to just about everyone demanding my attention and then walked away.

It was late and the stars were out. I found myself sitting on the top of some inn and reading the scroll I had gotten from Yingwen. For the first time in days, I had some peace and quiet.

It was a note of thanks and apology, as well as, of all things, poetry. Some flowery stuff about a mountain blocking the cold wind from the north and how they would never forget the cloud's gentle shadow. Courtly language.

I think I got the gist of it, *maybe*.

I never was very good at poetry.

I sighed and put the scroll down just in time to hear a *thump* as Tigu jumped up from the ground floor as well. She had a bright smile on her face.

"There you are, Master!" she cheered, climbing onto me and wrapping me in a hug. I smiled at her and hugged her back.

"Hey, Tigu," I whispered. "Did you enjoy your time with your friends?" I asked her.

Tigu grinned and immediately started babbling away about Loud Boy and Rags, as well as "the Smaller Blade of Grass," having some kind of drinking contest.

I listened to her as she curled up into my lap and just talked. She wasn't too far into her story when there was a light flapping of wings; Big D landed beside me with Rizzo on his back. The little rat squealed a greeting and let me scratch at her head, leaning into my touch. I took a breath and just let Tigu's voice wash over me.

"So I added to its beauty!" Tigu enthused. "It's a treasure! Just ask the owner!"

'She carved it into the wall,' Ri Zu interjected. *'Then she had to apologise to the owner!'*

Tigu stuck her tongue out at the rat, who just responded in kind. I raised an eyebrow at the two girls squabbling like sisters. Seemed like they had grown closer. I couldn't help being happy at the thought.

Big D seemed just as amused as I felt. He hopped over and started preening Tigu's hair. The girl harrumphed and went still, but I could see the small smile of satisfaction on her face.

She . . . sounded like she had at least had a good time.

I stared up at the sky for a little bit longer letting the cool night air soothe me, until I finally said what was on my mind.

"What do you think about heading home soon?" I asked.

Tigu paused and looked up at me. She considered the question.

A smaller, softer smile spread across her face. "Home sounds amazing," she stated simply.

"Yeah, it does, doesn't it?"

CHAPTER 62

FRAGMENTS OF A BROKEN SOUL

E*ight days ago . . .*

Tianlan was so happy when she managed to finish the road. She pulled off her yellow helmet and wiped her brow, staring with pride at her construction. It had been hard work, but she had managed it, forging ahead of her Connected One, instead of having to catch up to him. Also, she'd gotten to see her little ones who had been missing for a while, out of her web. Her people.

Tigu, Ri Zu, Gou Ren, and Yun Ren. Perhaps even the grass girl, who felt . . . familiar, sometimes. It was good to feel them again after days of building. She carefully guided the little cracks of gold, taking care to avoid the bulk of the sleeping energy under the mountain. Some of her energy bled and touched the mountain, causing it to stir . . . but it didn't do more than sluggishly churn.

She breathed a sigh of relief as nothing happened and ruffled Chun Ke's mane. Her touch caressed what was hers, spreading out along golden cracks. They were safe and whole. Smiling, she let out a breath as the energy she had been using to create the connections dispersed back down the link she had with her Connected One. He felt very tired. So she gave some of herself back, perking him up again so he could get here and play with his friends—

And then there was terror, she felt it, from the little connections she had to what was hers. The terror and the pain.

What was hers was in danger. Tianlan tried to send Qi down the link, but the newly built roads were still too fragile—they were not meant to have such power coursing through them. They would need to be bigger.

But to make them bigger, she would have to touch the mountain. She would have to feel it. The ball of memories and screaming pain within.

More fear came down her link. More determination. What was hers was fighting. Hurting.

Chun Ke was there, a stable rock against her back. Tianlan swallowed thickly. She would not stand for it.

She strengthened the connections. The little gold roads thickened and surged, burrowing into a rotting piece of herself.

It was like a spike had been driven into her skull.

Memories. Remembrance. *Pain.*

She fell to her knees and grabbed at her eye, screaming as the thoughts surged and threatened to overwhelm her.

She did not let them. She had to help. She shoved her own Qi down the connections. Tiny golden cracks in their souls, proof of their bonds, opened up. It was a bare trickle of power that she could give them, but it did its work, reinforcing their bodies and letting them fight long past when they should have fallen over in exhaustion.

Her Connected One's strides grew in length, covering the distance of a hundred steps with every one he took, pulling him towards her along a golden road.

Her people held the line. Moment by agonizing moment. She felt the little Blade of Grass *burn*. She felt Tigu's turmoil, screaming as she forced her body back into its original form.

And then her Connected One arrived.

His resolve burned. Tianlan could feel his determination shining through her, along with his sorrow. The disgusting, wriggling thing that had been attacking the grass girl stood before her Connected One. It was a cancer that needed to be excised, and it felt oddly familiar.

Her Connected One asked. His Qi brushed up against hers.

Tianlan answered.

Her head pounded with the sudden influx of memories rampaging through her, but she managed to hold off sinking into oblivion.

Just a little longer. She had to help her Connected One.

She gave of herself without hesitation, Wood and Earth mingling together. She spoke the old, old words, blending together with her Connected One's movements. Gold burned in the darkness, flooding everything with light.

"And so the Great Ancestor, Shennong, commanded his disciple in the ways of preparing the fields. Till the land. Fell the trees. Divert the waters—"

Old memories. Old pain. The feeling of being drained. Tianlan sang it. Tianlan screamed it as the two of them put their all into the blow.

[Break the Rocks]

And then, nothing at all.

□

"Something for all of us. A place for music, culture, and arts. A place to see our future defenders," a man said with conviction, staring at the mountain that had been split in two by his struggle.

The thousands behind him nodded their heads.

"Let's get to work," he commanded.

□

When Tianlan returned to consciousness, the first thing she felt was an old sensation.

Exhaustion. Bone-deep, weary exhaustion. It was something Tianlan knew all too well. She knew it so well that it was a return to normalcy.

She reached to her chest to pull down the rags that were her clothes . . . though this time with both hands. She stared at the new limb. Where before there had been a stump of gold, there now was cracked flesh. The gold was dull. It had lost its luster. But . . . to her surprise, no new wounds had opened up. The Qi of her Connected One had held fast, binding her wounds closed.

She glanced around at her surroundings. It looked like she was in a dilapidated bedroom. There was an ancient stone bedframe, bare of any covers.

It felt familiar—

Another spike of pain pressed through her head. She grimaced and walked towards the door.

The hall was . . . ancient. It was filled with levers, pipes, and machinery.

Her hands ghosted along pathways and mechanisms. Some powered on, but those . . . those were in the minority. Most stayed dark. Some, when they turned on, tried to move, only to break themselves completely.

Tianlan grimaced as the knowledge of how these worked once more assaulted her, and she shook her head to clear the haze.

She clambered out of the depths of the mountain. The Earthly Arena, the Palace of the—

She cut the thought off as she grabbed her head, alone in the darkness. But then, a snout touched her.

Chun Ke chuffed happily at her. He grinned, taking some of the pain she felt into himself like he always did. Bearing some of her nightmares to give her a modicum of peace.

Shaking, she pressed her forehead to his nose and climbed onto his back.

Chun Ke needed no other direction. He cantered out of the old hallways, rising back into the sun so she could feel her other ones. They were safe. She breathed a sigh of relief.

Well, most of them. She could feel Xiulan still on fire. For a moment, she considered leaving the girl. The overly familiar woman who'd dared to trespass again and again . . . but the others would be sad if she died.

And Chun Ke had already started trotting in the girl's direction.

The girl had grown on Tianlan as well. Like a mushroom.

Tianlan took a breath as they arrived at the connection. It was hot to the touch. She slid off the boar's back and pressed into it.

In a field full of ashes, the girl danced a familiar dance. Something Tianlan could remember, would always remember, no matter how broken she was. It was something she had loved.

Her feet touched the ground, and the two of them danced together. The girl danced well this time. She had learned to cast off the rigid, wrong forms.

The mushroom had learned. She no longer felt . . . wrong. Tianlan could feel her resolve to give her life for the little ones. It was enough.

Tianlan joined her. It always felt so right, dancing with the girl. Though having to teach her had felt wrong. For some reason, Tianlan had always felt she should have been the better of the two of them. But there was none of that hesitation now.

Xiulan danced, the lessons of the Cycle surging through her soul and repairing the ruined ground within her.

Their familiar dance ended.

Cai Xiulan opened her eyes and smiled at Tianlan.

It caused a dull ache. But . . . the woman was so happy to see her.

As Tianlan pulled her head down to claim her as her own, another familiar face flashed over the top.

Her lips touched Xiulan's forehead. The girl woke up. But Tianlan, still exhausted, fell asleep.

□

"What are these for?" Tianlan asked, raising an eyebrow at the bundle in Ruolan's hands.

Ruolan grinned. Her eyes were outlined in red and her robes were the finest silk. Tianlan tried not to be jealous of the other woman's perfect grace. Her stunning beauty and crystal-blue eyes were the envy of all . . . even Tianlan.

The opera singer and dancer smiled brilliantly at Tianlan and posed, as she was wont to do, flicking her silky brown hair behind her.

"This one's performance needs them!" the woman decreed, her fans floating behind her. "A work must have props to deepen the immersion!"

"Swords, though?"

"The character is a warrior! A fierce one! This Ruolan would never forgive herself if the performance was anything less than perfect! The Verdant Fan Opera Troupe provides only the best, and these Jade Grass Blades will take this Ruolan's performance to new heights!"

Tianlan rolled her eyes at the woman's antics.

"Just don't make the mistake of having people think you can actually fight now," Tianlan teased.

Ruolan seemed affronted. "Who would *dare* sully the Thirty-Two Fans of Grass with something as base as *combat*?" she demanded.

Tianlan shrugged. "Dunno," she said, before shaking her head. "Enough about those. Do you have what I asked for?

"I do indeed. The Essence of Wood is coming along, I do think. My Lord shall be pleased. The Cycle of the Elements shall be my magnum opus!" Her eyes shone with passion.

Tianlan laughed and stood. Her feet got into position and the other woman smiled at her.

"Shoulders set. Eyes forward. *Plant that lead foot.*" Ruolan began as she always did, a little grin on her face.

Together, they crafted a masterpiece.

◻

The moments where she was awake . . . stuttered. More and more. Each time she saw somebody through her Connected One's eyes.

People she didn't know, yet knew.

A man with a bandana and tattoos.

◻

Gatai Altan, who had taken the name Guo Daxian like he was some kind of bandit. Enduring dishonour to keep his people safe. They fought together. They laughed together. And when Altan called her Sister, Tianlan smiled.

Tianlan looked at her hand, the one that had been recently repaired; there was the outline of what looked like a design of a faded tattoo upon it.

◻

Tie Jun, the mason nodding sagely as he carved characters into massive stone pillars, followed the designs laid out for him. Slow and steady in all he did. He always said that stone was more talkative than metal, eschewing his ancestors' craft.

Even walking with him, along the halls of a place that was so strange and so familiar. Everything reacted to them. Igniting. Bowing to her Qi.

It was unnerving and relieving. Like she was coming home to a place she no longer remembered could be home.

A stone chair. A band of light formed like a crown, which brought the light of happiness and the darkness of despair at the same time.

"My Lord. My Lady. We humbly receive you!"

◻

Tianlan looked away, only glancing back when she could feel her Connected One's distaste for them visiting. The feeling of their Qi was . . . disgusting.

The feeling of them reaching inside and plundering. Grasping hands, tearing sensations. Why weren't they helping? Why were they ignoring her desperate pleas? She was begging them for help—

Her Qi surged without her consent, pinning them with her fury.

◻

The days continued.

She was . . . uncomfortable. The place here had filled her head with memories, fragments of who she used to be. Things she had forgotten clicked into place. Friends long since dead, yet in some form still existing.

She couldn't help seeing the similarities. The looks the tattooed man gave her Connected One. Xiulan, who looked so much like an old friend.

Why had they forgotten? Why had *she* forgotten? Why was a mason working like a smith? Why was a graceful dancer's body heavier with muscle meant for war?

It hurt and confused in equal measure.

And all she could do was watch on. Watch on, as a blazing crown of light formed over her Connected One's head, like it had done in the past.

Fear seized her heart for a moment. Would the past repeat? Would what happened before happen again?

Would they break her again?

It was an insidious thought. She took her breath in great gasps as she curled up into a ball. Nervous, worried, and—

A hand on her head.

She looked up.

"You okay, shortstop?" her Connected One asked. He stared down at her with concern, his Qi gently touching the gold in her body and wrapping around her. Concern. Worry.

A boar chuffed at her, and she pouted at Chun Ke as the man picked her up and placed her in his lap.

She curled into him, feeling his heartbeat. She shook her head.

Her Connected One sighed when he held her. "Well, I can't speak for everybody . . . But getting home always makes me feel better, you know? I can't wait. Everything is too . . . complicated here."

Tianlan hiccuped a sob as she hugged him. His hands ghosted over her scars. Resolve filled his voice.

"Shh . . . shh," he soothed her. "Hey, don't worry, kiddo. Nothing like what happened to you will ever happen again. I'll make sure of it."

His voice stopped the shaking.

She clung to him. She believed in him.

Just like she had once believed in somebody else—

A nose touched her side. Chun Ke chuffed. And another hand joined the one on her back. Yet another set of hands embraced her.

She lifted her head to see Meiling's smile.

Not just two of them. But three. Or was it four? Or was it everybody else the little golden strands had connected to?

She buried her face back down, tears streaming from her eyes.

CHAPTER 63

COMIN' HOME

Cai Xi Kong sipped his tea as he studied the man across from him; Master Rou's eyes were closed as he smelled the tea before him. Xi Kong frowned. He could almost detect . . . discomfort from the expert. His face had been stone during the last meeting. He had received the reports of the Lord Director on their reparations, and he had listened to the testimony of the Sects upon the resources given to those who had participated in the defence of Tigu.

Then he, calmly and matter-of-factly, had nodded his head and announced his intention to leave the next day. Xi Kong had already known. The man had discussed it with his disciples last night and offered to allow this "Rags" and "Loud Boy" to accompany him. To Xi Kong's surprise, though, Loud Boy had politely declined for the moment.

His statement to the Elders had been taken in stride. Who would dare to argue with the man? Lines of communication for emergencies were set up . . . and that was it.

When asked if he had any guidelines for them to follow, the man had simply raised an eyebrow and stated:

"Protect the people and live virtuous lives. Otherwise, it's hardly any of my business."

And that was that. The halo of light upon the chair went out, and Master Rou had left with that simple edict.

Xi Kong knew that there would be many, many discussions over the months and years about Master Rou's actions and words. But there was one thing that was certain.

The Azure Hills had a new Master, one who ruled by might and with benevolence.

And now Xi Kong was having tea with the Master as the younger generation vented the last of their rowdiness. The buildings were awash in the colours of Yun Ren's murals and the shouts of Tigu. The Young Masters and Mistresses spoke in hushed voices with his daughter, nodding solemnly and pledging to whatever she was saying.

All his disciples were in the thick of it, as the servants delayed their departure for one last night.

Xi Kong stared at the man for a moment longer. The days had been busy and full of meetings before, so he'd barely gotten any time to truly sit down and have a personal conversation with his daughter's saviour.

"Master Rou?" he asked. The man opened his eyes and shook his head.

"Please, call me Jin," he said.

Xi Kong inclined his head. "Then I hope you would do the honour of calling this one Xi Kong." The man nodded and Xi Kong continued, "My daughter told me of your actions in saving her life. This Xi Kong has not yet had an opportunity to thank you."

The man sipped his tea. "It was the least I could do. The first thing she did on seeing us was warn us of a dangerous monster."

"Still, we are in your debt—"

"The debt has been paid," he said with finality. "We are friends now, and that is all that matters."

Xi Kong nodded. It was as the rooster said. His daughter was in good hands.

"Master Rou . . . Jin. I entrust my daughter to you," he said, bowing his head.

"I think . . . you should entrust her with herself," Master Rou returned.

Xi Kong looked up at the man. The absolute confidence he had in Xiulan. "Yes, I think she has learned quite well how to take care of herself," he said quietly. "She will be a fine Elder of our Sect when she returns. A new dawn for the grass upon the plains."

The man chuckled and took a drink. "Xiulan definitely has some ideas, I think."

They returned to silence for a moment, both of them amused, until Xi Kong recomposed himself. This was a rare opportunity to speak with a Master like this, and so he decided upon the opening question that his father had liked to use. His father had told him it allowed one to get a quick measure of a man. To see his priorities and what he valued at a glance.

"Jin, what do you believe is the most important thing to remember?" Xi Kong asked.

The man's lips twitched. "You know, Xiulan asked me the exact same question once," the man stated.

"Oh?" Xi Kong asked, curious.

"Always remember a clean pair of socks," he replied. Xi Kong paused, then barked out a laugh and felt some of the tension fade.

They sipped their tea and made small talk about their plans. Jin spoke at length about his "still," which looked curiously like the contraption in Pale Moon Lake City that Xi Kong had seen once, some thirty years ago, when the troubles in the mortal capital had required his attention.

It was an interesting subject, and he was surprised the man would share his profound secrets so easily.

Or perhaps that was just his nature? Xi Kong knew some men taught as many as they could instead of hoarding their knowledge, but those instructors were few and far between.

Truly, his daughter had found a one-of-a-kind man.

↔

Tie Delun swallowed thickly and glanced at the setting sun. He had missed most of the goodbyes as he rushed to finish this and had only just managed it.

He shifted the box he was carrying under his arm and pondered Master Rou's words. Perhaps . . . perhaps he *was* too suddenly devoted. Tigu had been the only woman to . . . well, ever compliment his appearance instead of calling him an ugly brute. The splotches on his nose, the deep tan of his skin, and his bulging muscles were hardly considered attractive to most other cultivators.

But thinking on Master Rou's words . . . well, he was right. Tigu seemed completely oblivious, even with her calling him handsome. She'd demanded he take off his shirt so she could carve him with pure eyes.

It hurt to think about it, but he would persevere!

He entered the open gates of the Verdant Blade Sect's manor.

Even if this wasn't an official courting gift like he intended it to be . . . it was still fine. It would be his parting gift instead.

Most people had left already, going out into the town with Yun Ren to record their images onto stone. He had seen Xianghua dragging Gou Ren off again.

So when he was guided in by the servants into the room, there were very few people to greet him. Tigu, Xiulan, the Petals, and the two annoyances, Loud Boy and Rags.

Tie Delun pushed them out of his mind and focused on the one who mattered.

"Handsome Man!" Tigu enthused upon seeing him—and he felt his face immediately flush. "Finally! I was going to come hunt you down if you had remained hidden for too much longer!"

Delun chuckled and scratched the back of his head. "Sorry. I just had to finish this up. It's . . . it's for you," he said, holding the lacquered box out to Tigu.

Tigu's eyes widened as she opened the box, revealing two shiny silver armguards. They would cover her knuckles and go up her forearms to her elbows. One was carved with the designs of his family, and the other was blank, so she could add her own.

Tears sprang up in Tigu's eyes as she stared at the carvings. She swallowed thickly and flushed crimson.

"Handsome Man! These are masterpieces!" the young woman declared. "You dare shame me by giving me a better gift than this Tigu is about to give to you?!"

Delun's eyes widened as Tigu pulled out her own gift. She handed him a wooden pendant carved in the shape of a strange hammer. It had intricate knotwork upon it and it was flanked by two blue feathers that felt of Qi—

Delun's eyes shot to the Spirit Beast rooster, the rooster that had the same blue colouration on his wings.

"I couldn't find any good feathers, so I asked Senior Brother to give me some!" she stated.

The feathers of a Profound Realm Spirit Beast, given willingly. The rooster turned to Tie Delun and offered him a bow.

"Hey look, we're brothers!" Rags japed, showing his own pendant, which appeared to have the design of a boar. Loud Boy had what looked like an oddly plump and fishy dragon.

Tie Delun for a brief moment felt a twinge of jealousy but crushed it down. Instead, he nodded to the two others, who nodded back.

Then Tigu slammed into him and started talking about how great it would be to see his home and more of his carvings before inviting him over.

Tie Delun couldn't help it. At her earnestness, he fell in love all over again.

Waiting . . . wouldn't be too bad, would it?

↔

Zang Wei, known to most as Loud Boy, stared fondly at the pendant. It joined the other one around his neck: a piece of dull blue horn, inlaid with jade.

"What is the nature of this world?" the booming voice asked.

He shook his head and started packing up. He was amused at how quickly his world had changed. Who would have ever thought that things would have come to this? Certainly not him. He kept up his packing, staring around at the room.

"Are you certain of this?" Miss Cai asked. "Master Jin would welcome you with open arms."

Wei paused at her gentle words. She was concerned for him, he could tell that much.

The young man hesitated before eventually nodding.

"Yes, I'm sure. The manual said that to achieve the best effects one must travel to a place significant to their cultivation, to reconnect with their past and bring it to the present. And there's only one place I can think of."

Back to a hidden old alcove and a nest of dragon bones. He clutched his necklace under his shirt. His resolve firmed.

"Besides! I finally have an answer to a question somebody asked me, long ago." He smiled at her. "I gotta give it to the old bastard, yanno?"

"And it ain't like he's headin' out alone," Rags said, staggering in and clapping Loud Boy on the shoulder. "I'll take good care of my little brother!"

Wei shoved at him, glaring. Deep inside, though, his heart felt . . . warm.

How long had it been since people had touched him with affection? He tried to think back as far as he could . . . and nothing came to mind.

Wei rolled his eyes, then said, "I beat you when we fought the first time! I'll be the Senior Brother!" Rags laughed and ruffled Wei's hair.

"We've got to go back to our old stomping grounds, anyway," the other man said. "Got some unfinished business! We'll get Loud Boy his cultivation back, and then come and visit!"

Miss Cai nodded before her face turned serious. "Dong Chou. Zang Wei. You will forever be friends of the Verdant Blade Sect. Honour and nobility can come from any, no matter how ragged they look."

Before he'd gotten to know her . . . he never would have realised that Cai Xiulan would have a sense of humour.

Nor that she hummed along to the song about the whore and the donkey.

Rags grabbed his chest with mock pain, groaning as he leaned back.

Rags laughed at her words—and then cut off when he saw what she was handing out to them: a vial with two pills in it.

It was the prize from the tournament. The Profound Breakthrough Pills.

"Just in case that which you have gained from the Shrouded Mountain Sect is not enough," she said, smiling at them.

"You . . . you were hurt too. Your cultivation is—" Wei began, but Xiulan just shook her head.

"Indeed, it probably could bring me back up to the Profound Realm, or at least knock upon the door to it. But a good friend taught me to treasure a slower path. They were useless to me when I earned them, and I would rather they go to you."

Her words were soft and full of conviction. There was no pity in her words. Only that she believed them worth the reward.

Tears gathered at the corners of Wei's eyes. He remembered his master, asking him the question that would form the basis of his cultivation.

"What is the truth of this world?" the Dragon Spirit had demanded.

"The truth of this world is cruelty," Wei had replied.

And yet that answer had changed.

He took a breath and clasped his hands in front of himself. "I will never forget what you did for me, Cai Xiulan."

Rags too stared at the pills, his hands shaking.

"You know . . . when I came here, I didn't expect any of this to happen," he muttered.

"And I will never forget your courage," Miss Cai returned. She studied them for a moment before clasping her hands in front of her. "Live well, Rags, Loud Boy. I look forward to seeing you again soon."

They returned her salute.

And then Tigu stormed into the room, carrying a bottle of alcohol.

"We forgot to do this!" she shouted out, both men jumping in surprise. "Rags! Loud Boy! Will you be my sworn brothers?" Tigu asked the two of them. They both looked at each other.

"I get to be the Senior Brother!" Rags declared.

Both Tigu and Wei objected to that, even as they clasped their hands together.

Miss Cai smiled at them.

Wei had come to the tournament for glory. To cast aside his sorry past and embark upon the lonely path to the heavens.

He looked around, and two grins met him. One from a ragged-looking man and another from an orange-haired girl.

He had lost everything that he had come here with. A lesser man would be broken. Wei had *almost* broken, but as he looked at the Profound Breakthrough Pills, he found himself musing on the pendant around his neck.

Putting the pills away, Wei thumbed the feathers of the pendant and smiled at what he had gained and *would regain*.

He would get his cultivation back. And then he would give the old dragon his answer.

↔

I thought back to the first time I had left the world of cultivation. The lonely mountain above, the Cloudy Sword Sect, hadn't cared. I'd had nothing but a backpack while I'd wandered alone across the Empire in a mad dash to get away from it all.

There had been nobody who'd even really noticed I had left.

It was a far cry from this.

"Bye!" Tigu shouted, jumping up and down and waving both arms. "Goodbye, Brother Loud Boy, Brother Rags, and Handsome Man! Smaller Blade of Grass, practise what I showed you and match the Blade of Grass! Fish Eyes, hug your little sister for me! Head of Grass, remember to practise! Smallest Blade of Grass, grow taller!"

She shouted out a barrage of nicknames for nearly every single person, dashing from one to another. From Blue Man, to Bright Smile, to Hairpin, each one with something directed at them. For all that she seemingly couldn't remember most people's actual names, she did seem to know at least something about them, shouting for them to get better or be stronger, challenging some of them to fights later on.

It was cute how bouncy she was being . . . and how surprisingly sociable. Who would have thought that a cat would turn out to be good at making friends.

Ri Zu was watching fondly from up on Big D's back. She had already said her goodbyes, and out of all of us she surprisingly had the most luggage. Satchels of herbs and several scrolls she had come across were the main thing, but she also had a crapload of bottles of alcohol that she had *no* idea what to do with. Presents from Rags, I was told.

Gou Ren suddenly burst out from the crowd, his face flushed and Bowu on his shoulders. The kid was laughing his head off as Gou Ren dashed forwards. From out of the crowd appeared Xianghua, a languid smile on her face—before she too got accosted by Tigu as the girl rubbed their cheeks together.

Yun Ren chortled and hopped down off the cart, putting away his recording crystal and checking over everything one last time.

Gou skidded to a stop before us and set Bowu down in the carriage. Xianghua herself would be along later.

We did have two extra people coming along, though: a kid who knew what steam engines were and a monkey.

I looked up at the sky, then back down to the people.

As one, the line of cultivators bowed their heads to us.

"May the Heavens favour you!" the people shouted.

I raised my hands and bowed back.

A rooster let out an earsplitting crow.

I chuckled.

"You tell 'em, Big D," I said, as we started marching.

Finally, marching back home.

CHAPTER 64

PRESSURE CRACKS

The warm sunlight streamed through the windows of his office as the Lord Magistrate worked. The beads of the abacus he was using clicked across the frame in rapid succession. He was in the middle of confirming the upkeep for Verdant Hill, a routine task. Seeing his numbers line up with what was already written down by his clerk, Tingfeng, he nodded in satisfaction.

His subordinates were by and large competent, yet he always made sure everything was in order himself before he commanded it be done. Patience was a bitter plant to grow, but its fruit was sweet.

He let out a sigh and turned back to look out of the window, reflecting on the past several weeks. With most of the cultivators gone, it had been largely quiet. No sudden roads appearing out of nowhere, no new reports of tainted wells, and no Spirit Beasts walking around doing who knows what, but Hong Meiling, or "Sister Medical Fairy," had visited his wife last week. Out of all of them, she was the least concerning. He could at least still pretend that she was just a villager, and his wife enjoyed her visits, so he turned a blind eye.

Also, the girl had been treating his beloved. He'd do more than turn a blind eye since she'd achieved the results she had.

The Medical Fairy had brought along a new medicinal draught in her most recent visit. It had improved his dear's condition immensely. He had watched as some of her old vigor returned to her. His wife was downright energetic, which was both surprising and welcome. It was good to go on walks through the town with her as a more daily occurrence, rather than something reserved for special occasions. She had even made noises about taking up riding again, instead of being carried in a palanquin.

For that, Hong Meiling would have his eternal gratitude. Her husband was a gut-churning menace, but she was obviously the milder, more gentle of the two, no matter what the rumours about her "poison tongue" said. They were obviously mistaken. The girl was a gentle healer, and likely as mild in temperament as her father. A good man. Anyone who spoke badly of her were fools, the lot of them!

Indeed, her visit had been most pleasant. Not just for the healing his wife received but for the other gift she had given his wife in private.

That *wonderful* outfit.

He didn't know why it had rabbit ears, but the overall effect was quite appealing—er—of course, cultivators were deviants, one and all. The girl had obviously been corrupted by Rou Jin. No wonder they had such . . . depraved garments. He had to admit the fishnets on the legs were an inspired idea, however.

It would be a bit awkward to commission the fishnets in that manner, though. Perhaps he could try his hand at it. He had made most of their ropes to his exacting standards.

He was wondering how such a thing would look on his own legs when a gentle rap at the door alerted him to his head dispatcher, Muyang. The man came in with the reports from the transmission stone. While the larger towns and the cities normally had messages come in at all hours of the day, unless it was an emergency the stone at Verdant Hill only got messages once a week. His town was too far away and the stone too unreliable to handle more than that.

What followed was a standard report from Pale Moon Lake City. The Lord Magistrate listened with half an ear to his man as he summarized things. Reports on what the predicted tax total would be, several obituaries of more prominent clerks or members of the court, a report on several areas that had been experiencing weather difficulty. Following this was a reminder to file taxes appropriately, and that the following year a random sampling of villages would be visited by the auditors.

All very standard and nothing to be concerned about.

"That concludes the official governmental reports. On to other matters of importance. There was a transmission from the Azure Jade Trading Company. They say that they will be sending an important representative to the north and will be seeking an audience with yourself."

That was mildly concerning. But the fact of the matter was that if they were coming for the reason the Lord Magistrate thought . . . it would probably be for the gold-grade rice.

"Is that everything for today?" the Lord Magistrate asked.

"There was one last report, sir," Muyang said. "The results of the Dueling Peaks Tournament."

For a moment he considered just waving his man off. He didn't particularly *care* who won what, but it was good to be informed just in case one of them decided to visit or something. In the past he would have thought it impossible . . . but that was the past. Now he had an entire Sect's worth of cultivators barely a week away.

"Let us hear which of our virtuous protectors gained merit, then," he decided.

"In first place was Cai Xiulan, the Demon-Slaying Orchid."

The Lord Magistrate nodded and picked up his tea to take a sip.

"And in second . . . a Rou Tigu."

Every muscle in his body clenched, but the Lord Magistrate managed to resist the urge to spit out his tea; instead, he forced himself to swallow.

"From the—ah, no Sect listed, Lord Magistrate."

Rou Tigu. The cultivator's *cat* had placed second in the Dueling Peaks Tournament. The heavens truly wished to see him cry, did they not?

"Hmm. Interesting," the Lord Magistrate said, feeling sweat bead on his forehead.

"Finally, there was some kind of minor altercation? The reports are a bit unclear, but there was some manner of drunken brawl that was resolved before it could do any damage."

"Thank you, Muyang," he said, dismissing the man before leaning back into his seat and groaning. The Azure Jade Trading Company wanted to talk to him, and the cat had nearly won the biggest tournament in the Azure Hills—!

The Lord Magistrate reached out and poured some wine into his tea. He groaned. Maybe he *should* have become a farmer. Then he wouldn't have to deal with any of this. He had seen Rou Jin's home; it was quite idyllic, and he probably could have created something just as beautiful.

It was good land, now that it was cleared. And it would be quiet, with a mild woman like Hong Meiling tending to it . . .

Ah, well, a man could dream.

↔

"If you please, Wa Shi!" Meiling commanded. The dragon obliged her by opening his mouth and issuing forth a torrent of lightning. The blue bolts of energy split the air with a loud *crack* and left the vessel he had hit steaming.

It had been mostly an accident at first. Meiling had asked Wa Shi to start a fire for her when she'd been experimenting with Jin's Spiritual Herbs. The lazy fish had just blasted the general direction with lightning, and some of the Qi discharge had struck the herbs.

Instead of being ruined, however, the resulting extract took on a greenish glow as if lit from within. The extract had much more potency . . . or at least seemed to work faster. It almost felt like Meiling's own Medicinal Qi, though purifying in a different way. After several tests on herself—and some unfortunate fish—she had deemed the mixture suitable enough to attempt to purge the last dregs of foreign Qi out of Lady Wu's system.

The results had been better than even Meiling could hope for once administered through acupuncture deep into the woman's muscles.

Now Meiling was achieving what Jin always said was important: repeatable, consistent results.

"Hmmm. It's consistently different from using fire; it produces more liquid, for one thing. Mark down the Hairroot fungus for this one, please, Pi Pa," she asked, and the pig obligingly wrote something down on a piece of paper. "I think I know what Ancestor Hong Xian the Thirty-Second was saying about the liquid. He must have gotten a batch that was struck by lightning, or at least was in proximity to the strike." She trailed off as she examined the fungus.

Another question lingered: what else changes if struck by lightning? Most of the time she ended up with nothing but charred remains, but she had an inkling that perhaps she could get better results out of some of the herbs with a lower, more consistent application. A lower charge over a longer period of time.

She had little idea how to go about that, though. Well, Wa Shi had been sufficiently motivated with her cooking practice, so maybe she could ask her to help figure it out?

Meiling sighed and sat back, humming as she thought on what to have for lunch . . . then froze when a scent was carried to her on the breeze. Or several scents.

The warmth and the harvest. The slightly medicinal smell of Hong Yaowu. An undercurrent of fox. High notes of the moon.

A smile broke out across Meiling's face and she sprang back up, her grin widening.

'Home! Home!' Chun Ke oinked happily.

Meiling grinned and scratched his mane.

"Yes, home very soon," Meiling agreed as she pulled off the thick mask she'd been using to cover the bottom of her face. They were right outside Hong Yaowu, or maybe even in it. The range at which smells came to her was a bit . . . inconsistent at times, but she was getting better at guessing the distances.

She paused and sniffed the air again as the smell came to her. Her heart clenched when she noticed the scent of Jin's Qi. It was . . . off. It once more smelled like boiled peat.

Something had happened.

She restrained herself from running to him, though. She had work to do! Everybody was coming back home!

Meiling planned a feast for everyone and began by pulling the fermenting "pizza" dough from the river. Wa Shi filled pots for boiling. Pi Pa scurried around, placing ingredients for Meiling to cut and stirring pots for stew. Chun Ke helped as best as he could, shuffling around cheerily.

With most of the prep work done, Meiling set out of the house, took a seat on the porch, and simply waited.

She did not have to wait long.

With what seemed like a sigh, a breeze flowed through the farm. As one, the bees buzzed into the air. The cows and the sheep ceased their play.

Meiling stood up as Jin crested the hill, pulling his enormous wagon. His eyes were tired, yet they widened with happiness at his home. His gaze, after jumping around the farm, settled squarely on her.

The look he gave her was filled with pure love and relief, and it washed away some of the tiredness in his eyes. He leaned on the handles of the cart, and they smiled at each other across the hill.

Chun Ke was off like a rocket as he squealed happily, the land thundering beneath his trotters.

From Jin's party came an equal squeal.

"Miiiiiiissssstrrrreeeeessss!" Tigu yowled as she shot down the hill, her legs pumping. Both she and Chun Ke leapt at the same time.

Jin caught a boar bigger than he was with a laugh, and Meiling opened her arms at the same time.

Tigu slammed into her, though lighter than she'd been expecting. There was enough momentum that Meiling could spin the girl around but not enough to knock her over. Tigu, however, didn't let go, so Meiling shifted her arms, resting the girl who was just barely shorter than her on her hip as Tigu rubbed her cheek against Meiling's. Ri Zu hit next, squeaking happily.

Meiling giggled when Ri Zu leapt off Tigu to run circles around Meiling's shoulders before burying herself into Meiling's hair.

Gou Ren and Yun Ren were trotting past Jin as well, having greeted Wa Shi and the rest.

She received their hugs with grace, as well as one from her own little brother, who had evidently tagged along with the cart.

"Hey, Meimei," Yun Ren whispered gently when he hugged her, almost desperately. Gou Ren said nothing, simply leaning in and pressing Tigu more forcefully into their side.

They stayed for a moment before they released her, going off to talk to Wa Shi and dragging Tigu with them, the girl grumbling for only a moment before heading off to shout at "that fishy bastard!"

Meiling shook her head when a wall of water slammed into Tigu.

They were back for only a moment, and already chaos had broken out.

It was fun.

Next was Xiulan. She had her hair styled differently, a single, long braid down her back. She also smelled different. No longer was blade oil part of her scent—just pleasing wildflowers and fresh grass . . . But it was a lot less intense than Meiling remembered it being.

They embraced for a moment, then pulled back.

"It's good to see you again, Meiling," the other woman whispered. Her eyes seemed a bit watery.

Meiling's smile brightened. "Oh? No Senior Sister?" she teased, even as her hands lifted to cup the other woman's face. Xiulan let out a throaty chuckle, then laid her hand on top of the one on her cheek.

They pressed their foreheads together, and then Xiulan slid out of her grasp too.

She bent down to greet the cheerful-looking rabbit and the old snake who was riding upon her. They bowed politely, but they were still a bit distant—Meiling would have to fix that. Bi De, a package upon his back, swept into a bow.

Finally . . . finally there was one last hug waiting for her.

Jin scooped her up into his arms. He buried his nose in her hair for a brief moment, as they both inhaled with contentment, and then he pulled back. They gazed into each other's eyes.

His smile at seeing her was bright . . . but she could nearly feel his exhaustion.

"I missed you," he whispered, leaning in for a kiss.

Meiling obliged him.

Heavens, she had missed this. For a brief moment, everything was perfect. Cradled in Jin's arms, until he pulled away with a sigh.

He kept one arm around her shoulder as he turned though, and Meiling got a look at the cart.

Sitting within it were a monkey and a boy.

"Oh? More strays?" she whispered in Jin's ear with a teasing lilt. First Yin the Rabbit, and Miantiao the Snake. Now a monkey and a boy. "Are we going to add to our house after every journey?"

"Maybe," Jin said with a shrug. "That one is Huo Ten, and this is Bowu." He gestured to the boy, who was carefully getting out of the cart. Meiling nodded to the monkey, who nodded back politely, then turned her attention back to the boy. One of his legs looked to be injured, though the injury itself appeared to be quite old already. Meiling frowned at the injury as the boy went to bow deeply.

"This Liu Bowu greets you, Great Healing Sage," the boy intoned. "It is an honour to meet your . . . august self?" he was definitely stretching, saying the last part like that.

Meiling remembered Xiulan's story, during her wedding, about fighting a woman named Liu Xianghua . . .

"It's nice to meet you," she said, returning the bow. *I wonder why he's he—*

"He's Gou's woman's little brother," Yun Ren called from the side. "Or rather than her being *his* woman, he's *her* man."

Meiling whipped around to stare at the brothers.

Gou Ren flushed, yet he didn't deny it. Meiling's eyes widened.

"Yup! Little Brother has become a man! I'm so proud," Yun Ren heckled again.

Things devolved from there. Bowu looked a bit lost as to what to do . . . until he was scooped up onto the back of a boar and held on for dear life as they went cantering around the field.

There was laughter and cheers. Yun Ren went sailing into the river, Xiulan tossing him in for some backhanded words.

It was loud, and chaotic, and, heavens . . . it was *home.* She leaned into Jin's side for a moment longer, despite the tang of his Qi. It was already fading a bit as they held each other.

"Now. I think everybody is going to be hungry," she declared.

"Do you need any help—" Jin started to ask, but she just pushed him away.

"*Go and sit,* husband. You look like you've had a long hard road—so just let me take care of everything, okay?"

It seemed like he wanted to object, but when they hit the house, she pushed Jin into their hanging seat, brewed him some tea, and went to get everything ready.

He didn't get up. He still seemed a bit tense . . . but he watched the others play: Tigu stripped down and tackled the dragon into the river. Yun Ren managed to get Gou Ren into a headlock before the flailing dragon hit all of them. Chun Ke aided the apprehensive Bowu into the water, far away from the roughhousing, while Xiulan sat on the edge of the river . . . and lay down, apparently deciding to take a nap.

At least until Tigu grabbed Xiulan's leg and pulled her in. Even Bi De and Ri Zu decided to join the fun, while Miantiao the snake was deposited beside Jin, watching on with fatherly eyes.

Jin exhaled and slowly leaned back into the cushions.

It didn't take very long to finish everything up, anyway. The stews, the potatoes, even the cheese for the pizza. She completed the dish, no matter how . . . *fragrant* the cheese was.

Meiling called everybody in to eat. Jin looked like he was going to cry when he took the first piece of cheese and sauce.

They were ravenous. Every last scrap of food was eaten. Their guests were quick to compliment the chef, and they even liked the cheese. Meiling tried a slice—and nearly spat it out, much to the others' amusement.

They also brought some food back with them from the tournament. Wa Shi loved the preserved spider legs, the fish slapping the side of his trough as Tigu presented to him his spoils. Even Meiling had to admit they tasted pretty good.

For dessert they had ice cream.

Finally, only after they were all full and Tigu was resting her head in Meiling's lap, did Meiling ask the question that was burning in her mind.

"So what happened at the tournament?"

The good mood paused; Jin took a deep breath.

And then he started to tell the story.

→

Meiling sighed as she put on her nightgown, the details of Jin's account still swimming around in her head.

The tale she had been told was terrifying. The attack of the Shrouded Mountain Sect. What they had done to Tigu and Xiulan—

The rage had made her mind go blank . . . then utterly focused as recipes and half-baked ideas for poisons started swimming around in her head.

She had checked all of them over after that. Aside from the strange, golden crack on Xiulan's chest, and her diminished scent, there was no evidence of the battles that had happened. Ri Zu had done a good job patching everybody up. The little rat had made Meiling proud.

They had spoken calmly, almost clinically about the attack and everything that had happened around it, getting the bad news out of the way first.

They had obviously talked about how they should tell her . . . and she was kind of annoyed at them that it worked. The bad news first had certainly dulled her mood . . . but the bright images coming from Yun Ren's recording crystal cheered her up in equal measure, showing her murals and smiling faces.

Her lips had quirked up at the image of Gou Ren kissing a beautiful, willowy woman, and then she'd laughed out loud at the next image of him looking outraged.

In the end . . . her family had come back safe.

Still, she was not quite willing to let things go so easily. She would be spending some time in her workshop. Her husband had given her a new library, and she would put it to good use—after she healed Bowu's leg, of course.

She finished her evening preparations while listening to the sounds coming from downstairs. Tigu was still awake, gushing to Chun Ke about her new friends and how she was such a good big sister. Meiling decided she would like to meet Rags and Loud Boy. They sounded like fun.

And "Handsome Man" as well. Just to make sure he was good enough for her Tigu—

There was a sudden clatter behind her as Jin dropped something. Meiling turned around, curious.

"What fell—" she started, freezing at the sight of Jin.

He looked . . . *lost.* His eyes were wide, and there was a slight tremor that shuddered through his body. His Qi was bubbling out like a spring from a crack.

Jin bent down, and it took him two attempts to pick up the dropped comb, and then he turned to her.

He tried to smile, but it didn't work. The corners of his mouth quirked and fell.

"Ha. Sorry. Just feeling a bit off, yanno?" he said, turning away from her. "It's all catching up to me."

He was trying to deflect, despite all his conversations about talking things out? She raised an eyebrow at him, and he shuffled uncomfortably.

She sighed, then clambered into bed. She patted the covers next to her, and Jin climbed in after her; she grabbed his head, pulling him down into her bosom. Meiling gently stroked his hair and said nothing for a moment, humming a soft song.

At first, nothing happened. His hands simply came up to rest on her back . . . and then they started shaking.

"Sorry," he whispered again. "Supposed to be stronger than this." His bark of laughter was thick with emotion. She could feel the brittleness of her husband's composure.

He said nothing as he simply held her. Held her like a drowning man who had finally been thrown a rope—like a man who had been forced to shoulder all the weight of the world. Golden lines appeared on his right arm, like cracks. They spread down to his chest—like something that had been so compressed one couldn't see the cracks until the pressure was released.

"It was hard, wasn't it?" she asked.

". . . yeah," he answered after a moment.

"Was it scary?"

"Terrifying."

"But you did it."

"Yeah."

"None of our friends got hurt after you showed up, did they?"

Jin shuffled as she kept stroking his hair. "No."

"They all got home safely?"

He nodded.

Meiling hummed. "You did everything you could," she whispered. "Everybody is safe. You won. So let it all out. I'm here. We're all here. Safe, because of you."

Her shirt got damp after that. She stayed with him, humming an old song her mother had taught her, until the shaking stopped.

"Thanks, Meimei," he whispered finally, as he calmed down. He pulled his head from her chest. He still looked exhausted, but there was a spark again. His lips curled into his smile properly this time.

She leaned forwards and kissed him. Slowly, he seemed to regain some of his steadiness. He took a breath, seeming to expand, his presence filling the room. His eyes were pure and clear as he stared into hers.

Meiling stared back into them. They were a field of jade green, interspersed with tiny veins of gold. So filled with love.

What sort of woman would she be if she didn't return that wholeheartedly?

They lay there together, embracing, until they fell asleep.

CHAPTER 65

RESET

How do you go back to the way things were?

Can you?

It was a question I grappled with as I wandered the hills in my backyard. The worst-case scenario had come to pass, in my mind. Well, not *the* worst-case scenario, but it was pretty up there. The cat was out of the bag. The cultivators knew who I was. And not just the Cloudy Sword Sect, who I guess I could trust to be discreet or at least leave me alone, but every Sect in the Azure Hills and the Shrouded Mountain Sect knew who I was.

I was no longer an anonymous farmer. I was a *person of interest.*

This had been coming, I'd known it was, but I hadn't wanted to admit it to myself. My rice was getting too good. I was expanding the roads too much. There was no way I could have remained hidden forever.

Maybe I could have said no to Tigu when she had asked if she could go to the tournament. Maybe I could have tried not to grow my rice as well as it was doing. Maybe if I had done nothing at all, I could have prevented the chain of events that had been set in motion. But it had happened, and no one can change the past.

I couldn't change the fact that I had killed a man and effectively taken charge of an entire province.

I had killed somebody. I couldn't say I really regretted it. Some men needed killing. Taking charge of the Azure Hills? Well, that was downright terrifying, but I think it had to be done too.

The question was, what was I going to do *now*? I had a responsibility to my family. I had things that needed to get done.

What was I going to do about this whole thing? I was clueless. My mind kept on replaying and inventing new scenarios. People taking me up on my offer of emergency aid. Having to host some kind of cultivator get-together. Having to fully return to that life through some quirk of fate.

I sighed and kicked the ground, trying to settle my mind, then heard Big D sound the call for lunch.

Pondering the conundrum before me, I wandered back home. Everybody else seemed in a relatively good mood. Meimei was already poring over the new medical scrolls with fervor. Bowu apparently had bone shards in his cartilage and needed his kneecap broken and reset—both things Meiling never would have attempted without the Lowly Spiritual Herbs. Nothing else in the Azure Hills healed people fast enough or repaired damage like those unassuming green sprigs. She glanced up with an unreadable expression on her face as I approached. Meiling hummed at my appearance, her brow furrowing for a brief instant before she gave me a smile.

Bowu was sitting off to the side on the veranda. The young man hesitantly reached out a hand and patted Chunky. Bowu didn't really seem to know how to interact with everybody yet. He was quiet and skittish . . . though Chunky seemed to be winning him over with sheer dogged friendliness.

Yun Ren was practising with his sword in the courtyard, cursing at it occasionally. "So, like *hwa!* And not *haacha!* Right?" he demanded of the sword. He paused, like he was listening to it. "Yeah, yeah, interesting, approval. I get it."

I kept walking. I saw Babe come over with a look of interest from the fields, staring at Yun with curiosity on his normally placid face.

I entered the house, walking into the main room. Huo Ten was checking over the crystal with Big D. The annoying chunk of rock was apparently nearly ready . . . after it had nearly been destabilized. Apparently it would be ready to view at the solstice.

I slowly sat down at the table, mulling things over. A second later I jumped a little as a plate was placed in front of me.

Xiulan and Gou Ren were both on food duty today, whipping up a light lunch for us all. It was tasty, but I spent most of lunch thinking about things again. I muttered my thanks for the food, then went out to the fields, doing the chores I had neglected in the morning.

I spent the time lost in thought. And when I finished with my chores . . . I leaned up against the fence. Mulling over the paths available to me and getting steadily more frustrated.

My dark mood was interrupted by a voice.

"Oi! Jin!" Yun Ren called, holding one of my makeshift lacrosse sticks. I raised an eyebrow at him, then sighed at the expression on his and his brother's faces. I kind of wanted to, but I had too much crap to think about.

"Not today, guys. I—"

"*Chiiickennnn,*" Gou Ren called. *"Bok bok bok bok!"* I froze and raised an eyebrow at him. *Really?*

"Old Man is just tired, I get it. Too infirm to go at it with the boys, makes sense." He shrugged and smirked at me.

My eye twitched. *Seriously? They're really doing this?*

Their boasts were poor and annoying . . . but I kind of did need some stress relief. Smacking the two asshats around the field would probably be fun.

"Gimme a stick," I commanded, and my two friends whooped. I couldn't help the smile that came to my face.

It was . . . surprisingly normal. Neither of the Xong brothers evidently wanted to escalate the situation, so there were no illusions . . . though Yun Ren had great footwork. Maybe it was all the sword practice he was doing? Gou was getting more and more solid too, to the point where he could take my cross-checks, even when I gave them a little bit of *oomph*.

It was . . . well. It was just like old times. Until we were interrupted.

"Ah! Can I play?!" Tigu asked hopefully, jogging up to us.

I immediately seized the opportunity, saying, "Yeah, you can be on my team."

Tigu's eyes widened happily, and both brothers cursed.

I'd been losing to the Xong brothers, but with Tigu the tide turned instantly against them. Tigu was just way too fast for them to handle, though Gou Ren just tanked her checks and Yun could occasionally dodge, which was no easy feat.

In the end, though, we were too much for them. I was actually starting to feel a little bad when Yun Ren hit the emergency button. "Washy! I'll bring you with me to Pale Moon Lake City the next time I go, and you can pick out whatever you want to eat!" he howled.

The sky darkened. Thunder cracked. A smattering of rain fell from the sky.

Washy descended from the heavens, his eyes burning with greed.

Things . . . devolved from there. Our little game grew quickly into an all-out Fa Ram battle to end all battles, then started getting a bit out of hand. Chunky and Peppa joined our team, while Xiulan decided that she wanted to face off against Tigu again.

It was pure wild chaos, and I couldn't help but laugh. Especially when Yin and Big D started trying to figure out how to use the sticks. It was super unwieldy for them, and we didn't have that many to begin with. So instead we switched to some kind of bastard love child of soccer and rugby.

Eventually, the teams dissolved completely, each person just trying to grab the ball and run with it. Off on the sidelines, Meiling, Noodle, and Bowu watched with varying degrees of interest. Bowu finally let loose a bit, hollering and cheering on Gou Ren, while Meimei cheerfully asked me to kick their asses.

Chunky got a bit too excited, and with a mighty swing of his head he slammed the ball into the air so high it became practically a speck. Everybody paused, trying to see where it would come down . . . except for Washy, who flew up after it. I got an idea.

"Tigu," I called as I crouched down, cupping my hands.

She turned to me, and then confusion turned to elation. The dragon spiked the ball back down. Tigu's foot caught into my cupped hand and I launched her into the air.

The girl howled with laughter as she spun around like a top before putting all her momentum and strength into her leg, smashing a shot straight into one of the goals.

The ball hit the ground so hard it exploded. The game stopped at that point.

Tigu looked at her handiwork. "That was worth more points, right?" she asked hopefully.

I burst out laughing and ruffled her hair.

Then I took a breath and let it out, grinning all the while.

That . . . that had been fun.

→

It kept going. Bit by bit, little by little, I settled back into my life.

Chunky and Washy showed me around the mushroom farm that they'd been tending to, the logs so covered with fungus it looked like we were on an alien planet.

Big D performed the cognitive tests on the chickens with me and greeted each day.

I spent time with Yin, trying to find something around the farm that she truly enjoyed doing.

Helping Gou Ren expand his house had me thinking about the tools that I would need in the future. I'd ended up talking about steam engines to a steadily more enthusiastic Bowu.

At some point Yun Ren somehow found Meiling's bunny costume . . . and then tramped downstairs singing a musical number while illusioned to look like a woman.

At night I had long chats with an old snake, sometimes about nothing and sometimes about healing wounds.

I lost terribly to Xiulan at answer go, and had to tell her a few more embarrassing stories. The girl was merciless!

I reconnected with Meiling, with our silly talks in the morning . . . and our . . . *activities*.

The little things brought me back home, to the place I was building.

One night, a week after, we all decided to camp out under the stars together. We lay down with our backs somehow all fitting against Chunky. The massive boar huffed happily.

Yun Ren told us the stories of his tribe as he traced the constellations above.

It wasn't that I wasn't thinking about it . . . I just wasn't obsessing anymore. No longer was I constantly thinking about the worst-case scenarios, the consequences, and the responsibilities.

I knew what I had to do. I had to ask the Lord Magistrate for lessons. I had to . . . well, I should probably look over Gramps's martial arts scroll.

And then take things as they come. Or if I could, head them off before they began.

I took a breath and closed my eyes, humming. I could also desensitize myself a bit. Go on another adventure, but this time . . . a place with lower stakes. A little place all of us could go. It was something to think about.

Whatever I did, though, I wasn't alone. A rooster on top of a boar. Xiulan, her head on Meiling's shoulder. Tigu, listening raptly to Yun Ren. Gou Ren pulling a blanket over Bowu.

This was my path. I'd started going down it when I decided I wanted nothing to do with the heavens. *This* is my heaven.

It was a pretty good one, if you ask me.

CHAPTER 66

THE ROCK

River warm.

Farm peaceful.

Life good.

A hand scratched his mane absently, Big Brother lying on Chunky's back and dozing. Chunky nearly filled the river, so he was big enough to give Big Brother a bed.

Being big, very fun.

Sister Xiulan shouted and splashed into the river. Sister Tigger danced on the poles, laughing about winning.

Brother Washy went zap, and Sister Tigger fell into the water too.

Very peaceful. Very good.

Chunky chuffed, putting his head under the water and coming up with a mouthful of plants and lotus roots.

River grass tasty too.

Little fish swam around Chunky's belly, hiding from the sun. Funny creatures. They know Chunky not harm. Birdies too, as they landed on his tusks.

Big Brother on top of him shifted and yawned. His head came up for a moment, and then he fell back asleep.

Big Brother sleep a lot. Very tired. Big Little Sister sleep a lot too.

Big Brother use lots of energy, with Big Little Sister. Swing hard. Beat bad man. Very good. Chunky praise both, both laugh and give scratches.

Good.

Still hurt, still tired . . . but smiles were always good.

They were tense. Scared. But time and family starting to heal. Time, family, and sleep.

All the best things, so friends heal fast!

"Thanks, Big Guy," Big Brother and Big Little Sister said at the same time, and they scratched through his mane.

Laughter too.

Sister Tigger laughed a lot. But train harder than ever. Apologised to Chunky for being mean so long ago. Apologised to Wife too. Peppa accept. Chunky happy better friends.

Chunky looked around the farm. At fuzzy friends, chewing on grass. At Friend Babe, honing his cuts. Good friend, Babe. Quiet. Chunky talk for both. Very good listener. Very good road builder.

Back at house was Big Sister Mei and Sister Rizzo.

Right now Big Sister Mei very busy! Very busy, working with Sister Rizzo on healing new friend Bowu's leg. Take many notes, devise many things that make Chunky's head spin. New friend quiet and polite and lost, so Chunky help. New friend small and bitter creature. Expect little. A long time pain, like Chunky. But only one friend, so he healed wrong.

□

"I am not a heavenly doctor, or anything of the sort. I'm not the best doctor in the province, either. To be blunt, the only reason I'm even attempting to fix this is because of the Spiritual Herbs. Otherwise, the only thing I could do is numb the pain, and even that comes with its own problems," Big Sister explained to her new friend.

The boy listened intently before nodding his head.

"Now, here is what I believe the problem is, and these are the steps we need to do to fix it. Tell me if you don't understand anything, okay?"

Big Sister Mei easy to understand, even for Chunky. Bones in cartilage bad. Knee needed to be rebroken, set properly.

"You're the first doctor to actually explain things like that," new friend said.

Big Sister Mei's eyes softened.

"All I can promise you is my best. "

□

Chunky know that pain. Easy make friends, when know same hurt. Friend Noodle talk about hurt with Chunky. Noodle say Chunky wise; Chunky just think Friend Noodle overthinks things. Gave Chunky pot to store treasures, and helped Chunky decorate.

Chunky's pot had a smiling sun, and all friends on it. Three rows, with space for even more friends!

New friend smile and help, after Chunky gave ride, and asked Bowu to draw on Chunky's pot. Helped Big Brother with big thing of copper pipes. His hands were quick, and his mind quicker. Like Brother Washy, but not as lazy.

Lazy, lazy fishdragon.

Other new friend too.

Friend monkey helped all. Curious and quiet friend. Young, but voice was old and sounded like gravel. Helped with Brother Big D's new crystal. Huo Ten say new crystal inferior to old one, even though old one was broken. New one needs time to settle to watch memory. Friend Huo Ten say ready by solstice. Or the new year. Then strange crystal questions be answered.

Brother Big D say crystal can wait. Other things more important anyway.

Brother Big D talk a lot about time with Big Brother. Say he learned a lot. Say he knows how big world is, how cruel. Ask for Chunky opinion on what should do.

Chunky said to do what Big D thinks is best, and Chunky help.

Brother Big D give Chunky pat, say Chunky is good friend.

□

Bi De gazed upon the conclave of the disciples. Sister Tigu was to his right; Sister Ri Zu was to his left. The rest were gathered around the table.

"We are not alone. Others now know of our Lord, and though his might is a barrier . . ." Bi De trailed off.

This is not our Lord's dream alone.

'What shall we do?' Ri Zu squeaked.

'Help,' the boar stated simply.

□

Chunky turned his eyes further.

Brother Gou Ren was working on his house. Say wife come soon, make house better. Little Sun helped him. Little Sun from very far away, still trying to figure out what she was. Still trying to find her place, outside war and battle.

Could dance, but wanted something else. Something like Sister Tigger carving, or Washy math.

Brother Yun Ren was further along. Practising with sword and training illusion technique. Big Sister Mei see new drawings of body. Ask Brother Yun Ren to record medical plants, put in scroll for others.

Finally: Wife. Pretty lady nuzzle against Chunky, her eyes full of warmth. Chunky scared Wife, helping Big Little Sister build roads. Walking out of body felt strange. Went into forest for week. Slept a lot. Big Sister Mei very worried too.

Wife stay by Chunky side while he dreamed. She took care of Chunky. Her eyes scared away any who got too close, too fast back when Chunky was . . . less.

But now . . . Wife happy again. Wife pleased family back home.

Chunky took a breath and nuzzled into Wife. He watched the silly bees. He watched the clouds come across the sky.

He watched as friends sat, and talked, and played. Big Brother even sat up too, finishing his nap. He looked around the farm and sighed.

"It's beautiful, isn't it?" he asked.

Chunky nodded.

'Hmmm. Life good,' he replied, and Big Brother laughed, before going quiet.

But good must be worked on to stay good.

Friends had to keep doing good. Sometimes, it was hard. But Chunky believed.

Future uncertain. Future scary.

But Chunky help. Friends help.

All lift together, and make Big Brother and Big Little Sister's load lighter.

"Life good . . . yeah. Yeah, I think it is," Big Brother said. "Or I hope it will be."

They stayed together until Big Brother spoke again.

"You know what we need? A vacation. Hey, Big D! Where did you say your student was from again?"

CHAPTER 67

THE EMPIRE AND THE VILLAGE

The soldiers stared dispassionately down at their foes. They howled and raged, clumping together, and gathering courage. Their black armour was tarnished and their lances crooked and broken. With a roar, they suddenly surged forwards, slamming into the ranks of the soldiers.

Blades flashed. Armour held firm. For the third time, the enemy assaulted the gleaming, near-iridescent phalanx. For the third time, they were repelled, bodies falling to earth and lying unmoving.

Desperation and blood tinged the air.

The soldiers advanced, closing the entrapment. Each movement was perfect and drilled relentlessly. There could be no mistakes as they felt the weight of their commander's stare upon them.

The auxiliaries, smaller, weaker, and less armoured, milled about in holding patterns, their formations imperfect, hemming the last of these rebels in.

This last band was all that was left of the raiders who had once seemed without number. The grasslands had been scoured. The forests, purged. The duels among the reeds ended. Corpses littered the countryside, as far as the eye could see.

Though they would return next year, in greater numbers, this was their duty.

For the enemy had committed the ultimate sin in raising their lances against the Emperor.

The largest of the rebels roared a challenge. Her black armour gleamed; her lance was still sharp. She raged, waving her weapon about, as her body swirled with Qi.

A command was given.

Blades' keen edges shone. The loyal soldiers' eyes gleamed with heavy intent.

The soldiers descended upon the enemy, power rising about them.

Their charge was met by the greatest rebel. Her speed was beyond the soldiers.

For the first time, a warrior fell as she shot past and to the side, lancing straight through the armoured form of the soldier.

There was little reaction to their comrade falling. No thought, just the simple calculation of war.

For the rebel "queen" fought alone. As the auxiliaries and the rest of the cohort butchered the disorganised, fleeing creatures, these warriors closed in. Their formations and tactics were unstoppable, commanded as they were by one who had fought a thousand battles.

The rebel's spear slashed and lanced; it struck and it battered. Legs flew off. Heads were severed. Blood sprayed in the air, yet the relentless attack continued.

A nick to the leg. A strike to her midsection. Her speed and agility were superlative.

But she was slowing. She was tiring.

One of her limbs sailed through the air, her black armour cracking. One soldier rammed bodily into her, slamming her into the earth. Armour splintered, and black lance erupted from flesh.

The soldiers gave thanks for their comrade's sacrifice.

The rebel screamed as she was pierced through. Her entrails spilled onto the ground. Her eyes were filled with hate as a second blade rose high and stabbed down, ending her life and removing her head. Her face was fixed into a rictus of hate.

The cohort rose again, their numbers reduced, and turned their eyes to the still ongoing battle. To call it a battle was giving the rebels too much credit.

It was simply butchery.

No quarter was given to the enemy.

The Great Queen Vajra reclined upon her throne, gazing contemptuously upon the broken forms of her enemies. These damnable blood suckers, who dared attempt to sully the Emperor's flesh with their proboscises. Death was too good for them!

She waved her abdomen, and her soldiers obeyed, carrying the bodies of the wretched creatures off to the river. How apt. Those that dared attempt to sup upon the Emperor would now be eaten in turn.

She rose from her seat to tour her fortress. The golden walls of honey stretched high and heavy. The pollen stores were packed full.

And in each and every comb, in every cell, she felt the slight charge of the Emperor's power. Nourishing them. Empowering them.

Mayhap in a few years she would be more powerful than any queen before her. It was a heady thought. To go from a half-dead wretch to a queen, an empress in truth.

For that to happen, however, a sacrifice had to be made.

She carefully eyed her brood, looking for ones that fit her needs. She directed the caretakers to lead her to the fattest and plumpest specimens.

She nodded her head. These would make a fine tribute for her Emperor. Though it was always painful to sacrifice brood this way, she had declared no expense would be spared. The Emperor would receive only their finest when he came to collect his due. None of her brood would dare raise their stingers to him.

And . . . it seemed that that day was today. A warning spread into her mind that the Emperor was approaching, with the valiant and beautiful Bi De, as well as the glorious and powerful Chun Ke.

There was another human with him, a servant, but Vajra disregarded him, instead focusing upon the Emperor.

He approached one of Vajra's servant hives, the lesser bees, and with a mental command, she quelled their burgeoning nervousness. With a slow movement he opened it to the elements. He gazed upon the lesser creatures' work and nodded.

He carefully removed three of the frames, all filled with only honey . . . and then closed the box again.

No brood was taken. Not a single larva. Just the honey, the frames replaced by new ones.

She was stunned. Dumbfounded even. How little tribute the Emperor took! How benevolent was his hand!

She was so stunned she barely noticed his approach as he opened her own hive, gaining access to her fortress.

"Yeah, definitely a different kind of bee. Look, they arranged the honey by what they harvested it from, I think. That's pine, that one looks like peach blossom . . ." The Emperor's voice was booming as both he and Bi De gazed upon her work.

"Good work, Vajra," he praised, as he collected his meagre tribute from her.

"Definitely going to need to expand this, though. They grew way faster than I was expecting. I'll need ten, no, twenty more hive boxes if they continue like this," he said, and it was all Vajra could do to remain conscious. More fortresses?

How powerful was the Emperor to grant them such a bounty?

The queen bowed her head, then danced her supplication. Her mind whirling with desire.

"This'll make a good snack for when we meet Bi De's disciple. Let's go!"

From the fortresses, she would not just have a new kingdom. She would have an unstoppable Empire. An Empire that would spread across the whole of the Azure Hills!

□

Two forms slunk through the shadows, moving from rock to rock. There was little cover in the Gutter, save for the stones. They moved with purpose, slinking towards the flocks of sheep, with the shadowed moon providing them cover.

"Are you sure this place is a good mark?" one of the men asked. He was lanky and twitchy, clad in rough, ill-fitting clothes. His voice was nervous as his eyes leapt around. "Don't they have some guardian Spirit Beast here?"

There was a snort of derision as the men continued on their path.

"Don't tell me you actually *believe* that story," the other man said, his voice mocking. "A Spirit Beast? Some tall tale to ward off any foolish enough to believe them. Like a Spirit Beast is going to guard sheep."

The twitchy man nodded hesitantly. It did sound like some manner of a fool's tale. *Beware of Chicken*. They could at least make it believable.

"Look at 'em," the more rotund of the two muttered, as they peeked over a rock, gazing down at the balls of fluff. "They barely have any dogs. Simple in and out. We grab one of the sheep and eat well for a couple of days. They probably won't even notice one is missing."

Two sets of eyes glanced around, noting the lack of shepherds or other visible defenders. A few of the sheep had wandered this way, separating themselves from the flock. The men looked at each other and grinned.

It was rather easy to skirt the rock to head directly for the animals. They were fat and dopey-looking. Their dumb eyes glancing at the humans before dismissing them as not anything to worry about. One of the beasts even approached, looking like it was going to attempt to beg them for food.

Talk about easy. But . . . the twitchy man still felt like something was amiss. They wouldn't be that lax, would they?

But it seemed they were. A pair of hands grasped the sheep firmly and started coaxing it away from the herd. The surprisingly docile beast accepted this treatment. They had gotten perhaps a quarter of a li up the hill when the relative silence of the night was shattered.

There was a yip. It was angry and aggressive-sounding, but tiny.

Both men nearly jumped out of their skins, their heads whipping around, as they beheld what had caught them.

A small white-furred puppy glared at them. Its entire chest expanded as it sucked in another breath and put its whole body behind a yip that couldn't carry far.

The rotund man snorted at the little yips. He shook his head and attempted to coax the sheep farther away but nearly ran into his partner. The twitchy man was still staring at the dog, his face pale. His lip was trembling.

"What are you—" the man asked as he turned back around, looking to where his partner was staring, which wasn't at the dog, but at the *rock*.

Or more accurately, at the shadow on the rock.

A slightly hunched, inhuman figure, a long spear held upright.

A cloud moved from the moon, revealing the shadow into sharp relief.

The slightly too long arms. The grey fur running over its back.

And the rooster's head that glared balefully down at them.

The rotund man did not freeze like his companion.

He dropped the sheep and turned, sprinting up the hill as fast as his legs could carry him.

There was a viscous-sounding smack of flesh on flesh and a gurgle from his friend, but the man kept running, his eyes wild, scrambling up the Gutter.

It was all for naught.

The shadowy, demonic rooster-beast cut in front of him, skidding to a stop. The man tried to change direction and instead landed on his ass.

The hunched creature cocked its head to the side at him, slowly rising up to its full height. Its baleful red eyes reflected the light of the moon.

Beware of Chicken the sign had said.

That was no chicken, it was some manner of horrid beast! Did they sacrifice travellers to it?

Something wet the grass between his legs. His heart was thundering in his ears.

The demonic rooster-beast stalked forwards. The last thing the man saw was a foot hammering into his face. His head spun as he hit the grass.

□

The great rooster stood atop a house as he watched the Magistrate's men recede into the distance. He balanced on the edge of the roof, his eyes taking in and surveying his whole domain. It was protected, as it would be. Interlopers in the night were unwelcome.

The great defender soared through the air as he began his training, leaping and flipping, as only such a creature that commanded the sky could. His spear struck in an expert pattern, his form was impeccable, his balance sublime—

"Zhang Fei! Your father is asking for you!" his mother shouted. The great rooster staggered and fell off the roof.

He managed a landing in the hay. With a groan, Zhang Fei pushed up his rooster mask.

There was a happy yip as a small white puppy landed on his chest, licking excitedly at him.

He sighed and gently pushed the puppy away, and it hopped down to his feet. The puppy's tail began to wag so hard it was having trouble standing.

The boy chuckled as he set his spear and his mask against the wall. He smiled fondly at the thing, wondering how his Master was doing.

A smaller part asked when he would return, or when Zhang Fei would go and visit this Fa Ram. It wasn't too far away. And people were already saying that the Lord Magistrate was building more roads.

"Come on, Shaggy Two. Let's go see what Dad wants," he said.

The dog yipped happily and pranced after him.

→

The next day was very boring. The sheep were out to pasture and the sun was beating down.

Zhang Fei the Torrent Rider sighed. He practised his kata. He swung his stick, like he had every day for the last three months. But even that was starting to get old. He fell onto his back and sighed.

He was interrupted by Shaggy, who started barking. Visitors? He pulled his mask down and ascended to the roof, crawling to hide his form. His eyes scanned the horizon for—

His eyes lit up as he beheld a magnificent form.

"Master!" he shouted happily. Zhang Fei the Torrent Rider scrambled to his feet and jumped off the roof, landing on the ground. His eyes widened when he realised his Master wasn't alone.

There was an entire group of people with him. There was a short woman with green hair, two pigs, and the prettiest girl Zhang Fei had ever seen—who was carrying a fish in a jar?

"Greetings, my disciple. Are you well?" Master Bi De asked aloud. "I have abided by my promise. We have met again, haven't we?"

Zhang Fei smiled brilliantly and dropped into a bow. Shaggy Two yipped.

"So, you're my disciple's disciple, huh?" asked one of the people who had come with his Master, amused. The man was staring incredulously at Zhang Fei's mask of power, clearly jealous of it. He was huge! The biggest person Zhang Fei had ever seen! He had a long piece of wood in his hand, curved into an oblong oval. "I heard there was something called torrent riding here, and we decided to check it out."

Zhang Fei nodded, distracted.

"Ah, yes! This way to the village!" he said, waving them onwards and towards the gate guarded by the Master's talisman.

The group saw the talisman and stopped in shock.

A sign that proudly proclaimed one thing:

Beware of Chicken

The giant of a man, the Master of Zhang Fei's Master, began to roar with laughter.

The rooster preened.

CHAPTER 68

EPILOGUE: OMENS

In a secure storage room in the Shrouded Mountain Sect, two Inquisitors worked in grim silence, dissecting a ruined corpse. Their bodies were completely covered in cloth, faces hidden with protective masks and defensive talismans on their bodies, just in case. Notes were written down, hypotheses created, and counter-techniques devised and discarded.

They worked with precision, their eyes completely focused upon the subject, for they could produce only the best results for their Masters and the Sect.

When they were done, they placed seals upon the corpse and called in their relief. Two new Inquisitors entered the room as the others exited, then took their places standing guard.

The room was silent and cold, but they were unaffected. They had the utmost vigilance in their duties. Lightning crackled around their bodies intermittently, ready to dispel illusions.

Until suddenly their eyes went blank, though they still stood at attention.

The shadows of the room started to bubble and a woman slid out of them. She was clad entirely in black, with a veil over her face, Qi suppressors worn upon her body. She took a moment to look at the guards and smirk in satisfaction. Of course the poison had worked. It was a technique of the Master's. However, it did come with some drawbacks; namely, it was utterly useless in direct combat. The only reason it was working at all at the moment was the stable Qi of the room—if she moved even a little too fast, if a bare breeze ghosted across their skin, the technique would fail.

She carefully approached the corpse, acting with the utmost subtlety. Her fingers flashed through arcane signs, and one of the seals peeled back slightly.

The woman let out a breath. The most delicate stage of the operation was over.

It was time to collect the wayward disciple.

The woman pressed her fingers against the corpse, directing her Qi to gather the remnants of Lu Ban and shake what was left of him out of his torpor—the woman paused as her sense extended through the corpse. It felt . . . odd. She pushed her ghostly Qi farther into the body.

Pulling her fingers back, the woman stared at the tiny motes of oil and blood clinging to them.

"You're . . . actually dead?" she asked, half-amused and half-incredulous. Really, he hadn't internalized even the basest of Master's abilities? The little bastard should still be alive.

There was only a tiny, lingering feeling, a grudge, and nothing more. Not enough to reconstruct anything. There was no true part of what was once Lu Ban.

The woman sighed in irritation. At first she had gone to Yellow Rock Plateau, the site of the impact. There had been nothing there but scorched rock. She had then checked the populace in the immediate surrounding area . . . and no peasant had suddenly decided to up and leave after coming back from the mountain, Lu Ban's essence having taken them over.

She had expected that, even if captured, he would be able to survive after feigning his own death. One who had learned the Twilight Cuckoo's Triumph was said to have a hundred lives.

The woman scoffed. He'd been a waste of resources and time.

She placed the little piece of grudge residue in a vial. Perhaps it could still be useful. A poison for a father? Zang Zeng of the Shrouded Mountain Sect, poked and prodded to avenge the wrongful death of his son? That could work. Still, how utterly *disappointing*, to come all this way for what amounted to nothing more than a simple ingredient. She placed the vial within her robes. Master would have been disappointed.

He had once had high hopes for Lu Ban.

It took over an hour to replace the broken seals to perfection, exactly as they had been upon the corpse. She swept the room for any sign of her passing. Then she melted back into the shadows.

The men's eyes returned to focus. Their watch resumed, uninterrupted. Then, six hours later, they were relieved in turn.

□

The village of Hong Yaowu was beginning to bring in the last of the harvest. The trees looked to be starting to turn, and the air had notes of cold in it. Mist clung to everything. Summer was finally ending.

Xong Ten Ren and his wife worked together, without their sons, for the first time in twenty years. They dressed the hides and sorted out cuts of dried meat.

It was a bit lonely, but their boys had said that they would be around soon.

And that was enough.

The day had been a quiet one so far, a routine they had done for decades.

Then there was a bit of commotion at the road leading to Verdant Hill. The children noticed the stranger first, but unlike when Jin had arrived, they were apprehensive. A form slid out of the mists, gliding like a wraith along the ground. A large hat on her head, like fishermen wore, contrasted heavily with the robes of finest silk draped over her frame, yet the strangest thing about the mist-clad woman was the bulbous contraption on her back, the vents on it glowing with heat.

She strode in without hesitation, unstoppable and indomitable, moving with absolute purpose much like an incoming fog bank.

The people stared with trepidation at this stranger, and she paused in the center of the village. She pulled off her hat, revealing beautiful, sharp features and wavy hair.

Several people gasped at her beauty as her eyes scanned the villagers. Ten Ren watched curiously . . . until her searching gaze landed on him.

The woman's eyes narrowed and her march resumed, striding directly towards him and his wife. She ignored absolutely everybody else, and several people stepped out of her way as she neared Ten Ren's house.

The woman stopped in front of them.

"Are you Xong Ten Ren and Nezin Hu Li?" the woman asked imperiously. "The parents of Xong Gou Ren?"

Ten Ren swallowed at the haughty expression on the cultivator and the blunt question. She had a presence about her, a physical weight that could not be denied. He noticed one of the villagers starting to slink in the direction of the road to Jin's house.

Ten Ren licked his lips. He made a motion to his wife; should things go wrong, she would attempt to run. "I am Ten Ren. Who asks for me?"

The woman nodded . . . and then bowed at ninety degrees.

"This Liu Xianghua asks to court your son!" her voice boomed. "Allow me to call you Mother and Father!"

There was silence in the village. Hu Li dropped the hides she was holding.

Pandemonium erupted.

□

Two old men stood upon a mountain. Their faces were carved from stone as they rested together.

Shen Yu handed Brother Ge a scroll.

"Unfortunate," the man muttered, staring at the crossed-off locations.

Even with Shen Yu cutting loose, the demons were annoyingly tenacious, and they'd gotten good at hiding. From inhospitable mountaintops to poisonous bogs, the two had ventured everywhere they could think of, laying waste to their enemies as they went.

It had been surprisingly liberating, almost like old times. Ge by his side, going on a grand adventure.

They had even found a Silver Yin Lotus! They'd shared a cup of its dew together, finally indulging in a treasure that had eluded them all those years ago. Shen Yu chuckled. What had once been a grand quest of their youth was a mere distraction now.

It was still taking a very, very long time. *Too long*, Shen Yu worried.

"Are you sure your man will find him?" Shen Yu asked.

"I have faith in the Senior Disciple. He withstood the full force of my intent without flinching. He will not rest until his mission is—"

There was a swirl of shadow and a messenger stepped forth, dropping to one knee before them and raising up a message tube.

"Masters. This one brings word from Disciple Lu Ri. He has accomplished his mission and returns with a missive from Jin Rou."

Shen Yu's eyes widened. Elder Ge nodded, vindicated.

"See? Speak of a man and he shall appear."

"Lu Ri, you said his name was? I shall reward him personally for this," Shen Yu declared.

He held out his hand and the message tube was carefully placed in his hand.

Shen Yu wondered what it would say. Rou had been injured badly as a result of Shen Yu's advice and the Cloudy Sword Sect. Would the letter be full of vitriol? Would it be a condemnation? He would not blame Little Rou if it was. Shen Yu opened the tube—

And horse dung popped out, some trick causing it to spray all over his robes.

Elder Ge and the messenger froze, while Shen Yu stared at the droppings. The smell hit his nose as he picked up a scrap of paper that had come out with the dung, a stylized smiling face upon it.

His stern façade cracked.

Shen Yu began to howl with laughter.

ABOUT THE AUTHOR

Casualfarmer started writing after listening to his parents' stories on their long drives to visit relatives. He had been saving money from his food-service-industry job to go to college for teaching when the COVID-19 pandemic hit. *Beware of Chicken* is Casualfarmer's first original story. He lives in Ontario, Canada.